ZANE GREY

THREE COMPLETE NOVELS

ZANE GREY

THREE COMPLETE NOVELS

Riders of the Purple Sage

The Rainbow Trail

The Lone Star Ranger

PORTLAND HOUSE

This edition is published by Portland House, a division of Random House Value
Publishing, Inc., 40 Engelhard Avenue, Avenel, New Jersey 07001.

Printed and bound in the United States of America

ISBN 0-517-19005-2

8 7 6 5 4 3 2 1

CONTENTS

INTRODUCTION

Z ANE G REY (1875–1939) wrote scores of best-selling western-adventure novels, many of which have been adapted for motion pictures. His depictions of the people and places of the Old West set the standard by which all other tales of this genre have since been measured.

The three novels included in this book are perhaps the finest and best known of Zane Grey's stories. *Riders of the Purple Sage* and its sequel, *The Rainbow Trail*, are set among the Mormon communities in Utah and involve rustlers, a hidden canyon, polygamy and a secret village of "sealed wives," relentless searches for loved ones, tension-filled romance, and outcasts yearning for redemption. The central character of *The Lone Star Ranger* is Buck Duane, the archetypal western gunfighter, whose background and skills propel him into the life of an outlaw, always on the run and always challenged, because of his fame, to kill.

While their immense popularity may be due to Grey's extraordinary power as a storyteller, these tales are also impressive explorations of character and personal motivation. Figuring prominently in the stories are such themes as salvation through love, individual integrity in the face of society's pressures, the conflict between religious faith and personal conscience, strength through sacrifice, and adherence to duty.

Riders of the Purple Sage introduces Jane Withersteen, the strong-willed and wealthy daughter of the founder of Cottonwoods, a Mormon village in southern Utah. Withersteen is an independent woman who refuses to capitulate to the moral admonitions of the Mormon elders. She further alienates the community leaders by her friendship with Venters, a hired hand and master rider, and with Lassiter, a gunman from Texas who is searching for the grave of a woman named Milly Erne—and for those responsible for her death. Venters encounters Bess, a woman outlaw associated with the notorious gang of rustlers led by Oldring, and together they hide out in Surprise Valley, while Lassiter and Jane Withersteen face an increasingly hostile Mormon leadership.

The passage recounting Venters's race—to reclaim Jane Withersteen's two stolen horses—with Jerry Card, a member of Oldring's gang renowned for his riding skill, is a masterpiece of action description. In this riveting episode, page after page of exciting narration pulls the reader headlong into a blur of speeding horses and emotional frenzy and, in impact, rivals anything that may be seen in a motion picture. A similar suspense-filled chase concludes the book, with Venters, Bess, Jane Withersteen, Lassiter, and Jane's adopted daughter, Fay, drawn to Surprise Valley.

The Rainbow Trail follows the journey of Shefford, an ex-minister who has lost his faith and seeks redemption by wandering through Utah and searching for Jane Withersteen's daughter, Fay Larkin. Shefford discovers true religion and brotherhood with the help of an Indian friend, Nas Ta Bega, and charms the inhabitants of a hidden village of "sealed wives"—the other women of polygamous Mormon men, who visit the community only occasionally, like predators in the night. Shefford makes enemies of the Mormon authorities and of the outlaws Joe Lake and Shadd, and finds his salvation through his protection of, and love for, the woman who had been the object of his obsession.

The Lone Star Ranger is the story of a decent man whose strength, gun skills, and family background force him into the life of a hunted outlaw. In Buck Duane, Grey created the prototype of the fictional western hero: the noble gunfighter, hounded unjustly, always on the run, decent and honest but able to kill if necessary. Haunted by his past and unable to stop killing because of his reputation, Duane is a man who travels in a dangerous world, with its own code—one that respects the skills of riding, gunslinging, cooking, gambling, and climbing, and that values honesty, generosity, friendship, loyalty, and honor. But in Grey's stories there is always an added dimension of psychological drama and final redemption. Duane is haunted by the men he's shot; he fears that something within him relishes killing, and wonders, "Am I an inborn murderer or not?" Duane's own salvation comes through his association with the Texas Rangers and through the faith and love of a strong woman.

Full of action and suspense, cinematic and fast-moving, the three masterful novels in this book can be enjoyed for their gripping action, their rapturous descriptions of western landscapes, their nail-biting suspense, their myriad surprises, and their unforgettable characters. But these are also tales of complex emotions. In Zane Grey's Old West, people tormented by inner conflicts and harrowing physical contests discover decency beneath brutishness, and ultimately find peace through courage, sacrifice, and love.

JOHN GABRIEL HUNT

New York
1994

RIDERS
OF THE
PURPLE SAGE

CONTENTS

❧1❧

LASSITER

A SHARP clip-clop of iron-shod hoofs deadened and died away, and clouds of yellow dust drifted from under the cottonwoods out over the sage.

Jane Withersteen gazed down the wide purple slope with dreamy and troubled eyes. A rider had just left her and it was his message that held her thoughtful and almost sad, awaiting the churchmen who were coming to resent and attack her right to befriend a Gentile.

She wondered if the unrest and strife that had lately come to the little village of Cottonwoods was to involve her. And then she sighed, remembering that her father had founded this remotest border settlement of southern Utah and that he had left it to her. She owned all the ground and many of the cottages. Withersteen House was hers, and the great ranch, with its thousands of cattle, and the swiftest horses of the sage. To her belonged Amber Spring, the water which gave verdure and beauty to the village and made living possible on that wild purple upland waste. She could not escape being involved by whatever befell Cottonwoods.

That year, 1871, had marked a change which had been gradually coming in the lives of the peace-loving Mormons of the border. Glaze—Stone Bridge—Sterling, villages to the north, had risen against the invasion of Gentile settlers and the forays of rustlers. There had been opposition to the one and fighting with the other. And now Cottonwoods had begun to wake and bestir itself and grow hard.

Jane prayed that the tranquillity and sweetness of her life would not be permanently disrupted. She meant to do so much more for her people than she had done. She wanted the sleepy quiet pastoral days to last always. Trouble between the Mormons and the Gentiles of the community would make her unhappy. She was Mormon-born, and she was a

5

friend to poor and unfortunate Gentiles. She wished only to go on doing good and being happy. And she thought of what that great ranch meant to her. She loved it all—the grove of cottonwoods, the old stone house, the amber-tinted water, and the droves of shaggy, dusty horses and mustangs, the sleek, clean-limbed, blooded racers, and the browsing herds of cattle and the lean, sun-browned riders of the sage.

While she waited there she forgot the prospect of untoward change. The bray of a lazy burro broke the afternoon quiet, and it was comfortingly suggestive of the drowsy farmyard, and the open corrals, and the green alfalfa fields. Her clear sight intensified the purple sage-slope as it rolled before her. Low swells of prairie-like ground sloped up to the west. Dark, lonely cedar trees, few and far between, stood out strikingly, and at long distances ruins of red rocks. Farther on, up the gradual slope, rose a broken wall, a huge monument, looming dark purple and stretching its solitary, mystic way, a wavering line that faded in the north. Here to the west was the light and color and beauty. Northward the slope descended to a dim line of canyons from which rose an upflinging of the earth, not mountainous, but a vast heave of purple uplands, with ribbed and fan-shaped walls, castle-crowned cliffs, and gray escarpments. Over it all crept the lengthening, waning afternoon shadows.

The rapid beat of hoofs recalled Jane Withersteen to the question at hand. A group of riders cantered up the lane, dismounted, and threw their bridles. They were seven in number, and Tull, the leader, a tall, dark man, was an elder of Jane's church.

"Did you get my message?" he asked, curtly.

"Yes," replied Jane.

"I sent word I'd give that rider Venters half an hour to come down to the village. He didn't come."

"He knows nothing of it," said Jane. "I didn't tell him. I've been waiting here for you."

"Where is Venters?"

"I left him in the courtyard."

"Here, Jerry," called Tull, turning to his men, "take the gang and fetch Venters out here if you have to rope him."

The dusty-booted and long-spurred riders clanked noisily into the grove of cottonwoods and disappeared in the shade.

"Elder Tull, what do you mean by this?" demanded Jane. "If you must arrest Venters you might have the courtesy to wait till he leaves my home. And if you do arrest him it will be adding insult to injury. It's absurd to accuse Venters of being mixed up in that shooting fray in the village last night. He was with me at the time. Besides, he let me take charge of his guns. You're only using this as a pretext. What do you mean to do to Venters?"

"I'll tell you presently," replied Tull. "But first tell me why you defend this worthless rider?"

"Worthless!" exclaimed Jane, indignantly. "He's nothing of the kind. He was the best rider I ever had. There's not a reason why I shouldn't champion him and every reason why I should. It's no little shame to me, Elder Tull, that through my friendship he has roused the enmity of my people and become an outcast. Besides, I owe him eternal gratitude for saving the life of little Fay."

"I've heard of your love for Fay Larkin and that you intend to adopt her. But—Jane Withersteen, the child is a Gentile!"

"Yes. But, Elder, I don't love the Mormon children any less because I love a Gentile child. I shall adopt Fay if her mother will give her to me."

"I'm not so much against that. You can give the child Mormon teaching," said Tull. "But I'm sick of seeing this fellow Venters hang around you. I'm going to put a stop to it. You've so much love to throw away on these beggars of Gentiles that I've an idea you might love Venters."

Tull spoke with the arrogance of a Mormon whose power could not be brooked and with the passion of a man in whom jealousy had kindled a consuming fire.

"Maybe I do love him," said Jane. She felt both fear and anger stir her heart. "I'd never thought of that. Poor fellow! He certainly needs someone to love him."

"This'll be a bad day for Venters unless you deny that," returned Tull, grimly.

Tull's men appeared under the cottonwoods and led a young man out into the lane. His ragged clothes were those of an outcast. But he stood tall and straight, his wide shoulders flung back, with the muscles of his bound arms rippling and a blue flame of defiance in the gaze he bent on Tull.

For the first time Jane Withersteen felt Venters's real spirit. She wondered if she would love this splendid youth. Then her emotion cooled to the sobering sense of the issue at stake.

"Venters, will you leave Cottonwoods at once and forever?" asked Tull, tensely.

"Why?" rejoined the rider.

"Because I order it."

Venters laughed in cool disdain.

The red leaped to Tull's dark cheek.

"If you don't go it means your ruin," he said, sharply.

"Ruin!" exclaimed Venters, passionately. "Haven't you already ruined me? What do you call ruin? A year ago I was a rider. I had horses and cattle of my own. I had a good name in Cottonwoods. And now when I come into the village to see this woman you set your men on me. You hound me. You trail me as if I were a rustler. I have no more to lose— except my life."

"Will you leave Utah?"

"Oh! I know," went on Venters, tauntingly, "it galls you, the idea of beautiful Jane Withersteen being friendly to a poor Gentile. You want her all yourself. You're a wiving Mormon. You have use for her—and Withersteen House and Amber Spring and seven thousand head of cattle!"

Tull's hard jaw protruded, and rioting blood corded the veins of his neck.

"Once more. Will you go?"

"No!"

"Then I'll have you whipped within an inch of your life," replied Tull, harshly. "I'll turn you out in the sage. And if you ever come back you'll get worse."

Venters's agitated face grew coldly set and the bronze changed to gray.

Jane impulsively stepped forward. "Oh! Elder Tull!" she cried. "You won't do that!"

Tull lifted a shaking finger toward her.

"That'll do from you. Understand, you'll not be allowed to hold this boy to a friendship that's offensive to your bishop. Jane Withersteen, your father left you wealth and power. It has turned your head. You haven't yet come to see the place of Mormon women. We've reasoned with you, borne with you. We've patiently waited. We've let you have your fling, which is more than I ever saw granted to a Mormon woman. But you haven't come to your senses. Now, once and for all, you can't have any further friendship with Venters. He's going to be whipped, and he's got to leave Utah!"

"Oh! Don't whip him! It would be dastardly!" implored Jane, with slow certainty of her failing courage.

Tull always blunted her spirit, and she grew conscious that she had feigned a boldness which she did not possess. He loomed up now in different guise, not as a jealous suitor, but embodying the mysterious despotism she had known from childhood—the power of her creed.

"Venters, will you take your whipping here or would you rather go out in the sage?" asked Tull. He smiled a flinty smile that was more than inhuman, yet seemed to give out of its dark aloofness a gleam of righteousness.

"I'll take it here—if I must," said Venters. "But by God!—Tull, you'd better kill me outright. That'll be a dear whipping for you and your praying Mormons. You'll make me another Lassiter!"

The strange glow, the austere light which radiated from Tull's face, might have been a holy joy at the spiritual conception of exalted duty. But there was something more in him, barely hidden, a something personal and sinister, a deep of himself, an engulfing abyss. As his religious mood was fanatical and inexorable, so would his physical hate be merciless.

"Elder, I—I repent my words," Jane faltered. The religion in her, the long habit of obedience, of humility, as well as agony of fear, spoke in her voice. "Spare the boy!" she whispered.

"You can't save him now," replied Tull, stridently.

Her head was bowing to the inevitable. She was grasping the truth, when suddenly there came, in inward constriction, a hardening of gentle forces within her breast. Like a steel bar it was, stiffening all that had been soft and weak in her. She felt a birth in her of something new and unintelligible. Once more her strained gaze sought the sage-slopes. Jane Withersteen loved that wild and purple wilderness. In times of sorrow it had been her strength, in happiness its beauty was her continual delight. In her extremity she found herself murmuring, "Whence cometh my help!" It was a prayer, as if forth from those lonely purple reaches and walls of red and clefts of blue might ride a fearless man, neither creed-bound nor creed-mad, who would hold up a restraining hand in the faces of her ruthless people.

The restless movements of Tull's men suddenly quieted down. Then followed a low whisper, a rustle, a sharp exclamation.

"Look!" said one, pointing to the west.

"A rider!"

Jane Withersteen wheeled and saw a horseman, silhouetted against the western sky, coming riding out of the sage. He had ridden down from the left, in the golden glare of the sun, and had been unobserved till close at hand. An answer to her prayer!

"Do you know him? Does anyone know him?" questioned Tull, hurriedly.

His men looked and looked, and one by one shook their heads.

"He's come from far," said one.

"Thet's a fine hoss," said another.

"A strange rider."

"Huh! He wears black leather," added a fourth.

With a wave of his hand, enjoining silence, Tull stepped forward in such a way that he concealed Venters.

The rider reined in his mount, and with a lithe forward-slipping action appeared to reach the ground in one long step. It was a peculiar movement in its quickness and inasmuch that while performing it the rider did not swerve in the slightest from a square front to the ground before him.

"Look!" hoarsely whispered one of Tull's companions. "He packs two black-butted guns—low down—they're hard to see—black agin them black chaps."

"A gunman!" whispered another. "Fellers, careful now about movin' your hands."

The stranger's slow approach might have been a mere leisurely manner of gait or the cramped short steps of a rider unused to walking; yet, as well, it could have been the guarded advance of one who took no chances with men.

"Hello, stranger!" called Tull. No welcome was in this greeting, only a gruff curiosity.

The rider responded with a curt nod. The wide brim of a black sombrero cast a dark shade over his face. For a moment he closely regarded Tull and his comrades, and then halting in his slow walk, he seemed to relax.

"Evenin', ma'am," he said to Jane, and removed his sombrero with quaint grace.

Jane, greeting him, looked up into a face that she trusted instinctively and which riveted her attention. It had all the characteristics of the range riders—the leanness, the red burn of the sun, and the set changelessness that came from years of silence and solitude. But it was not these which held her—rather the intensity of his gaze, a strained wearinesss, a piercing wistfulness of keen, gray sight, as if the man was forever looking for that which he never found. Jane's subtle woman's intuition, even in that brief instant, felt a sadness, a hungering, a secret.

"Jane Withersteen, ma'am?" he inquired.

"Yes," she replied.

"The water here is yours?"

"Yes."

"May I water my horse?"

"Certainly. There's the trough."

"But mebbe if you knew who I was—" He hesitated, with his glance on the listening men. "Mebbe you wouldn't let me water him—though I ain't askin' none for myself."

"Stranger, it doesn't matter who you are. Water your horse. And if you are thirsty and hungry come into my house."

"Thanks, ma'am. I can't accept for myself—but for my tired horse—"

Trampling of hoofs interrupted the rider. More restless movements on the part of Tull's men broke up the little circle, exposing the prisoner Venters.

"Mebbe I've kind of hindered somethin'—for a few moments, perhaps?" inquired the rider.

"Yes," replied Jane Withersteen, with a throb in her voice.

She felt the drawing power of his eyes; and then she saw him look at the bound Venters, and at the men who held him, and their leader.

"In this here country all the rustlers an' thieves an' cutthroats an' gunthrowers an' all-round no-good men jest happen to be Gentiles. Ma'am, which of the no-good class does that young feller belong to?"

"He belongs to none of them. He's an honest boy."

"You *know* that, ma'am?"

"Yes—yes."

"Then what has he done to get tied up that way?"

His clear and distinct question, meant for Tull as well as for Jane Withersteen, stilled the restlessness and brought a momentary silence.

"Ask him," replied Jane, her voice rising high.

The rider stepped away from her, moving out with the same slow, measured stride in which he had approached, and the fact that his action placed her wholly to one side, and him no nearer to Tull and his men, had a penetrating significance.

"Young feller, speak up," he said to Venters.

"Here, stranger, this's none of your mix," began Tull. "Don't try any interference. You've been asked to drink and eat. That's more than you'd have got in any other village on the Utah border. Water your horse and be on your way."

"Easy—easy—I ain't interferin' yet," replied the rider. The tone of his voice had undergone a change. A different man had spoken. Where, in addressing Jane he had been mild and gentle, now, with his first speech to Tull, he was dry, cool, biting. "I've jest stumbled onto a queer deal. Seven Mormons all packin' guns an' a Gentile tied with a rope, an' a woman who swears by his honesty! Queer, ain't that?"

"Queer or not, it's none of your business," retorted Tull.

"Where I was raised a woman's word was law. I 'ain't quite outgrowed that yet."

Tull fumed between amaze and anger.

"Meddler, we have a law here something different from a woman's whim—Mormon law! . . . Take care you don't transgress it."

"To hell with your Mormon law!"

The deliberate speech marked the rider's further change, this time from kindly interest to an awakening menace. It produced a transformation in Tull and his companions. The leader gasped and staggered backward at a blasphemous affront to an institution he held most sacred. The man Jerry, holding the horses, dropped the bridles and froze in his tracks. Like posts the other men stood, watchful-eyed, arms hanging rigid, all waiting.

"Speak up now, young man. What have you done to be roped that way?"

"It's a damned outrage!" burst out Venters. "I've done no wrong. I've offended this Mormon elder by being a friend to that woman."

"Ma'am, is it true—what he says?" asked the rider of Jane; but his quiveringly alert eyes never left the little knot of quiet men.

"True? Yes, perfectly true," she answered.

"Well, young man, it seems to me that bein' a friend to such a woman would be what you wouldn't want to help an' couldn't help. . . . What's to be done to you for it?"

"They intend to whip me. You know what that means—in Utah!"

"I reckon," replied the rider, slowly.

With his gray glance cold on the Mormons, with the restive bit-champing of the horses, with Jane failing to repress her mounting agitation, with Venters standing pale and still, the tension of the moment tightened. Tull broke the spell with a laugh, a laugh without mirth, a laugh that was only a sound betraying fear.

"Come on, men!" he called.

Jane Withersteen turned again to the rider.

"Stranger, can you do nothing to save Venters?"

"Ma'am, you ask me to save him—from your own people?"

"Ask you? I beg of you!"

"But you don't dream who you're askin'."

"Oh, sir, I pray you—save him!"

"These are Mormons, an' I . . ."

"At—at any cost—save him. For I—I care for him!"

Tull snarled. "You lovesick fool! Tell your secrets. There'll be a way to teach you what you've never learned. . . . Come men, out of here!"

"Mormon, the young man stays," said the rider.

Like a shot his voice halted Tull.

"What!"

"He stays."

"Who'll keep him? He's my prisoner!" cried Tull, hotly. "Stranger, again I tell you—don't mix here. You've meddled enough Go your way now or—"

"Listen! . . . He stays."

Absolute certainty, beyond any shadow of doubt breathed in the rider's low voice.

"Who are you? We are seven here."

The rider dropped his sombrero and made a rapid movement, singular in that it left him somewhat crouched, arms bent and stiff, with the big black gun-sheaths swung round to the fore.

"Lassiter!"

It was Venters's wondering, thrilling cry that bridged the fateful connection between the rider's singular position and the dreaded name.

Tull put out a groping hand. The life of his eyes dulled to the gloom with which men of his fear saw the approach of death. But death, while it hovered over him, did not descend, for the rider waited for the twitching fingers, the downward flash of hand that did not come. Tull, gathering himself together, turned to the horses, attended by his pale comrades.

❧2❧

COTTONWOODS

VENTERS appeared too deeply moved to speak the gratitude his face expressed. And Jane turned upon the rescuer and gripped his hands. Her smiles and tears seemingly dazed him. Presently, as something like calmness returned, she went to Lassiter's weary horse.

"I will water him myself," she said, and she led the horse to a trough under a huge old cottonwood. With nimble fingers she loosened the bridle and removed the bit. The horse snorted and bent his head. The trough was of solid stone, hollowed out, moss-covered and green and wet and cool, and the clear brown water that fed it spouted and splashed from a wooden pipe.

"He has brought you far today?"

"Yes, ma'am, a matter of over sixty miles, mebbe seventy."

"A long ride—a ride that— Ah, he is blind!"

"Yes, ma'am," replied Lassiter.

"What blinded him?"

"Some men once roped an' tied him, an' then held white-iron close to his eyes."

"Oh! Men? You mean devils. . . . Were they your enemies—Mormons?"

"Yes, ma'am."

"To take revenge on a horse! Lassiter, the men of my creed are unnaturally cruel. To my everlasting sorrow I confess it. They have been driven, hated, scourged till their hearts have hardened. But we women hope and pray for the time when our men will soften."

"Beggin' your pardon, ma'am—that time will never come."

"Oh, it will! . . . Lassiter, do you think Mormon women wicked? Has your hand been against them, too?"

"No. I believe Mormon women are the best and noblest, the most long-sufferin', and the blindest, unhappiest women on earth."

"Ah!" She gave him a grave, thoughtful look. "Then you will break bread with me?"

Lassiter had no ready response, and he uneasily shifted his weight from one leg to another, and turned his sombrero round and round in his hands. "Ma'am," he began, presently, "I reckon your kindness of heart makes you overlook things. Perhaps I ain't well known hereabouts, but

13

back up North there's Mormons who'd rest uneasy in their graves at the idea of me sittin' to table with you."

"I dare say. But—will you do it, anyway?" she asked.

"Mebbe you have a brother or relative who might drop in an' be offended, an' I wouldn't want to—"

"I've not a relative in Utah that I know of. There's no one with a right to question my actions." She turned smilingly to Venters. "You will come in, Bern, and Lassiter will come in. We'll eat and be merry while we may."

"I'm only wonderin' if Tull an' his men'll raise a storm down in the village," said Lassiter, in his last weakening stand.

"Yes, he'll raise the storm—after he has prayed," replied Jane. "Come."

She led the way, with the bridle of Lassiter's horse over her arm. They entered a grove and walked down a wide path shaded by great low-branching cottonwoods. The last rays of the setting sun sent golden bars through the leaves. The grass was deep and rich, welcome contrast to sage-tired eyes. Twittering quail darted across the path, and from a tree-top somewhere a robin sang its evening song, and on the still air floated the freshness and murmur of flowing water.

The home of Jane Withersteen stood in a circle of cottonwoods, and was a flat, long, red-stone structure with a covered court in the center through which flowed a lively stream of amber-colored water. In the massive blocks of stone and heavy timbers and solid doors and shutters showed the hand of a man who had built against pillage and time; and in the flowers and mosses lining the stone-bedded stream, in the bright colors of rugs and blankets on the court floor, and the cozy corner with hammock and books, and the clean-linened table, showed the grace of a daughter who lived for happiness and the day at hand.

Jane turned Lassiter's horse loose in the thick grass. "You will want him to be near you," she said, "or I'd have him taken to the alfalfa fields." At her call appeared women who began at once to bustle about, hurrying to and fro, setting the table. Then Jane, excusing herself, went within.

She passed through a huge low-ceiled chamber, like the inside of a fort, and into a smaller one where a bright wood-fire blazed in an old open fireplace, and from this into her own room. It had the same comfort as was manifested in the homelike outer court; moreover, it was warm and rich in soft hues.

Seldom did Jane Withersteen enter her room without looking into her mirror. She knew she loved the reflection of that beauty which since early childhood she had never been allowed to forget. Her relatives and friends, and later a horde of Mormon and Gentile suitors, had fanned the flame of natural vanity in her. So that at twenty-eight she scarcely thought at all of her wonderful influence for good in the little community where her father had left her practically its beneficent landlord; but cared most for the dream and the assurance and the allurement of her beauty. This time, however, she gazed into her glass with more than the usual happy motive, without the usual slight conscious smile. For she was thinking of more than the desire to be fair in her own eyes, in those of her friend; she wondered if she were to seem fair in the eyes of this Lassiter, this man whose name had crossed the long, wild brakes of stone and plains of sage, this gentle-voiced, sad-faced man who was a hater and a killer of Mormons. It was not now her usual half-conscious vain obsession that actuated her as she hurriedly changed her riding-dress to one of white, and then looked long at the stately form with its gracious contours, at the fair face with its strong chin and full firm lips, at the dark-blue, proud, and passionate eyes.

"If by some means I can keep him here a few days, a week—he will never kill another Mormon," she mused. "Lassiter! . . . I shudder when I think of that name, of him. But when I look at the man I forget who he is—I almost like him. I remember only that he saved Bern. He has suffered. I wonder what it was—did he love a Mormon woman once? How splendidly he championed us poor misunderstood souls! Somehow he knows—much."

Jane Withersteen joined her guests and bade them to her board. Dismissing her woman, she waited upon them with her own hands. It was a bountiful supper and a strange company. On her right sat the ragged and half-starved Venters; and though blind eyes could have seen what he counted for in the sum of her happiness, yet he looked the gloomy outcast his allegiance had made him, and about him there was the shadow of the ruin presaged by Tull. On her left sat the black-leather-garbed Lassiter looking like a man in a dream. Hunger was not with him, nor composure, nor speech, and when he twisted in frequent unquiet movements the heavy guns that he had not removed knocked against the table-legs. If it had been otherwise possible to forget the presence of Lassiter those telling little jars would have rendered it unlikely. And Jane Withersteen talked and smiled and laughed with all the dazzling play of lips and eyes that a beautiful, daring woman could summon to her purpose.

When the meal ended, and the men pushed back their chairs, she leaned closer to Lassiter and looked square into his eyes.

"Why did you come to Cottonwoods?"

Her question seemed to break a spell. The rider arose as if he had just remembered himself and had tarried longer than his wont.

"Ma'am, I have hunted all over southern Utah and Nevada for—somethin'. An' through your name I learned where to find it—here in Cottonwoods."

"My name! Oh, I remember. You did know my name when you spoke first. Well, tell me where you heard it and from whom?"

"At the little village—Glaze, I think it's called—some fifty miles or more west of here. An' I heard it from a Gentile, a rider who said you'd know where to tell me to find—"

"What?" she demanded, imperiously, as Lassiter broke off.

"Milly Erne's grave," he answered low, and the words came with a wrench.

Venters wheeled in his chair to regard Lassiter in amazement, and Jane slowly raised herself in white, still wonder.

"Milly Erne's grave?" she echoed, in a whisper. "What do you know of Milly Erne, my best-beloved friend—who died in my arms? What were you to her?"

"Did I claim to be anythin'?" he inquired. "I know people—relatives—who have long wanted to know where she's buried. That's all."

"Relatives? She never spoke of relatives, except a brother who was shot in Texas. Lassiter, Milly Erne's grave is in a secret burrying-ground on my property."

"Will you take me there? . . . You'll be offendin' Mormons worse than by breakin' bread with me."

"Indeed yes, but I'll do it. Only we must go unseen. Tomorrow, perhaps."

"Thank you, Jane Withersteen," replied the rider, and he bowed to her and stepped backward out of the court.

"Will you not stay—sleep under my roof?" she asked.

"No, ma'am, an' thanks again. I never sleep indoors. An' even if I did there's that gatherin' storm in the village below. No, no. I'll go to the sage. I hope you won't suffer none for your kindness to me."

"Lassiter," said Venters, with a half-bitter laugh, "my bed, too, is the sage. Perhaps we may meet out there."

"Mebbe so. But the sage is wide an' I won't be near. Good night."

At Lassiter's low whistle the black horse whinnied, and carefully picked his blind way out of the grove. The rider did not bridle him, but walked beside him, leading him by touch of hand, and together they passed slowly into the shade of the cottonwoods.

"Jane, I must be off soon," said Venters. "Give me my guns. If I'd had my guns—"

"Either my friend or the Elder of my church would be lying dead," she interposed.

"Tull would be—surely."

"Oh, you fierce-blooded, savage youth! Can't I teach you forbearance, mercy? Bern, it's divine to forgive your enemies. 'Let not the sun go down upon thy wrath.' "

"Hush! Talk to me no more of mercy or religion—after today. Today this strange coming of Lassiter left me still a man, and now I'll die a man! . . . Give me my guns."

Silently she went into the house, to return with a heavy cartridge-belt and gun-filled sheath and a long rifle; these she handed to him, and as he buckled on the belt she stood before him in silent eloquence.

"Jane," he said, in gentler voice, "don't look so. I'm not going out to murder your churchman. I'll try to avoid him and all his men. But can't you see I've reached the end of my rope? Jane, you're a wonderful woman. Never was there a woman so unselfish and good. Only you're blind in one way. . . . Listen!"

From behind the grove came the clicking sound of horses in rapid trot.

"Some of your riders," he continued. "It's getting time for the night shift. Let us go out to the bench in the grove and talk there."

It was still daylight in the open, but under the spreading cottonwoods shadows were obscuring the lanes. Venters drew Jane off from one of these into a shrub-lined trail, just wide enough for the two to walk abreast, and in a roundabout way led her far from the house to a knoll on the edge of the grove. Here in a secluded nook was a bench from which, through an opening in the treetops, could be seen the sage-slope and the wall of rock and the dim lines of canyons. Jane had not spoken since Venters had shocked her with his first harsh speech; but all the way she had clung to his arm, and now, as he stopped and laid his rifle against the bench, she still clung to him.

"Jane, I'm afraid I must leave you."

"Bern!" she cried.

"Yes, it looks that way. My position is not a happy one—I can't feel right—I've lost all—"

"I'll give you anything you—"

"Listen, please. When I say loss I don't mean what you think. I mean loss of goodwill, good name—that which would have enabled me to stand up in this village without bitterness. Well, it's too late. . . . Now, as to the future, I think you'd do best to give me up. Tull is implacable. You ought to see from his intention today that— But you can't see. Your blindness—your damned religion! . . . Jane, forgive me—I'm sore within and something rankles. Well, I fear that invisible hand will turn its hidden work to your ruin."

"Invisible hand? Bern!"

"I mean your bishop." Venters said it deliberately and would not release her as she started back. "He's the law. The edict went forth to ruin me. Well, look at me! It'll now go forth to compel you to the will of the church."

"You wrong Bishop Dyer. Tull is hard, I know. But then he has been in love with me for years."

"Oh, your faith and your excuses! You can't see what I know—and if you did see it you'd not admit it to save your life. That's the Mormon of you. These elders and bishops will do absolutely any deed to go on building up the power and wealth of their church, their empire. Think of what they've done to the Gentiles here, to me—think of Milly Erne's fate!"

"What do you know of her story?"

"I know enough—all, perhaps, except the name of the Mormon who brought her here. But I must stop this kind of talk."

She pressed his hand in response. He helped her to a seat beside him on the bench. And he respected a silence that he divined was full of woman's deep emotion, beyond his understanding.

It was the moment when the last ruddy rays of the sunset brightened momentarily before yielding to twilight. And for Venters the outlook before him was in some sense similar to a feeling of his future, and with searching eyes he studied the beautiful purple, barren waste of sage. Here was the unknown and the perilous. The whole scene impressed Venters as a wild, austere, and mighty manifestation of nature. And as it somehow reminded him of his prospect in life, so it suddenly resembled the woman near him, only in her there were greater beauty and peril, a mystery more unsolvable, and something nameless that numbed his heart and dimmed his eye.

"Look! A rider!" exclaimed Jane, breaking the silence. "Can that be Lassiter?"

Venters moved his glance once more to the west. A horseman showed dark on the skyline, then merged into the color of the sage.

"It might be. But I think not—that fellow was coming in. One of your riders, more likely. Yes, I see him clearly now. And there's another."

"I see them, too."

"Jane, your riders seem as many as the bunches of sage. I ran into five yesterday 'way down near the trail to Deception Pass. They were with the white herd."

"You still go to that canyon? Bern, I wish you wouldn't. Oldring and his rustlers live somewhere down there."

"Well, what of that?"

"Tull has already hinted of your frequent trips into Deception Pass."

"I know." Venters uttered a short laugh. "He'll make a rustler of me next. But, Jane, there's no water for fifty miles after I leave here, and that nearest is in the canyon. I must drink and water my horse. There! I see more riders. They are going out."

"The red herd is on the slope, toward the Pass."

Twilight was fast falling. A group of horsemen crossed the dark line of low ground to become more distinct as they climbed the slope. The silence broke to a clear call from an incoming rider, and, almost like the peal of a hunting-horn, floated back the answer. The outgoing riders moved swiftly, came sharply into sight as they topped a ridge to show wild and black above the horizon, and then passed down, dimming into the purple of the sage.

"I hope they don't meet Lassiter," said Jane.

"So do I," replied Venters. "By this time the riders of the night shift know what happened today. But Lassiter will likely keep out of their way."

"Bern, who is Lassiter? He's only a name to me—a terrible name."

"Who is he? I don't know, Jane. Nobody I ever met knows him. He talks a little like a Texan, like Milly Erne. Did you note that?"

"Yes. How strange of him to know of her! And she lived here ten years and has been dead two. Bern, what do you know of Lassiter? Tell me what he has done—why you spoke of him to Tull—threatening to become another Lassiter yourself?"

"Jane, I only heard things, rumors, stories, most of which I disbelieved. At Glaze his name was known, but none of the riders or ranchers I knew there ever met him. At Stone Bridge I never heard him mentioned. But at Sterling and villages north of there he was spoken of often. I've never been in a village which he had been known to visit. There were many conflicting stories about him and his doings. Some said he had shot up this and that Mormon village, and others denied it. I'm inclined to believe he has, and you know how Mormons hide the truth. But there was one feature about Lassiter upon which all agree—that he was what riders in this country call a gunman. He's a man with marvelous quickness and accuracy in the use of a Colt. And now that I've seen him I know more. Lassiter was born without fear. I watched him with eyes which saw him my friend. I'll never forget the moment I recognized him from what had been told me of his crouch before the draw. It was then I yelled his name. I believe that yell saved Tull's life. At any rate, I know this, between Tull and death then there was not the breadth of the littlest hair. If he or any of his men had moved a finger downward . . ."

Venters left his meaning unspoken, but at the suggestion Jane shuddered.

The pale afterglow in the west darkened with the merging of twilight into night. The sage now spread out black and gloomy. One dim star glimmered in the southwest sky. The sound of trotting horses had ceased, and there was silence broken only by a faint, dry pattering of cottonwood leaves in the soft night wind.

Into this peace and calm suddenly broke the high-keyed yelp of a coyote, and from far off in the darkness came the faint answering note of a trailing mate.

"Hello! the sage-dogs are barking," said Venters.

"I don't like to hear them," replied Jane. "At night, sometimes, when I lie awake, listening to the long mourn or breaking bark or wild howl, I think of you asleep somewhere in the sage, and my heart aches."

"Jane, you couldn't listen to sweeter music, nor could I have a better bed."

"Just think! Men like Lassiter and you have no home, no comfort, no rest, no place to lay your weary heads. Well! . . . Let us be patient. Tull's anger may cool, and time may help us. You might do some service to the village—who can tell? Suppose you discovered the long-unknown hiding-place of Oldring and his band, and told it to my riders? That would disarm Tull's ugly hints and put you in favor. For years my riders have trailed the tracks of stolen cattle. You know as well as I how dearly we've paid for our ranges in this wild country. Oldring drives our cattle down into that network of deceiving canyons, and somewhere far to the north or east he drives them up and out to Utah markets. If you will spend time in Deception Pass, try to find the trails."

"Jane, I've thought of that. I'll try."

"I must go now. And it hurts, for now I'll never be sure of seeing you again. But tomorrow, Bern?"

"Tomorrow surely. I'll watch for Lassiter and ride in with him."

"Good night."

Then she left him and moved away, a white, gliding shape that soon vanished in the shadows.

Venters waited until the faint slam of a door assured him she had reached the house; and then, taking up his rifle, he noiselessly slipped through the bushes, down the knoll, and on under the dark trees to the edge of the grove. The sky was now turning from gray to blue: stars had begun to lighten the earlier blackness; and from the wide flat sweep before him blew a cool wind, fragrant with the breath of sage. Keeping close to the edge of the cottonwoods, he went swiftly and silently westward. The grove was long, and he had not reached the end when he heard something that brought him to a halt. Low padded thuds told him horses were coming his way. He sank down in the gloom, waiting, listening. Much before he had expected, judging from sound, to his amazement he descried horsemen near at hand. They were riding along the border of the sage, and instantly he knew the hoofs of the horses were muffled. Then the pale starlight afforded him indistinct sight of the riders. But his eyes were keen and used to the dark, and by peering closely he recognized the huge bulk and black-bearded visage of Oldring and the lithe, supple form of the rustler's lieutenant, a masked rider. They passed on; the darkness swallowed them. Then, farther out on the sage, a dark, compact body of horsemen went by, almost without sound, almost like specters, and they, too, melted into the night.

⁊3⁊

AMBER SPRING

N O UNUSUAL circumstance was it for Oldring and some of his men
to visit Cottonwoods in the broad light of day, but for him to prowl
about in the dark with the hoofs of his horses muffled meant that mischief
was brewing. Moreover, to Venters the presence of the masked rider with
Oldring seemed especially ominous. For about this man there was mystery: he seldom rode through the village, and when he did ride through, it
was swiftly; riders seldom met him by day on the sage, but wherever he
rode there always followed deeds as dark and mysterious as the mask he
wore. Oldring's band did not confine themselves to the rustling of cattle.

Venters lay low in the shade of the cottonwoods, pondering this
chance meeting, and not for many moments did he consider it safe to
move on. Then, with sudden impulse, he turned the other way and went
back along the grove. When he reached the path leading to Jane's home
he decided to go down to the village. So he hurried onward, with quick
soft steps. Once beyond the grove he entered the one and only street. It
was wide, lined with tall poplars, and under each row of trees, inside the
footpath, were ditches where ran the water from Jane Withersteen's
spring.

Between the trees twinkled lights of cottage candles, and far down
flared bright windows of the village stores. When Venters got closer to
these he saw knots of men standing together in earnest conversation. The
usual lounging on the corners and benches and steps was not in evidence.
Keeping in the shadow, Venters went closer and closer until he could hear
voices. But he could not distinguish what was said. He recognized many
Mormons, and looked hard for Tull and his men, but looked in vain.
Venters concluded that the rustlers had not passed along the village
street. No doubt these earnest men were discussing Lassiter's coming. But
Venters felt positive that Tull's intention toward himself that day had not
been and would not be revealed.

So Venters, seeing there was little for him to learn, began retracing his
steps. The church was dark, Bishop Dyer's home next to it was also dark,
and likewise Tull's cottage. Upon almost any night at this hour there
would be lights here, and Venters marked the unusual omission.

As he was about to pass out of the street to skirt the grove, he once
more slunk down at the sound of trotting horses. Presently he descried

two mounted men riding toward him. He hugged the shadow of a tree. Again the starlight, brighter now, aided him, and he made out Tull's stalwart figure, and beside him the short, froglike shape of the rider Jerry. They were silent, and they rode on to disappear.

Venters went his way with busy, gloomy mind, revolving events of the day, trying to reckon those brooding in the night. His thoughts overwhelmed him. Up in that dark grove dwelt a woman who had been his friend. And he skulked about her home, gripping a gun stealthily as an Indian, a man without place or people or purpose. Above her hovered the shadow of grim, hidden, secret power. No queen could have given more royally out of a bounteous store than Jane Withersteen gave her people, and likewise to those unfortunates whom her people hated. She asked only the divine right of all women—freedom; to love and to live as her heart willed. And yet prayer and her hope were vain.

"For years I've seen a storm clouding over her and the village of Cottonwoods," muttered Venters, as he strode on. "Soon it'll burst. I don't like the prospect." That night the villagers whispered in the street —and night-riding rustlers muffled horses—and Tull was at work in secret —and out there in the sage hid a man who meant something terrible— Lassiter!

Venters passed the black cottonwoods, and, entering the sage, climbed the gradual slope. He kept his direction in line with a western star. From time to time he stopped to listen and heard only the usual familiar bark of coyote and sweep of wind and rustle of sage. Presently a low jumble of rocks loomed up darkly somewhat to his right, and, turning that way, he whistled softly. Out of the rocks glided a dog that leaped and whined about him. He climbed over rough, broken rock, picking his way carefully, and then went down. Here it was darker, and sheltered from the wind. A white object guided him. It was another dog, and this one was asleep, curled up between a saddle and a pack. The animal awoke and thumped his tail in greeting. Venters placed the saddle for a pillow, rolled in his blankets, with his face upward to the stars. The white dog snuggled close to him. The other whined and pattered a few yards to the rise of ground and there crouched on guard. And in that wild covert Venters shut his eyes under the great white stars and intense vaulted blue, bitterly comparing their loneliness to his own, and fell asleep.

When he awoke, day had dawned and all about him was bright steelgray. The air had a cold tang. Arising, he greeted the fawning dogs and stretched his cramped body, and then, gathering together bunches of dead sage sticks, he lighted a fire. Strips of dried beef held to the blaze for a moment served him and the dogs. He drank from a canteen. There was nothing else in his outfit; he had grown used to a scant fare. Then he sat over the fire, palms outspread, and waited. Waiting had been his chief occupation for months, and he scarcely knew what he waited for, unless it was the passing of the hours. But now he sensed action in the immediate present; the day promised another meeting with Lassiter and Jane, perhaps news of the rustlers; on the morrow he meant to take the trail to Deception Pass.

And while he waited he talked to his dogs. He called them Ring and Whitie; they were sheepdogs, half collie, half deerhound, superb in build, perfectly trained. It seemed that in his fallen fortunes these dogs understood the nature of their value to him, and governed their affection and faithfulness accordingly. Whitie watched him with somber eyes of love, and Ring, crouched on the little rise of ground above, kept tireless guard. When the sun rose, the white dog took the place of the other, and Ring went to sleep at his master's feet.

By and by Venters rolled up his blankets and tied them and his meager pack together, then climbed out to look for his horse. He saw him, presently, a little way off in the sage, and went to fetch him. In that country, where every rider boasted of a fine mount and was eager for a race, where thoroughbreds dotted the wonderful grazing ranges, Venters rode a horse that was sad proof of his misfortunes.

Then, with his back against a stone, Venters faced the east, and, stick in hand and idle blade, he waited. The glorious sunlight filled the valley with purple fire. Before him, to left, to right, waving, rolling, sinking, rising, like low swells of a purple sea, stretched the sage. Out of the grove of cottonwoods, a green patch on the purple, gleamed the dull red of Jane Withersteen's old stone house. And from there extended the wide green of the village gardens and orchards marked by the graceful poplars; and farther down shone the deep, dark richness of the alfalfa fields. Numberless red and black and white dots speckled the sage, and these were cattle and horses.

So, watching and waiting, Venters let the time wear away. At length he saw a horse rise above a ridge, and he knew it to be Lassiter's black. Climbing to the highest rock, so that he would show against the skyline, he stood and waved his hat. The almost instant turning of Lassiter's horse attested to the quickness of that rider's eye. Then Venters climbed down, saddled his horse, tied on his pack, and, with a word to his dogs, was about to ride out to meet Lassiter, when he concluded to wait for him there, on higher ground, where the outlook was commanding.

It had been long since Venters had experienced friendly greeting from a man. Lassiter's warmed in him something that had grown cold from neglect. And when he had returned it, with a strong grip of the iron hand that held his, and met the gray eyes, he knew that Lassiter and he were to be friends.

"Venters, let's talk awhile before we go down there," said Lassiter, slipping his bridle. "I ain't in no hurry. Them's sure fine dogs you've got." With a rider's eye he took in the points of Venters's horse, but did not speak his thought. "Well, did anythin' come off after I left you last night?"

Venters told him about the rustlers.

"I was snug hid in the sage," replied Lassiter, "an' didn't see or hear no one. Oldrin's got a high hand here, I reckon. It's no news up in Utah how he holes in canyons an' leaves no track." Lassiter was silent a moment. "Me an' Oldrin' wasn't exactly strangers some years back when he drove cattle into Bostil's Ford, at the head of the Rio Virgin. But he got harassed there an' now he drives someplace else."

"Lassiter, you knew him? Tell me, is he Mormon or Gentile?"

"I can't say. I've knowed Mormons who pretended to be Gentiles."

"No Mormon ever pretended that unless he was a rustler," declared Venters.

"Mebbe so."

"It's a hard country for anyone, but hardest for Gentiles. Did you ever know or hear of a Gentile prospering in a Mormon community?"

"I never did."

"Well, I want to get out of Utah. I've a mother living in Illinois. I want to go home. It's eight years now."

The older man's sympathy moved Venters to tell his story. He had left Quincy, run off to seek his fortune in the gold fields, had never gotten any farther than Salt Lake City, wandered here and there as helper, teamster, shepherd, and drifted southward over the divide and across the barrens and up the rugged plateau through the passes to the last border settlements. Here he became a rider of the sage, had stock of his own, and for a time prospered, until chance threw him in the employ of Jane Withersteen.

"Lassiter, I needn't tell you the rest."

"Well, it'd be no news to me. I know Mormons. I've seen their women's strange love an' patience an' sacrifice an' silence an' what I call madness for their idea of God. An' over against that I've seen the tricks of the men. They work hand in hand, all together, an' in the dark. No man can hold out against them, unless he takes to packin' guns. For Mormons are slow to kill. That's the only good I ever seen in their religion. Venters, take this from me, these Mormons ain't just right in their minds. Else could a Mormon marry one woman when he already had a wife, an' call it duty?"

"Lassiter, you think as I think," returned Venters.

"How'd it come then that you never threw a gun on Tull or some of them?" inquired the rider, curiously.

"Jane pleaded with me, begged me to be patient, to overlook. She even took my guns from me. I lost all before I knew it," replied Venters, with the red color in his face. "But, Lassiter, listen. Out of the wreck I saved a Winchester, two Colts, and plenty of shells. I packed these down into Deception Pass. There, almost every day for six months, I have practiced with my rifle till the barrel burnt my hands. Practiced the draw—the firing of a Colt, hour after hour!"

"Now that's interestin' to me," said Lassiter, with a quick uplift of his head and a concentration of his gray gaze on Venters. "Could you throw a gun before you began that practisin'?"

"Yes. And now . . ." Venters made a lightning-swift movement.

Lassiter smiled, and then his bronzed eyelids narrowed till his eyes seemed mere gray slits. "You'll kill Tull!" He did not question; he affirmed.

"I promised Jane Withersteen I'd try to avoid Tull. I'll keep my word. But sooner or later Tull and I will meet. As I feel now, if he even looks at me I'll draw!"

"I reckon so. There'll be hell down there, presently." He paused a moment and flicked a sage-brush with his quirt. "Venters, seein' as you're considerable worked up, tell me Milly Erne's story."

Venters's agitation stilled to the trace of suppressed eagerness in Lassiter's query.

"Milly Erne's story? Well, Lassiter, I'll tell you what I know. Milly Erne had been in Cottonwoods years when I first arrived there, and most of what I tell you happened before my arrival. I got to know her pretty well. She was a slip of a woman, and crazy on religion. I conceived an idea that I never mentioned—I thought she was at heart more Gentile than Mormon. But she passed as a Mormon, and certainly she had the Mormon woman's locked lips. You know, in every Mormon village there are women who seem mysterious to us, but about Milly there was more than the ordinary mystery. When she came to Cottonwoods she had a beautiful little girl whom she loved passionately. Milly was not known openly in Cottonwoods as a Mormon wife. That she really was a Mormon wife I have no doubt. Perhaps the Mormon's other wife or wives would not acknowledge Milly. Such things happen in these villages. Mormon wives wear yokes, but they get jealous. Well, whatever had brought Milly to this country—love or madness of religion—she repented of it. She gave up teaching the village school. She quit the church. And she began to fight Mormon upbringing for her baby girl. Then the Mormons put on the screws—slowly, as is their way. At last the child disappeared. Lost, was the report. The child was stolen, I know that. So do you. That wrecked Milly Erne. But she lived on in hope. She became a slave. She worked her heart and soul and life out to get back her child. She never heard of it again. Then she sank. . . . I can see her now, a frail thing, so transparent you could almost look through her—white like ashes—and her eyes! . . . Her eyes have always haunted me. She had one real friend— Jane Withersteen. But Jane couldn't mend a broken heart, and Milly died."

For moments Lassiter did not speak, or turn his head.

"The man!" he exclaimed, presently, in husky accents.

"I haven't the slightest idea who the Mormon was," replied Venters, "nor has any Gentile in Cottonwoods."

"Does Jane Withersteen know?"

"Yes. But a red-hot running-iron couldn't burn that name out of her!"

Without further speech Lassiter started off, walking his horse, and Venters followed with his dogs. Half a mile down the slope they entered a luxuriant growth of willows, and soon came into an open space carpeted with grass like deep green velvet. The rushing of water and singing of birds filled their ears. Venters led his comrade to a shady bower and showed him Amber Spring. It was a magnificent outburst of clear, amber water pouring from a dark, stone-lined hole. Lassiter knelt and drank, lingered there to drink again. He made no comment, but Venters did not need words. Next to his horse a rider of the sage loved a spring. And this spring was the most beautiful and remarkable known to the upland riders of southern Utah. It was the spring that made old Withersteen a feudal lord and now enabled his daughter to return the toll which her father had exacted from the toilers of the sage.

The spring gushed forth in a swirling torrent, and leaped down joyously to make its swift way along a willow-skirted channel. Moss and ferns and lilies overhung its green banks. Except for the rough-hewn stones that held and directed the water, this willow thicket and glade had been left as nature had made it.

Below were artificial lakes, three in number, one above the other in banks of raised earth; and round about them rose the lofty green-foliaged shafts of poplar trees. Ducks dotted the glassy surface of the lakes; a blue heron stood motionless on a water-gate; kingfishers darted with shrieking flight along the shady banks; a white hawk sailed above; and from the trees and shrubs came the song of robins and cat-birds. It was all in strange contrast to the endless slopes of lonely sage and the wild rock environs beyond. Venters thought of the woman who loved the birds and the green of the leaves and the murmur of water.

Next on the slope, just below the third and largest lake, were corrals and a wide stone barn and open sheds and coops and pens. Here were clouds of dust, and cracking sounds of hoofs, and romping colts and hee-hawing burros. Neighing horses trampled to the corral fences. And from the little windows of the barn projected bobbing heads of bays and blacks and sorrels. When the two men entered the immense barnyard, from all around the din increased. This welcome, however, was not seconded by the several men and boys who vanished on sight.

Venters and Lassiter were turning toward the house when Jane appeared in the lane leading a horse. In riding-skirt and blouse she seemed to have lost some of her statuesque proportions, and looked more like a girl-rider than the mistress of Withersteen. She was bright smiling, and her greeting was warmly cordial.

"Good news," she announced. "I've been to the village. All is quiet. I expected—I don't know what. But there's no excitement. And Tull has ridden out on his way to Glaze."

"Tull gone?" inquired Venters, with surprise. He was wondering what could have taken Tull away. Was it to avoid another meeting with Lassiter that he went? Could it have any connection with the probable nearness of Oldring and his gang?

"Gone, yes, thank goodness," replied Jane. "Now I'll have peace for a while. Lassiter, I want you to see my horses. You are a rider, and you must be a judge of horseflesh. Some of mine have Arabian blood. My father got his best strain in Nevada from Indians who claimed their horses were bred down from the original stock left by the Spaniards."

"Well, ma'am, the one you've been ridin' takes my eye," said Lassiter, as he walked round the racy, clean-limbed, and fine-pointed roan.

"Where are the boys?" she asked, looking about. "Jerd, Paul, where are you? Here, bring out the horses."

The sound of dropping bars inside the barn was the signal for the horses to jerk their heads in the windows, to snort and stamp. Then they came pounding out of the door, a file of thoroughbreds, to plunge about the barnyard, heads and tails up, manes flying. They halted afar off, squared away to look, came slowly forward with whinnies for their mistress, and doubtful snorts for the strangers and their horses.

"Come—come—come," called Jane, holding out her hands. "Why Bells—Wrangle, where are your manners? Come, Black Star—come, Night. Ah, you beauties! My racers of the sage!"

Only two came up to her; those she called Night and Black Star. Venters never looked at them without delight. The first was soft dead black, the other glittering black, and they were perfectly matched in size, both being high and long-bodied, wide through the shoulders, with lithe, powerful legs. That they were a woman's pets showed in the gloss of skin, the fineness of mane. It showed, too, in the light of big eyes and the gentle reach of eagerness.

"I never seen their like," was Lassiter's encomium, "an' in my day I've seen a sight of horses. Now, ma'am, if you was wantin' to make a long an' fast ride across the sage—say to elope—"

Lassiter ended there with dry humor, yet behind that was meaning. Jane blushed and made arch eyes at him.

"Take care, Lassiter, I might think that a proposal," she replied, gaily. "It's dangerous to propose elopement to a Mormon woman. Well, I was expecting you. Now will be a good hour to show you Milly Erne's grave. The day-riders have gone, and the night-riders haven't come in. Bern, what do you make of that? Need I worry? You know I have to be made worry."

"Well, it's not usual for the night shift to ride in so late," replied Venters, slowly, and his glance sought Lassiter's. "Cattle are usually quiet after dark. Still, I've known even a coyote to stampede your white herd."

"I refuse to borrow trouble. Come," said Jane.

They mounted, and, with Jane in the lead, rode down the lane, and, turning off into a cattle trail, proceeded westward. Venters's dogs trotted behind them. On this side of the ranch the outlook was different from that on the other; the immediate foreground was rough and the sage more rugged and less colorful; there were no dark-blue lines of canyons to hold the eye, nor any uprearing rock walls. It was a long roll and slope into gray obscurity. Soon Jane left the trail and rode into the sage, and presently she dismounted and threw her bridle. The men did likewise. Then, on foot, they followed her, coming out at length on the rim of a low escarpment. She passed by several little ridges of earth to halt before a faintly defined mound. It lay in the shade of a sweeping sage-brush close to the edge of the promontory; and a rider could have jumped his horse over it without recognizing a grave.

"Here!"

She looked sad as she spoke, but she offered no explanation for the neglect of an unmarked, uncared-for grave. There was a little bunch of pale, sweet lavender daisies, doubtless planted there by Jane.

"I only come here to remember and to pray," she said. "But I leave no trail!"

A grave in the sage! How lonely this resting-place of Milly Erne! The cottonwoods or the alfalfa fields were not in sight, nor was there any rock or ridge or cedar to lend contrast to the monotony. Gray slopes, tinging the purple, barren and wild, with the wind waving the sage, swept away to the dim horizon.

Lassiter looked at the grave and then out into space. At that moment he seemed a figure of bronze.

Jane touched Venters's arm and led him back to the horses.

"Bern!" cried Jane, when they were out of hearing. "Suppose Lassiter were Milly's husband—the father of that little girl lost so long ago!"

"It might be, Jane. Let us ride on. If he wants to see us again he'll come."

So they mounted and rode out to the cattle trail and began to climb. From the height of the ridge, where they had started down, Venters looked back. He did not see Lassiter, but his glance, drawn irresistibly farther out on the gradual slope, caught sight of a moving cloud of dust.

"Hello, a rider!"

"Yes, I see," said Jane.

"That fellow's riding hard. Jane, there's something wrong."

"Oh yes, there must be. . . . How he rides!"

The horse disappeared in the sage, and then puffs of dust marked his course.

"He's short-cut on us—he's making straight for the corrals."

Venters and Jane galloped their steeds and reined in at the turning of the lane. This lane led down to the right of the grove. Suddenly into its lower entrance flashed a bay horse. Then Venters caught the fast rhythmic beat of pounding hoofs. Soon his keen eye recognized the swing of the rider in his saddle.

"It's Judkins, your Gentile rider!" he cried. "Jane, when Judkins rides like that it means hell!"

❖4❖

DECEPTION PASS

THE RIDER thundered up and almost threw his foam-flecked horse in the sudden stop. He was of giant form, and with fearless eyes.

"Judkins, you're all bloody!" cried Jane, in affright. "Oh, you've been shot!"

"Nothin' much, Miss Withersteen. I got a nick in the shoulder. I'm some wet an' the hoss's been throwin' lather, so all this ain't blood."

"What's up?" queried Venters, sharply.

"Rustlers sloped off with the red herd."

"Where are my riders?" demanded Jane.

"Miss Withersteen, I was alone all night with the herd. At daylight this mornin' the rustlers rode down. They began to shoot at me on sight. They chased me hard an' far, burnin' powder all the time, but I got away."

"Jud, they meant to kill you," declared Venters.

"Now I wonder," returned Judkins. "They wanted me bad. An' it ain't regular for rustlers to waste time chasin' one rider."

"Thank heaven you got away," said Jane. "But my riders—where are they?"

"I don't know. The night-riders weren't there last night when I rode down, an' this mornin' I met no day-riders."

"Judkins! Bern, they've been set upon—killed by Oldring's men!"

"I don't think so," replied Venters, decidedly. "Jane, your riders haven't gone out in the sage."

"Bern, what do you mean?" Jane Withersteen turned deathly pale.

"You remember what I said about the unseen hand?"

"Oh! . . . Impossible!"

"I hope so. But I fear—" Venters finished, with a shake of his head.

"Bern, you're bitter; but that's only natural. We'll wait to see what's happened to my riders. Judkins, come to the house with me. Your wound must be attended to."

"Jane, I'll find out where Oldring drives the herd," vowed Venters.

"No, no! Bern, don't risk it now—when the rustlers are in such shooting mood."

"I'm going. Jud, how many cattle in that red herd?"

"Twenty-five hundred head."

"Whew! What on earth can Oldring do with so many cattle? Why, a hundred head is a big steal. I've got to find out."

"Don't go," implored Jane.

"Bern, you want a hoss that can run. Miss Withersteen, if it's not too bold of me to advise, make him take a fast hoss or don't let him go."

"Yes, yes, Judkins. He must ride a horse that can't be caught. Which one—Black Star—Night?"

"Jane, I won't take either," said Venters, emphatically. "I wouldn't risk losing one of your favorites."

"Wrangle, then?"

"Thet's the hoss," replied Judkins. "Wrangle can outrun Black Star an' Night. You'd never believe it, Miss Withersteen, but I know. Wrangle's the biggest an' fastest hoss on the sage."

"Oh no, Wrangle can't beat Black Star. But, Bern, take Wrangle, if you will go. Ask Jerd for anything you need. Oh, be watchful, careful. . . . God speed you!"

She clasped his hand, turned quickly away, and went down the lane with the rider.

Venters rode to the barn, and, leaping off, shouted for Jerd. The boy came running. Venters sent him for meat, bread, and dried fruits, to be packed in saddle-bags. His own horse he turned loose into the nearest corral. Then he went for Wrangle. The giant sorrel had earned his name for a trait the opposite of amiability. He came readily out of the barn, but once in the yard he broke from Venters, and plunged about with ears laid back. Venters had to rope him, and then he kicked down a section of fence, stood on his hind legs, crashed down and fought the rope. Jerd returned to lend a hand.

"Wrangle don't git enough work," said Jerd, as the big saddle went on. "He's unruly when he's corralled, an' wants to run. Wait till he smells the sage!"

"Jerd, this horse is an iron-jawed devil. I never straddled him but once. Run? Say, he's swift as wind!"

When Venters's boot touched the stirrup the sorrel bolted, giving him the rider's flying mount. The swing of this fiery horse recalled to Venters days that were not really long past, when he rode into the sage as the leader of Jane Withersteen's riders. Wrangle pulled hard on a tight rein. He galloped out of the lane, down the shady border of the grove, and hauled up at the watering trough, where he pranced and champed his bit.

Venters got off and filled his canteen while the horse drank. The dogs, Ring and Whitie, came trotting up for their drink. Then Venters remounted and turned Wrangle toward the sage.

A wide, white trail wound away down the slope. One keen, sweeping glance told Venters that there was neither man nor horse nor steer within the limit of his vision, unless they were lying down in the sage. Ring loped in the lead and Whitie loped in the rear. Wrangle settled gradually into an easy swinging canter, and Venters's thoughts, now that the rush and flurry of the start were past, and the long miles stretched before him, reverted to a calm reckoning of late singular coincidences.

There was the night ride of Tull's, which, viewed in the light of subsequent events, had a look of his covert machinations; Oldring and his Masked Rider and his rustlers riding muffled horses; the report that Tull had ridden out that morning with his man Jerry on the trail to Glaze, the strange disappearance of Jane Withersteen's riders, the unusually determined attempt to kill the one Gentile still in her employ, an intention frustrated, no doubt, only by Judkins's magnificent riding on her racer, and lastly the driving of the red herd. These events, to Venters's color of mind, had a dark relationship. Remembering Jane's accusation of bitterness, he tried hard to put aside his rancor in judging Tull. But it was bitter knowledge that made him see the truth. He had felt the shadow of an unseen hand; he had watched till he saw its dim outline, and then he had traced it to a man's hate, to the rivalry of a Mormon Elder, to the power of a bishop, to the long, far-reaching arm of a terrible creed. That unseen hand had made its first move against Jane Withersteen. Her riders had been called in, leaving her without help to drive seven thousand head of cattle. But to Venters it seemed extraordinary that the power which had called in these riders had left so many cattle to be driven by rustlers and harried by wolves. For hand in glove with that power was an insatiate greed; they were one and the same.

"What can Oldring do with twenty-five hundred head of cattle?" muttered Venters. "Is he a Mormon? Did he meet Tull last night? It looks like a black plot to me. But Tull and his churchmen wouldn't ruin Jane Withersteen unless the church was to profit by that ruin. Where does Oldring come in? I'm going to find out about these things."

Wrangle did twenty-five miles in three hours and walked little of the way. When he had gotten warmed up he had been allowed to choose his own gait. The afternoon had well advanced when Venters struck the trail of the red herd and found where it had grazed the night before. Then Venters rested the horse and used his eyes. Near at hand were a cow and a calf and several yearlings, and farther out in the sage some straggling steers. He caught a glimpse of coyotes skulking near the cattle. The slow, sweeping gaze of the rider failed to find other living things within the field of sight. The sage about him was breast-high to his horse, oversweet with its warm, fragrant breath, gray where it waved to the light, darker where

the wind left it still, and beyond the wonderful haze-purple lent by distance. Far across that wide waste began the slow lift of uplands through
which Deception Pass cut its tortuous many-canyoned way.

Venters raised the bridle of his horse and followed the broad cattle
trail. The crushed sage resembled the path of a monster snake. In a few
miles of travel he passed several cows and calves that had escaped the
drive. Then he stood on the last high bench of the slope with the floor of
the valley beneath. The opening of the canyon showed in a break of the
sage, and the trail paralleled it as far as he could see. That trail led to an
undiscovered point where Oldring drove cattle into the pass, and many a
rider who had followed it had never returned. Venters satisfied himself
that the rustlers had not deviated from their usual course, and then he
turned at right angles off the cattle trail and made for the head of the pass.

The sun lost its heat and wore down to the western horizon, where it
changed from white to gold and rested like a huge ball about to roll on its
golden shadows down the slope. Venters watched the lengthening of the
rays and bars, and marveled at his own league-long shadow. The sun sank.
There was instant shading of brightness about him, and he saw a kind of
cold purple bloom creep ahead of him to cross the canyon, to mount the
opposite slope and chase and darken and bury the last golden flare of
sunlight.

Venters rode into a trail that he always took to get down into the
canyon. He dismounted and found no tracks but his own made several
days previous. Nevertheless he sent the dog Ring ahead and waited. In a
little while Ring returned. Whereupon Venters led his horse on to the
break in the ground.

The opening into Deception Pass was one of the remarkable natural
phenomena in a country remarkable for vast slopes of sage, uplands insulated by gigantic red walls, and deep canyons of mysterious source and
outlet. Here the valley floor was level, and here opened a narrow chasm, a
ragged vent in yellow walls of stone. The trail down the five hundred feet
of sheer depth always tested Venters's nerve. It was bad going for even a
burro. But Wrangle, as Venters led him, snorted defiance or disgust rather
than fear, and, like a hobbled horse on the jump, lifted his ponderous
iron-shod fore hoofs and crashed down over the first rough step. Venters
warmed to greater admiration of the sorrel; and, giving him a loose bridle,
he stepped down foot by foot. Oftentimes the stones and shale started by
Wrangle buried Venters to his knees; again he was hard put to it to dodge
a rolling boulder; there were times when he could not see Wrangle for
dust, and once he and the horse rode a sliding shelf of yellow, weathered
cliff. It was a trail on which there could be no stops, and, therefore, if
perilous, it was at least one that did not take long in the descent.

Venters breathed lighter when that was over, and felt a sudden assurance in the success of his enterprise. For at first it had been a reckless
determination to achieve something at any cost, and now it resolved itself

into an adventure worthy of all his reason and cunning, and keenness of eye and ear.

Pinyon pines clustered in little clumps along the level floor of the Pass. Twilight had gathered under the walls. Venters rode into the trail and up the canyon. Gradually the trees and caves and objects low down turned black, and this blackness moved up the walls till night enfolded the Pass, while day still lingered above. The sky darkened; and stars began to show, at first pale and then bright. Sharp notches of the rim-wall, biting like teeth into the blue, were landmarks by which Venters knew where his camping site lay. He had to feel his way through a thicket of slender oaks to a spring where he watered Wrangle and drank himself. Here he unsaddled and turned Wrangle loose, having no fear that the horse would leave the thick, cool grass adjacent to the spring. Next he satisfied his own hunger, fed Ring and Whitie, and, with them curled beside him, composed himself to await sleep.

There had been a time when night in the high altitude of these Utah uplands had been satisfying to Venters. But that was before the oppression of enemies had made the change in his mind. As a rider guarding the herd he had never thought of the night's wildness and loneliness; as an outcast, now when the full silence set in, and the deep darkness, and trains of radiant stars shone cold and calm, he lay with an ache in his heart. For a year he had lived as a black fox, driven from his kind. He longed for the sound of a voice, the touch of a hand. In the daytime there was riding from place to place, and the gun practice to which something drove him, and other tasks that at least necessitated action; at night, before he won sleep, there was strife in his soul. He yearned to leave the endless sage slopes, the wilderness of canyons; and it was in the lonely night that this yearning grew unbearable. It was then that he reached forth to feel Ring or Whitie, immeasurably grateful for the love and companionship of two dogs.

On this night the same old loneliness beset Venters, the old habit of sad thought and burning unquiet had its way. But from it evolved a conviction that his useless life had undergone a subtle change. He had sensed it first when Wrangle swung him up to the high saddle, he knew it now when he lay in the gateway of Deception Pass. He had no thrill of adventure, rather a gloomy perception of great hazard, perhaps death. He meant to find Oldring's retreat. The rustlers had fast horses, but none that could catch Wrangle. Venters knew no rustler could creep upon him at night when Ring and Whitie guarded his hiding-place. For the rest, he had eyes and ears, and a long rifle and an unerring aim, which he meant to use. Strangely his foreshadowing of change did not hold a thought of the killing of Tull. It related only to what was to happen to him in Deception Pass; and he could no more lift the veil of that mystery than tell where the trails led to in that unexplored canyon. Moreover, he did not care. And at length, tired out by stress of thought, he fell asleep.

When his eyes unclosed, day had come again, and he saw the rim of the opposite wall tipped with the gold of sunrise. A few moments sufficed for the morning's simple camp duties. Near at hand he found Wrangle, and to his surprise the horse came to him. Wrangle was one of the horses that left his viciousness in the home corral. What he wanted was to be free of mules and burros and steers, to roll in dust-patches, and then to run down the wide, open, windy sage-plains, and at night browse and sleep in the cool, wet grass of a springhole. Jerd knew the sorrel when he said of him, "Wait till he smells the sage!"

Venters saddled and led him out of the oak thicket, and, leaping astride, rode up the canyon, with Ring and Whitie trotting behind. An old grass-grown trail followed the course of a shallow wash where flowed a thin stream of water. The canyon was a hundred rods wide; its yellow walls were perpendicular; it had abundant sage and a scant growth of oak and pinyon. For five miles it held to a comparatively straight bearing, and then began a heightening of rugged walls and a deepening of the floor. Beyond this point of sudden change in the character of the canyon Venters had never explored, and here was the real door to the intricacies of Deception Pass.

He reined Wrangle to a walk, halted now and then to listen, and then proceeded cautiously with shifting and alert gaze. The canyon assumed proportions that dwarfed those of its first ten miles. Venters rode on and on, not losing in the interest of his wide surroundings any of his caution or keen search for tracks or sight of living thing. If there ever had been a trail here, he could not find it. He rode through sage and clumps of pinyon trees and grassy plots where long-petaled purple lilies bloomed. He rode through a dark constriction of the pass no wider than the lane in the grove at Cottonwoods. And he came out into a great amphitheater into which jutted huge towering corners of a confluence of intersecting canyons.

Venters sat his horse, and, with a rider's eye, studied this wild cross-cut of huge stone gullies. Then he went on, guided by the course of running water. If it had not been for the main stream of water flowing north he would never have been able to tell which of those many openings was a continuation of the pass. In crossing this amphitheater he went by the mouths of five canyons, fording little streams that flowed into the larger one. Gaining the outlet which he took to be the pass, he rode on again under overhanging walls. One side was dark in shade, the other light in sun. This narrow passageway turned and twisted and opened into a valley that amazed Venters.

Here again was a sweep of purple sage, richer than upon the higher levels. The valley was miles long, several wide, and enclosed by unscalable walls. But it was the background of this valley that so forcibly struck him. Across the sage-flat rose a strange up-flinging of yellow rocks. He could not tell which were close and which were distant. Scrawled mounds of stone, like mountain waves, seemed to roll up to steep bare slopes and towers.

In this plain of sage Venters flushed birds and rabbits, and when he had proceeded about a mile he caught sight of the bobbing white tails of a herd of running antelope. He rode along the edge of the stream which wound toward the western end of the slowly looming mounds of stone. The high slope retreated out of sight behind the nearer projection. To Venters the valley appeared to have been filled in by a mountain of melted stone that had hardened in strange shapes of rounded outline. He followed the stream till he lost it in a deep cut. Therefore Venters quit the dark slit which baffled further search in that direction, and rode out along the curved edge of stone where it met the sage. It was not long before he came to a low place, and here Wrangle readily climbed up.

All about him was ridgy roll of wind-smoothed, rain-washed rock. Not a tuft of grass or a bunch of sage colored the dull rust-yellow. He saw where, to the right, this uneven flow of stone ended in a blunt wall. Leftward, from the hollow that lay at his feet, mounted a gradual slow-swelling slope to a great height topped by leaning, cracked, and ruined crags. Not for some time did he grasp the wonder of that acclivity. It was no less than a mountainside, glistening in the sun like polished granite, with cedar trees springing as if by magic out of the denuded surface. Winds had swept it clear of weathered shale, and rains had washed it free of dust. Far up the curved slope its beautiful lines broke to meet the vertical rim-wall, to lose its grace in a different order and color of rock, a stained yellow cliff of cracks and caves and seamed crags. And straight before Venters was a scene less striking but more significant to his keen survey. For beyond a mile of the bare, hummocky rock began the valley of sage, and the mouths of canyons, one of which surely was another gateway into the Pass.

He got off his horse, and, giving the bridle to Ring to hold, he commenced a search for the cleft where the stream ran. He was not successful and concluded the water dropped into an underground passage. Then he returned to where he had left Wrangle, and led him down off the stone to the sage. It was a short ride to the opening canyons. There was no reason for a choice of which one to enter. The one he rode into was a clear, sharp shaft in yellow stone a thousand feet deep, with wonderful wind-worn caves low down and high above buttressed and turreted ramparts. Farther on Venters came into a region where deep indentations marked the line of canyon walls. These were huge, covelike blind pockets extending back to a sharp corner with a dense growth of underbrush and trees.

Venters penetrated into one of these offshoots, and, as he had hoped, he found abundant grass. He had to bend the oak saplings to get his horse through. Deciding to make this a hiding-place if he could find water, he worked back to the limit of the shelving walls. In a little cluster of silver spruces he found a spring. This inclosed nook seemed an ideal place to leave his horse and to camp at night, and from which to make stealthy trips on foot. The thick grass hid his trail; the dense growth of oaks in the opening would serve as a barrier to keep Wrangle in, if, indeed, the luxuriant browse would not suffice for that. So Venters, leaving Whitie with the horse, called Ring to his side, and, rifle in hand, worked his way out to the open. A careful photographing in mind of the formation of the bold outlines of rimrock assured him he would be able to return to his retreat even in the dark.

Bunches of scattered sage covered the center of the canyon, and among these Venters threaded his way with the step of an Indian. At intervals he put his hand on the dog and stopped to listen. There was a drowsy hum of insects, but no other sound disturbed the warm midday stillness. Venters saw ahead a turn, more abrupt than any yet. Warily he rounded this corner, once again to halt bewildered.

The canyon opened fan-shaped into a great oval of green and gray growths. It was the hub of an oblong wheel, and from it, at regular distances, like spokes, ran the outgoing canyons. Here a dull red color predominated over the fading yellow. The corners of wall bluntly rose, scarred and scrawled, to taper into towers and serrated peaks and pinnacled domes.

Venters pushed on more heedfully than ever. Toward the center of this circle the sage-brush grew smaller and farther apart. He was about to sheer off to the right, where thickets and jumbles of fallen rock would afford him cover, when he ran right upon a broad cattle trail. Like a road it was, more than a trail; and the cattle tracks were fresh. What surprised him more, they were wet! He pondered over this feature. It had not rained. The only solution to this puzzle was that the cattle had been driven through water, and water deep enough to wet their legs.

Suddenly Ring growled low. Venters rose cautiously and looked over the sage. A band of straggling horsemen were riding across the oval. He sank down, startled and trembling. "Rustlers!" he muttered. Hurriedly he glanced about for a place to hide. Near at hand there was nothing but sage-brush. He dared not risk crossing the open patches to reach the rocks. Again he peeped over the sage. The rustlers—four—five—seven— eight in all, were approaching, but not directly in line with him. That was relief for a cold deadness which seemed to be creeping inward along his veins. He crouched down with bated breath and held the bristling dog.

He heard the click of iron-shod hoofs on stone, the coarse laughter of men, and then voices gradually dying away. Long moments passed. Then he rose. The rustlers were riding into a canyon. Their horses were tired, and they had several pack animals; evidently they had traveled far. Venters doubted that they were the rustlers who had driven the red herd. Oldring's band had split. Venters watched these horsemen disappear under a bold canyon wall.

The rustlers had come from the northwest side of the oval. Venters kept a steady gaze in that direction, hoping, if there were more, to see from what canyon they rode. A quarter of an hour went by. Reward for his vigilance came when he descried three more mounted men, far over to the north. But out of what canyon they had ridden it was too late to tell. He watched the three ride across the oval and round the jutting red corner where the others had gone.

"Up that canyon!" exclaimed Venters. "Oldring's den! I've found it!"

A knotty point for Venters was the fact that the cattle tracks all pointed west. The broad trail came from the direction of the canyon into which the rustlers had ridden, and undoubtedly the cattle had been driven out of it across the oval. There were no tracks pointing the other way. It had been in his mind that Oldring had driven the red herd toward the rendezvous, and not from it. Where did that broad trail come down into the Pass, and where did it lead? Venters knew he wasted time in pondering the question, but it held a fascination not easily dispelled. For many years Oldring's mysterious entrance and exit to Deception Pass had been all-absorbing topics to sage-riders.

All at once the dog put an end to Venters's pondering. Ring sniffed the air, turned slowly in his tracks with a whine, and then growled. Venters wheeled. Two horsemen were within a hundred yards, coming straight at him. One, lagging behind the other, was Oldring's Masked Rider.

Venters cunningly sank, slowly trying to merge into sage-brush. But, guarded as his action was, the first horse detected it. He stopped short, snorted, and shot up his ears. The rustler bent forward, as if keenly peering ahead. Then, with a swift sweep, he jerked a gun from its sheath and fired.

The bullet zipped through the sage-brush. Flying bits of wood struck Venters, and the hot, stinging pain seemed to lift him in one leap. Like a flash the blue barrel of his rifle gleamed level and he shot once—twice.

The foremost rustler dropped his weapon and toppled from his saddle, to fall with his foot catching in a stirrup. The horse snorted wildly and plunged away, dragging the rustler through the sage.

The Masked Rider huddled over his pommel, slowly swaying to one side, and then, with a faint, strange cry slipped out of the saddle.

⁙5⁙

THE MASKED RIDER

VENTERS looked quickly from the fallen rustlers to the canyon where the others had disappeared. He calculated on the time needed for running horses to return to the open, if their riders heard shots. He waited breathlessly. But the estimated time dragged by and no riders appeared. Venters began presently to believe that the rifle reports had not penetrated into the recesses of the canyon, and felt safe for the immediate present.

He hurried to the spot where the first rustler had been dragged by his horse. The man lay in deep grass, dead, jaw fallen, eyes protruding—a sight that sickened Venters. The first man at whom he had ever aimed a weapon he had shot through the heart. With the clammy sweat oozing from every pore Venters dragged the rustler in among some boulders and covered him with slabs of rock. Then he smoothed out the crushed trail in grass and sage. The rustler's horse had stopped a quarter of a mile off and was grazing.

When Venters rapidly strode toward the Masked Rider not even the cold nausea that gripped him could wholly banish curiosity. For he had shot Oldring's infamous lieutenant, whose face had never been seen. Venters experienced a grim pride in the feat. What would Tull say to this achievement of the outcast who rode too often to Deception Pass?

Venters's curious eagerness and expectation had not prepared him for the shock he received when he stood over a slight, dark figure. The rustler wore the black mask that had given him his name, but he had no weapons. Venters glanced at the drooping horse; there were no gun-sheaths on the saddle.

"A rustler who didn't pack guns!" muttered Venters. "He wears no belt. He couldn't pack guns in that rig. . . . Strange!"

A low, gasping intake of breath and a sudden twitching of body told Venters the rider still lived.

"He's alive! . . . I've got to stand here and watch him die. And I shot an unarmed man."

Shrinkingly Venters removed the rider's wide sombrero and the black cloth mask. This action disclosed bright chestnut hair, inclined to curl, and a white, youthful face. Along the lower line of cheek and jaw was a clear demarcation, where the brown of tanned skin met the white that had been hidden from the sun.

"Oh, he's only a boy! . . . What! Can he be Oldring's Masked Rider?"

The boy showed signs of returning consciousness. He stirred; his lips moved; a small brown hand clenched in his blouse.

Venters knelt with a gathering horror of his deed. His bullet had entered the rider's right breast, high up to the shoulder. With hands that shook, Venters untied a black scarf and ripped open the blood-wet blouse.

First he saw a gaping hole, dark red against a whiteness of skin, from which welled a slender red stream. Then the graceful, beautiful swell of a woman's breast!

"A woman!" he cried. "A girl! . . . I've killed a girl!"

She suddenly opened eyes that transfixed Venters. They were fathomless blue. Consciousness of death was there, a blended terror and pain, but no consciousness of sight. She did not see Venters. She stared into the unknown.

Then came a spasm of vitality. She writhed in a torture of reviving strength, and in her convulsions she almost tore from Venters's grasp. Slowly she relaxed and sank partly back. The ungloved hand sought the wound, and pressed so hard that her wrist half buried itself in her bosom. Blood trickled between her spread fingers, and she looked at Venters with eyes that saw him.

He cursed himself and the unerring aim of which he had been so proud. He had seen that look in the eyes of a crippled antelope which he was about to finish with his knife. But in her it had infinitely more—a revelation of mortal spirit. The instinctive clinging to life was there, and the divining helplessness and the terrible accusation of the stricken.

"Forgive me! I didn't know!" burst out Venters.

"You shot me—you've killed me!" she whispered, in panting gasps. Upon her lips appeared a fluttering, bloody froth. By that Venters knew the air in her lungs was mixing with blood. "Oh, I knew—it would—come—some day! . . . Oh, the burn! . . . Hold me—I'm sinking—it's all dark. . . . Ah, God! . . . Mercy—"

Her rigidity loosened in one long quiver and she lay back limp, still, white as snow, with closed eyes.

Venters thought then that she died. But the faint pulsation of her breast assured him that life yet lingered. Death seemed only a matter of moments, for the bullet had gone clear through her. Nevertheless, he tore sage-leaves from a bush, and, pressing them tightly over her wounds, he bound the black scarf round her shoulder, tying it securely under her arm. Then he closed the blouse, hiding from his sight that blood-stained, accusing breast.

"What—now?" he questioned, with flying mind. "I must get out of here. She's dying—but I can't leave her."

He rapidly surveyed the sage to the north and made out no animate object. Then he picked up the girl's sombrero and the mask. This time the mask gave him as great a shock as when he first removed it from her face. For in the woman he had forgotten the rustler, and this black strip of felt-cloth established the identity of Oldring's Masked Rider. Venters had solved the mystery. He slipped his rifle under her, and, lifting her carefully upon it, he began to retrace his steps. The dog trailed in his shadow. And the horse, that had stood drooping by, followed without a call. Venters chose the deepest tufts of grass and clumps of sage on his return. From time to time he glanced over his shoulder. He did not rest. His concern was to avoid jarring the girl and to hide his trail. Gaining the narrow canyon, he turned and held close to the wall till he reached his hiding-place. When he entered the dense thicket of oaks he was hard put to it to force a way through. But he held his burden almost upright, and by slipping sidewise and bending the saplings he got in. Through sage and grass he hurried to the grove of silver spruces.

He laid the girl down, almost fearing to look at her. Though marble pale and cold, she was living. Venters then appreciated the tax that long carry had been to his strength. He sat down to rest. Whitie sniffed at the pale girl and whined and crept to Venters's feet. Ring lapped the water in the runway of the spring.

Presently Venters went out to the opening, caught the horse, and, leading him through the thicket, unsaddled him and tied him with a long halter. Wrangle left his browsing long enough to whinny and toss his head. Venters felt that he could not rest easily till he had secured the other rustler's horse; so, taking his rifle and calling for Ring, he set out. Swiftly yet watchfully he made his way through the canyon to the oval and out to the cattle trail. What few tracks might have betrayed him he obliterated, so only an expert tracker could have trailed him. Then, with many a wary backward glance across the sage, he started to round up the rustler's horse. This was unexpectedly easy. He led the horse to lower ground, out of sight from the opposite side of the oval, along the shadowy western wall, and so on into his canyon and secluded camp.

The girl's eyes were open; a feverish spot burned in her cheeks; she moaned something unintelligible to Venters, but he took the movement of her lips to mean that she wanted water. Lifting her head, he tipped the canteen to her lips. After that she again lapsed into unconsciousness or a weakness which was its counterpart. Venters noted, however, that the burning flush had faded into the former pallor.

The sun set behind the high canyon rim, and a cool shade darkened the walls. Venters fed the dogs and put a halter on the dead rustler's horse. He allowed Wrangle to browse free. This done, he cut spruce boughs and made a lean-to for the girl. Then, gently lifting her upon a blanket, he folded the sides over her. The other blanket he wrapped about his shoulders and found a comfortable seat against a spruce tree that upheld the little shack. Ring and Whitie lay near at hand, one asleep, the other watchful.

Venters dreaded the night's vigil. At night his mind was active, and this time he had to watch and think and feel beside a dying girl whom he had all but murdered. A thousand excuses he invented for himself, yet not one made any difference in his act or his self-reproach.

It seemed to him that when night fell black he could see her white face so much more plainly.

"She'll go, presently," he said, "and be out of agony—thank God!"

Every little while certainty of her death came to him with a shock; and then he would bend over and lay his ear on her breast. Her heart still beat.

The early night blackness cleared to the cold starlight. The horses were not moving, and no sound disturbed the deathly silence of the canyon.

"I'll bury her here," thought Venters, "and let her grave be as much a mystery as her life was."

For the girl's few words, the look of her eyes, the prayer, had strangely touched Venters.

"She was only a girl," he soliloquized. "What was she to Oldring? Rustlers don't have wives nor sisters nor daughters. She was bad—that's all. But somehow . . . well, she may not have willingly become the companion of rustlers. That prayer of hers to God for mercy! . . . Life is strange and cruel. I wonder if other members of Oldring's gang are women? Likely enough. But what was his game? Oldring's Masked Rider! A name to make villagers hide and lock their doors. A name credited with a dozen murders, a hundred forays, and a thousand stealings of cattle. What part did the girl have in this? It may have served Oldring to create mystery."

Hours passed. The white stars moved across the narrow strip of dark-blue sky above. The silence awoke to the low hum of insects. Venters watched the immovable white face, and as he watched, hour by hour waiting for death, the infamy of her passed from his mind. He thought only of the sadness, the truth of the moment. Whoever she was—whatever she had done—she was young and she was dying.

The after-part of the night wore on interminably. The starlight failed and the gloom blackened to the darkest hour. "She'll die at the gray of dawn," muttered Venters, remembering some old woman's fancy. The blackness paled to gray, and the gray lightened and day peeped over the eastern rim. Venters listened at the breast of the girl. She still lived. Did he only imagine that her heart beat stronger, ever so slightly, but stronger? He pressed his ear closer to her breast. And he rose with his own pulse quickening.

"If she doesn't die soon—she's got a chance—the barest chance—to live," he said.

He wondered if the internal bleeding had ceased. There was no more film of blood upon her lips. But no corpse could have been whiter. Opening her blouse, he untied the scarf, and carefully picked away the sage-leaves from the wound in her shoulder. It had closed. Lifting her lightly, he ascertained that the same was true of the hole where the bullet had come out. He reflected on the fact that clean wounds closed quickly in the healing upland air. He recalled instances of riders who had been cut and shot, apparently to fatal issues; yet the blood had clotted, the wounds closed, and they had recovered. He had no way to tell if internal hemorrhage still went on, but he believed that it had stopped. Otherwise she would surely not have lived so long. He marked the entrance of the bullet, and concluded that it had just touched the upper lobe of her lung. Perhaps the wound in the lung had also closed. As he began to wash the blood stains from her breast and carefully rebandage the wound, he was vaguely conscious of a strange, grave happiness in the thought that she might live.

Broad daylight and a hint of sunshine high on the cliff-rim to the west brought him to consideration of what he had better do. And while busy with his few camp tasks he revolved the thing in this mind. It would not be wise for him to remain long in his present hiding-place. And if he intended to follow the cattle trail and try to find the rustlers he had better make a move at once. For he knew that rustlers, being riders, would not make much of a day's or night's absence from camp for one or two of their number; but when the missing ones failed to show up in reasonable time there would be a search. And Venters was afraid of that.

"A good tracker could trail me," he muttered. "And I'd be cornered here. Let's see. Rustlers are a lazy set when they're not on the ride. I'll risk it. Then I'll change my hiding-place."

He carefully cleaned and reloaded his guns. When he rose to go he bent a long glance down upon the unconscious girl. Then, ordering Whitie and Ring to keep guard, he left the camp.

The safest cover lay close under the wall of the canyon, and here through the dense thickets Venters made his slow, listening advance toward the oval. Upon gaining the wide opening he decided to cross it and follow the left wall till he came to the cattle trail. He scanned the oval as keenly as if hunting for antelope. Then, stooping, he stole from one cover to another, taking advantage of rocks and bunches of sage, until he had reached the thickets under the opposite wall. Once there, he exercised extreme caution in his surveys of the ground ahead, but increased his speed when moving. Dodging from bush to bush, he passed the mouths of two canyons, and in the entrance of a third canyon he crossed a wash of swift, clear water, to come abruptly upon the cattle trail.

It followed the low bank of the wash, and, keeping it in sight, Venters hugged the line of sage and thicket. Like the curves of a serpent the canyon wound for a mile or more and then opened into a valley. Patches of red showed clear against the purple of sage, and farther out on the level dotted strings of red led away to the wall of rock.

"Ha, the red herd!" exclaimed Venters.

Then dots of white and black told him there were cattle of other colors in this inclosed valley. Oldring, the rustler, was also a rancher. Venters's calculating eye took count of stock that outnumbered the red herd.

"What a range!" went on Venters. "Water and grass enough for fifty thousand head, and no riders needed!"

After his first burst of surprise and rapid calculation Venters lost no time there, but slunk again into the sage on his back trail. With the discovery of Oldring's hidden cattle-range had come enlightenment on several problems. Here the rustler kept his stock; here was Jane Withersteen's red herd; here were the few cattle that had disappeared from the Cottonwoods slopes during the last two years. Until Oldring had driven the red herd his thefts of cattle for that time had not been more than enough to supply meat for his men. Of late no drives had been reported from Sterling or the villages north. And Venters knew that the riders had wondered at Oldring's inactivity in that particular field. He and his band had been active enough in their visits to Glaze and Cottonwoods; they always had gold; but of late the amount gambled away and drunk and thrown away in the villages had given rise to much conjecture. Oldring's more frequent visits had resulted in new saloons, and where there had formerly been one raid or shooting fray in the little hamlets there were now many. Perhaps Oldring had another range farther on up the Pass, and from there drove the cattle to distant Utah towns where he was little known. But Venters came finally to doubt this. And, from what he had learned in the last few days, a belief began to form in Venters's mind that Oldring's intimidations of the villages and the mystery of the Masked Rider, with his alleged evil deeds, and the fierce resistance offered any trailing riders, and the rustling of cattle—these things were only the craft of the rustler-chief to conceal his real life and purpose and work in Deception Pass.

And like a scouting Indian, Venters crawled through the sage of the oval valley, crossed trail after trail on the north side, and at last entered the canyon out of which headed the cattle trail, and into which he had watched the rustlers disappear.

If he had used caution before, now he strained every nerve to force himself to creeping stealth and to sensitiveness of ear. He crawled along so hidden that he could not use his eyes except to aid himself in the toilsome progress through the brakes and ruins of cliff wall. Yet from time to time, as he rested, he saw the massive red walls growing higher and wilder, more looming and broken. He made note of the fact that he was turning and climbing. The sage and thickets of oak and brakes of alder gave place to pinyon pine growing out of rocky soil. Suddenly a low, dull murmur assailed his ears. At first he thought it was thunder, then the slipping of a weathered slope of rock. But it was incessant, and as he progressed it filled out deeper and from a murmur changed into a soft roar.

"Falling water," he said. "There's volume to that. I wonder if it's the stream I lost."

The roar bothered him, for he could hear nothing else. Likewise, however, no rustlers could hear him. Emboldened by this, and sure that nothing but a bird could see him, he arose from his hands and knees to hurry on. An opening in the pinyons warned him that he was nearing the height of slope.

He gained it, and dropped low with a burst of astonishment. Before him stretched a short canyon with rounded stone floor bare of grass or sage or tree, and with curved, shelving walls. A broad rippling stream flowed toward him, and at the back of the canyon a waterfall burst from a wide rent in the cliff, and, bounding down in two green steps, spread into a long white sheet.

If Venters had not been indubitably certain that he had entered the right canyon his astonishment would not have been so great. There had been no breaks in the walls, no side canyons entering this one where the rustlers' tracks and the cattle trail had guided him, and, therefore, he could not be wrong. But here the canyon ended, and presumably the trails also.

"That cattle trail headed out of here," Venters kept saying to himself. "It headed out. Now what I want to know is how on earth did cattle ever get in here?"

If he could be sure of anything it was of the careful scrutiny he had given that cattle track, every hoofmark of which headed straight west. He was now looking east at an immense round boxed corner of canyon down which tumbled a thin, white veil of water, scarcely twenty yards wide. Somehow, somewhere, his calculations had gone wrong. For the first time in years he found himself doubting his rider's skill in finding tracks, and his memory of what he had actually seen. In his anxiety to keep under cover he must have lost himself in this offshoot of Deception Pass, and thereby, in some unaccountable manner, missed the canyon with the trails. There was nothing else for him to think. Rustlers could not fly, nor cattle jump down thousand-foot precipices. He was only proving what the sage-riders had long said of this labyrinthine system of deceitful canyons and valleys—trails led down into Deception Pass, but no rider had ever followed them.

On a sudden he heard above the soft roar of the waterfall an unusual sound that he could not define. He dropped flat behind a stone and listened. From the direction he had come swelled something that resembled a strange muffled pounding and splashing and ringing. Despite his nerve the chill sweat began to dampen his forehead. What might not be possible in this stone-walled maze of mystery? The unnatural sound passed beyond him as he lay gripping his rifle and fighting for coolness. Then from the open came the sound, now distinct and different. Venters recognized a hobble-bell of a horse, and the cracking of iron on submerged stones, and the hollow splash of hoofs in water.

Relief surged over him. His mind caught again at realities, and curiosity prompted him to peep from behind the rock.

In the middle of the stream waded a long string of packed burros driven by three superbly mounted men. Had Venters met these dark-clothed, dark-visaged, heavily armed men anywhere in Utah, let alone in this robbers' retreat, he would have recognized them as rustlers. The discerning eye of a rider saw the signs of a long, arduous trip. These men were packing in supplies from one of the northern villages. They were tired, and their horses were almost played out, and the burros plodded on, after the manner of their kind when exhausted, faithful and patient, but as if every weary, splashing, slipping step would be their last.

All this Venters noted in one glance. After that he watched with a thrilling eagerness. Straight at the waterfall the rustlers drove the burros, and straight through the middle, where the water spread into a fleecy, thin film like dissolving smoke. Following closely, the rustlers rode into this white mist, showing in bold black relief for an instant, and then they vanished.

Venters drew a full breath that rushed out in brief and sudden utterance.

"Good heaven! Of all the holes for a rustler! . . . There's a cavern under that waterfall, and a passageway leading out to a canyon beyond. Oldring hides in there. He needs only to guard a trail leading down from the sage-flat above. Little danger of this outlet to the Pass being discovered. I stumbled on it by luck, after I had given up. And now I know the truth of what puzzled me most—why that cattle trail was wet!"

He wheeled and ran down the slope, and out to the level of the sage-brush. Returning, he had no time to spare, only now and then, between dashes, a moment when he stopped to cast sharp eyes ahead. The abundant grass left no trace of his trail. Short work he made of the distance to the circle of canyons. He doubted that he would ever see it again; he knew he never wanted to; yet he looked at the red corners and towers with the eyes of a rider picturing landmarks never to be forgotten.

Here he spent a panting moment in a slow-circling gaze of the sage-oval and the gaps between the bluffs. Nothing stirred except the gentle wave of the tips of the brush. Then he pressed on past the mouths of several canyons and over ground new to him, now close under the eastern wall. This latter part proved to be easy traveling, well screened from possible observation from the north and west, and he soon covered it and felt safer in the deepening shade of his own canyon. Then the huge, notched bulge of red rim loomed over him, a mark by which he knew again the deep cove where his camp lay hidden. As he penetrated the thicket, safe again for the present, his thoughts reverted to the girl he had left there. The afternoon had far advanced. How would he find her? He ran into camp, frightening the dogs.

The girl lay with wide-open, dark eyes, and they dilated when he knelt beside her. The flush of fever shone in her cheeks. He lifted her and held water to her dry lips, and felt an inexplicable sense of lightness as he saw her swallow in a slow, choking gulp. Gently he laid her back.

"Who—are—you?" she whispered, haltingly.

"I'm the man who shot you," he replied.

"You'll—not—kill me—now?"

"No, no."

"What—will—you—do—with me?"

"When you get better—strong enough—I'll take you back to the canyon where the rustlers ride through the waterfall."

As with a faint shadow from a flitting wing overhead, the marble whiteness of her face seemed to change.

"Don't—take—me—back—there!"

THE MILL WHEEL
OF STEERS

MEANTIME, at the ranch, when Judkins's news had sent Venters on the trail of the rustlers, Jane Withersteen led the injured man to her house and with skilled fingers dressed the gunshot wound in his arm.

"Judkins, what do you think happened to my riders?"

"I—I'd rather not say," he replied.

"Tell me. Whatever you'll tell me I'll keep to myself. I'm beginning to worry about more than the loss of a herd of cattle. Venters hinted of—but tell me, Judkins."

"Well, Miss Withersteen, I think as Venters thinks—your riders have been called in."

"Judkins! . . . By whom?"

"You know who handles the reins of your Mormon riders."

"Do you dare insinuate that my churchmen have ordered in my riders?"

"I ain't insinuatin' nothin', Miss Withersteen," answered Judkins, with spirit. "I know what I'm talking about. I didn't want to tell you."

"Oh, I can't believe that! I'll not believe it! Would Tull leave my herds at the mercy of rustlers and wolves just because—because—? No, no! It's unbelievable."

"Yes, thet particular thing's onheard of around Cottonwoods. But, beggin' pardon, Miss Withersteen, there never was any other rich Mormon woman here on the border, let alone one thet's taken the bit between her teeth."

That was a bold thing for the reserved Judkins to say, but it did not anger her. This rider's crude hint of her spirit gave her a glimpse of what others might think. Humility and obedience had been hers always. But had she taken the bit between her teeth? Still she wavered. And then, with a quick spurt of warm blood along her veins, she thought of Black Star when he got the bit fast between his iron jaws and ran wild in the sage. If she ever started to run! Jane smothered the glow and burn within her, ashamed of a passion for freedom that opposed her duty.

"Judkins, go to the village," she said, "and when you have learned anything definite about my riders please come to me at once."

When he had gone Jane resolutely applied her mind to a number of tasks that of late had been neglected. Her father had trained her in the management of a hundred employees and the working of gardens and fields; and to keep record of the movements of cattle and riders. And beside the many duties she had added to this work was one of extreme delicacy, such as required all her tact and ingenuity. It was an unobtrusive, almost secret aid which she rendered to the Gentile families of the village. Though Jane Withersteen never admitted so to herself, it amounted to no less than a system of charity. But for her invention of numberless kinds of employment, for which there was no actual need, these families of Gentiles, who had failed in a Mormon community, would have starved.

In aiding these poor people Jane thought she deceived her keen churchmen, but it was a kind of deceit for which she did not pray to be forgiven. Equally as difficult was the task of deceiving the Gentiles, for they were as proud as they were poor. It had been a great grief to her to discover how these people hated her people; and it had been a source of great joy that through her they had come to soften in hatred. At any time this work called for a clearness of mind that precluded anxiety and worry; but under the present circumstances it required all her vigor and obstinate tenacity to pin her attention upon her task.

Sunset came, bringing with the end of her labor a patient calmness and power to wait that had not been hers earlier in the day. She expected Judkins, but he did not appear. Her house was always quiet; tonight, however, it seemed unusually so. At supper her women served her with a silent assiduity; it spoke what their sealed lips could not utter—the sym-

pathy of Mormon women. Jerd came to her with the key of the great door
of the stone stable, and to make his daily report about the horses. One of
his daily duties was to give Black Star and Night and the other racers a
ten-mile run. This day it had been omitted, and the boy grew confused in
explanations that she had not asked for. She did inquire if he would
return on the morrow, and Jerd, in mingled surprise and relief, assured her
he would always work for her. Jane missed the rattle and trot, canter and
gallop of the incoming riders on the hard trails. Dusk shaded the grove
where she walked; the birds ceased singing; the wind sighed through the
leaves of the cottonwoods, and the running water murmured down its
stone-bedded channel. The glimmering of the first star was like the peace
and beauty of the night. Her faith welled up in her heart and said that all
would soon be right in her little world. She pictured Venters about his
lonely campfire sitting between his faithful dogs. She prayed for his safety,
for the success of his undertaking.

Early the next morning one of Jane's women brought in word that
Judkins wished to speak to her. She hurried out, and in her surprise to see
him armed with rifle and revolver, she forgot her intention to inquire
about his wound.

"Judkins! Those guns? You never carried guns."

"It's high time, Miss Withersteen," he replied. "Will you come into the
grove? It ain't jest exactly safe for me to be seen here."

She walked with him into the shade of the cottonwoods.

"What do you mean?"

"Miss Withersteen, I went to my mother's house last night. While
there, someone knocked, an' a man asked for me. I went to the door. He
wore a mask. He said I'd better not ride anymore for Jane Withersteen.
His voice was hoarse an' strange, disguised, I reckon, like his face. He said
no more, an' ran off in the dark."

"Did you know who he was?" asked Jane, in a low voice.

"Yes."

Jane did not ask to know; she did not want to know; she feared to
know. All her calmness fled at a single thought.

"Thet's why I'm packin' guns," went on Judkins. "For I'll never quit
ridin' for you, Miss Withersteen, till you let me go."

"Judkins, do you want to leave me?"

"Do I look thet way? Give me a hoss—a fast hoss, an' send me out on
the sage."

"Oh, thank you, Judkins! You're more faithful than my own people. I
ought not accept your loyalty—you might suffer more through it. But
what in the world can I do? My head whirls. The wrong to Venters—the
stolen herd—these masks, threats, this coil in the dark! I can't understand! But I feel something dark and terrible closing in around me."

"Miss Withersteen, it's all simple enough," said Judkins, earnestly.
"Now please listen—an' beggin' your pardon—jest turn that deaf Mor-

mon ear aside, an' let me talk clear an' plain in the other. I went around to the saloons an' the stores an' the loafin' places yesterday. All your riders are in. There's talk of a vigilance band organized to hunt down rustlers. They call themselves The Riders. Thet's the report—thet's the reason given for your riders leavin' you. Strange thet only a few riders of other ranchers joined the band! An' Tull's man, Jerry Card—he's the leader. I seen him an' his hoss. He 'ain't been to Glaze. I'm not easy to fool on the looks of a hoss thet's traveled the sage. Tull an' Jerry didn't ride to Glaze! . . . Well, I met Blake an' Dorn, both good friends of mine, usually, as far as their Mormon lights will let 'em go. But these fellers couldn't fool me, an' they didn't try very hard. I asked them, straight out like a man, why they left you like thet. I didn't forget to mention how you nursed Blake's poor old mother when she was sick, an' how good you was to Dorn's kids. They looked ashamed, Miss Wither-steen. An' they jest froze up—thet dark set look thet makes them strange an' different to me. But I could tell the difference between thet first natural twinge of conscience an' the later look of some secret thing. An' the difference I caught was thet they couldn't help themselves. They hadn't no say in the matter. They looked as if their bein' unfaithful to you was bein' faithful to a higher duty. An' there's the secret. Why, it's as plain as—as sight of my gun here."

"Plain! . . . My herds to wander in the sage—to be stolen! Jane Withersteen a poor woman! Her head to be brought low and her spirit broken! . . . Why, Judkins, it's plain enough."

"Miss Withersteen, let me get what boys I can gather, an' hold the white herd. It's on the slope now, not ten miles out—three thousand head, an' all steers. They're wild, an' likely to stampede at the pop of a jackrabbit's ears. We'll camp right with them an' try to hold them."

"Judkins, I'll reward you some day for your service, unless all is taken from me. Get the boys and tell Jerd to give you pick of my horses, except Black Star and Night. But—do not shed blood for my cattle nor heed-lessly risk your lives."

Jane Withersteen rushed to the silence and seclusion of her room, and there could not longer hold back the bursting of her wrath. She went stone-blind in the fury of a passion that had never before showed its power. Lying upon her bed, sightless, voiceless, she was a writhing, living flame. And she tossed there while her fury burned and burned, and finally burned itself out.

Then, weak and spent, she lay thinking, not of the oppression that would break her, but of this new revelation of self. Until the last few days there had been little in her life to rouse passions. Her forefathers had been Vikings, savage chieftains who bore no cross and brooked no hindrance to their will. Her father had inherited that temper; and at times, like ante-lope fleeing before fire on the slope, his people fled from his red rages. Jane Withersteen realized that the spirit of wrath and war had lain dormant in her. She shrank from black depths hitherto unsuspected. The one thing in man or woman that she scorned above all scorn, and which she could not forgive, was hate. Hate headed a flaming pathway straight to hell. All in a flash, beyond her control there had been in her a birth of fiery hate. And the man who had dragged her peaceful and loving spirit to this degradation was a minister of God's word, an elder of her church, the counselor of her beloved bishop.

The loss of herds and ranges, even of Amber Spring and the Old Stone House, no longer concerned Jane Withersteen; she faced the foremost thought of her life, what she now considered the mightiest problem—the salvation of her soul.

She knelt by her bedside and prayed; she prayed as she had never prayed in all her life—prayed to be forgiven for her sin; to be immune from that dark, hot hate; to love Tull as her minister, though she could not love him as a man; to do her duty by her church and people and those dependent upon her bounty; to hold reverence of God and womanhood inviolate.

When Jane Withersteen rose from that storm of wrath and prayer for help she was serene, calm, sure—a changed woman. She would do her duty as she saw it, live her life as her own truth guided her. She might never be able to marry a man of her choice, but she certainly never would become the wife of Tull. Her churchmen might take her cattle and horses, ranges and fields, her corrals and stables, the house of Withersteen and the water that nourished the village of Cottonwoods; but they could not force her to marry Tull, they could not change her decision or break her spirit. Once resigned to further loss, and sure of herself, Jane Withersteen attained a peace of mind that had not been hers for a year. She forgave Tull, and felt a melancholy regret over what she knew he considered duty, irrespective of his personal feeling for her. First of all, Tull, as he was a man, wanted her for himself; and secondly, he hoped to save her and her riches for his church. She did not believe that Tull had been actuated solely by his minister's zeal to save her soul. She doubted her interpretation of one of his dark sayings—that if she were lost to him she might as well be lost to heaven. Jane Withersteen's common sense took arms against the binding limits of her religion; and she doubted that her bishop, whom she had been taught had direct communication with God —would damn her soul for refusing to marry a Mormon. As for Tull and his churchmen, when they had harassed.her, perhaps made her poor, they would find her unchangeable, and then she would get back most of what she had lost. So she reasoned, true at last to her faith in all men, and in their ultimate goodness.

The clank of iron hoofs upon the stone courtyard drew her hurriedly from her retirement. There, beside his horse, stood Lassiter, his dark apparel and the great black gun-sheaths contrasting singularly with his gentle smile. Jane's active mind took up her interest in him and her half-determined desire to use what charm she had to foil his evident design in visiting Cottonwoods. If she could mitigate his hatred of Mormons, or at least keep him from killing more of them, not only would she be saving her people, but also be leading back this blood-spiller to some semblance of the human.

"Mornin', ma'am," he said, black sombrero in hand.

"Lassiter, I'm not an old woman, or even a madam," she replied, with her bright smile. "If you can't say Miss Withersteen—call me Jane."

"I reckon Jane would be easier. First names are always handy for me."

"Well, use mine, then. Lassiter, I'm glad to see you. I'm in trouble."

Then she told him of Judkins's return, of the driving of the red herd, of Venters's departure on Wrangle, and the calling-in of her riders.

" 'Pears to me you're some smilin' an' pretty for a woman with so much trouble," he remarked.

"Lassiter! Are you paying me compliments? But, seriously, I've made up my mind not to be miserable. I've lost much, and I'll lose more. Nevertheless, I won't be sour, and I hope I'll never be unhappy—again."

Lassiter twisted his hat round and round, as was his way, and took his time in replying.

"Women are strange to me. I got to back-trailin' myself from them long ago. But I'd like a game woman. Might I ask, seein' as how you take this trouble, if you're goin' to fight?"

"Fight! How? Even if I would, I haven't a friend except that boy who doesn't dare stay in the village."

"I make bold to say, ma'am—Jane—that there's another, if you want him."

"Lassiter! . . . Thank you. But how can I accept you as a friend? Think! Why, you'd ride down into the village with those terrible guns and kill my enemies—who are also my churchmen."

"I reckon I might be riled up to jest about that," he replied, dryly.

She held out both hands to him.

"Lassiter! I'll accept your friendship—be proud of it—return it—if I may keep you from killing another Mormon."

"I'll tell you one thing," he said, bluntly, as the gray lightning formed in his eyes. "You're too good a woman to be sacrificed as you're goin' to be. . . . No, I reckon you an' me can't be friends on such terms."

In her earnestness she stepped closer to him, repelled yet fascinated by the sudden transition of his moods. That he would fight for her was at once horrible and wonderful.

"You came here to kill a man—the man whom Milly Erne—"

"The man who dragged Milly Erne to hell—put it that way! . . . Jane Withersteen, yes, that's why I came here. I'd tell so much to no other livin' soul. . . . There're things such a woman as you'd never dream of— so don't mention her again. Not till you tell me the name of the man!"

"Tell you! I? Never!"

"I reckon you will. An' I'll never ask you. I'm a man of strange beliefs an' ways of thinkin', an' I seem to see into the future an' feel things hard to explain. The trail I've been followin' for so many years was twisted an' tangled, but it's straightenin' out now. An', Jane Withersteen, you crossed it long ago to ease poor Milly's agony. That, whether you want or not, makes Lassiter your friend. But you cross it now strangely to mean somethin' to me—God knows what!—unless by your noble blindness to incite me to greater hatred of Mormon men."

Jane felt swayed by a strength that far exceeded her own. In a clash of wills with this man she would go to the wall. If she were to influence him it must be wholly through womanly allurement. There was that about Lassiter which commanded her respect; she had abhorred his name; face to face with him, she found she feared only his deeds. His mystic suggestion, his foreshadowing of something that she was to mean to him, pierced deep into her mind. She believed fate had thrown in her way the lover or husband of Milly Erne. She believed that through her an evil man might be reclaimed. His allusion to what he called her blindness terrified her. Such a mistaken idea of his might unleash the bitter, fatal mood she sensed in him. At any cost she must placate this man; she knew the die was cast, and that if Lassiter did not soften to a woman's grace and beauty and wiles, then it would be because she could not make him.

"I reckon you'll hear no more such talk from me," Lassiter went on, presently. "Now, Miss Jane, I rode in to tell you that your herd of white steers is down on the slope behind them big ridges. An' I seen somethin' goin' on that'd be mighty interestin' to you, if you could see it. Have you a field glass?"

"Yes, I have two glasses. I'll get them and ride out with you. Wait, Lassiter, please," she said, and hurried within. Sending word to Jerd to saddle Black Star and fetch him to the court, she then went to her room and changed to the riding-clothes she always donned when going into the sage. In this male attire her mirror showed her a jaunty, handsome rider. If she expected some little meed of admiration from Lassiter, she had no cause for disappointment. The gentle smile that she liked, which made of him another person, slowly overspread his face.

"If I didn't take you for a boy!" he exclaimed. "It's powerful queer what difference clothes make. Now I've been some scared of your dignity, like when the other night you was all in white, but in this rig—"

Black Star came pounding into the court, dragging Jerd half off his feet, and he whistled at Lassiter's black. But at sight of Jane all his defiant lines seemed to soften, and with tosses of his beautiful head he whipped his bridle.

"Down, Black Star, down," said Jane.

He dropped his head, and, slowly lengthening, he bent one foreleg, then the other, and sank to his knees. Jane slipped her left foot in the stirrup, swung lightly into the saddle, and Black Star rose with a ringing stamp. It was not easy for Jane to hold him to a canter through the grove, and like the wind he broke when he saw the sage. Jane let him have a couple of miles of free running on the open trail, and then she coaxed him in and waited for her companion. Lassiter was not long in catching up, and presently they were riding side by side. It reminded her how she used to ride with Venters. Where was he now? She gazed far down the slope to the curved purple lines of Deception Pass, and involuntarily shut her eyes with a trembling stir of nameless fear.

"We'll turn off here," Lassiter said, "an' take to the sage a mile or so. The white herd is behind them big ridges."

"What are you going to show me?" asked Jane. "I'm prepared—don't be afraid."

He smiled as if he meant that bad news came swiftly enough without being presaged by speech.

When they reached the lee of a rolling ridge Lassiter dismounted, motioning her to do likewise. They left the horses standing, bridles down. Then Lassiter, carrying the field glasses, began to lead the way up the slow rise of ground. Upon nearing the summit he halted her with a gesture.

"I reckon we'd see more if we didn't show ourselves against the sky," he said. "I was here less than a hour ago. Then the herd was seven or eight miles south, an' if they 'ain't bolted yet—"

"Lassiter! . . . Bolted?"

"That's what I said. Now let's see."

Jane climbed a few more paces behind him and then peeped over the ridge. Just beyond began a shallow swale that deepened and widened into a valley and then swung to the left. Following the undulating sweep of sage, Jane saw the straggling lines and then the great body of the white herd. She knew enough about steers, even at a distance of four or five miles, to realize that something was in the wind. Bringing her field glass into use, she moved it slowly from left to right, which action swept the whole herd into range. The stragglers were restless; the more compactly massed steers were browsing. Jane brought the glass back to the big sentinels of the herd, and she saw them trot with quick steps, stop short and toss wide horns, look everywhere, and then trot in another direction.

"Judkins hasn't been able to get his boys together yet," said Jane. "But he'll be there soon. I hope not too late. Lassiter, what's frightening those big leaders?"

"Nothin' jest on the minute," replied Lassiter. "Them steers are quietin' down. They've been scared, but not bad yet. I reckon the whole herd has moved a few miles this way since I was here."

"They didn't browse that distance—not in less than an hour. Cattle aren't sheep."

"No, they jest run it, an' that looks bad."

"Lassiter, what frightened them?" repeated Jane, impatiently.

"Put down your glass. You'll see at first better with a naked eye. Now look along them ridges on the other side of the herd, the ridges where the sun shines bright on the sage. . . . That's right. Now look an' look hard an' wait."

Long-drawn moments of straining sight rewarded Jane with nothing save the low, purple rim of ridge and the shimmering sage.

"It's begun again!" whispered Lassiter, and he gripped her arm. "Watch. . . . There, did you see that?"

"No, no. Tell me what to look for?"

"A white flash—a kind of pinpoint of quick light—a gleam as from sun shinin' on somethin' white."

Suddenly Jane's concentrated gaze caught a fleeting glint. Quickly she brought her glass to bear on the spot. Again the purple sage, magnified in color and size and wave, for long moments irritated her with its monotony. Then from out of the sage on the ridge flew up a broad, white object, flashed in the sunlight, and vanished. Like magic it was, and bewildered Jane.

"What on earth is that?"

"I reckon there's someone behind that ridge throwin' up a sheet or a white blanket to reflect the sunshine."

"Why?" queried Jane, more bewildered than ever.

"To stampede the herd," replied Lassiter, and his teeth clicked.

"Ah!" She made a fierce, passionate movement, clutched the glass tightly, shook as with the passing of a spasm, and then dropped her head. Presently she raised it to greet Lassiter with something like a smile.

"My righteous brethren are at work again," she said, in scorn. She had stifled the leap of her wrath, but for perhaps the first time in her life a bitter derision curled her lips. Lassiter's cool gray eyes seemed to pierce her. "I said I was prepared for anything; but that was hardly true. But why would they—anybody stampede my cattle?"

"That's a Mormon's godly way of bringin' a woman to her knees."

"Lassiter, I'll die before I ever bend my knees. I might be led; I won't be driven. Do you expect the herd to bolt?"

"I don't like the looks of them big steers. But you can never tell. Cattle sometimes stampede as easily as buffalo. Any little flash or move will start them. A rider gettin' down an' walkin' toward them sometimes will make them jump and fly. Then again nothin' seems to scare them. But I reckon that white flare will do the biz. It's a new one on me, an' I've seen some ridin' an' rustlin'. It jest takes one of them God-fearin' Mormons to think of devilish tricks."

"Lassiter, might not this trick be done by Oldring's men?" asked Jane, ever grasping at straws.

"It might be, but it ain't," replied Lassiter. "Oldrin's an honest thief. He don't skulk behind ridges to scatter your cattle to the four winds. He rides down on you, an' if you don't like it you can throw a gun."

Jane bit her tongue to refrain from championing men who at the very moment were proving to her that they were little and mean compared even with rustlers.

"Look! . . . Jane, them leadin' steers have bolted! They're drawin' the stragglers, an' that'll pull the whole herd."

Jane was not quick enough to catch the details called out by Lassiter, but she saw the line of cattle lengthening. Then, like a stream of white bees pouring from a huge swarm, the steers stretched out from the main body. In a few moments, with astonishing rapidity, the whole herd got into motion. A faint roar of trampling hoofs came to Jane's ears, and gradually swelled; low, rolling clouds of dust began to rise above the sage.

"It's a stampede, an' a hummer," said Lassiter.

"Oh, Lassiter! The herd's running with the valley! It leads into the canyon! There's a straight jump-off!"

"I reckon they'll run into it, too. But that's a good many miles yet. An' Jane, this valley swings round almost north before it goes east. That stampede will pass within a mile of us."

The long, white, bobbing line of steers streaked swiftly through the sage, and a funnel-shaped dust cloud arose at a low angle. A dull rumbling filled Jane's ears.

"I'm thinkin' of millin' that herd," said Lassiter. His gray glance swept up the slope to the west. "There's some specks an' dust way off toward the village. Mebbe that's Judkins an' his boys. It ain't likely he'll get here in time to help. You'd better hold Black Star here on this high ridge."

He ran to his horse and, throwing off saddle-bags and tightening the cinches, he leaped astride and galloped straight down across the valley.

Jane went for Black Star and, leading him to the summit of the ridge, she mounted and faced the valley with excitement and expectancy. She had heard of milling stampeded cattle, and knew it was a feat accomplished by only the most daring riders.

The white herd was now strung out in a line two miles long. The dull rumble of thousands of hoofs deepened into continuous low thunder, and as the steers swept swiftly closer the thunder became a heavy roll. Lassiter crossed in a few moments the level of the valley to the eastern rise of ground and there waited the coming of the herd. Presently, as the head of the white line reached a point opposite to where Jane stood, Lassiter spurred his black into a run.

Jane saw him take a position on the off side of the leaders of the stampede, and there he rode. It was like a race. They swept on down the valley, and when the end of the white line neared Lassiter's first stand the head had begun to swing round to the west. It swung slowly and stubbornly, yet surely, and gradually assumed a long, beautiful curve of moving white. To Jane's amaze she saw the leaders swinging, turning till they headed back toward her and up the valley. Out to the right of these wild, plunging steers ran Lassiter's black, and Jane's keen eye appreciated the fleet stride and sure-footedness of the blind horse. Then it seemed that the herd moved in a great curve, a huge half-moon, with the points of head and tail almost opposite, and a mile apart. But Lassiter relentlessly crowded the leaders, sheering them to the left, turning them little by little. And the dust-blinded wild followers plunged on madly in the tracks of their leaders. This ever-moving, ever-changing curve of steers rolled toward Jane, and when below her, scarce half a mile, it began to narrow and close into a circle. Lassiter had ridden parallel with her position, turned toward her, then aside, and now he was riding directly away from her, all the time pushing the head of that bobbing line inward.

It was then that Jane, suddenly understanding Lassiter's feat, stared and gasped at the riding of this intrepid man. His horse was fleet and tireless, but blind. He had pushed the leaders around and around till they were about to turn in on the inner side of the end of that line of steers. The leaders were already running in a circle; the end of the herd was still running almost straight. But soon they would be wheeling. Then, when Lassiter had the circle formed, how would he escape? With Jane Withersteen prayer was as ready as praise; and she prayed for this man's safety. A circle of dust began to collect. Dimly, as through a yellow veil, Jane saw Lassiter press the leaders inward to close the gap in the sage. She lost sight of him in the dust; again she thought she saw the black, riderless now, rear and drag himself and fall. Lassiter had been thrown—lost! Then he reappeared running out of the dust into the sage. He had escaped, and she breathed again.

Spellbound, Jane Withersteen watched this stupendous mill wheel of steers. Here was the milling of the herd. The white running circle closed in upon the open space of sage. And the dust circles closed above into a pall. The ground quaked and the incessant thunder of pounding hoofs rolled on. Jane felt deafened, yet she thrilled to a new sound. As the circle of sage lessened the steers began to bawl, and when it closed entirely there came a great upheaval in the center, and a terrible thumping of heads and clicking of horns. Bawling, climbing, goring, the great mass of steers on the inside wrestled in a crashing din, heaved and groaned under the pressure. Then came a deadlock. The inner strife ceased, and the hideous roar and crash. Movement went on in the outer circle, and that, too, gradually stilled. The white herd had come to a stop, and the pall of yellow dust began to drift away on the wind.

Jane Withersteen waited on the ridge with full and grateful heart. Lassiter appeared, making his weary way toward her through the sage. And up on the slope Judkins rode into sight with his troop of boys. For the present, at least, the white herd would be looked after.

When Lassiter reached her and laid his hand on Black Star's mane, Jane could not find speech.

"Killed—my—hoss," he panted.

"Oh! I'm sorry," cried Jane. "Lassiter! I know you can't replace him, but I'll give you any one of my racers—Bells, or Night, even Black Star."

"I'll take a fast hoss, Jane, but not one of your favorites," he replied. "Only—will you let me have Black Star now an' ride him over there an' head off them fellers who stampeded the herd?"

He pointed to several moving specks of black and puffs of dust in the purple sage.

"I can head them off with this hoss, an' then—"

"Then, Lassiter?"

"They'll never stampede no more cattle."

"Oh! No! No! . . . Lassiter, I won't let you go!"

But a flush of fire flamed in her cheeks, and her trembling hands shook Black Star's bridle, and her eyes fell before Lassiter's.

⚜7⚜

THE DAUGHTER
OF WITHERSTEEN

LASSITER, will you be my rider?" Jane had asked him.

"I reckon so," he had replied.

Few as the words were, Jane knew how infinitely much they implied. She wanted him to take charge of her cattle and horses and ranges, and save them if that were possible. Yet, though she could not have spoken aloud all she meant, she was perfectly honest with herself. Whatever the price to be paid, she must keep Lassiter close to her; she must shield from him the man who had lured Milly Erne to Cottonwoods. In her fear she so controlled her mind that she did not whisper this Mormon's name to her own soul, she did not even think it. Besides, beyond this thing she regarded as a sacred obligation thrust upon her, was the need of a helper, of a friend, of a champion in this critical time. If she could rule this gunman, as Venters had called him, if she could even keep him from shedding blood, what strategy to play his name and his presence against the game of oppression her churchmen were waging against her? Never would she forget the effect upon Tull and his men when Venters shouted Lassiter's name. If she could not wholly control Lassiter, then what she could do might put off the fatal day.

One of her sage-racers was a dark bay, and she called him Bells because of the way he struck his iron shoes on the stones. When Jerd led out this slender, beautifully built horse Lassiter suddenly became all eyes. A rider's love of a thoroughbred shone in them. Round and round Bells he walked, plainly weakening all the time in his determination not to take one of Jane's favorite racers.

"Lassiter, you're half horse, and Bells sees it already," said Jane, laughing. "Look at his eyes. He likes you. He'll love you, too. How can you resist him? Oh, Lassiter, but Bells can run! It's nip and tuck between him and Wrangle, and only Black Star can beat him. He's too spirited a horse for a woman. Take him. He's yours."

"I jest am weak where a hoss's concerned," said Lassiter. "I'll take him, an' I'll take your orders, ma'am."

"Well, I'm glad, but never mind the ma'am. Let it still be Jane."

From that hour, it seemed Lassiter was always in the saddle, riding early and late; and coincident with his part in Jane's affairs the days assumed their old tranquillity. Her intelligence told her this was only the lull before the storm, but her faith would not have it so.

She resumed her visits to the village, and upon one of these she encountered Tull. He greeted her as he had before any trouble came between them, and she, responsive to peace if not quick to forget, met him halfway with manner almost cheerful. He regretted the loss of her cattle; he assured her that the vigilantes which had been organized would soon rout the rustlers; when that had been accomplished her riders would likely return to her.

"You've done a headstrong thing to hire this man Lassiter," Tull went on, severely. "He came to Cottonwoods with evil intent."

"I had to have somebody. And perhaps making him my rider may turn out best in the end for the Mormons of Cottonwoods."

"You mean to stay his hand?"

"I do—if I can."

"A woman like you can do anything with a man. That would be well, and would atone in some measure for the errors you have made."

He bowed and passed on. Jane resumed her walk with conflicting thoughts. She resented Elder Tull's cold, impassive manner that looked down upon her as one who had incurred his just displeasure. Otherwise he would have been the same calm, dark-browed, impenetrable man she had known for ten years. In fact, except when he had revealed his passion in the matter of the seizing of Venters, she had never dreamed he could be other than the grave, reproving preacher. He stood out now a strange, secretive man. She would have thought better of him if he had picked up the threads of their quarrel where they had parted. Was Tull what he appeared to be? The question flung itself involuntarily over Jane Withersteen's inhibitive habit of faith without question. And she refused to answer it. Tull could not fight in the open. Venters had said, Lassiter had said, that her elder shirked fight and worked in the dark. Just now in this meeting Tull had ignored the fact that he had sued, exhorted, demanded that she marry him. He made no mention of Venters. His manner was that of the minister who had been outraged, but who overlooked the frailties of a woman. Beyond question he seemed unutterably aloof from all knowledge of pressure being brought to bear upon her, absolutely guiltless of any connection with secret power over riders, with night journeys, with rustlers and stampedes of cattle. And that convinced her again of unjust suspicions. But it was convincement through an obstinate faith. She shuddered as she accepted it, and that shudder was the nucleus of a terrible revolt.

Jane turned into one of the wide lanes leading from the main street and entered a huge, shady yard. Here were sweet-smelling clover, alfalfa, flowers, and vegetables, all growing in happy confusion. And like these fresh green things were the dozens of babies, tots, toddlers, noisy urchins, laughing girls, a whole multitude of children of one family. For Collier Brandt, the father of all this numerous progeny, was a Mormon with four wives.

The big house where they lived was old, solid, picturesque, the lower part built of logs, the upper of rough clapboards, with vines growing up the outside stone chimneys. There were many wooden-shuttered windows, and one pretentious window of glass, proudly curtained in white. As this house had four mistresses, it likewise had four separate sections, not one of which communicated with another, and all had to be entered from the outside.

In the shade of a wide, low, vine-roofed porch Jane found Brandt's wives entertaining Bishop Dyer. They were motherly women, of comparatively similar ages, and plain-featured, and just at this moment anything but grave. The bishop was rather tall, of stout build, with iron-gray hair and beard, and eyes of light blue. They were merry now; but Jane had seen them when they were not, and then she feared him as she had feared her father.

The women flocked around her in welcome.

"Daughter of Withersteen," said the Bishop, gaily, as he took her hand, "you have not been prodigal of your gracious self of late. A Sabbath without you at service! I shall reprove Elder Tull."

"Bishop, the guilt is mine. I'll come to you and confess," Jane replied, lightly; but she felt the undercurrent of her words.

"Mormon love-making!" exclaimed the bishop, rubbing his hands. "Tull keeps you all to himself."

"No. He is not courting me."

"What? The laggard! If he does not make haste I'll go a-courting myself up to Withersteen House."

There was laughter and further bantering by the bishop, and then mild talk of village affairs, after which he took his leave, and Jane was left with her friend, Mary Brandt.

"Jane, you're not yourself. Are you sad about the rustling of the cattle? But you have so many, you are so rich."

Then Jane confided in her, telling much, yet holding back her doubts and fears.

"Oh, why don't you marry Tull and be one of us?"

"But, Mary, I don't love Tull," said Jane, stubbornly.

"I don't blame you for that. But, Jane Withersteen, you've got to choose between the love of man and love of God. Often we Mormon women have to do that. It's not easy. The kind of happiness you want I wanted once. I never got it, nor will you, unless you throw away your soul. We've all watched your affair with Venters in fear and trembling. Some dreadful thing will come of it. You don't want him hanged or shot—or treated worse, as that Gentile boy was treated in Glaze for fooling round a Mormon woman. Marry Tull. It's your duty as a Mormon. You'll feel no rapture as his wife—but think of heaven! Mormon women don't marry for what they expect on earth. Take up the cross, Jane. Remember your father found Amber Spring, built these old houses, brought Mormons here, and fathered them. You are the daughter of Withersteen!"

Jane left Mary Brandt and went to call upon other friends. They received her with the same glad welcome as had Mary, lavished upon her the pent-up affection of Mormon women, and let her go with her ears ringing of Tull, Venters, Lassiter, of duty to God and glory in heaven.

"Verily," murmured Jane, "I don't know myself when, through all this, I remain unchanged—nay, more fixed of purpose."

She returned to the main street and bent her thoughtful steps toward the center of the village. A string of wagons drawn by oxen was lumbering along. These "sage-freighters," as they were called, hauled grain and flour and merchandise from Sterling; and Jane laughed suddenly in the midst of her humility at the thought that they were her property, as was one of the three stores for which they freighted goods. The water that flowed along the path at her feet, and turned into each cottage-yard to nourish garden and orchard, also was hers, no less her private property because she chose to give it free. Yet in this village of Cottonwoods, which her father had founded and which she maintained, she was not her own mistress; she was not to abide by her own choice of a husband. She was the daughter of Withersteen. Suppose she proved it, imperiously! But she quelled that proud temptation at its birth.

Nothing could have replaced the affection which the village people had for her; no power could have made her happy as the pleasure her presence gave. As she went on down the street, past the stores with their rude platform entrances, and the saloons, where tired horses stood with bridles dragging, she was again assured of what was the bread and wine of life to her—that she was loved. Dirty boys playing in the ditch, clerks, teamsters, riders, loungers on the corners, ranchers on dusty horses, little girls running errands, and women hurrying to the stores all looked up at her coming with glad eyes.

Jane's various calls and wandering steps at length led her to the Gentile quarter of the village. This was at the extreme southern end, and here some thirty Gentile families lived in huts and shacks and log cabins and several dilapidated cottages. The fortunes of these inhabitants of Cottonwoods could be read in their abodes. Water they had in abundance, and therefore grass and fruit trees and patches of alfalfa and vegetable gardens. Some of the men and boys had a few stray cattle, others obtained such intermittent employment as the Mormons reluctantly tendered them. But none of the families was prosperous, many were very poor, and some lived only by Jane Withersteen's beneficence.

As it made Jane happy to go among her own people, so it saddened her to come in contact with these Gentiles. Yet that was not because she was unwelcome; here she was gratefully received by the women, passionately by the children. But poverty and idleness, with their attendant wretchedness and sorrow, always hurt her. That she could alleviate this distress more now than ever before proved the adage that it was an ill wind that blew nobody good. While her Mormon riders were in her employ she had found few Gentiles who could stay with her, and now she was able to find employment for all the men and boys. No little shock was it to have man after man tell her that he dare not accept her kind offer.

"It won't do," said one Carson, an intelligent man who had seen better days. "We've had our warning. Plain and to the point! Now there's Judkins, he packs guns, and he can use them, and so can the daredevil boys he's hired. But they've little responsibility. Can we risk having our homes burned in our absence?"

Jane felt the stretching and chilling of the skin of her face as the blood left it.

"Carson, you and the others rent these houses?" she asked.

"You ought to know, Miss Withersteen. Some of them are yours."

"I know? . . . Carson, I never in my life took a day's labor for rent or a yearling calf or a bunch of grass, let alone gold."

"Bivens, your storekeeper, sees to that."

"Look here, Carson," went on Jane, hurriedly, and now her cheeks were burning. "You and Black and Willet pack your goods and move your families up to my cabins in the grove. They're far more comfortable than these. Then go to work for me. And if aught happens to you there I'll give you money—gold enough to leave Utah!"

The man choked and stammered, and then, as tears welled into his eyes, he found the use of his tongue and cursed. No gentle speech could ever have equaled that curse in eloquent expression of what he felt for Jane Withersteen. How strangely his look and tone reminded her of Lassiter!

"No, it won't do," he said, when he had somewhat recovered himself.

"Miss Withersteen, there are things that you don't know, and there's not a soul among us who can tell you."

"I seem to be learning many things, Carson. Well, then, will you let me aid you—say, till better times?"

"Yes, I will," he replied, with his face lighting up. "I see what it means to you, and you know what it means to me. Thank you! And if better times ever come I'll be only too happy to work for you."

"Better times will come. I trust God and have faith in man. Good day, Carson."

The lane opened out upon the sage-inclosed alfalfa fields, and the last habitation, at the end of that lane of hovels, was the meanest. Formerly it had been a shed; now it was a home. The broad leaves of a wide-spreading cottonwood sheltered the sunken roof of weathered boards. Like an Indian hut, it had one floor. Round about it were a few scanty rows of vegetables, such as the hand of a weak woman had time and strength to cultivate. This little dwelling-place was just outside the village limits, and the widow who lived there had to carry her water from the nearest irrigation ditch. As Jane Withersteen entered the unfenced yard a child saw her, shrieked with joy, and came tearing toward her with curls flying. This child was a little girl of four called Fay. Her name suited her, for she was an elf, a sprite, a creature so fairylike and beautiful that she seemed unearthly.

"Muvver sended for oo," cried Fay, as Jane kissed her, "an' oo never tome."

"I didn't know, Fay; but I've come now."

Fay was a child of outdoors, of the garden and ditch and field, and she was dirty and ragged. But rags and dirt did not hide her beauty. The one thin little bedraggled garment she wore half covered her fine, slim body. Red as cherries were her cheeks and lips; her eyes were violet blue, and the crown of her childish loveliness was the curling golden hair. All the children of Cottonwoods were Jane Withersteen's friends; she loved them all. But Fay was dearest to her. Fay had few playmates, for among the Gentile children there were none near her age, and the Mormon children were forbidden to play with her. So she was a shy, wild, lonely child.

"Muvver's sick," said Fay, leading Jane toward the door of the hut.

Jane went in. There was only one room, rather dark and bare, but it was clean and neat. A woman lay upon a bed.

"Mrs. Larkin, how are you?" asked Jane, anxiously.

"I've been pretty bad for a week, but I'm better now."

"You haven't been here all alone—with no one to wait on you?"

"Oh no! My women neighbors are kind. They take turns coming in."

"Did you send for me?"

"Yes, several times."

"But I had no word—no messages ever got to me."

"I sent the boys, and they left word with your women that I was ill and would you please come."

A sudden deadly sickness seized Jane. She fought the weakness, as she fought to be above suspicious thoughts, and it passed, leaving her conscious of her utter impotence. That, too, passed as her spirit rebounded. But she had again caught a glimpse of dark underhand domination, running its secret lines this time into her own household. Like a spider in the blackness of night an unseen hand had begun to run these dark lines, to turn and twist them about her life, to plait and weave a web. Jane Withersteen knew it now, and in the realization further coolness and sureness came to her, and the fighting courage of her ancestors.

"Mrs. Larkin, you're better, and I'm so glad," said Jane. "But may I not do something for you—a turn at nursing, or send you things, or take care of Fay?"

"You're so good. Since my husband's been gone what would have become of Fay and me but for you? It was about Fay that I wanted to speak to you. This time I thought surely I'd die, and I was worried about Fay. Well, I'll be around all right shortly, but my strength's gone and I won't live long. So I may as well speak now. You remember you've been asking me to let you take Fay and bring her up as your daughter?"

"Indeed yes, I remember. I'll be happy to have her. But I hope the day—"

"Never mind that. The day'll come—sooner or later. I refused your offer, and now I'll tell you why."

"I know why," interposed Jane. "It's because you don't want her brought up as a Mormon."

"No, it wasn't altogether that." Mrs. Larkin raised her thin hand and laid it appealingly on Jane's. "I don't like to tell you. But—it's this: I told all my friends what you wanted. They know you, care for you, and they said for me to trust Fay to you. Women will talk, you know. It got to the ears of Mormons—gossip of your love for Fay and your wanting her. And it came straight back to me, in jealousy, perhaps, that you wouldn't take Fay as much for love of her as because of your religious duty to bring up another girl for some Mormon to marry."

"That's a damnable lie!" cried Jane Withersteen.

"It was what made me hesitate," went on Mrs. Larkin, "but I never believed it at heart. And now I guess I'll let you—"

"Wait! Mrs. Larkin, I may have told little white lies in my life, but never a lie that mattered, that hurt anyone. Now believe me. I love little Fay. If I had her near me I'd grow to worship her. When I asked for her I thought only of that love. . . . Let me prove this. You and Fay come to live with me. I've such a big house, and I'm so lonely. I'll help nurse you, take care of you. When you're better you can work for me. I'll keep little Fay and bring her up—without Mormon teaching. When she's grown, if she should want to leave me, I'll send her, and not empty-handed, back to Illinois where you came from. I promise you."

"I knew it was a lie," replied the mother, and she sank back upon her pillow with something of peace in her white, worn face. "Jane Withersteen, may heaven bless you! I've been deeply grateful to you. But because you're a Mormon I never felt close to you till now. I don't know much about religion as religion, but your God and my God are the same."

※8※

SURPRISE VALLEY

Back in that strange canyon, which Venters had found indeed a valley of surprises, the wounded girl's whispered appeal, almost a prayer, not to take her back to the rustlers crowned the events of the last few days with a confounding climax. That she should not want to return to them staggered Venters. Presently, as logical thought returned, her appeal confirmed his first impression—that she was more unfortunate than bad—and he experienced a sensation of gladness. If he had known before that Oldring's Masked Rider was a woman his opinion would have been formed and he would have considered her abandoned. But his first knowledge had come when he lifted a white face quivering in a convulsion of agony; he had heard God's name whispered by blood-stained lips; through her solemn and awful eyes he had caught a glimpse of her soul. And just now had come the entreaty to him, "Don't—take—me—back—there!"

Once and for all Venters's quick mind formed a permanent conception of this poor girl. He based it, not upon what the chances of life had made her, but upon the revelation of dark eyes that pierced the infinite, upon a few pitiful, halting words that betrayed failure and wrong and misery, yet breathed the truth of a tragic fate rather than a natural leaning to evil.

"What's your name?" he inquired.

"Bess," she answered.

"Bess what?"

"That's enough—just Bess."

The red that deepened in her cheeks was not all the flush of fever. Venters marveled anew, and this time at the tint of shame in her face, at the momentary drooping of long lashes. She might be a rustler's girl, but she was still capable of shame; she might be dying, but she still clung to some little remnant of honor.

"Very well, Bess. It doesn't matter," he said. "But this matters—what shall I do with you?"

"Are—you—a rider?" she whispered.

"Not now. I was once. I drove the Withersteen herds. But I lost my place—lost all I owned—and now I'm—I'm a sort of outcast. My name's Bern Venters."

"You won't—take me—to Cottonwoods—or Glaze? I'd be—hanged."

"No, indeed. But I must do something with you. For it's not safe for me here. I shot that rustler who was with you. Sooner or later he'll be found, and then my tracks. I must find a safer hiding-place where I can't be trailed."

"Leave me—here."

"Alone—to die!"

"Yes."

"I will not." Venters spoke shortly with a kind of ring in his voice.

"What—do you want—to do—with me?" Her whispering grew difficult, so low and faint that Venters had to stoop to hear her.

"Why, let's see," he replied, slowly. "I'd like to take you some place where I could watch by you, nurse you, till you're all right again."

"And—then?"

"Well, it'll be time to think of that when you're cured of your wound. It's a bad one. And—Bess, if you don't want to live—if you don't fight for life—you'll never—"

"Oh! I want—to live! I'm afraid—to die. But I'd rather—die—than go back—to—to—"

"To Oldring?" asked Venters, interrupting her in turn.

Her lips moved in an affirmative.

"I promise not to take you back to him or to Cottonwoods or to Glaze."

The mournful earnestness of her gaze suddenly shone with unutterable gratitude and wonder. And as suddenly Venters found her eyes beautiful as he had never seen or felt beauty. They were as dark blue as the sky at night. Then the flashing changed to a long, thoughtful look, in which there was wistful, unconscious searching of his face, a look that trembled on the verge of hope and trust.

"I'll try—to live," she said. The broken whisper just reached his ears. "Do what—you want—with me."

"Rest then—don't worry—sleep," he replied.

Abruptly he arose, as if her words had been decision for him, and with a sharp command to the dogs he strode from the camp. Venters was conscious of an indefinite conflict of change within him. It seemed to be a vague passing of old moods, a dim coalescing of new forces, a moment of inexplicable transition. He was both cast down and uplifted. He wanted to think and think of the meaning, but he resolutely dispelled emotion. His imperative need at present was to find a safe retreat, and this called for action.

So he set out. It still wanted several hours before dark. This trip he turned to the left and wended his skulking way southward a mile or more to the opening of the valley, where lay the strange scrawled rocks. He did not, however, venture boldly out into the open sage, but clung to the right-hand wall and went along that till its perpendicular line broke into the long incline of bare stone.

Before proceeding farther he halted, studying the strange character of this slope and realizing that a moving black object could be seen far against such background. Before him ascended a gradual swell of smooth stone. It was hard, polished, and full of pockets worn by centuries of eddying rainwater. A hundred yards up began a line of grotesque cedar trees, and they extended along the slope clear to its most southerly end. Beyond that end Venters wanted to get, and he concluded the cedars, few as they were, would afford some cover.

Therefore he climbed swiftly. The trees were farther up than he had estimated, though he had from long habit made allowance for the deceiving nature of distances in that country. When he gained the cover of cedars he paused to rest and look, and it was then he saw how the trees sprang from holes in the bare rock. Ages of rain had run down the slope, circling, eddying in depressions, wearing deep round holes. There had been dry seasons, accumulations of dust, wind-blown seeds, and cedars rose wonderfully out of solid rock. But these were not beautiful cedars. They were gnarled, twisted into weird contortions, as if growth were torture, dead at the tops, shrunken, gray, and old. Theirs had been a bitter fight, and Venters felt a strange sympathy for them. This country was hard on trees—and men.

He slipped from cedar to cedar, keeping them between him and the open valley. As he progressed, the belt of trees widened, and he kept to its upper margin. He passed shady pockets half full of water, and, as he marked the location for possible future need, he reflected that there had been no rain since the winter snows. From one of these shady holes a rabbit hopped out and squatted down, laying its ears flat.

Venters wanted fresh meat now more than when he had only himself to think of. But it would not do to fire his rifle there. So he broke off a cedar branch and threw it. He crippled the rabbit, which started to flounder up the slope. Venters did not wish to lose the meat, and he never allowed crippled game to escape, to die lingeringly in some covert. So after a careful glance below, and back toward the canyon, he began to chase the rabbit.

The fact that rabbits generally ran uphill was not new to him. But it presently seemed singular why this rabbit, that might have escaped downward, chose to ascend the slope. Venters knew then that it had a burrow higher up. More than once he jerked over to seize it, only in vain, for the rabbit by renewed effort eluded his grasp. Thus the chase continued on up the bare slope. The farther Venters climbed the more determined he grew to catch his quarry. At last, panting and sweating, he captured the rabbit at the foot of a steeper grade. Laying his rifle on the bulge of rising stone, he killed the animal and slung it from his belt.

Before starting down he waited to catch his breath. He had climbed far up that wonderful smooth slope, and had almost reached the base of yellow cliff that rose skyward, a huge scarred and cracked bulk. It frowned down upon him as if to forbid further ascent. Venters bent over for his rifle, and, as he picked it up from where it leaned against the steeper grade, he saw several little nicks cut in the solid stone.

They were only a few inches deep and about a foot apart. Venters began to count them—one—two—three—four—on up to sixteen. That number carried his glance to the top of this first bulging bench of cliff-base. Above, after a more level offset, was still steeper slope, and the line of nicks kept on, to wind round a projecting corner of wall.

A casual glance would have passed by these little dents; if Venters had not known what they signified he would never have bestowed upon them the second glance. But he knew they had been cut there by hand and, though age-worn, he recognized them as steps cut in the rock by the cliff-dwellers. With a pulse beginning to beat and hammer away his calmness, he eyed that indistinct line of steps, up to where the buttress of wall hid further sight of them. He knew that behind the corner of stone would be a cave or a crack which could never be suspected from below. Chance, that had sported with him of late, now directed him to a probable hiding-place. Again he laid aside his rifle, and, removing boots and belt, he began to walk up the steps. Like a mountain goat, he was agile, sure-footed, and he mounted the first bench without bending to use his hands. The next ascent took grip of fingers as well as toes, but he climbed steadily, swiftly, to reach the projecting corner, and slipped around it. Here he faced a notch in the cliff. At the apex he turned abruptly into a ragged vent that split the ponderous wall clear to the top, showing a narrow streak of blue sky.

At the base this vent was dark, cool, and smelled of dry, musty dust. It zigzagged so that he could not see ahead more than a few yards at a time. He noticed tracks of wildcats and rabbits in the dusty floor. At every turn he expected to come upon a huge cavern full of little square stone houses, each with a small aperture like a staring dark eye. The passage lightened and widened, and opened at the foot of a narrow, steep, ascending chute. Venters had a moment's notice of the rock, which was of the same

smoothness and hardness as the slope below, before his gaze went irresistibly upward to the precipitous walls of this wide ladder of granite. These
were ruined walls of yellow sandstone, and so split and splintered, so
overhanging with great sections of balancing rim, so impending with
tremendous crumbling crags, that Venters caught his breath sharply, and,
appalled, he instinctively recoiled as if a step upward might jar the ponderous cliffs from their foundation. Indeed, it seemed that these ruined
cliffs were but awaiting a breath of wind to collapse and come tumbling
down. Venters hesitated. It would be a foolhardy man who risked his life
under the leaning, waiting avalanches of rock in that gigantic split. Yet
how many years had they leaned there without falling! At the bottom of
the incline was an immense heap of weathered sandstone all crumbling to
dust, but there were no huge rocks as large as houses, such as rested so
lightly and frightfully above, waiting patiently and inevitably to crash
down. Slowly split from the parent rock by the weathering process, and
carved and sculptured by ages of wind and rain, they waited their moment. Venters felt how foolish it was for him to fear these broken walls—
to fear that, after they had endured for thousands of years, the moment of
his passing should be the one for them to slip. Yet he feared it.

"What a place to hide!" muttered Venters. "I'll climb—I'll see where
this thing goes. If only I can find water!"

With teeth tight shut he essayed the incline. And as he climbed he
bent his eyes downward. This, however, after a little grew impossible; he
had to look to obey his eager, curious mind. He raised his glance and saw
light between row on row of shafts and pinnacles and crags that stood out
from the main wall. Some leaned against the cliff, others against each
other; many stood sheer and alone; all were crumbling, cracked, rotten. It
was a place of yellow, ragged ruin. The passage narrowed as he went up; it
became a slant, hard for him to stick on; it was smooth as marble. Finally
he surmounted it, surprised to find the walls still several hundred feet
high, and a narrow gorge leading down on the other side. This was a
divide between two inclines, about twenty yards wide. At one side stood
an enormous rock. Venters gave it a second glance, because it rested on a
pedestal. It attracted closer attention. It was like a colossal pear of stone
standing on its stem. Around the bottom were thousands of little nicks
just distinguishable to the eye. They were marks of stone hatchets. The
cliff-dwellers had chipped and chipped away at this boulder till it rested
its tremendous bulk upon a mere pinpoint of its surface. Venters pondered. Why had the little stone-men hacked away at that big boulder? It
bore no semblance to a statue or an idol or a godhead or a sphinx.
Instinctively he put his hands on it and pushed; then his shoulder and
heaved. The stone seemed to groan, to stir, to grate, and then to move. It
tipped a little downward and hung balancing for a long instant, slowly
returned, rocked slightly, groaned, and settled back to its former position.

Venters divined its significance. It had been meant for defense. The cliff-dwellers, driven by dreaded enemies to this last stand, had cunningly cut the rock until it balanced perfectly, ready to be dislodged by strong hands. Just below it leaned a tottering crag that would have toppled, starting an avalanche on an acclivity where no sliding mass could stop. Crags and pinnacles, splintered cliffs, and leaning shafts and monuments, would have thundered down to block forever the outlet to Deception Pass.

"That was a narrow shave for me," said Venters, soberly. "A balancing rock! The cliff-dwellers never had to roll it. They died, vanished, and here the rock stands, probably little changed. . . . But it might serve another lonely dweller of the cliffs. I'll hide up here somewhere, if I can only find water."

He descended the gorge on the other side. The slope was gradual, the space narrow, the course straight for many rods. A gloom hung between the up-sweeping walls. In a turn the passage narrowed to scarce a dozen feet, and here was darkness of night. But light shone ahead; another abrupt turn brought day again, and then wide open space.

Above Venters loomed a wonderful arch of stone bridging the canyon rims, and through the enormous round portal gleamed and glistened a beautiful valley shining under sunset gold reflected by surrounding cliffs. He gave a start of surprise. The valley was a cove a mile long, half that wide, and its enclosing walls were smooth and stained, and curved inward, forming great caves. He decided that its floor was far higher than the level of Deception Pass and the intersecting canyons. No purple sage colored this valley floor. Instead there were the white of aspens, streaks of branch and slender trunk glistening from the green of leaves, and the darker green of oaks, and through the middle of this forest, from wall to wall, ran a winding line of brilliant green which marked the course of cottonwoods and willows.

"There's water here—and this is the place for me," said Venters. "Only birds can peep over those walls. I've gone Oldring one better."

Venters waited no longer, and turned swiftly to retrace his steps. He named the canyon Surprise Valley and the huge boulder that guarded the outlet Balancing Rock. Going down he did not find himself attended by such fears as had beset him in the climb; still, he was not easy in mind and could not occupy himself with plans of moving the girl and his outfit until he had descended to the notch. There he rested a moment and looked about him. The pass was darkening with the approach of night. At the corner of the wall, where the stone steps turned, he saw a spur of rock that would serve to hold the noose of a lasso. He needed no more aid to scale that place. As he intended to make the move under cover of darkness, he wanted most to be able to tell where to climb up. So, taking several small stones with him, he stepped and slid down to the edge of the slope where he had left his rifle and boots. Here he placed the stones some yards apart. He left the rabbit lying upon the bench where the steps began. Then he addressed a keen-sighted, remembering gaze to the rim-wall above. It was serrated, and between two spears of rock, directly in line with his position, showed a zigzag crack that at night would let through the gleam of sky. This settled, he put on his belt and boots and prepared to descend. Some consideration was necessary to decide whether or not to leave his rifle there. On the return, carrying the girl and a pack, it would be added encumbrance; and after debating the matter he left the rifle leaning against the bench. As he went straight down the slope he halted every few rods to look up at his mark on the rim. It changed, but he fixed each change in his memory. When he reached the first cedar tree, he tied his scarf upon a dead branch, and then hurried toward camp, having no more concern about finding his trail upon the return trip.

Darkness soon emboldened and lent him greater speed. It occurred to him, as he glided into the grassy glade near camp and heard the whinny of a horse, that he had forgotten Wrangle. The big sorrel could not be gotten into Surprise Valley. He would have to be left here.

Venters determined at once to lead the other horses out through the thicket and turn them loose. The farther they wandered from this canyon the better it would suit him. He easily descried Wrangle through the gloom, but the others were not in sight. Venters whistled low for the dogs, and when they came trotting to him he sent them out to search for the horses, and followed. It soon developed that they were not in the glade nor the thicket. Venters grew cold and rigid at the thought of rustlers having entered his retreat. But the thought passed, for the demeanor of Ring and Whitie reassured him. The horses had wandered away.

Under the clump of silver spruces hung a denser mantle of darkness, yet not so thick that Venters's night-practiced eyes could not catch the white oval of a still face. He bent over it with a slight suspension of breath that was both caution lest he frighten her and chill uncertainty of feeling lest he find her dead. But she slept, and he arose to renewed activity.

He packed his saddle-bags. The dogs were hungry, they whined about him and nosed his busy hands; but he took no time to feed them nor to satisfy his own hunger. He slung the saddle-bags over his shoulders and made them secure with his lasso. Then he wrapped the blankets closer about the girl and lifted her in his arms. Wrangle whinnied and thumped the ground as Venters passed him with the dogs. The sorrel knew he was being left behind, and was not sure whether he liked it or not. Venters went on and entered the thicket. Here he had to feel his way in pitch blackness and to wedge his progress between the close saplings. Time meant little to him now that he had started, and he edged along with slow side movement till he got clear of the thicket. Ring and Whitie stood waiting for him. Taking to the open aisles and patches of the sage, he walked guardedly, careful not to stumble or step in dust or strike against spreading sage-branches.

If he were burdened he did not feel it. From time to time, when he passed out of the black lines of shade into the wan starlight, he glanced at the white face of the girl lying in his arms. She had not awakened from her sleep or stupor. He did not rest until he cleared the black gate of the canyon. Then he leaned against a stone breast-high to him and gently released the girl from his hold. His brow and hair and the palms of his hands were wet, and there was a kind of nervous contraction of his muscles. They seemed to ripple and string tense. He had a desire to hurry and no sense of fatigue. A wind blew the scent of sage in his face. The first early blackness of night passed with the brightening of the stars. Somewhere back on his trail a coyote yelped, splitting the dead silence. Venters's faculties seemed singularly acute.

He lifted the girl again and pressed on. The valley afforded better traveling than the canyon. It was lighter, freer of sage, and there were no rocks. Soon, out of the pale gloom shone a still paler thing, and that was the low swell of slope. Venters mounted it, and his dogs walked beside him. Once upon the stone he slowed to snail pace, straining his sight to avoid the pockets and holes. Foot by foot he went up. The weird cedars, like great demons and witches chained to the rock and writhing in silent anguish, loomed up with wide and twisting naked arms. Venters crossed this belt of cedars, skirted the upper border, and recognized the tree he had marked, even before he saw his waving scarf.

Here he knelt and deposited the girl gently, feet first, and slowly laid her out full length. What he feared was to reopen one of her wounds. If he gave her a violent jar, or slipped and fell! But the supreme confidence so strangely felt that night admitted of no such blunders.

The slope before him seemed to swell into obscurity, to lose its definite outline in a misty, opaque cloud that shaded into the over-shadowing wall. He scanned the rim where the serrated points speared the sky, and he found the zigzag crack. It was dim, only a shade lighter than the dark ramparts; but he distinguished it, and that served.

Lifting the girl, he stepped upward, closely attending to the nature of the path under his feet. After a few steps he stopped to mark his line with the crack in the rim. The dogs clung closer to him. While chasing the rabbit this slope had appeared interminable to him; now, burdened as he was, he did not think of length or height or toil. He remembered only to avoid a misstep and to keep his direction. He climbed on, with frequent stops to watch the rim, and before he dreamed of gaining the bench he bumped his knees into it, and saw, in the dim gray light, his rifle and the rabbit. He had come straight up without mishap or swerving off his course, and his shut teeth unlocked.

As he laid the girl down in the shallow hollow of the little ridge, with

her white face upturned, she opened her eyes. Wide, staring, black, at
once like both the night and the stars, they made her face seem still
whiter.

"Is—it—you?" she asked, faintly.

"Yes," replied Venters.

"Oh! Where—are we?"

"I'm taking you to a safe place where no one will ever find you. I must
climb a little here and call the dogs. Don't be afraid. I'll soon come for
you."

She said no more. Her eyes watched him steadily for a moment and
then closed. Venters pulled off his boots and then felt for the little steps
in the rock. The shade of the cliff above obscured the point he wanted to
gain, but he could see dimly a few feet before him. What he had attempted with care he now went at with surpassing lightness. Buoyant,
rapid, sure, he attained the corner of wall and slipped around it. Here he
could not see a hand before his face, so he groped along, found a little flat
space, and there removed the saddle-bags. The lasso he took back with
him to the corner and looped the noose over the spur of rock.

"Ring—Whitie—come," he called, softly.

Low whines came up from below.

"Here! Come, Whitie—Ring," he repeated, this time sharply.

Then followed scraping of claws and pattering of feet; and out of the
gray gloom below him swiftly climbed the dogs to reach his side and pass
beyond.

Venters descended, holding to the lasso. He tested its strength by
throwing all his weight upon it. Then he gathered the girl up, and,
holding her securely in his left arm, he began to climb, at every few steps
jerking his right hand upward along the lasso. It sagged at each forward
movement he made, but he balanced himself lightly during the interval
when he lacked the support of a taut rope. He climbed as if he had wings,
the strength of a giant, and knew not the sense of fear. The sharp corner
of cliff seemed to cut out of the darkness. He reached it and the protruding shelf, and then, entering the black shade of the notch, he moved
blindly but surely to the place where he had left the saddle-bags. He heard
the dogs, though he could not see them. Once more he carefully placed
the girl at his feet. Then, on hands and knees, he went over the little flat
space, feeling for stones. He removed a number, and, scraping the deep
dust into a heap, he unfolded the outer blanket from around the girl and
laid her upon this bed. Then he went down the slope again for his boots,
rifle, and the rabbit, and, bringing also his lasso with him, he made short
work of that trip.

"Are—you—there?" The girl's voice came low from the blackness.

"Yes," he replied, and was conscious that his laboring breast made
speech difficult.

"Are we—in a cave?"

"Yes."

"Oh, listen! . . . The waterfall! . . . I hear it! You've brought me back!"

Venters heard a murmuring moan that one moment swelled to a pitch almost softly shrill and the next lulled to a low, almost inaudible sigh.

"That's—wind blowing—in the—cliffs," he panted. "You're far—from Oldring's—canyon."

The effort it cost him to speak made him conscious of extreme lassitude following upon great exertion. It seemed that when he lay down and drew his blanket over him the action was the last before utter prostration. He stretched inert, wet, hot, his body one great strife of throbbing, stinging nerves and bursting veins. And there he lay for a long while before he felt that he had begun to rest.

Rest came to him that night, but no sleep. Sleep he did not want. The hours of strained effort were now as if they had never been, and he wanted to think. Earlier in the day he had dismissed an inexplicable feeling of change; but now, when there was no longer demand on his cunning and strength and he had time to think, he could not catch the elusive thing that had sadly perplexed as well as elevated his spirit.

Above him, through a V-shaped cleft in the dark rim of the cliff, shone the lustrous stars that had been his lonely accusers for a long, long year. Tonight they were different. He studied them. Larger, whiter, more radiant they seemed; but that was not the difference he meant. Gradually it came to him that the distinction was not one he saw, but one he felt. In this he divined as much of the baffling change as he thought would be revealed to him then. And as he lay there, with the singing of the cliff-winds in his ears, the white stars above the dark, bold vent, the difference which he felt was that he was no longer alone.

⁙ 9 ⁙

SILVER SPRUCE
AND ASPENS

T HE REST of that night seemed to Venters only a few moments of
starlight, a dark overcasting of sky, an hour or so of gray gloom, and
then the lighting of dawn.

When he had bestirred himself, feeding the hungry dogs and breaking
his long fast, and had repacked his saddle-bags, it was clear daylight,
though the sun had not tipped the yellow wall in the east. He concluded
to make the climb and descent into Surprise Valley in one trip. To that
end he tied his blanket upon Ring and gave Whitie the extra lasso and
the rabbit to carry. Then, with the rifle and saddle-bags slung upon his
back, he took up the girl. She did not awaken from heavy slumber.

That climb up under the rugged, menacing brows of the broken cliffs,
in the face of a grim, leaning boulder that seemed to be weary of its age-
long wavering, was a tax on strength and nerve that Venters felt equally
with something sweet and strangely exulting in its accomplishment. He
did not pause until he gained the narrow divide and there he rested.
Balancing Rock loomed huge, cold in the gray light of dawn, a thing
without life, yet it spoke silently to Venters: "I am waiting to plunge
down, to shatter and crash, roar and boom, to bury your trail, and close
forever the outlet to Deception Pass!"

On the descent of the other side Venters had easy going, but was
somewhat concerned because Whitie appeared to have succumbed to
temptation, and while carrying the rabbit was also chewing on it. And
Ring evidently regarded this as an injury to himself, especially as he had
carried the heavier load. Presently he snapped at one end of the rabbit
and refused to let go. But his action prevented Whitie from further misdo-
ing, and then the two dogs pattered down, carrying the rabbit between
them.

Venters turned out of the gorge, and suddenly paused stock-still, astounded at the scene before him. The curve of the great stone bridge had
caught the sunrise, and through the magnificent arch burst a glorious
stream of gold that shone with a long slant down into the center of
Surprise Valley. Only through the arch did any sunlight pass, so that all

the rest of the valley lay still asleep, dark green, mysterious, shadowy, merging its level into walls as misty and soft as morning clouds.

Venters then descended, passing through the arch, looking up at its tremendous height and sweep. It spanned the opening to Surprise Valley, stretching in almost perfect curve from rim to rim. Even in his hurry and concern Venters could not but feel its majesty, and the thought came to him that the cliff-dwellers must have regarded it as an object of worship.

Down, down, down Venters strode, more and more feeling the weight of his burden as he descended, and still the valley lay below him. As all other canyons and coves and valleys had deceived him, so had this deep, nestling oval. At length he passed beyond the slope of weathered stone that spread fan-shape from the arch, and encountered a grassy terrace running to the right and about on a level with the tips of the oaks and cottonwoods below. Scattered here and there upon this shelf were clumps of aspens, and he walked through them into a glade that surpassed, in beauty and adaptability for a wild home, any place he had ever seen. Silver spruces bordered the base of a precipitous wall that rose loftily. Caves indented its surface, and there were no detached ledges or weathered sections that might dislodge a stone. The level ground, beyond the spruces, dropped down into a little ravine. This was one dense line of slender aspens from which came the low splashing of water. And the terrace, lying open to the west, afforded unobstructed view of the valley of green treetops.

For his camp Venters chose a shady, grassy plot between the silver spruces and the cliff. Here, in the stone wall, had been wonderfully carved by wind or washed by water several deep caves above the level of the terrace. They were clean, dry, roomy. He cut spruce boughs and made a bed in the largest cave and laid the girl there. The first intimation that he had of her being aroused from sleep or lethargy was a low call for water.

He hurried down into the ravine with his canteen. It was a shallow, grass-green place with aspens growing up everywhere. To his delight he found a tiny brook of swift-running water. Its faint tinge of amber reminded him of the spring at Cottonwoods, and the thought gave him a little shock. The water was so cold it made his fingers tingle as he dipped the canteen. Having returned to the cave, he was glad to see the girl drink thirstily. This time he noted that she could raise her head slightly without his help.

"You were thirsty," he said. "It's good water. I've found a fine place. Tell me—how do you feel?"

"There's pain—here," she replied, and moved her hand to her left side.

"Why, that's strange! Your wounds are on your right side. I believe you're hungry. Is the pain a kind of dull ache—a gnawing?"

"It's like—that."

"Then it's hunger." Venters laughed, and suddenly caught himself with a quick breath and felt again the little shock. When had he laughed? "It's hunger," he went on. "I've had that gnaw many a time. I've got it now. But you mustn't eat. You can have all the water you want, but no food just yet."

"Won't I—starve?"

"No, people don't starve easily. I've discovered that. You must lie perfectly still and rest and sleep—for days."

"My hands—are dirty; my face feels—so hot and sticky; my boots hurt." It was her longest speech as yet, and it trailed off in a whisper.

"Well, I'm a fine nurse!"

It annoyed him that he had never thought of these things. But then, awaiting her death and thinking of her comfort were vastly different matters. He unwrapped the blanket which covered her. What a slender girl she was! No wonder he had been able to carry her miles and pack her up that slippery ladder of stone. Her boots were of soft, fine leather, reaching clear to her knees. He recognized the make as one of a boot-maker in Sterling. Her spurs, that he had stupidly neglected to remove, consisted of silver frames and gold chains, and the rowels, large as silver dollars, were fancifully engraved. The boots slipped off rather hard. She wore heavy woollen rider's stockings, half length, and these were pulled up over the ends of her short trousers. Venters took off the stockings to note her little feet were red and swollen. He bathed them. Then he removed his scarf and bathed her face and hands.

"I must see your wounds now," he said, gently.

She made no reply, but watched him steadily as he opened her blouse and untied the bandage. His strong fingers trembled a little as he removed it. If the wounds had reopened! A chill struck him as he saw the angry red bullet-mark, and a tiny stream of blood winding from it down her white breast. Very carefully he lifted her to see that the wound in her back had closed perfectly. Then he washed the blood from her breast, bathed the wound, and left it unbandaged, open to the air.

Her eyes thanked him.

"Listen," he said, earnestly. "I've had some wounds, and I've seen many. I know a little about them. The hole in your back has closed. If you lie still three days the one in your breast will close and you'll be safe. The danger from hemorrhage will be over."

He had spoken with earnest sincerity, almost eagerness.

"Why—do you—want me—to get well?" she asked, wonderingly.

The simple question seemed unanswerable except on grounds of humanity. But the circumstances under which he had shot this strange girl, the shock and realization, the waiting for death, the hope, had resulted in a condition of mind wherein Venters wanted her to live more than he had ever wanted anything. Yet he could not tell why. He believed the killing of the rustler and the subsequent excitement had disturbed him. For how else could he explain the throbbing of his brain, the heat of his blood, the undefined sense of full hours, charged, vibrant with pulsating mystery where once they had dragged in loneliness?

"I shot you," he said, slowly, "and I want you to get well so I shall not have killed a woman. But—for your own sake, too—"

A terrible bitterness darkened her eyes, and her lips quivered.

"Hush," said Venters. "You've talked too much already."

In her unutterable bitterness he saw a darkness of mood that could not have been caused by her present weak and feverish state. She hated the life she had led, that she probably had been compelled to lead. She had suffered some unforgivable wrong at the hands of Oldring. With that conviction Venters felt a flame throughout his body, and it marked the rekindling of fierce anger and ruthlessness. In the past long year he had nursed resentment. He had hated the wilderness—the loneliness of the uplands. He had waited for something to come to pass. It had come. Like an Indian stealing horses he had skulked into the recesses of the canyons. He had found Oldring's retreat; he had killed a rustler; he had shot an unfortunate girl, then had saved her from this unwitting act, and he meant to save her from the consequent wasting of blood, from fever and weakness. Starvation he had to fight for her and for himself. Where he had been sick at the letting of blood, now he remembered it in grim, cold calm. And as he lost that softness of nature, so he lost his fear of men. He would watch for Oldring, biding his time, and he would kill this great black-bearded rustler who had held a girl in bondage, who had used her to his infamous ends.

Venters surmised this much of the change in him—idleness had passed; keen, fierce vigor flooded his mind and body; all that had happened to him at Cottonwoods seemed remote and hard to recall; the difficulties and perils of the present absorbed him, held him in a kind of spell.

First, then, he fitted up the little cave adjoining the girl's room for his own comfort and use. His next work was to build a fireplace of stones and to gather a store of wood. That done, he spilled the contents of his saddle-bags upon the grass and took stock. His outfit consisted of a small-handled axe, a hunting-knife, a large number of cartridges for rifle or revolver, a tin plate, a cup, and a fork and spoon, a quantity of dried beef and dried fruits, and small canvas bags containing tea, sugar, salt, and pepper. For him alone this supply would have been bountiful to begin a sojourn in the wilderness, but he was no longer alone. Starvation in the uplands was not an unheard-of thing; he did not, however, worry at all on that score, and feared only his possible inability to supply the needs of a woman in a weakened and extremely delicate condition.

If there was no game in the valley—a contingency he doubted—it would not be a great task for him to go by night to Oldring's herd and pack out a calf. The exigency of the moment was to ascertain if there were game in Surprise Valley. Whitie still guarded the dilapidated rabbit, and Ring slept nearby under a spruce. Venters called Ring and went to the edge of the terrace, and there halted to survey the valley.

He was prepared to find it larger than his unstudied glanced had made it appear; for more than a casual idea of dimensions and a hasty conception of oval shape and singular beauty he had not had time. Again the felicity of the name he had given the valley struck him forcibly. Around the red perpendicular walls, except under the great arc of stone, ran a terrace fringed at the cliff-base by silver spruces; below that first terrace sloped another wider one densely overgrown with aspens, and the center of the valley was a level circle of oaks and alders, with the glittering green line of willows and cottonwood dividing it in half. Venters saw a number and variety of birds flitting among the trees. To his left, facing the stone bridge, an enormous cavern opened in the wall; and low down, just above the treetops, he made out a long shelf of cliff-dwellings, with little black, staring windows or doors. Like eyes they were, and seemed to watch him. The few cliff-dwellings he had seen—all ruins—had left him with haunting memory of age and solitude and of something past. He had come, in a way, to be a cliff-dweller himself, and those silent eyes would look down upon him, as if in surprise that after thousands of years a man had invaded the valley. Venters felt sure that he was the only white man who had ever walked under the shadow of the wonderful stone bridge, down into that wonderful valley with its circle of caves and its terraced rings of silver spruce and aspens.

The dog growled below and rushed into the forest. Venters ran down the declivity to enter a zone of light shade streaked with sunshine. The oak trees were slender, none more than half a foot thick, and they grew close together, intermingling their branches. Ring came running back with a rabbit in his mouth. Venters took the rabbit and, holding the dog near him, stole softly on. There were fluttering of wings among the branches and quick bird-notes, and rustling of dead leaves and rapid patterings. Venters crossed well-worn trails marked with fresh tracks; and when he had stolen on a little farther he saw many birds and running quail, and more rabbits than he could count. He had not penetrated the forest of oaks for a hundred yards, had not approached anywhere near the line of willows and cottonwoods which he knew grew along a stream. But he had seen enough to know that Surprise Valley was the home of many wild creatures.

Venters returned to camp. He skinned the rabbits, and gave the dogs the one they had quarreled over, and the skin of this he dressed and hung up to dry, feeling that he would like to keep it. It was a particularly rich, furry pelt with a beautiful white tail. Venters remembered that but for the bobbing of that white tail catching his eye he would never have discovered Surprise Valley. Little incidents of chance like this had turned him here and there in Deception Pass; and now they had assumed to him the significance and direction of destiny.

His good fortune in the matter of game at hand brought to his mind the necessity of keeping it in the valley. Therefore, he took the axe and cut bundles of aspens and willows, and packed them up under the bridge to the narrow outlet of the gorge. Here he began fashioning a fence, by driving aspens into the ground and lacing them fast with willows. Trip after trip he made down for more building material, and the afternoon had passed when he finished the work to his satisfaction. Wildcats might scale the fence, but no coyote could come in to search for prey, and no rabbits or other small game could escape from the valley.

Upon returning to camp he set about getting his supper at ease, around a fine fire, without hurry or fear of discovery. After hard work that had definite purpose, this freedom and comfort gave him peculiar satisfaction. He caught himself often, as he kept busy round the campfire, stopping to glance at the quiet form in the cave, and at the dogs stretched cozily near him, and then out across the beautiful valley. The present was not yet real to him.

While he ate, the sun set beyond a dip in the rim of the curved wall. As the morning sun burst wondrously through a grand arch into this valley, in a golden, slanting shaft, so the evening sun, at the moment of setting, shone through a gap of cliffs, sending down a broad red burst to brighten the oval with a blaze of fire. To Venters both sunrise and sunset were unreal.

A cool wind blew across the oval, waving the tips of oaks, and, while the light lasted, fluttering the aspen leaves into millions of facets of red, and sweeping the graceful spruces. Then with the wind soon came a shade and a darkening, and suddenly the valley was gray. Night came there quickly after the sinking of the sun. Venters went softly to look at the girl. She slept, and her breathing was quiet and slow. He lifted Ring into the cave, with a stern whisper for him to stay there on guard. Then he drew the blanket carefully over her and returned to the campfire.

Though exceedingly tired, he was yet loath to yield to lassitude, but this night it was not from listening, watchful vigilance; it was from a desire to realize his position. The details of his wild environment seemed the only substance of a strange dream. He saw the darkening rims, the gray oval turning black, the undulating surface of forest, like a rippling lake, and the spear-pointed spruces. He heard the flutter of aspen leaves and the soft, continuous splash of falling water. The melancholy note of a canyon bird broke clear and lonely from the high cliffs. Venters had no name for this night singer, and he had never seen one; but the few notes, always pealing out just at darkness, were as familiar to him as the canyon silence. Then they ceased, and the rustle of leaves and the murmur of water hushed in a growing sound that Venters fancied was not of earth.

Neither had he a name for this, only it was inexpressibly wild and sweet. The thought came that it might be a moan of the girl in her last outcry of life, and he felt a tremor shake him. But no! This sound was not human, though it was like despair. He began to doubt his sensitive perceptions, to believe that he half-dreamed what he thought he heard. Then the sound swelled with the strengthening of the breeze, and he realized it was the singing of the wind in the cliffs.

By and by a drowsiness overcame him, and Venters began to nod, half asleep, with his back against a spruce. Rousing himself and calling Whitie, he went to the cave. The girl lay barely visible in the dimness. Ring crouched beside her, and the patting of his tail on the stone assured Venters that the dog was awake and faithful to his duty. Venters sought his own bed of fragrant boughs; and as he lay back, somehow grateful for the comfort and safety, the night seemed to steal away from him and he sank softly into intangible space and rest and slumber.

Venters awakened to the sound of melody that he imagined was only the haunting echo of dream music. He opened his eyes to another surprise of this valley of beautiful surprises. Out of his cave he saw the exquisitely fine foliage of the silver spruces crossing a round space of blue morning sky; and in this lacy leafage fluttered a number of gray birds with black and white stripes and long tails. They were mockingbirds, and they were singing as if they wanted to burst their throats. Venters listened. One long, silver-tipped branch drooped almost to his cave, and upon it, within a few yards of him, sat one of the graceful birds. Venters saw the swelling and quivering of its throat in song. He arose, and when he slid down out of his cave the birds fluttered and flew farther away.

Venters stepped before the opening of the other cave and looked in. The girl was awake, with wide eyes and listening look, and she had a hand on Ring's neck.

"Mockingbirds!" she said.

"Yes," replied Venters, "and I believe they like our company."

"Where are we?"

"Never mind now. After a little I'll tell you."

"The birds woke me. When I heard them—and saw the shiny trees— and the blue sky—and then a blaze of gold dropping down—I wondered—"

She did not complete her fancy, but Venters imagined he understood her meaning. She appeared to be wandering in mind. Venters felt her face and hands and found them burning with fever. He went for water, and was glad to find it almost as cold as if flowing from ice. That water was the only medicine he had, and he put faith in it. She did not want to drink, but he made her swallow, and then he bathed her face and head and cooled her wrists.

The day began with a heightening of the fever. Venters spent the time reducing her temperature, cooling her hot cheeks and temples. He kept close watch over her, and at the least indication of restlessness, that he knew led to tossing and rolling of the body, he held her tightly, so no violent move could reopen her wounds. Hour after hour she babbled and laughed and cried and moaned in delirium; but whatever her secret was she did not reveal it. Attended by something somber for Venters, the day passed. At night in the cool winds the fever abated and she slept.

The second day was a repetition of the first. On the third he seemed to see her wither and waste away before his eyes. That day he scarcely went from her side for a moment, except to run for fresh, cool water; and he did not eat. The fever broke on the fourth day and left her spent and shrunken, a slip of a girl with life only in her eyes. They hung upon Venters with a mute observance, and he found hope in that.

To rekindle the spark that had nearly flickered out, to nourish the little life and vitality that remained in her, was Venters's problem. But he had little resource other than the meat of the rabbits and quail; and from these he made broths and soups as best he could, and fed her with a spoon. It came to him that the human body, like the human soul, was a strange thing and capable of recovering from terrible shocks. For almost immediately she showed faint signs of gathering strength. There was one more waiting day, in which he doubted, and spent long hours by her side as she slept, and watched the gentle swell of her breast rise and fall in breathing, and the wind stir the tangled chestnut curls. On the next day he knew that she would live.

Upon realizing it he abruptly left the cave and sought his accustomed seat against the trunk of a big spruce, where once more he let his glance stray along the sloping terraces. She would live, and the somber gloom lifted out of the valley, and he felt relief that was pain. Then he roused to the call of action, to the many things he needed to do in the way of making camp fixtures and utensils, to the necessity of hunting food, and the desire to explore the valley.

But he decided to wait a few more days before going far from camp, because he fancied that the girl rested easier when she could see him near at hand. And on the first day her languor appeared to leave her in a renewed grip of life. She awoke stronger from each short slumber; she ate greedily, and she moved about in her bed of boughs; and always, it seemed to Venters, her eyes followed him. He knew now that her recovery would be rapid. She talked about the dogs, about the caves, the valley, about how hungry she was, till Venters silenced her, asking her to put off further talk till another time. She obeyed, but she sat up in her bed, and her eyes roved to and fro, and always back to him.

Upon the second morning she sat up when he awakened her, and would not permit him to bathe her face and feed her, which actions she performed for herself. She spoke little, however, and Venters was quick to catch in her the first intimations of thoughtfulness and curiosity and appreciation of her situation. He left camp and took Whitie out to hunt for rabbits. Upon his return he was amazed and somewhat anxiously concerned to see his invalid sitting with her back to a corner of the cave and her bare feet swinging out. Hurriedly he approached, intending to advise her to lie down again, to tell her that perhaps she might overtax her strength. The sun shone upon her, glinting on the little head with its tangle of bright hair and the small, oval face with its pallor, and dark-blue eyes underlined by dark-blue circles. She looked at him and he looked at her. In that exchange of glances he imagined each saw the other in some different guise. It seemed impossible to Venters that this frail girl could be Oldring's Masked Rider. It flashed over him that he had made a mistake which presently she would explain.

"Help me down," she said.

"But—are you well enough?" he protested. "Wait—a little longer."

"I'm weak—dizzy. But I want to get down."

He lifted her—what a light burden now!—and stood her upright beside him, and supported her as she essayed to walk with halting steps. She was like a stripling of a boy; the bright, small head scarcely reached his shoulder. But now, as she clung to his arm, the rider's costume she wore did not contradict, as it had done at first, his feeling of her femininity. She might be the famous Masked Rider of the uplands, she might resemble a boy; but her outline, her little hands and feet, her hair, her big eyes and tremulous lips, and especially a something that Venters felt as a subtle essence rather than what he saw, proclaimed her sex.

She soon tired. He arranged a comfortable seat for her under the spruce that overspread the campfire.

"Now tell me—everything," she said.

He recounted all that had happened from the time of his discovery of the rustlers in the canyon up to the present moment.

"You shot me—and now you've saved my life?"

"Yes. After almost killing you I've pulled you through."

"Are you glad?"

"I should say so!"

Her eyes were unusually expressive, and they regarded him steadily; she was unconscious of that mirroring of her emotions, and they shone with gratefulness and interest and wonder and sadness.

"Tell me—about yourself?" she asked.

He made this a briefer story, telling of his coming to Utah, his various occupations till he became a rider, and then how the Mormons had practically driven him out of Cottonwoods, an outcast.

Then, no longer able to withstand his own burning curiosity, he questioned her in turn.

"Are you Oldring's Masked Rider?"

"Yes," she replied, and dropped her eyes.

"I knew it—I recognized your figure—and mask, for I saw you once. Yet I can't believe it! . . . But you never *were* really that rustler, as we riders knew him? A thief—a marauder—a kidnapper of women—a murderer of sleeping riders!"

"No! I never stole—or harmed anyone—in all my life. I only rode and rode—"

"But why—why?" he burst out. "Why the name? I understand Oldring made you ride. But the black mask—the mystery—the things laid to your hands—the threats in your infamous name—the night-riding credited to you—the evil deeds deliberately blamed on you and acknowledged by rustlers—even Oldring himself! Why? Tell me why?"

"I never knew that," she answered low. Her drooping head straightened, and the large eyes, larger now and darker, met Venters's with a clear, steadfast gaze in which he read truth. It verified his own conviction.

"Never knew? That's strange! Are you a Mormon?"

"No."

"Is Oldring a Mormon?"

"No."

"Do you—care for him?"

"Yes. I hate his men—his life—sometimes I almost hate him!"

Venters paused in his rapid-fire questioning, as if to brace himself to ask for a truth that would be abhorrent for him to confirm, but which he seemed driven to hear.

"What are—what *were* you to Oldring?"

Like some delicate thing suddenly exposed to blasting heat, the girl wilted; her head dropped, and into her white, wasted cheeks crept the red of shame.

Venters would have given anything to recall that question. It seemed so different—his thought when spoken. Yet her shame established in his mind something akin to the respect he had strangely been hungering to feel for her.

"D——n that question! Forget it!" he cried, in a passion of pain for her and anger at himself. "But once and for all—tell me—I know it, yet I want to hear you say so—you couldn't help yourself?"

"Oh no."

"Well, that makes it all right with me," he went on, honestly. "I—I want you to feel that . . . you see—we've been thrown together—and—and I want to help you—not hurt you. I thought life had been cruel to me, but when I think of yours I feel mean and little for my complaining. Anyway, I was a lonely outcast. And now! . . . I don't see very clearly what it all means. Only we are here—together. We've got to stay here, for long, surely till you are well. But you'll never go back to Oldring. And I'm sure helping you will help me, for I was sick in mind. There's something now for me to do. And if I can win back your strength—then get you away, out of this wild country—help you somehow to a happier life—just think how good that'll be for me!"

⁑10⁑

LOVE

DURING all these waiting days Venters, with the exception of the afternoon when he had built the gate in the gorge, had scarcely gone out of sight of camp and never out of hearing. His desire to explore Surprise Valley was keen, and on the morning after his long talk with the girl he took his rifle and, calling Ring, made a move to start. The girl lay back in a rude chair of boughs he had put together for her. She had been watching him, and when he picked up the gun and called the dog Venters thought she gave a nervous start.

"I'm only going to look over the valley," he said.

"Will you be gone long?"

"No," he replied, and started off. The incident set him thinking of his former impression that, after her recovery from fever, she did not seem at ease unless he was close at hand. It was fear of being alone, due, he concluded, most likely to her weakened condition. He must not leave her much alone.

As he strode down the sloping terrace, rabbits scampered before him, and the beautiful valley quail, as purple in color as the sage on the uplands, ran fleetly along the ground into the forest. It was pleasant under the trees, in the gold-flecked shade, with the whistle of quail and twittering of birds everywhere. Soon he had passed the limit of his former excursions and entered new territory. Here the woods began to show open glades and brooks running down from the slope, and presently he emerged from shade into the sunshine of a meadow. The shaking of the high grass told him of the running of animals, what species he could not tell, but from Ring's manifest desire to have a chase they were evidently some kind wilder than rabbits. Venters approached the willow and cottonwood belt that he had observed from the height of slope. He penetrated it to find a considerable stream of water and great half-submerged mounds of brush and sticks, and all about him were old and new gnawed circles at the base of the cottonwoods.

"Beaver!" he exclaimed. "By all that's lucky! The meadow's full of beaver. How did they ever get here?"

Beaver had not found a way into the valley by the trail of the cliff-dwellers, of that he was certain; and he began to have more than curiosity as to the outlet or inlet of the stream. When he passed some dead water, which he noted was held by a beaver-dam, there was a current in the stream, and it flowed west. Following its course, he soon entered the oak forest again, and passed through to find himself before massed and jumbled ruins of cliff wall. There were tangled thickets of wild plum trees and other thorny growths that made passage extremely laborsome. He found innumerable tracks of wildcats and foxes. Rustlings in the thick undergrowth told him of stealthy movements of these animals. At length his further advance appeared futile, for the reason that the stream disappeared in a split at the base of immense rocks over which he could not climb. To his relief he concluded that though beaver might work their way up the narrow chasm where the water rushed, it would be impossible for men to enter the valley there.

This western curve was the only part of the valley where the walls had been split asunder, and it was a wildly rough and inaccessible corner. Going back a little way, he leaped the stream and headed toward the southern wall. Once out of the oaks he found again the low terrace of aspens, and above that the wide, open terrace fringed by silver spruces. This side of the valley contained the wind- or water-worn caves. As he pressed on, keeping to the upper terrace, cave after cave opened out of the cliff; now a large one, now a small one. Then yawned, quite suddenly and wonderfully above him, the great cavern of the cliff-dwellers.

It was still a goodly distance, and he tried to imagine, if it appeared so huge from where he stood, what it would be when he got there. He climbed the terrace and then faced a long, gradual ascent of weathered rock and dust, which made climbing too difficult for attention to anything else. At length he entered a zone of shade, and looked up. He stood just within the hollow of a cavern so immense that he had no conception of its real dimensions. The curved roof, stained by ages of leakage, with buff and black and rust-colored streaks, swept up and loomed higher and seemed to soar to the rim of the cliff. Here again was a magnificent arch, such as formed the grand gateway to the valley, only in this instance it formed the dome of a cave instead of the span of a bridge.

Venters passed onward and upward. The stones he dislodged rolled down with strange, hollow crack and roar. He had climbed a hundred rods inward, and yet he had not reached the base of the shelf where the cliff-dwellings rested, a long half-circle of connected stone house, with little dark holes that he had fancied were eyes. At length he gained the base of the shelf, and here found steps cut in the rock. These facilitated climbing,

and as he went up he thought how easily this vanished race of men might
once have held that stronghold against an army. There was only one
possible place to ascend, and this was narrow and steep.

Venters had visited cliff-dwellings before, and they had been in ruins,
and of no great character or size but this place was of proportions that
stunned him, and it had not been desecrated by the hand of man, nor had
it been crumbled by the hand of time. It was a stupendous tomb. It had
been a city. It was just as it had been left by its builders. The little houses
were there, the smoke-blackened stains of fires, the pieces of pottery
scattered about cold hearths, the stone hatchets; and stone pestles and
mealing-stones lay beside round holes polished by years of grinding maize
—lay there as if they had been carelessly dropped yesterday. But the cliff-
dwellers were gone!

Dust! They were dust on the floor or at the foot of the shelf, and their
habitations and utensils endured. Venters felt the sublimity of that marvelous vaulted arch, and it seemed to gleam with a glory of something
that was gone. How many years had passed since the cliff-dwellers gazed
out across the beautiful valley as he was gazing now? How long had it
been since women ground grain in those polished holes? What time had
rolled by since men of an unknown race lived, loved, fought, and died
there? Had an enemy destroyed them? Had disease destroyed them, or
only that greatest destroyer—time? Venters saw a long line of blood-red
hands painted low down upon the yellow roof of stone. Here was strange
portent, if not an answer to his queries. The place oppressed him. It was
light, but full of a transparent gloom. It smelled of dust and musty stone,
of age and disuse. It was sad. It was solemn. It had the look of a place
where silence had become master and was now irrevocable and terrible
and could not be broken. Yet, at the moment, from high up in the carved
crevices of the arch, floated down the low, strange wail of wind—a knell
indeed for all that had gone.

Venters, sighing, gathered up an armful of pottery, such pieces as he
thought strong enough and suitable for his own use, and bent his steps
toward camp. He mounted the terrace at an opposite point to which he
had left. He saw the girl looking in the direction he had gone. His
footsteps made no sound in the deep grass, and he approached close
without her being aware of his presence. Whitie lay on the ground near
where she sat, and he manifested the usual actions of welcome, but the
girl did not notice them. She seemed to be oblivious to everything near at
hand. She made a pathetic figure drooping there, with her sunny hair
contrasting so markedly with her white, wasted cheeks and her hands
listlessly clasped and her little bare feet propped in the framework of the
rude seat. Venters could have sworn and laughed in one breath at the idea
of the connection between this girl and Oldring's Masked Rider. She was
the victim of more than accident or fate—a victim to some deep plot the
mystery of which burned him. As he stepped forward with a half-formed

thought that she was absorbed in watching for his return, she turned her head and saw him. A swift start, a change rather than rush of blood under her white cheeks, a flashing of big eyes that fixed their glance upon him, transformed her face in that single instant of turning; and he knew she had been watching for him, that his return was the one thing in her mind. She did not smile; she did not flush; she did not look glad. All these would have meant little compared to her indefinite expression. Venters grasped the peculiar, vivid, vital something that leaped from her face. It was as if she had been in a dead, hopeless clamp of inaction and feeling, and had been suddenly shot through and through with quivering animation. Almost it was as if she had returned to life.

And Venters thought with lightning swiftness, "I've saved her—I've unlinked her from that old life—she was watching as if I were all she had left on earth—she belongs to me!" The thought was startlingly new. Like a blow it was in an unprepared moment. The cheery salutation he had ready for her died unborn and he tumbled the pieces of pottery awkwardly on the grass, while some unfamiliar, deep-seated emotion, mixed with pity and glad assurance of his power to succor her, held him dumb.

"What a load you had!" she said. "Why, they're pots and crocks! Where did you get them?"

Venters laid down his rifle, and, filling one of the pots from his canteen, he placed it on the smoldering campfire.

"Hope it'll hold water," he said, presently. "Why, there's an enormous cliff-dwelling just across here. I got the pottery there. Don't you think we needed something? That tin cup of mine has served to make tea, broth, soup—everything."

"I noticed we hadn't a great deal to cook in."

She laughed. It was the first time. He liked that laugh, and though he was tempted to look at her, he did not want to show his surprise or his pleasure.

"Will you take me over there, and all around in the valley—pretty soon when I'm well?" she added.

"Indeed I shall. It's a wonderful place. Rabbits so thick you can't step without kicking one out. And quail, beaver, foxes, wildcats. We're in a regular den. But—haven't you ever seen a cliff-dwelling?"

"No. I've heard about them, though. The—the men say the Pass is full of old houses and ruins."

"Why, I should think you'd have run across one in all your riding around," said Venters. He spoke slowly, choosing his words carefully, and he essayed a perfectly casual manner, and pretended to be busy assorting pieces of pottery. She must have no cause again to suffer shame for curiosity of his. Yet never in all his days had he been so eager to hear the details of anyone's life.

"When I rode—I rode like the wind," she replied, "and never had time to stop for anything."

"I remember that day I—I met you in the Pass—how dusty you were, how tired your horse looked. Were you always riding?"

"Oh, no. Sometimes not for months, when I was shut up in the cabin." Venters tried to subdue a hot tingling.

"You were shut up, then?" he asked, carelessly.

"When Oldring went away on his long trips—he was gone for months sometimes—he shut me up in the cabin."

"What for?"

"Perhaps to keep me from running away. I always threatened that. Mostly, though, because the men got drunk at the villages. But they were always good to me. I wasn't afraid."

"A prisoner! That must have been hard on you?"

"I liked that. As long as I can remember I've been locked up there at times, and those times were the only happy ones I ever had. It's a big cabin, high up on a cliff, and I could look out. Then I had dogs and pets I had tamed, and books. There was a spring inside, and food stored, and the men brought me fresh meat. Once I was there one whole winter."

It now required deliberation on Venters's part to persist in his unconcern and to keep at work. He wanted to look at her, to volley questions at her.

"As long as you can remember—you've lived in Deception Pass?" he went on.

"I've a dim memory of some other place, and women and children; but I can't make anything of it. Sometimes I think till I'm weary."

"Then you can read—you have books?"

"Oh yes, I can read, and write, too, pretty well. Oldring is educated. He taught me, and years ago an old rustler lived with us, and he had been something different once. He was always teaching me."

"So Oldring takes long trips," mused Venters. "Do you know where he goes?"

"No. Every year he drives cattle north of Sterling—then does not return for months. I heard him accused once of living two lives—and he killed the man. That was at Stone Bridge."

Venters dropped his apparent task and looked up with an eagerness he no longer strove to hide.

"Bess," he said, using her name for the first time, "I suspected Oldring was something besides a rustler. Tell me, what's his purpose here in the Pass? I believe much that he has done was to hide his real work here."

"You're right. He's more than a rustler. In fact, as the men say, his rustling cattle is now only a bluff. There's gold in the canyons!"

"Ah!"

"Yes, there's gold, not in great quantities, but gold enough for him and his men. They wash for gold week in and week out. Then they drive a few cattle and go into the villages to drink and shoot and kill—to bluff the riders."

"Drive a few cattle! But, Bess, the Withersteen herd, the red herd—twenty-five hundred head! That's not a few. And I tracked them into a valley near here."

"Oldring never stole the red herd. He made a deal with Mormons. The riders were to be called in, and Oldring was to drive the herd and keep it till a certain time—I don't know when—then drive it back to the range. What his share was I didn't hear."

"Did you hear *why* that deal was made?" queried Venters.

"No. But it was a trick of Mormons. They're full of tricks. I've heard Oldring's men tell about Mormons. Maybe the Withersteen woman wasn't minding her halter! I saw the man who made the deal. He was a little, queer-shaped man, all humped up. He sat his horse well. I heard one of our men say afterward there was no better rider on the sage than this fellow. What was the name? I forget."

"Jerry Card?" suggested Venters.

"That's it. I remember—it's a name easy to remember—and Jerry Card appeared to be on fair terms with Oldring's men."

"I shouldn't wonder," replied Venters, thoughtfully. Verification of his suspicions in regard to Tull's underhand work—for the deal with Oldring made by Jerry Card assuredly had its inception in the Mormon elder's brain, and had been accomplished through his orders—revived in Venters a memory of hatred that had been smothered by press of other emotions. Only a few days had elapsed since the hour of his encounter with Tull, yet they had been forgotten and now seemed far off, and the interval one that now appeared large and profound with incalculable change in his feelings. Hatred of Tull still existed in his heart; but it had lost its white heat. His affection for Jane Withersteen had not changed in the least; nevertheless, he seemed to view it from another angle and see it as another thing—what, he could not exactly define. The recalling of these two feelings was to Venters like getting glimpses into a self that was gone; and the wonder of them—perhaps the change which was too elusive for him—was the fact that a strange irritation accompanied the memory and a desire to dismiss it from mind. And straightway he did dismiss it, to return to thoughts of his significant present.

"Bess, tell me one more thing," he said. "Haven't you known any women—any young people?"

"Sometimes there were women with the men; but Oldring never let me know them. And all the young people I ever saw in my life was when I rode fast through the villages."

Perhaps that was the most puzzling and thought-provoking thing she had yet said to Venters. He pondered, more curious the more he learned, but he curbed his inquisitive desires, for he saw her shrinking on the verge of that shame, the causing of which had occasioned him such self-reproach. He would ask no more. Still he had to think, and he found it difficult to think clearly. This sad-eyed girl was so utterly different from what it would have been reason to believe such a remarkable life would have made her. On this day he had found her simple and frank, as natural as any girl he had ever known. About her there was something sweet. Her voice was low and well modulated. He could not look into her face, meet her steady, unabashed, yet wistful eyes, and think of her as the woman she had confessed herself. Oldring's Masked Rider sat before him, a girl dressed as a man. She had been made to ride at the head of infamous forays and drives. She had been imprisoned for many months of her life in an obscure cabin. At times the most vicious of men had been her companions; and the vilest of women, if they had not been permitted to approach her, had, at least, cast their shadows over her. But—but in spite of all this—there thundered at Venters some truth that lifted its voice higher than the clamoring facts of dishonor, some truth that was the very life of her beautiful eyes; and it was innocence.

In the days that followed, Venters balanced perpetually in mind this haunting conception of innocence over against the cold and sickening fact of an unintentional yet actual guilt. How could it be possible for the two things to be true? He believed the latter to be true, and he would not relinquish his conviction of the former; and these conflicting thoughts augmented the mystery that appeared to be a part of Bess. In those ensuing days, however, it became clear as clearest light that Bess was rapidly regaining strength; that, unless reminded of her long association with Oldring, she seemed to have forgotten it; that, like an Indian who lives solely from moment to moment, she was utterly absorbed in the present.

Day by day Venters watched the white of her face slowly change to brown, and the wasted cheeks fill out by imperceptible degrees. There came a time when he could just trace the line of demarcation between the part of her face once hidden by a mask and that left exposed to wind and sun. When that line disappeared in clear bronze tan it was as if she had been washed clean of the stigma of Oldring's Masked Rider. The suggestion of the mask always made Venters remember; now that it was gone he seldom thought of her past. Occasionally he tried to piece together the several stages of strange experience and to make a whole. He had shot a masked outlaw the very sight of whom had been ill omen to riders; he had carried off a wounded woman whose bloody lips quivered in prayer; he had nursed what seemed a frail, shrunken boy; and now he watched a girl whose face had become strangely sweet, whose dark-blue eyes were ever upon him without boldness, without shyness, but with a steady, grave, and growing light. Many times Venters found the clear gaze embarrassing to him, yet, like wine, it had an exhilarating effect. What did she think when she looked at him so? Almost he believed she had no thought at all. All about her and the present there in Surprise Valley, and the dim yet subtly impending future, fascinated Venters and made him thoughtful as all his lonely vigils in the sage had not.

Chiefly it was the present that he wished to dwell upon; but it was the call of the future which stirred him to action. No idea had he of what that future had in store for Bess and him. He began to think of improving Surprise Valley as a place to live in, for there was no telling how long they would be compelled to stay there. Venters stubbornly resisted the entering into his mind of an insistent thought that, clearly realized, might have made it plain to him that he did not want to leave Surprise Valley at all. But it was imperative that he consider practical matters; and whether or not he was destined to stay long there, he felt the immediate need of a change of diet. It would be necessary for him to go farther afield for a variety of meat, and also that he soon visit Cottonwoods for a supply of food.

It occurred again to Venters that he could go to the canyon where Oldring kept his cattle, and at little risk he could pack out some beef. He wished to do this, however, without letting Bess know of it till after he had made the trip. Presently he hit upon the plan of going while she was asleep.

That very night he stole out of camp, climbed up under the stone bridge, and entered the outlet to the Pass. The gorge was full of luminous gloom. Balancing Rock loomed dark and leaned over the pale descent. Transformed in the shadowy light, it took shape and dimensions of a spectral god waiting—waiting for the moment to hurl himself down upon the tottering walls and close forever the outlet to Deception Pass. At night more than by day Venters felt something fearful and fateful in that rock, and that it had leaned and waited through a thousand years to have somehow to deal with his destiny.

"Old man, if you must roll, wait till I get back to the girl, and then roll!" he said, aloud, as if the stones were indeed a god.

And those spoken words, in their grim note to his ear, as well as contents to his mind, told Venters that he was all but drifting on a current which he had not power nor wish to stem.

Venters exercised his usual care in the matter of hiding tracks from the outlet, yet it took him scarcely an hour to reach Oldring's cattle. Here sight of many calves changed his original intention, and instead of packing out meat he decided to take a calf out alive. He roped one, securely tied its feet, and swung it up over his shoulder. Here was an exceedingly heavy burden, but Venters was powerful—he could take up a sack of grain and with ease pitch it over a pack-saddle—and he made long distance without resting. The hardest work came in the climb up to the outlet and on through to the valley. When he had accomplished it, he became fired with another idea that again changed his intention. He would not kill the calf, but keep it alive. He would go back to Oldring's herd and pack out more calves. Thereupon he secured the calf in the best available spot for the moment and turned to make a second trip.

When Venters got back to the valley with another calf, it was close upon daybreak. He crawled into his cave and slept late. Bess had no inkling that he had been absent from camp nearly all night, and only remarked solicitously that he appeared to be more tired than usual, and more in the need of sleep. In the afternoon Venters built a gate across a small ravine near camp, and here corralled the calves; and he succeeded in completing his task without Bess being any the wiser.

That night he made two more trips to Oldring's range, and again on the following night, and yet another on the next. With eight calves in his corral, he concluded that he had enough; but it dawned upon him then that he did not want to kill one. "I've rustled Oldring's cattle," he said, and laughed. He noted then that all the calves were red. "Red!" he exclaimed. "From the red herd. I've stolen Jane Withersteen's cattle! . . . That's about the strangest thing yet."

One more trip he undertook to Oldring's valley, and this time he roped a yearling steer and killed it and cut out a small quarter of beef. The howling of coyotes told him he need have no apprehension that the work of his knife would be discovered. He packed the beef back to camp and hung it upon a spruce tree. Then he sought his bed.

On the morrow he was up bright and early, glad that he had a surprise for Bess. He could hardly wait for her to come out. Presently she appeared and walked under the spruce. Then she approached the campfire. There was a tinge of healthy red in the bronze of her cheeks, and her slender form had begun to round out in graceful lines.

"Bess, didn't you say you were tired of rabbit?" inquired Venters. "And quail and beaver?"

"Indeed I did."

"What would you like?"

"I'm tired of meat, but if we have to live on it I'd like some beef."

"Well, how does that strike you?" Venters pointed to the quarter hanging from the spruce tree. "We'll have fresh beef for a few days, then we'll cut the rest into strips and dry it."

"Where did you get that?" asked Bess, slowly.

"I stole that from Oldring."

"You went back to the canyon—you risked—" While she hesitated the tinge of bloom faded out of her cheeks.

"It wasn't any risk, but it was hard work."

"I'm sorry I said I was tired of rabbit. Why! How—When did you get that beef?"

"Last night."

"While I was asleep?"

"Yes."

"I woke last night sometime—but I didn't know."

Her eyes were widening, darkening with thought, and whenever they did so the steady, watchful, seeing gaze gave place to the wistful light. In the former she saw as the primitive woman without thought; in the latter she looked inward, and her gaze was the reflection of a troubled mind. For long Venters had not seen that dark change, that deepening of blue, which he thought was beautiful and sad. But now he wanted to make her think.

"I've done more than pack in that beef," he said. "For five nights I've been working while you slept. I've got eight calves corralled near a ravine. Eight calves, all alive and doing fine!"

"You went five nights!"

All that Venters could make of the dilation of her eyes, her slow pallor, and her exclamation, was fear—fear for herself or for him.

"Yes. I didn't tell you, because I knew you were afraid to be left alone."

"Alone?" She echoed his word, but the meaning of it was nothing to her. She had not even thought of being left alone. It was not, then, fear for herself, but for him. This girl, always slow of speech and action, now seemed almost stupid. She put forth a hand that might have indicated the groping of her mind. Suddenly she stepped swiftly to him, with a look and touch that drove from him any doubt of her quick intelligence or feeling.

"Oldring has men watch the herds—they would kill you. You must never go again!"

When she had spoken, the strength and the blaze of her died, and she swayed toward Venters.

"*Bess, I'll not go again,*" he said, catching her.

She leaned against him, and her body was limp and vibrated to a long, wavering tremble. Her face was upturned to his. Woman's face, woman's eyes, woman's lips—all acutely and blindly and sweetly and terribly truthful in their betrayal! But as her fear was instinctive, so was her clinging to this one and only friend.

Venters gently put her from him and steadied her upon her feet; and all the while his blood raced wild, and a thrilling tingle unsteadied his nerve, and something—that he had seen and felt in her—that he could not understand—seemed very close to him, warm and rich as a fragrant breath, sweet as nothing had ever before been sweet to him.

With all his will Venters strove for calmness and thought and judgment unbiased by pity, and reality unswayed by sentiment. Bess's eyes were still fixed upon him with all her soul bright in that wistful light. Swiftly, resolutely he put out of mind all of her life except what had been spent with him. He scorned himself for the intelligence that made him still doubt. He meant to judge her as she had judged him. He was face to face with the inevitableness of life itself. He saw destiny in the dark, straight path of her wonderful eyes. Here was the simplicity, the sweetness of a girl contending with new and strange and enthralling emotions; here the living truth of innocence; here the blind terror of a woman confronted with the thought of death to her savior and protector. All this Venters saw, but, besides, there was in Bess's eyes a slow-dawning consciousness that seemed about to break out in glorious radiance.

"Bess, are you thinking?" he asked.

"Yes—oh yes!"

"Do you realize we are here alone—man and woman?"

"Yes."

"Have you thought that we may make our way out to civilization, or we may have to stay here—alone—hidden from the world all our lives?"

"I never thought—till now."

"Well, what's your choice—to go—or to stay here—alone with me?"

"Stay!" Newborn thought of self, ringing vibrantly in her voice, gave her answer singular power.

Venters trembled, and then swiftly turned his gaze from her face—from her eyes. He knew what she had only half divined—that she loved him.

❧11❧

FAITH AND UNFAITH

AT JANE WITHERSTEEN'S home the promise made to Mrs. Larkin to care for little Fay had begun to be fulfilled. Like a gleam of sunlight through the cottonwoods was the coming of the child to the gloomy house of Withersteen. The big, silent halls echoed with childish laughter. In the shady court, where Jane spent many of the hot July days, Fay's tiny feet pattered over the stone flags and splashed in the amber stream. She prattled incessantly. What difference, Jane thought, a child made in her home! It had never been a real home, she discovered. Even the tidiness and neatness she had so observed, and upon which she had insisted to her women, became, in the light of Fay's smile, habits that now lost their importance. Fay littered the court with Jane's books and papers, and other toys her fancy improvised, and many a strange craft when floating down the little brook.

And it was owing to Fay's presence that Jane Withersteen came to see more of Lassiter. The rider had for the most part kept to the sage. He rode for her, but he did not seek her except on business; and Jane had to acknowledge in pique that her overtures had been made in vain. Fay, however, captured Lassiter the moment he first laid eyes on her.

Jane was present at the meeting, and there was something about it which dimmed her sight and softened her toward this foe of her people.

The rider had clanked into the court, a tired yet wary man, always looking for the attack upon him that was inevitable and might come from any quarter; and he had walked right upon little Fay. The child had been beautiful even in her rags and amid the surroundings of the hovel in the sage, but now, in a pretty white dress, with her shining curls brushed and her face clean and rosy, she was lovely. She left her play and looked up at Lassiter.

If there was not an instinct for all three of them in that meeting, an unreasoning tendency toward a closer intimacy, then Jane Withersteen believed she had been subject to a queer fancy. She imagined any child would have feared Lassiter. And Fay Larkin had been a lonely, a solitary elf of the sage, not at all an ordinary child, and exquisitely shy with strangers. She watched Lassiter with great, round, grave eyes, but showed no fear. The rider gave Jane a favorable report of cattle and horses; and as he took the seat to which she invited him, little Fay edged as much as half an inch nearer. Jane replied to his look of inquiry and told Fay's story. The rider's gray, earnest gaze troubled her. Then he turned to Fay and smiled in a way that made Jane doubt her sense of the true relation of things. How could Lassiter smile so at a child when he had made so many children fatherless? But he did smile, and to the gentleness she had seen a few times he added something that was infinitely sad and sweet. Jane's intuition told her that Lassiter had never been a father; but if life ever so blessed him he would be a good one. Fay, also, must have found that smile singularly winning. For she edged closer and closer, and then, by way of feminine capitulation, went to Jane, from whose side she bent a beautiful glance upon the rider.

Lassiter only smiled at her.

Jane watched them, and realized that now was the moment she should seize, if she was ever to win this man from his hatred. But the step was not easy to take. The more she saw of Lassiter the more she respected him, and the greater her respect the harder it became to lend herself to mere coquetry. Yet as she thought of her great motive, of Tull, and of that other whose name she had schooled herself never to think of in connection with Milly Erne's avenger, she suddenly found she had no choice. And her creed gave her boldness far beyond the limit to which vanity would have led her.

"Lassiter, I see so little of you now," she said, and was conscious of heat in her cheeks.

"I've been ridin' hard," he replied.

"But you can't live in the saddle. You come in sometimes. Won't you come here to see me—oftener?"

"Is that an order?"

"Nonsense! I simply ask you to come to see me when you find time."

"Why?"

The query once heard was not so embarrassing to Jane as she might have imagined. Moreover, it established in her mind a fact that there existed actually other than selfish reasons for her wanting to see him. And as she had been bold, so she determined to be both honest and brave.

"I've reasons—only one of which I need mention," she answered. "If it's possible I want to change you toward my people. And on the moment I can conceive of little I wouldn't do to gain that end."

How much better and freer Jane felt after that confession! She meant to show him that there was one Mormon who could play a game or wage a fight in the open.

"I reckon," said Lassiter, and he laughed.

It was the best in her, if the most irritating, that Lassiter always aroused.

"Will you come?" She looked into his eyes, and for the life of her could not quite subdue an imperiousness that rose with her spirit. "I never asked so much of any man—except Bern Venters."

" 'Pears to me that you'd run no risk, or Venters, either. But mebbe that doesn't hold good for me."

"You mean it wouldn't be safe for you to be often here? You look for ambush in the cottonwoods?"

"Not that so much."

At this juncture little Fay sidled over to Lassiter.

"Has oo a little dirl?" she inquired.

"No, lassie," replied the rider.

Whatever Fay seemed to be searching for in Lassiter's sun-reddened face and quiet eyes she evidently found. "Oo tan tum to see me," she added, and with that, shyness gave place to friendly curiosity. First his sombrero with its leather band and silver ornaments commanded her attention; next his quirt, and then the clinking, silver spurs. These held her for some time, but presently, true to childish fickleness, she left off playing with them to look for something else. She laughed in glee as she ran her little hands down the slippery, shiny surface of Lassiter's leather chaps. Soon she discovered one of the hanging gun-sheaths, and she dragged it up and began tugging at the huge black handle of the gun. Jane Withersteen repressed an exclamation. What significance there was to her in the little girl's efforts to dislodge that heavy weapon! Jane Withersteen saw Fay's play and her beauty and her love as most powerful allies to her own woman's part in a game that suddenly had acquired a strange zest and a hint of danger. And as for the rider, he appeared to have forgotten Jane in the wonder of this lovely child playing about him. At first he was much the shyer of the two. Gradually her confidence overcame his backwardness, and he had the temerity to stroke her golden curls with a great hand. Fay rewarded his boldness with a smile, and when he had gone to the extreme of closing that great hand over her little brown one, she said, simply, "I like oo!"

Sight of his face then made Jane oblivious for the time to his character

as a hater of Mormons. Out of the mother longing that swelled her breast
she divined the child hunger in Lassiter.

He returned the next day, and the next; and upon the following he
came both at morning and at night. Upon the evening of this fourth day
Jane seemed to feel the breaking of a brooding struggle in Lassiter. During
all these visits he had scarcely a word to say, though he watched her and
played absent-mindedly with Fay. Jane had contented herself with silence. Soon little Fay substituted for the expression of regard, "I like oo,"
a warmer and more generous one, "I love oo."

Thereafter Lassiter came oftener to see Jane and her little protégée.
Daily he grew more gentle and kind, and gradually developed a quaintly
merry mood. In the morning he lifted Fay upon his horse and let her ride
as he walked beside her to the edge of the sage. In the evening he played
with the child at an infinite variety of games she invented, and then,
oftener than not, he accepted Jane's invitation to supper. No other visitor
came to Withersteen House during those days. So that in spite of watchfulness he never forgot, Lassiter began to show he felt at home there.
After the meal they walked into the grove of cottonwoods or up by the
lakes, and little Fay held Lassiter's hand as much as she held Jane's. Thus
a strange relationship was established, and Jane liked it. At twilight they
always returned to the house, where Fay kissed them and went in to her
mother. Lassiter and Jane were left alone.

Then, if there were anything that a good woman could do to win a
man and still preserve her self-respect, it was something which escaped
the natural subtlety of a woman determined to allure. Jane's vanity, that
after all was not great, was soon satisfied with Lassiter's silent admiration.
And her honest desire to lead him from his dark, blood-stained path
would never have blinded her to what she owed herself. But the driving
passion of her religion, and its call to save Mormons' lives, one life in
particular, bore Jane Withersteen close to an infringement of her womanhood. In the beginning she had reasoned that her appeal to Lassiter
must be through the senses. With whatever means she possessed in the
way of adornment she enhanced her beauty. And she stooped to artifices
that she knew were unworthy of her, but which she deliberately chose to
employ. She made of herself a girl in every variable mood wherein a girl
might be desirable. In those moods she was not above the methods of an
inexperienced though natural flirt. She kept close to him whenever opportunity afforded; and she was forever playfully, yet passionately underneath the surface, fighting him for possession of the great black guns.
These he would never yield to her. And so in that manner their hands
were often and long in contact. The more of simplicity that she sensed in
him the greater the advantage she took.

She had a trick of changing—and it was not altogether voluntary—
from this gay, thoughtless, girlish coquettishness to the silence and the
brooding, burning mystery of a woman's mood. The strength and passion

and fire of her were in her eyes, and she so used them that Lassiter had to see this depth in her, this haunting promise more fitted to her years than to the flaunting guise of a willful girl.

The July days flew by. Jane reasoned that if it were possible for her to be happy during such a time, then she was happy. Little Fay completely filled a long aching void in her heart. In fettering the hands of this Lassiter she was accomplishing the greatest good of her life, and to do good even in a small way rendered happiness to Jane Withersteen. She had attended the regular Sunday services of her church; otherwise she had not gone to the village for weeks. It was unusual that none of her church- men or friends had called upon her of late; but it was neglect for which she was glad. Judkins and his boy riders had experienced no difficulty in driving the white herd. So these warm July days were free of worry, and soon Jane hoped she had passed the crisis; and for her to hope was presently to trust, and then to believe. She thought often of Venters, but in a dreamy, abstract way. She spent hours teaching and playing with little Fay. And the activity of her mind centered around Lassiter. The direction she had given her will seemed to blunt any branching off of thought from that straight line. The mood came to obsess her.

In the end, when her awakening came, she learned that she had built better than she knew. Lassiter, though kinder and gentler than ever, had parted with his quaint humor and his coldness and his tranquillity to become a restless and unhappy man. Whatever the power of his deadly intent toward Mormons, that passion now had a rival, and one equally burning and consuming. Jane Withersteen had one moment of exultation before the dawn of a strange uneasiness. What if she had made of herself a lure, at tremendous cost to him and to her, and all in vain!

That night in the moonlit grove she summoned all her courage and, turning suddenly in the path, she faced Lassiter and leaned close to him, so that she touched him and her eyes looked up to his.

"Lassiter! . . . Will you do anything for me?"

In the moonlight she saw his dark, worn face change, and by that change she seemed to feel him immovable as a wall of stone.

Jane slipped her hands down to the swinging gun-sheaths, and when she had locked her fingers around the huge, cold handles of the guns, she trembled as with a chilling ripple over all her body.

"May I take your guns?"

"Why?" he asked, and for the first time to her his voice carried a harsh note. Jane felt his hard, strong hands close round her wrists. It was not wholly with intent that she leaned toward him, for the look of his eyes and the feel of his hands made her weak.

"It's no trifle—no woman's whim—it's deep—as my heart. Let me take them?"

"Why?"

"I want to keep you from killing more men—Mormons. You must let me save you from more wickedness—more wanton bloodshed—" Then the truth forced itself falteringly from her lips. "You must—let—me—help me to keep my vow to Milly Erne. I swore to her—as she lay dying—that if ever anyone came here to avenge her—I swore I would stay his hand. Perhaps I—I alone can save the—the man who—who—Oh, Lassiter! . . . I feel that if I can't change you—then soon you'll go out to kill—and you'll kill by instinct—and among the Mormons you kill will be the one—who . . . Lassiter, if you care a little for me—let me—for my sake—let me take your guns!"

As if her hands had been those of a child, he unclasped their clinging grip from the handles of his guns, and, pushing her away, he turned his gray face to her in one look of terrible realization and then strode off into the shadows of the cottonwoods.

When the first shock of her futile appeal to Lassiter had passed, Jane took his cold, silent condemnation and abrupt departure not so much as a refusal to her entreaty as a hurt and stunned bitterness for her attempt at his betrayal. Upon further thought and slow consideration of Lassiter's past actions, she believed he would return and forgive her. The man could not be hard to a woman, and she doubted that he could stay away from her. But at the point where she had hoped to find him vulnerable she now began to fear he was proof against all persuasion. The iron and stone quality that she had early suspected in him had actually cropped out as an impregnable barrier. Nevertheless, if Lassiter remained in Cottonwoods she would never give up her hope and desire to change him. She would change him if she had to sacrifice everything dear to her except hope of heaven. Passionately devoted as she was to her religion, she had yet refused to marry a Mormon. But a situation had developed wherein self paled in the great white light of religious duty of the highest order. That was the leading motive, the divinely spiritual one; but there were other motives, which, like tentacles, aided in drawing her will to the acceptance of a possible abnegation. And through the watches of that sleepless night Jane Withersteen, in fear and sorrow and doubt, came finally to believe that if she must throw herself into Lassiter's arms to make him abide by "Thou shalt not kill," she would yet do well.

In the morning she expected Lassiter at the usual hour, but she was not able to go at once to the court, so she sent little Fay. Mrs. Larkin was ill and required attention. It appeared that the mother, from the time of her arrival at Withersteen House, had relaxed and was slowly losing her hold on life. Jane had believed that absence of worry and responsibility coupled with good nursing and comfort would mend Mrs. Larkin's broken health. Such, however, was not the case.

When Jane did get out to the court, Fay was there alone, and at the moment embarking on a dubious voyage down the stone-lined amber stream upon a craft of two brooms and a pillow. Fay was as delightfully wet as she could possibly wish to get.

Clatter of hoofs distracted Fay and interrupted the scolding she was gleefully receiving from Jane. The sound was not the light-spirited trot that Bells made when Lassiter rode him into the outer court. This was slower and heavier, and Jane did not recognize in it any of her other horses. The appearance of Bishop Dyer startled Jane. He dismounted with his rapid, jerky motion, flung the bridle, and, as he turned toward the inner court and stalked up on the stone flags, his boots rang. In his authoritative front, and in the red anger unmistakably flaming in his face, he reminded Jane of her father.

"Is that the Larkin pauper?" he asked, brusquely, without any greeting to Jane.

"It's Mrs. Larkin's little girl," replied Jane, slowly.

"I hear you intend to raise the child?"

"Yes."

"Of course you mean to give her Mormon bringing-up?"

"No!"

His questions had been swift. She was amazed at a feeling that someone else was replying for her.

"I've come to say a few things to you." He stopped to measure her with stern, speculative eye.

Jane Withersteen loved this man. From earliest childhood she had been taught to revere and love bishops of her church. And for ten years Bishop Dyer had been the closest friend and counselor of her father, and for the greater part of that period her own friend and scriptural teacher. Her interpretation of her creed and her religious activity in fidelity to it, her acceptance of mysterious and holy Mormon truths, were all invested in this bishop. Bishop Dyer as an entity was next to God. He was God's mouthpiece to the little Mormon community at Cottonwoods. God revealed himself in secret to this mortal.

And Jane Withersteen suddenly suffered a paralyzing affront to her consciousness of reverence by some strange, irresistible twist of thought wherein she saw this bishop as a man. And the train of thought hurdled the rising, crying protests of that other self whose poise she had lost. It was not her bishop who eyed her in curious measurement. It was a man who tramped into her presence without removing his hat, who had no greeting for her, who had no semblance of courtesy. In looks, as in action, he made her think of a bull stamping cross-grained into a corral. She had heard of Bishop Dyer forgetting the minister in the fury of a common man, and now she was to feel it. The glance by which she measured him in turn momentarily veiled the divine in the ordinary. He looked a rancher; he was booted, spurred, and covered with dust; he carried a gun at his hip, and she remembered that he had been known to use it. But during the long moment while he watched her there was nothing commonplace in the slow-gathering might of his wrath.

"Brother Tull has talked to me," he began. "It was your father's wish that you marry Tull, and my order. You refused him?"

"Yes."

"You would not give up your friendship with that tramp Venters?"

"No."

"But you'll do as *I* order!" he thundered. "Why, Jane Withersteen, you are in danger of becoming a heretic! You can thank your Gentile friends for that. You face the damning of your soul to perdition."

In the flux and reflux of the whirling torture of Jane's mind, that new, daring spirit of hers vanished in the old habitual order of her life. She was a Mormon, and the bishop regained ascendance.

"It's well I got you in time, Jane Withersteen. What would your father have said to these goings-on of yours? He would have put you in a stone cage on bread and water. He would have taught you something about Mormonism. Remember, you're a *born* Mormon. There have been Mormons who turned heretic—damn their souls!—but no born Mormon ever left us yet. Ah, I see your shame. Your faith is not shaken. You are only a wild girl." The bishop's tone softened. "Well, it's enough that I got to you in time. . . . Now tell me about this Lassiter. I hear strange things."

"What do you wish to know?" queried Jane.

"About this man. You hired him?"

"Yes, he's riding for me. When my riders left me I had to have anyone I could get."

"Is it true what I hear—that he's a gunman, a Mormon-hater, steeped in blood?"

"True—terribly true, I fear."

"But what's he doing here in Cottonwoods? This place isn't notorious enough for such a man. Sterling and the villages north, where there's universal gun-packing and fights every day—where there are more men like him, it seems to me they would attract him most. We're only a wild, lonely border settlement. It's only recently that the rustlers have made killings here. Nor have there been saloons till lately, nor the drifting in of outcasts. Has not this gunman some special mission here?"

Jane maintained silence.

"Tell me," ordered Bishop Dyer, sharply.

"Yes," she replied.

"Do you know what it is?"

"Yes."

"Tell me that."

"Bishop Dyer, I don't want to tell."

He waved his hand in an imperative gesture of command. The red once more leaped to his face, and in his steel-blue eyes glinted a pinpoint of curiosity.

"That first day," whispered Jane, "Lassiter said he came here to find—Milly Erne's grave!"

With downcast eyes Jane watched the swift flow of the amber water. She saw it and tried to think of it, of the stones, of the ferns; but, like her body, her mind was in a leaden vise. Only the bishop's voice could release her. Seemingly there was silence of longer duration than all her former life.

"For what—else?" When Bishop Dyer's voice did cleave the silence it was high, curiously shrill, and on the point of breaking. It released Jane's tongue, but she could not lift her eyes.

"To kill the man who persuaded Milly Erne to abandon her home and her husband—and her God!"

With wonderful distinctness Jane Withersteen heard her own clear voice. She heard the water murmur at her feet and flow on to the sea; she heard the rushing of all the waters in the world. They filled her ears with low, unreal murmurings—these sounds that deadened her brain and yet could not break the long and terrible silence. Then, from somewhere— from an immeasurable distance—came a slow, guarded, clinking, clanking step. Into her it shot electrifying life. It released the weight upon her numbed eyelids. Lifting her eyes she saw—ashen, shaken, stricken—not the bishop but the man! And beyond him, from round the corner came that soft, silvery step. A long black boot with a gleaming spur swept into sight—and then Lassiter! Bishop Dyer did not see, did not hear: he stared at Jane in the throes of sudden revelation.

"Ah, I understand!" he cried, in hoarse accents. "That's why you made love to this Lassiter—to bind his hands!"

It was Jane's gaze riveted upon the rider that made Bishop Dyer turn. Then clear sight failed her. Dizzily, in a blur, she saw the bishop's hand jerk to his hip. She saw a gleam of blue and spout of red. In her ears burst a thundering report. The court floated in darkening circles around her, and she fell into utter blackness.

The darkness lightened, turned to slow-drifting haze, and lifted. Through a thin film of blue smoke she saw the rough-hewn timbers of the court roof. A cool, damp touch moved across her brow. She smelled powder, and it was that which galvanized her suspended thought. She moved, to see that she lay prone upon the stone flags with her head on Lassiter's knee, and he was bathing her brow with water from the stream. The same swift glance, shifting low, brought into range of her sight a smoking gun and splashes of blood.

"Ah-h!" she moaned, and was drifting, sinking again into darkness, when Lassiter's voice arrested her.

"It's all right, Jane. It's all right."

"Did—you—kill—him?" she whispered.

"Who? That fat party who was here? No. I didn't kill him."

"Oh! . . . Lassiter!"

"Say! It was queer for you to faint. I thought you were such a strong woman, not faintish like that. You're all right now—only some pale. I thought you'd never come to. But I'm awkward round women folks. I couldn't think of anythin'."

"Lassiter! . . . the gun there! . . . the blood!"

"So that's troublin' you. I reckon it needn't. You see it was this way. I come round the house an' seen that fat party an' heard him talkin' loud. Then he seen me, an' very impolite goes straight for his gun. He oughtn't have tried to throw a gun on me—whatever his reason was. For that's meetin' me on my own grounds. I've seen runnin' molasses that was quicker'n him. Now I didn't know who he was, visitor or friend or relation of yours, though I seen he was a Mormon all over, an' I couldn't get serious about shootin'. So I winged him—put a bullet through his arm as he was pullin' at his gun. An' he dropped the gun there, and a little blood. I told him he'd introduced himself sufficient, an' to please move out of my vicinity. An' he went."

Lassiter spoke with slow, cool, soothing voice, in which there was a hint of levity, and his touch, as he continued to bathe her brow, was gentle and steady. His impassive face, and the kind, gray eyes, further stilled her agitation.

"He drew on you first, and you deliberately shot to cripple him—you wouldn't kill him—you—*Lassiter?*"

"That's about the size of it."

Jane kissed his hand.

All that was calm and cool about Lassiter instantly vanished.

"Don't do that! I won't stand it! An' I don't care a d——n who that fat party was."

He helped Jane to her feet and to a chair. Then with the wet scarf he had used to bathe her face he wiped the blood from the stone flags and, picking up the gun, he threw it upon a couch. With that he began to pace the court, and his silver spurs jangled musically, and the great gun-sheaths softly brushed against his leather chaps.

"So—it's true—what I heard him say?" Lassiter asked, presently halting before her. "You made love to me—to bind my hands?"

"Yes," confessed Jane. It took all her woman's courage to meet the gray storm of his glance.

"All these days that you've been so friendly an' like a pardner—all these evenin's that have been so bewilderin' to me—your beauty—an'— an' the way you looked an' came close to me—they were woman's tricks to bind my hands?"

"Yes."

"An' your sweetness that seemed so natural, an' your throwin' little Fay an' me so much together—to make me love the child—all that was for the same reason?"

"Yes."

Lassiter flung his arms—a strange gesture for him.

"Mebbe it wasn't much in your Mormon thinkin', for you to play that game. But to ring the child in—that was hellish!"

Jane's passionate, unheeding zeal began to loom darkly.

"Lassiter, whatever my intention in the beginning, Fay loves you dearly—and I—I've grown to—to like you."

"That's powerful kind of you, now," he said. Sarcasm and scorn made his voice that of a stranger. "An' you sit there an' look me straight in the eyes! You're a wonderful strange woman, Jane Withersteen."

"I'm not ashamed, Lassiter. I told you I'd try to change you."

"Would you mind tellin' me just what you tried?"

"I tried to make you see beauty in me and be softened by it. I wanted you to care for me so that I could influence you. It wasn't easy. At first you were stone-blind. Then I hoped you'd love little Fay, and through that come to feel the horror of making children fatherless."

"Jane Withersteen, either you're a fool or noble beyond my understandin'. Mebbe you're both. I know you're blind. What you meant is one thing—what you *did* was to make me love you."

"Lassiter!"

"I reckon I'm a human bein', though I never loved anyone but my sister, Milly Erne. That was long—"

"Oh, are you Milly's brother?"

"Yes, I was, an' I loved her. There never was anyone but her in my life till now. Didn't I tell you that long ago I back-trailed myself from women? I was a Texas ranger till—till Milly left home, an' then I became somethin' else—Lassiter! For years I've been a lonely man set on one thing. I came here an' met you. An' now I'm not the man I was. The change was gradual, an' I took no notice of it. I understand now that never-satisfied longin' to see you, listen to you, watch you, feel you near me. It's plain now why you were never out of my thoughts. I've had no thoughts but of you. I've lived an' breathed for you. An' now when I know what it means —what you've done—I'm burnin' up with hell's fire!"

"Oh, Lassiter—no—no—you don't love me that way!" Jane cried.

"If that's what love is, then I do."

"Forgive me! I didn't mean to make you love me like that. Oh, what a tangle of our lives! You—Milly Erne's brother! And I—heedless, mad to melt your heart toward Mormons. Lassiter, I may be wicked, but not wicked enough to hate. If I couldn't hate Tull, could I hate you?"

"After all, Jane, mebbe you're only blind—Mormon blind. That only can explain what's close to selfishness—"

"I'm not selfish. I despise the very word. If I were free—"

"But you're not free. Not free of Mormonism. An' in playin' this game with me you've been unfaithful."

"Un-faithful!" faltered Jane.

"Yes, I said unfaithful. You're faithful to your bishop an' unfaithful to yourself. You're false to your womanhood an' true to your religion. But for a savin' innocence you'd have made yourself low an' vile—betrayin' yourself, betrayin' me—all to bind my hands an' keep me from snuffin' out Mormon life. It's your damned Mormon blindness."

"Is it vile—is it blind—is it only Mormonism to save human life? No, Lassiter, that's God's law, divine, universal for all Christians."

"The blindness I mean is blindness that keeps you from seein' the truth. I've known many good Mormons. But some are blacker than hell. You won't see that even when you know it. Else, why all this blind passion to save the life of that—that. . . ."

Jane shut out the light, and the hands she held over her eyes trembled and quivered against her face.

"Blind—yes, an' let me make it clear an' simple to you," Lassiter went on, his voice losing its tone of anger. "Take, for instance, that idea of yours last night when you wanted my guns. It was good an' beautiful, an' showed your heart—but—why, Jane, it was crazy. Mind I'm assumin' that life to me is as sweet as to any other man. An' to preserve that life is each man's first an' closest thought. Where would any man be on this border without guns? Where, especially, would Lassiter be? Well, I'd be under the sage with thousands of other men now livin' an' sure better men than me. Gun-packin' in the West since the Civil War has growed into a kind of moral law. An' out here on this border it's the difference between a man an' somethin' not a man. Look what your takin' Venters's guns from him all but made him! Why, your churchmen carry guns. Tull has killed a man an' drawed on others. Your bishop has shot a half-dozen men, an' it wasn't through prayers of his that they recovered. An' today he'd have shot me if he'd been quick enough on the draw. Could I walk or ride down into Cottonwoods without my guns? This is a wild time, Jane Withersteen, this year of our Lord eighteen seventy-one."

"No time—for a woman!" exclaimed Jane, brokenly. "Oh, Lassiter, I feel helpless—lost—and don't know where to turn. If I *am* blind—then—I need some one—a friend—you, Lassiter—more than ever!"

"Well, I didn't say nothin' about goin' back on you, did I?"

❧12❧

THE INVISIBLE HAND

JANE received a letter from Bishop Dyer, not in his own handwriting, which stated that the abrupt termination of their interview had left him in some doubt as to her future conduct. A slight injury had incapacitated him from seeking another meeting at present, the letter went on to say, and ended with a request which was virtually a command—that she call upon him at once.

The reading of the letter acquainted Jane Withersteen with the fact that something within her had all but changed. She sent no reply to Bishop Dyer nor did she go to see him. On Sunday she remained absent from the service—for the second time in years—and though she did not actually suffer there was a deadlock of feelings deep within her, and the waiting for a balance to fall on either side was almost as bad as suffering. She had a gloomy expectancy of untoward circumstances, and with it a keen-edged curiosity to watch developments. She had a half-formed conviction that her future conduct—as related to her churchmen—was beyond her control and would be governed by their attitude toward her. Something was changing in her, forming, waiting for decision to make it a real and fixed thing. She had told Lassiter that she felt helpless and lost in the fateful tangle of their lives; and now she feared that she was approaching the same chaotic condition of mind in regard to her religion. It appalled her to find that she questioned phases of that religion. Absolute faith had been her serenity. Though leaving her faith unshaken, her serenity had been disturbed, and now it was broken by open war between her and her ministers. That something within her—a whisper—which she had tried in vain to hush had become a ringing voice, and it called to her to wait. She had transgressed no laws of God. Her churchmen, however, invested with the power and the glory of a wonderful creed, however they sat in inexorable judgment of her, must now practice toward her the simple, common, Christian virtue they professed to preach, "Do unto others as you would have others do unto you!"

Jane Withersteen, waiting in darkness of mind, remained faithful still. But it was darkness that must soon be pierced by light. If her faith were justified, if her churchmen were trying only to intimidate her, the fact would soon be manifest, as would their failure, and then she would redouble her zeal toward them and toward what had been the best work of her life—work for the welfare and happiness of those among whom she lived, Mormon and Gentile alike. If that secret, intangible power closed its toils round her again, if that great invisible hand moved here and there and everywhere, slowly paralyzing her with its mystery and its inconceivable sway over her affairs, then she would know beyond doubt that it was not chance, nor jealousy, nor intimidation, nor ministerial wrath at her revolt, but a cold and calculating policy thought out long before she was born, a dark, immutable will of whose empire she and all that was hers was but an atom.

Then might come her ruin. Then might come her fall into black storm. Yet she would rise again, and to the light. God would be merciful to a driven woman who had lost her way.

A week passed. Little Fay played and prattled and pulled at Lassiter's big black guns. The rider came to Withersteen House oftener than ever. Jane saw a change in him, though it did not relate to his kindness and gentleness. He was quieter and more thoughtful. While playing with Fay or conversing with Jane he seemed to be possessed of another self that watched with cool, roving eyes, that listened, listened always as if the murmuring amber stream brought messages, and the moving leaves whispered something. Lassiter never rode Bells into the court anymore, nor did he come by the lane or the paths. When he appeared it was suddenly and noiselessly out of the dark shadow of the grove.

"I left Bells out in the sage," he said, one day at the end of that week. "I must carry water to him."

"Why not let him drink at the trough or here?" asked Jane, quickly.

"I reckon it'll be safer for me to slip through the grove. I've been watched when I rode in from the sage."

"Watched? By whom?"

"By a man who thought he was well hid. But my eyes are pretty sharp. An', Jane," he went on, almost in a whisper, "I reckon it'd be a good idea for us to talk low. You're spied on here by your women."

"Lassiter!" she whispered in turn. "That's hard to believe. My women love me."

"What of that?" he asked. "Of course they love you. But they're Mormon women."

Jane's old, rebellious loyalty clashed with her doubt.

"I won't believe it," she replied stubbornly.

"Well then, just act natural an' talk natural, an' pretty soon—give them time to hear us—pretend to go over there to the table an' then quick-like make a move for the door an' open it."

"I will," said Jane, with heightened color. Lassiter was right; he never made mistakes; he would not have told her unless he positively knew. Yet Jane was so tenacious of faith that she had to see with her own eyes, and so constituted that to employ even such small deceit toward her women made her ashamed, and angry for her shame as well as theirs. Then a singular thought confronted her that made her hold up this simple ruse—which hurt her, though it was well justified—against the deceit she had wittingly and eagerly used toward Lassiter. The difference was staggering in its suggestion of that blindness of which he had accused her. Fairness and justice and mercy, that she had imagined were anchor-cables to hold fast her soul to righteousness, had not been hers in the strange, biased duty that had so exalted and confounded her.

Presently Jane began to act her little part, to laugh and play with Fay, to talk of horses and cattle to Lassiter. Then she made deliberate mention of a book in which she kept records of all pertaining to her stock, and she walked slowly toward the table, and when near the door she suddenly whirled and thrust it open. Her sharp action nearly knocked down a woman who had undoubtedly been listening.

"Hester," said Jane, sternly, "you may go home, and you need not come back."

Jane shut the door and returned to Lassiter. Standing unsteadily, she put her hand on his arm. She let him see that doubt had gone, and how this stab of disloyalty pained her.

"Spies! My own women! . . . Oh, miserable!" she cried, with flashing, tearful eyes.

"I hate to tell you," he replied. By that she knew he had long spared her. "It's begun again—that work in the dark."

"Nay, Lassiter—it never stopped!"

So bitter certainty claimed her at last, and trust fled Withersteen House and fled forever. The women who owed much to Jane Withersteen changed not in love for her, nor in devotion to their household work, but they poisoned both by a thousand acts of stealth and cunning and duplicity. Jane broke out once and caught them in strange, stone-faced, unhesitating falsehood. Thereafter she broke out no more. She forgave them because they were driven. Poor, fettered, and sealed Hagars, how she pitied them! What terrible thing bound them and locked their lips, when they showed neither consciousness of guilt toward their benefactress nor distress at the slow wearing apart of long-established and dear ties?

"The blindness again!" cried Jane Withersteen. "In my sisters as in me! . . . O God!"

There came a time when no words passed between Jane and her women. Silently they went about their household duties, and secretly they went about the underhand work to which they had been bidden. The gloom of the house and the gloom of its mistress, which darkened even the bright spirit of little Fay, did not pervade these women. Happiness was not among them, but they were aloof from gloom. They spied and listened; they received and sent secret messengers; and they stole Jane's books and records, and finally the papers that were deeds of her possessions. Through it all they were silent, rapt in a kind of trance. Then one by one, without leave or explanation or farewell, they left Withersteen House, and never returned.

Coincident with this disappearance Jane's gardeners and workers in the alfalfa fields and stable men quit her, not even asking for their wages. Of all her Mormon employees about the great ranch only Jerd remained. He went on with his duty, but talked no more of the change than if it had never occurred.

"Jerd," said Jane, "what stock you can't take care of turn out in the sage. Let your first thought be for Black Star and Night. Keep them in perfect condition. Run them every day and watch them always."

Though Jane Withersteen gave with such liberality, she loved her possessions. She loved the rich, green stretches of alfalfa, and the farms, and the grove, and the old stone house, and the beautiful, ever-faithful amber spring, and every one of a myriad of horses and colts and burros and fowls down to the smallest rabbit that nipped her vegetables; but she loved best her noble Arabian steeds. In common with all riders of the upland sage Jane cherished two material things—the cold, sweet, brown water that made life possible in the wilderness and the horses which were a part of that life. When Lassiter asked her what Lassiter would be without his guns he was assuming that his horse was part of himself. So Jane loved Black Star and Night because it was her nature to love all beautiful creatures—perhaps all living things; and then she loved them because she herself was of the sage and in her had been born and bred the rider's instinct to rely on his four-footed brother. And when Jane gave Jerd the order to keep her favorites trained down to the day it was a half-conscious admission that presaged a time when she would need her fleet horses.

Jane had now, however, no leisure to brood over the coils that were closing round her. Mrs. Larkin grew weaker as the August days began; she required constant care; there was little Fay to look after; and such household work as was imperative. Lassiter put Bells in the stable with the other racers, and directed his efforts to a closer attendance upon Jane. She welcomed the change. He was always at hand to help, and it was her fortune to learn that his boast of being awkward around women had its root in humility and was not true.

His great, brown hands were skilled in a multiplicity of ways which a woman might have envied. He shared Jane's work, and was of especial help to her in nursing Mrs. Larkin. The woman suffered most at night, and this often broke Jane's rest. So it came about that Lassiter would stay by Mrs. Larkin during the day, when she needed care, and Jane would make up the sleep she lost in night-watches. Mrs. Larkin at once took kindly to the gentle Lassiter, and, without ever asking who or what he was, praised him to Jane. "He's a good man and loves children," she said. How sad to hear this truth spoken of a man whom Jane thought lost beyond all redemption! Yet ever and ever Lassiter towered above her, and behind or through his black, sinister figure shone something luminous that strangely affected Jane. Good and evil began to seem incomprehensibly blended in her judgment. It was her belief that evil could not come forth from good; yet here was a murderer who dwarfed in gentleness, patience, and love any man she had ever known.

She had almost lost track of her more outside concerns when early one morning Judkins presented himself before her in the courtyard.

Thin, hard, burnt, bearded, with the dust and sage thick on him, with his leather wrist-bands shining from use, and his boots worn through on the stirrup side, he looked the rider of riders. He wore two guns and carried a Winchester.

Jane greeted him with surprise and warmth, set meat and bread and drink before him, and called Lassiter out to see him. The men exchanged glances, and the meaning of Lassiter's keen inquiry and Judkins's bold reply, both unspoken, was not lost upon Jane.

"Where's your hoss?" asked Lassiter, aloud.

"Left him down the slope," answered Judkins. "I footed it in a ways, an' slept last night in the sage. I went to the place you told me you 'most always slept, but didn't strike you."

"I moved up some, near the spring, an' now I go there nights."

"Judkins—the white herd?" queried Jane, hurriedly.

"Miss Withersteen, I make proud to say I've not lost a steer. Fer a good while after thet stampede Lassiter milled we hed no trouble. Why, even the sage dogs left us. But it's begun agin—thet flashin' of lights over ridge tips, an' queer puffin' of smoke, an' then at night strange whistles an' noises. But the herd's acted magnificent. An' my boys, say, Miss Withersteen, they're only kids, but I ask no better riders. I got the laugh in the village for takin' them out. They're a wild lot, an' you know boys hev more nerve than grown men, because they don't know what danger is. I'm not denyin' there's danger. But they glory in it, an' mebbe I like it myself —anyway, we'll stick. We're goin' to drive the herd on the far side of the first break of Deception Pass. There's a great round valley over there, an' no ridges or piles of rocks to aid these stampeders. The rains are due. We'll hev plenty of water for a while. An' we can hold thet herd from anybody except Oldrin'. I come in fer supplies. I'll pack a couple of burros an' drive out after dark tonight."

"Judkins, take what you want from the storeroom. Lassiter will help you. I—I can't thank you enough . . . but—wait."

Jane went to the room that had once been her father's, and from a secret chamber in the thick stone wall she took a bag of gold, and, carrying it back to the court, she gave it to the rider.

"There, Judkins, and understand that I regard it as little for your loyalty. Give what is fair to your boys, and keep the rest. Hide it. Perhaps that would be wisest."

"Oh . . . Miss Withersteen!" ejaculated the rider. "I couldn't earn so much in—in ten years. It's not right—I oughtn't take it."

"Judkins, you know I'm a rich woman. I tell you I've few faithful friends. I've fallen upon evil days. God only knows what will become of me and mine! So take the gold."

She smiled in understanding of his speechless gratitude, and left him with Lassiter. Presently she heard him speaking low at first, then in louder accents emphasized by the thumping of his rifle on the stones. "As infernal a job as even you, Lassiter, ever heerd of."

"Why, son," was Lassiter's reply, "this breakin' of Miss Withersteen may seem bad to you, but it ain't bad—yet. Some of these wall-eyed fellers who look jest as if they was walkin' in the shadow of Christ himself, right down the sunny road, now they can think of things an' do things that are really hell-bent."

Jane covered her ears and ran to her own room, and there like a caged lioness she paced to and fro till the coming of little Fay reversed her dark thoughts.

The following day, a warm and muggy one threatening rain, while Jane was resting in the court, a horseman clattered through the grove and up to the hitching-rack. He leaped off and approached Jane with the manner of a man determined to execute a difficult mission, yet fearful of its reception. In the gaunt, wiry figure and the lean, brown face Jane recognized one of her Mormon riders, Blake. It was he of whom Judkins had long since spoken. Of all the riders ever in her employ Blake owed her the most, and as he stepped before her, removing his hat and making manly efforts to subdue his emotion, he showed that he remembered.

"Miss Withersteen, Mother's dead," he said.

"Oh—Blake!" exclaimed Jane, and she could say no more.

"She died free from pain in the end, and she's buried—resting at last, thank God! . . . I've come to ride for you again, if you'll have me. Don't think I mentioned Mother to get your sympathy. When she was living and your riders quit, I had to also. I was afraid of what might be done—said to her. . . . Miss Withersteen, we can't talk of—of what's going on now—"

"Blake, do you know?"

"I know a great deal. You understand, my lips are shut. But without explanation or excuse I offer my services. I'm a Mormon—I hope a good one. But—there are some things! . . . It's no use, Miss Withersteen, I can't say anymore—what I'd like to. But will you take me back?"

"Blake! . . . You know what it means?"

"I don't care. I'm sick of—of—I'll show you a Mormon who'll be true to you!"

"But, Blake—how terribly you might suffer for that!"

"Maybe. Aren't you suffering now?"

"God knows indeed I am!"

"Miss Withersteen, it's a liberty on my part to speak so, but I know you pretty well—know you'll never give in. I wouldn't if I were you. And I—I must— Something makes me tell you the worst is yet to come. That's all. I absolutely can't say more. Will you take me back—let me ride for you— show everybody what I mean?"

"Blake, it makes me happy to hear you. How my riders hurt me when they quit!" Jane felt the hot tears well to her eyes and splash down upon her hands. "I thought so much of them—tried so hard to be good to them. And not one was true. You've made it easy to forgive. Perhaps many of them really feel as you do, but dare not return to me. Still, Blake, I hesitate to take you back. Yet I want you so much."

"Do it, then. If you're going to make your life a lesson to Mormon women, let me make mine a lesson to the men. Right is right. I believe in you, and here's my life to prove it."

"You hint it may mean your life!" said Jane, breathless and low.

"We won't speak of that. I want to come back. I want to do what every rider aches in his secret heart to do for you. . . . Miss Withersteen, I hoped it'd not be necessary to tell you that my mother on her deathbed told me to have courage. She knew how the thing galled me—she told me to come back. . . . Will you take me?"

"God bless you, Blake! Yes, I'll take you back. And will you—will you accept gold from me?"

"Miss Withersteen!"

"I just gave Judkins a bag of gold. I'll give you one. If you will not take it you must not come back. You might ride for me a few months—weeks —days till the storm breaks. Then you'd have nothing, and be in disgrace with your people. We'll forearm you against poverty, and me against endless regret. I'll give you gold which you can hide—till some future time."

"Well, if it pleases you," replied Blake. "But you know I never thought of pay. Now, Miss Withersteen, one thing more. I want to see this man Lassiter. Is he here?"

"Yes, but, Blake—what— Need you see him? Why?" asked Jane, instantly worried. "I can speak to him—tell him about you."

"That won't do. I want to—I've got to tell him myself. Where is he?"

"Lassiter is with Mrs. Larkin. She is ill. I'll call him," answered Jane, and going to the door she softly called for the rider. A faint, musical jingle preceded his step—then his tall form crossed the threshold.

"Lassiter, here's Blake, an old rider of mine. He has come back to me and he wishes to speak to you."

Blake's brown face turned exceedingly pale.

"Yes, I had to speak to you," he said, swiftly. "My name's Blake. I'm a Mormon and a rider. Lately I quit Miss Withersteen. I've come to beg her to take me back. Now I don't know you, but I know—what you are. So I've this to say to your face. It would never occur to this woman to imagine—let alone suspect me to be a spy. She couldn't think it might just be a low plot to come here and shoot you in the back. Jane Withersteen hasn't that kind of a mind. . . . Well, I've not come for that. I want to help her—to pull a bridle along with Judkins and—and you. The thing is—do you believe me?"

"I reckon I do," replied Lassiter. How this slow, cool speech contrasted with Blake's hot, impulsive words! "You might have saved some of your breath. See here, Blake, cinch this in your mind. Lassiter has met some square Mormons! An' mebbe—"

"Blake," interrupted Jane, nervously anxious to terminate a colloquy that she perceived was an ordeal for him. "Go at once and fetch me a report of my horses."

"Miss Withersteen! . . . You mean the big drove—down in the sage-cleared fields?"

"Of course," replied Jane. "My horses are all there, except the blooded stock I keep here."

"Haven't you heard—then?"

"Heard? No! What's happened to them?

"They're gone, Miss Withersteen, gone these ten days past. Dorn told me, and I rode down to see for myself."

"Lassiter—did you know?" asked Jane, whirling to him.

"I reckon so. . . . But what was the use to tell you?"

It was Lassiter turning away his face and Blake studying the stone flags at his feet that brought Jane to the understanding of what she betrayed. She strove desperately, but she could not rise immediately from such a blow.

"My horses! My horses! What's become of them?"

"Dorn said the riders report another drive by Oldring. . . . And I trailed the horses miles down the slope toward Deception Pass."

"My red herd's gone! My horses gone! The white herd will go next. I can stand that. But if I lost Black Star and Night, it would be like parting with my own flesh and blood. Lassiter—Blake—am I in danger of losing my racers?"

"A rustler—or—or anybody stealin' hosses of yours would most of all want the blacks," said Lassiter. His evasive reply was affirmative enough. The other rider nodded gloomy acquiescence.

"Oh! Oh!" Jane Withersteen choked, with violent utterance.

"Let me take charge of the blacks?" asked Blake. "One more rider won't be any great help to Judkins. But I might hold Black Star and Night, if you put such store on their value."

"Value! Blake, I love my racers. Besides, there's another reason why I mustn't lose them. You go to the stables. Go with Jerd every day when he runs the horses, and don't let them out of your sight. If you would please me, win my gratitude—guard my black racers."

When Blake had mounted and ridden out of the court Lassiter regarded Jane with the smile that was becoming rarer as the days sped by.

" 'Pears to me, as Blake says, you do put some store on them hosses.

Now I ain't gainsayin' that the Arabians are the handsomest hosses I ever seen. But Bells can beat Night, an' run neck an' neck with Black Star."

"Lassiter, don't tease me now. I'm miserable—sick. Bells is fast, but he can't stay with the blacks, and you know it. Only Wrangle can do that."

"I'll bet that big raw-boned brute can more'n show his heels to your black racers. Jane, out there in the sage, on a long chase, Wrangle could kill your favorites."

"No, no," replied Jane, impatiently. "Lassiter, why do you say that so often? I know you've teased me at times, and I believe it's only kindness. You're always trying to keep my mind off worry. But you mean more by this repeated mention of my racers?"

"I reckon so." Lassiter paused, and for the thousandth time in her presence moved his black sombrero round and round, as if counting the silver pieces on the band. "Well, Jane, I've sort of read a little that's passin' in your mind."

"You think I might fly from my home—from Cottonwoods—from the Utah border?"

"I reckon. An' if you ever do an' get away with the blacks I wouldn't like to see Wrangle left here on the sage. Wrangle could catch you. I know Venters had him. But you can never tell. Mebbe he hasn't got him now. . . . Besides—things are happenin', an' somethin' of the same queer nature might have happened to Venters."

"God knows you're right! . . . Poor Bern, how long he's gone! In my trouble I've been forgetting him. But, Lassiter, I've little fear for him. I've heard my riders say he's as keen as a wolf. . . . As to your reading my thoughts—well, your suggestion makes an actual thought of what was only one of my dreams. I believe I dreamed of flying from this wild borderland, Lassiter. I've strange dreams. I'm not always practical and thinking of my many duties, as you said once. For instance—if I dared—if I dared I'd ask you to saddle the blacks and ride away with me—and hide me."

"Jane!"

The rider's sunburnt face turned white. A few times Jane had seen Lassiter's cool calm broken—when he had met little Fay, when he had learned how and why he had come to love both child and mistress, when he had stood beside Milly Erne's grave. But one and all they could not be considered in the light of his present agitation. Not only did Lassiter turn white—not only did he grow tense, not only did he lose his coolness, but also he suddenly, violently, hungrily took her into his arms and crushed her to his breast.

"Lassiter!" cried Jane, trembling. It was an action for which she took sole blame. Instantly, as if dazed, weakened, he released her. "Forgive me!" went on Jane. "I'm always forgetting your—your feelings. I thought of you as my faithful friend. I'm always making you out more than human

. . . only, let me say—I meant that—about riding away. I'm wretched, sick of this—this— Oh, something bitter and black grows on my heart!"

"Jane, the hell—of it," he replied, with deep intake of breath, "is you *can't* ride away. Mebbe realizin' it accounts for my grabbin' you—that way, as much as the crazy boy's rapture your words gave me. I don't understand myself. . . . But the hell of this game is—you *can't* ride away."

"Lassiter! . . . What on earth do you mean? I'm an absolutely free woman."

"You ain't absolutely anythin' of the kind. . . . I reckon I've got to tell you!"

"Tell me all. It's uncertainty that makes me a coward. It's faith and hope—blind love, if you will, that makes me miserable. Every day I awake believing—still believing. The day grows, and with it doubts, fears, and that black bat hate that bites hotter and hotter into my heart. Then comes night—I pray—I pray for all, and for myself—I sleep—and I awake free once more, trustful, faithful, to believe—to hope! Then, oh my God! I grow and live a thousand years till night again! . . . But if you want to see me a woman, tell me why I can't ride away—tell me what more I'm to lose—tell me the worst."

"Jane, you're watched. There's no single move of yours, except when you're hid in your house, that ain't seen by sharp eyes. The cottonwood grove's full of creepin', crawlin' men. Like Indians in the grass. When you rode, which wasn't often lately, the sage was full of sneakin' men. At night they crawl under your windows, into the court, an' I reckon into the house. Jane Withersteen, you know, never locked a door! This here grove's a hummin' beehive of mysterious happenin's. Jane, it ain't so much that these spies keep out of my way as me keepin' out of theirs. They're goin' to try to kill me. That's plain. But mebbe I'm as hard to shoot in the back as in the face. So far I've seen fit to watch only. This all means, Jane, that you're a marked woman. You can't get away—not now. Mebbe later, when you're broken, you might. But that's sure doubtful. Jane, you're to lose the cattle that's left—your home an' ranch—an' Amber Spring. You can't even hide a sack of gold! For it couldn't be slipped out of the house, day or night, an' hid or buried, let alone be rid off with. You may lose all. I'm tellin' you, Jane, hopin' to prepare you, if the worst does come. I told you once before about that strange power I've got to feel things."

"Lassiter, what can I do?"

"Nothin', I reckon, except know what's comin' an' wait an' be game. If you'd let me make a call on Tull, an' a long-deferred call on—"

"Hush! . . . Hush!" she whispered.

"Well, even that wouldn't help you any in the end."

"What does it mean? Oh, what does it mean? I am my father's daughter —a Mormon, yet I can't see! I've not failed in religion—in duty. For years

I've given with a free and full heart. When my father died I was rich. If I'm still rich it's because I couldn't find enough ways to become poor. What am I, what are my possessions to set in motion such intensity of secret oppression?"

"Jane, the mind behind it all is an empire builder."

"But, Lassiter, I would give freely—all I own to avert this—this wretched thing. If I gave—that would leave me with faith still. Surely my —my churchmen think of my soul? If I lose my trust in them—"

"Child, be still!" said Lassiter, with a dark dignity that had in it something of pity. "You are a woman, fine an' big an' strong, an' your heart matches your size. But in mind you're a child. I'll say a little more—then I'm done. I'll never mention this again. Among many thousands of women you're one who has bucked against your churchmen. They tried you out, an' failed of persuasion, an' finally of threats. You meet now the cold steel of a will as far from Christlike as the universe is wide. You're to be broken. Your body's to be held, given to some man, made, if possible, to bring children into the world. But your soul? . . . What do they care for your soul?"

⁓ 13 ⁓

SOLITUDE AND STORM

I N HIS HIDDEN VALLEY Venters awakened from sleep, and his ears rang with innumerable melodies from full-throated mockingbirds, and his eyes opened wide upon the glorious golden shaft of sunlight shining through the great stone bridge. The circle of cliffs surrounding Surprise Valley lay shrouded in morning mist, a dim blue low down along the terraces, a creamy, moving cloud along the ramparts. The oak forest in the center was a plumed and tufted oval of gold.

He saw Bess under the spruces. Upon her complete recovery of strength she always rose with the dawn. At the moment she was feeding the quail she had tamed. And she had begun to tame the mockingbirds. They fluttered among the branches overhead, and some left off their songs to flit down and shyly hop near the twittering quail. Little gray and white rabbits crouched in the grass, now nibbling, now laying long ears flat and watching the dogs.

Venters's swift glance took in the brightening valley, and Bess and her pets, and Ring and Whitie. It swept over all to return again and rest upon the girl. She had changed. To the dark trousers and blouse she had added moccasins of her own make, but she no longer resembled a boy. No eye could have failed to mark the rounded contours of a woman. The change had been to grace and beauty. A glint of warm gold gleamed from her hair, and a tint of red shone in the clear dark brown of cheeks. The haunting sweetness of her lips and eyes, that earlier had been elusive, a promise, had become a living fact. She fitted harmoniously into that wonderful setting; she was like Surprise Valley—wild and beautiful.

Venters leaped out of his cave to begin the day.

He had postponed his journey to Cottonwoods until after the passing of the summer rains. The rains were due soon. But until their arrival and the necessity for his trip to the village he sequestered in a far corner of mind all thought of peril, of his past life, and almost that of the present. It was enough to live. He did not want to know what lay hidden in the dim and distant future. Surprise Valley had enchanted him. In this home of the cliff-dwellers there were peace and quiet and solitude, and another thing, wondrous as the golden morning shaft of sunlight, that he dared not ponder over long enough to understand.

The solitude he had hated when alone he had now come to love. He was assimilating something from this valley of gleams and shadows. From this strange girl he was assimilating more.

The day at hand resembled many days gone before. As Venters had no tools with which to build, or to till the terraces, he remained idle. Beyond the cooking of the simple fare there were no tasks. And as there were no tasks, there was no system. He and Bess began one thing, to leave it; to begin another, to leave that; and then do nothing but lie under the spruces and watch the great cloud-sails majestically move along the ramparts, and dream and dream. The valley was a golden, sunlit world. It was silent. The sighing wind and the twittering quail and the singing birds, even the rare and seldom-occurring hollow crack of a sliding weathered stone, only thickened and deepened that insulated silence.

Venters and Bess had vagrant minds.

"Bess, did I tell you about my horse Wrangle?" inquired Venters.

"A hundred times," she replied.

"Oh, have I? I'd forgotten. I want you to see him. He'll carry us both."

"I'd like to ride him. Can he run?"

"Run? He's a demon. Swiftest horse on the sage! I hope he'll stay in that canyon."

"He'll stay."

They left camp to wander along the terraces, into the aspen ravines, under the gleaming walls. Ring and Whitie wandered in the fore, often turning, often trotting back, open-mouthed and solemn-eyed and happy. Venters lifted his gaze to the grand archway over the entrance to the valley, and Bess lifted hers to follow his, and both were silent. Sometimes the bridge held their attention for a long time. Today a soaring eagle attracted them.

"How he sails!" exclaimed Bess. "I wonder where his mate is?"

"She's at the nest. It's on the bridge in a crack near the top. I see her often. She's almost white."

They wandered on down the terrace, into the shady, sun-flecked forest. A brown bird fluttered crying from a bush. Bess peeped into the leaves.

"Look! A nest and four little birds. They're not afraid of us. See how they open their mouths. They're hungry."

Rabbits rustled the dead brush and pattered away. The forest was full of a drowsy hum of insects. Little darts of purple, that were running quail, crossed the glades. And a plaintive, sweet peeping came from the coverts. Bess's soft step disturbed a sleeping lizard that scampered away over the leaves. She gave chase and caught it, a slim creature of nameless color but of exquisite beauty.

"Jewel eyes," she said. "It's like a rabbit—afraid. We won't eat you. There—go."

Murmuring water drew their steps down into a shallow shaded ravine where a brown brook brawled softly over mossy stones. Multitudes of strange, gray frogs with white spots and black eyes lined the rocky bank and leaped only at close approach. Then Venters's eye descried a very thin, very long green snake coiled round a sapling. They drew closer and closer till they could have touched it. The snake had no fear and watched them with scintillating eyes.

"It's pretty," said Bess. "How tame! I thought snakes always ran."

"No. Even the rabbits didn't run here till the dogs chased them."

On and on they wandered to the wild jumble of massed and broken fragments of cliff at the west end of the valley. The roar of the disappearing stream dinned in their ears. Into this maze of rocks they threaded a tortuous way, climbing, descending, halting to gather wild plums and great lavender lilies, and going on at the will of fancy. Idle and keen perceptions guided them equally.

"Oh, let us climb there!" cried Bess, pointing upward to a small space of terrace left green and shady between huge abutments of broken cliff. And they climbed to the nook and rested and looked out across the valley to the curling column of blue smoke from their campfire. But the cool shade and the rich grass and the fine view were not what they had climbed for. They could not have told, although whatever had drawn them was all-satisfying. Light, sure-footed as a mountain goat, Bess pattered down at Venters's heels; and they went on, calling the dogs, eyes dreamy and wide, listening to the wind and the bees and the crickets and the birds.

Part of the time Ring and Whitie led the way, then Venters, then Bess; and the direction was not an object. They left the sun-streaked shade of the oaks, brushed the long grass of the meadows, entered the green and fragrant swaying willows, to stop, at length, under the huge old cottonwoods where the beavers were busy.

Here they rested and watched. A dam of brush and logs and mud and stones backed the stream into a little lake. The round, rough beaver houses projected from the water. Like the rabbits, the beavers had become shy. Gradually, however, as Venters and Bess knelt low, holding the dogs, the beavers emerged to swim with logs and gnaw at cottonwoods and pat mud walls with their paddlelike tails, and, glossy and shiny in the sun, to go on with their strange, persistent industry. They were the builders. The lake was a mudhole, and the immediate environment a scarred and dead region, but it was a wonderful home of wonderful animals.

"Look at that one—he puddles in the mud," said Bess. "And there! See him dive! Hear them gnawing! I'd think they'd break their teeth. How's it they can stay out of the water and under the water?"

And she laughed.

Then Venters and Bess wandered farther, and, perhaps not all unconsciously this time, wended their slow steps to the cave of the cliff-dwellers, where she liked best to go.

The tangled thicket and the long slant of dust and little chips of weathered rock and the steep bench of stone and the worn steps all were arduous work for Bess in the climbing. But she gained the shelf, gasping, hot of cheek, glad of eye, with her hand in Venters's. Here they rested. The beautiful valley glittered below with its millions of wind-turned leaves bright-faced in the sun, and the mighty bridge towered heavenward, crowned with blue sky. Bess, however, never rested for long. Soon she was exploring, and Venters followed; she dragged forth from corners and shelves a multitude of crudely fashioned and painted pieces of pottery, and he carried them. They peeped down into the dark holes of the kivas, and Bess gleefully dropped a stone and waited for the long-coming hollow sound to rise. They peeped into the little globular houses, like mud-wasp nests, and wondered if these had been store-places for grain, or baby cribs, or what; and they crawled into the larger houses and laughed when they bumped their heads on the low roofs, and they dug in the dust of the floors. And they brought from dust and darkness armloads of treasure which they carried to the light. Flints and stones and strange curved sticks and pottery they found; and twisted grass rope that crumbled in their hands, and bits of whitish stone which crushed to powder at a touch and seemed to vanish in the air.

"That white stuff was bone," said Venters, slowly. "Bones of a cliff-dweller."

"No!" exclaimed Bess.

"Here's another piece. Look! . . . Whew! dry, powdery smoke! That's bone."

Then it was that Venters's primitive, childlike mood, like a savage's, seeing, yet unthinking, gave way to the encroachment of civilized thought. The world had not been made for a single day's play or fancy or idle watching. The world was old. Nowhere could be gotten a better idea of its age than in this gigantic silent tomb. The gray ashes in Venters's hand had once been bone of a human being like himself. The pale gloom of the cave had shadowed people long ago. He saw that Bess had received the same shock—could not in moments such as this escape her feeling, living, thinking destiny.

"Bern, people have *lived* here," she said, with wide, thoughtful eyes.

"Yes," he replied.

"How long ago?"

"A thousand years and more."

"What were they?"

"Cliff-dwellers. Men who had enemies and made their homes high out of reach."

"They had to fight?"

"Yes."

"They fought for—what?"

"For life. For their homes, food, children, parents—for their women!"

"Has the world changed any in a thousand years?"

"I don't know—perhaps very little."

"Have men?"

"I hope so—I think so."

"Things crowd into my mind," she went on, and the wistful light in her eyes told Venters the truth of her thoughts. "I've ridden the border of Utah. I've seen people—know how they live—but they must be few of all who are living. I had my books and I studied them. But all that doesn't help me anymore. I want to go out into the big world and see it. Yet I want to stay here more. What's to become of us? Are we cliff-dwellers? We're alone here. I'm happy when I don't think. These—these bones that fly into dust—they make me sick and a little afraid. Did the people who lived here once have the same feelings as we have? What was the good of their living at all? They're gone! What's the meaning of it all—of us?"

"Bess, you ask more than I can tell. It's beyond me. Only there was laughter here once—and now there's silence. There was life—and now there's death. Men cut these little steps, made these arrowheads and mealing-stones, plaited the ropes we found, and left their bones to crumble in our fingers. As far as time is concerned it might all have been yesterday. We're here today. Maybe we're higher in the scale of human beings—in intelligence. But who knows? We can't be any higher in the things for which life is lived at all."

"What are they?"

"Why—I suppose relationship, friendship—love."

"Love!"

"Yes. Love of man for woman—love of woman for man. That's the nature, the meaning, the best of life itself."

She said no more. Wistfulness of glance deepened into sadness.

"Come, let us go," said Venters.

Action brightened her. Beside him, holding his hand, she slipped down the shelf, ran down the long, steep slant of sliding stones, out of the cloud of dust, and likewise out of the pale gloom.

"We beat the slide," she cried.

The miniature avalanche cracked and roared, and rattled itself into an inert mass at the base of the incline. Yellow dust like the gloom of the cave, but not so changeless, drifted away on the wind; the roar clapped in echo from the cliff, returned, went back, and came again to die in the hollowness. Down on the sunny terrace there was a different atmosphere. Ring and Whitie leaped around Bess. Once more she was smiling, gay, and thoughtless, with the dream-mood in the shadow of her eyes.

"Bess, I haven't seen that since last summer. Look!" said Venters, pointing to the scalloped edge of rolling purple clouds that peeped over the western wall. "We're in for a storm."

"Oh, I hope not. I'm afraid of storms."

"Are you? Why?"

"Have you ever been down in one of these walled-up pockets in a bad storm?"

"No, now I think of it, I haven't."

"Well, it's terrible. Every summer I get scared to death and hide somewhere in the dark. Storms up on the sage are bad, but nothing to what they are down here in the canyons. And in this little valley—why, echoes can rap back and forth so quick they'll split our ears."

"We're perfectly safe here, Bess."

"I know. But that hasn't anything to do with it. The truth is I'm afraid of lightning and thunder, and thunderclaps hurt my head. If we have a bad storm, will you stay close by me?"

"Yes."

When they got back to camp the afternoon was closing, and it was exceedingly sultry. Not a breath of air stirred the aspen leaves, and when these did not quiver the air was indeed still. The dark-purple clouds moved almost imperceptibly out of the west.

"What have we for supper?" asked Bess.

"Rabbit."

"Bern, can't you think of another new way to cook rabbit?" went on Bess, with earnestness.

"What do you think I am—a magician?" retorted Venters.

"I wouldn't dare tell you. But, Bern, do you want me to turn into a rabbit?"

There was a dark-blue, merry flashing of eyes and a parting of lips; then she laughed. In that moment she was naïve and wholesome.

"Rabbit seems to agree with you," replied Venters. "You are well and strong—and growing very pretty."

Anything in the nature of compliment he had never before said to her, and just now he responded to a sudden curiosity to see its effect. Bess stared as if she had not heard aright, slowly blushed, and completely lost her poise in happy confusion.

"I'd better go right away," he continued, "and fetch supplies from Cottonwoods."

A startlingly swift change in the nature of her agitation made him reproach himself for his abruptness.

"No, no, don't go!" she said. "I didn't mean—that about the rabbit. I —I was only trying to be—funny. Don't leave me all alone!"

"Bess, I must go sometime."

"Wait then. Wait till after the storms."

The purple cloud-bank darkened the lower edge of the setting sun, crept up and up, obscuring its fiery red heart, and finally passed over the last ruddy crescent of its upper rim.

The intense dead silence awakened to a long, low, rumbling roll of thunder.

"Oh!" cried Bess, nervously.

"We've had big black clouds before this without rain," said Venters. "But there's no doubt about that thunder. The storms are coming. I'm glad. Every rider on the sage will hear that thunder with glad ears."

Venters and Bess finished their simple meal and the few tasks around the camp, then faced the open terrace, the valley, and the west, to watch and await the approaching storm.

It required keen vision to see any movement whatever in the purple clouds. By infinitesimal degrees the dark cloud-line merged upward into the golden-red haze of the afterglow of sunset. A shadow lengthened from under the western wall across the valley. As straight and rigid as steel rose the delicate spear-pointed silver spruces; the aspen leaves, by nature pendant and quivering, hung limp and heavy; no slender blade of grass moved. A gentle plashing of water came from the ravine. Then again from out of the west sounded the low, dull, and rumbling roll of thunder.

A wave, a ripple of light, a trembling and turning of the aspen leaves, like the approach of a breeze on the water, crossed the valley from the west; and the lull and the deadly stillness and the sultry air passed away on a cool wind.

The night bird of the canyon, with his clear and melancholy notes, announced the twilight. And from all along the cliffs rose the faint murmur and moan and mourn of the wind singing in the caves. The bank of clouds now swept hugely out of the western sky. Its front was purple and black, with gray between, a bulging, mushrooming, vast thing instinct with storm. It had a dark, angry, threatening aspect. As if all the power of the winds were pushing and piling behind, it rolled ponderously across the sky. A red flare burned out instantaneously, flashed from west to east, and died. Then from the deepest black of the purple cloud burst a boom. It was like the bowling of a huge boulder along the crags and ramparts, and seemed to roll on and fall into the valley to bound and bang and boom from cliff to cliff.

"Oh!" cried Bess, with her hands over her ears. "What did I tell you?"

"Why, Bess, be reasonable!" said Venters.

"I'm a coward."

"Not quite that, I hope. It's strange you're afraid. I love a storm."

"I tell you a storm down in these canyons is an awful thing. I know Oldring hated storms. His men were afraid of them. There was one who went deaf in a bad storm, and never could hear again."

"Maybe I've lots to learn, Bess. I'll lose my guess if this storm isn't bad enough. We're going to have heavy wind first, then lightning and thunder, then the rain. Let's stay out as long as we can."

The tips of the cottonwoods and the oaks waved to the east, and the rings of aspens along the terraces twinkled their myriad of bright faces in fleet and glancing gleam. A low roar rose from the leaves of the forest, and the spruces swished in the rising wind. It came in gusts, with light breezes between. As it increased in strength the lulls shortened in length till there was a strong and steady blow all the time, and violent puffs at intervals, and sudden whirling currents. The clouds spread over the valley, rolling swiftly and low, and twilight faded into a sweeping darkness. Then the singing of the wind in the caves drowned the swift roar of rustling leaves; then the song swelled to a mourning, moaning wail; then with the gathering power of the wind the wail changed to a shriek. Steadily the wind strengthened and constantly the strange sound changed.

The last bit of blue sky yielded to the onsweep of clouds. Like angry surf the pale gleams of gray, amid the purple of that scudding front, swept beyond the eastern rampart of the valley. The purple deepened to black. Broad sheets of lightning flared over the western wall. There were not yet any ropes or zigzag streaks darting down through the gathering darkness. The storm center was still beyond Surprise Valley.

"Listen! . . . Listen!" cried Bess, with her lips close to Venters's ear. "You'll hear Oldring's knell!"

"What's that?"

"Oldring's knell. When the wind blows a gale in the caves it makes what the rustlers call Oldring's knell. They believe it bodes his death. I think he believes so, too. It's not like any sound on earth. . . . It's beginning. Listen!"

The gale swooped down with a hollow unearthly howl. It yelled and

pealed and shrilled and shrieked. It was made up of a thousand piercing
cries. It was a rising and a moving sound. Beginning at the western break
of the valley, it rushed along each gigantic cliff, whistling into the caves
and cracks, to mount in power, to bellow a blast through the great stone
bridge. Gone, as into an engulfing roar of surging waters, it seemed to
shoot back and begin all over again.

It was only wind, thought Venters. Here sped and shrieked the sculptor
that carved out the wonderful caves in the cliffs. It was only a gale, but as
Venters listened, as his ears became accustomed to the fury and strife, out
of it all or through it or above it pealed low and perfectly clear and
persistently uniform a strange sound that had no counterpart in all the
sounds of the elements. It was not of earth or of life. It was the grief and
agony of the gale. A knell of all upon which it blew!

Black night enfolded the valley. Venters could not see his companion,
and knew of her presence only through the tightening hold of her hand
on his arm. He felt the dogs huddle closer to him. Suddenly the dense,
black vault overhead split asunder to a blue-white, dazzling streak of
lightning. The whole valley lay vividly clear and luminously bright in his
sight. Upreared, vast, and magnificent, the stone bridge glimmered like
some grand god of storm in the lightning's fire. Then all flashed black
again—blacker than pitch—a thick, impenetrable coal-blackness. And
there came a ripping, crashing report. Instantly an echo resounded with a
clapping crash. The initial report was nothing to the echo. It was a
terrible, living, reverberating, detonating crash. The wall threw the sound
across, and could have made no greater roar if it had slipped in avalanche.
From cliff to cliff the echo went in crashing retort and banged in lessening
power, and boomed in thinner volume, and clapped weaker and weaker
till a final clap could not reach across to waiting cliff.

In the pitchy darkness Venters led Bess, and, groping his way, by feel of
hand found the entrance to her cave and lifted her up. On the instant a
blinding flash of lightning illumined the cave and all about him. He saw
Bess's face white now, with dark, frightened eyes. He saw the dogs leap
up, and he followed suit. The golden glare vanished; all was black; then
came the splitting crack and the infernal din of echoes.

Bess shrank closer to him and closer, found his hands, and pressed
them tightly over her ears, and dropped her face upon his shoulder, and
hid her eyes.

Then the storm burst with a succession of ropes and streaks and shafts
of lightning, playing continuously, filling the valley with a broken radiance; and the cracking shots followed each other swiftly till the echoes
blended in one fearful, deafening crash.

Venters looked out upon the beautiful valley—beautiful now as never
before—mystic in its transparent, luminous gloom, weird in the quivering, golden haze of lightning. The dark spruces were tipped with glimmer-

ing lights; the aspens bent low in the winds, as waves in a tempest at sea; the forest of oaks tossed wildly and shone with gleams of fire. Across the valley the huge cavern of the cliff-dwellers yawned in the glare, every little black window as clear as at noonday; but the night and the storm added to their tragedy. Flung arching to the black clouds, the great stone bridge seemed to bear the brunt of the storm. It caught the full fury of the rushing wind. It lifted its noble crown to meet the lightnings. Venters thought of the eagles and their lofty nest in a niche under the arch. A driving pall of rain, black as the clouds, came sweeping on to obscure the bridge and the gleaming walls and the shining valley. The lightning played incessantly, streaking down through opaque darkness of rain. The roar of the wind, with its strange knell and the recrashing echoes, mingled with the roar of the flooding rain, and all seemingly were deadened and drowned in a world of sound.

In the dimming pale light Venters looked down upon the girl. She had sunk into his arms, upon his breast, burying her face. She clung to him. He felt the softness of her, and the warmth, and the quick heave of her breast. He saw the dark, slender, graceful outline of her form. A woman lay in his arms! And he held her closer. He who had been alone in the sad, silent watches of the night was not now and never must be again alone. He who had yearned for the touch of a hand felt the long tremble and the heartbeat of a woman. By what strange chance had she come to love him! By what change—by what marvel had she grown into a treasure!

No more did he listen to the rush and roar of the thunderstorm. For with the touch of clinging hands and the throbbing bosom he grew conscious of an inward storm—the tingling of new chords of thought, strange music of unheard, joyous bells, sad dreams dawning to wakeful delight, dissolving doubt, resurging hope, force, fire, and freedom, unutterable sweetness of desire. A storm in his breast—a storm of real love.

❀14❀

WEST WIND

WHEN THE STORM abated Venters sought his own cave, and late in the night, as his blood cooled and the stir and throb and thrill subsided, he fell asleep.

With the breaking of dawn his eyes unclosed. The valley lay drenched and bathed, a burnished oval of glittering green. The rain-washed walls glistened in the morning light. Waterfalls of many forms poured over the rims. One, a broad, lacy sheet, thin as smoke, slid over the western notch and struck a ledge in its downward fall, to bound into broader leap, to burst far below into white and gold and rosy mist.

Venters prepared for the day, knowing himself a different man.

"It's a glorious morning," said Bess, in greeting.

"Yes. After the storm the west wind," he replied.

"Last night was I—very much of a baby?" she asked, watching him.

"Pretty much."

"Oh, I couldn't help it!"

"I'm glad you were afraid."

"Why?" she asked, in slow surprise.

"I'll tell you some day," he answered, soberly. Then around the camp-fire and through the morning meal he was silent; afterward he strolled thoughtfully off alone along the terrace. He climbed a great yellow rock raising its crest among the spruces, and there he sat down to face the valley and the west.

"I love her!"

Aloud he spoke—unburdened his heart—confessed his secret. For an instant the golden valley swam before his eyes, and the walls waved, and all about him whirled with tumult within.

"I love her! . . . I understand now."

Reviving memory of Jane Withersteen and thought of the complications of the present amazed him with proof of how far he had drifted from his old life. He discovered that he hated to take up the broken threads, to delve into dark problems and difficulties. In this beautiful valley he had been living a beautiful dream. Tranquillity had come to him, and the joy of solitude, and interest in all the wild creatures and crannies of this incomparable valley—and love. Under the shadow of the great stone bridge God had revealed Himself to Venters.

126

"The world seems very far away," he muttered, "but it's there—and I'm not yet done with it. Perhaps I never shall be. . . . Only—how glorious it would be to live here always and never think again!"

Whereupon the resurging reality of the present, as if in irony of his wish, steeped him instantly in contending thought. Out of it all he presently evolved these things: he must go to Cottonwoods; he must bring supplies back to Surprise Valley; he must cultivate the soil and raise corn and stock, and, most imperative of all, he must decide the future of the girl who loved him and whom he loved. The first of these things required tremendous effort, the last one, concerning Bess, seemed simply and naturally easy of accomplishment. He would marry her. Suddenly, as from roots of poisonous fire, flamed up the forgotten truth concerning her. It seemed to wither and shrivel up all his joy on its hot, tearing way to his heart. She had been Oldring's Masked Rider. To Venters's question, "What were you to Oldring?" she had answered with scarlet shame and drooping head.

"What do I care who she is or what she was!" he cried, passionately. And he knew it was not his old self speaking. It was this softer, gentler man who had awakened to new thoughts in the quiet valley. Tenderness, masterful in him now, matched the absence of joy and blunted the knife-edge of entering jealousy. Strong and passionate effort of will, surprising to him, held back the poison from piercing his soul.

"Wait! . . . Wait!" he cried, as if calling. His hand pressed his breast, and he might have called to the pang there. "Wait! It's all so strange—so wonderful. Anything can happen. Who am I to judge her? I'll glory in my love for her. But I can't tell it—can't give up to it."

Certainly he could not then decide her future. Marrying her was impossible in Surprise Valley and in any village south of Sterling. Even without the mask she had once worn she would easily have been recognized as Oldring's Rider. No man who had ever seen her would forget her, regardless of his ignorance as to her sex. Then more poignant than all other argument was the fact that he did not want to take her away from Surprise Valley. He resisted all thought of that. He had brought her to the most beautiful and wildest place of the uplands; he had saved her, nursed her back to strength, watched her bloom as one of the valley lilies; he knew her life there to be pure and sweet—she belonged to him, and he loved her. Still these were not all the reasons why he did not want to take her away. Where could they go? He feared the rustlers—he feared the riders—he feared the Mormons. And if he should ever succeed in getting Bess safely away from these immediate perils, he feared the sharp eyes of women and their tongues, the big outside world with its problems of existence. He must wait to decide her future, which, after all, was deciding his own. But between her future and his something hung impending. Like Balancing Rock, which waited darkly over the steep gorge, ready to close forever the outlet to Deception Pass, that nameless thing, as certain

yet intangible as fate, must fall and close forever all doubts and fears of
the future.

"I've dreamed," muttered Venters, as he rose. "Well, why not? . . . To
dream is happiness! But let me just once see this clearly, wholly; then I
can go on dreaming till the thing falls. I've got to tell Jane Withersteen.
I've dangerous trips to take. I've work here to make comfort for this girl.
She's mine. I'll fight to keep her safe from that old life. I've already seen
her forget it. I love her. And if a beast ever rises in me I'll burn my hand
off before I lay it on her with shameful intent. And, by God! Sooner or
later I'll kill the man who hid her and kept her in Deception Pass!"

As he spoke the west wind softly blew in his face. It seemed to soothe
his passion. That west wind was fresh, cool, fragrant, and it carried a
sweet, strange burden of far-off things—tidings of life in other climes, of
sunshine asleep on other walls—of other places where reigned peace. It
carried, too, sad truth of human hearts and mystery—of promise and hope
unquenchable. Surprise Valley was only a little niche in the wide world
whence blew that burdened wind. Bess was only one of millions at the
mercy of unknown motive in nature and life. Content had come to
Venters in the valley; happiness had breathed in the slow, warm air; love
as bright as light had hovered over the walls and descended to him; and
now on the west wind came a whisper of the eternal triumph of faith over
doubt.

"How much better I am for what has come to me!" he exclaimed. "I'll
let the future take care of itself. Whatever falls, I'll be ready."

Venters retraced his steps along the terrace back to camp, and found
Bess in the old familiar seat, waiting and watching for his return.

"I went off by myself to think a little," he explained.

"You never looked that way before. What—what is it? Won't you tell
me?"

"Well, Bess, the fact is I've been dreaming a lot. This valley makes a
fellow dream. So I forced myself to think. We can't live this way much
longer. Soon I'll simply have to go to Cottonwoods. We need a whole
pack train of supplies. I can get—"

"Can you go safely?" she interrupted.

"Why, I'm sure of it. I'll ride through the Pass at night. I haven't any
fear that Wrangle isn't where I left him. And once on him—Bess, just
wait till you see that horse!"

"Oh, I want to see him—to ride him. But—but, Bern, this is what
troubles me," she said. "Will—will you come back?"

"Give me four days. If I'm not back in four days you'll know I'm dead.
For that only shall keep me."

"Oh!"

"Bess, I'll come back. There's danger—I wouldn't lie to you—but I can
take care of myself."

"Bern, I'm sure—oh, I'm sure of it! All my life I've watched hunted men. I can tell what's in them. And I believe you can ride and shoot and see with any rider of the sage. It's not—not that I—fear."

"Well, what is it, then?"

"Why—why—why should you come back at all?"

"I couldn't leave you here alone."

"You might change your mind when you get to the village—among old friends—"

"I won't change my mind. As for old friends—" He uttered a short, expressive laugh.

"Then—there—there must be a—a woman!" Dark red mantled the clear tan of temple and cheek and neck. Her eyes were eyes of shame, upheld a long moment by intense, straining search for the verification of her fear. Suddenly they drooped, her head fell to her knees, her hands flew to her hot cheeks.

"Bess—look here," said Venters, with a sharpness due to the violence with which he checked his quick, surging emotion.

As if compelled against her will—answering to an irresistible voice— Bess raised her head, looked at him with sad, dark eyes, and tried to whisper with tremulous lips.

"There's no woman," went on Venters, deliberately holding her glance with his. "Nothing on earth, barring the chances of life, can keep me away."

Her face flashed and flushed with the glow of a leaping joy; but like the vanishing of a gleam it disappeared to leave her as he had never beheld her.

"I am nothing—I am lost—I am nameless!"

"Do you *want* me to come back?" he asked, with sudden stern coldness. "Maybe *you* want to go back to Oldring!"

That brought her erect, trembling and ashy pale, with dark, proud eyes and mute lips refuting his insinuation.

"Bess, I beg your pardon. I shouldn't have said that. But you angered me. I intend to work—to make a home for you here—to be a—a brother to you as long as ever you need me. And you must forget what you are— were—I mean, and be happy. When you remember that old life you are bitter, and it hurts me."

"I was happy—I shall be very happy. Oh, you're so good that—that it kills me! If I think, I can't believe it. I grow sick with wondering *why*. I'm only a—*let me say it*— only a lost, nameless—girl of the rustlers. *Oldring's Girl*, they called me. That you should save me—be so good and kind— want to make me happy—why, it's beyond belief. No wonder I'm wretched at the thought of your leaving me. But I'll be wretched and bitter no more. I promise you. If only I could repay you even a little—"

"You've repaid me a hundredfold. Will you believe me?"

"Believe you! I couldn't do else."

"Then listen! . . . Saving you, I saved myself. Living here in this valley with you, I've found myself. I've learned to think while I was dreaming. I never troubled myself about God. But God, or some wonderful spirit, has whispered to me here. I absolutely deny the truth of what you say about yourself. I can't explain it. There are things too deep to tell. Whatever the terrible wrongs you've suffered, God holds you blameless. I see that—feel that in you every moment you are near me. I've a mother and a sister 'way back in Illinois. If I could I'd take you to them—to-morrow."

"*If it were true!* Oh, I might—I might lift my head!" she cried.

"Lift it then—you child. For I swear it's true."

She did lift her head with the singular wild grace always a part of her actions, with that old unconscious intimation of innocence which always tortured Venters, but now with something more—a spirit rising from the depths that linked itself to his brave words.

"I've been thinking—too," she cried, with quivering smile and swelling breast. "I've discovered myself—too. I'm young—I'm alive—I'm so full—oh! I'm a woman!"

"Bess, I believe I can claim credit of that last discovery—before you," Venters said, and laughed.

"Oh, there's more—there's something I must tell you."

"Tell it, then."

"When will you go to Cottonwoods?"

"As soon as the storms are past, or the worst of them."

"I'll tell you before you go. I can't now. I don't know how I shall then. But it must be told. I'd never let you leave me without knowing. For in spite of what you say there's a chance you mightn't come back."

Day after day the west wind blew across the valley. Day after day the clouds clustered gray and purple and black. The cliffs sang and the caves rang with Oldring's knell, and the lightning flashed, the thunder rolled, the echoes crashed and crashed, and the rains flooded the valley. Wild flowers sprang up everywhere, swaying with the lengthening grass on the terraces, smiling wanly from shady nooks, peeping wondrously from year-dry crevices of the walls. The valley bloomed into a paradise. Every single moment, from the breaking of the gold bar through the bridge at dawn on to the reddening of rays over the western wall, was one of colorful change. The valley swam in thick, transparent haze, golden at dawn, warm and white at noon, purple in the twilight. At the end of every storm a rainbow curved down into the leaf-bright forest to shine and fade and leave lingeringly some faint essence of its rosy iris in the air.

Venters walked with Bess, once more in a dream, and watched the lights change on the walls, and faced the wind from out of the west.

Always it brought softly to him strange, sweet tidings of far-off things.

It blew from a place that was old and whispered of youth. It blew down the grooves of time. It brought a story of the passing hours. It breathed low of fighting men and praying women. It sang clearly the song of love. That ever was the burden of its tidings—youth in the shady woods, waders through the wet meadows, boy and girl at the hedgerow stile, bathers in the booming surf, sweet, idle hours on grassy, windy hills, long strolls down moonlit lanes—everywhere in far-off lands, fingers locked and bursting hearts and longing lips—from all the world tidings of unquenchable love.

Often, in these hours of dreams he watched the girl, and asked himself of what was she dreaming? For the changing light of the valley reflected its gleam and its color and its meaning in the changing light of her eyes. He saw in them infinitely more than he saw in his dreams. He saw thought and soul and nature—strong vision of life. All tidings the west wind blew from distance and age he found deep in those dark-blue depths, and found them mysteries solved. Under their wistful shadow he softened, and in the softening felt himself grow a sadder, a wiser, and a better man.

While the west wind blew its tidings, filling his heart full, teaching him a man's part, the days passed, the purple clouds changed to white, and the storms were over for that summer.

"I must go now," he said.

"When?" she asked.

"At once—tonight."

"I'm glad the time has come. It dragged at me. Go—for you'll come back the sooner."

Late in the afternoon, as the ruddy sun split its last flame in the ragged notch of the western wall, Bess walked with Venters along the eastern terrace, up the long, weathered slope, under the great stone bridge. They entered the narrow gorge to climb around the fence long before built there by Venters. Farther than this she had never been. Twilight had already fallen in the gorge. It brightened to waning shadow in the wider ascent. He showed her Balancing Rock, of which he had often told her, and explained its sinister leaning over the outlet. Shuddering, she looked down the long, pale incline with its closed-in, toppling walls.

"What an awful trail! Did you carry me up here?"

"I did, surely," replied he.

"It frightens me, somehow. Yet I never was afraid of trails. I'd ride anywhere a horse could go, and climb where he couldn't. But there's something fearful here. I feel as—as if the place was watching me."

"Look at this rock. It's balanced here—balanced perfectly. You know I told you the cliff-dwellers cut the rock, and why. But they're gone and the rock waits. Can't you see—feel how it waits here? I moved it once, and I'll never dare again. A strong heave would start it. Then it would fall and bang, and smash that crag, and jar the walls, and close forever the outlet to Deception Pass!"

"Ah! When you come back I'll steal up here and push and push with all my might to roll the rock and close forever the outlet to the Pass!" She said it lightly, but in the undercurrent of her voice was a heavier note, a ring deeper than any ever given mere play of words.

"Bess! . . . You can't dare me! Wait till I come back with supplies—then roll the stone."

"I—was—in—fun." Her voice now throbbed low. "Always you must be free to go when you will. Go now . . . this place presses on me—stifles me."

"I'm going—but you had something to tell me?"

"Yes. . . .Will you—come back?"

"I'll come if I live."

"But—but you mightn't come?"

"That's possible, of course. It'll take a good deal to kill me. A man couldn't have a faster horse or keener dog. And, Bess, I've guns, and I'll use them if I'm pushed. But don't worry."

"I've faith in you. I'll not worry until after four days. Only—because you mightn't come—I *must* tell you—"

She lost her voice. Her pale face, her great, glowing, earnest eyes, seemed to stand alone out of the gloom of the gorge. The dog whined, breaking the silence.

"I *must* tell you—because you mightn't come back," she whispered. "You *must* know what—what I think of your goodness—of you. Always I've been tongue-tied. I seemed not to be grateful. It was deep in my heart. Even now—if I were other than I am—I couldn't tell you. But I'm nothing—only a rustler's girl—nameless—infamous. You've saved me—and I'm—I'm yours to do with as you like. . . . With all my heart and soul—I love you!"

:15:

SHADOWS ON
THE SAGE-SLOPE

I N THE CLOUDY, threatening, waning summer days shadows lengthened down the sage-slope, and Jane Withersteen likened them to the
shadows gathering and closing in around her life.

Mrs. Larkin died, and little Fay was left an orphan with no known
relative. Jane's love redoubled. It was the saving brightness of a darkening
hour. Fay turned now to Jane in childish worship. And Jane at last found
full expression for the mother-longing in her heart. Upon Lassiter, too,
Mrs. Larkin's death had some subtle reaction. Before, he had often, without explanation, advised Jane to send Fay back to any Gentile family that
would take her in. Passionately and reproachfully and wonderingly Jane
had refused even to entertain such an idea. And now Lassiter never
advised it again, grew sadder and quieter in his contemplation of the
child, and infinitely more gentle and loving. Sometimes Jane had a cold,
inexplicable sensation of dread when she saw Lassiter watching Fay.
What did the rider see in the future? Why did he, day by day, grow more
silent, calmer, cooler, yet sadder in prophetic assurance of something to
be?

No doubt, Jane thought, the rider, in his almost superhuman power of
foresight, saw behind the horizon the dark, lengthening shadows that
were soon to crowd and gloom over him and her and little Fay. Jane
Withersteen awaited the long-deferred breaking of the storm with a courage and embittered calm that had come to her in her extremity. Hope had
not died. Doubt and fear, subservient to her will, no longer gave her
sleepless nights and tortured days. Love remained. All that she had loved
she now loved the more. She seemed to feel that she was defiantly flinging
the wealth of her love in the face of misfortune and of hate. No day
passed but she prayed for all—and most fervently for her enemies. It
troubled her that she had lost, or had never gained, the whole control of
her mind. In some measure reason and wisdom and decision were locked
in a chamber of her brain, awaiting a key. Power to think of some things
was taken from her. Meanwhile, abiding a day of judgment, she fought
ceaselessly to deny the bitter drops in her cup, to tear back the slow, the
intangibly slow growth of a hot, corrosive lichen eating into her heart.

On the morning of August 10, Jane, while waiting in the court for Lassiter, heard a clear, ringing report of a rifle. It came from the grove, somewhere toward the corrals. Jane glanced out in alarm. The day was dull, windless, soundless. The leaves of the cottonwoods drooped, as if they had foretold the doom of Withersteen House and were now ready to die and drop and decay. Never had Jane seen such shade. She pondered on the meaning of the report. Revolver shots had of late cracked from different parts of the grove—spies taking snap-shots at Lassiter from a cowardly distance! But a rifle report meant more. Riders seldom used rifles. Judkins and Venters were the exceptions she called to mind. Had the men who hounded her hidden in her grove, taken to the rifle to rid her of Lassiter, her last friend? It was probable—it was likely. And she did not share his cool assumption that his death would never come at the hands of a Mormon. Long had she expected it. His constancy to her, his singular reluctance to use the fatal skill for which he was famed—both now plain to all Mormons—laid him open to inevitable assassination. Yet what charm against ambush and aim and enemy he seemed to bear about him! No, Jane reflected, it was not charm; only a wonderful training of eye and ear, and sense of impending peril. Nevertheless that could not forever avail against secret attack.

That moment a rustling of leaves attracted her attention; then the familiar clinking accompaniment of a slow, soft, measured step, and Lassiter walked into the court.

"Jane, there's a fellow out there with a long gun," he said, and, removing his sombrero, showed his head bound in a bloody scarf.

"I heard the shot; I knew it was meant for you. Let me see—you can't be badly injured?"

"I reckon not. But mebbe it wasn't a close call . . . I'll sit here in this corner where nobody can see me from the grove." He untied the scarf and removed it to show a long, bleeding furrow above his left temple.

"It's only a cut," said Jane. "But how it bleeds! Hold your scarf over it just a moment till I come back."

She ran into the house and returned with bandages; and while she bathed and dressed the wound Lassiter talked.

"That fellow had a good chance to get me. But he must have flinched when he pulled the trigger. As I dodged down I saw him run through the trees. He had a rifle. I've been expectin' that kind of gun play. I reckon now I'll have to keep a little closer hid myself. These fellers all seem to get chilly or shaky when they draw a bead on me, but one of them might jest happen to hit me."

"Won't you go away—leave Cottonwoods as I've begged you to—before someone does happen to hit you?" she appealed to him.

"I reckon I'll stay."

"But, oh, Lassiter—your blood will be on my hands!"

"See here, lady, look at your hands now, right now. Aren't they fine, firm, white hands? Aren't they bloody now? Lassiter's blood! That's a queer thing to stain your beautiful hands. But if you could only see deeper you'd find a redder color of blood. Heart color, Jane!"

"Oh! . . . My friend!"

"No, Jane, I'm not one to quit when the game grows hot, no more than you. This game, though, is new to me, an' I don't know the moves yet, else I wouldn't have stepped in front of that bullet."

"Have you no desire to hunt the man who fired at you—to find him—and—and kill him?"

"Well, I reckon I haven't any great hankerin' for that."

"Oh, the wonder of it! . . . I knew—I prayed—I trusted. Lassiter, I almost gave—all myself to soften you to Mormons. Thank God, and thank you, my friend. . . . But, selfish woman that I am, this is no great test. What's the life of one of those sneaking cowards to such a man as you? I think of your great hate toward him who—I think of your life's implacable purpose. Can it be—"

"Wait! . . . Listen!" he whispered. "I hear a hoss."

He rose noiselessly, with his ear to the breeze. Suddenly he pulled his sombrero down over his bandaged head and, swinging his gun-sheaths round in front, he stepped into the alcove.

"It's a hoss—comin' fast," he added.

Jane's listening ear soon caught a faint, rapid, rhythmic beat of hoofs. It came from the sage. It gave her a thrill that she was at a loss to understand. The sound rose stronger, louder. Then came a clear, sharp difference when the horse passed from the sage trail to the hard-packed ground of the grove. It became a ringing run—swift in its bell-like clatterings, yet singular in longer pause than usual between the hoofbeats of a horse.

"It's Wrangle! . . . It's Wrangle!" cried Jane Withersteen. "I'd know him from a million horses!"

Excitement and thrilling expectancy flooded out all Jane Withersteen's calm. A tight band closed round her breast as she saw the giant sorrel flit in reddish-brown flashes across the openings in the green. Then he was pounding down the lane—thundering into the court—crashing his great iron-shod hoofs on the stone flags. Wrangle it was surely, but shaggy and wild-eyed, and sage-streaked, with dust-caked lather staining his flanks. He reared and crashed down and plunged. The rider leaped off, threw the bridle, and held hard on a lasso looped round Wrangle's head and neck. Jane's heart sank as she tried to recognize Venters in the rider. Something familiar struck her in the lofty stature, in the sweep of powerful shoulders. But this bearded, long-haired, unkempt man, who wore ragged clothes patched with pieces of skin, and boots that showed bare legs and feet—this dusty, dark, and wild rider could not possibly be Venters.

"Whoa, Wrangle, old boy! Come down. Easy now. So—so—so. You're home, old boy, and presently you can have a drink of water you'll remember."

In the voice Jane knew the rider to be Venters. He tied Wrangle to the hitching-rack and turned to the court.

"Oh, Bern! . . . You wild man!" she exclaimed.

"Jane—Jane, it's good to see you! Hello, Lassiter! Yes, it's Venters."

Like rough iron his hard hand crushed Jane's. In it she felt the difference she saw in him. Wild, rugged, unshorn—yet how splendid! He had gone away a boy—he had returned a man. He appeared taller, wider of shoulder, deeper-chested, more powerfully built. But was that only her fancy—he had always been a young giant—was the change one of spirit? He might have been absent for years, proven by fire and steel, grown like Lassiter, strong and cool and sure. His eyes—were they keener, more flashing than before?—met hers with clear, frank, warm regard, in which perplexity was not, nor discontent, nor pain.

"Look at me long as you like," he said, with a laugh. "I'm not much to look at. And, Jane, neither you nor Lassiter can brag. You're paler than I ever saw you. Lassiter, here, he wears a bloody bandage under his hat. That reminds me. Someone took a flying shot at me down in the sage. It made Wrangle run some. . . . Well, perhaps you've more to tell me than I've got to tell you."

Briefly, in few words, Jane outlined the circumstances of her undoing in the weeks of his absence.

Under his beard and bronze she saw his face whiten in terrible wrath. "Lassiter—what held you back?"

No time in the long period of fiery moments and sudden shocks had Jane Withersteen ever beheld Lassiter as calm and serene and cool as then.

"Jane had gloom enough without my addin' to it by shootin' up the village," he said.

As strange as Lassiter's coolness was Venters's curious, intent scrutiny of them both, and under it Jane felt a flaming tide wave from bosom to temples.

"Well—you're right," he said, with slow pause. "It surprises me a little, that's all."

Jane sensed then a slight alteration in Venters, and what it was, in her own confusion, she could not tell. It had always been her intention to acquaint him with the deceit she had fallen to in her zeal to move Lassiter. She did not mean to spare herself. Yet now, at the moment, before these riders, it was an impossibility to explain.

Venters was speaking somewhat haltingly, without his former frankness. "I found Oldring's hiding-place and your red herd. I learned—I know—I'm sure there was a deal between Tull and Oldring." He paused and shifted his position and his gaze. He looked as if he wanted to say something that he found beyond him. Sorrow and pity and shame seemed to contend for mastery over him. Then he raised himself and spoke with effort. "Jane, I've cost you too much. You've almost ruined yourself for me. It was wrong, for I'm not worth it. I never deserved such friendship. Well, maybe it's not too late. You must give me up. Mind, I haven't changed. I am just the same as ever. I'll see Tull while I'm here, and tell him to his face."

"Bern, it's too late," said Jane.

"I'll *make* him believe!" cried Venters, violently.

"You ask me to break our friendship?"

"Yes. If you don't, I shall!"

"Forever?"

"Forever!"

Jane sighed. Another shadow had lengthened down the sage-slope to cast further darkness upon her. A melancholy sweetness pervaded her resignation. The boy who had left her had returned a man, nobler, stronger, one in whom she divined something unbending as steel. There might come a moment later when she would wonder why she had not fought against his will, but just now she yielded to it. She liked him as well—nay, more, she thought, only her emotions were deadened by the long, menacing wait for the bursting storm.

Once before she had held out her hand to him—when she gave it; now she stretched it tremblingly forth in acceptance of the decree circumstance had laid upon them. Venters bowed over it, kissed it, pressed it hard, and half stifled a sound very like a sob. Certain it was that when he raised his head tears glistened in his eyes.

"Some—women—have a hard lot," he said, huskily. Then he shook his powerful form, and his rags lashed about him. "I'll say a few things to Tull—when I meet him."

"Bern—you'll not draw on Tull? Oh, that must not be! Promise me—"

"I promise you this," he interrupted, in stern passion that thrilled while it terrorized her. "If you say one more word for that plotter I'll kill him as I would a mad coyote!"

Jane clasped her hands. Was this fire-eyed man the one whom she had once made as wax to her touch? Had Venters become Lassiter and Lassiter Venters?

"I'll—say no more," she faltered.

"Jane, Lassiter once called you blind," said Venters. "It must be true. But I won't upbraid you. Only don't rouse the devil in me by praying for Tull! I'll try to keep cool when I meet him. That's all. Now there's one more thing I want to ask of you—the last. I've found a valley down in the Pass. It's a wonderful place. I intend to stay there. It's so hidden I believe no one can find it. There's good water, and browse, and game. I want to raise corn and stock. I need to take in supplies. Will you give them to me?"

"Assuredly. The more you take the better you'll please me—and perhaps the less my—my enemies will get."

"Venters, I reckon you'll have trouble packin' anythin' away," put in Lassiter.

"I'll go at night."

"Mebbe that wouldn't be best. You'd sure be stopped. You'd better go early in the mornin'—say, just after dawn. That's the safest time to move round here."

"Lassiter, I'll be hard to stop," returned Venters, darkly.

"I reckon so."

"Bern," said Jane, "go first to the riders' quarters and get yourself a complete outfit. You're a—a sight. Then help yourself to whatever else you need—burros, packs, grain, dried fruits, and meat. You must take coffee and sugar and flour—all kinds of supplies. Don't forget corn and seeds. I remember how you used to starve. Please—please take all you can pack away from here. I'll make a bundle for you, which you mustn't open till you're in your valley. How I'd like to see it! To judge by you and Wrangle, how wild it must be!"

Jane walked down into the outer court and approached the sorrel. Upstarting, he laid back his ears and eyed her.

"Wrangle—dear old Wrangle," she said, and put a caressing hand on his matted mane. "Oh, he's wild, but he knows me! Bern, can he run as fast as ever?"

"Run? Jane, he's done sixty miles since last night at dark, and I could make him kill Black Star right now in a ten-mile race."

"He never could," protested Jane. "He couldn't even if he was fresh."

"I reckon mebbe the best hoss'll prove himself yet," said Lassiter, "an', Jane, if it ever comes to that race I'd like you to be on Wrangle."

"I'd like that, too," rejoined Venters. "But, Jane, maybe Lassiter's hint is extreme. Bad as your prospects are, you'll surely never come to the running point."

"Who knows!" she replied, with mournful smile.

"No, no, Jane, it can't be so bad as all that. Soon as I see Tull there'll be a change in your fortunes. I'll hurry down to the village. . . . Now don't worry."

Jane retired to the seclusion of her room. Lassiter's subtle forecasting of disaster, Venters's forced optimism, neither remained in mind. Material loss weighed nothing in the balance with other losses she was sustaining. She wondered dully at her sitting there, hands folded listlessly, with a kind of numb deadness to the passing of time and the passing of her riches. She thought of Venters's friendship. She had not lost that, but she had lost him. Lassiter's friendship—that was more than love—it would endure, but soon he, too, would be gone. Little Fay slept dreamlessly upon the bed, her golden curls streaming over the pillow. Jane had the child's worship. Would she lose that, too? And if she did, what then would be left? Conscience thundered at her that there was left her religion. Conscience thundered that she should be grateful on her knees for this baptism of fire; that through misfortune, sacrifice, and suffering her soul might be fused pure gold. But the old, spontaneous, rapturous spirit no more exalted her. She wanted to be a woman—not a martyr. Like the saint of old who mortified his flesh, Jane Withersteen had in her the temper for heroic martyrdom, if by sacrificing herself she could save the souls of others. But here the damnable verdict blistered her that the more she sacrificed herself the blacker grew the souls of her churchmen. There was something terribly wrong with her soul, something terribly wrong with her churchmen and her religion. In the whirling gulf of her thought there was yet one shining light to guide her, to sustain her in her hope; and it was that, despite her errors and her frailties and her blindness, she had one absolute and unfaltering hold on ultimate and supreme justice. That was love. "Love your enemies as yourself!" was a divine word, entirely free from any church or creed.

Jane's meditations were disturbed by Lassiter's soft, tinkling step in the court. Always he wore the clinking spurs. Always he was in readiness to ride. She passed out and called him into the huge, dim hall.

"I think you'll be safer here. The court is too open," she said.

"I reckon," replied Lassiter. "An' it's cooler here. The day's sure muggy. Well, I went down to the village with Venters."

"Already! Where is he?" queried Jane, in quick amaze.

"He's at the corrals. Blake's helpin' him get the burros an' packs ready. That Blake is a good fellow."

"Did—did Bern meet Tull?"

"I guess he did," answered Lassiter, and he laughed dryly.

"Tell me! Oh, you exasperate me! You're so cool, so calm! For heaven's sake, tell me what happened!"

"First time I've been in the village for weeks," went on Lassiter, mildly. "I reckon there 'ain't been more of a show for a long time. Me an' Venters walkin' down the road! It was funny. I 'ain't sayin' anybody was particular glad to see us. I'm not much thought of hereabouts, an' Venters he sure looks like what you called him, a wild man. Well, there was some runnin' of folks before we got to the stores. Then everybody vamoosed except some surprised rustlers in front of a saloon. Venters went right in the stores an' saloons, an' of course I went along. I don't know which tickled me the most—the actions of many fellers we met, or Venters's nerve. Jane, I was downright glad to be along. You see *that* sort of thing is my element, an' I've been away from it for a spell. But we didn't find Tull in one of them places. Some Gentile feller at last told Venters he'd find Tull in that long buildin' next to Parsons's store. It's a kind of meetin'-room; and sure enough, when we peeped in, it was half full of men.

"Venters yelled: 'Don't anybody pull guns! We ain't come for that!' Then he tramped in, an' I was some put to keep alongside him. There was a hard, scrapin' sound of feet, a loud cry, an' then some whisperin', an' after that stillness you could cut with a knife. Tull was there, an' that fat party who once tried to throw a gun on me, an' other important-lookin' men, an' that little frog-legged feller who was with Tull the day I rode in here. I wish you could have seen their faces, 'specially Tull's an' the fat party's. But there ain't no use of me tryin' to tell you how they looked.

"Well, Venters an' I stood there in the middle of the room, with that batch of men all in front of us, an' not a blamed one of them winked an eyelash or moved a finger. It was natural, of course, for me to notice many of them packed guns. That's a way of mine, first noticin' them things. Venters spoke up, an' his voice sort of chilled an' cut, an' he told Tull he had a few things to say."

Here Lassiter paused while he turned his sombrero round and round, in his familiar habit, and his eyes had the look of a man seeing over again some thrilling spectacle, and under his red bronze there was strange animation.

"Like a shot, then, Venters told Tull that the friendship between you an' him was all over, an' he was leaving your place. He said you'd both of you broken off all the hope of propitiatin' your people, but you hadn't changed your mind otherwise, an' never would.

"Next he spoke up for you. I ain't goin' to tell you what he said. Only —no other woman who ever lived ever had such tribute! You had a champion, Jane, an' never fear that those thick-skulled men don't know you now. It couldn't be otherwise. He spoke the ringin', lightnin' truth. . . . Then he accused Tull of the underhand, miserable robbery of a helpless woman. He told Tull where the red herd was, of a deal made with Oldrin', that Jerry Card had made the deal. I thought Tull was goin' to drop, an' that little frog-legged cuss, he looked some limp an' white. But Venters's voice would have kept anybody's legs from bucklin'. I was stiff myself. He went on an' called Tull—called him every bad name ever known to a rider, an' then some. He cursed Tull. I never hear a man get such a cursin'. He laughed in scorn at the idea of Tull bein' a minister. He said Tull an' a few more dogs of hell built their empire out of the hearts of such innocent an' God-fearin' women as Jane Withersteen. He called Tull a binder of women, a callous beast who hid behind a mock mantle of righteousness—an' the last an' lowest coward on the face of the earth. To prey on weak women through their religion—that was the last unspeakable crime!

"Then he finished, an' by this time he'd almost lost his voice. But his whisper was enough. 'Tull,' he said, '*she* begged me not to draw on you today. *She* would pray for you if you burned her at the stake. . . . But listen! . . . I swear if you and I ever come face to face again, I'll kill you!'

"We backed out of the door then, an' up the road. But nobody follered us."

Jane found herself weeping passionately. She had not been conscious of it till Lassiter ended his story, and she experienced exquisite pain and relief in shedding tears. Long had her eyes been dry, her grief deep; long had her emotions been dumb. Lassiter's story put her on the rack; the appalling nature of Venters's act and speech had no parallel as an outrage; it was worse than bloodshed. Men like Tull had been shot, but had one ever been so terribly denounced in public? Overmounting her horror, an uncontrollable, quivering passion shook her very soul. It was sheer human glory in the deed of a fearless man. It was hot, primitive instinct to live— to fight. It was a kind of mad joy in Venters's chivalry. It was close to the wrath that had first shaken her in the beginning of this war waged upon her.

"Well, well, Jane, don't take it that way," said Lassiter, in evident distress. "I had to tell you. There's some things a feller jest can't keep. It's strange you give up on hearin' that, when all this long time you've been the gamest woman I ever seen. But I don't know women. Mebbe there's reason for you to cry. I know this—nothin' ever rang in my soul an' so filled it as what Venters did. I'd like to have done it, but—I'm only good for throwin' a gun, an' it seems you hate that. . . . Well, I'll be goin' now."

"Where?"

"Venters took Wrangle to the stable. The sorrel's shy a shoe, an' I've got to help hold the big devil an' put on another."

"Tell Bern to come for the pack I want to give him—and—and to say goodbye," called Jane, as Lassiter went out.

Jane passed the rest of that day in a vain endeavor to decide what and what not to put in the pack for Venters. This task was the last she would ever perform for him, and the gifts were the last she would ever make him. So she picked and chose and rejected, and chose again, and often paused in sad revery, and began again, till at length she filled the pack.

It was about sunset, and she and Fay had finished supper and were sitting in the court, when Venters's quick steps rang on the stones. She scarcely knew him, for he had changed the tattered garments, and she missed the dark beard and long hair. Still he was not the Venters of old. As he came up the steps she felt herself pointing to the pack, and heard herself speaking words that were meaningless to her. He said goodbye; he kissed her, released her, and turned away. His tall figure blurred in her sight, grew dim through dark, streaked vision, and then he vanished.

Twilight fell around Withersteen House, and dusk and night. Little Fay slept; but Jane lay with strained, aching eyes. She heard the wind moaning in the cottonwoods and mice squeaking in the walls. The night was interminably long, yet she prayed to hold back the dawn. What would another day bring forth? The blackness of her room seemed blacker for the sad, entering gray of morning light. She heard the chirp of awakening birds, and fancied she caught a faint clatter of hoofs. Then low, dull, distant, throbbed a heavy gunshot. She had expected it, was waiting for it; nevertheless, an electric shock checked her heart, froze the very living fiber of her bones. That vise-like hold on her faculties apparently did not relax for a long time, and it was a voice under her window that released her.

"Jane! . . . Jane!" softly called Lassiter.

She answered somehow.

"It's all right. Venters got away. I thought mebbe you'd heard that shot, an' I was worried some."

"What was it—who fired?"

"Well—some fool feller tried to stop Venters out there in the sage—an' he only stopped lead! . . . I think it'll be all right. I haven't seen or heard of any other fellers round. Venters'll go through safe. An', Jane, I've got Bells saddled, an' I'm going to trail Venters. Mind, I won't show myself unless he falls foul of somebody an' needs me. I want to see if this place where he's goin' is safe for him. He says nobody can track him there. I never seen the place yet I couldn't track a man to. Now, Jane, you stay indoors while I'm gone, an' keep close watch on Fay. Will you?"

"Yes! Oh yes!"

"An' another thing, Jane," he continued, then paused for long—"another thing—if you ain't here when I come back—if you're *gone*—don't fear, I'll trail you—I'll find you."

"My dear Lassiter, where could I be gone—as you put it?" asked Jane, in curious surprise.

"I reckon you might be somewhere. Mebbe tied in an old barn—or corralled in some gulch—or chained in a cave! *Milly Erne was*— till she give in! Mebbe that's news to you. . . . Well, if you're gone I'll hunt for you."

"No, Lassiter," she replied, sadly and low. "If I'm gone just forget the unhappy woman whose blinded, selfish deceit you repaid with kindness and love."

She heard a deep, muttering curse, under his breath, and then the silvery tinkling of his spurs as he moved away.

Jane entered upon the duties of that day with a settled, gloomy calm. Disaster hung in the dark clouds, in the shade, in the humid west wind. Blake, when he reported, appeared without his usual cheer; and Jerd wore a harassed look of a worn and worried man. And when Judkins put in appearance, riding a lame horse, and dismounted with the cramp of a rider, his dust-covered figure and his darkly grim, almost dazed expression told Jane of dire calamity. She had no need of words.

"Miss Withersteen, I have to report—loss of the—white herd," said Judkins, hoarsely.

"Come, sit down; you look played out," replied Jane, solicitously. She brought him brandy and food, and while he partook of refreshments, of which he appeared badly in need, she asked no questions.

"No one rider—could hev done more—Miss Withersteen," he went on, presently.

"Judkins, don't be distressed. You've done more than any other rider.

I've long expected to lose the white herd. It's no surprise. It's in line with other things that are happening. I'm grateful for your service."

"Miss Withersteen, I knew how you'd take it. But if anythin', that makes it harder to tell. You see, a feller wants to do so much fer you, an' I'd got fond of my job. We hed the herd a ways off to the north of the break in the valley. There was a big level an' pools of water an' tip-top browse. But the cattle was in a high nervous condition. Wild—as wild as antelope! You see, they'd been so scared they never slept. I ain't a-goin' to tell you of the many tricks that were pulled off out there in the sage. But there wasn't a day fer weeks thet the herd didn't get started to run. We allus managed to ride 'em close an' drive 'em back an' keep 'em bunched. Honest, Miss Withersteen, them steers was *thin*. They was *thin* when water and grass was everywhere. *Thin* at this season—thet'll tell you how your steers was pestered. Fer instance, one night a strange runnin' streak of fire run right through the herd. That streak was a coyote—*with an oiled an' blazin' tail!* Fer I shot it an' found out. We hed hell with the herd that night, an' if the sage an' grass hedn't been wet—we, hosses, steers, an' all would hev burned up. But I said I wasn't goin' to tell you any of the tricks. . . . Strange now, Miss Withersteen; when the stampede did come it was from natural cause—jest a whirlin' devil of dust. You've seen the like often. An' this wasn't no big whirl, fer the dust was mostly settled. It had dried out in a little swale, an' ordinarily no steer would ever hev run fer it. But the herd was nervous an' wild. An' jest as Lassiter said, when that bunch of white steers got to movin' they was as bad as buffalo. I've seen some buffalo stampedes back in Nebraska, an' this bolt of the steers was the same kind.

"I tried to mill the herd jest as Lassiter did. But I wasn't equal to it, Miss Withersteen. I don't believe the rider lives who could hev turned thet herd. We kept along of the herd fer miles, an' more'n one of my boys tried to get the steers a-millin'. It wasn't no use. We got off level ground, goin' down, an' then the steers ran somethin' fierce. We left the little gullies an' washes level-full of dead steers. Finally I saw the herd was makin' to pass a kind of low pocket between ridges. There was a hog-back —as we used to call 'em—a pile of rocks stickin' up, an I saw the herd was goin' to split round it, or swing out to the left. An' I wanted 'em to go to the right so mebbe we'd be able to drive 'em into the pocket. So, with all my boys except three, I rode hard to turn the herd a little to the right. We couldn't budge 'em. They went on an' split round the rocks, an' the most of 'em was turned sharp to the left by a deep wash we hedn't seen—hed no chance to see.

"The other three boys—Jimmy Vail, Joe Wills, an' thet little Cairns boy, a nervy kid!—they, with Cairns leadin', tried to buck thet herd round to the pocket. It was a wild, fool idee. I couldn't do nothin'. The boys got hemmed in between the steers an' the wash—thet they hedn't no chance to see, either. Vail an' Wills was run down right before our eyes. An' Cairns, who rode a fine hoss, he did some ridin' I never seen equaled, an' would hev beat the steers if there'd been any room to run in. I was high up an' could see how the steers kept spillin' by twos an' threes over into the wash. Cairns put his hoss to a place thet was too wide fer any hoss, an' broke his neck an' the hoss's too. We found that out after, an' as fer Vail an' Wills—two thousand steers ran over the poor boys. There wasn't much left to pack home fer buryin'! . . . An', Miss Withersteen, thet all happened yesterday, an' I believe, if the white herd didn't run over the wall of the Pass, it's runnin' yet."

On the morning of the second day after Judkins's recital, during which time Jane remained indoors a prey to regret and sorrow for the boy riders, and a new and now strangely insistent fear for her own person, she again heard what she had missed more than she dared honestly confess—the soft, jingling step of Lassiter. Almost overwhelming relief surged through her, a feeling as akin to joy as any she could have been capable of in those gloomy hours of shadow, and one that suddenly stunned her with the significance of what Lassiter had come to mean to her. She had begged him, for his own sake, to leave Cottonwoods. She might yet beg that, if her weakening courage permitted her to dare absolute loneliness and helplessness, but she realized now that if she were left alone her life would become one long, hideous nightmare.

When his soft steps clinked into the hall, in answer to her greeting, and his tall, black-garbed form filled the door, she felt an inexpressible sense of immediate safety. In his presence she lost her fear of the dim passageways of Withersteen House and of every sound. Always it had been that, when he entered the court or the hall, she had experienced a distinctly sickening but gradually lessening shock at sight of the huge black guns swinging at his sides. This time the sickening shock again visited her; it was, however, because a revealing flash of thought told her that it was not Lassiter alone who was thrillingly welcome, but also his fatal weapons. They meant so much. How she had fallen—how broken and spiritless must she be—to have still the same old horror of Lassiter's guns and his name, yet feel somehow a cold, shrinking protection in their law and might and use.

"Did you trail Venters—find his wonderful valley?" she asked, eagerly.

"Yes, an' I reckon it's sure a wonderful place."

"Is he safe there?"

"That's been botherin' me some. I tracked him an' part of the trail was the hardest I ever tackled. Mebbe there's a rustler or somebody in this country who's as good at trackin' as I am. If that's so Venters ain't safe."

"Well—tell me all about Bern and his valley."

To Jane's surprise Lassiter showed disinclination for further talk about his trip. He appeared to be extremely fatigued. Jane reflected that 120 miles, with probably a great deal of climbing on foot, all in three days, was enough to tire any rider. Moreover, it presently developed that Lassiter had returned in a mood of singular sadness and preoccupation. She put it down to a moodiness over the loss of her white herd and the now precarious condition of her fortune.

Several days passed, and, as nothing happened, Jane's spirits began to brighten. Once in her musings she thought that this tendency of hers to rebound was as sad as it was futile. Meanwhile, she had resumed her walks through the grove with little Fay.

One morning she went as far as the sage. She had not seen the slope since the beginning of the rains, and now it bloomed a rich deep purple. There was a high wind blowing, and the sage tossed and waved and colored beautifully from light to dark. Clouds scudded across the sky and their shadows sailed darkly down the sunny slope.

Upon her return toward the house she went by the lane to the stables, and she had scarcely entered the great open space with its corrals and sheds when she saw Lassiter hurriedly approaching. Fay broke from her and, running to a corral fence, began to pat and pull the long, hanging ears of a drowsy burro.

One look at Lassiter armed her for a blow.

Without a word he led her across the wide yard to the rise of the ground upon which the stable stood.

"Jane—look!" he said, and pointed to the ground.

Jane glanced down, and again, and upon steadier vision made out splotches of blood on the stones, and broad, smooth marks in the dust, leading out toward the sage.

"What made these?" she asked.

"I reckon somebody has dragged dead or wounded men out to where there was hosses in the sage."

"Dead—or—wounded—men!"

"I reckon—Jane, are you strong? Can you bear up?"

His hands were gently holding hers, and his eyes—suddenly she could no longer look into them. "Strong?" she echoed, trembling. "I—I will be."

Up on the stone-flag drive, nicked with the marks made by the iron-shod hoofs of her racers, Lassiter led her, his grasp ever growing firmer.

"Where's Blake—and—and Jerd?" she asked, haltingly.

"I don't know where Jerd is. Bolted, most likely," replied Lassiter, as he took her through the stone door. "But Blake—poor Blake! He's gone forever! . . . Be prepared, Jane."

With a cold prickling of her skin, with a queer thrumming in her ears, with fixed and staring eyes, Jane saw a gun lying at her feet with chamber swung and empty, and discharged shells scattered near.

Outstretched upon the stable floor lay Blake, ghastly white—dead—one hand clutching a gun and the other twisted in his bloody blouse.

"Whoever the thieves were, whether your people or rustlers—Blake killed some of them!" said Lassiter.

"Thieves?" whispered Jane.

"I reckon. Hoss-thieves! . . . Look!" Lassiter waved his hand toward the stalls.

The first stall—Bell's stall—was empty. All the stalls were empty. No racer whinnied and stamped greeting to her. Night was gone! Black Star was gone!

⋇16⋇

GOLD

A S LASSITER had reported to Jane, Venters "went through" safely, and after a toilsome journey reached the peaceful shelter of Surprise Valley. When finally he lay wearily down under the silver spruces, resting from the strain of dragging packs and burros up the slope and through the entrance to Surprise Valley, he had leisure to think, and a great deal of the time went in regretting that he had not been frank with his loyal friend, Jane Withersteen.

But, he kept continually recalling, when he had stood once more face to face with her and had been shocked at the change in her and had heard the details of her adversity, he had not had the heart to tell her of the closer interest which had entered his life. He had not lied; yet he had kept silence.

Bess was in transports over the stores of supplies and the outfit he had packed from Cottonwoods. He had certainly brought a hundred times more than he had gone for; enough, surely, for years, perhaps to make permanent home in the valley. He saw no reason why he need ever leave there again.

After a day of rest he recovered his strength and shared Bess's pleasure in rummaging over the endless packs, and began to plan for the future. And in this planning, his trip to Cottonwoods, with its revived hate of Tull and consequent unleashing of fierce passions, soon faded out of mind. By slower degrees his friendship for Jane Withersteen and his contrition drifted from the protective preoccupation of his present thought to a place of memory, with more and more infrequent recalls.

And as far as the state of his mind was concerned, upon the second day of his return, the valley, with its golden hues and purple shades, the speaking west wind and the cool, silent night, and Bess's watching eyes with their wonderful light, so wrought upon Venters that he might never have left them at all.

That very afternoon he set to work. Only one thing hindered him upon beginning, though it in no wise checked his delight, and that was that in the multiplicity of tasks planned to make a paradise out of the valley he could not choose the one with which to begin. He had grown into the habit of passing from one dreamy pleasure to another, like a bee going from flower to flower in the valley, and he found this wandering habit likely to extend to his labors. Nevertheless, he made a start.

At the outset he discovered Bess to be both a considerable help in some ways and a very great hindrance in others. Her excitement and joy were spurs, inspirations; but she was utterly impracticable in her ideas, and she flitted from one plan to another with bewildering vacillation. Moreover, he fancied that she grew more eager, youthful, and sweet; and he marked that it was far easier to watch her and listen to her than it was to work. Therefore he gave her tasks that necessitated her going often to the cave where he had stored his packs.

Upon the last of these trips, when he was some distance down the terrace and out of sight of camp, he heard a scream, and then the barking of the dogs.

For an instant he straightened up, amazed. Danger for her had been absolutely out of his mind. She had seen a rattlesnake—or a wildcat. Still she would not have been likely to scream at sight of either; and the barking of the dogs was ominous. Dropping his work, he dashed back along the terrace. Upon breaking through a clump of aspens he saw the dark form of a man in the camp. Cold, then hot, Venters burst into frenzied speed to reach his guns. He was cursing himself for a thoughtless fool when the man's tall form became familiar and he recognized Lassiter. Then the reversal of emotions changed his run to a walk; he tried to call out, but his voice refused to carry; when he reached camp there was Lassiter staring at the white-face girl. By that time Ring and Whitie had recognized him.

"Hello, Venters! I'm makin' you a visit," said Lassiter, slowly. "An' I'm some surprised to see you've a—a young feller for company."

One glance had sufficed for the keen rider to read Bess's real sex, and for once his cool calm had deserted him. He stared till the white of Bess's cheeks flared into crimson. That, if it were needed, was the concluding evidence of her femininity; for it went fittingly with her sun-tinted hair and darkened, dilated eyes, the sweetness of her mouth, and the striking symmetry of her slender shape.

"Heavens! Lassiter!" panted Venters, when he caught his breath. "What relief—it's only you! How—in the name of all—that's wonderful —did you ever get here!"

"I trailed you. We—I wanted to know where you was, if you had a safe place. So I trailed you."

"Trailed me!" cried Venters, bluntly.

"I reckon. It was some of a job after I got to them smooth rocks. I was all day trackin' you up to them little cut steps in the rock. The rest was easy."

"Where's your hoss? I hope you hid him."

"I tied him in them queer cedars down on the slope. He can't be seen from the valley."

"That's good. Well, well! I'm completely dumfounded. It was my idea that no man could track me in here."

"I reckon. But if there's a tracker in these uplands as good as me he can find you."

"That's bad. That'll worry me. But, Lassiter, now you're here I'm glad to see you. And—and my companion here is not a young fellow! . . . Bess, this is a friend of mine. He saved my life once."

The embarrassment of the moment did not extend to Lassiter. Almost at once his manner, as he shook hands with Bess, relieved Venters and put the girl at ease. After Venters's words and one quick look at Lassiter, her agitation stilled, and, though she was shy, if she were conscious of anything out of the ordinary in the situation, certainly she did not show it.

"I reckon I'll only stay a little while," Lassiter was saying. "An' if you don't mind troublin', I'm hungry. I fetched some biscuits along, but they're gone. Venters, this place is sure the wonderfullest ever seen. Them cut steps on the slope! That outlet into the gorge! An' it's like climbin' up through hell into heaven to climb through that gorge into this valley! There's a queer-lookin' rock at the top of the passage. I didn't have time to stop. I'm wonderin' how you ever found this place. It's sure interestin'."

During the preparation and eating of dinner Lassiter listened mostly, as was his wont, and occasionally he spoke in his quaint and dry way. Venters noted, however, that the rider showed an increasing interest in Bess. He asked her no questions, and only directed his attention to her while she was occupied and had no opportunity to observe his scrutiny. It seemed to Venters that Lassiter grew more and more absorbed in his study of Bess, and that he lost his coolness in some strange, softening sympathy. Then, quite abruptly, he arose and announced the necessity for his early departure. He said goodbye to Bess in a voice gentle and somewhat broken, and turned hurriedly away. Venters accompanied him, and they had traversed the terrace, climbed the weathered slope, and passed under the stone bridge before either spoke again.

Then Lassiter put a great hand on Venters's shoulder and wheeled him to meet a smoldering fire of gray eyes.

"Lassiter, I couldn't tell Jane! I couldn't," burst out Venters, reading his friend's mind. "I tried. But I couldn't. She wouldn't understand, and she has troubles enough. And I love the girl!"

"Venters, I reckon this beats me. I've seen some queer things in my time, too. This girl—who is she?"

"I don't know."

"Don't know! What is she, then?"

"I don't know that, either. Oh, it's the strangest story you ever heard. I must tell you. But you'll never believe."

"Venters, women were always puzzles to me. But for all that, if this girl ain't a child, an' as innocent, I'm no fit person to think of virtue an' goodness in anybody. Are you goin' to be square with her?"

"I am—so help me God!"

"I reckoned so. Mebbe my temper oughtn't led me to make sure. But, man, she's a woman in all but years. She's sweeter'n the sage."

"Lassiter, I know, I know. And the *hell* of it is is that in spite of her innocence and charm she's—she's not what she seems!"

"I wouldn't want to—of course, I couldn't call you a liar, Venters," said the older man.

"What's more, she was Oldring's Masked Rider!"

Venters expected to floor his friend with that statement, but he was not in any way prepared for the shock his words gave. For an instant he was astounded to see Lassiter stunned; then his own passionate eagerness to unbosom himself, to tell the wonderful story, precluded any other thought.

"Son, tell me all about this," presently said Lassiter as he seated himself on a stone and wiped his moist brow.

Thereupon Venters began his narrative at the point where he had shot the rustler and Oldring's Masked Rider, and he rushed through it, telling all, not holding back even Bess's unreserved avowal of her love or his deepest emotions.

"That's the story," he said, concluding. "I love her, though I've never told her. If I did tell her I'd be ready to marry her, and that seems impossible in this country. I'd be afraid to risk taking her anywhere. So I intend to do the best I can for her here."

"The longer I live the stranger life is," mused Lassiter, with downcast eyes. "I'm reminded of somethin' you once said to Jane about hands in her game of life. There's that unseen hand of power, an' Tull's black hand, an' my red one, an' your indifferent one, an' the girl's little brown, helpless one. An', Venters, there's another one that's all-wise an' all-wonderful. *That's* the hand guidin' Jane Withersteen's game of life! . . . Your story's one to daze a far clearer head than mine. I can't offer no advice, even if you asked for it. Mebbe I can help you. Anyway, I'll hold Oldrin' up when he comes to the village, an' find out about this girl. I knew the rustler years ago. He'll remember me."

"Lassiter, if I ever meet Oldring I'll kill him!" cried Venters, with sudden intensity.

"I reckon that'd be perfectly natural," replied the rider.

"Make him think Bess is dead—as she is to him and that old life."

"Sure, sure, son. Cool down now. If you're goin' to begin pullin' guns on Tull an' Oldrin' you want to be cool. I reckon, though, you'd better keep hid here. Well, I must be leavin'."

"One thing, Lassiter. You'll not tell Jane about Bess? Please don't!"

"I reckon not. But I wouldn't be afraid to bet that after she'd got over anger at your secrecy—Venters, she'd be furious once in her life!—she'd think more of you. I don't mind sayin' for myself that I think you're a good deal of a man."

In the further ascent Venters halted several times with the intention of saying goodbye, yet he changed his mind and kept on climbing till they reached Balancing Rock. Lassiter examined the huge rock, listened to Venters's idea of its position and suggestion, and curiously placed a strong hand upon it.

"Hold on!" cried Venters. "I heaved at it once and have never gotten over my scare."

"Well, you do seem oncommon nervous," replied Lassiter, much amused. "Now, as for me, why I always had the funniest notion to roll stones! When I was a kid I did it, an' the bigger I got the bigger stones I'd roll. Ain't that funny? Honest—even now I often get off my hoss just to tumble a big stone over a precipice, an' watch it drop, an' listen to it bang an' boom. I've started some slides in my time, an' don't you forget it. I never seen a rock I wanted to roll as bad as this one! Wouldn't there jest be roarin', crashin' hell down that trail?"

"You'd close the outlet forever!" exclaimed Venters. "Well, goodbye, Lassiter. Keep my secret and don't forget me. And be mighty careful how you get out of the valley below. The rustlers' canyon isn't more than three miles up the Pass. Now you've tracked me here, I'll never feel safe again."

In his descent to the valley, Venters's emotion, roused to stirring pitch by the recital of his love story, quieted gradually, and in its place came a sober, thoughtful mood. All at once he saw that he was serious, because he would never more regain his sense of security while in the valley. What Lassiter could do another skillful cracker might duplicate. Among the many riders with whom Venters had ridden he recalled no one who could have taken his trail at Cottonwoods and have followed it to the edge of the bare slope in the Pass, let alone up that glistening smooth stone. Lassiter, however, was not an ordinary rider. Instead of hunting cattle tracks he had likely spent a goodly portion of his life tracking men. It was not improbable that among Oldring's rustlers there was one who shared Lassiter's gift for-trailing. And the more Venters dwelt on this possibility the more perturbed he grew.

Lassiter's visit, moreover, had a disquieting effect upon Bess, and Venters fancied that she entertained the same thought as to future seclusion. The breaking of their solitude, though by a well-meaning friend, had not only dispelled all its dream and much of its charm, but had instilled a canker of fear. Both had seen the footprint in the sand.

Venters did no more work that day. Sunset and twilight gave way to night, and the canyon bird whistled its melancholy notes, and the wind sang softly in the cliffs, and the campfire blazed and burned down to red embers. To Venters a subtle difference was apparent in all of these, or else the shadowy change had been in him. He hoped that on the morrow this slight depression would have passed away.

In that measure, however, he was doomed to disappointment. Furthermore, Bess reverted to a wistful sadness that he had not observed in her since her recovery. His attempt to cheer her out of it resulted in dismal failure, and consequently in a darkening of his own mood. Hard work relieved him; still, when the day had passed, his unrest returned. Then he set to deliberate thinking, and there came to him the startling conviction that he must leave Surprise Valley and take Bess with him. As a rider he had taken many chances, and as an adventurer in Deception Pass he had unhesitatingly risked his life; but now he would run no preventable hazard of Bess's safety and happiness, and he was too keen not to see that hazard. It gave him a pang to think of leaving the beautiful valley just when he had the means to establish a permanent and delightful home there. One flashing thought tore in hot temptation through his mind—why not climb up into the gorge, roll Balancing Rock down the trail, and close forever the outlet to Deception Pass? "That was the beast in me—showing his teeth!" muttered Venters, scornfully. "I'll just kill him good and quick! I'll be fair to this girl, if it's the last thing I do on earth!"

Another day went by, in which he worked less and pondered more and all the time covertly watched Bess. Her wistfulness had deepened into downright unhappiness, and that made his task to tell her all the harder. He kept the secret another day, hoping by some chance she might grow less moody, and to his exceeding anxiety she fell into far deeper gloom. Out of his own secret and the torment of it he divined that she, too, had a secret and the keeping of it was torturing her. As yet he had no plan thought out in regard to how or when to leave the valley, but he decided to tell her the necessity of it and to persuade her to go. Furthermore, he hoped his speaking out would induce her to unburden her own mind.

"Bess, what's wrong with you?" he asked.

"Nothing," she answered, with averted face.

Venters took hold of her and gently, though masterfully, forced her to meet his eyes.

"You can't look at me and lie," he said. "Now—what's wrong with you? You're keeping something from me. Well, I've got a secret, too, and I intend to tell it presently."

"Oh—I *have* a secret. I was crazy to tell you when you came back.

That's why I was so silly about everything. I kept holding my secret back —gloating over it. But when Lassiter came I got an idea—that changed my mind. Then I hated to tell you."

"Are you going to now?"

"Yes—yes. I was coming to it. I tried yesterday, but you were so cold. I was afraid. I couldn't keep it much longer."

"Very well, most mysterious lady, tell your wonderful secret."

"You needn't laugh," she retorted, with a first glimpse of reviving spirit. "I can take the laugh out of you in one second."

"It's a go."

She ran through the spruces to the cave, and returned carrying something which was manifestly heavy. Upon nearer view he saw that whatever she held with such evident importance had been bound up in a black scarf he well remembered. That alone was sufficient to make him tingle with curiosity.

"Have you any idea what I did in your absence?" she asked.

"I imagine you lounged about, waiting and watching for me," he replied, smiling. "I've my share of conceit, you know."

"You're wrong. I worked. Look at my hands." She dropped on her knees close to where he sat, and, carefully depositing the black bundle, she held out her hands. The palms and inside of her fingers were white, puckered, and worn.

"Why, Bess, you've been fooling in the water," he said.

"Fooling? Look here!" With deft fingers she spread open the black scarf, and the bright sun shone upon a dull, glittering heap of gold.

"Gold" he ejaculated.

"Yes, gold! See, pounds of gold! I found it—washed it out of the stream —picked it out grain by grain, nugget by nugget!"

"Gold!" he cried.

"Yes. Now—now laugh at my secret!"

For a long minute Venters gazed. Then he stretched forth a hand to feel if the gold was real.

"*Gold!*" he almost shouted. "Bess, there are hundreds—thousands of dollars' worth here!"

He leaned over to her, and put his hand, strong and clenching now, on hers.

"Is there more where this came from?" he whispered.

"Plenty of it, all the way up the stream to the cliff. You know I've often washed for gold. Then I've heard the men talk. I think there's no great quantity of gold here, but enough for—for a fortune for *you.*"

"That—was—your—secret!"

"Yes. I hate gold. For it makes men mad. I've seen them drunk with joy and dance and fling themselves around. I've seen them curse and rave. I've seen them fight like dogs and roll in the dust. I've seen them kill each other for gold."

"Is that why you hated to tell me?"

"Not—not altogether." Bess lowered her head. "It was because I knew you'd never stay here long after you found gold."

"You were afraid I'd leave you?"

"Yes."

"Listen! . . . You great, simple child! Listen . . . You sweet, wonderful, wild, blue-eyed girl! I was tortured by my secret. It was that I knew we—*we* must leave the valley. We can't stay here much longer. I couldn't think how we'd get away—out of the country—or how we'd live, if we ever got out. I'm a beggar. That's why I kept my secret. I'm poor. It takes money to make way beyond Sterling. We couldn't ride horses or burros or walk forever. So while I knew we must go, I was distracted over how to go and what to do. *Now!* We've gold! Once beyond Sterling, we'll be safe from rustlers. We've no others to fear.

"Oh! Listen! Bess!" Venters now heard his voice ringing high and sweet, and he felt Bess's cold hands in in his crushing grasp as she leaned toward him, pale, breathless. "This is how much I'd leave you! You made me live again! I'll take you away—far away from this wild country. You'll begin a new life. You'll be happy. You shall see cities, ships, people. You shall have anything your heart craves. All the shame and sorrow of your life shall be forgotten—as if they had never been. This is how much I'd leave you here alone—you sad-eyed girl. I love you! Didn't you know it? How could you fail to know it! I love you! I'm free! I'm a man—a man you've made—no more a beggar! . . . Kiss me! This is how much I'd leave you here alone—you beautiful, strange, unhappy girl. But I'll make you happy. What—what do I care for—your past! I love you! I'll take you home to Illinois—to my mother. Then I'll take you to far places. I'll make up all you've lost. Oh, I know you love me—knew it before you told me. And it changed my life. And you'll go with me, not as my companion as you are here, nor my sister, but, Bess, darling! . . . *As my wife!*"

❧17❧

WRANGLE'S RACE RUN

THE PLAN eventually decided upon by the lovers was for Venters to go to the village, secure a horse and some kind of a disguise for Bess, or at least less striking apparel than her present garb, and to return post-haste to the valley. Meanwhile, she would add to their store of gold. Then they would strike the long and perilous trail to ride out of Utah. In the event of his inability to fetch back a horse for her, they intended to make the giant sorrel carry double. The gold, a little food, saddle blankets, and Venters's guns were to compose the light outfit with which they would make the start.

"I love this beautiful place," said Bess. "It's hard to think of leaving it."

"Hard! Well, I should think so," replied Venters. "Maybe—in years—" But he did not complete in words his thought that it might be possible to return after many years of absence and change.

Once again Bess bade Venters farewell under the shadow of Balancing Rock, and this time it was with whispered hope and tenderness and passionate trust. Long after he had left her, all down through the outlet to the Pass, the clinging clasp of her arms, the sweetness of her lips, and the sense of a new and exquisite birth of character in her remained haunt-ingly and thrillingly in his mind. The girl who had sadly called herself nameless and nothing had been marvelously transformed in the moment of his avowal of love. It was something to think over, something to warm his heart, but for the present it had absolutely to be forgotten so that all his mind could be addressed to the trip so fraught with danger.

He carried only his rifle, revolver, and a small quantity of bread and meat; and thus lightly burdened, he made swift progress down the slope and out into the valley. Darkness was coming on, and he welcomed it. Stars were blinking when he reached his old hiding-place in the split of canyon wall, and by their aid he slipped through the dense thickets to the grassy enclosure. Wrangle stood in the center of it with his head up, and he appeared black and of gigantic proportions in the dim light. Venters whistled softly, began a slow approach, and then called. The horse snorted and, plunging away with dull, heavy sound of hoofs, he disap-peared in the gloom. "Wilder than ever!" muttered Venters. He followed the sorrel into the narrowing split between the walls, and presently had to desist because he could not see a foot in advance. As he went back toward the open, Wrangle jumped out of an ebony shadow of cliff and like a thunderbolt shot huge and black past him down into the starlit glade. Deciding that all attempts to catch Wrangle at night would be useless, Venters repaired to the shelving rock where he had hidden saddle and blanket, and there went to sleep.

The first peep of day found him stirring, and as soon as it was light enough to distinguish objects, he took his lasso off his saddle and went out to rope the sorrel. He espied Wrangle at the lower end of the cove and approached him in a perfectly natural manner. When he got near enough, Wrangle evidently recognized him, but was too wild to stand. He ran up the glade and on into the narrow lane between the walls. This favored Venters's speedy capture of the horse, so, coiling his noose ready to throw, he hurried on. Wrangle let Venters get to within a hundred feet and then he broke. But as he plunged by, rapidly getting into his stride, Venters made a perfect throw with the rope. He had time to brace himself for the shock; nevertheless, Wrangle threw him and dragged him several yards before halting.

"You wild devil," said Venters, as he slowly pulled Wrangle up. "Don't you know me? Come now—old fellow—so—so—"

Wrangle yielded to the lasso and then to Venters's strong hand. He was as straggly and wild-looking as a horse left to roam free in the sage. He dropped his long ears and stood readily to be saddled and bridled. But he was exceedingly sensitive, and quivered at every touch and sound. Venters led him to the thicket, and, bending the close saplings to let him squeeze through, at length reached the open. Sharp survey in each direction assured him of the usual lonely nature of the canyon; then he was in the saddle, riding south.

Wrangle's long, swinging canter was a wonderful ground-gainer. His stride was almost twice that of an ordinary horse, and his endurance was equally remarkable. Venters pulled him in occasionally, and walked him up the stretches of rising ground and along the soft washes. Wrangle had never yet shown any indication of distress while Venters rode him. Nevertheless, there was now reason to save the horse; therefore Venters did not resort to the hurry that had characterized his former trip. He camped at the last water in the Pass. What distance that was to Cottonwoods he did not know; he calculated, however, that it was in the neighborhood of fifty miles.

Early in the morning he proceeded on his way, and about the middle of the forenoon reached the constricted gap that marked the southerly end of the Pass, and through which led the trail up to the sage-level. He spied out Lassiter's tracks in the dust, but no others, and, dismounting, he straightened out Wrangle's bridle and began to lead him up the trail. The short climb, more severe on beast than on man, necessitated a rest on the level above, and during this he scanned the wide purple reaches of slope. Wrangle whistled his pleasure at the smell of the sage. Remounting,

Venters headed up the white trail with the fragrant wind in his face. He had proceeded for perhaps a couple of miles when Wrangle stopped with a suddenness that threw Venters heavily against the pommel.

"What's wrong, old boy?" called Venters, looking down for a loose shoe or a snake or a foot lamed by a picked-up stone. Unrewarded, he raised himself from his scrutiny. Wrangle stood stiff, head high, with his long ears erect. Thus guided, Venters swiftly gazed ahead to make out a dust-clouded, dark group of horsemen riding down the slope. If they had seen him, it apparently made no difference in their speed or direction.

"Wonder who they are!" exclaimed Venters. He was not disposed to run. His cool mood tightened under grip of excitement as he reflected that, whoever the approaching riders were, they could not be friends. He slipped out of the saddle and led Wrangle behind the tallest sage-brush. It might serve to conceal them until the riders were close enough for him to see who they were; after that he would be indifferent to how soon they discovered him.

After looking to his rifle and ascertaining that it was in working order, he watched, and as he watched, slowly the force of a bitter fierceness, long dormant, gathered ready to flame into life. If those riders were not rustlers he had forgotten how rustlers looked and rode. On they came, a small group, so compact and dark that he could not tell their number. How unusual that their horses did not see Wrangle! But such failure, Venters decided, was owing to the speed with which they were traveling. They moved at a swift canter affected more by rustlers than by riders. Venters grew concerned over the possibility that these horsemen would actually ride down on him before he had a chance to tell what to expect. When they were within three hundred yards he deliberately led Wrangle out into the trail.

Then he heard shouts, and the hard scrape of sliding hoofs, and saw horses rear and plunge back with up-flung heads and flying manes. Several little white puffs of smoke appeared sharply against the black background of riders and horses, and shots rang out. Bullets struck far in front of Venters, and whipped up the dust and then hummed low into the sage. The range was great for revolvers, but whether the shots were meant to kill or merely to check advance, they were enough to fire that waiting ferocity in Venters. Slipping his arm through the bridle, so that Wrangle could not get away, Venters lifted his rifle and pulled the trigger twice.

He saw the first horseman lean sideways and fall. He saw another lurch in his saddle and heard a cry of pain. Then Wrangle, plunging in fright, lifted Venters and nearly threw him. He jerked the horse down with a powerful hand and leaped into the saddle. Wrangle plunged again, dragging his bridle, that Venters had not had time to throw in place. Bending over with a swift movement, he secured it and dropped the loop over the pommel. Then, with grinding teeth, he looked to see what the issue would be.

The band had scattered so as not to afford such a broad mark for bullets. The riders faced Venters, some with red-belching guns. He heard a sharper report, and just as Wrangle plunged again he caught the whizz of a leaden missile that would have hit him but for Wrangle's sudden jump. A swift, hot wave, turning cold, passed over Venters. Deliberately he picked out the one rider with a carbine, and killed him. Wrangle snorted shrilly and bolted into the sage. Venters let him run a few rods, then with iron arm checked him.

Five riders, surely rustlers, were left. One leaped out of the saddle to secure his fallen comrade's carbine. A shot from Venters, which missed the man but sent the dust flying over him, made him run back to his horse. Then they separated. The crippled rider went one way; the one frustrated in his attempt to get the carbine rode another; Venters thought he made out a third rider, carrying a strange-appearing bundle and disappearing in the sage. But in the rapidity of action and vision he could not discern what it was. Two riders with three horses swung out to the right. Afraid of the long rifle—a burdensome weapon seldom carried by rustlers or riders—they had been put to rout.

Suddenly Venters discovered that one of the two men last noted was riding Jane Withersteen's horse Bells—the beautiful bay racer she had given to Lassiter. Venters uttered a savage outcry. Then the small, wiry, froglike shape of the second rider, and the ease and grace of his seat in the saddle—things so strikingly incongruous—grew more and more familiar in Venters's sight.

"Jerry Card!" cried Venters.

It was indeed Tull's right-hand man. Such a white-hot wrath inflamed Venters that he fought himself to see with clearer gaze.

"It's Jerry Card!" he exclaimed, instantly, *"And he's riding Black Star and leading Night!"*

The long-kindled, stormy fire in Venters's heart burst into flame. He spurred Wrangle, and as the horse lengthened his stride Venters slipped cartridges into the magazine of his rifle till it was once again full. Card and his companion were now half a mile or more in advance, riding easily down the slope. Venters marked the smooth gait, and understood it when Wrangle galloped out of the sage into the broad cattle trail, down which Venters had once tracked Jane Withersteen's red herd. This hard-packed trail, from years of use, was as clean and smooth as a road. Venters saw Jerry Card look back over his shoulder; the other rider did likewise. Then the three racers lengthened their stride to the point where the swinging canter was ready to break into a gallop.

"Wrangle, the race's on," said Venters, grimly. "We'll canter with them and gallop with them and run with them. We'll let them set the pace."

Venters knew he bestrode the strongest, swiftest, most tireless horse ever ridden by any rider across the Utah uplands. Recalling Jane Withersteen's devoted assurance that Night could run neck and neck with

Wrangle, and Black Star could show his heels to him, Venters wished that
Jane were there to see the race to recover her blacks and the unqualified
superiority of the giant sorrel. Then Venters found himself thankful that
she was absent, for he meant that race to end in Jerry Card's death. The
first flush, the raging of Venters's wrath, passed, to leave him in sullen,
almost cold possession of his will. It was a deadly mood, utterly foreign to
his nature, engendered, fostered, and released by the wild passions of wild
men in a wild country. The strength in him then—the thing rife in him
that was not hate, but something as remorseless—might have been the
fiery fruition of a whole lifetime of vengeful quest. Nothing could have
stopped him.

Venters thought out the race shrewdly. The rider on Bells would probably drop behind and take to the sage. What he did was of little moment to
Venters. To stop Jerry Card, his evil, hidden career as well as his present
flight, and then to catch the blacks—that was all that concerned Venters.
The cattle trail wound for miles and miles down the slope. Venters saw
with a rider's keen vision ten, fifteen, twenty miles of clear purple sage.
There were no on-coming riders or rustlers to aid Card. His only chance
to escape lay in abandoning the stolen horses and creeping away in the
sage to hide. In ten miles Wrangle could run Black Star and Night off
their feet, and in fifteen he could kill them outright. So Venters held the
sorrel in, letting Card make the running. It was a long race that would
save the blacks.

In a few miles of that swinging canter Wrangle had crept appreciably
closer to the three horses. Jerry Card turned again, and when he saw how
the sorrel had gained, he put Black Star to a gallop. Night and Bells, on
either side of him, swept into his stride.

Venters loosened the rein on Wrangle and let him break into a gallop.
The sorrel saw the horses ahead and wanted to run. But Venters restrained him. And in the gallop he gained more than in the canter. Bells
was fast in that gait, but Black Star and Night had been trained to run.
Slowly Wrangle closed the gap down to a quarter of a mile, and crept
closer and closer.

Jerry Card wheeled once more. Venters distinctly saw the red flash of
his red face. This time he looked long. Venters laughed. He knew what
passed in Card's mind. The rider was trying to make out what horse it
happened to be that thus gained on Jane Withersteen's peerless racers.
Wrangle had so long been away from the village that not improbably Jerry
had forgotten. Besides, whatever Jerry's qualifications for his fame as the
greatest rider of the sage, certain it was that his best point was not far-
sightedness. He had not recognized Wrangle. After what must have been
a searching gaze he got his comrade to face about. This action gave
Venters amusement. It spoke so surely of the fact that neither Card nor
the rustler actually knew their danger. Yet if they kept to the trail—and

the last thing such men would do would be to leave it—they were both doomed.

This comrade of Card's whirled far around in his saddle, and he even shaded his eyes from the sun. He, too, looked long. Then, all at once, he faced ahead again and, bending lower in the saddle, began to fling his right arm up and down. That flinging Venters knew to be the lashing of Bells. Jerry also became active. And the three racers lengthened out into a run.

"Now, Wrangle!" cried Venters. "Run, you big devil!" Run!"

Venters laid the reins on Wrangle's neck and dropped the loop over the pommel. The sorrel needed no guiding on that smooth trail. He was surer-footed in a run than at any other fast gait, and his running gave the impression of something devilish. He might now have been actuated by Venters's spirit; undoubtedly his savage running fitted the mood of his rider. Venters bent forward, swinging with the horse, and gripped his rifle. His eye measured the distance between him and Jerry Card.

In less than two miles of running Bells began to drop behind the blacks, and Wrangle began to overhaul him. Venters anticipated that the rustler would soon take to the sage. Yet he did not. Not improbably he reasoned that the powerful sorrel could more easily overtake Bells in the heavier going outside of the trail. Soon only a few hundred yards lay between Bells and Wrangle. Turning in his saddle, the rustler began to shoot, and the bullets beat up little whiffs of dust. Venters raised his rifle, ready to take snap shots, and waited for favorable opportunity when Bells was out of line with the forward horses. Venters had it in him to kill these men as if they were skunk-bitten coyotes, but also he had restraint enough to keep from shooting one of Jane's beloved Arabians.

No great distance was covered, however, before Bells swerved to the left, out of line with Black Star and Night. Then Venters, aiming high and waiting for the pause between Wrangle's great strides, began to take snap shots at the rustler. The fleeing rider presented a broad target for a rifle, but he was moving swiftly forward and bobbing up and down. Moreover, shooting from Wrangle's back was shooting from a thunderbolt. And added to that was the danger of a low-placed bullet taking effect on Bells. Yet, despite these considerations, making the shot exceedingly difficult, Venters's confidence, like his implacability, saw a speedy and fatal termination of that rustler's race. On the sixth shot the rustler threw up his arms and took a flying tumble off his horse. He rolled over and over, hunched himself to a half-erect position, fell, and then dragged himself into the sage. As Venters went thundering by he peered keenly into the sage, but caught no sign of the man. Bells ran a few hundred yards, slowed up, and had stopped when Wrangle passed him.

Again Venters began slipping fresh cartridges into the magazine of his rifle, and his hand was so sure and steady that he did not drop a single cartridge. With the eye of a rider and the judgment of a marksman he once more measured the distance between him and Jerry Card. Wrangle had gained, bringing him into rifle range. Venters was hard put to it now not to shoot, but thought it better to withhold his fire. Jerry, who, in anticipation of a running fusillade, had huddled himself into a little twisted ball on Black Star's neck, now surmising that this pursuer would make sure of not wounding one of the blacks, rose to his natural seat in the saddle.

In his mind perhaps, as certainly as in Venters's, this moment was the beginning of the real race.

Venters leaned forward to put his hand on Wrangle's neck; then backward to put it on his flank. Under the shaggy, dusty hair trembled and vibrated and rippled a wonderful muscular activity. But Wrangle's flesh was still cold. What a cold-blooded brute, thought Venters, and felt in him a love for the horse he had never given to any other. It would not have been humanly possible for any rider, even though clutched by hate or revenge or a passion to save a loved one or fear of his own life, to be astride the sorrel, to swing with his swing, to see his magnificent stride and hear the rapid thunder of his hoofs, to ride him in that race and not glory in the ride.

So, with his passion to kill still keen and unabated, Venters lived out that ride, and drank a rider's sage-sweet cup of wildness to the dregs.

When Wrangle's long mane, lashing in the wind, stung Venters in the cheek, the sting added a beat to his flying pulse. He bent a downward glance to try to see Wrangle's actual stride, and saw only twinkling, darting streaks and the white rush of the trail. He watched the sorrel's savage head, pointed level, his mouth still closed and dry, but his nostrils distended as if he were snorting unseen fire. Wrangle was the horse for a race with death. Upon each side Venters saw the sage merged into a sailing, colorless wall. In front sloped the lay of ground with its purple breadth split by the white trail. The wind, blowing with heavy, steady blast into his face, sickened him with enduring, sweet odor, and filled his ears with a hollow, rushing roar.

Then for the hundredth time he measured the width of space separating him from Jerry Card. Wrangle had ceased to gain. The blacks were proving their fleetness. Venters watched Jerry Card, admiring the little rider's horsemanship. He had the incomparable seat of the upland rider, born in the saddle. It struck Venters that Card had changed his position, or the position of the horses. Presently Venters remembered positively that Jerry had been leading Night on the right-hand side of the trail. The racer was now on the side to the left. No—it was Black Star. But, Venters argued in amaze, Jerry had been mounted on Black Star. Another clearer, keener gaze assured Venters that Black Star was really riderless. Night now carried Jerry Card.

"He's changed from one to the other!" ejaculated Venters, realizing the astounding feat with unstinted admiration. "Changed at full speed! Jerry Card, that's what you've done unless I'm drunk on the smell of sage. But I've got to see the trick before I believe it."

Thenceforth, while Wrangle sped on, Venters glued his eyes to the little rider. Jerry Card rode as only he could ride. Of all the daring horsemen of the uplands, Jerry was the one rider fitted to bring out the greatness of the blacks in that long race. He had them on a dead run, but not yet at the last strained and killing pace. From time to time he glanced backward, as a wise general in retreat calculating his chances and the power and speed of pursuers, and the moment for the last desperate burst. No doubt, Card, with his life at stake, gloried in that race, perhaps more wildly than Venters. For he had been born to the sage and the saddle and the wild. He was more than half horse. Not until the last call—the sudden up-flashing instinct of self-preservation—would he lose his skill and judgment and nerve and the spirit of the race. Venters seemed to read Jerry's mind. That little crime-stained rider was actually thinking of his horses, husbanding their speed, handling them with knowledge of years, glorying in their beautiful, swift, racing stride, and wanting them to win the race when his own life hung suspended in quivering balance. Again Jerry whirled in his saddle and the sun flashed red on his face. Turning, he drew Black Star closer and closer toward Night, till they ran side by side, as one horse. Then Card raised himself in the saddle, slipped out of the stirrups, and, somehow twisting himself, leaped upon Black Star. He did not even lose the swing of the horse. Like a leech he was there in the other saddle, and as the horses separated, his right foot, that had been apparently doubled under him, shot down to catch the stirrup. The grace and dexterity and daring of that rider's act won something more than admiration from Venters.

For the distance of a mile Jerry rode Black Star and then changed back to Night. But all Jerry's skill and the running of the blacks could avail little more against the sorrel.

Venters peered far ahead, studying the lay of the land. Straightaway for five miles the trail stretched, and then it disappeared in hummocky ground. To the right, some few rods, Venters saw a break in the sage, and this was the rim of Deception Pass. Across the dark cleft gleamed the red of the opposite wall. Venters imagined that the trail went down into the Pass somewhere north of those ridges. And he realized that he must and would overtake Jerry Card in this straight course of five miles.

Cruelly he struck his spurs into Wrangle's flanks. A light touch of spur was sufficient to make Wrangle plunge. And now, with a ringing, wild snort, he seemed to double up in muscular convulsions and to shoot forward with an impetus that almost unseated Venters. The sage blurred by, the trail flashed by, and the wind robbed him of breath and hearing.

Jerry Card turned once more. And the way he shifted to Black Star showed he had to make his last desperate running. Venters aimed to the side of the trail and sent a bullet puffing the dust beyond Jerry. Venters hoped to frighten the rider and get him to take to the sage. But Jerry returned the shot, and his ball struck dangerously close in the dust at Wrangle's flying feet. Venters held his fire then, while the rider emptied his revolver. For a mile, with Black Star leaving Night behind and doing his utmost, Wrangle did not gain; for another mile he gained little, if at all. In the third he caught up with the now galloping Night and began to gain rapidly on the other black.

Only a few hundred yards now stretched between Black Star and Wrangle. The giant sorrel thundered on—and on—and on. In every yard he gained a foot. He was whistling through his nostrils, wringing wet, flying lather, and as hot as fire. Savage as ever, strong as ever, fast as ever, but each tremendous stride jarred Venters out of the saddle! Wrangle's power and spirit and momentum had begun to run him off his legs. Wrangle's great race was nearly won—and run. Venters seemed to see the expanse before him as a vast, sheeted, purple plain sliding under him. Black Star moved in it as a blur. The rider, Jerry Card, appeared a mere dot bobbing dimly. Wrangle thundered on—on—on! Venters felt the increase in quivering, straining shock after every leap. Flecks of foam flew into Venters's eyes, burning him, making him see all the sage as red. But in that red haze he saw, or seemed to see, Black Star suddenly riderless and with broken gait. Wrangle thundered on to change his pace with a violent break. Then Venters pulled him hard. From run to gallop, gallop to canter, canter to trot, trot to walk, and walk to stop, the great sorrel ended his race.

Venters looked back. Black Star stood riderless in the trail. Jerry Card had taken to the sage. Far up the white trail Night came trotting faithfully down. Venters leaped off, still half blind, reeling dizzily. In a moment he had recovered sufficiently to have a care for Wrangle. Rapidly he took off the saddle and bridle. The sorrel was reeking, heaving, whistling, shaking. But he had still the strength to stand, and for him Venters had no fears.

As Venters ran back to Black Star he saw the horse stagger on shaking legs into the sage and go down in a heap. Upon reaching him Venters removed the saddle and bridle. Black Star had been killed on his legs, Venters thought. He had no hope for the stricken horse. Black Star lay flat, covered with bloody froth, mouth wide, tongue hanging, eyes glaring, and all his beautiful body in convulsions.

Unable to stay there to see Jane's favorite racer die, Venters hurried up the trail to meet the other black. On the way he kept a sharp lookout for Jerry Card. Venters imagined the rider would keep well out of range of the rifle, but, as he would be lost on the sage without a horse, not improbably he would linger in the vicinity on the chance of getting back one of the blacks. Night soon came trotting up, hot and wet and run out. Venters led him down near the others, and, unsaddling him, let him loose to rest. Night wearily lay down in the dust and rolled, proving himself not yet spent.

Then Venters sat down to rest and think. Whatever the risk, he was compelled to stay where he was, or comparatively near, for the night. The horses must rest and drink. He must find water. He was now seventy miles from Cottonwoods, and, he believed, close to the canyon where the cattle trail must surely turn off and go down into the Pass. After a while he rose to survey the valley.

He was very near to the ragged edge of a deep canyon into which the trail turned. The ground lay in uneven ridges divided by washes, and these sloped into the canyon. Following the canyon line, he saw where its rim was broken by other intersecting canyons, and farther down red walls and yellow cliffs leading toward a deep blue cleft that he made sure was Deception Pass. Walking out a few rods to a promontory, he found where the trail went down. The descent was gradual, along a stone-walled trail, and Venters felt sure that this was the place where Oldring drove cattle into the Pass. There was, however, no indication at all that he ever had driven cattle out at this point. Oldring had many holes to his burrow.

In searching round in the little hollows Venters, much to his relief, found water. He composed himself to rest and eat some bread and meat, while he waited for a sufficient time to elapse so that he could safely give the horses a drink. He judged the hour to be somewhere around noon. Wrangle lay down to rest and Night followed suit. So long as they were down Venters intended to make no move. The longer they rested the better, and the safer it would be to give them water. By and by he forced himself to go over to where Black Star lay, expecting to find him dead. Instead he found the racer partially if not wholly recovered. There was recognition, even fire, in his big black eyes. Venters was overjoyed. He sat by the black for a long time. Black Star presently labored to his feet with a heave and a groan, shook himself, and snorted for water. Venters repaired to the little pool he had found, filled his sombrero, and gave the racer a drink. Black Star gulped it at one draught, as if it were but a drop, and pushed his nose into the hat and snorted for more. Venters now led Night down to drink, and after a further time Black Star also. Then the blacks began to graze.

The sorrel had wandered off down the sage between the trail and the canyon. Once or twice he disappeared in little swales. Finally Venters concluded Wrangle had grazed far enough, and, taking his lasso, he went to fetch him back. In crossing from one ridge to another he saw where the horse had made muddy a pool of water. It occurred to Venters then that Wrangle had drunk his fill, and did not seem the worse for it, and might be anything but easy to catch. And, true enough, he could not come within roping reach of the sorrel. He tried for an hour, and gave up in disgust. Wrangle did not seem so wild as simply perverse. In a quandary Venters returned to the other horses, hoping much, yet doubting more, that when Wrangle had grazed to suit himself he might be caught.

As the afternoon wore away Venters's concern diminished, yet he kept close watch on the blacks and the trail and the sage. There was no telling of what Jerry Card might be capable. Venters sullenly acquiesced to the idea that the rider had been too quick and too shrewd for him. Strangely and doggedly, however, Venters clung to his foreboding of Card's downfall.

The wind died away; the red sun topped the far distant western rise of slope; and the long, creeping purple shadows lengthened. The rims of the canyons gleamed crimson and the deep clefts appeared to belch forth blue smoke. Silence enfolded the scene.

It was broken by a horrid, long-drawn scream of a horse and the thudding of heavy hoofs. Venters sprang erect and wheeled south. Along the canyon rim, near the edge, came Wrangle, once more in thundering flight.

Venters gasped in amazement. Had the wild sorrel gone mad? His head was high and twisted, in a most singular position for a running horse. Suddenly Venters descried a froglike shape clinging to Wrangle's neck. Jerry Card! Somehow he had straddled Wrangle and now stuck like a huge burr. But it was his strange position and the sorrel's wild scream that shook Venters's nerves. Wrangle was pounding toward the turn where the trail went down. He plunged onward like a blind horse. More than one of his leaps took him to the very edge of the precipice.

Jerry Card was bent forward with his teeth fast in the front of Wrangle's nose! Venters saw it, and there flashed over him a memory of this trick of a few desperate riders. He even thought of one rider who had worn off his teeth in this terrible hold to break or control desperate horses. Wrangle had indeed gone mad. The marvel was what guided him. Was it the half-brute, the more than half-horse instinct of Jerry Card? Whatever the mystery, it was true. And in a few more rods Jerry would have the sorrel turning into the trail leading down into the canyon.

"No—Jerry!" whispered Venters, stepping forward and throwing up the rifle. He tried to catch the little humped, froglike shape over the sights. It was moving too fast; it was too small. Yet Venters shot once . . . twice . . . the third time . . . four times . . . five! All wasted shots and precious seconds!

With a deep-muttered curse Venters caught Wrangle through the sights and pulled the trigger. Plainly he heard the bullet thud. Wrangle uttered a horrible strangling sound. In swift death action he whirled, and with one last splendid leap he cleared the canyon rim. And he whirled downward with the little froglike shape clinging to his neck!

There was a pause which seemed never-ending, a shock, and an instant's silence.

Then up rolled a heavy crash, a long roar of sliding rocks dying away in distant echo, then silence unbroken.

Wrangle's race was run.

✦18✦

OLDRING'S KNELL

SOME FORTY HOURS or more later Venters created a commotion in Cottonwoods by riding down the main street on Black Star and leading Bells and Night. He had come upon Bells grazing near the body of a dead rustler, the only incident of his quick ride into the village.

Nothing was farther from Venters's mind than bravado. No thought came to him of the defiance and boldness of riding Jane Withersteen's racers straight into the arch-plotter's stronghold. He wanted men to see the famous Arabians; he wanted men to see them dirty and dusty, bearing all the signs of having been driven to their limit; he wanted men to see and to know that the thieves who had ridden them out into the sage had not ridden them back. Venters had come for that and for more—he wanted to meet Tull face to face; if not Tull, then Dyer; if not Dyer, then anyone in the secret of these master conspirators. Such was Venters's passion. The meeting with the rustlers, the unprovoked attack upon him, the spilling of blood, the recognition of Jerry Card and the horses, the race, and that last plunge of mad Wrangle—all these things, fuel on fuel to the smoldering fire, had kindled and swelled and leaped into living flame. He could have shot Dyer in the midst of his religious services at the altar; he could have killed Tull in front of wives and babes.

He walked the three racers down the broad, green-bordered village road. He heard the murmur of running water from Amber Spring. Bitter waters for Jane Withersteen! Men and women stopped to gaze at him and the horses. All knew him; all knew the blacks and the bay. As well as if it had been spoken, Venters read in the faces of men the intelligence that Jane Withersteen's Arabians had been known to have been stolen. Venters reined in and halted before Dyer's residence. It was a low, long, stone structure resembling Witherst House. The spacious front yard was green and luxuriant with grass and flowers; gravel walks led to the huge porch; a well-trimmed hedge of purple sage separated the yard from the church grounds; birds sang in the trees; water flowed musically along the walks, and there were glad, careless shouts of children. For Venters the beauty of this home, and the serenity and its apparent happiness, all turned red and black. For Venters a shade overspread the lawn, the flowers, the old vine-clad stone house. In the music of the singing birds, in the murmur of the running water, he heard an ominous sound. Quiet beauty —sweet music—innocent laughter! By what monstrous abortion of fate did these abide in the shadow of Dyer?

Venters rode on and stopped before Tull's cottage. Women stared at him with white faces and then flew from the porch. Tull himself appeared at the door, bent low, craning his neck. His dark face flashed out of sight; the door banged; a heavy bar dropped with a hollow sound.

Then Venters shook Black Star's bridle, and, sharply trotting, led the other horses to the center of the village. Here at the intersecting streets and in front of the stores he halted once more. The usual lounging atmosphere of that prominent corner was not now in evidence. Riders and ranchers and villagers broke up what must have been absorbing conversation. There was a rush of many feet, and then the walk was lined with faces.

Venters's glance swept down the line of silent stone-faced men. He recognized many riders and villagers, but none of those he had hoped to meet. There was no expression in the faces turned toward him. All of them knew him, most were inimical, but there were few who were not burning with curiosity and wonder in regard to the return of Jane Withersteen's racers. Yet all were silent. Here were the familiar characteristics— masked feeling—strange secretiveness—expressionless expression of mystery and hidden power.

"Has anybody here seen Jerry Card?" queried Venters, in a loud voice.

In reply there came not a word, not a nod or shake of head, not so much as dropping eye or twitching lip—nothing but a quiet, stony stare.

"Been under the knife? You've a fine knife-wielder here—one Tull, I believe! . . . Maybe you've all had your tongues cut out?"

This passionate sarcasm of Venters brought no response, and the stony calm was as oil on the fire within him.

"I see some of you pack guns, too!" he added, in biting scorn. In the long, tense pause, strung keenly as a tight wire, he sat motionless on Black Star. "All right," he went on. "Then let some of you take this message to Tull. Tell him I've seen Jerry Card! . . . Tell him Jerry Card *will never return!*"

Thereupon, in the same dead calm, Venters backed Black Star away from the curb, into the street, and out of range. He was ready now to ride up to Withersteen House and turn the racers over to Jane.

"Hello, Venters!" a familiar voice cried, hoarsely, and he saw a man running toward him. It was the rider Judkins who came up and gripped Venters's hand. "Venters, I could hev dropped when I seen them hosses. But thet sight ain't a marker to the looks of you. What's wrong? Hev you gone crazy? You must be crazy to ride in here this way—with them hosses —talkin' thet way about Tull an' Jerry Card."

"Jud, I'm not crazy—only mad clean through," replied Venters.

"Wal, now, Bern, I'm glad to hear some of your old self in your voice. Fer when you come up you looked like the corpse of a dead rider with fire fer eyes. You hed thet crowd too stiff fer throwin' guns. Come, we've got to hev a talk. Let's go up the lane. We ain't much safe here."

Judkins mounted Bells and rode with Venters up to the cottonwood grove. Here they dismounted and went among the trees.

"Let's hear from you first," said Judkins. "You fetched back them hosses. Thet is the trick. An', of course, you got Jerry the same as you got Horne."

"Horne!"

"Sure. He was found dead yesterday all chewed by coyotes, an' he'd been shot plumb center."

"Where was he found?"

"At the split down the trail—you know where Oldrin's cattle trail runs off north from the trail to the Pass."

"That's where I met Jerry and the rustlers. What was Horne doing with them? I thought Horne was an honest cattle-man."

"Lord—Bern, don't ask me thet! I'm all muddled now tryin' to figure things."

Venters told of the fight and the race with Jerry Card and its tragic conclusion.

"I knowed it! I knowed all along that Wrangle was the best hoss!" exclaimed Judkins, with his lean face working and his eyes lighting. "Thet was a race! Lord, I'd like to hev seen Wrangle jump the cliff with Jerry. An' thet was goodbye to the grandest hoss an' rider ever on the sage! . . . But, Bern, after you got the hosses why'd you want to bolt right in Tull's face?"

"I want him to know. An' if I can get to him I'll—"

"You can't get near Tull," interrupted Judkins. "Thet vigilante bunch hev taken to bein' bodyguard for Tull an' Dyer, too."

"Hasn't Lassiter made a break yet?" inquired Venters, curiously.

"Naw!" replied Judkins, scornfully. "Jane turned his head. He's mad in love over her—follers her like a dog. He ain't no more Lassiter! He's lost his nerve; he doesn't look like the same feller. It's village talk. Everybody knows it. He hasn't thrown a gun, an' he won't!"

"Jud, I'll bet he does," replied Venters, earnestly. "Remember what I say. This Lassiter is something more than a gunman. Jud, he's big—he's great! . . . I feel that in him. God help Tull and Dyer when Lassiter does go after them. For horses and riders and stone walls won't save them."

"Wal, hev it your way, Bern. I hope you're right. Nat'rully I've been some sore on Lassiter fer gittin' soft. But I ain't denyin' his nerve, or whatever's great in him thet sort of paralyzes people. No later 'n this mornin' I seen him saunterin' down the lane, quiet an' slow. An' like his guns he comes black—*black*, thet's Lassiter. Wal, the crowd on the corner never batted an eye, an' I'll gamble my hoss thet there wasn't one who hed a heartbeat till Lassiter got by. He went in Snell's saloon, an' as there wasn't no gun play I had to go in, too. An' there, darn my pictures, if Lassiter wasn't standin' to the bar, drinkin' an' talkin' with Oldrin'."

"*Oldring!*" whispered Venters. His voice, as all fire and pulse within him, seemed to freeze.

"Let go my arm!" exclaimed Judkins. "Thet's my bad arm. Sure it was Oldrin'. What the hell's wrong with you, anyway? Venters, I tell you somethin's wrong. You're whiter'n a sheet. You can't be *scared* of the rustler. I don't believe you've got a scare in you. Wal, now, jest let me talk. You know I like to talk, an' if I'm slow I allus git there sometime. As I said, Lassiter was talkin' chummy with Oldrin'. There wasn't no hard feelin's. An' the gang wasn't payin' no pertic'lar attention. But like a cat watchin' a mouse I hed my eyes on them two fellers. It was strange to me, thet confab. I'm gittin' to think a lot, fer a feller who doesn't know much. There's been some queer deals lately an' this seemed to me the queerest. These men stood to the bar alone, an' so close their big gun-hilts butted together. I seen Oldrin' was some surprised at first, an' Lassiter was cool as ice. They talked, an' presently at somethin' Lassiter said the rustler bawled out a curse, an' then he jest fell up against the bar, an' sagged there. The gang in the saloon looked around an' laughed, an' thet's about all. Finally Oldrin' turned, and it was easy to see somethin' hed shook him. Yes, sir, thet big rustler—you know he's as broad as he is long, an' the powerfulest build of a man—yes, sir, the nerve had been taken out of him. Then, after a little, he began to talk an' said a lot to Lassiter, an' by an' by it didn't take much of an eye to see thet Lassiter was gittin' hit hard. I never seen him anyway but cooler 'n ice—till then. He seemed to be hit harder 'n Oldrin', only he didn't roar out thet way. He jest kind of sunk in, an' looked an' looked, an' he didn't see a livin' soul in thet saloon. Then he sort of come to, an' shakin' hands—mind you, *shakin' hands* with Oldrin'—he went out. I couldn't help thinkin' how easy even a boy could hev dropped the great gunman then! . . . Wal, the rustler stood at the bar fer a long time, an' he was seein' things far off, too; then he come to an' roared fer whisky, an' gulped a drink thet was big enough to drown me."

"Is Oldring here now?" whispered Venters. He could not speak above a whisper. Judkins's story had been meaningless to him.

"He's at Snell's yet. Bern, I hevn't told you yet thet the rustlers hev been raisin' hell. They shot up Stone Bridge an' Glaze, an' fer three days they've been here drinkin' an' gamblin' an' throwin' of gold. These rustlers hev a pile of gold. If it was gold dust or nugget gold I'd hev reason to think, but it's new coin gold, as if it had jest come from the United States treasury. An' the coin's genuine. Thet's all been proved. The truth is Oldrin's on a rampage. A while back he lost his Masked Rider, an' they say he's wild about thet. I'm wonderin' if Lassiter could hev told the rustler anythin' about thet little masked, hard-ridin' devil. Ride! He was most as good as Jerry Card. An', Bern, I've been wonderin' if you know—"

"Judkins, you're a good fellow," interrupted Venters. "Some day I'll tell you a story. I've no time now. Take the horses to Jane."

Judkins stared, and then, muttering to himself, he mounted Bells, and stared again at Venters, and then, leading the other horses, he rode into the grove and disappeared.

Once, long before, on the night Venters had carried Bess through the canyon and up into Surprise Valley, he had experienced the strangeness of faculties singularly, tinglingly acute. And now the same sensation recurred. But it was different in that he felt cold, frozen, mechanical, incapable of free thought, and all about him seemed unreal, aloof, remote. He hid his rifle in the sage, marking its exact location with extreme care. Then he faced down the lane and strode toward the center of the village. Perceptions flashed upon him, the faint, cold touch of the breeze, a cold, silvery tinkle of flowing water, a cold sun shining out of a cold sky, song of birds and laugh of children, coldly distant. Cold and intangible were all things in earth and heaven. Colder and tighter stretched the skin over his face; colder and harder grew the polished butts of his guns; colder and steadier became his hands as he wiped the clammy sweat from his face or reached low to his gunsheaths. Men meeting him in the walk gave him wide berth. In front of Bevin's store a crowd melted apart for his passage, and their faces and whispers were faces and whispers of a dream. He turned a corner to meet Tull face to face, eye to eye. As once before he had seen this man pale to a ghastly, livid white, so again he saw the change. Tull stopped in his tracks, with right hand raised and shaking. Suddenly it dropped, and he seemed to glide aside, to pass out of Venters's sight. Next he saw many horses with bridles down—all clean-limbed, dark bays or blacks—rustlers' horses! Loud voices and boisterous laughter, rattle of dice and scrape of chair and clink of gold, burst in mingled din from an open doorway. He stepped inside.

With the sight of smoke-hazed room and drinking, cursing, gambling, dark-visaged men, reality once more dawned upon Venters.

His entrance had been unnoticed, and he bent his gaze upon the drinkers at the bar. Dark-clothed, dark-faced men they all were, burned by the sun, bow-legged as were most riders of the sage, but neither lean nor gaunt. Then Venters's gaze passed to the tables, and swiftly it swept over the hard-featured gamesters, to alight upon the huge, shaggy, black head of the rustler chief.

"Oldring!" he cried, and to him his voice seemed to split a bell in his ears.

It stilled the din.

That silence suddenly broke to the scrape and crash of Oldring's chair as he rose; and then, while he passed, a great gloomy figure, again the thronged room stilled in silence yet deeper.

"Oldring, a word with you!" continued Venters.

"Ho! What's this?" boomed Oldring, in frowning scrutiny.

"Come outside, alone. A word for you—*from your Masked Rider!*"

Oldring kicked a chair out of his way and lunged forward with a stamp of heavy boot that jarred the floor. He waved down his muttering, rising men.

Venters backed out of the door and waited, hearing, as no sound had ever before struck into his soul, the rapid, heavy steps of the rustler.

Oldring appeared, and Venters had one glimpse of his great breadth and bulk, his gold-buckled belt with hanging guns, his high-top boots with gold spurs. In that moment Venters had a strange, unintelligible curiosity to see Oldring alive. The rustler's broad brow, his large black eyes, his sweeping beard, as dark as the wing of a raven, his enormous width of shoulder and depth of chest, his whole splendid presence so wonderfully charged with vitality and force and strength, seemed to afford Venters an unutterable fiendish joy because for that magnificent manhood and life he meant cold and sudden death.

"Oldring, Bess is alive! But she's dead to you—dead to the life you made her lead—dead as you will be in one second!"

Swift as lightning Venters's glance dropped from Oldring's rolling eyes to his hands. One of them, the right, swept out, then toward his gun— and Venters shot him through the heart.

Slowly Oldring sank to his knees, and the hand, dragging at the gun, fell away. Venters's strangely acute faculties grasped the meaning of that limp arm, of the swaying hulk, of the gasp and heave, of the quivering beard. But was that awful spirit in the black eyes only one of vitality?

"Man—why—didn't—you—wait? Bess—was—" Oldring's whisper died under his beard, and with a heavy lurch he fell forward.

Bounding swiftly away, Venters fled around the corner, across the street, and, leaping a hedge, he ran through yard, orchard, and garden to the sage. Here, under cover of the tall brush, he turned west and ran on to the place where he had hidden his rifle. Securing that, he again set out into a run, and, circling through the sage, came up behind Jane Withersteen's stable and corrals. With laboring, dripping chest, and pain as of a knife thrust in his side, he stopped to regain his breath, and while resting his eyes roved around in search of a horse. Doors and windows of the stable were open wide and had a deserted look. One dejected, lonely burro stood in the near corral. Strange indeed was the silence brooding over the once happy, noisy home of Jane Withersteen's pets.

He went into the corral, exercising care to leave no tracks, and led the burro to the watering-trough. Venters, though not thirsty, drank till he could drink no more. Then, leading the burro over hard ground, he struck into the sage and down the slope.

He strode swiftly, turning from time to time to scan the slope for riders. His head just topped the level of sage-brush, and the burro could not have been seen at all. Slowly the green of Cottonwoods sank behind the slope, and at last a wavering line of purple sage met the blue of sky.

To avoid being seen, to get away, to hide his trail—these were the sole ideas in his mind as he headed for Deception Pass; and he directed all his acuteness of eye and ear, and the keenness of a rider's judgment for distance and ground, to stern accomplishment of the task. He kept to the sage far to the left of the trail leading into the Pass. He walked ten miles and looked back a thousand times. Always the graceful, purple wave of sage remained wide and lonely, a clear, undotted waste. Coming to a stretch of rocky ground, he took advantage of it to cross the trail and then continued down on the right. At length he persuaded himself that he would be able to see riders mounted on horses before they could see him on the little burro, and he rode bareback.

Hour by hour the tireless burro kept to his faithful, steady trot. The sun sank and the long shadows lengthened down the slope. Moving veils of purple twilight crept out of the hollows and, mustering and forming on the levels, soon merged and shaded into night. Venters guided the burro nearer to the trail, so that he could see its white line from the ridges, and rode on through the hours.

Once down in the Pass without leaving a trail, he would hold himself safe for the time being. When late in the night he reached the break in the sage, he sent the burro down ahead of him, and started an avalanche that all but buried the animal at the bottom of the trail. Bruised and battered as he was, he had a moment's elation, for he had hidden his tracks. Once more he mounted the burro and rode on. The hour was the blackest of the night when he made the thicket which inclosed his old camp. Here he turned the burro loose in the grass near the spring, and then lay down on his old bed of leaves.

He felt only vaguely, as outside things, the ache and burn and throb of the muscles of his body. But a dammed-up torrent of emotion at last burst its bounds, and the hour that saw his release from immediate action was one that confounded him in the reaction of his spirit. He suffered without understanding why. He caught glimpses into himself, into unlit darkness of soul. The fire that had blistered him and the cold which had frozen him now united in one torturing possession of his mind and heart, and like a fiery steed with ice-shod feet, ranging his being, ran rioting through his blood, trampling the resurging good, dragging ever at the evil.

Out of the subsiding chaos came a clear question. What had happened?

He had left the valley to go to Cottonwoods. Why? It seemed that he had gone to kill a man—Oldring! The name riveted his consciousness upon the one man of all men upon earth whom he had wanted to meet. He had met the rustler. Venters recalled the smoky haze of the saloon, the dark-visaged men, the huge Oldring. He saw him step out of the door, a splendid specimen of manhood, a handsome giant with purple-black and sweeping beard. He remembered inquisitive gaze of falcon eyes. He heard himself repeating: *"Oldring, Bess is alive! But she's dead to you,"* and he felt himself jerk, and his ears throbbed to the thunder of a gun, and he saw the giant sink slowly to his knees. Was that only the vitality of him—that awful light in the eyes—only the hard-dying life of a tremendously powerful brute? A broken whisper, strange as death: *"Man—why—didn't—you —wait! Bess—was—"* And Oldring plunged face forward, dead.

"I killed him," cried Venters, in remembering shock. "But it wasn't *that*. Ah, the look in his eyes and his whisper!"

Herein lay the secret that had clamored to him through all the tumult and stress of his emotions. What a look in the eyes of a man shot through the heart! It had been neither hate nor ferocity nor fear of men nor fear of death. It had been no passionate, glinting spirit of a fearless foe, willing shot for shot, life for life, but lacking physical power. Distinctly recalled now, never to be forgotten, Venters saw in Oldring's magnificent eyes the rolling of great, glad surprise—softness—love! Then came a shadow and the terrible superhuman striving of his spirit to speak. Oldring, shot through the heart, had fought and forced back death, not for a moment in which to shoot or curse, but to whisper strange words.

What words for a dying man to whisper! Why had not Venters waited? For what? That was no plea for life. It was regret that there was not a moment of life left in which to speak. Bess was—Herein lay renewed torture for Venters. What had Bess been to Oldring? The old question, like a specter, stalked from its grave to haunt him. He had overlooked, he had forgiven, he had loved, and he had forgotten; and now, out of the mystery of a dying man's whisper rose again that perverse, unsatisfied, jealous uncertainty. Bess had loved that splendid, black-crowned giant— by her own confession she had loved him; and in Venters's soul again flamed up the jealous hell. Then into the clamoring hell burst the shot that had killed Oldring, and it rang in a wild, fiendish gladness, a hateful, vengeful joy. That passed to the memory of the love and light in Oldring's eyes and the mystery in his whisper. So the changing, swaying emotions fluctuated in Venters's heart.

This was the climax of his year of suffering and the crucial struggle of his life. And when the gray dawn came he rose, a gloomy, almost heart-broken man, but victor over evil passions. He could not change the past; and, even if he had not loved Bess with all his soul, he had grown into a man who would not change the future he had planned for her. Only, and once and for all, he must know the truth, know the worst, stifle all these insistent doubts and subtle hopes and jealous fancies, and kill the past by knowing truly what Bess had been to Oldring. For that matter he knew—he had always known, but he must hear it spoken. Then, when they had safely gotten out of that wild country to take up a new and an absorbing life, she would forget, she would be happy, and through that, in the years to come, he could not but find life worth living.

All day he rode slowly and cautiously up the Pass, taking time to peer around corners, to pick out hard ground and grassy patches, and to make sure there was no one in pursuit. In the night sometime he came to the smooth, scrawled rocks dividing the valley, and here set the burro at liberty. He walked beyond, climbed the slope and the dim, starlit gorge. Then, weary to the point of exhaustion, he crept into a shallow cave and fell asleep.

In the morning, when he descended the trail, he found the sun was pouring a golden stream of light through the arch of the great stone bridge. Surprise Valley, like a valley of dreams, lay mystically soft and beautiful, awakening to the golden flood which was rolling away its slumberous bands of mist, brightening its walled faces.

While yet far off he discerned Bess moving under the silver spruces, and soon the barking of the dogs told him that they had seen him. He heard the mockingbirds singing in the trees, and then the twittering of the quail. Ring and Whitie came bounding toward him, and behind them ran Bess, her hands outstretched.

"Bern! You're back! You're back!" she cried, in joy that rang of her loneliness.

"Yes, I'm back," he said, as she rushed to meet him.

She had reached out for him when suddenly, as she saw him closely, something checked her, and as quickly all her joy fled, and with it her color, leaving her pale and trembling.

"Oh! What's happened?"

"A good deal has happened, Bess. I don't need to tell you what. And I'm played out. Worn out in mind more than body."

"Dear—you look strange to me!" faltered Bess.

"Never mind that. I'm all right. There's nothing for you to be scared about. Things are going to turn out just as we have planned. As soon as I'm rested we'll make a break to get out of the country. Only now, right now, I must know the truth about you."

"Truth about me?" echoed Bess, shrinkingly. She seemed to be casting back into her mind for a forgotten key. Venters himself, as he saw her, received a pang.

"Yes—the truth. Bess, don't misunderstand. I haven't changed that way. I love you still. I'll love you more afterward. Life will be just as sweet —sweeter to us. We'll be—be married as soon as ever we can. We'll be happy—but there's a devil in me. A perverse, jealous devil! Then I've queer fancies. I forgot for a long time. Now all those fiendish little whispers of doubt and faith and fear and hope come torturing me again. I've got to kill them with the truth."

"I'll tell you anything you want to know," she replied, frankly.

"Then, by heaven! we'll have it over and done with! . . . Bess—did Oldring love you?"

"Certainly he did."

"Did—did you love him?"

"Of course. I told you so."

"How can you tell it so lightly?" cried Venters, passionately. "Haven't you any sense of—of—" He choked back speech. He felt the rush of pain and passion. He seized her in rude, strong hands and drew her close. He looked straight into her dark-blue eyes. They were shadowing with the old wistful light, but they were as clear as the limpid water of the spring. They were earnest, solemn in unutterable love and faith and abnegation. Venters shivered. He knew he was looking into her soul. He knew she could not lie in that moment; but that she might tell the truth, looking at him with those eyes, almost killed his belief in purity.

"What are—what were you to—to Oldring?" he panted, fiercely.

"I am his daughter," she replied, instantly.

Venters slowly let go of her. There was a violent break in the force of his feeling—then creeping blankness.

"What—was it—you said?" he asked, in a kind of dull wonder.

"I am his daughter."

"Oldring's daughter?" queried Venters, with life gathering in his voice.

"Yes."

With a passionately awakening start he grasped her hands and drew her close.

"All the time—you've been Oldring's daughter?"

"Yes, of course all the time—always."

"But Bess, you told me—you let me think—I made out you were—a—so—so ashamed."

"It is my shame," she said, with voice deep and full, and now the scarlet fired her cheek. "I told you—I'm nothing—nameless—just Bess, Oldring's girl!"

"I know—I remember. But I never thought—" he went on, hurriedly, huskily. "That time—when you lay dying—you prayed—you—somehow I got the idea you were bad."

"Bad?" she asked, with a little laugh.

She looked up with a faint smile of bewilderment and the absolute unconsciousness of a child. Venters gasped in the gathering might of the truth. She did not understand his meaning.

"Bess! Bess!" He clasped her in his arms, hiding her eyes against his breast. She must not see his face in that moment. And he held her while he looked out across the valley. In his dim and blinded sight, in the blur of golden light and moving mist, he saw Oldring. She was the rustler's nameless daughter. Oldring had loved her. He had so guarded her, so kept her from women and men and knowledge of life that her mind was as a child's. That was part of the secret—part of the mystery. That was the wonderful truth. Not only was she not bad, but good, pure, innocent above all innocence in the world—the innocence of lonely girlhood.

He saw Oldring's magnificent eyes, inquisitive, searching—softening. He saw them flare in amaze, in gladness, with love, then suddenly strain in terrible effort of will. He heard Oldring whisper and saw him sway like a log and fall. Then a million bellowing, thundering voices—gunshots of conscience, thunderbolts of remorse—dinned horribly in his ears. He had killed Bess's father. Then a rushing wind filled his ears like the moan of wind in the cliffs, a knell indeed—Oldring's knell.

He dropped to his knees and hid his face against Bess, and grasped her with the hands of a drowning man.

"My God! . . . My God! . . . Oh, Bess! . . . Forgive me! Never mind what I've done—what I've thought. But forgive me. I'll give you my life. I'll live for you. I'll love you. Oh, I do love you as no man ever loved a woman. I want you to know—to remember that I fought a fight for you—however blind I was. I thought—I thought—never mind what I thought—but I loved you—I asked you to marry me. Let that—let me have that to hug to my heart. Oh, Bess, I was driven! And I might have known! I could not rest nor sleep till I had this mystery solved. God! how things work out!"

"Bern, you're weak—trembling—you talk wildly," cried Bess. "You've overdone your strength. There's nothing to forgive. There's no mystery except your love for me. You have come back to me!"

And she clasped his head tenderly in her arms and pressed it closely to her throbbing breast.

❦19❧

FAY

A<small>T THE HOME</small> of Jane Withersteen little Fay was climbing Lassiter's knee.

"Does oo love me?" she asked.

Lassiter, who was as serious with Fay as he was gentle and loving, assured her in earnest and elaborate speech that he was her devoted subject. Fay looked thoughtful and appeared to be debating the duplicity of men or searching for a supreme test to prove this cavalier.

"Does oo love my new muvver?" she asked, with bewildering suddenness.

Jane Withersteen laughed, and for the first time in many a day she felt a stir of her pulse and warmth in her cheek.

It was a still drowsy afternoon of summer, and the three were sitting in the shade of the wooded knoll that faced the sage-slope. Little Fay's brief spell of unhappy longing for her mother—the childish, mystic gloom—had passed, and now where Fay was there were prattle and laughter and glee. She had emerged from sorrow to be the incarnation of joy and loveliness. She had grown supernaturally sweet and beautiful. For Jane Withersteen the child was an answer to prayer, a blessing, a possession infinitely more precious than all she had lost. For Lassiter, Jane divined that little Fay had become a religion.

"Does oo love my new muvver?" repeated Fay.

Lassiter's answer to this was a modest and sincere affirmative.

"Why don't oo marry my new muvver an' be my favver?"

Of the thousands of questions put by little Fay to Lassiter that was the first he had been unable to answer.

"Fay—Fay, don't ask questions like that," said Jane.

"Why?"

"Because," replied Jane. And she found it strangely embarrassing to meet the child's gaze. It seemed to her that Fay's violet eyes looked through her with piercing wisdom.

"Oo love him, don't oo?"

"Dear child—run and play," said Jane, "but don't go too far. Don't go from this little hill."

Fay pranced off wildly, joyous over freedom that had not been granted her for weeks.

"Jane, why are children more sincere than grown-up persons?" asked Lassiter.

"Are they?"

"I reckon so. Little Fay there—she sees things as they appear on the face. An Indian does that. So does a dog. An' an Indian an' a dog are most of the time right in what they see. Mebbe a child is always right."

"Well, what does Fay see?" asked Jane.

"I reckon you know. I wonder what goes on in Fay's mind when she sees part of the truth with the wise eyes of a child, an' wantin' to know more, meets with strange falseness from you? Wait! You are false in a way, though you're the best woman I ever knew. What I want to say is this. Fay has taken your pretendin' to—to care for me for the thing it looks on the face. An' her little formin' mind asks questions. An' the answers she gets are different from the looks of things. So she'll grow up, gradually takin' on that falseness, an' be like the rest of women, an' men, too. An' the truth of this falseness to life is proved by your appearin' to love me when you don't. Things aren't what they seem."

"Lassiter, you're right. A child should be told the absolute truth. But— is that possible? I haven't been able to do it, and all my life I've loved the truth, and I've prided myself upon being truthful. Maybe that was only egotism. I'm learning much, my friend. Some of those blinding scales have fallen from my eyes. And—and as to caring for you, I think I care a great deal. How much, how little, I couldn't say. My heart is almost broken, Lassiter. So now is not a good time to judge of affection. I can still play and be merry with Fay. I can still dream. But when I attempt serious thought I'm dazed. I don't think. I don't care anymore. I don't pray! . . . Think of that, my friend! But in spite of my numb feeling I believe I'll rise out of all this dark agony a better woman, with greater love of man and God. I'm on the rack now; I'm senseless to all but pain, and growing dead to that. Sooner or later I shall rise out of this stupor. I'm waiting the hour."

"It'll soon come, Jane," replied Lassiter, soberly. "Then I'm afraid for you. Years are terrible things, an' for years you've been bound. Habit of years is strong as life itself. Somehow, though, I believe as you—that you'll come out of it all a finer woman. I'm waitin', too. An' I'm wonderin' —I reckon, Jane, that marriage between us is out of all human reason?"

"Lassiter! . . . My dear friend! . . . It's impossible for us to marry."

"Why—as Fay says?" inquired Lassiter, with gentle persistence.

"Why! I never thought why. But it's not possible. I am Jane, daughter of Withersteen. My father would rise out of his grave. I'm of Mormon birth. I'm being broken. But I'm still a Mormon woman. And you—you are Lassiter!"

"Mebbe I'm not so much Lassiter as I used to be."

"What was it you said? Habit of years is strong as life itself! You can't change the one habit—the purpose of your life. For you still pack those black guns! You still nurse your passion for blood."

A smile, like a shadow, flickered across his face.

"No."

"Lassiter, I lied to you. But I beg of you—don't you lie to me. I've great respect for you. I believe you're softened toward most, perhaps all, my people except— But when I speak of your purpose, your hate, your guns, I have only him in mind. I don't believe you've changed."

For answer he unbuckled the heavy cartridge-belt, and laid it with the heavy, swing gun-sheaths in her lap.

"Lassiter!" Jane whispered, as she gazed from him to the black, cold guns. Without them he appeared shorn of strength, defenseless, a smaller man. Was she Delilah? Swiftly, conscious of only one motive—refusal to see this man called craven by his enemies—she rose, and with blundering fingers buckled the belt around his waist where it belonged.

"Lassiter, I am the coward."

"Come with me out of Utah—where I can put away my guns an' be a man," he said. "I reckon I'll prove it to you then! Come! You've got Black Star back, an' Night an' Bells. Let's take the racers an' little Fay, an' ride out of Utah. The hosses an' the child are all you have left. Come!"

"No, no, Lassiter. I'll never leave Utah. What would I do in the world with my broken fortunes and my broken heart? I'll never leave these purple slopes I love so well."

"I reckon I ought to've knowed that. Presently you'll be livin' down here in a hovel, an' presently Jane Withersteen will be a memory. I only wanted to have a chance to show you how a man—*any* man—can be better'n he was. If we left Utah I could prove—I reckon I could prove this thing you call love. It's strange, an' hell an' heaven at once, Jane Withersteen. 'Pears to me that you've thrown away your big heart on love—love of religion an' duty an' churchmen, an' riders an' poor families an' poor children! Yet you can't see what love is—how it changes a person! . . . Listen, an' in tellin' you Milly Erne's story I'll show you how love changed her.

"Milly an' me was children when our family moved from Missouri to Texas, an' we growed up in Texas ways same as if we'd been born there. We had been poor, an' there we prospered. In time the little village where we went became a town, an' strangers an' new families kept movin' in. Milly was the belle them days. I can see her now, a little girl no bigger'n a bird, an' as pretty. She had the finest eyes, dark blue-black when she was excited, an' beautiful all the time. You remember Milly's eyes! An' she had light-brown hair with streaks of gold, an' a mouth that every feller wanted to kiss.

"An' about the time Milly was the prettiest an' the sweetest, along came a young minister who began to ride some of a race with the other fellers for Milly. An' he won. Milly had always been strong on religion, an' when she met Frank Erne she went in heart an' soul for the salvation of souls. Fact was, Milly, through study of the Bible an' attendin' church an' revivals, went a little out of her head. It didn't worry the old folks none, an' the only worry to me was Milly's everlastin' prayin' an' workin' to save my soul. She never converted me, but we was the best of comrades, an' I reckon no brother an' sister ever loved each other better. Well, Frank Erne an' me hit up a great friendship. He was a strappin' feller, good to look at, an' had the most pleasin' ways. His religion never bothered me, for he could hunt an' fish an' ride an' be a good feller. After buffalo once, he come pretty near to savin' my life. We got to be thick as brothers, an' he was the only man I ever seen who I thought was good enough for Milly. An' the day they were married I got drunk for the only time in my life.

"Soon after that I left home—it seems Milly was the only one who could keep me home—an' I went to the bad, as to prosperin'. I saw some pretty hard life in the Pan Handle, an' then I went north. In them days Kansas an' Nebraska was as bad, come to think of it, as these days right here on the border of Utah. I got to be pretty handy with guns. An' there wasn't many riders as could beat me ridin'. An' I can say all modest-like that I never seen the white man who could track a hoss or a steer or a man with me. Afore I knowed it two years slipped by, an' all at once I got homesick, an' pulled a bridle south.

"Things at home had changed. I never got over that homecomin'. Mother was dead an' in her grave. Father was a silent, broken man, killed already on his feet. Frank Erne was a ghost of his old self, through with workin', through with preachin', almost through with livin', an' Milly was gone! . . . It was a long time before I got the story. Father had no mind left, an' Frank Erne was *afraid* to talk. So I had to pick up what'd happened from different people.

"It 'pears that soon after I left home another preacher come to the little town. An' he an' Frank become rivals. This feller was different from Frank. He preached some other kind of religion, and he was quick an' passionate, where Frank was slow an' mild. He went after people, women specially. In looks he couldn't compare to Frank Erne, but he had power over women. He had a voice, an' he talked an' talked an' preached an' preached. Milly fell under his influence. She became mightily interested in his religion. Frank had patience with her, as was his way, an' let her be as interested as she liked. All religions were devoted to one God, he said, an' it wouldn't hurt Milly none to study a different point of view. So the new preacher often called on Milly, an' sometimes in Frank's absence. Frank was a cattle-man between Sundays.

"Along about this time an incident come off that I couldn't get much light on. A stranger come to town, an' was seen with the preacher. This stranger was a big man with an eye like blue ice, an' a beard of gold. He had money, an' he 'peared a man of mystery, an' the town went to buzzin' when he disappeared about the same time as a young woman known to be mightily interested in the new preacher's religion. Then, presently, along comes a man from somewheres in Illinois, an' he up an' spots this preacher as a famous Mormon proselyter. That ri'led Frank Erne as nothin' ever before, an' from rivals they come to be bitter enemies. An' it ended in Frank goin' to the meetin'-house where Milly was listenin', an' before her an' everybody else he called that preacher—called him, well, almost as hard as Venters called Tull here sometime back. An' Frank followed up that call with a hoss-whippin', an' he drove the proselyter out of town.

"People noticed, so 'twas said, that Milly's sweet disposition changed. Some said it was because she would soon become a mother, an' others said she was pinin' after the new religion. An' there was women who said right out that she was pinin' after the Mormon. Anyway, one mornin' Frank rode in from one of his trips, to find Milly gone. He had no real near neighbors—livin' a little out of town—but those who was nearest said a wagon had gone by in the night, an' they thought it stopped at her door. Well, tracks always tell, an' there was the wagon tracks an' hoss tracks an' man tracks. The news spread like wildfire that Milly had run off from her husband. Everybody but Frank believed it an' wasn't slow in tellin' why she run off. Mother had always hated that strange streak of Milly's, takin' up with the new religion as she had, an' she believed Milly ran off with the Mormon. That hastened mother's death, an' she died unforgivin'. Father wasn't the kind to bow down under disgrace or misfortune, but he had surpassin' love for Milly, an' the loss of her broke him.

"From the minute I heard of Milly's disappearance I never believed she went off of her own free will. I knew Milly, an' I knew she *couldn't* have done that. I stayed at home awhile, tryin' to make Frank Erne talk. But if he knowed anythin' then he wouldn't tell it. So I set out to find Milly. An' I tried to get on the trail of that proselyter. I knew if I ever struck a town he'd visited that I'd get a trail. I knew, too, that nothin' short of hell would stop his proselytin'. An' I rode from town to town. I had a blind faith that somethin' was guidin' me. An' as the weeks an' months went by I growed into a strange sort of a man, I guess. Anyway, people were afraid of me. Two years after that, way over in a corner of Texas, I struck a town where my man had been. He'd jest left. People said he came to that town *without* a woman. I back-trailed my man through Arkansas an' Mississippi, an' the old trail got hot again in Texas. I found the town where he first went after leavin' home. An' here I got track of Milly. I found a cabin where she had given birth to her baby. There was no way to tell whether she'd been kept a prisoner or not. The feller who owned the place was a mean, silent sort of a skunk, an' as I was leavin' I jest took a chance an' left my mark on him. Then I went home again.

"It was to find I hadn't any home, no more. Father had been dead a year. Frank Erne still lived in the house where Milly had left him. I stayed with him awhile, an' I grew old watchin' him. His farm had gone to weed, his cattle had strayed or been rustled, his house weathered till it wouldn't keep out rain nor wind. An' Frank set on the porch and whittled sticks, an' day by day wasted away. There was times when he ranted about like a crazy man, but mostly he was always sittin' an' starin' with eyes that made a man curse. I figured Frank had a secret fear that I needed to know. An' when I told him I'd trailed Milly for near three years an' had got trace of her, an' saw where she'd had her baby, I thought he would drop dead at my feet. An' when he'd come round more natural-like he begged me to *give up* the trail. But he wouldn't explain. So I let him alone, an' watched him day an' night.

"An' I found there was one thing still precious to him, an' it was a little drawer where he kept his papers. This was in the room where he slept. An' it 'peared he seldom slept. But after bein' patient I got the contents of that drawer an' found two letters from Milly. One was a long letter written a few months after her disappearance. She had been bound an' gagged an' dragged away from her home by three men, an' she named them—Hurd, Metzger, Slack. They was strangers to her. She was taken to the little town where I found trace of her two years after. But she didn't send the letter from that town. There she was penned in. 'Peared that the proselyter, who had, of course, come on the scene, was not runnin' any risks of losin' her. She went on to say that for a time she was out of her head, an' when she got right again, all that kept her alive was the baby. It was a beautiful baby, she said, an' all she thought an' dreamed of was somehow to get the baby back to its father, an' then she'd thankfully lay down and die. An' the letter ended abrupt, in the middle of a sentence, an' it wasn't signed.

"The second letter was written more than two years after the first. It was from Salt Lake City. It simply said that Milly had heard her brother was on her trail. She asked Frank to tell her brother to give up the search because if he didn't she would suffer in a way too horrible to tell. She didn't beg. She just stated a fact an' made the simple request. An' she ended that letter by sayin' she would soon leave Salt Lake City with the man she had come to love, an' would never be heard of again.

"I recognized Milly's handwritin', an' I recognized her way of puttin' things. But that second letter told me of some great change in her. Ponderin' over it, I felt at last she'd either come to love that feller an' his religion, or some terrible fear made her lie an' say so. I couldn't be sure which. But, of course, I meant to find out. I'll say here, if I'd known Mormons then as I do now I'd left Milly to her fate. For mebbe she was right about what she'd suffer if I kept on her trail. But I was young an' wild them days. First I went to the town where she'd first been taken, an' I went to the place where she'd been kept. I got that skunk who owned the place, an' took him out in the woods, an' made him tell all he knowed. That wasn't much as to length, but it was pure hell's-fire in substance.

This time I left him some incapacitated for any more skunk work short of hell. Then I hit the trail for Utah.

"That was fourteen years ago. I saw the incomin' of most of the Mormons. It was a wild country an' a wild time. I rode from town to town, village to village, ranch to ranch, camp to camp. I never stayed long in one place. I never had but one idea. I never rested. Four years went by, an' I knowed every trail in northern Utah. I kept on an' as time went by, an' I'd begun to grow old in my search, I had firmer, blinder faith in whatever was guidin' me. Once I read about a feller who sailed the seven seas an' traveled the world, an' he had a story to tell, an' whenever he seen the man to whom he must tell that story he knowed him on sight. I was like that, only I had a question to ask. An' always I knew the man of whom I must ask. So I never really lost the trail, though for years it was the dimmest trail ever followed by any man.

"Then come a change in my luck. Along in central Utah I rounded up Hurd, an' I whispered somethin' in his ear, an' watched his face, an' then throwed a gun against his bowels. An' he died with his teeth so tight shut I couldn't have pried them open with a knife. Slack an' Metzger that same year both heard me whisper the same question, an' neither would they speak a word when they lay dyin'. Long before I'd learned no man of this breed or class—or God knows what—would give up any secrets! I had to see in a man's fear of death the connections with Milly Erne's fate. An' as the years passed at long intervals I would find such a man.

"So as I drifted on the long trail down into southern Utah my name preceded me, an' I had to meet a people prepared for me, an' ready with guns. They made me a gunman. An' that suited me. In all this time signs of the proselyter an' the giant with the blue-ice eyes an' the gold beard seemed to fade dimmer out of the trail. Only twice in ten years did I find a trace of that mysterious man who had visited the proselyter at my home village. What he had to do with Milly's fate was beyond all hope for me to learn, unless my guidin' spirit led me to him! As for the other man, I knew, as sure as I breathed an' the stars shone an' the wind blew, that I'd meet him some day.

"Eighteen years I've been on the trail. An' it led me to the last lonely villages of the Utah border. Eighteen years! . . . I feel pretty old now. I was only twenty when I hit that trail. Well, as I told you, back here a ways a Gentile said Jane Withersteen could tell me about Milly Erne an' show me her grave!"

The low voice ceased, and Lassiter slowly turned his sombrero round and round, and appeared to be counting the silver ornaments on the band. Jane, leaning toward him, sat as if petrified, listening intently, waiting to hear more. She could have shrieked, but power of tongue and lips were denied her. She saw only this sad, gray, passion-worn man, and she heard only the faint rustling of the leaves.

"Well, I came to Cottonwoods," went on Lassiter, "an' you showed me

Milly's grave. An' though your teeth have been shut tighter 'n them of all the dead men lyin' back along that trail, jest the same you told me the secret I've lived these eighteen years to hear! Jane, I said you'd tell me without ever me askin'. I didn't need to ask my question here. The day, you remember, when that fat party throwed a gun on me in your court, an'—"

"Oh! Hush!" whispered Jane, blindly holding up her hands.

"I seen in your face that Dyer, now a bishop, was the proselyter who ruined Milly Erne!"

For an instant Jane Withersteen's brain was a whirling chaos, and she recovered to find herself grasping at Lassiter like one drowning. And as if by a lightning stroke she sprang from her dull apathy into exquisite torture.

"It's a lie! Lassiter! No, no!" she moaned. "I swear—you're wrong!"

"Stop! You'd perjure yourself! But I'll spare you that. You poor woman! Still blind! Still faithful! . . . Listen. I *know*. Let that settle it. An' I give up my purpose!"

"What is it—you say?"

"I give up my purpose. I've come to see an' feel differently. I can't help poor Milly. An' I've outgrowed revenge. I've come to see I can be no judge for men. I can't kill a man jest for hate. Hate ain't the same with me since I loved you and little Fay."

"Lassiter! You mean you won't kill him?" Jane whispered.

"No."

"For my sake?"

"I reckon. I can't understand, but I'll respect your feelin's."

"Because you—oh, because you love me? . . . Eighteen years! You were that terrible Lassiter! And *now*— because you love me?"

"That's it, Jane."

"Oh, you'll make me love you! How can I help but love you? My heart must be stone. But—oh, Lassiter, wait, wait! Give me time. I'm not what I was. Once it was so easy to love. Now it's easy to hate. Wait! My faith in God—*some* God—still lives. By it I see happier times for you, poor passion-swayed wanderer! For me—a miserable, broken woman. I loved your sister Milly. I *will* love you. I can't have fallen so low—I can't be so abandoned by God—that I've no love left to give you. Wait! Let us forget Milly's sad life. Ah, I knew it as no one else on earth! There's one thing I shall tell you—if you are at my deathbed, but I can't speak now."

"I reckon I don't want to hear no more," said Lassiter.

Jane leaned against him; as if some pent-up force had rent its way out, she fell into a paroxysm of weeping. Lassiter held her in silent sympathy. By degrees she regained composure, and she was rising, sensible of being relieved of a weighty burden, when a sudden start on Lassiter's part alarmed her.

"I heard hosses—hosses with muffled hoofs!" he said; and he got up guardedly.

"Where's Fay?" asked Jane, hurriedly glancing round the shady knoll. The bright-haired child, who had appeared to be close all the time, was not in sight.

"Fay!" called Jane.

No answering shout of glee. No patter of flying feet. Jane saw Lassiter stiffen.

"Fay—oh—Fay!" Jane almost screamed.

The leaves quivered and rustled; a lonesome cricket chirped in the grass; a bee hummed by. The silence of the waning afternoon breathed hateful portent. It terrified Jane. When had silence been so infernal?

"She's—only—strayed—out—of—earshot," faltered Jane, looking at Lassiter.

Pale, rigid as a statue, the rider stood, not in listening, searching posture, but in one of doomed certainty. Suddenly he grasped Jane with an iron hand, and, turning his face from her gaze, he strode with her from the knoll.

"See—Fay played here last—a house of stones an' sticks. . . . An' here's a corral of pebbles with leaves for hosses," said Lassiter, stridently, and pointed to the ground. "Back an' forth she trailed here . . . See, she's buried somethin'—a dead grasshopper—there's a tombstone . . . here she went, chasin' a lizard—see the tiny streaked trail . . . she pulled bark off this cottonwood . . . look in the dust of the path—the letters you taught her—she's drawn pictures of birds an' hosses an' people. . . . Look, a cross! Oh, Jane, *your* cross!"

Lassiter dragged Jane on, and as if from a book read the meaning of little Fay's trail. All the way down the knoll, through the shrubbery, round and round a cottonwood, Fay's vagrant fancy left records of her sweet musings and innocent play. Long had she lingered round a bird-nest to leave therein the gaudy wing of a butterfly. Long had she played beside the running stream, sending adrift vessels freighted with pebbly cargo. Then she had wandered through the deep grass, her tiny feet scarcely turning a fragile blade, and she had dreamed beside some old faded flowers. Thus her steps led her into the broad lane. The little dimpled imprints of her bare feet showed clean-cut in the dust; they went a little way down the lane; and then, at a point where they stopped, the great tracks of a man led out from the shrubbery and returned.

❧20❧

LASSITER'S WAY

OOTPRINTS told the story of little Fay's abduction. In anguish Jane Withersteen turned speechlessly to Lassiter, and, confirming her fears, she saw him gray-faced, aged all in a moment, stricken as if by a mortal blow.

Then all her life seemed to fall about her in wreck and ruin.

"It's all over," she heard her voice whisper. "It's ended. I'm going—I'm going—"

"Where?" demanded Lassiter, suddenly looming darkly over her.

"To—to those cruel men—"

"Speak names!" thundered Lassiter.

"To Bishop Dyer—to Tull," went on Jane, shocked into obedience.

"Well—what for?"

"I want little Fay. I can't live without her. They've stolen her as they stole Milly Erne's child. I must have little Fay. I want only her. I give up. I'll go and tell Bishop Dyer—I'm broken. I'll tell him I'm ready for the yoke—only give me back Fay—and—and I'll marry Tull!"

"*Never!*" hissed Lassiter.

His long arm leaped at her. Almost running, he dragged her under the cottonwoods, across the court, into the huge hall of Withersteen House, and he shut the door with a force that jarred the heavy walls. Black Star and Night and Bells, since their return, had been locked in this hall, and now they stamped on the stone floor.

Lassiter released Jane and like a dizzy man swayed from her with a hoarse cry and leaned shaking against a table where he kept his rider's accoutrements. He began to fumble in his saddle-bags. His action brought a clinking, metallic sound—the rattling of gun-cartridges. His fingers trembled as he slipped cartridges into an extra belt. But as he buckled it over the one he habitually wore his hands became steady. This second belt contained two guns, smaller than the black ones swinging low, and he slipped them round so that his coat hid them. Then he fell to swift action. Jane Withersteen watched him, fascinated but uncomprehending; and she saw him rapidly saddle Black Star and Night. Then he drew her into the light of the huge window, standing over her, gripping her arm with fingers like cold steel.

"Yes, Jane, it's ended—but you're not goin' to Dyer! . . . *I'm goin' instead!*"

Looking at him—he was so terrible of aspect—she could not comprehend his words. Who was this man with the face gray as death, with eyes that would have made her shriek had she the strength, with the strange, ruthlessly bitter lips? Where was the gentle Lassiter? What was this presence in the hall, about him, about her—this cold, invisible presence?

"Yes, it's ended, Jane," he was saying, so awfully quiet and cool and implacable, "an' I'm goin' to make a little call. I'll lock you in here, an' when I get back have the saddle-bags full of meat an' bread. An' be ready to ride!"

"Lassiter!" cried Jane.

Desperately she tried to meet his gray eyes, in vain; desperately she tried again, fought herself as feeling and thought resurged in torment, and she succeeded; and then she knew.

"No—no—no!" she wailed. "You said you'd foregone your vengeance. You promised not to kill Bishop Dyer."

"If you want to talk to me about him—leave off the bishop. I don't understand that name, or its use."

"Oh, hadn't you foregone your vengeance on—on Dyer?"

"Yes."

"But—your actions—your words—your guns—your terrible looks! . . . They don't seem foregoing vengeance?"

"Jane, now it's justice."

"You'll—kill him?"

"If God lets me live another hour! If not God—then the devil who drives me!"

"You'll kill him—for yourself—for your vengeful hate?"

"No!"

"For Milly Erne's sake?"

"No."

"For little Fay's?"

"No!"

"Oh—for whose?"

"*For yours!*"

"His blood on my soul!" whispered Jane, and she fell to her knees. This was the long-pending hour of fruition. And the habit of years—the religious passion of her life—leaped from lethargy, and the long months of gradual drifting to doubt were as if they had never been. "If you spill his blood it'll be on my soul—and on my father's. Listen." And she clasped his knees, and clung there as he tried to raise her. "Listen. Am I nothing to you?"

"Woman—don't trifle at words! I love you! An' I'll soon prove it!"

"I'll give myself to you—I'll ride away with you—marry you, if only you'll spare him?"

His answer was a cold, ringing, terrible laugh.

"Lassiter—I'll love you. Spare him!"

"No!"

She sprang up in despairing, breaking spirit, and encircled his neck with her arms, and held him in an embrace that he strove vainly to loosen. "Lassiter, would you kill me? I'm fighting my last fight for the principles of my youth—love of religion, love of father. You don't know—you can't guess the truth, and I can't speak it! I'm losing all. I'm changing. All I've gone through is nothing to this hour. Pity me—help me in my weakness. You're strong again—oh, so cruelly, coldly strong! You're killing me. I see you—feel you as some other Lassiter! My master, be merciful—spare him!"

His answer was a ruthless smile.

She clung the closer to him, and leaned her panting breast on him, and lifted her face to his. "Lassiter, *I do love you!* It's leaped out of my agony. It comes suddenly with a terrible blow of truth. You are a man! I never knew it till now. Some wonderful change came to me when you buckled on those guns and showed that gray, awful face. I loved you then. All my life I've loved, but never as now. No woman can love like a broken woman. If it were not for one thing—just one thing—and yet! I *can't* speak it—I'd glory in your manhood—the lion in you that means to slay for me. Believe me—and spare Dyer. Be merciful—great as it's in you to be great. . . . Oh, listen and believe—I have nothing, but I'm a woman—a beautiful woman, Lassiter—a passionate, loving woman—and I love you! Take me—hide me in some wild place—and love me and mend my broken heart. Spare him and take me away."

She lifted her face closer and closer to his, until their lips nearly touched, and she hung upon his neck, and with strength almost spent pressed and still pressed her palpitating body to his.

"Kiss me!" she whispered, blindly.

"No—not at your price!" he answered. His voice had changed or she had lost clearness of hearing.

"Kiss me! . . . Are you a man? Kiss me and save me!"

"Jane, you never played fair with me. But now you're blisterin' your lips—blackenin' your soul with lies!"

"By the memory of my mother—by my Bible—no! No, I *have* no Bible! But by my hope of heaven I swear I love you!"

Lassiter's gray lips formed soundless words that meant even her love could not avail to bend his will. As if the hold of her arms was that of a child's he loosened it and stepped away.

"Wait! Don't go! Oh, hear a last word! . . . May a more just and merciful God than the God I was taught to worship judge me—forgive me—save me! For I can no longer keep silent! . . . Lassiter, in pleading for Dyer I've been pleading more for my father. My father was a Mormon master, close to the leaders of the church. It was my father who sent Dyer out to proselyte. It was my father who had the blue-ice eye and the beard of gold. It was my father you got trace of in the past years. Truly, Dyer ruined Milly Erne—dragged her from her home—to Utah—to Cottonwoods. *But it was for my father!* If Milly Erne was ever wife of a Mormon that Mormon was my father! I never knew—never will know whether or not she was a wife. Blind I may be, Lassiter—fanatically faithful to a false religion I may have been, but I know justice, and my father is beyond human justice. Surely he is meeting just punishment—somewhere. Always it has appalled me—the thought of your killing Dyer for my father's sins. So I have prayed!"

"Jane, the past is dead. In my love for you I forgot the past. This thing I'm about to do ain't for myself or Milly or Fay. It's not because of anythin' that ever happened in the past, but for what is happenin' right *now*. *It's for you!* . . . An' listen. Since I was a boy I've never thanked God for anythin'. If there is a God—an' I've come to believe it—I thank Him now for the years that made me Lassiter! . . . I can reach down an' feel these big guns, an' know what I can do with them. An', Jane, only one of the miracles Dyer professes to believe in can save him!"

Again for Jane Withersteen came the spinning of her brain in darkness, and as she whirled in endless chaos she seemed to be falling at the feet of a luminous figure—a man—Lassiter—who had saved her from herself, who could not be changed, who would slay rightfully. Then she slipped into utter blackness.

When she recovered from her faint she became aware that she was lying on a couch near the window in her sitting room. Her brow felt damp and cold and wet; someone was chafing her hands; she recognized Judkins, and then saw that his lean, hard face wore the hue and look of excessive agitation.

"Judkins!" Her voice broke weakly.

"Aw, Miss Withersteen, you're comin' round fine. Now jest lay still a little. You're all right; everythin's all right."

"Where is—he?"

"Who?"

"Lassiter!"

"You needn't worry none about him."

"Where is he? Tell me—instantly."

"Wal, he's in the other room patchin' up a few triflin' bullet holes."

"Ah! . . . Bishop Dyer?"

"When I seen him last—a matter of half an hour ago, he was on his knees. He was some busy, *but* he wasn't prayin'!"

"How strangely you talk! I'll sit up. I'm—well, strong again. Tell me. Dyer on his knees! What was he doing?"

"Wal, beggin' your pardon fer blunt talk, Miss Withersteen, Dyer was on his knees an' *not* prayin'. You remember his big, broad hands? You've seen 'em raised in blessin' over old gray men an' little curly-headed children like—like Fay Larkin! Come to think of thet, I disremember ever hearin' of his liftin' his big hands in blessin' over a *woman*. Wal, when I seen him last—jest a little while ago—he was on his knees, *not* prayin', as I remarked—an' he was pressin' his big hands over some bigger wounds."

"Man, you drive me mad! Did Lassiter kill Dyer?"

"Yes."

"Did he kill Tull?"

"No. Tull's out of the village with most of his riders. He's expected back before evenin'. Lassiter will hev to git away before Tull an' his riders come in. It's sure death fer him here. An' wuss fer you, too, Miss Withersteen. There'll be some of an uprisin' when Tull gits back."

"I shall ride away with Lassiter. Judkins, tell me all you saw—all you know about this killing." She realized, without wonder or amaze, how Judkins's one word, affirming the death of Dyer—that the catastrophe had fallen—had completed the change whereby she had been molded or beaten or broken into another woman. She felt calm, slightly cold, strong as she had not been strong since the first shadow fell upon her.

"I jest saw about all of it, Miss Withersteen, an' I'll be glad to tell you if you'll only hev patience with me," said Judkins, earnestly. "You see, I've been pecooliarly interested, an' nat'rully I'm some excited. An' I talk a lot thet mebbe ain't necessary, but I can't help thet.

"I was at the meetin'-house where Dyer was holdin' court. You know he allus acts as magistrate an' judge when Tull's away. An' the trial was fer tryin' what's left of my boy riders—thet helped me hold your cattle—fer a lot of hatched-up things the boys never did. We're used to thet, an' the boys wouldn't hev minded bein' locked up fer a while, or hevin' to dig ditches, or whatever the judge laid down. You see, I divided the gold you give me among all my boys, an' they all hid it, an' they all feel rich. Howsomever, court was adjourned before the judge passed sentence. Yes, ma'am, court was adjourned some strange an' quick, much as if lighthin' hed struck the meetin'-house.

"I hed trouble attendin' the trial, but I got in. There was a good many people there, all my boys, an' Judge Dyer with his several clerks. Also he hed with him the five riders who've been guardin' him pretty close of late. They was Carter, Wright, Jengessen, an' two new riders from Stone Bridge. I didn't hear their names, but I heard they was handy men with guns an' they looked more like rustlers than riders. Anyway, there they was, the five all in a row.

"Judge Dyer was tellin' Willie Kern, one of my best an' steadiest boys— Dyer was tellin' him how there was a ditch opened near Willie's home lettin' water through his lot, where it hadn't ought to go. An' Willie was tryin' to get a word in to prove he wasn't at home all the day it happened —which was true, as I know—but Willie couldn't git a word in, an' then Judge Dyer went on layin' down the law. An' all to onct he happened to look down the long room. An' if ever any man turned to stone he was thet man.

"Nat'rully I looked back to see what hed acted so powerful strange on the judge. An' there, halfway up the room, in the middle of the wide aisle, stood Lassiter! All white an' black he looked, an' I can't think of anythin' he resembled, onless it's death. Venters made thet same room some still an' chilly when he called Tull; but this was different. I give my word, Miss Withersteen, thet I went cold to my very marrow. I don't know why. But Lassiter has a way about him thet's awful. He spoke a word—a name—I couldn't understand it, though he spoke clear as a bell. I was too excited, mebbe. Judge Dyer must hev understood it, an' a lot more thet was mystery to me, fer he pitched forward out of his chair right onto the platform.

"Then them five riders, Dyer's bodyguards, they jumped up, an' two of them thet I found out afterward were the strangers from Stone Bridge, they piled right out of a winder, so quick you couldn't catch your breath. It was plain they wasn't Mormons.

"Jengessen, Carter, an' Wright eyed Lassiter, for what must hev been a second an' seemed like an hour, an' they went white an' strung. But they didn't weaken nor lose their nerve.

"I hed a good look at Lassiter. He stood sort of stiff, bendin' a little, an' both his arms were crooked, an' his hands looked like a hawk's claws. But there ain't no tellin' how his eyes looked. I know this, though, an' thet is his eyes could read the mind of any man about to throw a gun. An' in watchin' him, of course, I couldn't see the three men go fer their guns. An' though I was lookin' right at Lassiter—lookin' hard—I couldn't see how he drawed. He was quicker 'n eyesight—thet's all. But I seen the red spurtin' of his guns, an' heard his shots jest the very littlest instant before I heard the shots of the riders. An' when I turned, Wright an' Carter was down, an' Jengessen, who's tough like a steer, was pullin' the trigger of a wabblin' gun. But it was plain he was shot through, plumb center. An' sudden he fell with a crash, an' his gun clattered on the floor.

"Then there was a hell of a silence. Nobody breathed. Sartin I didn't, anyway. I saw Lassiter slip a smokin' gun back in a belt. But he hadn't throwed either of the big black guns, an' I thought thet strange. An' all this was happenin' quick—you can't imagine how quick.

"There come a scrapin' on the floor an' Dyer got up, his face like lead. I wanted to watch Lassiter, but Dyer's face, onct I seen it like thet, glued my eyes. I seen him go fer his gun—why, I could hev done better, quicker —an' then there was a thunderin' shot from Lassiter, an' it hit Dyer's right arm, an' his gun went off as it dropped. He looked at Lassiter like a cornered sage-wolf, an' sort of howled, an' reached down fer his gun. He'd jest picked it off the floor an' was raisin' it when another thunderin' shot almost tore thet arm off—so it seemed to me. The gun dropped again an' he went down on his knees, kind of flounderin' after it. It was some strange an' terrible to see his awful earnestness. Why would such a man cling so to life? Anyway, he got the gun with left hand an' was raisin' it, pullin' trigger in his madness, when the third thunderin' shot hit his left arm, an' he dropped the gun again. But thet left arm wasn't useless yet, fer he grabbed up the gun, an' with a shakin' aim thet would hev been pitiful to me—in any other man—he began to shoot. One wild bullet struck a man twenty feet from Lassiter. An' it killed thet man, as I seen afterward. Then come a bunch of thunderin' shots—nine I calkilated after, fer they come so quick I couldn't count them—an' I knew Lassiter hed turned the black guns loose on Dyer.

"I'm tellin' you straight, Miss Withersteen, fer I want you to know. Afterward you'll get over it. I've seen some soul-rackin' scenes on this Utah border, but this was the awfulest. I remember I closed my eyes, an' fer a minute I thought of the strangest things, out of place there, such as you'd never dream would come to mind. I saw the sage, an' runnin' hosses—an' thet's the beautifulest sight to me—an' I saw dim things in the dark, an' there was a kind of hummin' in my ears. An' I remember distinctly—fer it was what made all these things whirl out of my mind an' opened my eyes—I remember distinctly it was the smell of gunpowder.

"The court had about adjourned fer thet judge. He was on his knees, an' he wasn't prayin'. He was gaspin' an' tryin' to press his big, floppin', crippled hands over his body. Lassiter had sent all those last thunderin' shots through his body. Thet was Lassiter's way.

"An' Lassiter spoke, an' if I ever forgit his words I'll never forgit the sound of his voice.

" '*Proselyter*, I reckon you'd better call quick on thet God who reveals Hisself to you on earth, because He won't be visitin' the place you're goin' to!'

"An' then I seen Dyer look at his big, hangin' hands thet wasn't big enough fer the last work he set them to. An' he looked up at Lassiter. An' then he stared horrible at somethin' thet wasn't Lassiter, nor anyone there, nor the room, nor the branches of purple sage peepin' into the winder. Whatever he seen, it was with the look of a man who *discovers* somethin' too late. Thet's a terrible look! . . . An' with a horrible *understandin'* cry he slid forrard on his face."

Judkins paused in his narrative, breathing heavily while he wiped his perspiring brow.

"Thet's about all," he concluded. "Lassiter left the meetin'-house an' I hurried to catch up with him. He was bleedin' from three gunshots, none of them much to bother him. An' we come right up here. I found you layin' in the hall, an' I hed to work some over you."

Jane Withersteen offered up no prayer for Dyer's soul.

Lassiter's step sounded in the hall—the familiar soft, silver-clinking step—and she heard it with thrilling new emotions in which was a vague joy in her very fear of him. The door opened, and she saw him, the old

Lassiter, slow, easy, gentle, cool, yet not exactly the same Lassiter. She rose, and for a moment her eyes blurred and swam in tears.

"Are you—all—all right?" she asked, tremulously.

"I reckon."

"Lassiter, I'll ride away with you. Hide me till danger is past—till we are forgotten—then take me where you will. Your people shall be my people, and your God my God!"

He kissed her hand with the quaint grace and courtesy that came to him in rare moments.

"Black Star an' Night are ready," he said, simply.

His quiet mention of the black racers spurred Jane to action. Hurrying to her room, she changed to her rider's suit, packed her jewelry, and the gold that was left, and all the woman's apparel for which there was space in the saddle-bags, and then returned to the hall. Black Star stamped his iron-shod hoofs and tossed his beautiful head, and eyed her with knowing eyes.

"Judkins, I give Bells to you," said Jane. "I hope you will always keep him and be good to him."

Judkins mumbled thanks that he could not speak fluently, and his eyes flashed.

Lassiter strapped Jane's saddle-bags upon Black Star, and led the racers out into the court.

"Judkins, you ride with Jane out into the sage. If you see any riders comin' shout quick twice. An', Jane, *don't look back!* I'll catch up soon. We'll get to the break into the Pass before midnight, an' then wait until mornin' to go down."

Black Star bent his graceful neck and bowed his noble head, and his broad shoulders yielded as he knelt for Jane to mount.

She rode out of the court beside Judkins, through the grove, across the wide lane into the sage, and she realized that she was leaving Withersteen House forever, and she did not look back. A strange, dreamy, calm peace pervaded her soul. Her doom had fallen upon her, but, instead of finding life no longer worth living she found it doubly significant, full of sweetness as the western breeze, beautiful and unknown as the sage-slope stretching its purple sunset shadows before her. She became aware of Judkins's hand touching hers; she heard him speak a husky goodbye; then into the place of Bells shot the dead-black, keen, racy nose of Night, and she knew Lassiter rode beside her.

"Don't—look—back!" he said, and his voice, too, was not clear.

Facing straight ahead, seeing only the waving, shadowy sage, Jane held out her gauntleted hand, to feel it enclosed in strong clasp. So she rode on without a backward glance at the beautiful grove of Cottonwoods. She did not seem to think of the past, of what she left forever, but of the color and mystery and wildness of the sage-slope leading down to Deception Pass, and of the future. She watched the shadows lengthen down the slope; she felt the cool west wind sweeping by from the rear; and she wondered at low, yellow clouds sailing swiftly over her and beyond.

"*Don't—look—back!*" said Lassiter.

Thick-driving belts of smoke traveled by on the wind, and with it came a strong, pungent odor of burning wood.

Lassiter had fired Withersteen House! But Jane did not look back.

A misty veil obscured the clear, searching gaze she had kept steadfastly upon the purple slope and the dim lines of canyons. It passed, as passed the rolling clouds of smoke, and she saw the valley deepening into the shades of twilight. Night came on, swift as the fleet racers, and stars peeped out to brighten and grow, and the huge, windy, eastern heave of sage-level paled under a rising moon and turned to silver. Blanched in moonlight, the sage yet seemed to hold its hue of purple and was infinitely more wild and lonely. So the night hours wore on, and Jane Withersteen never once looked back.

⁘21⁘

BLACK STAR
AND NIGHT

THE TIME had come for Venters and Bess to leave their retreat. They were at great pains to choose the few things they would be able to carry with them on the journey out of Utah.

"Bern, whatever kind of a pack's this, anyhow?" questioned Bess, rising from her work with reddened face.

Venters, absorbed in his own task, did not look up at all, and in reply said he had brought so much from Cottonwoods that he did not recollect the half of it.

"A woman packed this!" Bess exclaimed.

He scarcely caught her meaning, but the peculiar tone of her voice caused him instantly to rise, and he saw Bess on her knees before an open pack which he recognized as the one given him by Jane.

"By George!" he ejaculated, guiltily, and then at sight of Bess's face he laughed outright.

"A woman packed this," she repeated, fixing woeful, tragic eyes on him.

"Well, is that a crime?"

"There—there *is* a woman, after all!"

"Now Bess—"

"You've lied to me!"

Then and there Venters found it imperative to postpone work for the present. All her life Bess had been isolated, but she had inherited certain elements of the eternal feminine.

"But there *was* a woman and you *did* lie to me," she kept repeating, after he had explained.

"What of that? Bess, I'll get angry at you in a moment. Remember you've been pent up all your life. I venture to say that if you'd been out in the world you'd have had a dozen sweethearts and have told many a lie before this."

"I wouldn't anything of the kind," declared Bess, indignantly.

"Well—perhaps not lie. But you'd have had the sweethearts. You couldn't have helped that—being so pretty."

This remark appeared to be a very clever and fortunate one; and the work of selecting and then of stowing all the packs in the cave went on without further interruption.

Venters closed up the opening of the cave with a thatch of willows and aspens, so that not even a bird or a rat could get into the sacks of grain. And this work was in order with the precaution habitually observed by him. He might not be able to get out of Utah, and have to return to the valley. But he owed it to Bess to make the attempt, and in case they were compelled to turn back he wanted to find that fine store of food and grain intact. The outfit of implements and utensils he packed away in another cave.

"Bess, we have enough to live here all our lives," he said once, dreamily.

"Shall I go roll Balancing Rock?" she asked, in light speech, but with deep-blue fire in her eyes.

"No—no."

"Ah, you don't forget the gold and the world," she sighed.

"Child, you forget the beautiful dresses and the travel—and everything."

"Oh, I want to go. But I want to stay!"

"I feel the same way."

They let the eight calves out of the corral, and kept only two of the burros Venters had brought from Cottonwoods. These they intended to hide. Bess freed all her pets—the quail and rabbits and foxes.

The last sunset and twilight and night were both the sweetest and saddest they had ever spent in Surprise Valley. Morning brought keen exhilaration and excitement. When Venters had saddled the two burros, strapped on the light packs and the two canteens, the sunlight was dispersing the lazy shadows from the valley. Taking a last look at the caves and the silver spruces, Venters and Bess made a reluctant start, leading the burros. Ring and Whitie looked keen and knowing. Something seemed to drag at Venters's feet and he noticed Bess lagged behind. Never had the climb from terrace to bridge appeared so long.

Not till they reached the opening of the gorge did they stop to rest and take one last look at the valley. The tremendous arch of stone curved clear and sharp in outline against the morning sky. And through it streaked the golden shaft. The valley seemed an enchanted circle of glorious veils of gold and wraiths of white and silver haze and dim, blue, moving shade—beautiful and wild and unreal as a dream.

"We—we can—th—think of it—always—re—remember," sobbed Bess.

"Hush! Don't cry. Our valley has only fitted us for a better life somewhere. Come!"

They entered the gorge and he closed the willow gate. From rosy, golden morning light they passed into cool, dense gloom. The burros pattered up the trail with little hollow-cracking steps. And the gorge widened to narrow outlet and the gloom lightened to gray. At the divide they halted for another rest. Venters's keen, remembering gaze searched Balancing Rock, and the long incline, and the cracked toppling walls, but failed to note the slightest change.

The dogs led the descent; then came Bess leading her burro; then Venters leading his. Bess kept her eyes bent downward. Venters, however, had an irresistible desire to look upward at Balancing Rock. It had always haunted him, and now he wondered if he were really to get through the outlet before the huge stone thundered down. He fancied that would be a miracle. Every few steps he answered to the strange, nervous fear and turned to make sure the rock still stood like a giant statue. And, as he descended, it grew dimmer in his sight. It changed form; it swayed; it nodded darkly; and at last, in his heightened fancy, he saw it heave and roll. As in a dream when he felt himself falling yet knew he would never fall, so he saw this long-standing thunderbolt of the little stone-men plunge down to close forever the outlet to Deception Pass.

And while he was giving way to unaccountable dread imaginations the descent was accomplished without mishap.

"I'm glad that's over," he said, breathing more freely. "I hope I'm by that hanging rock for good and all. Since almost the moment I first saw it I've had an idea that it was waiting for me. Now, when it does fall, if I'm thousands of miles away, I'll hear it."

With the first glimpses of the smooth slope leading down to the grotesque cedars and out to the Pass, Venters's cool nerve returned. One long survey to the left, then one to the right, satisfied his caution. Leading the burros down to the spur of rock, he halted at the steep incline.

"Bess, here's the bad place, the place I told you about, with the cut steps. You start down, leading your burro. Take your time and hold on to him if you slip. I've got a rope on him and a half-hitch on this point of rock, so I can get him down safely. Coming up here was a killing job. But it'll be easy going down."

Both burros passed down the difficult stairs cut by the cliff-dwellers, and did it without a misstep. After that the descent down the slope and over the mile of scrawled, ribbed, and ridged rock required only careful guidance, and Venters got the burros to level ground in a condition that caused him to congratulate himself.

"Oh, if we only had Wrangle!" exclaimed Venters. "But we're lucky. That's the worst of our trail passed. We've only men to fear now. If we get up in the sage we can hide and slip along like coyotes."

They mounted and rode west through the valley and entered the canyon. From time to time Venters walked, leading his burro. When they got by all the canyons and gullies opening into the Pass they went faster and with fewer halts. Venters did not confide in Bess the alarming fact that he had seen horses and smoke less than a mile up one of the intersecting canyons. He did not talk at all. And long after he had passed this canyon and felt secure once more in the certainty that they had been unobserved he never relaxed his watchfulness. But he did not walk anymore, and he kept the burros at a steady trot. Night fell before they reached the last water in the Pass and they made camp by starlight. Venters did not want the burros to stray, so he tied them with long halters in the grass near the spring. Bess, tired out and silent, laid her head in a saddle and went to sleep between the two dogs. Venters did not close his eyes. The canyon silence appeared full of the low, continuous hum of insects. He listened until the hum grew into a roar, and then, breaking the spell, once more he heard it low and clear. He watched the stars and the moving shadows, and always his glance returned to the girl's dimly pale face. And he remembered how white and still it had once looked in the starlight. And again stern thought fought his strange fancies. Would all his labor and his love be for naught? Would he lose her, after all? What did the dark shadow around her portend? Did calamity lurk on that long upland trail through the sage? Why should his heart swell and throb with nameless fear? He listened to the silence, and told himself that in the broad light of day he could dispel this leaden-weighted dread.

At the first hint of gray over the eastern rim he awoke Bess, saddled the burros, and began the day's travel. He wanted to get out of the Pass before there was any chance of riders coming down. They gained the break as the first red rays of the rising sun colored the rim.

For once, so eager was he to get up to level ground, he did not send

Ring or Whitie in advance. Encouraging Bess to hurry, pulling at his patient, plodding burro, he climbed the soft, steep trail.

Brighter and brighter grew the light. He mounted the last broken edge of rim to have the sun-fired, purple sage-slope burst upon him as a glory. Bess panted up to his side, tugging on the halter of her burro.

"We're up!" he cried joyously. "There's not a dot on the sage. We're safe. We'll not be seen! Oh, Bess—"

Ring growled and sniffed the keen air and bristled. Venters clutched at his rifle. Whitie sometimes made a mistake, but Ring never. The dull thud of hoofs almost deprived Venters of power to turn and see from where disaster threatened. He felt his eyes dilate as he stared at Lassiter leading Black Star and Night out of the sage, with Jane Withersteen, in rider's costume, close beside them.

For an instant Venters felt himself whirl dizzily in the center of vast circles of sage. He recovered partially, enough to see Lassiter standing with a glad smile and Jane riveted in astonishment.

"Why, Bern!" she exclaimed. "How good it is to see you! We're riding away, you see. The storm burst—and I'm a ruined woman! . . . I thought you were alone."

Venters, unable to speak for consternation, and bewildered out of all sense of what he ought or ought not to do, simply stared at Jane.

"Son, where are you bound for?" asked Lassiter.

"Not safe—where I was. I'm—we're going out of Utah—back East," he found tongue to say.

"I reckon this meetin's the luckiest thing that ever happened to you an' to me—an' to Jane—an' to Bess," said Lassiter, coolly.

"*Bess!*" cried Jane, with a sudden leap of blood to her pale cheek.

It was entirely beyond Venters to see any luck in that meeting.

Jane Withersteen took one, flashing, woman's glance at Bess's scarlet face, at her slender, shapely form.

"Venters! Is this a girl—a woman?" she questioned, in a voice that stung.

"Yes."

"Did you have her in that wonderful valley?"

"Yes, but Jane—"

"All the time you were gone?"

"Yes, but I couldn't tell—"

"Was is for *her* you asked me to give you supplies? Was it for *her* that you wanted to make your valley a paradise?"

"Oh—Jane—"

"Answer me."

"Yes."

"Oh, you liar!" And with these passionate words Jane Withersteen succumbed to fury. For the second time in her life she fell into the ungovernable rage that had been her father's weakness. And it was worse than his, for she was a jealous woman—jealous even of her friends.

As best he could, he bore the brunt of her anger. It was not only his deceit to her that she visited upon him, but her betrayal by religion, by life itself.

Her passion, like fire at white heat, consumed itself in little time. Her physical strength failed, and still her spirit attempted to go on in magnificent denunciation of those who had wronged her. Like a tree cut deep into its roots, she began to quiver and shake, and her anger weakened into despair. And her ringing voice sank into a broken, husky whisper. Then, spent and pitiable, upheld by Lassiter's arm, she turned and hid her face in Black Star's mane.

Numb as Venters was when at length Jane Withersteen lifted her head and looked at him, he yet suffered a pang.

"Jane, this girl is innocent!" he cried.

"Can you expect me to believe that?" she asked, with weary, bitter eyes.

"I'm not that kind of a liar. And you know it. If I lied—if I kept silent when honor should have made me speak, it was to spare you. I came to Cottonwoods to tell you. But I couldn't add to your pain. I intended to tell you I had come to love this girl. But, Jane, I hadn't forgotten how good you were to me. I haven't changed at all toward you. I prize your friendship as I always have. But, however it may look to you—don't be unjust. The girl is innocent. Ask Lassiter."

"Jane, she's jest as sweet an' innocent as little Fay," said Lassiter. There was a faint smile upon his face and a beautiful light.

Venters saw, and knew that Lassiter saw, how Jane Withersteen's tortured soul wrestled with hate and threw it—with scorn, doubt, suspicion, and overcame all.

"Bern, if in my misery I accused you unjustly, I crave forgiveness," she said. "I'm not what I once was. Tell me—who is this girl?"

"Jane, she is Oldring's daughter, and his Masked Rider. Lassiter will tell you how I shot her for a rustler, saved her life—all the story. It's a strange story, Jane, as wild as the sage. But it's true—true as her innocence. That you must believe!"

"Oldring's Masked Rider! Oldring's daughter!" exclaimed Jane. "And she's innocent! You ask me to believe much. If this girl is—is what you say, how could she be going away with the man who killed her father?"

"Why did you tell that?" cried Venters, passionately.

Jane's question had roused Bess out of stupefaction. Her eyes suddenly darkened and dilated. She stepped toward Venters and held up both hands as if to ward off a blow.

"Did—did you kill Oldring?"

"I did, Bess, and I hate myself for it. But you know I never dreamed he was your father. I thought he'd wronged you. I killed him when I was madly jealous."

For a moment Bess was shocked into silence.

"But he was my father!" she broke out, at last. "And now I must go back—I can't go with you. It's all over—that beautiful dream. Oh, I *knew* it couldn't come true. You can't take me now."

"If you forgive me, Bess, it'll all come right in the end!" implored Venters.

"It can't be right. I'll go back. After all, I loved him. He was good to me. I can't forget that."

"If you go back to Oldring's men I'll follow you, and then they'll kill me," said Venters, hoarsely.

"Oh no, Bern, you'll not come. Let me go. It's best for you to forget me. I've brought you only pain and dishonor."

She did not weep. But the sweet bloom and life died out of her face. She looked haggard and sad, all at once stunted; and her hands dropped listlessly; and her head drooped in slow, final acceptance of a hopeless fate.

"Jane, look there!" cried Venters, in despairing grief. "Need you have told her? Where was all your kindness of heart? This girl has had a wretched, lonely life. And I'd found a way to make her happy. You've killed it. You've killed something sweet and pure and hopeful, just as sure as you breathe."

"Oh, Bern! It was a slip. I never thought—I never thought!" replied Jane. "How could I tell she didn't know?"

Lassiter suddenly moved forward, and with the beautiful light on his face now strangely luminous, he looked at Jane and Venters and then let his soft, bright gaze rest on Bess.

"Well, I reckon you've all had your say, an' now it's Lassiter's turn. Why, I was jest prayin' for this meetin'. Bess, jest look here."

Gently he touched her arm and turned her to face the others, and then outspread his great hand to disclose a shiny, battered gold locket.

"Open it," he said, with a singularly rich voice.

Bess complied, but listlessly.

"Jane—Venters—come closer," went on Lassiter. "Take a look at the picture. Don't you know the woman?"

Jane, after one glance, drew back.

"Milly Erne!" she cried, wonderingly.

Venters, with tingling pulse, with something growing on him, recognized in the faded miniature portrait the eyes of Milly Erne.

"Yes, that's Milly," said Lassiter, softly. "Bess, did you ever see her face —look hard—with all your heart an' soul?"

"The eyes seem to haunt me," whispered Bess. "Oh, I can't remember —they're eyes of my dreams—but—but—"

Lassiter's strong arm went round her and he bent his head.

"Child, I thought you'd remember her eyes. They're the same beautiful eyes you'd see if you looked in a mirror or a clear spring. They're your mother's eyes. You are Milly Erne's child. Your name is Elizabeth Erne. You're not Oldring's daughter. You're the daughter of Frank Erne, a man once my best friend. Look! Here's his picture beside Milly's. He was handsome, an' as fine an' gallant a Southern gentleman as I ever seen. Frank come of an old family. You come of the best of blood, lass, an' blood tells."

Bess slipped through his arm to her knees and hugged the locket to her bosom, and lifted wonderful, yearning eyes.

"It—can't—be—true!"

"Thank God, lass, it *is* true," replied Lassiter. "Jane an' Bern here— they both recognize Milly. They see Milly in you. They're so knocked out they can't tell you, that's all."

"Who are you?" whispered Bess.

"I reckon I'm Milly's brother an' your uncle! . . . Uncle Jim! Ain't that fine?"

"Oh, I can't believe— Don't raise me! Bern, let me kneel. I see truth in your face—in Miss Withersteen's. But let me hear it all—all on my knees. Tell me *how* it's true!"

"Well, Elizabeth, listen," said Lassiter. "Before you was born your father made a mortal enemy of a Mormon named Dyer. They was both ministers an' come to be rivals. Dyer stole your mother away from her home. She gave birth to you in Texas eighteen years ago. Then she was taken to Utah, from place to place, an' finally to the last border settlement—Cottonwoods. You was about three years old when you was taken away from Milly. She never knew what had become of you. But she lived a good while hopin' and prayin' to have you again. Then she gave up an' died. An' I may as well put in here your father died ten years ago. Well, I spent my time tracin' Milly, an' some months back I landed in Cottonwoods. An' jest lately I learned all about you. I had a talk with Oldrin' an' told him you was dead, an' he told me what I had so long been wantin' to know. It was Dyer, of course, who stole you from Milly. Part reason he was sore because Milly refused to give you Mormon teachin', but mostly he still hated Frank Erne so infernally that he made a deal with Oldrin' to take you an' bring you up as an infamous rustler an' rustler's girl. The idea was to break Frank Erne's heart if he ever came to Utah—to show him his daughter with a band of low rustlers. Well—Oldrin' took you, brought you up from childhood, an' then made you his Masked Rider. He made you infamous. He kept that part of the contract, but he learned to love you as a daughter an' never let any but his own men know you was a girl. I heard him say that with my own ears, an' I saw his big eyes grow dim. He told me how he had guarded you always, kept you locked up in his absence, was always at your side or near you on those rides that made you famous on the sage. He said he an' an old rustler whom he trusted had taught you how to read an' write. They selected the books for you. Dyer had wanted you brought up the vilest of the vile! An' Oldrin' brought you up the innocentest of the innocent. He said you didn't know what vileness was. I can hear his big voice tremble now as he said it. He told me how the men—rustlers an' outlaws—who from time to time tried to approach you familiarly—he told me how he shot them dead. I'm tellin' you this 'specially because you've showed such shame—sayin' you was nameless an' all that. Nothin' on earth can be wronger than that idea of yours. An' the truth of it is here. Oldrin' swore to me that if Dyer died, releasin' the contract, he intended to hunt up your father an' give you back to him. It seems Oldrin' wasn't all bad, an' he sure loved you."

Venters leaned forward in passionate remorse.

"Oh, Bess! I know Lassiter speaks the truth. For when I shot Oldring he dropped to his knees and fought with unearthly power to speak. And he said: 'Man—why—didn't—you—wait? Bess was—' Then he fell dead. And I've been haunted by his look and words. Oh, Bess, what a strange, splendid thing for Oldring to do! It all seems impossible. But, dear, you really are not what you thought."

"Elizabeth Erne!" cried Jane Withersteen. "I loved your mother and I see her in you!"

What had been incredible from the lips of men became, in the tone, look, and gesture of a woman, a wonderful truth for Bess. With little tremblings of all her slender body she rocked to and fro on her knees. The yearning wistfulness of her eyes changed to solemn splendor of joy. She believed. She was realizing happiness. And as the process of thought was slow, so were the variations of her expression. Her eyes reflected the transformation of her soul. Dark, brooding, hopeless belief—clouds of gloom—drifted, paled, vanished in glorious light. An exquisite rose flush —a glow—shone from her face as she slowly began to rise from her knees. A spirit uplifted her. All that she had held as base dropped from her.

Venters watched her in joy too deep for words. By it he divined something of what Lassiter's revelation meant to Bess, but he knew he could only faintly understand. That moment when she seemed to be lifted by some spiritual transfiguration was the most beautiful moment of his life. She stood with parted, quivering lips, with hands tightly clasping the locket to her heaving breast. A new conscious pride of worth dignified the old wild, free grace and poise.

"Uncle Jim!" she said, tremulously, with a different smile from any Venters had ever seen on her face.

Lassiter took her into his arms.

"I reckon. It's powerful fine to hear that," replied Lassiter, unsteadily.

Venters, feeling his eyes grow hot and wet, turned away, and found

himself looking at Jane Withersteen. He had almost forgotten her presence. Tenderness and sympathy were fast hiding traces of her agitation.
Venters read her mind—felt the reaction of her noble heart—saw the joy
she was beginning to feel at the happiness of others. And suddenly
blinded, choked by his emotions, he turned from her also. He knew what
she would do presently; she would make some magnificent amend for her
anger; she would give some manifestation of her love; probably all in a
moment, as she had loved Milly Erne, so would she love Elizabeth Erne.

" 'Pears to me, folks, that we'd better talk a little serious now," remarked Lassiter, at length. "Time flies."

"You're right," replied Venters, instantly. "I'd forgotten time—place—
danger. Lassiter, you're riding away. Jane's leaving Withersteen House?"

"Forever," replied Jane.

"I fired Withersteen House," said Lassiter.

"Dyer?" questioned Venters, sharply.

"I reckon where Dyer's gone there won't be any kidnappin' of girls."

"Ah! I knew it. I told Judkins— And Tull?" went on Venters, passionately.

"Tull wasn't around when I broke loose. By now he's likely on our trail
with his riders."

"Lassiter, you're going into the Pass to hide till all this storm blows
over?"

"I reckon that's Jane's idea. I'm thinkin' the storm'll be a powerful long
time blowin' over. I was comin' to join you in Surprise Valley. You'll go
back now with me?"

"No. I want to take Bess out of Utah. Lassiter, Bess found gold in the
valley. We've a saddle-bag full of gold. If we can reach Sterling—"

"Man! How're you ever goin' to do that? Sterlin' is a hundred miles."

"My plan is to ride on, keeping sharp lookout. Somewhere up the trail
we'll take to the sage and go round Cottonwoods and then hit the trail
again."

"It's a bad plan. You'll kill the burros in two days."

"Then we'll walk."

"That's more bad an' worse. Better go back down the Pass with me."

"Lassiter, this girl has been hidden all her life in that lonely place,"
went on Venters. "Oldring's men are hunting me. We'd not be safe there
any longer. Even if we would be I'd take this chance to get her out. I want
to marry her. She shall have some of the pleasures of life—see cities and
people. We've gold—we'll be rich. Why, life opens sweet for both of us.
And, by Heaven! I'll get her out or lose my life in the attempt!"

"I reckon if you go on with them burros you'll lose your life all right.
Tull will have riders all over this sage. You can't get out on them burros.
It's a fool idea. That's not doin' best by the girl. Come with me an' take
chances on the rustlers."

Lassiter's cool argument made Venters waver, not in determination to go, but in hope of success.

"Bess, I want you to know. Lassiter says the trip's almost useless now. I'm afraid he's right. We've got about one chance in a hundred to go through. Shall we take it? Shall we go on?"

"We'll go on," replied Bess.

"That settles it, Lassiter."

Lassiter spread wide his hands, as if to signify he could do no more, and his face clouded.

Venters felt a touch on his elbow. Jane stood beside him with a hand on his arm. She was smiling. Something radiated from her, and like an electric current accelerated the motion of his blood.

"Bern, you'd be right to die rather than not take Elizabeth out of Utah —out of this wild country. You must do it. You'll show her the great world, with all its wonders. Think how little she has seen! Think what delight is in store for her! You have gold; you will be free; you will make her happy. What a glorious prospect! I share it with you. I'll think of you —dream of you—pray for you."

"Thank you, Jane," replied Venters, trying to steady his voice. "It does look bright. Oh, if we were only across that wide, open waste of sage!"

"Bern, the trip's as good as made. It'll be safe—easy. It'll be a glorious ride," she said, softly.

Venters stared. Had Jane's troubles made her insane? Lassiter, too, acted queerly, all at once beginning to turn his sombrero round with hands that actually shook.

"You are a rider. She is a rider. This will be the ride of your lives," added Jane, in that same soft undertone, almost as if she were musing to herself.

"Jane!" he cried.

"I give you Black Star and Night!"

"Black Star and Night!" he echoed.

"It's done. Lassiter, put our saddle-bags on the burros."

Only when Lassiter moved swiftly to execute her bidding did Venters's clogged brain grasp at literal meanings. He leaped to catch Lassiter's busy hands.

"No, no! What are you doing?" he demanded, in a kind of fury. "I won't take her racers. What do you think I am? It'd be monstrous. Lassiter! Stop it, I say! . . . You've got her to save. You've miles and miles to go. Tull is trailing you. There are rustlers in the Pass. Give me back that saddle-bag!"

"Son—cool down," returned Lassiter, in a voice he might have used to a child. But the grip with which he tore away Venters's grasping hands was that of a giant. "Listen—you fool boy! Jane's sized up the situation. The burros'll do for us. We'll sneak along an' hide. I'll take your dogs an' your rifle. Why, it's the trick. The blacks are yours, an' sure as I can throw a gun you're goin' to ride safe out of the sage."

"Jane—stop him—please stop him," gasped Venters. "I've lost my strength. I can't do—anything. This's hell for me! Can't you see that? I've ruined you—it was through me you lost all. You've only Black Star and Night left. You love these horses. Oh! I know how you must love them now! And—you're trying to give them to me. To help me out of Utah! To save the girl I love!"

"That will be my glory."

Then in the white, rapt face, in the unfathomable eyes, Venters saw Jane Withersteen in a supreme moment. This moment was one wherein she reached up to the height for which her noble soul had ever yearned. He, after disrupting the calm tenor of her peace, after bringing down on her head the implacable hostility of her churchmen, after teaching her a bitter lesson in life—he was to be her salvation. And he turned away again, this time shaken to the core of his soul. Jane Withersteen was the incarnation of selflessness. He experienced wonder and terror, exquisite pain and rapture. What were all the shocks life had dealt him compared to the thought of such loyal and generous friendship?

And instantly, as if by some divine insight, he knew himself in the remaking—tried, found wanting; but stronger, better, surer—and he wheeled to Jane Withersteen, eager, joyous, passionate, wild, exalted. He bent to her; he left tears and kisses on her hands.

"Jane, I—I can't find words—now," he said. "I'm beyond words. Only —I understand. And I'll take the blacks."

"Don't be losin' no more time," cut in Lassiter. "I ain't certain, but I think I seen a speck up the sage-slope. Mebbe I was mistaken. But, anyway, we must all be movin'. I've shortened the stirrups on Black Star. Put Bess on him."

Jane Withersteen held out her arms.

"Elizabeth Erne!" she cried, and Bess flew to her.

How inconceivably strange and beautiful it was for Venters to see Bess clasped to Jane Withersteen's breast!

Then he leaped astride Night.

"Venters, ride straight on up the slope," Lassiter was saying, "an' if you don't meet any riders keep on till you're a few miles from the village, then cut off in the sage an' go round to the trail. But you'll most likely meet riders with Tull. Jest keep right on till you're jest out of gunshot an' then make your cut-off into the sage. They'll ride after you, but it won't be no use. You can ride, an' Bess can ride. When you're out of reach turn on round to the west, an' hit the trail somewhere. Save the hosses all you can, but don't be afraid. Black Star and Night are good for a hundred miles before sundown, if you have to push them. You can get to Sterlin' by night if you want. But better make it along about tomorrow mornin'.

When you get through the notch on the Glaze trail, swing to the right. You'll be able to see both Glaze an' Stone Bridge. Keep away from them villages. You won't run no risk of meetin' any of Oldrin's rustlers from Sterlin' on. You'll find water in them deep hollows north of the Notch. There's an old trail there, not much used, an' it leads to Sterlin'. That's your trail. An' one thing more. If Tull pushes you—or keeps on persistent-like, for a few miles—jest let the blacks out an' lose him an' his riders."

"Lassiter, may we meet again!" said Venters, in a deep voice.

"Son, it ain't likely—it ain't likely. Well, Bess Oldrin'—Masked Rider —Elizabeth Erne—now you climb on Black Star. I've heard you could ride. Well, every rider loves a good hoss. An', lass, there never was but one that could beat Black Star."

"Ah, Lassiter, there never was any horse that could beat Black Star," said Jane, with the old pride.

"I often wondered—mebbe Venters rode out that race when he brought back the blacks. Son, was Wrangle the best hoss?"

"No, Lassiter," replied Venters. For this lie he had his reward in Jane's quick smile.

"Well, well, my hoss-sense ain't always right. An' here I'm talkin' a lot, wastin' time. It ain't so easy to find an' lose a pretty niece all in one hour! Elizabeth—goodbye!"

"Oh, Uncle Jim! . . . Goodbye!"

"Elizabeth Erne, be happy! Goodbye," said Jane.

"Goodbye—oh—goodbye!"

In lithe, supple action Bess swung up to Black Star's saddle.

"Jane Withersteen! . . . Goodbye!" called Venters hoarsely.

"Bern—Bess—riders of the purple sage—goodbye!"

⁙22⁙

RIDERS OF
THE PURPLE SAGE

BLACK STAR AND NIGHT, answering to spur, swept swiftly west-ward along the white, slow-rising, sage-bordered trail. Venters heard a mournful howl from Ring, but Whitie was silent. The blacks settled into their fleet, long-striding gallop. The wind sweetly fanned Venters's hot face. From the summit of the first low-swelling ridge he looked back. Lassiter waved his hand; Jane waved her scarf. Venters replied by standing in his stirrups and holding high his sombrero. Then the dip of the ridge hid them. From the height of the next he turned once more. Lassiter, Jane, and the burros had disappeared. They had gone down into the Pass. Venters felt a sensation of irreparable loss.

"Bern—look!" called Bess, pointing up the long slope.

A small, dark, moving dot split the line where purple sage met blue sky. That dot was a band of riders.

"Pull the black, Bess."

They slowed from gallop to canter, then to trot. The fresh and eager horses did not like the check.

"Bern, Black Star has great eyesight."

"I wonder if they're Tull's riders. They might be rustlers. But it's all the same to us."

The black dot grew to a dark patch moving under low dust-clouds. It grew all the time, though very slowly. There were long periods when it was in plain sight, and intervals when it dropped behind the sage. The blacks trotted for half an hour, for another half-hour, and still the moving patch appeared to stay on the horizon line. Gradually, however, as time passed, it began to enlarge, to creep down the slope, to encroach upon the intervening distance.

"Bess, what do you make them out?" asked Venters. "I don't think they're rustlers."

"They're sage-riders," replied Bess. "I see a white horse and several grays. Rustlers seldom ride any horses but bays and blacks."

"That white horse is Tull's. Pull the black, Bess. I'll get down and cinch up. We're in for some riding. Are you afraid?"

"Not now," answered the girl, smiling.

"You needn't be. Bess, you don't weigh enough to make Black Star know you're on him. I won't be able to stay with you. You'll leave Tull and his riders as if they were standing still."

"How about you?"

"Never fear. If I can't stay with you I can still laugh at Tull."

"Look, Bern! They've stopped on that ridge. They see us."

"Yes. But we're too far yet for them to make out who we are. They'll recognize the blacks first. We've passed most of the ridges and the thickest sage. Now, when I give the word, let Black Star go and ride!"

Venters calculated that a mile or more still intervened between them and the riders. They were approaching at a swift canter. Soon Venters recognized Tull's white horse, and concluded that the riders had likewise recognized Black Star and Night. But it would be impossible for Tull yet to see that the blacks were not ridden by Lassiter and Jane. Venters noted that Tull and the line of horsemen, perhaps ten or twelve in number, stopped several times and evidently looked hard down the slope. It must have been a puzzling circumstance for Tull. Venters laughed grimly at the thought of what Tull's rage would be when he finally discovered the trick. Venters meant to sheer out into the sage before Tull could possibly be sure who rode the blacks.

The gap closed to a distance of half a mile. Tull halted. His riders came up and formed a dark group around him. Venters thought he saw him wave his arms, and was certain of it when the riders dashed into the sage, to right and left of the trail. Tull had anticipated just the move held in mind by Venters.

"Now Bess!" shouted Venters. "Strike north. Go round those riders and turn west."

Black Star sailed over the low sage, and in few leaps got into his stride and was running. Venters spurred Night after him. It was hard going in the sage. The horses could run as well there, but keen eyesight and judgment must constantly be used by the riders in choosing ground. And continuous swerving from aisle to aisle between the brush, and leaping little washes and mounds of the pack-rats, and breaking through sage, made rough riding. When Venters had turned into a long aisle he had time to look up at Tull's riders. They were now strung out into an extended line riding northeast. And, as Venters and Bess were holding due north, this meant, if the horses of Tull and his riders had the speed and the staying power, they would head the blacks and turn them back down the slope. Tull's men were not saving their mounts; they were driving them desperately. Venters feared only an accident to Black Star or Night, and skillful riding would mitigate possibility of that. One glance ahead served to show him that Bess could pick a course through the sage as well as he. She looked neither back nor at the running riders, and bent forward over Black Star's neck and studied the ground ahead.

It struck Venters, presently, after he had glanced up from time to time, that Bess was drawing away from him as he had expected. He had, however, only thought of the light weight Black Star was carrying and of his superior speed; he saw now that the black was being ridden as never before, except when Jerry Card lost the race to Wrangle. How easily, gracefully, naturally, Bess sat her saddle! She could ride! Suddenly Venters remembered she had said she could ride. But he had not dreamed she was capable of such superb horsemanship. Then all at once, flashing over him, thrilling him, came the recollection that Bess was Oldring's Masked Rider.

He forgot Tull—the running riders—the race. He let Night have a free rein and felt him lengthen out to suit himself, knowing he would keep to Black Star's course, knowing that he had been chosen by the best rider now on the upland sage. For Jerry Card was dead. And fame had rivaled him with only one rider, and that was the slender girl who now swung so easily with Black Star's stride. Venters had abhorred her notoriety, but

now he took passionate pride in her skill, her daring, her power over a
horse. And he delved into his memory, recalling famous rides which he
had heard related in the villages and round the campfires. Oldring's
Masked Rider! Many times this strange rider, at once well known and
unknown, had escaped pursuers by matchless riding. He had run the
gauntlet of vigilantes down the main street of Stone Bridge, leaving dead
horses and dead rustlers behind. He had jumped his horse over the Gerber
Wash, a deep, wide ravine separating the fields of Glaze from the wild
sage. He had been surrounded north of Sterling; and he had broken
through the line. How often had been told the story of day stampedes, of
night raids, of pursuit, and then how the Masked Rider, swift as the wind,
was gone in the sage! A fleet, dark horse—a slender, dark form—a black
mask—a driving run down the slope—a dot on the purple sage—a shadowy, muffled steed disappearing in the night!

And this Masked Rider of the uplands had been Elizabeth Erne!

The sweet sage wind rushed in Venters's face and sang a song in his
ears. He heard the dull, rapid beat of Night's hoofs; he saw Black Star
drawing away, farther and farther. He realized both horses were swinging
to the west. Then gunshots in the rear reminded him of Tull. Venters
looked back. Far to the side, dropping behind, trooped the riders. They
were shooting. Venters saw no puffs of dust, heard no whistling bullets.
He was out of range. When he looked back again Tull's riders had given
up pursuit. The best they could do, no doubt, had been to get near enough
to recognize who really rode the blacks. Venters saw Tull drooping in his
saddle.

Then Venters pulled Night out of his running stride. Those few miles
had scarcely warmed the black, but Venters wished to save him. Bess
turned, and, though she was far away, Venters caught the white glint of
her waving hand. He held Night to a trot and rode on, seeing Bess and
Black Star, and the sloping upward stretch of sage, and from time to time
the receding black riders behind. Soon they disappeared behind a ridge,
and he turned no more. They would go back to Lassiter's trail and follow
it, and follow in vain. So Venters rode on, with the wind growing sweeter
to taste and smell, and the purple sage richer and the sky bluer in his
sight; and the song in his ears ringing. By and by Bess halted to wait for
him, and he knew she had come to the trail. When he reached her it was
to smile at sight of her standing with arms around Black Star's neck.

"Oh, Bern! I love him!" she cried. "He's beautiful; he knows; and how
he can run! I've had fast horses. But Black Star! . . . Wrangle never
beat him!"

"I'm wondering if I didn't dream that. Bess, the blacks are grand. What
it must have cost Jane—ah!—well, when we get out of this wild country
with Star and Night, back to my old home in Illinois, we'll buy a beautiful
farm with meadows and springs and cool shade. There we'll turn the

horses free—free to roam and browse and drink—never to feel a spur again—never to be ridden!"

"I would like that," said Bess.

They rested. Then, mounting, they rode side by side up the white trail. The sun rose higher behind them. Far to the left a low line of green marked the site of Cottonwoods. Venters looked once and looked no more. Bess gazed only straight ahead. They put the blacks to the long, swinging rider's canter, and at times pulled them to a trot, and occasionally to a walk. The hours passed, the miles slipped behind, and the wall of rock loomed in the fore. The Notch opened wide. It was a rugged, stony pass, but with level and open trail, and Venters and Bess ran the blacks through it. An old trail led off to the right, taking the line of the wall, and this Venters knew to be the trail mentioned by Lassiter.

The little hamlet, Glaze, a white and green patch in the vast waste of purple, lay miles down a slope much like the Cottonwoods slope, only this descended to the west. And miles farther west a faint green spot marked the location of Stone Bridge. All the rest of that world was seemingly smooth, undulating sage, with no ragged lines of canyons to accentuate its wildness.

"Bess, we're safe—we're free!" said Venters. "We're alone on the sage. We're half way to Sterling."

"Ah, I wonder how it is with Lassiter and Miss Withersteen."

"Never fear, Bess. He'll outwit Tull. He'll get away and hide her safely. He might climb into Surprise Valley, but I don't think he'll go so far."

"Bern, will we ever find any place like our beautiful valley?"

"No. But, dear, listen. We'll go back some day, after years—ten years. Then we'll be forgotten. And our valley will be just as we left it."

"What if Balancing Rock falls and closes the outlet to the Pass?"

"I've thought of that. I'll pack in ropes and ropes. And if the outlet's closed we'll climb up the cliffs and over them to the valley and go down on rope ladders. It could be done. I know just where to make the climb, and I'll never forget."

"Oh yes, let us go back!"

"It's something sweet to look forward to. Bess, it's like all the future looks to me."

"Call me—Elizabeth," she said, shyly.

"Elizabeth Erne! It's a beautiful name. But I'll never forget Bess. Do you know—have you thought that very soon—by this time tomorrow— you will be Elizabeth Venters?"

So they rode on down the old trail. And the sun sloped to the west, and a golden sheen lay on the sage. The hours sped now; the afternoon waned. Often they rested the horses. The glisten of a pool of water in a hollow caught Venters's eye, and here he unsaddled the blacks and let them roll and drink and browse. When he and Bess rode up out of the hollow the sun was low, a crimson ball, and the valley seemed veiled in purple fire and smoke. It was that short time when the sun appeared to rest before setting, and silence, like a cloak of invisible life, lay heavy on all that shimmering world of sage.

They watched the sun begin to bury its red curve under the dark horizon.

"We'll ride on till late," he said. "Then you can sleep a little, while I watch and graze the horses. And we'll ride into Sterling early tomorrow. We'll be married! . . . We'll be in time to catch the stage. We'll tie Black Star and Night behind—and then—for a country not wild and terrible like this!"

"Oh, Bern! . . . But look! The sun is setting on the sage—the last time for us till we dare come again to the Utah border. Ten years! Oh, Bern, look, so you will never forget!"

Slumbering, fading purple fire burned over the undulating sage ridges. Long streaks and bars and shafts and spears fringed the far western slope. Drifting, golden veils mingled with low, purple shadows. Colors and shades changed in slow, wondrous transformation.

Suddenly Venters was startled by a low, rumbling roar—so low that it was like the roar in a seashell.

"Bess, did you hear anything?" he whispered.

"No."

"Listen! . . . Maybe I only imagined—*Ah!*"

Out of the east or north, from remote distance, breathed an infinitely low, continuously long sound—deep, weird, detonating, thundering, deadening—dying.

⸭23⸭

THE FALL OF BALANCING ROCK

THROUGH tear-blurred sight Jane Withersteen watched Venters and Elizabeth Erne and the black racers disappear over the ridge of sage. "They're gone!" said Lassiter. "An' they're safe now. An' there'll never be a day of their comin' happy lives but what they'll remember Jane

Withersteen an'—an' Uncle Jim! . . . I reckon, Jane, we'd better be on our way."

The burros obediently wheeled and started down the break with little, cautious steps, but Lassiter had to leash the whining dogs and lead them. Jane felt herself bound in a feeling that was neither listlessness nor indifference, yet which rendered her incapable of interest. She was still strong in body, but emotionally tired. That hour at the entrance to Deception Pass had been the climax of her suffering—the flood of her wrath—the last of her sacrifice—the supremity of her love—and the attainment of peace. She thought that if she had little Fay she would not ask any more of life.

Like an automaton she followed Lassiter down the steep trail of dust and bits of weathered stone; and when the little slides moved with her or piled around her knees she experienced no alarm. Vague relief came to her in the sense of being enclosed between dark stone walls, deep hidden from the glare of sun, from the glistening sage. Lassiter lengthened the stirrup straps on one of the burros and bade her mount and ride close to him. She was to keep the burro from cracking his little hard roofs on stones. Then she was riding on between dark, gleaming walls. There were quiet and rest and coolness in this canyon. She noted indifferently that they passed close under shady, bulging shelves of cliff, through patches of grass and sage and thicket and groves of slender trees, and over white, pebbly washes, and around masses of broken rock. The burros trotted tirelessly; the dogs, once more free, pattered tirelessly; and Lassiter led on with never a stop, and at every open place he looked back. The shade under the walls gave place to sunlight. And presently they came to a dense thicket of slender trees, through which they passed to rich, green grass and water. Here Lassiter rested the burros for a little while, but he was restless, uneasy, silent, always listening, peering under the trees. She dully reflected that enemies were behind them—before them; still the thought awakened no dread or concern or interest.

At his bidding she mounted and rode on close to the heels of his burro. The canyon narrowed; the walls lifted their rugged rims higher; and the sun shone down hot from the center of the blue stream of sky above. Lassiter traveled slower, with more exceeding care as to the ground he chose, and he kept speaking low to the dogs. They were now hunting-dogs—keen, alert, suspicious, sniffing the warm breeze. The monotony of the yellow walls broke in change of color and smooth surface, and the rugged outline of rims grew craggy. Splits appeared in deep breaks, and gorges running at right angles, and then the Pass opened wide at a junction of intersecting canyons.

Lassiter dismounted, led his burro, called the dogs close, and proceeded at snail pace through dark masses of rock and dense thickets under the left wall. Long he watched and listened before venturing to cross the mouths of side canyons. At length he halted, tied his burro, lifted a warning hand to Jane, and then slipped away among the boulders, and, followed by the stealthy dogs, disappeared from sight. The time he remained absent was neither short nor long to Jane Withersteen.

When he reached her side again he was pale, and his lips were set in a hard line, and his gray eyes glittered coldly. Bidding her dismount, he led the burros into a covert of stones and cedars, and tied them.

"Jane, I've run into the fellers I've been lookin' for, an' I'm goin' after them," he said.

"Why?" she asked.

"I reckon I won't take time to tell you."

"Couldn't we slip by without being seen?"

"Likely enough. But that ain't my game. An' I'd like to know, in case I don't come back, what you'll do."

"What can I do?"

"I reckon you can go back to Tull. Or stay in the Pass an' be taken off by rustlers. Which'll you do?"

"I don't know. I can't think very well. But I believe I'd rather be taken off by rustlers."

Lassiter sat down, put his head in his hands, and remained for a few moments in what appeared to be deep and painful thought. When he lifted his face it was haggard, lined, cold as sculptured marble.

"I'll go. I only mentioned that chance of my not comin' back. I'm pretty sure to come."

"Need you risk so much? Must you fight more? Haven't you shed enough blood?"

"I'd like to tell you why I'm goin'," he continued, in coldness he had seldom used to her. She remarked it, but it was the same to her as if he had spoken with his old gentle warmth. "But I reckon I won't. Only, I'll say that mercy an' goodness, such as is in you, though they're the grand things in human nature, can't be lived up to on this Utah border. Life's hell out here. You think—or you used to think—that your religion made this life heaven. Mebbe them scales on your eyes has dropped now. Jane, I wouldn't have you no different, an' that's why I'm goin' to try to hide you somewhere in this Pass. I'd like to hide many more women, for I've come to see there are more like you among your people. An' I'd like you to see jest how hard an' cruel this border life is. It's bloody. You'd think churches an' churchmen would make it better. They make it worse. You give names to things—bishops, elders, ministers, Mormonism, duty, faith, glory. You dream—or you're driven mad. I'm a man, an' I know. I name fanatics, followers, blind women, oppressors, thieves, ranchers, rustlers, riders. An' we have—what you've lived through these last months. It can't be helped. But it can't last always. An' remember this—someday the border'll be better, cleaner, for the ways of men like Lassiter!"

She saw him shake his tall form erect, look at her strangely and steadfastly, and then, noiselessly, stealthily slip away amid the rocks and trees.

Ring and Whitie, not being bidden to follow, remained with Jane. She felt extreme weariness, yet somehow it did not seem to be of her body. And she sat down in the shade and tried to think. She saw a creeping lizard, cactus flowers, the drooping burros, the resting dogs, an eagle high over a yellow crag. Once the meanest flower, a color, the flight of a bee, or any living thing had given her deepest joy. Lassiter had gone off, yielding to his incurable blood lust, probably to his own death; and she was sorry, but there was no feeling in her sorrow.

Suddenly from the mouth of the canyon just beyond her rang out a clear, sharp report of a rifle. Echoes clapped. Then followed a piercingly high yell of anguish, quickly breaking. Again echoes clapped, in grim imitation. Dull revolver shots—hoarse yells—pound of hoofs—shrill neighs of horses—commingling of echoes—and again silence! Lassiter must be busily engaged, thought Jane, and no chill trembled over her, no blanching tightened her skin. Yes, the border was a bloody place. But life had always been bloody. Men were blood-spillers. Phases of the history of the world flashed through her mind—Greek and Roman wars, dark, medieval times, the crimes in the name of religion. On sea, on land, everywhere—shooting, stabbing, cursing, clashing, fighting men! Greed, power, oppression, fanaticism, love, hate, revenge, justice, freedom—for these, men killed one another.

She lay there under the cedars, gazing up through the delicate lacelike foliage at the blue sky, and she thought and wondered and did not care.

More rattling shots disturbed the noonday quiet. She heard a sliding of weathered rock, a hoarse shout of warning, a yell of alarm, again the clear, sharp crack of the rifle, and another cry that was a cry of death. Then rifle reports pierced a dull volley of revolver shots. Bullets whizzed over Jane's hiding-place; one struck a stone and whined away in the air. After that, for a time, succeeded desultory shots; and then they ceased under long, thundering fire from heavier guns.

Sooner or later, then, Jane heard the cracking of horses' hoofs on the stones, and the sound came nearer and nearer. Silence intervened until Lassiter's soft, jingling step assured her of his approach. When he appeared he was covered with blood.

"All right, Jane," he said. "I come back. An' don't worry."

With water from a canteen he washed the blood from his face and hands.

"Jane, hurry now. Tear my scarf in two, an' tie up these places. That hole through my hand is some inconvenient, worse 'n this cut over my ear. There—you're doin' fine! Not a bit nervous—no tremblin'. I reckon I ain't done your courage justice. I'm glad you're brave jest now—you'll need to be. Well, I was hid pretty good, enough to keep them from shootin' me deep, but they was slingin' lead close all the time. I used up all the rifle shells, an' then I went after them. Mebbe you heard. It was then I got hit. I had to use up every shell in my own guns, an' they did, too, as I seen. Rustlers an' Mormons, Jane! An' now I'm packin' five bullet holes in my carcass, an' guns without shells. Hurry, now."

He unstrapped the saddle-bags from the burros, slipped the saddles and let them lie, turned the burros loose, and, calling the dogs, led the way through stones and cedars to an open where two horses stood.

"Jane, are you strong?" he asked.

"I think so. I'm not tired," Jane replied.

"I don't mean that way. Can you bear up?"

"I think I can bear anything."

"I reckon you look a little cold an' thick. So I'm preparin' you."

"For what?"

"I didn't tell you why I jest had to go after them fellers. I couldn't tell you. I believe you'd have died. But I can tell you now—if you'll bear up under a shock?"

"Go on, my friend."

"*I've got little Fay!* Alive—bad hurt—but she'll live!"

Jane Withersteen's dead-locked feeling, rent by Lassiter's deep, quivering voice, leaped into an agony of sensitive life.

"Here," he added, and showed her where little Fay lay on the grass.

Unable to speak, unable to stand, Jane dropped on her knees. By that long, beautiful golden hair Jane recognized the beloved Fay. But Fay's loveliness was gone. Her face was drawn and looked old with grief. But she was not dead—her heart beat—and Jane Withersteen gathered strength and lived again.

"You see I jest had to go after Fay," Lassiter was saying, as he knelt to bathe her little pale face. "But I reckon I don't want no more choices like the one I had to make. There was a crippled feller in that bunch, Jane. Mebbe Venters crippled him. Anyway, that's why they were holdin' up here. I seen little Fay first thing, an' was hard put to it to figure out a way to get her. An' I wanted hosses, too. I had to take chances. So I crawled close to their camp. One feller jumped a hoss with little Fay, an' when I shot him, of course she dropped. She's stunned an' bruised—she fell right on her head. Jane, she's comin' to! She ain't bad hurt!"

Fay's long lashes fluttered; her eyes opened. At first they seemed glazed over. They looked dazed by pain. Then they quickened, darkened, to shine with intelligence—bewilderment—memory—and sudden wonderful joy.

"Muvver—Jane!" she whispered.

"Oh, little Fay, little Fay!" cried Jane, lifting, clasping the child to her.

"*Now*, we've got to rustle!" said Lassiter, in grim coolness. "Jane, look down the pass!"

Across the mounds of rock and sage Jane caught sight of a band of riders filing out of the narrow neck of the Pass; and in the lead was a white horse, which, even at a distance of a mile or more, she knew.

"Tull!" she almost screamed.

"I reckon. But, Jane, we've still got the game in our hands. They're ridin' tired hosses. Venters likely give them a chase. He wouldn't forget that. An' we've fresh hosses."

Hurriedly he strapped on the saddle-bags, gave quick glance to girths and cinches and stirrups, then leaped astride.

"Lift little Fay up," he said.

With shaking arms Jane complied.

"Get back your nerve, woman! This's life or death now. Mind that. Climb up! Keep your wits. Stick close to me. Watch where your hoss 's goin' an' ride!"

Somehow Jane mounted—somehow found strength to hold the reins, to spur, to cling on, to ride. A horrible quaking, craven fear possessed her soul. Lassiter led the swift flight across the wide space, over washes, through sage, into a narrow canyon where the rapid clatter of hoofs rapped sharply from the walls. The wind roared in her ears; the gleaming cliffs swept by; trail and sage and grass moved under her. Lassiter's bandaged, blood-stained face turned to her; he shouted encouragement; he looked back down the Pass; he spurred his horse. Jane clung on, spurring likewise. And the horses settled from hard, furious gallop into a long-striding, driving run. She had never ridden at anything like that pace; desperately she tried to get the swing of the horse, to be of some help to him in that race, to see the best of the ground and guide him into it. But she failed of everything except to keep her seat in the saddle, and to spur and spur. At times she closed her eyes, unable to bear sight of Fay's golden curls streaming in the wind. She could not pray; she could not rail; she no longer cared for herself. All of life, of good, of use in the world, of hope in heaven centered in Lassiter's ride with little Fay to safety. She would have tried to turn the iron-jawed brute she rode; she would have given herself to that relentless, dark-browed Tull. But she knew Lassiter would turn with her, so she rode on and on.

Whether that run was of moments or hours Jane Withersteen could not tell. Lassiter's horse covered her with froth that blew back in white streams. Both horses ran their limit, were allowed to slow down in time to save them, and went on dripping, heaving, staggering.

"Oh, Lassiter, we must run—we must run!"

He looked back, saying nothing. The bandage had blown from his head, and blood trickled down his face. He was bowing under the strain of injuries, of the ride, of his burden. Yet how cool and gray he looked—how intrepid!

The horses walked, trotted, galloped, ran, to fall again to walk. Hours sped or dragged. Time was an instant—an eternity. Jane Withersteen felt hell pursuing her, and dared not look back for fear she would fall from her horse.

"Oh, Lassiter! Is he coming?"

The grim rider looked over his shoulder, but said no word. Little Fay's golden hair floated on the breeze. The sun shone; the walls gleamed; the sage glistened. And then it seemed the sun vanished, the walls shaded, the sage paled. The horses walked—trotted—galloped—ran—to fall again to walk. Shadows gathered under shelving cliffs. The canyon turned, brightened, opened into long, wide, wall-enclosed valley. Again the sun, lowering in the west, reddened the sage. Far ahead round, scrawled stone appeared to block the Pass.

"Bear up, Jane, bear up!" called Lassiter. "It's our game, if you don't weaken."

"Lassiter! Go on—*alone!* Save little Fay!"

"Only with you!"

"Oh!—I'm a coward—a miserable coward! I can't fight or think or hope or pray! I'm lost! Oh, Lassiter, look back! Is he coming? I'll not—hold out—"

"Keep your breath, woman, an' ride not for yourself or for me, but for Fay!"

A last breaking run across the sage brought Lassiter's horse to a walk.

"He's done," said the rider.

"Oh, no—no!" moaned Jane.

"Look back, Jane, look back. Three—four miles we've come across this valley, an' no Tull yet in sight. Only a few more miles!"

Jane looked back over the long stretch of sage, and found the narrow gap in the wall, out of which came a file of dark horses with a white horse in the lead. Sight of the riders acted upon Jane as a stimulant. The weight of cold, horrible terror lessened. And, gazing forward at the dogs, at Lassiter's limping horse, at the blood on his face, at the rocks growing nearer, last at Fay's golden hair, the ice left her veins, and slowly, strangely, she gained hold of strength that she believed would see her to the safety Lassiter promised. And, as she gazed, Lassiter's horse stumbled and fell.

He swung his leg and slipped from the saddle.

"Jane, take the child," he said, and lifted Fay up. Jane clasped her with arms suddenly strong. "They're gainin'," went on Lassiter, as he watched the pursuing riders. "But we'll beat 'em yet."

Turning with Jane's bridle in his hand, he was about to start when he saw the saddle-bag on the fallen horse.

"I've jest about got time," he muttered, and with swift fingers that did not blunder or fumble he loosened the bag and threw it over his shoulder. Then he started to run, leading Jane's horse, and he ran, and trotted, and walked, and ran again. Close ahead now Jane saw a rise of bare rock. Lassiter reached it, searched along the base, and, finding a low place, dragged the weary horse up and over round, smooth stone. Looking backward, Jane saw Tull's white horse not a mile distant, with riders strung out in a long line behind him. Looking forward, she saw more valley to the right, and to the left a towering cliff. Lassiter pulled the horse and kept on.

Little Fay lay in her arms with wide-open eyes—eyes which were still shadowed by pain, but no longer fixed, glazed in terror. The golden curls blew across Jane's lips; the little hands feebly clasped her arm; a ghost of a troubled, trustful smile hovered round the sweep lips. And Jane Withersteen awoke to the spirit of a lioness.

Lassiter was leading the horse up a smooth slope toward cedar trees of twisted and bleached appearance. Among these he halted.

"Jane, give me the girl an' get down," he said. As if it wrenched him he unbuckled the empty black guns with a strange air of finality. He then received Fay in his arms and stood a moment looking backward. Tull's white horse mounted the ridge of round stone, and several bays or blacks followed. "I wonder what he'll think when he sees them empty guns. Jane, bring your saddle-bag and climb after me."

A glistening, wonderful bare slope, with little holes, swelled up and up to lose itself in a frowning yellow cliff. Jane closely watched her steps and climbed behind Lassiter. He moved slowly. Perhaps he was only husbanding his strength. But she saw drops of blood on the stone, and then she knew. They climbed and climbed without looking back. Her breast labored; she began to feel as if little points of fiery steel were penetrating her side into her lungs. She heard the panting of Lassiter and the quicker panting of the dogs.

"Wait—here," he said.

Before her rose a bulge of stone, nicked with little cut steps, and above that a corner of yellow wall, and overhanging that a vast, ponderous cliff.

The dogs pattered up, disappeared round the corner. Lassiter mounted the steps with Fay, and he swayed like a drunken man, and he too disappeared. But instantly he returned alone, and half ran, half slipped down to her.

Then from below pealed up hoarse shouts of angry men. Tull and several of his riders had reached the spot where Lassiter had parted with his guns.

"You'll need that breath—mebbe!" said Lassiter, facing downward, with glittering eyes.

"Now, Jane, the last pull," he went on. "Walk up them little steps. I'll follow an' steady you. Don't think. Jest go. Little Fay's above. Her eyes are open. She jest said to me, 'Where's muvver Jane?' "

Without a fear or a tremor or a slip or a touch of Lassiter's hand Jane Withersteen walked up that ladder of cut steps.

He pushed her round the corner of wall. Fay lay with wide staring eyes, in the shade of a gloomy wall. The dogs waited. Lassiter picked up the child and turned into a dark cleft. It zigzagged. It widened. It opened. Jane was amazed at a wonderfully smooth and steep incline leading up between ruined, splintered, toppling walls. A red haze from the setting sun filled this passage. Lassiter climbed with slow, measured steps, and blood dripped from him to make splotches on the white stone. Jane tried not to step in his blood, but was compelled, for she found no other footing. The saddle-bag began to drag her down; she gasped for breath; she thought her heart was bursting. Slower, slower yet the rider climbed, whistling as he breathed. The incline widened. Huge pinnacles and monuments of stone stood alone, leaning fearfully. Red sunset haze shone through cracks where the wall had split. Jane did not look high, but she felt the overshadowing of broken rims above. She felt that it was a fearful, menacing place. And she climbed on in heartrending effort. And she fell beside Lassiter and Fay at the top of the incline in a narrow, smooth divide.

He staggered to his feet—staggered to a huge, leaning rock that rested on a small pedestal. He put his hand on it—the hand that had been shot through—and Jane saw blood drip from the ragged hole. Then he fell.

"Jane—I—can't—do—it!" he whispered.

"What?"

"Roll the—stone! . . . All my—life I've loved—to roll stones—an' now I—can't!"

"What of it? You talk strangely. Why roll that stone?"

"I planned to—fetch you here—to roll this stone. See! It'll smash the crags—loosen the walls—close the outlet!"

As Jane Withersteen gazed down that long incline, walled in by crumbling cliffs, awaiting only the slightest jar to make them fall asunder, she saw Tull appear at the bottom and begin to climb. A rider followed him—another—another.

"See! Tull! The riders!"

"Yes—they'll get us—now."

"Why? Haven't you strength left to roll the stone?"

"Jane—it ain't that—I've lost my nerve!"

"*You!* . . . Lassiter!"

"I wanted to roll it—meant to—but I—can't. Venters's valley is down behind here. We could—live there. But if I roll the stone—we're shut in for always. I don't dare. I'm thinkin' of you!"

"Lassiter! Roll the stone!" she cried.

He arose, tottering, but with set face, and again he placed the bloody hand on the Balancing Rock. Jane Withersteen gazed from him down the passageway. Tull was climbing. Almost, she thought, she saw his dark, relentless face. Behind him more riders climbed. What did they mean for Fay—for Lassiter—for herself?

"*Roll the stone! . . . Lassiter, I love you!*"

Under all his deathly pallor, and the blood, and the iron of seared cheek and lined brow, worked a great change. He placed both hands on the rock and then leaned his shoulder there and braced his powerful body.

"*Roll the stone!*"

It stirred, it groaned, it grated, it moved; and with a slow grinding, as of wrathful relief, began to lean. It had waited ages to fall, and now was slow in starting. Then, as if suddenly instinct with life, it leaped hurtlingly down to alight on the steep incline, to bound more swiftly into the air, to gather momentum, to plunge into the lofty leaning crag below. The crag thundered into atoms. A wave of air—a splitting shock! Dust shrouded the sunset red of shaking rims; dust shrouded Tull as he fell on his knees with uplifted arms. Shafts and monuments and sections of wall fell majestically.

From the depths there rose a long-drawn rumbling roar. The outlet to Deception Pass closed forever.

THE
RAINBOW
TRAIL

CONTENTS

1

RED LAKE

SHEFFORD halted his tired horse and gazed with slowly realizing eyes. A league-long slope of sage rolled and billowed down to Red Lake, a dry red basin, denuded and glistening, a hollow in the desert, a lonely and desolate door to the vast, wild and broken upland beyond.

All day Shefford had plodded onward with the clear horizon-line a thing unattainable; and for days before that he had ridden the wild bare flats and climbed the rocky desert benches. The great colored reaches and steps had led endlessly onward and upward through dim and deceiving distance.

A hundred miles of desert travel, with its mistakes and lessons and intimations, had not prepared him for what he now saw. He beheld what seemed a world that knew only magnitude. Wonder and awe fixed his gaze, and thought remained aloof. Then that dark and unknown north-land flung a menace at him. An irresistible call had drawn him to this seamed and peaked border of Arizona, this broken battlemented wilderness of Utah upland; and at first sight they frowned upon him, as if to warn him not to search for what lay hidden beyond the ranges. But Shefford thrilled with both fear and exultation. That was the country which had been described to him. Far across the red valley, far beyond the ragged line of black mesa and yellow range, lay the wild canyon with its haunting secret.

Red Lake must be his Rubicon. Either he must enter the unknown to seek, to strive, to find, or turn back and fail and never know and be always haunted. A friend's strange story had prompted his singular journey; a beautiful rainbow with its mystery and promise had decided him. Once in his life he had answered a wild call to the kingdom of adventure within him, and once in his life he had been happy. But here in the horizon-wide face of that up-flung and cloven desert he grew cold; he faltered even while he felt more fatally drawn.

As if impelled, Shefford started his horse down the sandy trail, but he checked his former far-reaching gaze. It was the month of April, and the waning sun lost heat and brightness. Long shadows crept down the slope ahead of him and the scant sage deepened its gray. He watched the lizards shoot like brown streaks across the sand, leaving their slender tracks; he heard the rustle of pack-rats as they darted into their brushy homes; the whir of a low-sailing hawk startled his horse.

Like ocean waves the slope rose and fell, its hollows choked with sand, its ridge-tops showing scantier growth of sage and grass and weed. The last ridge was a sand-dune, beautifully ribbed and scalloped and lined by the wind, and from its knife-sharp crest a thin wavering sheet of sand blew, almost like smoke. Shefford wondered why the sand looked red at a distance, for here it seemed almost white. It rippled everywhere, clean and glistening, always leading down.

Suddenly Shefford became aware of a house looming out of the bareness of the slope. It dominated that long white incline. Grim, lonely, forbidding, how strangely it harmonized with the surroundings! The structure was octagon-shaped, built of uncut stone, and resembled a fort. There was no door on the sides exposed to Shefford's gaze, but small apertures two-thirds the way up probably served as windows and portholes. The roof appeared to be made of poles covered with red earth.

Like a huge cold rock on a wide plain this house stood there on the windy slope. It was an outpost of the trader Presbrey, of whom Shefford had heard at Flagstaff and Tuba. No living thing appeared in the limit of Shefford's vision. He gazed shudderingly at the unwelcoming habitation, at the dark eyelike windows, at the sweep of barren slope merging into the vast red valley, at the bold, bleak bluffs. Could anyone live here? The nature of that sinister valley forbade a home there, and the spirit of the place hovered in the silence and space. Shefford thought irresistibly of how his enemies would have consigned him to just such a hell. He thought bitterly and mockingly of the narrow congregation that had proved him a failure in the ministry, that had repudiated his ideas of religion and immortality and God, that had driven him, at the age of twenty-four, from the calling forced upon him by his people. As a boy he had yearned to make himself an artist; his family had made him a clergyman; fate had made him a failure. A failure only so far in his life, something urged him to add—for in the lonely days and silent nights of the desert he had experienced a strange birth of hope. Adventure had called him, but it was a vague and spiritual hope, a dream of promise, a nameless attainment that fortified his wilder impulse.

As he rode around a corner of the stone house his horse snorted and stopped. A lean, shaggy pony jumped at sight of him, almost displacing a red long-haired blanket that covered an Indian saddle. Quick thuds of hoofs in sand drew Shefford's attention to a corral made of peeled poles, and here he saw another pony.

Shefford heard subdued voices. He dismounted and walked to an open door. In the dark interior he dimly descried a high counter, a stairway, a pile of bags of flour, blankets, and silver-ornamented objects, but the persons he had heard were not in that part of the house. Around another corner of the octagon-shaped wall he found another open door, and through it saw goat-skins and a mound of dirty sheep-wool, black and brown and white. It was light in this part of the building. When he crossed the threshold he was astounded to see a man struggling with a girl —an Indian girl. She was straining back from him, panting, and uttering low guttural sounds. The man's face was corded and dark with passion. This scene affected Shefford strangely. Primitive emotions were new to him.

Before Shefford could speak the girl broke loose and turned to flee. She was an Indian and this place was the uncivilized desert, but Shefford knew terror when he saw it. Like a dog the man rushed after her. It was instinct that made Shefford strike, and his blow laid the man flat. He lay stunned a moment, then raised himself to a sitting posture, his hand to his face, and the gaze he fixed upon Shefford seemed to combine astonishment and rage.

"I hope you're not Presbrey," said Shefford, slowly. He felt awkward, not sure of himself.

The man appeared about to burst into speech, but repressed it. There was blood on his mouth and his hand. Hastily he scrambled to his feet. Shefford saw this man's amaze and rage change to shame. He was tall and rather stout; he had a smooth tanned face, soft of outline, with a weak chin; his eyes were dark. The look of him and his corduroys and his soft shoes gave Shefford an impression that he was not a man who worked hard. By contrast with the few other worn and rugged desert men Shefford had met this stranger stood out strikingly. He stooped to pick up a soft felt hat and, jamming it on his head, he hurried out. Shefford followed him and watched him from the door. He went directly to the corral, mounted the pony, and rode out, to turn down the slope toward the south. When he reached the level of the basin, where evidently the sand was hard, he put the pony to a lope and gradually drew away.

"Well!" ejaculated Shefford. He did not know what to make of this adventure. Presently he became aware that the Indian girl was sitting on a roll of blankets near the wall. With curious interest Shefford studied her appearance. She had long, raven-black hair, tangled and disheveled, and she wore a soiled white band of cord above her brow. The color of her face struck him; it was dark, but not red nor bronzed; it almost had a tinge of gold. Her profile was clear-cut, bold, almost stern. Long black eyelashes hid her eyes. She wore a tight-fitting waist garment of material resembling velveteen. It was ripped along her side, exposing a skin still more richly

gold than that of her face. A string of silver ornaments and turquoise-and-
white beads encircled her neck, and it moved gently up and down with
the heaving of her full bosom. Her skirt was some gaudy print goods, torn
and stained and dusty. She had little feet, incased in brown moccasins,
fitting like gloves and buttoning over the ankles with silver coins.

"Who was that man? Did he hurt you?" inquired Shefford, turning to
gaze down the valley where a moving black object showed on the bare
sand.

"No savvy," replied the Indian girl.

"Where's the trader Presbrey?" asked Shefford.

She pointed straight down into the red valley.

"Toh," she said.

In the center of the basin lay a small pool of water shining brightly in
the sunset glow. Small objects moved around it, so small that Shefford
thought he saw several dogs led by a child. But it was the distance that
deceived him. There was a man down there watering his horses. That
reminded Shefford of the duty owing to his own tired and thirsty beast.
Whereupon he untied his pack, took off the saddle, and was about ready
to start down when the Indian girl grasped the bridle from his hand.

"Me go," she said.

He saw her eyes then, and they made her look different. They were as
black as her hair. He was puzzled to decide whether or not he thought her
handsome.

"Thanks, but I'll go," he replied, and, taking the bridle again, he
started down the slope. At every step he sank into the deep, soft sand.
Down a little way he came upon a pile of tin cans; they were everywhere,
buried, half buried, and lying loose; and these gave evidence of how the
trader lived. Presently Shefford discovered that the Indian girl was following him with her own pony. Looking upward at her against the light, he
thought her slender, lithe, picturesque. At a distance he liked her.

He plodded on, at length glad to get out of the drifts of sand to the
hard level floor of the valley. This, too, was sand, but dried and baked
hard, and red in color. At some season of the year this immense flat must
be covered with water. How wide it was, and empty! Shefford experienced again a feeling that had been novel to him—and it was that he was
loose, free, unanchored, ready to veer with the wind. From the foot of the
slope the water hole had appeared to be a few hundred rods out in the
valley. But the small size of the figures made Shefford doubt; and he had
to travel many times a few hundred rods before those figures began to
grow. Then Shefford made out that they were approaching him.

Thereafter they rapidly increased to normal proportions of man and
beast. When Shefford met them he saw a powerful, heavily built young
man leading two ponies.

"You're Mr. Presbrey, the trader?" inquired Shefford.

"Yes, I'm Presbrey, without the Mister," he replied.

"My name's Shefford. I'm knocking about on the desert. Rode from beyond Tuba today."

"Glad to see you," said Presbrey. He offered his hand. He was a stalwart man, clad in gray shirt, overalls, and boots. A shock of tumbled light hair covered his massive head; he was tanned, but not darkly, and there was red in his cheeks; under his shaggy eyebrows were deep, keen eyes; his lips were hard and set, as if occasion for smiles or words was rare; and his big, strong jaw seemed locked.

"Wish more travelers came knocking around Red Lake," he added. "Reckon here's the jumping-off place."

"It's pretty—lonesome," said Shefford, hesitating as if at a loss for words.

Then the Indian girl came up. Presbrey addressed her in her own language, which Shefford did not understand. She seemed shy and would not answer; she stood with downcast face and eyes. Presbrey spoke again, at which she pointed down the valley, and then moved on with her pony toward the water-hole.

Presbrey's keen eyes fixed on the receding black dot far down that oval expanse.

"That fellow left—rather abruptly," said Shefford, constrainedly. "Who was he?"

"His name's Willetts. He's a missionary. He rode in today with this Navajo girl. He was taking her to Blue Canyon, where he lives and teaches the Indians. I've met him only a few times. You see, not many white men ride in here. He's the first white man I've seen in six months, and you're the second. Both the same day! . . . Red Lake's getting popular! It's queer, though, his leaving. He expected to stay all night. There's no other place to stay. Blue Canyon is fifty miles away."

"I'm sorry to say—no, I'm not sorry, either—but I must tell you I was the cause of Mr. Willetts leaving," replied Shefford.

"How so?" inquired the other.

Then Shefford related the incident following his arrival.

"Perhaps my action was hasty," he concluded, apologetically. "I didn't think. Indeed, I'm surprised at myself."

Presbrey made no comment and his face was as hard to read as one of the distant bluffs.

"But what did the man mean?" asked Shefford, conscious of a little heat. "I'm a stranger out here. I'm ignorant of Indians—how they're controlled. Still I'm no fool. . . . If Willetts didn't mean evil, at least he was brutal."

"He was teaching her religion," replied Presbrey. His tone held faint scorn and implied a joke, but his face did not change in the slightest.

Without understanding just why, Shefford felt his conviction justified and his action approved. Then he was sensible of a slight shock of wonder and disgust.

"I am—I was a minister of the Gospel," he said to Presbrey. "What you hint seems impossible. I can't believe it."

"I didn't hint," replied Presbrey, bluntly, and it was evident that he was a sincere, but close-mouthed, man. "Shefford, so you're a preacher? . . . Did you come out here to try to convert the Indians?"

"No. I said I *was* a minister. I am no longer. I'm just a—a wanderer."

"I see. Well, the desert's no place for missionaries, but it's good for wanderers. . . . Go water your horse and take him up to the corral. You'll find some hay for him. I'll get grub ready."

Shefford went on with his horse to the pool. The water appeared thick, green, murky, and there was a line of salty crust extending around the margin of the pool. The thirsty horse splashed in and eagerly bent his head. But he did not like the taste. Many times he refused to drink, yet always lowered his nose again. Finally he drank, though not his fill. Shefford saw the Indian girl drink from her hand. He scooped up a handful and found it too sour to swallow. When he turned to retrace his steps she mounted her pony and followed him.

A golden flare lit up the western sky, and silhouetted dark and lonely against it stood the trading-post. Upon his return Shefford found the wind rising, and it chilled him. When he reached the slope thin gray sheets of sand were blowing low, rising, whipping, falling, sweeping along with soft silken rustle. Sometimes the gray veils hid his boots. It was a long, toilsome climb up that yielding, dragging ascent, and he had already been lame and tired. By the time he had put his horse away twilight was everywhere except in the west. The Indian girl left her pony in the corral and came like a shadow toward the house.

Shefford had difficulty in finding the foot of the stairway. He climbed to enter a large loft, lighted by two lamps. Presbrey was there, kneading biscuit dough in a pan.

"Make yourself comfortable," he said.

The huge loft was the shape of a half-octagon. A door opened upon the valley side, and here, too, there were windows. How attractive the place was in comparison with the impressions gained from the outside! The furnishings consisted of Indian blankets on the floor, two beds, a desk and table, several chairs and a couch, a gun-rack full of rifles, innumerable silver-ornamented belts, bridles, and other Indian articles upon the walls, and in one corner a wood-burning stove with teakettle steaming, and a great cupboard with shelves packed full of canned foods.

Shefford leaned in the doorway and looked out. Beneath him on a roll of blankets sat the Indian girl, silent and motionless. He wondered what was in her mind, what she would do, how the trader would treat her. The slope now was a long slant of sheeted moving shadows of sand. Dusk had gathered in the valley. The bluffs loomed black beyond. A pale star twinkled above. Shefford suddenly became aware of the intense nature of the stillness about him. Yet, as he listened to this silence, he heard an intermittent and immeasurably low moan, a fitful, mournful murmur. Assuredly it was only the wind. Nevertheless, it made his blood run cold. It was a different wind from that which had made music under the eaves of his Illinois home. This was a lonely, haunting wind, with desert hunger in it, and more which he could not name. Shefford listened to this spirit-brooding sound while he watched night envelop the valley. How black, how thick the mantle! Yet it brought no comforting sense of close-folded protection, of walls of soft sleep, of a home. Instead there was the feeling of space, of emptiness, of an infinite hall down which a mournful wind swept streams of murmuring sand.

"Well, grub's about ready," said Presbrey.

"Got any water?" asked Shefford.

"Sure. There in the bucket. It's rainwater. I have a tank here."

Shefford's sore and blistered face felt better after he had washed off the sand and alkali dust.

"Better not wash your face often while you're in the desert. Bad plan," went on Presbrey, noting how gingerly his visitor had gone about his ablutions. "Well, come and eat."

Shefford marked that if the trader did live a lonely life he fared well. There was more on the table than twice two men could have eaten. It was the first time in four days that Shefford had sat at a table, and he made up for lost opportunity. His host's actions indicated pleasure, yet the strange, hard face never relaxed, never changed. When the meal was finished Presbrey declined assistance, had a generous thought of the Indian girl, who, he said, could have a place to eat and sleep downstairs, and then with the skill and dispatch of an accomplished housewife cleared the table, after which work he filled a pipe and evidently prepared to listen.

It took only one question for Shefford to find that the trader was starved for news of the outside world; and for an hour Shefford fed that appetite, even as he had been done by. But when he had talked himself out there seemed indication of Presbrey being more than a good listener.

"How'd you come in?" he asked, presently.

"By Flagstaff—across the Little Colorado—and through Moencopie."

"Did you stop at Moen Ave?"

"No. What place is that?"

"A missionary lives there. Did you stop at Tuba?"

"Only long enough to drink and water my horse. That was a wonderful spring for the desert."

"You said you were a wanderer. . . . Do you want a job? I'll give you one."

"No, thank you, Presbrey."

"I saw your pack. That's no pack to travel with in this country. Your horse won't last, either. Have you any money?"

"Yes, plenty of money."

"Well, that's good. Not that a white man out here would ever take a dollar from you. But you can buy from the Indians as you go. Where are you making for, anyhow?"

Shefford hesitated, debating in mind whether to tell his purpose or not. His host did not press the question.

"I see. Just footloose and wandering around," went on Presbrey. "I can understand how the desert appeals to you. Preachers lead easy, safe, crowded, bound lives. They're shut up in a church with a Bible and good people. When once in a lifetime they get loose—they break out."

"Yes, I've broken out—beyond all bounds," replied Shefford, sadly. He seemed retrospective for a moment, unaware of the trader's keen and sympathetic glance, and then he caught himself. "I want to see some wild life. Do you know the country north of here?"

"Only what the Navajos tell me. And they're not much to talk. There's a trail goes north, but I've never traveled it. It's a new trail every time an Indian goes that way, for here the sand blows and covers old tracks. But few Navajos ride in from the north. My trade is mostly with Indians up and down the valley."

"How about water and grass?"

"We've had rain and snow. There's sure to be water. Can't say about grass, though the sheep and ponies from the north are always fat. . . . But, say, Shefford, if you'll excuse me for advising you—don't go north."

"Why?" asked Shefford, and it was certain that he thrilled.

"It's unknown country, terribly broken, as you can see from here, and there are bad Indians hiding in the canyons. I've never met a man who had been over the pass between here and Kayenta. The trip's been made, so there must be a trail. But it's a dangerous trip for any man, let alone a tenderfoot. You're not even packing a gun."

"What's this place Kayenta?" asked Shefford.

"It's a spring. Kayenta means Bottomless Spring. There's a little trading-post, the last and the wildest in northern Arizona. Withers, the trader who keeps it, hauls his supplies in from Colorado and New Mexico. He's never come down this way. I never saw him. Know nothing of him except hearsay. Reckon he's a nervy and strong man to hold that post. If you want to go there, better go by way of Keams Canyon, and then around the foot of Black Mesa. It'll be a long ride—maybe two hundred miles."

"How far straight north over the pass?"

"Can't say. Upward of seventy-five miles over rough trails, if there are trails at all. . . . I've heard rumors of a fine tribe of Navajos living in there, rich in sheep and horses. It may be true and it may not. But I do know there are bad Indians, half-breeds and outcasts, hiding in there.

Some of them have visited me here. Bad customers! More than that, you'll be going close to the Utah line, and the Mormons over there are unfriendly these days."

"Why?" queried Shefford, again with that curious thrill.

"They are being persecuted by the government."

Shefford asked no more questions and his host vouchsafed no more information on that score. The conversation lagged. Then Shefford inquired about the Indian girl and learned that she lived up the valley somewhere. Presbrey had never seen her before Willetts came with her to Red Lake. And this query brought out the fact that Presbrey was comparatively new to Red Lake and vicinity. Shefford wondered why a lonely six months there had not made the trader old in experience. Probably the desert did not readily give up its secrets. Moreover, this Red Lake house was only an occasionally used branch of Presbrey's main trading-post, which was situated at Willow Springs, fifty miles westward over the mesa.

"I'm closing up here soon for a spell," said Presbrey, and now his face lost its set hardness and seemed singularly changed. It was a difference of light and softness. "Won't be so lonesome over at Willow Springs. . . . I'm being married soon."

"That's fine," replied Shefford, warmly. He was glad for the sake of this lonely desert man. What good a wife would bring into a trader's life!

Presbrey's naïve admission, however, appeared to detach him from his present surroundings, and with his massive head enveloped by a cloud of smoke he lived in dreams.

Shefford respected his host's serene abstraction. Indeed, he was grateful for silence. Not for many nights had the past impinged so closely upon the present. The wound in his soul had not healed, and to speak of himself made it bleed anew. Memory was too poignant; the past was too close; he wanted to forget until he had toiled into the heart of this forbidding wilderness—until time had gone by and he dared to face his unquiet soul. Then he listened to the steadily rising roar of the wind. How strange and hollow! That wind was freighted with heavy sand, and he heard it sweep, sweep, sweep by in gusts, and then blow with dull, steady blast against the walls. The sound was provocative of thought. This moan and rush of wind was no dream—this presence of his in a night-enshrouded and sand-besieged house of the lonely desert was a reality—this adventure was not one of fancy. True indeed, then, must be the wild, strange story that had led him hither. He was going on to seek, to strive, to find. Somewhere northward in the broken fastnesses lay hidden a valley walled in from the world. Would they be there, those lost fugitives whose story had thrilled him? After twelve years would she be alive, a child grown to womanhood in the solitude of a beautiful canyon? Incredible! Yet he believed his friend's story and he indeed knew how strange and tragic life was. He fancied he heard her voice on the sweeping wind.

She called to him, haunted him. He admitted the improbability of her existence, but lost nothing of the persistent intangible hope that drove him. He believed himself a man stricken in soul, unworthy, through doubt of God, to minister to the people who had banished him. Perhaps a labor of Hercules, a mighty and perilous work of rescue, the saving of this lost and imprisoned girl, would help him in his trouble. She might be his salvation. Who could tell? Always as a boy and as a man he had fared forth to find the treasure at the foot of the rainbow.

⸰2⸰

THE SAGI

NEXT morning the Indian girl was gone and the tracks of her pony led north. Shefford's first thought was to wonder if he would overtake her on the trail; and this surprised him with the proof of how unconsciously his resolve to go on had formed.

Presbrey made no further attempt to turn Shefford back. But he insisted on replenishing the pack, and that Shefford take weapons. Finally Shefford was persuaded to accept a revolver. The trader bade him goodbye and stood in the door while Shefford led his horse down the slope toward the water-hole. Perhaps the trader believed he was watching the departure of a man who would never return. He was still standing at the door of the post when Shefford halted at the pool.

Upon the level floor of the valley lay thin patches of snow which had fallen during the night. The air was biting cold, yet stimulated Shefford while it stung him. His horse drank rather slowly and disgustedly. Then Shefford mounted and reluctantly turned his back upon the trading-post.

As he rode away from the pool he saw a large flock of sheep approaching. They were very closely, even densely, packed, in a solid slow-moving mass, and coming with a precision almost like a march. This fact surprised Shefford, for there was not an Indian in sight. Presently he saw that a dog was leading the flock, and a little later he discovered another dog in the rear of the sheep. They were splendid, long-haired dogs, of a wild-looking shepherd breed. He halted his horse to watch the procession pass by. The flock covered fully an acre of ground and the sheep were black, white, and brown. They passed him, making a little pattering roar on the hard-caked sand. The dogs were taking the sheep in to water.

Shefford went on and was drawing close to the other side of the basin, where the flat red level was broken by rising dunes and ridges, when he espied a bunch of ponies. A shrill whistle told him that they had seen him. They were wild, shaggy, with long manes and tails. They stopped, threw up their heads, and watched him. Shefford certainly returned the attention. There was no Indian with them. Presently, with a snort, the leader, which appeared to be a stallion, trotted behind the others, seemed to be driving them, and went clear round the band to get in the lead again. He was taking them in to water, the same as the dogs had taken the sheep.

These incidents were new and pleasing to Shefford. How ignorant he had been of life in the wilderness! Once more he received subtle intimations of what he might learn out in the open; and it was with a less weighted heart that he faced the gateway between the huge yellow bluffs on his left and the slow rise of ground to the black mesa on his right. He looked back in time to see the trading-post, bleak and lonely on the bare slope, pass out of sight behind the bluffs. Shefford felt no fear—he really had little experience of physical fear—but it was certain that he gritted his teeth and welcomed whatever was to come to him. He had lived a narrow, insulated life with his mind on spiritual things; his family and his congregation and his friends—except that one new friend whose story had enthralled him—were people of quiet religious habit; the man deep down in him had never had a chance. He breathed hard as he tried to imagine the world opening to him, and almost dared to be glad for the doubt that had sent him adrift.

The tracks of the Indian girl's pony were plain in the sand. Also there were other tracks, not so plain, and these Shefford decided had been made by Willetts and the girl the day before. He climbed a ridge, half soft sand and half hard, and saw right before him, rising in striking form, two great yellow buttes, like elephant legs. He rode between them, amazed at their height. Then before him stretched a slowly ascending valley, walled on one side by the black mesa and on the other by low bluffs. For miles a dark-green growth of greasewood covered the valley, and Shefford could see where the green thinned and failed, to give place to sand. He trotted his horse and made good time on this stretch.

The day contrasted greatly with any he had yet experienced. Gray clouds obscured the walls of rock a few miles to the west, and Shefford saw squalls of snow like huge veils dropping down and spreading out. The wind cut with the keenness of a knife. Soon he was chilled to the bone. A squall swooped and roared down upon him, and the wind that bore the driving white pellets of snow, almost like hail, was so freezing, bitter cold that the former wind seemed warm in comparison. The squall passed as

swiftly as it had come, and it left Shefford so benumbed he could not hold
the bridle. He tumbled off his horse and walked. By and by the sun came
out and soon warmed him and melted the thin layer of snow on the sand.
He was still on the trail of the Indian girl, but hers were now the only
tracks he could see.

All morning he gradually climbed, with limited view, until at last he
mounted to a point where the country lay open to his sight on all sides
except where the endless black mesa ranged on into the north. A rugged
yellow peak dominated the landscape to the fore, but it was far away. Red
and ragged country extended westward to a huge flat-topped wall of gray
rock. Lowering swift clouds swept across the sky, like drooping mantles,
and they darkened the sun. Shefford built a little fire out of dead greasewood sticks, and with his blanket round his shoulders he hung over the
blaze, scorching his clothes and hands. He had been cold before in his
life, but he had never before appreciated fire. This desert blast pierced
him. The squall enveloped him, thicker and colder and windier than the
other, but, being better fortified, he did not suffer so much. It howled
away, hiding the mesa and leaving a white desert behind. Shefford walked
on, leading his horse, until the exercise and the sun had once more
warmed him.

This last squall had rendered the Indian girl's trail difficult to follow.
The snow did not quickly melt, and, besides, sheep tracks and the tracks
of horses gave him trouble, until at last he was compelled to admit that he
could not follow her any longer. A faint path or trail led north, however,
and, following that, he soon forgot the girl. Every surmounted ridge held a
surprise for him. The desert seemed never to change in the vast whole
that encompassed him, yet near him it was always changing. From Red
Lake he had seen a peaked, walled, and canyoned country, as rough as a
stormy sea; but when he rode into that country the sharp and broken
features held to the distance.

He was glad to get out of the sand. Long narrow flats, gray with grass
and dotted with patches of greasewood, and lined by low bare ridges of
yellow rock, stretched away from him, leading toward the yellow peak
that seemed never to be gained upon.

Shefford had pictures in his mind, pictures of stone walls and wild
valleys and domed buttes, all of which had been painted in colorful and
vivid words by his friend Venters. He believed he would recognize the
distinctive and remarkable landmarks Venters had portrayed, and he was
certain that he had not yet come upon one of them. This was his second
lonely day of travel, and he had grown more and more susceptible to the
influence of horizon and the different prominent points. He attributed a
gradual change in his feelings to the loneliness and the increasing wildness. Between Tuba and Flagstaff he had met Indians and an occasional
prospector and teamster. Here he was alone, and though he felt some
strange gladness, he could not help but see the difference.

He rode on during the gray, lowering, chilly day, and toward evening the clouds broke in the west, and a setting sun shone through the rift, burnishing the desert to red and gold. Shefford's instinctive but deadened love of the beautiful in nature stirred into life, and the moment of its rebirth was a melancholy and sweet one. Too late for the artist's work, but not too late for his soul!

For a place to make camp he halted near a low area of rock that lay like an island in a sea of grass. There was an abundance of dead greasewood for a campfire, and, after searching over the rock, he found little pools of melted snow in the depressions. He took off the saddle and pack, watered his horse, and, hobbling him as well as his inexperience permitted, he turned him loose on the grass.

Then while he built a fire and prepared a meal the night came down upon him. In the lee of the rock he was well sheltered from the wind, but the air was bitter cold. He gathered all the dead greasewood in the vicinity, replenished the fire, and rolled in his blanket, back to the blaze. The loneliness and the coyotes did not bother him this night. He was too tired and cold. He went to sleep at once and did not awaken until the fire died out. Then he rebuilt it and went to sleep again. Every half-hour all night long he repeated this, and was glad indeed when the dawn broke.

The day began with misfortune. His horse was gone; it had been stolen, or had worked out of sight, or had broken the hobbles and made off. From a high stone ridge Shefford searched the grassy flats and slopes, all to no purpose. Then he tried to track the horse, but this was equally futile. He had expected disasters, and the first one did not daunt him. He tied most of his pack in the blanket, threw the canteen across his shoulder, and set forth, sure at least of one thing—that he was a very much better traveler on foot than on horseback.

Walking did not afford him the leisure to study the surrounding country; however, from time to time, when he surmounted a bench he scanned the different landmarks that had grown familiar. It took hours of steady walking to reach and pass the yellow peak that had been a kind of goal. He saw many sheep trails and horse tracks in the vicinity of this mountain, and once he was sure he espied an Indian watching him from a bold ridge-top.

The day was bright and warm, with air so clear it magnified objects he knew to be far away. The ascent was gradual; there were many narrow flats connected by steps; and the grass grew thicker and longer. At noon Shefford halted under the first cedar tree, a lonely, dwarfed shrub that seemed to have had a hard life. From this point the rise of ground was more perceptible, and straggling cedars led the eye on to a purple slope that merged into green of pinyon and pine. Could that purple be the sage Venters had so feelingly described, or was it merely the purple of deceiving distance? Whatever it might be, it gave Shefford a thrill and made him think of the strange, shy, and lovely woman Venters had won out here in this purple-sage country.

He calculated that he had ridden thirty miles the day before and had already traveled ten miles today, and therefore could hope to be in the pass before night. Shefford resumed his journey with too much energy and enthusiasm to think of being tired. And he discovered presently that the straggling cedars and the slope beyond were much closer than he had judged them to be. He reached the sage to find it gray instead of purple. Yet it was always purple a little way ahead, and if he half shut his eyes it was purple near at hand. He was surprised to find that he could not breathe freely, or it seemed so, and soon made the discovery that the sweet, pungent, penetrating fragrance of sage and cedar had this strange effect upon him. This was an exceedingly dry and odorous forest, where every open space between the clumps of cedars was choked with luxuriant sage. The pinyons were higher up on the mesa, and the pines still higher. Shefford appeared to lose himself. There were no trails; the black mesa on the right and the wall of stone on the left could not be seen; but he pushed on with what was either singular confidence or rash impulse. And he did not know whether that slope was long or short.

Once at the summit he saw with surprise that it broke abruptly and the descent was very steep and short on that side. Through the trees he once more saw the black mesa, rising to the dignity of a mountain; and he had glimpses of another flat, narrow valley, this time with a red wall running parallel with the mesa. He could not help but hurry down to get an unobstructed view. His eagerness was rewarded by a splendid scene, yet to his regret he could not force himself to believe it had any relation to the pictured scenes in his mind. The valley was half a mile wide, perhaps several miles long, and it extended in a curve between the cedar-sloped mesa and a looming wall of red stone. There was not a bird or a beast in sight. He found a well-defined trail, but it had not been recently used. He passed a low structure made of peeled logs and mud, with a dark opening like a door. It did not take him many minutes to learn that the valley was longer than he had calculated. He walked swiftly and steadily, in spite of the fact that the pack had become burdensome. What lay beyond the jutting corner of the mesa had increasing fascination for him and acted as a spur. At last he turned the corner, only to be disappointed at sight of another cedar slope. He had a glimpse of a single black shaft of rock rising far in the distance, and it disappeared as his striding forward made the crest of the slope rise toward the sky.

Again his view became restricted, and he lost the sense of a slow and gradual uplift of rock and an increase in the scale of proportion. Halfway up this ascent he was compelled to rest; and again the sun was slanting low when he entered the cedar forest. Soon he was descending, and he suddenly came into the open to face a scene that made his heart beat thick and fast.

He saw lofty crags and cathedral spires, and a wonderful canyon winding between huge beetling red walls. He heard the murmur of flowing water. The trail led down to the canyon floor, which appeared to be level and green and cut by deep washes in red earth. Could this canyon be the mouth of Deception Pass? It bore no resemblance to any place Shefford had heard described, yet somehow he felt rather than saw that it was the portal to the wild fastness he had traveled so far to enter.

Not till he had descended the trail and had dropped his pack did he realize how weary and footsore he was. Then he rested. But his eyes roved to and fro, and his mind was active. What a wild and lonesome spot! The low murmur of shallow water came up to him from a deep, narrow cleft. Shadows were already making the canyon seem full of blue haze. He saw a bare slope of stone out of which cedar trees were growing. And as he looked about him he became aware of a singular and very perceptible change in the lights and shades. The sun was setting; the crags were gold-tipped; the shadows crept upward; the sky seemed to darken swiftly; then the gold changed to red, slowly dulled, and the grays and purples stood out. Shefford was entranced with the beautiful changing effects, and watched till the walls turned black and the sky grew steely and a faint star peeped out. Then he set about the necessary camp tasks.

Dead cedars right at hand assured him a comfortable night with steady fire; and when he had satisfied his hunger he arranged an easy seat before the blazing logs, and gave his mind over to thought of his weird, lonely environment.

The murmur of running water mingled in harmonious accompaniment with the moan of the wind in the cedars—wild, sweet sounds that were balm to his wounded spirit! They seemed a part of the silence, rather than a break in it or a hindrance to the feeling of it. But suddenly that silence did break to the rattle of a rock. Shefford listened, thinking some wild animal was prowling around. He felt no alarm. Presently he heard the sound again, and again. Then he recognized the crack of unshod hoofs upon rock. A horse was coming down the trail. Shefford rather resented the interruption, though he still had no alarm. He believed he was perfectly safe. As a matter of fact, he had never in his life been anything but safe and padded around with wool; hence, never having experienced peril, he did not know what fear was.

Presently he saw a horse and rider come into dark prominence on the ridge just above his camp. They were silhouetted against the starry sky. The horseman stopped and he and his steed made a magnificent black statue, somehow wild and strange, in Shefford's sight. Then he came on, vanished in the darkness under the ridge, presently to emerge into the circle of campfire light.

He rode to within twenty feet of Shefford and the fire. The horse was dark, wild-looking, and seemed ready to run. The rider appeared to be an

240 Z A N E   G R E Y

Indian, and yet had something about him suggesting the cowboy. At once Shefford remembered what Presbrey had said about half-breeds. A little shock, inexplicable to Shefford, rippled over him.

He greeted his visitor, but received no answer. Shefford saw a dark, squat figure bending forward in the saddle. The man was tense. All about him was dark except the glint of a rifle across the saddle. The face under the sombrero was only a shadow. Shefford kicked the fire-logs and a brighter blaze lightened the scene. Then he saw this stranger a little more clearly, and made out an unusually large head, broad dark face, a sinister tight-shut mouth, and gleaming black eyes.

Those eyes were unmistakably hostile. They roved searchingly over Shefford's pack and then over his person. Shefford felt for the gun that Presbrey had given him. But it was gone. He had left it back where he had lost his horse, and had not thought of it since. Then a strange, slow-coming cold agitation possessed Shefford. Something gripped his throat.

Suddenly Shefford was stricken at a menacing movement on the part of the horseman. He had drawn a gun. Shefford saw it shine darkly in the firelight. The Indian meant to murder him. Shefford saw the grim, dark face in a kind of horrible amaze. He felt the meaning of that drawn weapon as he had never felt anything before in his life. And he collapsed back into his seat with an icy, sickening terror. In a second he was dripping wet with cold sweat. Lightning-swift thoughts flashed through his mind. It had been one of his platitudes that he was not afraid of death. Yet here he was a shaking, helpless coward. What had he learned about either life or death? Would this dark savage plunge him into the unknown? It was then that Shefford realized his hollow philosophy and the bittersweetness of life. He had a brain and a soul, and between them he might have worked out his salvation. But what were they to this ruthless night-wanderer, this raw and horrible wildness of the desert?

Incapable of voluntary movement, with tongue cleaving to the roof of his mouth, Shefford watched the horseman and the half-poised gun. It was not yet leveled. Then it dawned upon Shefford that the stranger's head was turned a little, his ear to the wind. He was listening. His horse was listening. Suddenly he straightened up, wheeled his horse, and trotted away into the darkness. But he did not climb the ridge down which he had come.

Shefford heard the click of hoofs upon the stony trail. Other horses and riders were descending into the canyon. They had been the cause of his deliverance, and in the relaxation of feeling he almost fainted. Then he sat there, slowly recovering, slowly ceasing to tremble, divining that this situation was somehow to change his attitude toward life.

Three horses, two with riders, moved in dark shapes across the skyline above the ridge, disappeared as had Shefford's first visitor, and then rode into the light. Shefford saw two Indians—a man and a woman—then with surprise recognized the latter to be the Indian girl he had met at Red Lake. He was still more surprised to recognize in the third horse the one he had lost at the last camp. Shefford rose, a little shaky on his legs, to thank these Indians for a double service. The man slipped from his saddle and his moccasined feet thudded lightly. He was tall, lithe, erect, a singularly graceful figure, and as he advanced Shefford saw a dark face and sharp, dark eyes. The Indian was bareheaded, with his hair bound in a band. He resembled the girl, but appeared to have a finer face.

"How do?" he said, in a voice low and distinct. He extended his hand, and Shefford felt a grip of steel. He returned the greeting. Then the Indian gave Shefford the bridle of the horse, and made signs that appeared to indicate the horse had broken his hobbles and strayed. Shefford thanked him. Thereupon the Indian unsaddled and led the horses away, evidently to water them. The girl remained behind. Shefford addressed her, but she was shy and did not respond. He then set about cooking a meal for his visitors, and was busily engaged at this when the Indian returned without the horses. Presently Shefford resumed his seat by the fire and watched the two eat what he had prepared. They certainly were hungry and soon had the pans and cups empty. Then the girl drew back a little into the shadow, while the man sat with his legs crossed and his feet tucked under him.

His dark face was smooth, yet it seemed to have lines under the surface. Shefford was impressed. He had never seen an Indian who interested him as this one. Looked at superficially, he appeared young, wild, silent, locked in his primeval apathy, just a healthy savage; but looked at more attentively, he appeared matured, even old, a strange, sad, brooding figure, with a burden on his shoulders. Shefford found himself growing curious.

"What place?" asked Shefford, waving his hand toward the dark opening between the black cliffs.

"Sagi," replied the Indian.

That did not mean anything to Shefford, and he asked if the Sagi was the pass, but the Indian shook his head.

"Wife?" asked Shefford, pointing to the girl.

The Indian shook his head again. *"Bi-la,"* he said.

"What you mean?" asked Shefford. "What *bi-la?"*

"Sister," replied the Indian. He spoke the word reluctantly, as if the white man's language did not please him, but the clearness and correct pronunciation surprised Shefford.

"What name—what call her?" he went on.

"Glen Naspa."

"What your name?" inquired Shefford, indicating the Indian.

"Nas Ta Bega," answered the Indian.

"Navajo?"

The Indian bowed with what seemed pride and stately dignity.

"My name John Shefford. Come far 'way back toward rising sun. Come stay here long."

Nas Ta Bega's dark eyes were fixed steadily upon Shefford. He reflected that he could not remember having felt so penetrating a gaze. But neither the Indian's eyes nor face gave any clue to his thoughts.

"Navajo no savvy Jesus Christ," said the Indian, and his voice rolled out low and deep.

Shefford felt both amaze and pain. The Indian had taken him for a missionary.

"No! . . . Me no missionary," cried Shefford, and he flung up a passionately repudiating hand.

A singular flash shot from the Indian's dark eyes. It struck Shefford even at this stinging moment when the past came back.

"Trade—buy wool—blanket?" queried Nas Ta Bega.

"No," replied Shefford. "Me want ride—walk far." He waved his hand to indicate a wide sweep of territory. "Me sick."

Nas Ta Bega laid a significant finger upon his lungs.

"No," replied Shefford. "Me strong. Sick here." And with motions of his hands he tried to show that his was a trouble of the heart.

Shefford received instant impression of this Indian's intelligent comprehension, but he could not tell just what had given him the feeling. Nas Ta Bega rose then and walked away into the shadow. Shefford heard him working around the dead cedar tree, where he had probably gone to get firewood. Then Shefford heard a splintering crash, which was followed by a crunching, bumping sound. Presently he was astounded to see the Indian enter the lighted circle dragging the whole cedar tree, trunk first. Shefford would have doubted the ability of two men to drag that tree, and here came Nas Ta Bega, managing it easily. He laid the trunk on the fire, and then proceeded to break off small branches, to place them advantageously where the red coals kindled them into a blaze.

The Indian's next move was to place his saddle, which he evidently meant to use for a pillow. Then he spread a goat-skin on the ground, lay down upon it, with his back to the fire, and, pulling a long-haired saddle-blanket over his shoulders, he relaxed and became motionless. His sister, Glen Naspa, did likewise, except that she stayed farther away from the fire, and she had a larger blanket, which covered her well. It appeared to Shefford that they went to sleep at once.

Shefford felt as tired as he had ever been, but he did not think he could soon drop into slumber, and in fact he did not want to.

There was something in the companionship of these Indians that he had not experienced before. He still had a strange and weak feeling—the aftermath of that fear which had sickened him with its horrible icy grip. Nas Ta Bega's arrival had frightened away that dark and silent prowler of the night; and Shefford was convinced the Indian had saved his life. The measure of his gratitude was a source of wonder to him. Had he cared so much for life? Yes—he had, when face to face with death. That was something to know. It helped him. And he gathered from his strange feelings that the romantic quest which had brought him into the wilderness might turn out to be an antidote for the morbid bitterness of heart.

With new sensations had come new thoughts. Right then it was very pleasant to sit in the warmth and light of the roaring cedar fire. There was a deep-seated ache of fatigue in his bones. What joy it was to rest! He had felt the dry scorch of desert thirst and the pang of hunger. How wonderful to learn the real meaning of water and food! He had just finished the longest, hardest day's work of his life! Had that anything to do with a something almost like peace which seemed to hover near in the shadows, trying to come to him? He had befriended an Indian girl, and now her brother had paid back the service. Both the giving and receiving were somehow sweet to Shefford. They opened up hitherto vague channels of thought. For years he had imagined he was serving people, when he had never lifted a hand. A blow given in the defense of an Indian girl had somehow operated to make a change in John Shefford's existence. It had liberated a spirit in him. Moreover, it had worked its influence outside his mind. The Indian girl and her brother had followed his trail to return his horse, perhaps to guide him safely, but, unknowingly perhaps, they had done infinitely more than that for him. As Shefford's eye wandered over the dark, still figures of the sleepers, he had a strange, dreamy premonition, or perhaps only a fancy, that there was to be more come of this fortunate meeting.

For the rest, it was good to be there in the speaking silence, to feel the heat on his outstretched palms and the cold wind on his cheek, to see the black wall lifting its bold outline and the crags reaching for the white stars.

⁌3⁍

KAYENTA

THE STAMPING of horses awoke Shefford. He saw a towering crag, rosy in the morning light, like a huge red spear splitting the clear blue of sky. He got up, feeling cramped and sore, yet with unfamiliar exhilaration. The whipping air made him stretch his hands to the fire. An odor of coffee and broiled meat mingled with the fragrance of wood smoke. Glen Naspa was on her knees broiling a rabbit on a stick over the red coals. Nas Ta Bega was saddling the ponies. The canyon appeared to be full of purple shadows under one side of dark cliffs and golden streaks of mist on the other where the sun struck high up on the walls.

"Good morning," said Shefford.

Glen Naspa shyly replied in Navajo.

"How," was Nas Ta Bega's greeting.

In daylight the Indian lost some of the dark somberness of face that had impressed Shefford. He had a noble head, in poise like that of an eagle, a bold, clean-cut profile, and stern, close-shut lips. His eyes were the most striking and attractive feature about him; they were coal-black and piercing; the intent look out of them seemed to come from a keen and inquisitive mind.

Shefford ate breakfast with the Indians, and then helped with the few preparations for departure. Before they mounted, Nas Ta Bega pointed to horse tracks in the dust. They were those that had been made by Shefford's threatening visitor of the night before. Shefford explained by word and sign, and succeeded at least in showing that he had been in danger. Nas Ta Bega followed the tracks a little way and presently returned.

"Shadd," he said, with an ominous shake of his head. Shefford did not understand whether he meant the name of his visitor or something else, but the menace connected with the word was clear enough.

Glen Naspa mounted her pony, and it was a graceful action that pleased Shefford. He climbed a little stiffly into his own saddle. Then Nas Ta Bega got up and pointed northward.

"Kayenta?" he inquired.

Shefford nodded and then they were off, with Glen Naspa in the lead. They did not climb the trail which they had descended, but took one leading to the right along the base of the slope. Shefford saw down into the red wash that bisected the canyon floor. It was a sheer wall of red clay or loam, a hundred feet high, and at the bottom ran a swift, shallow stream of reddish water. Then for a time a high growth of greasewood hid the surroundings from Shefford's sight. Presently the trail led out into the open, and Shefford saw that he was at the neck of a wonderful valley that gradually widened with great jagged red peaks on the left and the black mesa, now a mountain, running away to the right. He turned to find that the opening of the Sagi could no longer be seen, and he was conscious of a strong desire to return and explore that canyon.

Soon Glen Naspa put her pony to a long, easy, swinging canter and her followers did likewise. As they got outward into the valley Shefford lost the sense of being overshadowed and crowded by the nearness of the huge walls and crags. The trail appeared level underfoot, but at a distance it was seen to climb. Shefford found where it disappeared over the foot of a slope that formed a graceful rising line up to the cedared flank of the mesa. The valley floor, widening away to the north, remained level and green. Beyond rose the jagged range of red peaks, all strangely cut and slanting. These distant deceiving features of the country held Shefford's gaze until the Indian drew his attention to things near at hand. Then Shefford saw flocks of sheep dotting the gray-green valley, and bands of beautiful long-maned, long-tailed ponies.

For several miles the scene did not change except that Shefford imagined he came to see where the upland plain ended or at least broke its level. He was right, for presently the Indian pointed, and Shefford went on to halt upon the edge of a steep slope leading down into a valley vast in its barren gray reaches.

"Kayenta," said Nas Ta Bega.

Shefford at first saw nothing except the monotonous gray valley reaching far to the strange, grotesque monuments of yellow cliff. Then close under the foot of the slope he espied two squat stone houses with red roofs, and a corral with a pool of water shining in the sun.

The trail leading down was steep and sandy, but it was not long. Shefford's sweeping eyes appeared to take in everything at once—the crude stone structures with their earthen roofs, the piles of dirty wool, the Indians lolling around, the tents, and wagons, and horses, little lazy burros and dogs, and scattered everywhere saddles, blankets, guns, and packs.

Then a white man came out of the door. He waved a hand and shouted. Dust and wool and flour were thick upon him. He was muscular and weather-beaten, and appeared young in activity rather than face. A gun swung at his hip and a row of brass-tipped cartridges showed in his belt. Shefford looked into a face that he thought he had seen before, until he realized the similarity was only the bronze and hard line and rugged cast common to desert men. The gray searching eyes went right through him.

"Glad to see you. Get down and come in. Just heard from an Indian that you were coming. I'm the trader Withers," he said to Shefford. His voice was welcoming and the grip of his hand made Shefford's ache.

Shefford told his name and said he was as glad as he was lucky to arrive at Kayenta.

"Hello! Nas Ta Bega!" exclaimed Withers. His tone expressed a surprise his face did not show. "Did this Indian bring you in?"

Withers shook hands with the Navajo while Shefford briefly related what he owed to him. Then Withers looked at Nas Ta Bega and spoke to him in the Indian tongue.

"Shadd," said Nas Ta Bega.

Withers let out a dry little laugh and his strong hand tugged at his mustache.

"Who's Shadd?" asked Shefford.

"He's a half-breed Ute—bad Indian, outlaw, murderer. He's in with a gang of outlaws who hide in the San Juan country. . . . Reckon you're lucky. How'd you come to be there in the Sagi alone?"

"I traveled from Red Lake. Presbrey, the trader there, advised against it, but I came anyway."

"Well." Withers's gray glance was kind, if it did express the foolhardiness of Shefford's act. "Come into the house. . . . Never mind the horse. My wife will sure be glad to see you."

Withers led Shefford by the first stone house, which evidently was the trading-store, into the second. The room Shefford entered was large, with logs smoldering in a huge open fireplace, blankets covering every foot of floor space, and Indian baskets and silver ornaments everywhere, and strange Indian designs painted upon the whitewashed walls. Withers called his wife and made her acquainted with Shefford. She was a slight, comely little woman, with keen, earnest, dark eyes. She seemed to be serious and quiet, but she made Shefford feel at home immediately. He refused, however, to accept the room offered him, saying that he meant to sleep out under the open sky. Withers laughed at this and said he understood. Shefford, remembering Presbrey's hunger for news of the outside world, told this trader and his wife all he could think of; and he was listened to with that close attention a traveler always gained in the remote places.

"Sure am glad you rode in," said Withers, for the fourth time. "Now you make yourself at home. Stay here—come over to the store—do what you like. I've got to work. Tonight we'll talk."

Shefford went out with his host. The store was as interesting as Presbrey's, though much smaller and more primitive. It was full of everything, and smelled strongly of sheep and goats. There was a narrow aisle between sacks of flour and blankets on one side and a high counter on the other. Behind this counter Withers stood to wait upon the buying Indians. They sold blankets and skins and bags of wool, and in exchange took silver money. Then they lingered and with slow, staid reluctance bought one thing and then another—flour, sugar, canned goods, coffee, tobacco, ammunition. The counter was never without two or three Indians leaning on their dark, silver-braceleted arms. But as they were slow to sell and buy and go, so were others slow to come in. Their voices were soft and low and it seemed to Shefford they were whispering. He liked to hear them and to look at the banded heads, the long, twisted rolls of black hair tied with white cords, the still dark faces and watchful eyes, the silver earrings, the slender, shapely brown hands, the lean and sinewy shapes, the corduroys with a belt and gun, and the small, close-fitting buckskin moccasins buttoned with coins. These Indians all appeared young, and under the quiet, slow demeanor there was fierce blood and fire.

By and by two women came in, evidently squaw and daughter. The former was a huge, stout Indian with a face that was certainly pleasant if not jolly. She had the corners of a blanket tied under her chin and in the folds behind on her broad back was a naked Indian baby, round and black of head, brown-skinned, with eyes as bright as beads. When the youngster caught sight of Shefford he made a startled dive into the sack of the blanket. Manifestly, however, curiosity got the better of fear, for presently Shefford caught a pair of wondering dark eyes peeping at him.

"They're good spenders, but slow," said Withers. "The Navajos are careful and cautious. That's why they're rich. This squaw, Yan As Pa, has flocks of sheep and more mustangs than she knows about."

"Mustangs. So that's what you call the ponies?" replied Shefford.

"Yep. They're mustangs, and mostly wild as jackrabbits."

Shefford strolled outside and made the acquaintance of Withers's helper, a Mormon named Whisner. He was a stockily built man past maturity, and his sun-blistered face and watery eyes told of the open desert. He was engaged in weighing sacks of wool brought in by the Indians. Nearby stood a framework of poles from which an immense bag was suspended. From the top of this bag protruded the head and shoulders of an Indian who appeared to be stamping and packing wool with his feet. He grinned at the curious Shefford. But Shefford was more interested in the Mormon. So far as he knew, Whisner was the first man of that creed he had ever met, and he could scarcely hide his eagerness. Venters's stories had been of a long-past generation of Mormons, fanatical, ruthless, and unchangeable. Shefford did not expect to meet Mormons of this kind. But any man of that religion would have interested him. Besides this, Whisner seemed to bring him closer to that wild secret canyon he had come West to find. Shefford was somewhat amazed and discomfited to have his polite and friendly overtures repulsed. Whisner might have been an Indian. He was cold, incommunicative, aloof; and there was something about him that made the sensitive Shefford feel his presence was resented.

Presently Shefford strolled on to the corral, which was full of shaggy mustangs. They snorted and kicked at him. He had a half-formed wish that he would never be called upon to ride one of those wild brutes, and then he found himself thinking that he would ride one of them, and after a while any of them. Shefford did not understand himself, but he fought his natural instinctive reluctance to meet obstacles, peril, suffering.

He traced the white-bordered little stream that made the pool in the corral, and when he came to where it oozed out of the sand under the bluff he decided that was not the spring which had made Kayenta famous. Presently down below the trading-post he saw a trough from which burros were drinking. Here he found the spring, a deep well of eddying water walled in by stones, and the overflow made a shallow stream meandering away between its borders of alkali, like a crust of salt. Shefford tasted the water. It bit, but it was good.

Shefford had no trouble in making friends with the lazy sleepy-eyed burros. They let him pull their long ears and rub their noses, but the mustangs standing around were unapproachable. They had wild eyes; they raised long ears and looked vicious. He let them alone.

Evidently this trading-post was a great deal busier than Red Lake. Shefford counted a dozen Indians lounging outside, and there were others riding away. Big wagons told how the bags of wool were transported out of the wilds and how supplies were brought in. A wide, hard-packed road led off to the east, and another, not so clearly defined, wound away to the north. And Indian trails streaked off in all directions.

Shefford discovered, however, when he had walked off a mile or so across the valley to lose sight of the post, that the feeling of wildness and loneliness returned to him. It was a wonderful country. It held something for him besides the possible rescue of an imprisoned girl from a wild canyon.

That night after supper, when Withers and Shefford sat alone before the blazing logs in the huge fireplace, the trader laid his hand on Shefford's and said, with directness and force:

"I've lived my life in the desert. I've met many men and have been a friend to most. . . . You're no prospector or trader or missionary?"

"No," replied Shefford.

"You've had trouble?"

"Yes."

"Have you come in here to hide? Don't be afraid to tell me. I won't give you away."

"I didn't come to hide."

"Then no one is after you? You've done no wrong?"

"Perhaps I wronged myself, but no one else," replied Shefford, steadily.

"I reckoned so. Well, tell me, or keep your secret—it's all one to me."

Shefford felt a desire to unburden himself. This man was strong, persuasive, kindly. He drew Shefford.

"You're welcome in Kayenta," went on Withers. "Stay as long as you like. I take no pay from a white man. If you want work I have it aplenty."

"Thank you. That is good. I need to work. We'll talk of it later. . . . But just yet I can't tell you why I came to Kayenta, what I want to do, how long I shall stay. My thoughts put in words would seem so like dreams. Maybe they are dreams. Perhaps I'm only chasing a phantom—perhaps I'm only hunting the treasure at the foot of the rainbow."

"Well, this is the country for rainbows," laughed Withers. "In summer from June to August when it storms we have rainbows that'll make you think you're in another world. The Navajos have rainbow mountains, rainbow canyons, rainbow bridges of stone, rainbow trails. It sure is rainbow country."

That deep and mystic chord in Shefford thrilled. Here it was again—something tangible at the bottom of his dream.

Withers did not wait for Shefford to say anymore, and almost as if he read his visitor's mind he began to talk about the wild country he called home.

He had lived at Kayenta for several years—hard and profitless years by reason of marauding outlaws. He could not have lived there at all but for the protection of the Indians. His father-in-law had been friendly with the Navajos and Piutes for many years, and his wife had been brought up among them. She was held in peculiar reverence and affection by both tribes in that part of the country. Probably she knew more of the Indians' habits, religion, and life than any white person in the West. Both tribes were friendly and peaceable, but there were bad Indians, half-breeds, and outlaws that made the trading-post a venture Withers had long considered precarious, and he wanted to move and intended to some day. His nearest neighbors in New Mexico and Colorado were a hundred miles distant and at some seasons the roads were impassable. To the north, however, twenty miles or so, was situated a Mormon village named Stonebridge. It lay across the Utah line. Withers did some business with this village, but scarcely enough to warrant the risks he had to run. During the last year he had lost several pack-trains, one of which he had never heard of after it left Stonebridge.

"Stonebridge!" exclaimed Shefford, and he trembled. He had heard that name. In his memory it had a place beside the name of another village Shefford longed to speak of to this trader.

"Yes—Stonebridge," replied Withers. "Ever heard the name?"

"I think so. Are there other villages in—in that part of the country?"

"A few, but not close. Glaze is now only a waterhole. Bluff and Monticello are far north across the San Juan. . . . There used to be another village—but that wouldn't interest you."

"Maybe it would," replied Shefford, quietly.

But his hint was not taken by the trader. Withers suddenly showed a semblance to the aloofness Shefford had observed in Whisner.

"Withers, pardon an impertinence—I am deeply serious. . . . Are you a Mormon?"

"Indeed I'm not," replied the trader, instantly.

"Are you for the Mormons or against them?"

"Neither. I get along with them. I know them. I believe they are a misunderstood people."

"That's for them."

"No. I'm only fair-minded."

Shefford paused, trying to curb his thrilling impulse, but it was too strong.

"You said there used to be another village. . . . Was the name of it—Cottonwoods?"

Withers gave a start and faced round to stare at Shefford in blank astonishment.

"Say, did you give me a straight story about yourself?" he queried, sharply.

"So far as I went," replied Shefford.

"You're no spy on the lookout for sealed wives?"

"Absolutely not. I don't even know what you mean by sealed wives."

"Well, it's damn strange that you'd know the name Cottonwoods. . . . Yes, that's the name of the village I meant—the one that used to be. It's gone now, all except a few stone walls."

"What became of it?"

"Torn down by Mormons years ago. They destroyed it and moved away. I've heard Indians talk about a grand spring that was there once. It's gone, too. Its name was—let me see—"

"Amber Spring," interrupted Shefford.

"By George, you're right!" rejoined the trader, again amazed. "Shefford, this beats me. I haven't heard that name for ten years. I can't help seeing what a tenderfoot—stranger—you are to the desert. Yet, here you are—speaking of what you should know nothing of. . . . And there's more behind this."

Shefford rose, unable to conceal his agitation.

"Did you ever hear of a rider named Venters?"

"Rider? You mean a cowboy? Venters. No, I never heard that name."

"Did you ever hear of a gunman named Lassiter?" queried Shefford, with increasing emotion.

"No."

"Did you ever hear of a Mormon woman named—Jane Withersteen?"

"No."

Shefford drew his breath sharply. He had followed a gleam—he had caught a fleeting glimpse of it.

"Did you ever hear of a child—a girl—a woman—called Fay Larkin?"

Withers rose slowly with a paling face.

"If you're a spy it'll go hard with you—though I'm no Mormon," he said, grimly.

Shefford lifted a shaking hand.

"I *was* a clergyman. Now I'm nothing—a wanderer—least of all a spy."

Withers leaned closer to see into the other man's eyes; he looked long and then appeared satisfied.

"I've heard the name Fay Larkin," he said, slowly. "I reckon that's all I'll say till you tell your story."

Shefford stood with his back to the fire and he turned the palms of his hands to catch the warmth. He felt cold. Withers had affected him strangely. What was the meaning of the trader's somber gravity? Why was the very mention of Mormons attended by something austere and secret?

"My name is John Shefford. I am twenty-four," began Shefford. "My family—"

Here a knock on the door interrupted Shefford.

"Come in," called Withers.

The door opened and like a shadow Nas Ta Bega slipped in. He said something in Navajo to the trader.

"How," he said to Shefford, and extended his hand. He was stately, but there was no mistaking his friendliness. Then he sat down before the fire, doubled his legs under him after the Indian fashion, and with dark eyes on the blazing logs seemed to lose himself in meditation.

"He likes the fire," explained Withers. "Whenever he comes to Kayenta he always visits me like this. . . . Don't mind him. Go on with your story."

"My family were plain people, well-to-do, and very religious," went on Shefford. "When I was a boy we moved from the country to a town called Beaumont, Illinois. There was a college in Beaumont and eventually I was sent to it to study for the ministry. I wanted to be— But never mind that. . . . By the time I was twenty-two I was ready for my career as a clergyman. I preached for a year around at different places and then got a church in my hometown of Beaumont. I became exceedingly good friends with a man named Venters, who had recently come to Beaumont. He was a singular man. His wife was a strange, beautiful woman, very reserved, and she had wonderful dark eyes. They had money and were devoted to each other, and perfectly happy. They owned the finest horses ever seen in Illinois, and their particular enjoyment seemed to be riding. They were always taking long rides. It was something worth going far for to see Mrs. Venters on a horse.

"It was through my own love of horses that I became friendly with Venters. He and his wife attended my church, and as I got to see more of them, gradually we grew intimate. And it was not until I did get intimate with them that I realized that both seemed to be haunted by the past. They were sometimes sad even in their happiness. They drifted off into dreams. They lived back in another world. They seemed to be listening. Indeed, they were a singularly interesting couple, and I grew genuinely fond of them. By and by they had a little girl whom they named Jane. The coming of the baby made a change in my friends. They were happier, and I observed that the haunting shadow did not so often return.

"Venters had spoken of a journey west that he and his wife meant to take some time. But after the baby came he never mentioned his wife in connection with the trip. I gathered that he felt compelled to go to clear up a mystery or to find something—I did not make out just what. But eventually, and it was about a year ago, he told me his story—the strangest, wildest, and most tragic I ever heard.

"I can't tell it all now. It is enough to say that fifteen years before he had been a rider for a rich Mormon woman named Jane Withersteen, of this village Cottonwoods. She had adopted a beautiful Gentile child named Fay Larkin. Her interest in Gentiles earned the displeasure of her churchmen, and as she was proud there came a breach. Venters and a gunman named Lassiter became involved in her quarrel. Finally Venters took to the canyons. Here in the wilds he found the strange girl he eventually married. For a long time they lived in a wonderful hidden valley, the entrance to which was guarded by a huge balancing rock. Venters got away with the girl. But Lassiter and Jane Withersteen and the child Fay Larkin were driven into the canyon. They escaped to the valley where Venters had lived. Lassiter rolled the balancing rock, and, crashing down the narrow trail, it loosened the weathered walls and closed the narrow outlet forever."

⁂4⁂

NEW FRIENDS

SHEFFORD ended his narrative out of breath, pale, and dripping with sweat. Withers sat leaning forward with an expression of intense interest. Nas Ta Bega's easy, graceful pose had succeeded to one of strained rigidity. He seemed a statue of bronze. Could a few intelligible words, Shefford wondered, have created that strange, listening posture?

"Venters got out of Utah, of course, as you know," went on Shefford. "He got out, knowing—as I feel I would have known—that Jane, Lassiter, and little Fay Larkin were shut up, walled up in Surprise Valley. For years Venters considered it would not have been safe for him to venture to rescue them. He had no fears for their lives. They could live in Surprise Valley. But Venters always intended to come back with Bess and find the valley and his friends. No wonder he and Bess were haunted. However, when his wife had the baby that made a difference. It meant he had to go alone. And he was thinking seriously of starting when I—when there were developments that made it desirable for me to leave Beaumont. Venters's story haunted me as he had been haunted. I dreamed of that wild valley—of little Fay Larkin grown to womanhood—such a woman as Bess Venters was. And the longing to come was great. . . . And, Withers—here I am."

The trader reached out and gave Shefford the grip of a man in whom emotion was powerful, but deep and difficult to express.

"Listen to this. . . . I wish I could help you. Life is a queer deal. . . . Shefford, I've got to trust you. Over here in the wild canyon country there's a village of Mormons' sealed wives. It's in Arizona, perhaps twenty miles from here, and near the Utah line. When the United States government began to persecute, or prosecute, the Mormons for polygamy, the Mormons over here in Stonebridge took their sealed wives and moved them out of Utah, just across the line. They built houses, established a village there. I'm the only Gentile who knows about it. And I pack supplies every few weeks into these women. There are perhaps fifty women, mostly young—second or third or fourth wives of Mormons—sealed wives. And I want you to understand that sealed means *sealed* in all that religion or loyalty can get out of the word. There are also some old women and old men in the village, but they hardly count. And there's a flock of the finest children you ever saw in your life.

"The idea of the Mormons must have been to escape prosecution. The law of the government is one wife for each man—no more. All over Utah polygamists have been arrested. The Mormons are deeply concerned. I believe they are a good, law-abiding people. But this law is a direct blow at their religion. In my opinion they can't obey both. And therefore they have not altogether given up plural wives. Perhaps they will some day. I have no proof, but I believe the Mormons of Stonebridge pay secret night visits to their sealed wives across the line in the lonely, hidden village.

"Now once over in Stonebridge I overheard some Mormons talking about a girl who was named Fay Larkin. I never forgot the name. Later I heard the name in this sealed-wife village. But, as I told you, I never heard of Lassiter or Jane Withersteen. Still, if Mormons had found them I would never have heard of it. And Deception Pass—that might be the Sagi. . . . I'm not surprised at your rainbow-chasing adventure. It's a great story. . . . This Fay Larkin I've heard of *might* be your Fay Larkin —I almost believe so. Shefford, I'll help you find out."

"Yes, yes—I must know," replied Shefford. "Oh, I hope, I pray we can find her! But—I'd rather she was dead—if she's not still hidden in the valley."

"Naturally. You've dreamed yourself into rescuing this lost Fay Larkin. . . . But, Shefford, you're old enough to know life doesn't work out as you want it to. One way or another I fear you're in for a bitter disappointment."

"Withers, take me to the village."

"Shefford, you're liable to get in bad out here," said the trader, gravely.

"I couldn't be any more ruined than I am now," replied Shefford, passionately.

"But there's risk in this—risk such as you never had," persisted Withers.

"I'll risk anything."

"Reckon this 's a funny deal for a sheep-trader to have on his hands," continued Withers. "Shefford, I like you. I've a mind to see you through this. It's a damn strange story. . . . I'll tell you what—I will help you. I'll give you a job packing supplies into the village. I meant to turn that over to a Mormon cowboy—Joe Lake. The job shall be yours, and I'll go with you first trip. Here's my hand on it. . . . Now, Shefford, I'm more curious about you than I was before you told your story. What ruined you? As we're to be partners, you can tell me now. I'll keep your secret. Maybe I can do you good."

Shefford wanted to confess, yet it was hard. Perhaps, had he not been so agitated, he would not have answered to impulse. But this trader was a man—a man of the desert—he would understand.

"I told you I was a clergyman," said Shefford in low voice. "I didn't want to be one, but they made me one. I did my best. I failed. . . . I had doubts of religion—of the Bible—of God, as my church believed in them. As I grew older thought and study convinced me of the narrowness of religion as my congregation lived it. I preached what I believed. I alienated them. They put me out, took my calling from me, disgraced me, ruined me."

"So that's all!" exclaimed Withers, slowly. "You didn't believe in the God of the Bible. . . . Well, I've been in the desert long enough to know there *is* a God, but probably not the one your church worships. . . . Shefford, go to the Navajo for a faith!"

Shefford had forgotten the presence of Nas Ta Bega, and perhaps Withers had likewise. At this juncture the Indian rose to his full height, and he folded his arms to stand with the somber pride of a chieftain while his dark, inscrutable eyes were riveted upon Shefford. At that moment he seemed magnificent. How infinitely more he seemed than just a common Indian who had chanced to befriend a white man! The difference was obscure to Shefford. But he felt that it was there in the Navajo's mind.

Nas Ta Bega's strange look was not to be interpreted. Presently he turned and passed from the room.

"By George!" cried Withers, suddenly, and he pounded his knee with his fist. "I'd forgotten."

"What?" ejaculated Shefford.

"Why, that Indian understood every word we said. He knows English. He's educated. Well, if this doesn't beat me. . . . Let me tell you about Nas Ta Bega."

Withers appeared to be recalling something half forgotten.

"Years ago, in fifty-seven, I think, Kit Carson with his soldiers chased the Navajo tribes and rounded them up to be put on reservations. But he failed to catch all the members of one tribe. They escaped up into wild canyons like the Sagi. The descendants of these fugitives live there now and are the finest Indians on earth—the finest because unspoiled by the white man. Well, as I got the story, years after Carson's roundup one of his soldiers guided some interested travelers in here. When they left they took an Indian boy with them to educate. From what I know of Navajos I'm inclined to think the boy was taken against his parents' wish. Anyway, he was taken. That boy was Nas Ta Bega. The story goes that he was educated somewhere. Years afterward, and perhaps not long before I came in here, he returned to his people. There have been missionaries and other interested fools who have given Indians a white man's education. In all the instances I know of, these educated Indians returned to their tribes, repudiating the white man's knowledge, habits, life, and religion. I have heard that Nas Ta Bega came back, laid down the white man's clothes along with the education, and never again showed that he had known either.

"You have just seen how strangely he acted. It's almost certain he heard our conversation. Well, it doesn't matter. He won't tell. He can hardly be made to use an English word. Besides, he's a noble red man, if there ever was one. He has been a friend in need to me. If you stay long out here you'll learn something from the Indians. Nas Ta Bega has befriended you, too, it seems. I thought he showed unusual interest in you."

"Perhaps that was because I saved his sister—well, to be charitable, from the rather rude advances of a white man," said Shefford, and he proceeded to tell of the incident that occurred at Red Lake.

"Willetts!" exclaimed Withers, with much the same expression that Presbrey had used. "I never met him. But I know about him. He's—well, the Indians don't like him much. Most of the missionaries are good men —good for the Indians, in a way, but sometimes one drifts out here who is bad. A bad missionary teaching religion to savages! Queer, isn't it? The queerest part is the white people's blindness—the blindness of those who send the missionaries. Well, I dare say Willetts isn't very good. When Presbrey said that was Willetts's way of teaching religion he meant just what he said. If Willetts drifts over here he'll be risking much. . . . This you told me explains Nas Ta Bega's friendliness toward you, and also his bringing his sister Glen Naspa to live with relatives up in the Pass. She had been living near Red Lake."

"Do you mean Nas Ta Bega wants to keep his sister far removed from Willetts?" inquired Shefford.

"I mean that," replied Withers, "and I hope he's not too late."

Later Shefford went outdoors to walk and think. There was no moon, but the stars made light enough to cast his shadow on the ground. The dark, illimitable expanse of blue sky seemed to be glittering with numberless points of fire. The air was cold and still. A dreaming silence lay over the land. Shefford saw and felt all these things, and their effect was continuous and remained with him and helped calm him. He was conscious of a burden removed from his mind. Confession of his secret had been like tearing a thorn from his flesh, but, once done, it afforded him relief and a singular realization that out here it did not matter much. In a crowd of men all looking at him and judging him by their standards he had been made to suffer. Here, if he were judged at all, it would be by what he could do, how he sustained himself and helped others.

He walked far across the valley toward the low bluffs, but they did not seem to get any closer. And, finally, he stopped beside a stone and looked around at the strange horizon and up at the heavens. He did not feel utterly aloof from them, nor alone in a waste, nor a useless atom amid incomprehensible forces. Something like a loosened mantle fell from about him, dropping down at his feet; and all at once he was conscious of freedom. He did not understand in the least why abasement left him, but it was so. He had come a long way, in bitterness, in despair, believing himself to be what men had called him. The desert and the stars and the wind, the silence of the night, the loneliness of this vast country where there was room for a thousand cities—these somehow vaguely, yet surely, bade him lift his head. They withheld their secret, but they made a promise. The thing which he had been feeling every day and every night was a strange enveloping comfort. And it was at this moment that Shefford, divining whence his help was to come, embraced all that wild and speaking nature around and above him and surrendered himself utterly.

"I am young. I am free. I have my life to live," he said. "I'll be a man. I'll take what comes. Let me learn here!"

When he had spoken out, settled once and forever his attitude toward his future, he seemed to be born again, wonderfully alive to the influences around him, ready to trust what yet remained a mystery.

Then his thoughts reverted to Fay Larkin. Could this girl be known to the Mormons? It was possible. Fay Larkin was an unusual name. Deep into Shefford's heart had sunk the story Venters had told. Shefford found that he had unconsciously created a like romance—he had been loving a wild and strange and lonely girl, like beautiful Bess Venters. It was a shock to learn the truth, but, as it had been only a dream, it could hardly be vital.

Shefford retraced his steps toward the post. Halfway back he espied a tall, dark figure moving toward him, and presently the shape and the step seemed familiar. Then he recognized Nas Ta Bega. Soon they were face to face. Shefford felt that the Indian had been trailing him over the sand, and that this was to be a significant meeting. Remembering Withers's revelation about the Navajo, Shefford scarcely knew how to approach him now. There was no difference to be made out in Nas Ta Bega's dark face and inscrutable eyes, yet there was a difference to be felt in his presence. But the Indian did not speak, and turned to walk by Shefford's side. Shefford could not long be silent.

"Nas Ta Bega, were you looking for me?" he asked.

"You had no gun," replied the Indian.

But for his very low voice, his slow speaking of the words, Shefford would have thought him a white man. For Shefford there was indeed an instinct in this meeting, and he turned to face the Navajo.

"Withers told me you had been educated, that you came back to the desert, that you never showed your training. . . . Nas Ta Bega, did you understand all I told Withers?"

"Yes," replied the Indian.

"You won't betray me?"

"I am a Navajo."

"Nas Ta Bega, you trail me—you say I had no gun." Shefford wanted to ask this Indian if he cared to be the white man's friend, but the question was not easy to put, and, besides, seemed unnecessary. "I am alone and strange in this wild country. I must learn."

"Nas Ta Bega will show you the trails and the water-holes and how to hide from Shadd."

"For money—for silver you will do this?" inquired Shefford.

Shefford felt that the Indian's silence was a rebuke. He remembered Withers's singular praise of this red man. He realized he must change his idea of Indians.

"Nas Ta Bega, I know nothing. I feel like a child in the wilderness. When I speak it is out of the mouths of those who have taught me. I must find a new voice and a new life. . . . You heard my story to Withers. I am an outcast from my own people. If you will be my friend—be so."

The Indian clasped Shefford's hand and held it in a response that was more beautiful for its silence. So they stood for a moment in the starlight.

"Nas Ta Bega, what did Withers mean when he said go to the Navajo for a faith?" asked Shefford.

"He meant the desert is my mother. . . . Will you go with Nas Ta Bega into the canyons and the mountains?"

"Indeed I will."

They unclasped hands and turned toward the trading-post.

"Nas Ta Bega, have you spoken my tongue to any other white man since you returned to your home?" asked Shefford.

"No."

"Why do you—why are you different for me?"

The Indian maintained silence.

"Is it because of—of Glen Naspa?" inquired Shefford.

Nas Ta Bega stalked on, still silent, but Shefford divined that, although his service to Glen Naspa would never be forgotten, still it was not wholly responsible for the Indian's subtle sympathy.

"Bi Nai! The Navajo will call his white friend Bi Nai—brother," said Nas Ta Bega, and he spoke haltingly, not as if words were hard to find, but strange to speak. "I was stolen from my mother's hogan and taken to California. They kept me ten years in a mission at San Bernardino and four years in a school. They said my color and my hair were all that was left of the Indian in me. But they could not see my heart. They took fourteen years of my life. They wanted to make me a missionary among my own people. But the white man's ways and his life and his God are not the Indian's. They never can be."

How strangely productive of thought for Shefford to hear the Indian talk! What fatality in this meeting and friendship! Upon Nas Ta Bega had been forced education, training, religion, that had made him something more and something less than an Indian. It was something assimilated from the white man which made the Indian unhappy and alien in his own home—something meant to be good for him and his kind that had ruined him. For Shefford felt the passion and the tragedy of this Navajo.

"Bi Nai, the Indian is dying!" Nas Ta Bega's low voice was deep and wonderful with its intensity of feeling. "The white man robbed the Indian of lands and homes, drove him into the deserts, made him a gaunt and sleepless spiller of blood. . . . The blood is all spilled now, for the Indian is broken. But the white man sells him rum and seduces his daughters. . . . He will not leave the Indian in peace with his own God! . . . Bi Nai, the Indian is dying!"

That night Shefford lay in his blankets out under the open sky and the stars. The earth had never meant much to him, and now it was a bed. He had preached of the heavens, but until now had never studied them. An Indian slept beside him. And not until the gray of morning had blotted out the starlight did Shefford close his eyes.

With break of the next day came full, varied, and stirring incidents to Shefford. He was strong, though unskilled at most kinds of outdoor tasks. Withers had work for ten men, if they could have been found. Shefford dug and packed and lifted till he was so sore and tired that rest was a blessing.

He never succeeded in getting on a friendly footing with the Mormon Whisner, though he kept up his agreeable and kindly advances. He listened to the trader's wife as she told him about the Indians, and what he learned he did not forget. And his wonder and respect increased in proportion to his knowledge.

One day there rode into Kayenta the Mormon for whom Withers had been waiting. His name was Joe Lake. He appeared young, and slipped off his superb bay with a grace and activity that were astounding in one of his huge bulk. He had a still, smooth face, with the color of red bronze and the expression of a cherub; big, soft, dark eyes; and a winning smile. He was surprisingly different from Whisner or any Mormon character that Shefford had naturally conceived. His costume was that of the cowboy on active service; and he packed a gun at his hip. The handshake he gave Shefford was an ordeal for that young man and left him with his whole right side momentarily benumbed.

"I sure am glad to meet you," he said in a lazy, mild voice. And he was taking friendly stock of Shefford when the bay mustang reached with vicious muzzle to bite at him. Lake gave a jerk on the bridle that almost brought the mustang to his knees. He reared then, snorted, and came down to plant his forefeet wide apart, and watched his master with defiant eyes. This mustang was the finest horse Shefford had ever seen. He appeared quite large for his species, was almost red in color, had a racy and powerful build, and a fine thoroughbred head with dark, fiery eyes. He did not look mean, but he had spirit.

"Navvy, you've sure got bad manners," said Lake, shaking the mustang's bridle. He spoke as if he were chiding a refractory little boy. "Didn't I break you better 'n that? What's this gentleman goin' to think of you? Tryin' to bite my ear off!"

Lake had arrived about the middle of the forenoon, and Withers announced his intention of packing at once for the trip. Indians were sent out on the ranges to drive in burros and mustangs. Shefford had his thrilling expectancy somewhat chilled by what he considered must have been Lake's reception of the trader's plan. Lake seemed to oppose him, and evidently it took vehemence and argument on Withers's part to make the Mormon tractable. But Withers won him over, and then he called Shefford to his side.

"You fellows got to be good friends," he said. "You'll have charge of my pack-trains. Nas Ta Bega wants to go with you. I'll feel safer about my supplies and stock than I've ever been. . . . Joe, I'll back this stranger for all I'm worth. He's square. . . . And, Shefford, Joe Lake is a Mormon of the younger generation. I want to start you right. You can trust him as you trust me. He's white clean through. And he's the best horse-wrangler in Utah."

It was Lake who first offered his hand, and Shefford made haste to meet it with his own. Neither of them spoke. Shefford intuitively felt an alteration in Lake's regard, or at least a singular increase of interest. Lake had been told that Shefford had been a clergyman, was now a wanderer, without any religion. Again it seemed to Shefford that he owed a forming of friendship to this singular fact. And it hurt him. But strangely it came to him that he had taken a liking to a Mormon.

About one o'clock the pack-train left Kayenta. Nas Ta Bega led the way up the slope. Following him climbed half a dozen patient, plodding, heavily laden burros. Withers came next, and he turned in his saddle to wave goodbye to his wife. Joe Lake appeared to be busy keeping a red mule and a wild gray mustang and a couple of restive blacks in the trail. Shefford brought up in the rear.

His mount was a beautiful black mustang with three white feet, a white spot on his nose, and a mane that swept to his knees. "His name's Nack-yal," Withers had said. "It means two bits, or twenty-five cents. He ain't worth more." To look at Nack-yal had pleased Shefford very much indeed, but, once upon his back, he grew dubious. The mustang acted queer. He actually looked back at Shefford, and it was a look of speculation and disdain. Shefford took exception to Nack-yal's manner and to his reluctance to go, and especially to a habit the mustang had of turning off the trail to the left. Shefford had managed some rather spirited horses back in Illinois; and though he was willing and eager to learn all over again, he did not enjoy the prospect of Lake and Withers seeing this black mustang make a novice of him. And he guessed that was just what Nack-yal intended to do. However, once up over the hill, with Kayenta out of sight, Nack-yal trotted along fairly well, needing only now and then to be pulled back from his strange swinging to the left off the trail.

The pack-train traveled steadily and soon crossed the upland plain to descend into the valley again. Shefford saw the jagged red peaks with an emotion he could not name. The canyons between them were purple in the shadows, the great walls and slopes brightened to red, and the tips were gold in the sun. Shefford forgot all about his mustang and the trail.

Suddenly with a pound of hoofs Nack-yal seemed to rise. He leaped sidewise out of the trail, came down stiff-legged. Then Shefford shot out of the saddle. He landed so hard that he was stunned for an instant. Sitting up, he saw the mustang bent down, eyes and ears showing fight, and his forefeet spread. He appeared to be looking at something in the trail. Shefford got up and soon saw what had been the trouble. A long, crooked stick, rather thick and black and yellow, lay in the trail, and any mustang looking for an excuse to jump might have mistaken it for a rattlesnake. Nack-yal appeared disposed to be satisfied, and gave Shefford no trouble in mounting. The incident increased Shefford's dubiousness. These Arizona mustangs were unknown quantities.

Thereafter Shefford had an eye for the trail rather than the scenery, and this continued till the pack-train entered the mouth of the Sagi. Then those wonderful lofty cliffs, with their peaks and towers and spires, loomed so close and so beautiful that he did not care if Nack-yal did throw him. Along here, however, the mustang behaved well, and presently Shefford decided that if it had been otherwise he would have walked. The trail suddenly stood on end and led down into the deep wash, where some days before he had seen the stream of reddish water. This day there appeared to be less water and it was not so red. Nack-yal sank deep as he took short and careful steps down. The burros and other mustangs were drinking, and Nack-yal followed suit. The Indian, with a hand clutching his mustang's mane, rode up a steep, sandy slope on the other side that Shefford would not have believed any horse could climb. The burros plodded up and over the rim, with Withers calling to them. Joe Lake swung his rope and cracked the flanks of the gray mare and the red mule; and the way the two kicked was a revelation and a warning to Shefford. When his turn came to climb the trail he got off and walked, an action that Nack-yal appeared fully to appreciate.

From the head of this wash the trail wound away up the widening canyon, through greasewood flats and over greasy levels and across sandy stretches. The looming walls made the valley look narrow, yet it must have been half a mile wide. The slopes under the cliffs were dotted with huge stones and cedar trees. There were deep indentations in the walls, running back to form box canyons, choked with green of cedar and spruce and pinyon. These notches haunted Shefford, and he was ever on the lookout for more of them.

Withers came back to ride just in advance and began to talk.

"Reckon this Sagi Canyon is your Deception Pass," he said. "It's sure a queer hole. I've been lost more than once, hunting mustangs in here. I've an idea Nas Ta Bega knows all this country. He just pointed out a cliff-dwelling to me. See it? . . . There, 'way up in that cave of the wall."

Shefford saw a steep, rough slope leading up to a bulge of the cliff, and finally he made out strange little houses with dark, eyelike windows. He wanted to climb up there. Withers called his attention to more caves with what he believed were the ruins of cliff-dwellings. And as they rode along, the trader showed him remarkable formations of rock where the elements were slowly hollowing out a bridge. They came presently to a region of intersecting canyons, and here the breaking of the trail up and down the deep washes took Withers back to his task with the burros and gave Shefford more concern than he liked with Nack-yal. The mustang grew unruly and was continually turning to the left. Sometimes he tried to climb the steep slope. He had to be pulled hard away from the opening canyons on the left. It seemed strange to Shefford that the mustang never swerved to the right. This habit of Nack-yal's and the increasing caution needed on the trail took all of Shefford's attention. When he dismounted, however, he had a chance to look around, and more and more he was amazed at the increasing proportions and wildness of the Sagi.

He came at length to a place where a fallen tree blocked the trail. All of the rest of the pack-train had jumped the log. But Nack-yal balked. Shefford dismounted, pulled the bridle over the mustang's head, and tried to lead him. Nack-yal, however, refused to budge. Whereupon Shefford got a stick and, remounting, he gave the balky mustang a cut across the flank. Then something violent happened. Shefford received a sudden propelling jolt, and then he was rising into the air, and then falling. Before he alighted he had a clear image of Nack-yal in the air above him, bent double, and seemingly possessed of devils. Then Shefford hit the ground with no light thud. He was thoroughly angry when he got dizzily upon his feet, but he was not quick enough to catch the mustang. Nack-yal leaped easily over the log and went on ahead, dragging his bridle. Shefford hurried after him, and the faster he went just by so much the cunning Nack-yal accelerated his gait. As the pack-train was out of sight somewhere ahead, Shefford could not call to his companions to halt his mount, so he gave up trying, and walked on now with free and growing appreciation of his surroundings.

The afternoon had waned. The sun blazed low in the west in a notch of the canyon ramparts, and one wall was darkening into purple shadow while the other shone through a golden haze. It was a weird, wild world to Shefford, and every few strides he caught his breath and tried to realize actuality was not a dream.

Nack-yal kept about a hundred paces to the fore and ever and anon he looked back to see how his new master was progressing. He varied these occasions by reaching down and nipping a tuft of grass. Evidently he was too intelligent to go on fast enough to be caught by Withers. Also he kept continually looking up the slope to the left as if seeking a way to climb out of the valley in that direction. Shefford thought it was well the trail lay at the foot of a steep slope that ran up to unbroken bluffs.

The sun set and the canyon lost its red and its gold and deepened its purple. Shefford calculated he had walked five miles, and though he did not mind the effort, he would rather have ridden Nack-yal into camp. He mounted a cedar ridge, crossed some sandy washes, turned a corner of bold wall to enter a wide, green level. The mustangs were rolling and snorting. He heard the bray of a burro. A bright blaze of campfire greeted him, and the dark figure of the Indian approached to intercept and catch Nack-yal. When he stalked into camp Withers wore a beaming smile, and Joe Lake, who was on his knees making biscuit dough in a pan, stopped proceedings and drawled:

"Reckon Nack-yal bucked you off."

"Bucked! Was that it? Well, he separated himself from me in a new and somewhat painful manner—to me."

"Sure, I saw that in his eye," replied Lake; and Withers laughed with him.

"Nack-yal never was well broke," he said. "But he's a good mustang, nothing like Joe's Navvy or that gray mare Dynamite. All this Indian stock will buck on a man once in a while."

"I'll take the bucking along with the rest," said Shefford.

Both men liked his reply, and the Indian smiled for the first time.

Soon they all sat round a spread tarpaulin and ate like wolves. After supper came the rest and talk before the campfire. Joe Lake was droll; he said the most serious things in a way to make Shefford wonder if he was not joking. Withers talked about the canyon, the Indians, the mustangs, the scorpions running out of the heated sand; and to Shefford it was all like a fascinating book. Nas Ta Bega smoked in silence, his brooding eyes upon the fire.

⁑5⁑

ON THE TRAIL

SHEFFORD was awakened next morning by a sound he had never heard before—the plunging of hobbled horses on soft turf. It was clear daylight, with a ruddy color in the sky and a tinge of red along the canyon rim. He saw Withers, Lake, and the Indian driving the mustangs toward camp.

The burros appeared lazy, yet willing. But the mustangs and the mule Withers called Red and the gray mare Dynamite were determined not to be driven into camp. It was astonishing how much action they had, how much ground they could cover with their forefeet hobbled together. They were exceedingly skillful; they lifted both forefeet at once, and then plunged. And they all went in different directions. Nas Ta Bega darted in here and there to head off escape.

Shefford pulled on his boots and went out to help. He got too close to the gray mare and, warned by a yell from Withers, he jumped back just in time to avoid her vicious heels. Then Shefford turned his attention to Nack-yal and chased him all over the flat in a futile effort to catch him. Nas Ta Bega came to Shefford's assistance and put a rope over Nack-yal's head.

"Don't ever get behind one of these mustangs," said Withers, warningly, as Shefford came up. "You might be killed. . . . Eat your bite now. We'll soon be out of here."

Shefford had been late in awakening. The others had breakfasted. He found eating somewhat difficult in the excitement that ensued. Nas Ta Bega held ropes which were round the necks of Red and Dynamite. The mule showed his cunning and always appeared to present his heels to Withers, who tried to approach him with a pack-saddle. The patience of the trader was a revelation to Shefford. And at length Red was cornered by the three men, the pack-saddle was strapped on, and then the packs. Red promptly bucked the packs off, and the work had to be done over again. Then Red dropped his long ears and seemed ready to be tractable.

When Shefford turned his attention to Dynamite he decided that this was his first sight of a wild horse. The gray mare had fiery eyes that rolled and showed the white. She jumped straight up, screamed, pawed, bit, and then plunged down to shoot her hind hoofs into the air as high as her head had been. She was amazingly agile and she seemed mad to kill something. She dragged the Indian about, and when Joe Lake got a rope on her hind foot she dragged them both. They lashed her with the ends of the lassoes, which action only made her kick harder. She plunged into camp, drove Shefford flying for his life, knocked down two of the burros, and played havoc with the unstrapped packs. Withers ran to the assistance of Lake, and the two of them hauled back with all their strength and weight. They were both powerful and heavy men. Dynamite circled round and finally, after kicking the campfire to bits, fell down on her haunches in the hot embers. "Let—her—set—there!" panted Withers. And Joe Lake shouted, "Burn up, you durn coyote!" Both men appeared delighted that she had brought upon herself just punishment. Dynamite sat in the remains of the fire long enough to get burnt, and then she got up and meekly allowed Withers to throw a tarpaulin and a roll of blankets over her and tie them fast.

Lake and Withers were sweating freely when this job was finished.

"Say, is that a usual morning's task with the pack-animals?" asked Shefford.

"They're all pretty decent today, except Dynamite," replied Withers. "She's got to be worked out."

Shefford felt both amusement and consternation. The sun was just rising over the ramparts of the canyon, and he had already seen more difficult and dangerous work accomplished than half a dozen men of his type could do in a whole day. He liked the outlook of his new duty as Withers's assistant, but he felt helplessly inefficient. Still, all he needed was experience. He passed over what he anticipated would be pain and peril—the cost was of no moment.

Soon the pack-train was on the move, with the Indian leading. This morning Nack-yal began his strange swinging off to the left, precisely as he had done the day before. It got to be annoying to Shefford, and he lost patience with the mustang and jerked him sharply round. This, however, had no great effect upon Nack-yal.

As the train headed straight up the canyon Joe Lake dropped back to ride beside Shefford. The Mormon had been amiable and friendly.

"Flock of deer up that draw," he said, pointing up a narrow side canyon.

Shefford gazed to see a half-dozen small, brown, long-eared objects, very like burros, watching the pack-train pass.

"Are they deer?" he asked, delightedly.

"Sure are," replied Joe, sincerely. "Get down and shoot one. There's a rifle in your saddle-sheath."

Shefford had already discovered that he had been armed this morning, a matter which had caused him reflection. These animals certainly looked like deer; he had seen a few deer, though not in their native wild haunts; and he experienced the thrill of the hunter. Dismounting, he drew the rifle out of the sheath and started toward the little canyon.

"Hyar! Where you going with that gun?" yelled Withers. "That's a bunch of burros. . . . Joe's up to his old tricks. Shefford, look out for Joe!"

Rather sheepishly Shefford returned to his mustang and sheathed the rifle, and then took a long look at the animals up the draw. They resembled deer, but upon second glance they surely were burros.

"Durn me! Now if I didn't think they sure were deer!" exclaimed Joe. He appeared absolutely sincere and innocent. Shefford hardly knew how to take this likable Mormon, but vowed he would be on his guard in the future.

Nas Ta Bega soon led the pack-train toward the left wall of the canyon, and evidently intended to scale it. Shefford could not see any trail, and the wall appeared steep and insurmountable. But upon nearing the cliff he saw a narrow broken trail leading zigzag up over smooth rock, weathered slope, and through cracks.

"Spread out, and careful now!" yelled Withers.

The need of both advices soon became manifest to Shefford. The burros started stones rolling, making danger for those below. Shefford dismounted and led Nack-yal and turned aside many a rolling rock. The Indian and the burros, with the red mule leading, climbed steadily. But the mustangs had trouble. Joe's spirited bay had to be coaxed to face the ascent; Nack-yal balked at every difficult step; and Dynamite slipped on a flat slant of rock and slid down forty feet. Withers and Lake with ropes hauled the mare out of the dangerous position. Shefford, who brought up the rear, saw all the action, and it was exciting, but his pleasure in the climb was spoiled by sight of blood and hair on the stones. The ascent was crooked, steep, and long, and when Shefford reached the top of the wall he was glad to rest. It made him gasp to look down and see what he had surmounted. The canyon floor, green and level, lay a thousand feet below; and the wild burrows which had followed on the trail looked like rabbits.

Shefford mounted presently, and rode out upon a wide, smooth trail leading into a cedar forest. There were bunches of gray sage in the open places. The air was cool and crisp, laden with a sweet fragrance. He saw Lake and Withers bobbing along, now on one side of the trail, now on the other, and they kept to a steady trot. Occasionally the Indian and his bright-red saddle-blanket showed in an opening of the cedars.

It was level country, and there was nothing for Shefford to see except cedar and sage, an outcropping of red rock in places, and the winding trail. Mockingbirds made melody everywhere. Shefford seemed full of a strange pleasure, and the hours flew by. Nack-yal still wanted to be everlastingly turning off the trail, and, moreover, now he wanted to go faster. He was eager, restless, dissatisfied.

At noon the pack-train descended into a deep draw, well covered with cedar and sage. There was plenty of grass and shade, but no water. Shefford was surprised to see that every pack was removed; however, the roll of blankets was left on Dynamite.

The men made a fire and began to cook a noonday meal. Shefford, tired and warm, sat in a shady spot and watched. He had become all eyes. He had almost forgotten Fay Larkin; he had forgotten his trouble; and the present seemed sweet and full. Presently his ears were filled by a pattering roar and, looking up the draw, he saw two streams of sheep and goats coming down. Soon an Indian shepherd appeared, riding a fine mustang. A cream-colored colt bounded along behind, and presently a shaggy dog came in sight. The Indian dismounted at the camp, and his flock spread by in two white and black streams. The dog went with them. Withers and Joe shook hands with the Indian, whom Joe called "Navvy," and Shefford lost no time in doing likewise. Then Nas Ta Bega came in, and he and the Navajo talked. When the meal was ready all of them sat down round the canvas. The shepherd did not tie his horse.

Presently Shefford noticed that Nack-yal had returned to camp and was acting strangely. Evidently he was attracted by the Indian's mustang or the cream-colored colt. At any rate, Nack-yal hung around, tossed his head, whinnied in a low, nervous manner, and looked strangely eager and wild. Shefford was at first amused, then curious. Nack-yal approached too close to the mother of the colt, and she gave him a sounding kick in the ribs. Nack-yal uttered a plaintive snort and backed away, to stand, crestfallen, with all his eagerness and fire vanished.

Nas Ta Bega pointed to the mustang and said something in his own tongue. Then Withers addressed the visiting Indian, and they exchanged some words, whereupon the trader turned to Shefford.

"I bought Nack-yal from this Indian three years ago. This mare is Nack-yal's mother. He was born over here to the south. That's why he always swung left off the trail. He wanted to go home. Just now he recognized his mother and she whaled away and gave him a whack for his pains. She's got a colt now and probably didn't recognize Nack-yal. But he's broken-hearted."

The trader laughed, and Joe said, "You can't tell what these durn mustangs will do." Shefford felt sorry for Nack-yal, and when it came time to saddle him again found him easier to handle than ever before. Nack-yal stood with head down, broken-spirited.

Shefford was the first to ride up out of the draw, and once upon the top of the ridge he halted to gaze, wide-eyed and entranced. A rolling, endless plain sloped down beneath him, and led him on to a distant round-topped mountain. To the right a red canyon opened its jagged jaws, and away to the north rose a whorled and strange sea of curved ridges, crags, and domes.

Nas Ta Bega rode up then, leading the pack-train.

"Bi Nai, that is Na-tsis-an," he said, pointing to the mountain. "Navajo Mountain. And there in the north are the canyons."

Shefford followed the Indian down the trail and soon lost sight of that wide green-and-red wilderness. Nas Ta Bega turned at an intersecting trail, rode down into the canyon, and climbed out on the other side. Shefford got a glimpse now and then of the black dome of the mountain, but for the most part the distant points of the country were hidden. They crossed many trails, and went up and down the sides of many shallow canyons. Troops of wild mustangs whistled at them, stood on ridge-tops to watch, and then dashed away with manes and tails flying.

Withers rode forward presently and halted the pack-train. He had some conversation with Nas Ta Bega, whereupon the Indian turned his horse and trotted back, to disappear in the cedars.

"I'm some worried," explained Withers. "Joe thinks he saw a bunch of horsemen trailing us. My eyes are bad and I can't see far. The Indian will find out. I took a roundabout way to reach the village because I'm always dodging Shadd."

This communication lent an added zest to the journey. Shefford could hardly believe the truth that his eyes and his ears brought to his consciousness. He turned in behind Withers and rode down the rough trail, helping the mustang all in his power. It occurred to him that Nack-yal had been entirely different since that meeting with his mother in the draw. He turned no more off the trail; he answered readily to the rein; he did not look afar from every ridge. Shefford conceived a liking for the mustang.

Withers turned sidewise in his saddle and let his mustang pick the way.

"Another time we'll go up round the base of the mountain, where you can look down on the grandest scene in the world," said he. "Two hundred miles of wind-worn rock, all smooth and bare, without a single straight line—canyons, caves, bridges—the most wonderful country in the world! Even the Indians haven't explored it. It's haunted, for them, and they have strange gods. The Navajos will hunt on this side of the mountain, but not on the other. That north side is consecrated ground. My wife has long been trying to get the Navajos to tell her the secret of Nonnezoshe. Nonnezoshe means Rainbow Bridge. The Indians worship it, but as far as she can find out only a few have ever seen it. I imagine it'd be worth some trouble."

"Maybe that's the bridge Venters talked about—the one overarching the entrance to Surprise Valley," said Shefford.

"It might be," replied the trader. "You've got a good chance of finding out. Nas Ta Bega is the man. You stick to that Indian. . . . Well, we start down here into this canyon, and we go down *some*, I reckon. In half an hour you'll see sago-lilies and Indian paint-brush and vermilion cactus."

About the middle of the afternoon the pack-train and its drivers arrived at the hidden Mormon village. Nas Ta Bega had not returned from his scout back along the trail.

Shefford's sensibilities had all been overstrained, but he had left in him enthusiasm and appreciation that made the situation of this village a fairyland. It was a valley, a canyon floor, so long that he could not see the end, and perhaps a quarter of a mile wide. The air was hot, still, and sweetly odorous of unfamiliar flowers. Pinyon and cedar trees surrounded the little log and stone houses, and along the walls of the canyon stood sharp-pointed, dark-green spruce trees. These walls were singular of shape and color. They were not imposing in height, but they waved like the long, undulating swell of a sea. Every foot of surface was perfectly smooth, and the long curved lines of darker tinge that streaked the red followed the rounded line of the slope at the top. Far above, yet overhanging, were great yellow crags and peaks, and between these, still higher, showed the pine-fringed slope of Navajo Mountain with snow in the sheltered places, and glistening streams, like silver threads, running down.

All this Shefford noticed as he entered the valley from round a corner of wall. Upon nearer view he saw and heard a host of children, who, looking up to see the intruders, scattered like frightened quail. Long gray grass covered the ground, and here and there wide, smooth paths had been worn. A swift and murmuring brook ran through the middle of the valley, and its banks were bordered with flowers.

Withers led the way to one side near the wall, where a clump of cedar trees and a dark, swift spring boiling out of the rocks and banks of amber moss with purple blossoms made a beautiful camp site. Here the mustangs were unsaddled and turned loose without hobbles. It was certainly unlikely that they would leave such a spot. Some of the burros were un-packed, and the others Withers drove off into the village.

"Sure's pretty nice," said Joe, wiping his sweaty face. "I'll never want to leave. It suits me to lie on this moss. . . . Take a drink of that spring."

Shefford complied with alacrity and found the water cool and sweet, and he seemed to feel it all through him. Then he returned to the mossy bank. He did not reply to Joe. In fact, all his faculties were absorbed in watching and feeling, and he lay there long after Joe went off to the village. The murmur of water, the hum of bees, the songs of strange birds, the sweet, warm air, the dreamy summer somnolence of the valley—all these added drowsiness to Shefford's weary lassitude, and he fell asleep. When he awoke Nas Ta Bega was sitting near him and Joe was busy near a campfire.

"Hello, Nas Ta Bega!" said Shefford. "Was there anyone trailing us?"

The Navajo nodded.

Joe raised his head and with forceful brevity said, "Shadd."

"Shadd!" echoed Shefford, remembering the dark, sinister face of his visitor that night in the Sagi. "Joe, is it serious—his trailing us?"

"Well, I don't know how durn serious it is, but I'm scared to death," replied Lake. "He and his gang will hold us up somewhere on the way home."

Shefford regarded Joe with both concern and doubt. Joe's words were at variance with his looks.

"Say, pard, can you shoot a rifle?" queried Joe.

"Yes. I'm a fair shot at targets."

The Mormon nodded his head as if pleased. "That's good. These out-laws are all poor shots with a rifle. So'm I. But I can handle a six-shooter. I reckon we'll make Shadd sweat if he pushes us."

Withers returned, driving the burros, all of which had been unpacked down to the saddles. Two gray-bearded men accompanied him. One of them appeared to be very old and venerable, and walked with a stick. The other had a sad-lined face and kind, mild blue eyes. Shefford observed that Lake seemed unusually respectful. Withers introduced these Mor-mons merely as Smith and Henninger. They were very cordial and pleas-ant in their greetings to Shefford. Presently another, somewhat younger, man joined the group, a stalwart, jovial fellow with ruddy face. There was certainly no mistaking his kindly welcome as he shook Shefford's hand. His name was Beal. The three stood round the campfire for a while, evidently glad of the presence of fellow men and to hear news from the outside. Finally they went away, taking Joe with them. Withers took up the task of getting supper where Joe had been made to leave it.

"Shefford, listen," he said, presently, as he knelt before the fire. "I told them right out that you'd been a Gentile clergyman—that you'd gone back on your religion. It impressed them and you've been well received.

I'll tell the same thing over at Stonebridge. You'll get in right. Of course I don't expect they'll make a Mormon of you. But they'll try to. Meanwhile you can be square and friendly all the time you're trying to find your Fay Larkin. Tomorrow you'll meet some of the women. They're good souls, but, like any women, crazy for news. Think what it is to be shut up in here between these walls!"

"Withers, I'm intensely interested," replied Shefford, "and excited, too. Shall we stay here long?"

"I'll stay a couple of days, then go to Stonebridge with Joe. He'll come back here, and when you both feel like leaving, and if Nas Ta Bega thinks it safe, you'll take a trail over to some Indian hogans and pack me out a load of skins and blankets. . . . My boy, you've all the time there is, and I wish you luck. This isn't a bad place to loaf. I always get sentimental over here. Maybe it's the women. Some of them are pretty, and one of them— Shefford, they call her the Sago Lily. Her first name is Mary, I'm told. Don't know her last name. She's lovely. And I'll bet you forget Fay Larkin in a flash. Only—be careful. You drop in here with rather peculiar credentials, so to speak—as my helper and as a man with no religion! You'll not only be fully trusted, but you'll be welcome to these lonely women. So be careful. Remember it's my secret belief they are sealed wives and are visited occasionally at night by their husbands. I don't *know* this, but I believe it. And you're not supposed to dream of that."

"How many men in the village?" asked Shefford.

"Three. You met them."

"Have they wives?" asked Shefford, curiously.

"Wives! Well, I guess. But only one each that I know of. Joe Lake is the only unmarried Mormon I've met."

"And no men—strangers, cowboys, outlaws—ever come to this village?"

"Except to Indians, it seems to be a secret so far," replied the trader, earnestly. "But it can't be kept secret. I've said that time after time over in Stonebridge. With Mormons it's 'sufficient unto the day is the evil thereof.' "

"What'll happen when outsiders do learn and ride in here?"

"There'll be trouble—maybe bloodshed. Mormon women are absolutely good, but they're human, and want and need a little life. And, strange to say, Mormon men are pig-headedly jealous. . . . Why, if some of the cowboys I knew in Durango would ride over here there'd simply be hell. But that's a long way, and probably this village will be deserted before news of it ever reaches Colorado. There's more danger of Shadd and his gang coming in. Shadd's half Piute. He must know of this place. And he's got some white outlaws in his gang. . . . Come on. Grub's ready, and I'm too hungry to talk."

Later, when shadows began to gather in the valley and the lofty peaks above were gold in the sunset glow, Withers left camp to look after the straying mustangs, and Shefford strolled to and fro under the cedars. The lights and shades in the Sagi that first night had moved him to enthusiastic watchfulness, but here they were so weird and beautiful that he was enraptured. He actually saw great shafts of gold and shadows of purple streaming from the peaks down into the valley. It was day on the heights and twilight in the valley. The swiftly changing colors were like rainbows.

While he strolled up and down several women came to the spring and filled their buckets. They wore shawls or hoods and their garments were somber, but, nevertheless, they appeared to have youth and comeliness. They saw him, looked at him curiously, and then, without speaking, went back on the well-trodden path. Presently down the path appeared a woman—a girl in lighter garb. It was almost white. She was shapely and walked with free, graceful step, reminding him of the Indian girl, Glen Naspa. This one wore a hood shaped like a huge sunbonnet and it concealed her face. She carried a bucket. When she reached the spring and went down the few stone steps Shefford saw that she did not have on shoes. As she braced herself to lift the bucket her bare foot clung to the mossy stone. It was a strong, sinewy, beautiful foot, instinct with youth. He was curious enough, he thought, but the awakening artist in him made him more so. She dragged at the full bucket and had difficulty in lifting it out of the hole. Shefford strode forward and took the bucket-handle from her.

"Won't you let me help you?" he said, lifting the bucket. "Indeed—it's very heavy."

"Oh—thank you," she said, without raising her head. Her voice seemed singularly young and sweet. He had not heard a voice like it. She moved down the path and he walked beside her. He felt embarrassed, yet more curious than ever; he wanted to say something, to turn and look at her, but he kept on for a dozen paces without making up his mind.

Finally he said: "Do you really carry this heavy bucket? Why, it makes my arm ache."

"Twice every day—morning and evening," she replied. "I'm very strong."

Then he stole a look out of the corner of his eye, and, seeing that her face was hidden from him by the hood, he turned to observe her at better advantage. A long braid of hair hung down her back. In the twilight it gleamed dull gold. She came up to his shoulder. The sleeve nearest him was rolled up to her elbow, revealing a fine round arm. Her hand, like her foot, was brown, strong, and well shaped. It was a hand that had been developed by labor. She was full-bosomed, yet slender, and she walked with a free stride that made Shefford admire and wonder.

They passed several of the little stone and log houses, and women greeted them as they went by, and children peered shyly from the doors.

He kept trying to think of something to say, and, failing in that, determined to have one good look under the hood before he left her.

"You walk lame," she said, solicitously. "Let me carry the bucket now —please. My house is near."

"Am I lame? . . . Guess so, a little," he replied. "It was a hard ride for me. But I'll carry the bucket just the same."

They went on under some pinyon trees, down a path to a little house identical with the others, except that it had a stone porch. Shefford smelled fragrant wood-smoke and saw a column curling from the low, flat, stone chimney. Then he set the bucket down on the porch.

"Thank you, Mr. Shefford," she said.

"You know my name?" he asked.

"Yes. Mr. Withers spoke to my nearest neighbor and she told me."

"Oh, I see. And you—"

He did not go on and she did not reply. When she stepped upon the porch and turned he was able to see under the hood. The face there was in shadow, and for that very reason he answered to ungovernable impulse and took a step closer to her. Dark, grave, sad eyes looked down at him, and he felt as if he could never draw his own glance away. He seemed not to see the rest of her face, and yet felt that it was lovely. Then a downward movement of the hood hid from him the strange eyes and the shadowy loveliness.

"I—I beg your pardon," he said, quickly, drawing back. "I'm rude. . . . Withers told me about a girl he called—he said looked like a sago-lily. That's no excuse to stare under your hood. But I—I was curious. I wondered if—"

He hesitated, realizing how foolish his talk was. She stood a moment, probably watching him, but he could not be sure, for her face was hidden.

"They call me that," she said. "But my name is Mary."

"Mary—what?" he asked.

"Just Mary," she said, simply. "Good night."

He did not say good night and could not have told why. She took up the bucket and went into the dark house. Shefford hurried away into the gathering darkness.

⁖6⁖

IN THE HIDDEN VALLEY

SHEFFORD had hardly seen her face, yet he was more interested in a woman than he had ever been before. Still, he reflected, as he returned to camp, he had been under a long strain, he was unduly excited by this new and adventurous life, and these, with the mystery of this village, were perhaps accountable for a state of mind that could not last.

He rolled in his blankets on the soft bed of moss and he saw the stars through the needlelike fringe of the pinyons. It seemed impossible to fall asleep. The two domed peaks split the sky, and back of them, looming dark and shadowy, rose the mountain. There was something cold, austere, and majestic in their lofty presence, and they made him feel alone, yet not alone. He raised himself to see the quiet forms of Withers and Nas Ta Bega prone in the starlight, and their slow, deep breathing was that of tired men. A bell on a mustang rang somewhere off in the valley and gave out a low, strange, reverberating echo from wall to wall. When it ceased a silence set in that was deader than any silence he had ever felt, but gradually he became aware of the low murmur of the brook. For the rest there was no sound of wind, no bark of dog or yelp of coyote, no sound of voice in the village.

He tried to sleep, but instead thought of this girl who was called the Sago Lily. He recalled everything incident to their meeting and the walk to her home. Her swift, free step, her graceful poise, her shapely form—the long braid of hair, dull gold in the twilight, the beautiful bare foot and the strong round arm—these he thought of and recalled vividly. But of her face he had no idea except the shadowy, haunting loveliness, and that grew more and more difficult to remember. The tone of her voice and what she had said—how the one had thrilled him and the other mystified! It was her voice that had most attracted him. There was something in it besides music—what, he could not tell—sadness, depth, something like that in Nas Ta Bega's—a beauty springing from disuse. But this seemed absurd. Why should he imagine her voice one that had not been used as freely as any other woman's? She was a Mormon; very likely, almost surely, she was a sealed wife. His interest, too, was absurd, and he tried to throw it off, or imagine it one he might have felt in any other of these strange women of the hidden village.

But Shefford's intelligence and his good sense, which became operative

273

when he was fully roused and set the situation clearly before his eyes, had no effect upon his deeper, mystic, and primitive feelings. He saw the truth and he felt something that he could not name. He would not be a fool, but there was no harm in dreaming. And unquestionably, beyond all doubt, the dream and the romance that had lured him to the wilderness were here, hanging over him like the shadows of the great peaks. His heart swelled with emotion when he thought of how the black and incessant despair of the past was gone. So he embraced any attraction that made him forget and think and feel; some instinct stronger than intelligence bade him drift.

Joe's rolling voice awoke him next morning and he rose with a singular zest. When or where in his life had he awakened in such a beautiful place? Almost he understood why Venters and Bess had been haunted by memories of Surprise Valley. The morning was clear, cool, sweet; the peaks were dim and soft in rosy cloud; shafts of golden sunlight shot down into the purple shadows. Mockingbirds were singing. His body was sore and tired from the unaccustomed travel, but his heart was full, happy. His spirit wanted to run, and he knew there was something out there waiting to meet it. The Indian and the trader and the Mormon all meant more to him this morning. He had grown a little overnight. Nas Ta Bega's deep "Bi Nai" rang in his ears, and the smiles of Withers and Joe were greetings. He had friends; he had work; and there was rich, strange, and helpful life to live. There was even a difference in the mustang Nack-yal. He came readily; he did not look wild; he had a friendly eye; and Shefford liked him more.

"What is there to do?" asked Shefford, feeling equal to a hundred tasks.

"No work," replied the trader, with a laugh, and he drew Shefford aside. "I'm in no hurry. I like it here. And Joe never wants to leave. Today you can meet the women. Make yourself popular. I've already made you that. These women are most all young and lonesome. Talk to them. Make them like you. Then some day you may be safe to ask questions. Last night I wanted to ask old Mother Smith if she ever heard the name Fay Larkin. But I thought better of it. If there's a girl here or at Stonebridge of that name we'll learn it. If there's mystery we'd better go slow. Mormons are hell on secret and mystery, and to pry into their affairs is to queer yourself. My advice is—just be as nice as you can be, and let things happen."

Fay Larkin! All in a night Shefford had forgotten her. Why? He pondered over the matter, and then the old thrill, the old desire, came back.

"Shefford, what do you think Nas Ta Bega said to me last night?" asked Withers in lower voice.

"Haven't any idea," replied Shefford, curiously.

"We were sitting beside the fire. I saw you walking under the cedars. You seemed thoughtful. That keen Indian watched you, and he said to me in Navajo, 'Bi Nai has lost his God. He has come far to find a wife. Nas Ta

Bega is his brother.' . . . He meant he'll find both God and wife for you. I don't know about that, but I say take the Indian as he thinks he is—your brother. Long before I knew Nas Ta Bega well my wife used to tell me about him. He's a sage and a poet—the very spirit of this desert. He's worth cultivating for his own sake. But more—remember, if Fay Larkin is still shut in that valley the Navajo will find her for you."

"I shall take Nas Ta Bega as my brother—and be proud," replied Shefford.

"There's another thing. Do you intend to confide in Joe?"

"I hadn't thought of that."

"Well, it might be a good plan. But wait until you know him better and he knows you. He's ready to fight for you now. He's taken your trouble to heart. You wouldn't think Joe is deeply religious. Yet he is. He may never breathe a word about religion to you. . . . Now, Shefford, go ahead. You've struck a trail. It's rough, but it'll make a man of you. It'll lead somewhere."

"I'm singularly fortunate—I—who had lost all friends. Withers, I am grateful. I'll prove it. I'll show—"

Withers's upheld hand checked further speech, and Shefford realized that beneath the rough exterior of this desert trader there was fine feeling. These men of crude toil and wild surroundings were beginning to loom up large in Shefford's mind.

The day began leisurely. The men were yet at breakfast when the women of the village began to come one by one to the spring. Joe Lake made friendly and joking remarks to each. And as each one passed on down the path he poised a biscuit in one hand and a cup of coffee in the other, and with his head cocked sidewise like an owl he said, "Reckon I've got to get me a woman like her."

Shefford saw and heard, yet he was all the time half unconsciously watching with strange eagerness for a white figure to appear. At last he saw her—the same girl with the hood, the same swift step. A little shock or quiver passed over him, and at the moment all that was explicable about it was something associated with regret.

Joe Lake whistled and stared.

"I haven't met her," he muttered.

"That's the Sago Lily," said Withers.

"Reckon I'm going to carry that bucket," went on Joe.

"And queer yourself with all the other women who've been to the spring? Don't do it, Joe," advised the trader.

"But her bucket's bigger," protested Joe, weakly.

"That's true. But you ought to know Mormons. If she'd come first, all right. As she didn't—why, don't single her out."

Joe kept his seat. The girl came to the spring. A low "good morning" came from under the hood. Then she filled her bucket and started home. Shefford observed that this time she wore moccasins and she carried the heavy bucket with ease. When she disappeared he had again the vague, inexplicable sensation of regret.

Joe Lake breathed heavily. "Reckon I've got to get me a woman like her," he said. But the former jocose tone was lacking and he appeared thoughtful.

Withers first took Shefford to the building used for a school. It was somewhat larger than the other houses, had only one room with two doors and several windows. It was full of children of all sizes and ages, sitting on rude board benches.

There were half a hundred of them, sturdy, healthy, rosy boys and girls, clad in homemade garments. The young woman teacher was as embarrassed as her pupils were shy, and the visitors withdrew without having heard a word of lessons.

Withers then called upon Smith, Henninger, and Beal, and their wives. Shefford found himself cordially received, and what little he did say showed him how he would be listened to when he cared to talk. These folk were plain and kindly, and he found that there was nothing about them to dislike. The men appeared mild and quiet, and when not conversing seemed austere. The repose of the women was only on the surface; underneath he felt their intensity. Especially in many of the younger women, whom he met in the succeeding hour, did he feel this power of restrained emotion. This surprised him, as did also the fact that almost every one of them was attractive and some of them were exceedingly pretty. He became so interested in them all as a whole that he could not individualize one. They were as widely different in appearance and temperament as women of any other class, but it seemed to Shefford that one common trait united them—and it was a strange, checked yearning for something that he could not discover. Was it happiness? They certainly seemed to be happy, far more so than those millions of women who were chasing phantoms. Were they really sealed wives, as Withers believed, and was this unnatural wifehood responsible for the strange intensity? At any rate he returned to camp with the conviction that he had stumbled upon a remarkable situation.

He had been told the last names of only three women, and their husbands were in the village. The names of the others were Ruth, Rebecca, Joan—he could not recall them all. They were the mothers of these beautiful children. The fathers, as far as he was concerned, were as intangible as myths. Shefford was an educated clergyman, a man of the world, and, as such, knew women in his way. Mormons might be strange and different, yet the fundamental truth was that all over the world mothers of children were wives; there was a relation between wife and mother that did not need to be named to be felt; and he divined from this that, whatever the situation of these lonely and hidden women, they knew themselves to be wives. Shefford absolutely satisfied himself on that score. If they were miserable they certainly did not show it, and the question came to him how just was the criticism of uninformed men? His judgment of Mormons had been established by what he had heard and read, rather than what he knew. He wanted now to have an open mind. He had studied the totemism and exogamy of the primitive races, and here was his opportunity to understand polygamy. One wife for one man —that was the law. Mormons broke it openly; Gentiles broke it secretly. Mormons acknowledged all their wives and protected their children; Gentiles acknowledged one wife only. Unquestionably the Mormons were wrong, but were not the Gentiles still more wrong?

The following day Joe Lake appeared reluctant to start for Stonebridge with Withers.

"Joe, you'd better come along," said the trader, dryly. "I reckon you've seen a little too much of the Sago Lily."

Lake offered no reply, but it was evident from his sober face that Withers had not hit short of the mark. Withers rode off, with a parting word to Shefford, and finally Joe somberly mounted his bay and trotted down the valley. As Nas Ta Bega had gone off somewhere to visit Indians, Shefford was left alone.

He went into the village and made himself useful and agreeable. He made friends with the children and he talked to the women until he was hoarse. Their ignorance of the world was a spur to him, and never in his life had he had such an attentive audience. And as he showed no curiosity, asked no difficult questions, gradually what reserve he had noted wore away, and the end of the day saw him on a footing with them that Withers had predicted.

By the time several like days had passed it seemed from the interest and friendliness of these women that he might have lived long among them. He was possessed of wit and eloquence and information, which he freely gave, and not with selfish motive. He liked these women; he liked to see the somber shade pass from their faces, to see them brighten. He had met the girl Mary at the spring and along the path, but he had not yet seen her face. He was always looking for her, hoping to meet her, and confessed to himself that the best of the day for him were the morning and evening visits she made to the spring. Nevertheless, for some reason hard to divine, he was reluctant to seek her deliberately. Always while he had listened to her neighbors' talk, he had hoped they might let fall something about her. But they did not. He received an impression that she was not so intimate with the others as he had supposed. They all made one big family. Still, she seemed a little outside. He could bring no proofs to strengthen this idea. He merely felt it, and many of his feelings were independent of intelligent reason. Something had been added to curiosity, that was sure.

It was his habit to call upon Mother Smith in the afternoons. From the first her talk to him hinted of a leaning toward thought of making him a Mormon. Her husband and the other men took up her cue and spoke of their religion, casually at first, but gradually opening their minds to free and simple discussion of their faith. Shefford lent respectful attention. He would rather have been a Mormon than an atheist, and apparently they considered him the latter, and were earnest to save his soul. Shefford knew that he could never be one any more than the other. He was just at sea. But he listened, and he found them simple in faith, blind, perhaps, but loyal and good. It was noteworthy that Mother Smith happened to be the only woman in the village who had ever mentioned religion to him. She was old, of a past generation; the young women belonged to the present. Shefford pondered the significant difference.

Every day made more steadfast his impression of the great mystery that was like a twining shadow round these women, yet in the same time many little ideas shifted and many new characteristics became manifest. This last was of course the result of acquaintance; he was learning more about the villagers. He gathered from keen interpretation of subtle words and looks that here in this lonely village, the same as in all the rest of the world where women were together, there were cliques, quarrels, dislikes, loves, and jealousies. The truth, once known to him, made him feel natural and fortified his confidence to meet the demands of an increasingly interesting position. He discovered, with a somewhat grim amusement, that a clergyman's experience in a church full of women had not been entirely useless.

One afternoon he let fall a careless remark that was a subtle question in regard to the girl Mary, whom Withers called the Sago Lily. In response he received an answer couched in the sweet poisoned honey of woman's jealousy. He said no more. Certain ideas of his were strengthened, and straightway he became thoughtful.

That afternoon late, as he did his camp chores, he watched for her. But she did not come. Then he decided to go to see her. But even the decision and the strange thrill it imparted did not change his reluctance.

Twilight was darkening the valley when he reached her house, and the shadows were thick under the pinyons. There was no light in the door or window. He saw a white shape on the porch, and as he came down the path it rose. It was the girl Mary, and she appeared startled.

"Good evening," he said. "It's Shefford. May I stay and talk a little while?"

She was silent for so long that he began to feel awkward.

"I'd be glad to have you," she replied, finally.

There was a bench on the porch, but he preferred to sit upon a blanket on the step.

"I've been getting acquainted with everybody—except you," he went on.

"I have been here," she replied.

That might have been a woman's speech, but it certainly had been made in a girl's voice. She was neither shy nor embarrassed nor self-conscious. As she stood back from him he could not see her face in the dense twilight.

"I've been wanting to call on you."

She made some slight movement. Shefford felt a strange calm, yet he knew the moment was big and potent.

"Won't you sit here?" he asked.

She complied with his wish, and then he saw her face, though dimly, in the twilight. And it struck him mute. But he had no glimpse such as had flashed upon him from under her hood that other night. He thought of a white flower in shadow, and received his first impression of the rare and perfect lily Withers had said graced the wild canyons. She was only a girl. She sat very still, looking straight before her, and seemed to be waiting, listening. Shefford saw the quick rise and fall of her bosom.

"I want to talk," he began, swiftly, hoping to put her at her ease. "Everyone here has been good to me and I've talked—oh, for hours and hours. But the thing in my mind I haven't spoken of. I've never asked any questions. That makes my part so strange. I want to tell why I came out here. I need someone who will keep my secret, and perhaps help me. . . . Would you?"

"Yes, if I could," she replied.

"You see I've got to trust you, or one of these other women. You're all Mormons. I don't mean that's anything against you. I believe you're all good and noble. But the fact makes—well, makes a liberty of speech impossible. What can I do?"

Her silence probably meant that she did not know. Shefford sensed less strain in her and more excitement. He believed he was on the right track and did not regret his impulse. Even had he regretted it he would have gone on, for opposed to caution and intelligence was his driving mystic force.

Then he told her the truth about his boyhood, his ambition to be an artist, his renunciation to his father's hope, his career as a clergyman, his failure in religion, and the disgrace that had made him a wanderer.

"Oh—I'm sorry!" she said. The faint starlight shone on her face, in her eyes, and if he ever saw beauty and soul he saw them then. She seemed deeply moved. She had forgotten herself. She betrayed girlhood then—all the quick sympathy, the wonder, the sweetness of a heart innocent and untutored. She looked at him with great, starry, questioning eyes, as if they had just become aware of his presence, as if a man had been strange to her.

"Thank you. It's good of you to be sorry," he said. "My instinct guided me right. Perhaps you'll be my friend."

"I will be—if I can," she said.

"But *can* you be?"

"I don't know. I never had a friend. I . . . But, sir, I mustn't talk of myself. . . . Oh, I'm afraid I can't help you."

How strange the pathos of her voice! Almost he believed she was in need of help or sympathy or love. But he could not wholly trust a judgment formed from observation of a class different from hers.

"Maybe you *can* help me. Let's see," he said. "I don't seek to make you talk of yourself. But—you're a human being—a girl—almost a woman. You're not dumb. But even a nun can talk."

"A nun? What is that?"

"Well—a nun is a sister of mercy—a woman consecrated to God—who has renounced the world. In some ways you Mormon women here resemble nuns. It is sacrifice that nails you in this lonely valley. . . . You see—how I talk! One word, one thought brings another, and I speak what perhaps should be unsaid. And it's hard, because I feel I could unburden myself to you."

"Tell me what you want," she said.

Shefford hesitated, and became aware of the rapid pound of his heart. More than anything he wanted to be fair to this girl. He saw that she was warming to his influence. Her shadowy eyes were fixed upon him. The starlight, growing brighter, shone on her golden hair and white face.

"I'll tell you presently," he said. "I've trusted you. I'll trust you with all. . . . But let me have my own time. This is so strange a thing, my wanting to confide in you. It's selfish, perhaps. I have my own ax to grind. I hope I won't wrong you. That's why I'm going to be perfectly frank. I might wait for days to get better acquainted. But the impulse is on me. I've been so interested in all you Mormon women. The fact—the meaning of this hidden village is so—so terrible to me. But that's none of my business. I have spent my afternoons and evenings with these women at the different cottages. You do not mingle with them. They are lonely, but have not such loneliness as yours. I have passed here every night. No light —no sound. I can't help thinking. Don't censure me or be afraid or draw within yourself just because I must think. I may be all wrong. But I'm curious. I wonder about you. Who are you? Mary—Mary what? Maybe I really don't want to know. I came with selfish motive and now I'd like to —to—what shall I say? Make your life a little less lonely for the while I'm here. That's all. It needn't offend. And if you accept it, how much easier I can tell you my secret. You are a Mormon and I—well, I am only a wanderer in these wilds. But—we might help each other. . . . Have I made a mistake?"

"No—no," she cried, almost wildly.

"We can be friends then. You will trust me, help me?"

"Yes, if I dare."

"Surely you may dare what the other women would?"

She was silent.

And the wistfulness of her silence touched him. He felt contrition. He did not stop to analyze his own emotions, but he had an inkling that once this strange situation was ended he would have food for reflection. What struck him most now was the girl's blanched face, the strong, nervous clasp of her hands, the visible tumult of her bosom. Excitement alone could not be accountable for this. He had not divined the cause for such agitation. He was puzzled, troubled, and drawn irresistibly. He had not said what he had planned to say. The moment had given birth to his speech, and it had flowed. What was guiding him?

"Mary," he said, earnestly, "tell me—have you mother, father, sister, brother? Something prompts me to ask that."

"All dead—gone—years ago," she answered.

"How old are you?"

"Eighteen, I think. I'm not sure."

"You *are* lonely."

His words were gentle and divining.

"O God!" she cried. "Lonely!"

Then as a man in a dream he beheld her weeping. There was in her the unconsciousness of a child and the passion of a woman. He gazed out into the dark shadows and up at the white stars, and then at the bowed head with its mass of glinting hair. But her agitation was no longer strange to him. A few gentle and kind words had proved her undoing. He knew then that whatever her life was, no kindness or sympathy entered it. Presently she recovered, and sat as before, only whiter of face it seemed, and with something tragic in her dark eyes. She was growing cold and still again, aloof, more like those other Mormon women.

"I understand," he said. "I'm not sorry I spoke. I felt your trouble, whatever it is. . . . Do not retreat into your cold shell, I beg of you. . . . Let me trust you with my secret."

He saw her shake out of the cold apathy. She wavered. He felt an inexplicable sweetness in the power his voice seemed to have upon her. She bowed her head in acquiescence. And Shefford began his story. Did she grow still, like stone, or was that only his vivid imagination? He told her of Venters and Bess—of Lassiter and Jane—of little Fay Larkin—of the romance, and then the tragedy of Surprise Valley.

"So, when my church disowned me," he concluded, "I conceived the idea of wandering into the wilds of Utah to save Fay Larkin from that canyon prison. It grew to be the best and strongest desire of my life. I think if I could save her that it would save me. I never loved any girl. I can't say that I love Fay Larkin. How could I when I've never seen her— when she's only a dream girl? But I believe if she were to become a reality —a flesh-and-blood girl—that I would love her."

That was more than Shefford had ever confessed to anyone, and it stirred him to his depths. Mary bent her head on her hands in strange, stonelike rigidity.

"So here I am in the canyon country," he continued. "Withers tells me it is a country of rainbows, both in the evanescent air and in the change-less stone. Always as a boy there had been for me some haunting promise, some treasure at the foot of the rainbow. I shall expect the curve of a rainbow to lead me down into Surprise Valley. A dreamer, you will call me. But I have had strange dreams come true. . . . Mary, do you think *this* dream will come true?"

She was silent so long that he repeated his question.

"Only—in heaven," she whispered.

He took her reply strangely and a chill crept over him.

"You think my plan to seek to strive, to find—you think that idle, vain?"

"I think it noble. . . . Thank God I've met a man like you!"

"Don't praise me!" he exclaimed, hastily. "Only help me. . . . Mary, will you answer a few little questions, if I swear by my honor I'll never reveal what you tell me?"

"I'll try."

He moistened his lips. Why did she seem so strange, so far away? The hovering shadows made him nervous. Always he had been afraid of the dark. His mood now admitted of unreal fancies.

"Have you ever heard of Fay Larkin?" he asked, very low.

"Yes."

"Was there only one Fay Larkin?"

"Only one."

"Did you—ever see her?"

"Yes," came the faint reply.

He was grateful. How she might be breaking faith with creed or duty! He had not dared to hope so much. All his inner being trembled at the portent of his next query. He had not dreamed it would be so hard to put, or would affect him so powerfully. A warmth, a glow, a happiness per-vaded his spirit; and the chill, the gloom were as if they had never been.

"Where is Fay Larkin now?" he asked, huskily.

He bent over her, touched her, leaned close to catch her whisper.

"She is—dead!"

Slowly Shefford rose, with a sickening shock, and then in bitter pain he strode away into the starlight.

❧7❧

SAGO-LILIES

THE INDIAN returned to camp that night, and early the next day, which was Sunday, Withers rode in, accompanied by a stout, gray-bearded personage wearing a long black coat.

"Bishop Kane, this is my new man, John Shefford," said the trader.

Shefford acknowledged the introduction with the respectful courtesy evidently in order, and found himself being studied intently by clear blue eyes. The bishop appeared old, dry, and absorbed in thought; he spoke quaintly, using in every speech some biblical word or phrase; and he had an air of authority. He asked Shefford to hear him preach at the morning service, and then he went off into the village.

"Guess he liked your looks," remarked Withers.

"He certainly sized me up," replied Shefford.

"Well, what could you expect? Sure I never heard of a deal like this—a handsome young fellow left alone with a lot of pretty Mormon women! You'll understand when you learn to know Mormons. Bishop Kane's a square old chap. Crazy on religion, maybe, but otherwise he's a good fellow. I made the best stand I could for you. The Mormons over at Stonebridge were huffy because I hadn't consulted them before fetching you over here. If I had, of course you'd never have gotten here. It was Joe Lake who made it all right with them. Joe's well thought of, and he certainly stood up for you."

"I owe him something, then," replied Shefford. "Hope my obligations don't grow beyond me. Did you leave Joe at Stonebridge?"

"Yes. He wanted to stay, and I had work there that'll keep him awhile. Shefford, we got news of Shadd—bad news. The half-breed's cutting up rough. His gang shot up some Piutes over here across the line. Then he got run out of Durango a few weeks ago for murder. A posse of cowboys trailed him. But he slipped them. He's a fox. You know he was trailing us here. He left the trail, Nas Ta Bega said. I learned at Stonebridge that Shadd is well disposed toward Mormons. It takes the Mormons to handle Indians. Shadd knows of this village and that's why he shunted off our trail. But he might hang down in the pass and wait for us. I think I'd better go back to Kayenta alone, across country. You stay here till Joe and the Indian think it safe to leave. You'll be going up on the slope of Navajo to load a pack-train, and from there it may be well to go down West

Canyon to Red Lake, and home over the divide, the way you came. Joe'll decide what's best. And you might as well buckle on a gun and get used to it. Sooner or later you'll have to shoot your way through."

Shefford did not respond with his usual enthusiasm, and the omission caused the trader to scrutinize him closely.

"What's the matter?" he queried. "There's no light in your eye today. You look a little shady."

"I didn't rest well last night," replied Shefford. "I'm depressed this morning. But I'll cheer up directly."

"Did you get along with the women?"

"Very well indeed. And I've enjoyed myself. It's a strange, beautiful place."

"Do you like the women?"

"Yes."

"Have you seen much of the Sago Lily?"

"No. I carried her bucket one night—and saw her only once again. I've been with the other women most of the time."

"It's just as well you didn't run often into Mary. Joe's sick over her. I never saw a girl with a face and form to equal hers. There's danger here for any man, Shefford. Even for you who think you've turned your back on the world! Any of these Mormon women may fall in love with you. They *can't* love their husbands. That's how I figure it. Religion holds them, not love. And the peculiar thing is this: they're second, third, or fourth wives, all sealed. That means their husbands are old, have picked them out for youth and physical charms, have chosen the very opposite to their first wives, and then have hidden them here in this lonely hole. . . . Did you ever imagine so terrible a thing?"

"No, Withers, I did not."

"Maybe that's what depressed you. Anyway, my hunch is worth taking. Be as nice as you can, Shefford. Lord knows it would be good for these poor women if every last one of them fell in love with you. That won't hurt them so long as you keep your head. Savvy? Perhaps I seem rough and coarse to a man of your class. Well, that may be. But human nature is human nature. And in this strange and beautiful place you might love an Indian girl, let alone the Sago Lily. That's all. I sure feel better with that load off my conscience. Hope I don't offend."

"No indeed. I thank you, Withers," replied Shefford, with his hand on the trader's shoulder. "You are right to caution me. I seem to be wild—thirsting for adventure—chasing a gleam. In these unstable days I can't answer for my heart. But I can for my honor. These unfortunate women are as safe with me as—as they are with you and Joe."

Withers uttered a blunt laugh.

"See here, son, look things square in the eye. Men of violent, lonely, toilsome lives store up hunger for the love of woman. Love of a *strange* woman, if you want to put it that way. It's nature. It seems all the beautiful young women in Utah are corralled in this valley. When I come over here I feel natural, but I'm not happy. I'd like to make love to—to that flower-faced girl. And I'm not ashamed to own it. I've told Molly, my wife, and she understands. As for Joe, it's much harder for him. Joe never has had a wife or sweetheart. I tell you he's sick, and if I'd stay here a month I'd be sick."

Withers had spoken with fire in his eyes, with grim humor on his lips, with uncompromising brutal truth. What he admitted was astounding to Shefford, but, once spoken, not at all strange. The trader was a man who spoke his inmost thoughts. And what he said suddenly focused Shefford's mental vision clear and whole upon the appalling significance of the tragedy of those women, especially of the girl whose life was lonelier, sadder, darker than that of the others.

"Withers, trust me," replied Shefford.

"All right. Make the best of a bad job," said the trader, and went off about his tasks.

Shefford and Withers attended the morning service, which was held in the schoolhouse. Exclusive of the children every inhabitant of the village was there. The women, except the few eldest, were dressed in white and looked exceedingly well. Manifestly they had bestowed care upon this Sabbath morning's toilet. One thing surely this dress occasion brought out, and it was evidence that the Mormon women were not poor, what-ever their misfortunes might be. Jewelry was not wanting, nor fine lace. And they all wore beautiful wild flowers of a kind unknown to Shefford. He received many a bright smile. He looked for Mary, hoping to see her face for the first time in the daylight, but she sat far forward and did not turn. He saw her graceful white neck, the fine lines of her throat, and her colorless cheek. He recognized her, yet in the light she seemed a stranger.

The service began with a short prayer and was followed by the singing of a hymn. Nowhere had Shefford heard better music or sweeter voices. How deeply they affected him! Had any man ever fallen into a stranger adventure than this? He had only to shut his eyes to believe it all a creation of his fancy—the square log cabin with its red mud between the chinks and a roof like an Indian hogan—the old bishop in his black coat, standing solemnly, his hand beating time to the tune—the few old women, dignified and stately—the many young women, fresh and hand-some, lifting their voices.

Shefford listened intently to the bishop's sermon. In some respects it was the best he had ever heard. In others it was impossible for an intelli-gent man to regard seriously. It was very long, lasting an hour and a half, and the parts that were helpful to Shefford came from the experience and wisdom of a man who had grown old in the desert. The physical things that had molded characters of iron, the obstacles that only strong, patient men could have overcome, the making of homes in a wilderness, showed

the greatness of this alien band of Mormons. Shefford conceded greatness
to them. But the strange religion—the narrowing down of the world to
the soil of Utah, the intimations of prophets on earth who had direct
converse with God, the austere self-conscious omnipotence of this old
bishop—these were matters that Shefford felt he must understand better,
and see more favorably, if he were not to consider them impossible.

Immediately after the service, forgetting that his intention had been to
get the long-waited-for look at Mary in the light of the sun, Shefford
hurried back to camp and to a secluded spot among the cedars. Strikingly
it had come to him that the fault he had found in Gentile religion he now
found in the Mormon religion. An old question returned to haunt him—
were all religions the same in blindness? As far as he could see, religion
existed to uphold the founders of a church, a creed. The church of his
own kind was a place where narrow men and women went to think of
their own salvation. They did not go there to think of others. And now
Shefford's keen mind saw something of Mormonism and found it wanting.
Bishop Kane was a sincere, good, mistaken man. He believed what he
preached, but that would not stand logic. He taught blindness and mostly
it appeared to be directed at the women. Was there no religion divorced
from power, no religion as good for one man as another, no religion in the
spirit of brotherly love? Nas Ta Bega's "Bi Nai" (brother)—that was love,
if not religion, and perhaps the one and the other were the same. Shefford
kept in mind an intention to ask Nas Ta Bega what he thought of the
Mormons.

Later, when opportunity afforded, he did speak to the Indian. Nas Ta
Bega threw away his cigarette and made an impressive gesture that conveyed as much sorrow as scorn.

"The first Mormon said God spoke to him and told him to go to a
certain place and dig. He went there and found the Book of Mormon. It
said follow me, marry many wives, go into the desert and multiply, send
your sons out into the world and bring us young women, many young
women. And when the first Mormon became strong with many followers
he said again: Give to me part of your labor—of your cattle and sheep—of
your silver—that I may build me great cathedrals for you to worship in.
And I will commune with God and make it right and good that you have
more wives. That is what the bishop preached. That is Mormonism."

"Nas Ta Bega, you mean the Mormons are a great and good people
blindly following a leader?"

"Yes. And the leader builds for himself—not for them."

"That is not religion. He has no God but himself."

"They have no God. They are blind like the Mokis who have the
creeping growths on their eyes. They have no God they can see and hear
and feel, who is with them day and night."

It was late in the afternoon when Bishop Kane rode through the camp
and halted on his way to speak to Shefford. He was kind and fatherly.

"Young man, are you open to faith?" he questioned, gravely.

"I think I am," replied Shefford, thankful he could answer readily.

"Then come into the fold. You are a lost sheep. 'Away on the desert I heard its cry.' . . . God bless you. Visit me when you ride to Stonebridge."

He flicked his horse with a cedar branch and trotted away beside the trader, and presently the green-choked neck of the valley hid them from view. Shefford could not have said that he was glad to be left behind, and yet neither was he sorry.

That Sabbath evening as he sat quietly with Nas Ta Bega, watching the sunset gilding the peaks, he was visited by three of the young Mormon women—Ruth, Joan, and Hester. They deliberately sought him and merrily led him off to the village and to the evening service of singing and prayer. Afterward he was surrounded and made much of. He had been popular before, but this was different. When he thoughtfully wended his way campward under the quiet stars he realized that the coming of Bishop Kane had made a subtle change in the women. That change was at first hard to define, but from every point by which he approached it he came to the same conclusion—the bishop had not objected to his presence in the village. The women became natural, free, and unrestrained. A dozen or twenty young and attractive women thrown much into companionship with one man. He might become a Mormon. The idea made him laugh. But upon reflection it was not funny; it sobered him. What a situation! He felt instinctively that he ought to fly from this hidden valley. But he could not have done it, even had he not been in the trader's employ. The thing was provokingly seductive. It was like an Arabian Nights' tale. What would these strange, fatally bound women do? Would any one of them become involved in sweet toils such as were possible to him? He was no fool. Already eyes had flashed and lips had smiled.

A thousand like thoughts whirled through his mind. And when he had calmed down somewhat two things were not lost upon him—an intricate and fascinating situation, with no end to its possibilities, threatened and attracted him—and the certainty that, whatever change the bishop had inaugurated, it had made these poor women happier. The latter fact weighed more with Shefford than fears for himself. His word was given to Withers. He would have felt just the same without having bound himself. Still, in the light of the trader's blunt philosophy, and of his own assurance that he was no fool, Shefford felt it incumbent upon him to accept a belief that there were situations no man could resist without an anchor. The ingenuity of man could not have devised a stranger, a more enticing, a more overpoweringly fatal situation. Fatal in that it could not be left untried! Shefford gave in and clicked his teeth as he let himself go. And suddenly he thought of her whom these bitter women called the Sago Lily.

The regret that had been his returned with thought of her. The saddest disillusion of his life, the keenest disappointment, the strangest pain, would always be associated with her. He had meant to see her face once, clear in the sunlight, so that he could always remember it, and then never go near her again. And now it came to him that if he did see much of her these other women would find him like the stone wall in the valley. Folly! Perhaps it was, but she would be safe, maybe happier. When he decided, it was certain that he trembled.

Then he buried the memory of Fay Larkin.

Next day Shefford threw himself with all the boy left in him into the work and play of the village. He helped the women and made games for the children. And he talked or listened. In the early evening he called on Ruth, chatted awhile, and went on to see Joan, and from her to another. When the valley became shrouded in darkness he went unseen down the path to Mary's lonely home.

She was there, a white shadow against the black. When she replied to his greeting her voice seemed full, broken, eager to express something that would not come. She was happier to see him than she should have been, Shefford thought. He talked, swiftly, eloquently, about whatever he believed would interest her. He stayed long, and finally left, not having seen her face except in pale starlight and shadow; and the strong clasp of her hand remained with him as he went away under the pinyons.

Days passed swiftly. Joe Lake did not return. The Indian rode in and out of camp, watered and guarded the pack-burros and the mustangs. Shefford grew strong and active. He made garden for the women; he cut cords of firewood; he dammed the brook and made an irrigation ditch; he learned to love these fatherless children, and they loved him.

In the afternoons there was leisure for him and for the women. He had no favorites, and let the occasion decide what he should do and with whom he should be. They had little parties at the cottages and picnics under the cedars. He rode up and down the valley with Ruth, who could ride a horse as no other girl he had ever seen. He climbed with Hester. He walked with Joan. Mostly he contrived to include several at once in the little excursions, though it was not rare for him to be out alone with one.

It was not a game he was playing. More and more, as he learned to know these young women, he liked them better, he pitied them, he was good for them. It shamed him, hurt him, somehow, to see how they tried to forget something when they were with him. Not improbably a little of it was coquetry, as natural as a laugh to any pretty woman. But that was not what hurt him. It was to see Ruth or Rebecca, as the case might be, full of life and fun, thoroughly enjoying some jest or play, all of a sudden be strangely recalled from the wholesome pleasure of a girl to become a deep and somber woman. The crimes in the name of religion! How he thought of the blood and the ruin laid at the door of religion! He wondered if that were so with Nas Ta Bega's religion, and he meant to find out someday. The women he liked best he imagined the least religious, and they made less effort to attract him.

Every night in the dark he went to Mary's home and sat with her on the porch. He never went inside. For all he knew, his visits were unknown to her neighbors. Still, it did not matter to him if they found out. To her he could talk as he had never talked to anyone. She liberated all his thought and fancy. He filled her mind.

As there had been a change in the other women, so was there in Mary; however, it had no relation to the bishop's visit. The time came when Shefford could not but see that she lived and dragged through the long day for the sake of those few hours in the shadow of the stars with him. She seldom spoke. She listened. Wonderful to him—sometimes she laughed—and it seemed the sound was a ghost of childhood pleasure. When he stopped to consider that she might fall in love with him he drove the thought from him. When he realized that his folly had become sweet and that the sweetness imperiously drew him, he likewise cast off that thought. The present was enough. And if he had any treasures of mind and heart he gave them to her.

She never asked him to stay, but she showed that she wanted him to. That made it hard to go. Still, he never stayed late. The moment of parting was like a break. Her goodbye was sweet, low music; it lingered on his ear; it bade him come tomorrow night; and it sent him away into the valley to walk under the stars, a man fighting against himself.

One night at parting, as he tried to see her face in the wan glow of a clouded moon, he said:

"I've been trying to find a sago-lily."

"Have you never seen one?" she asked.

"No." He meant to say something with a double meaning, in reference to her face and the name of the flower, but her unconsciousness made him hold his tongue. She was wholly unlike the other women.

"I'll show you where the lilies grow," she said.

"When?"

"Tomorrow. Early in the afternoon I'll come to the spring. Then I'll take you."

Next morning Joe Lake returned and imparted news that was perturbing to Shefford. Reports of Shadd had come in to Stonebridge from different Indian villages; Joe was not inclined to linger long at the camp, and favored taking the trail with the pack-train.

Shefford discovered that he did not want to leave the valley, and the knowledge made him reflective. That morning he did not go into the village, and stayed in camp alone. A depression weighed upon him. It was dispelled, however, early in the afternoon by the sight of a slender figure in white swiftly coming down the path to the spring. He had an appointment with Mary to go to see the sago-lilies; everything else slipped his mind.

Mary wore the long black hood that effectually concealed her face. It made of her a woman, a Mormon woman, and strangely belied the lithe form and the braid of gold hair.

"Good day," she said, putting down her bucket. "Do you still want to go—to see the lilies?"

"Yes," replied Shefford, with a short laugh.

"Can you climb?"

"I'll go where you go."

Then she set off under the cedars and Shefford stalked at her side. He was aware that Nas Ta Bega watched them walk away. This day, so far, at least, Shefford did not feel talkative; and Mary had always been one who mostly listened. They came at length to a place where the wall rose in low, smooth swells, not steep, but certainly at an angle Shefford would not of his own accord have attempted to scale.

Light, quick, and sure as a mountain-sheep Mary went up the first swell to an offset above. Shefford, in amaze and admiration, watched the little moccasins as they flashed and held on to the smooth rock.

When he essayed to follow her he slipped and came to grief. A second attempt resulted in like failure. Then he backed away from the wall, to run forward fast and up the slope, only to slip, halfway up, and fall again.

He made light of the incident, but she was solicitous. When he assured her he was unhurt she said he had agreed to go where she went.

"But I'm not a—a bird," he protested.

"Take off your boots. Then you can climb. When we get over the wall it'll be easy," she said.

In his stocking-feet he had no great difficulty walking up the first bulge of the walls. And from there she led him up the strange waves of wind-worn rock. He could not attend to anything save the red, polished rock under him, and so saw little. The ascent was longer than he would have imagined, and steep enough to make him pant, but at last a huge round summit was reached.

From here he saw down into the valley where the village lay. But for the lazy columns of blue smoke curling up from the pinyons the place would have seemed uninhabited. The wall on the other side was about level with the one upon which he stood. Beyond rose other walls and cliffs, up and up to the great towering peaks between which the green-and-black mountain loomed. Facing the other way, Shefford had only a restricted view. There were low crags and smooth stone ridges, between which were aisles green with cedar and pinyon. Shefford's companion headed toward one of these, and when he had followed her a few steps he could no longer see down into the valley. The Mormon village where she lived was as if it were lost, and when it vanished Shefford felt a difference.

Scarcely had the thought passed when Mary removed the dark hood. Her small head glistened like gold in the sunlight.

Shefford caught up with her and walked at her side, but could not bring himself at once deliberately to look at her. They entered a narrow, low-walled lane where cedars and pinyons grew thickly, their fragrance heavy in the warm air, and flowers began to show in the grassy patches.

"This is Indian paint-brush," she said, pointing to little, low, scarlet flowers. A gray sage-bush with beautiful purple blossoms she called purple sage; another bush with yellow flowers she named buck-brush, and there were vermilion cacti and low, flat mounds of lavender daisies which she said had no name. A whole mossy bank was covered with lacelike green leaves and tiny blossoms the color of violets, which she called loco.

"Loco? Is this what makes the horses go crazy when they eat it?" he asked.

"It is, indeed," she said, laughing.

When she laughed it was impossible not to look at her. She walked a little in advance. Her white cheek and temple seemed framed in the gold of her hair. How white her skin! But it was like pearl, faintly veined and flushed. The profile, clear-cut and pure, appeared cold, almost stern. He knew now that she was singularly beautiful, though he had yet to see her full face.

They walked on. Quite suddenly the lane opened out between two rounded bluffs, and Shefford looked down upon a grander and more awe-inspiring scene than ever he had viewed in his dreams.

What appeared to be a green mountainside sloped endlessly down to a plain, and that rolled and billowed away to a boundless region of strangely carved rock. The greatness of the scene could not be grasped in a glance. The slope was long; the plain not as level as it seemed to be on first sight; here and there round, red rocks, isolated and strange, like lonely castles, rose out of the green. Beyond the green all the earth seemed naked, showing smooth, glistening bones. It was a formidable wall of rock that flung itself up in the distance, carved into a thousand canyons and walls and domes and peaks, and there was not a straight nor a broken nor a jagged line in all that wildness. The color low down was red, dark blue, and purple in the clefts, yellow upon the heights, and in the distance rainbow-hued. A land of curves and color!

Shefford uttered an exclamation.

"That's Utah," said Mary. "I come often to sit here, You see that winding blue line. There. . . . That's San Juan Canyon. And the other dark line, that's Escalante Canyon. They wind down into this great purple chasm—'way over here to the left—and that's the Grand Canyon. They say not even the Indians have been in there."

Shefford had nothing to say. The moment was one of subtle and vital assimilation. Such places as this to be unknown to men! What strength, what wonder, what help, what glory, just to sit there an hour, slowly and appallingly to realize! Something came to Shefford from the distance, out of the purple canyons and from those dim, wind-worn peaks. He resolved to come here to this promontory again and again, alone and in humble spirit, and learn to know why he had been silenced, why peace pervaded his soul.

It was with this emotion upon him that he turned to find his companion watching him. Then for the first time he saw her face fully, and was thrilled that chance had reserved the privilege for this moment. It was a girl's face he saw, flowerlike, lovely and pure as a Madonna's, and strangely, tragically sad. The eyes were large, dark gray, the color of the sage. They were as clear as the air which made distant things close, and yet they seemed full of shadows, like a ruffled pool under midnight stars. They disturbed him. Her mouth had the sweet curves and redness of youth, but it showed bitterness, pain, and repression.

"Where are the sago-lilies?" he asked, suddenly.

"Farther down. It's too cold up here for them. Come," she said.

He followed her down a winding trail—down and down till the green plain rose to blot out the scrawled wall of rock, down into a verdant canyon where a brook made swift music over stones, where the air was sultry and hot, laden with the fragrant breath of flower and leaf. This was a canyon of summer, and it bloomed.

The girl bent and plucked something from the grass.

"Here's a white lily," she said. "There are three colors. The yellow and pink ones are deeper down in the canyons."

Shefford took the flower and regarded it with great interest. He had never seen such an exquisite thing. It had three large petals, curving cuplike, of a whiteness purer than new-fallen snow, and a heart of rich, warm gold. Its fragrance was so faint as to be almost indistinguishable, yet of a haunting, unforgetable sweetness. And even while he looked at it the petals drooped and their whiteness shaded and the gold paled. In a moment the flower was wilted.

"I don't like to pluck the lilies," said Mary. "They die so swiftly."

Shefford saw the white flowers everywhere in the open, sunny places along the brook. They swayed with stately grace in the slow, warm wind. They seemed like three-pointed stars shining out of the green. He bent over one with a particularly lofty stem, and after a close survey of it he rose to look at her face. His action was plainly one of comparison. She laughed and said it was foolish for the women to call her the Sago Lily. She had no coquetry; she spoke as she would have spoken of the stones at her feet; she did not know that she was beautiful. Shefford imagined there was some resemblance in her to the lily—the same whiteness, the same rich gold, and, more striking than either, a strange, rare quality of beauty, of life, intangible as something fleeting, the spirit that had swiftly faded from the plucked flower. Where had the girl been born—what had her life been? Shefford was intensely curious about her. She seemed as different from any other women he had known as this rare canyon lily was different from the tame flowers at home.

On the return up the slope she outstripped him. She climbed lightly and tirelessly. When he reached her upon the promontory there was a stain of red in her cheeks and her expression had changed.

"Let's go back up over the rocks," she said. "I've not climbed for—for so long."

"I'll go where you go," he replied.

Then she was off, and he followed. She took to the curves of the bare rocks and climbed. He sensed a spirit released in her. It was so strange, so keen, so wonderful to be with her, and when he did catch her he feared to speak lest he break this mood. Her eyes grew dark and daring, and often she stopped to look away across the wavy sea of stones to something beyond the great walls. When they got high the wind blew her hair loose and it flew out, a golden stream, with the sun bright upon it. He saw that she changed her direction, which had been in line with the two peaks, and now she climbed toward the heights. They came to more difficult ascent, where the stone still held to the smooth curves, yet was marked by steep bulges and slants and crevices. Here she became a wild thing. She ran, she leaped, she would have left him far behind had he not called. Then she appeared to remember him and waited.

Her face had now lost its whiteness; it was flushed, rosy, warm.

"Where—did you—ever learn—to run over rocks—this way?" he panted.

"All my life I've climbed," she said. "Ah! It's so good to be up on the walls again—to feel the wind—to see!"

Thereafter he kept close to her, no matter what the effort. He would not miss a moment of her, if he could help it. She was wonderful. He imagined she must be like an Indian girl, or a savage who loved the lofty places and the silence. When she leaped she uttered a strange, low, sweet cry of wildness and exultation. Shefford guessed she was a girl freed from her prison, forgetting herself, living again youthful hours. Still she did not forget him. She waited for him at the bad places, lent him a strong hand, and sometimes let it stay long in his clasp. Tireless and agile, sure-footed as a goat, fleet and wild she leaped and climbed and ran until Shefford marveled at her. This adventure was indeed fulfillment of a dream. Perhaps she might lead him to the treasure at the foot of the rainbow. But that thought, sad with memory daring forth from its grave, was irrevocably linked with a girl who was dead. He could not remember her, in the presence of this wonderful creature who was as strange as she was beautiful. When Shefford reached for the brown hand stretched forth to help him in a leap, when he felt its strong clasp, the youth and vitality and life of it, he had the fear of a man who was running toward a precipice and who could not draw back. This was a climb, a lark, a wild race to the Mormon girl, bound now in the village, and by the very freedom of it she betrayed her bonds. To Shefford it was also a wild race, but toward one sure goal he dared not name.

They went on, and at length, hand in hand, even where no steep step or wide fissure gave reason for the clasp. But she seemed unconscious. They were nearing the last height, a bare eminence, when she broke from him and ran up the smooth stone. When he surmounted it she was standing on the very summit, her arms wide, her full breast heaving, her slender body straight as an Indian's, her hair flying in the wind and blazing in the sun. She seemed to embrace the west, to reach for something afar, to offer herself to the wind and distance. Her face was scarlet from the exertion of the climb, and her broad brow was moist. Her eyes had the piercing light of an eagle's, though now they were dark. Shefford instinctively grasped the essence of this strange spirit, primitive and wild. She was not the woman who had met him at the spring. She had dropped some side of her with that Mormon hood, and now she stood totally strange.

She belonged up here, he divined. She was a part of that wildness. She must have been born and brought up in loneliness, where the wind blew and the peaks loomed and silence held dominion. The sinking sun touched the rim of the distant wall, and as if in parting regret shone with renewed golden fire. And the girl was crowned as with a glory.

Shefford loved her then. Realizing it, he thought he might have loved her before, but that did not matter when he was certain of it now. He trembled a little, fearfully, though without regret. Everything pertaining to his desert experience had been strange—this the strangest of all.

The sun sank swiftly, and instantly there was a change in the golden light. Quickly it died out. The girl changed as swiftly. She seemed to remember herself, and sat down as if suddenly weary. Shefford went closer and seated himself beside her.

"The sun has set. We must go," she said. But she made no movement.

"Whenever you are ready," replied he.

Just as the blaze had died out of her eyes, so the flush faded out of her face. The whiteness stole back, and with it the sadness. He had to bite his tongue to keep from telling her what he felt, to keep from pouring out a thousand questions. But the privilege of having seen her, of having been with her when she had forgotten herself—that he believed was enough. It had been wonderful; it had made him love her. But it need not add to the tragedy of her life, whatever that was. He tried to eliminate himself. And he watched her.

Her eyes were fixed upon the gold-rimmed ramparts of the distant wall in the west. Plain it was how she loved that wild upland. And there seemed to be some haunting memory of the past in her gaze—some happy part of life, agonizing to think of now.

"We must go," she said, and rose.

Shefford rose to accompany her. She looked at him, and her haunting eyes seemed to want him to know that he had helped her to forget the present, to remember girlhood, and that somehow she would always associate a wonderful happy afternoon with him. He divined that her silence then was a Mormon seal on lips.

"Mary, this has been the happiest, the best, the most revealing day of my life," he said, simply.

Swiftly, as if startled, she turned and faced down the slope. At the top of the wall above the village she put on the dark hood, and with it that somber something which was Mormon.

Twilight had descended into the valley, and shadows were so thick Shefford had difficulty in finding Mary's bucket. He filled it at the spring, and made offer to carry it home for her, which she declined.

"You'll come tonight—later?" she asked.

"Yes," he replied, hurriedly promising. Then he watched her white form slowly glide down the path to disappear in the shadows.

Nas Ta Bega and Joe were busy at the campfire. Shefford joined them. This night he was uncommunicative. Joe peered curiously at him in the flare of the blaze. Later, after the meal, when Shefford appeared restless and strode to and fro, Joe spoke up gruffly:

"Better hang round camp tonight."

Shefford heard, but did not heed. Nevertheless, the purport of the remark, which was either jealousy or admonition, haunted him with the possibility of its meaning.

He walked away from the campfire, under the dark pinyons, out into the starry open; and every step was hard to take, unless it pointed toward the home of the girl whose beauty and sadness and mystery had bewitched him. After what seemed hours he took the well-known path toward her cabin and then every step seemed lighter. He divined he was rushing to some fate—he knew not what.

The porch was in shadow. He peered in vain for the white form against the dark background. In the silence he seemed to hear his heartbeats thick and muffled.

Some distance down the path he heard the sound of hoofs. Withdrawing into the gloom of a cedar, he watched. Soon he made out moving horses with riders. They filed past him to the number of half a score. Like a flash of fire the truth burned him. Mormons come for one of those mysterious night visits to sealed wives!

Shefford stalked far down the valley, into the lonely silence and the night shadows under the walls.

·8·

THE HOGAN
OF NAS TA BEGA

THE HOME of Nas Ta Bega lay far up the cedared slope, with the craggy yellow cliffs and the black canyons and the pine-fringed top of Navajo Mountain behind, and to the fore the vast, rolling descent of cedar groves and sage flats and sandy washes. No dim, dark range made bold outline along the horizon; the stretch of gray and purple and green extended to the blue line of sky.

Down the length of one sage level Shefford saw a long lane where the brush and the grass had been beaten flat. This, the Navajo said, was a track where the young braves had raced their mustangs and had striven for supremacy before the eyes of maidens and the old people of the tribe.

"Nas Ta Bega, did you ever race here?" asked Shefford.

"I am a chief by birth. But I was stolen from my home, and now I cannot ride well enough to race the braves of my tribe," the Indian replied, bitterly.

In another place Joe Lake halted his horse and called Shefford's attention to a big yellow rock lying along the trail. And then he spoke in Navajo to the Indian.

"I've heard of this stone—Isende Aha," said Joe, after Nas Ta Bega had spoken. "Get down, and let's see."

Shefford dismounted, but the Indian kept his seat in the saddle.

Joe placed a big hand on the stone and tried to move it. According to Shefford's eye measurement the stone was nearly oval, perhaps three feet high, by a little over two in width. Joe threw off his sombrero, took a deep breath, and, bending over, clasped the stone in his arms. He was an exceedingly heavy and powerful man, and it was plain to Shefford that he meant to lift the stone if that were possible. Joe's broad shoulders strained, flattened; his arms bulged, his joints cracked, his neck corded, and his face turned black. By gigantic effort he lifted the stone and moved it about six inches. Then as he released his hold he fell, and when he sat up his face was wet with sweat.

"Try it," he said to Shefford, with his lazy smile. "See if you can heave it."

Shefford was strong, and there had been a time when he took pride in his strength. Something in Joe's supreme effort and in the gloom of the Indian's eyes made Shefford curious about this stone. He bent over and grasped it as Joe had done. He braced himself and lifted with all his power, until a red blur obscured his sight and shooting stars seemed to explode in his head. But he could not even stir the stone.

"Shefford, maybe you'll be able to heft it some day," observed Joe. Then he pointed to the stone and addressed Nas Ta Bega.

The Indian shook his head and spoke for a moment.

"This is the Isende Aha of the Navajos," explained Joe. "The young braves are always trying to carry this stone. As soon as one of them can carry it he is a man. He who carries it farthest is the biggest man. And just so soon as any Indian can no longer lift it he is old. Nas Ta Bega says the stone has been carried two miles in his lifetime. His own father carried it the length of six steps."

"Well! It's plain to me that I am not a man," said Shefford, "or else I am old."

Joe Lake drawled his lazy laugh and, mounting, rode up the trail. But Shefford lingered beside the Indian.

"Bi Nai," said Nas Ta Bega, "I am a chief of my tribe, but I have never been a man. I never lifted that stone. See what the paleface education has done for the Indian!"

The Navajo's bitterness made Shefford thoughtful. Could greater injury be done to man than this—to rob him of his heritage of strength?

Joe drove the bobbing pack-train of burros into the cedars where the smoke of the hogans curled upward, and soon the whistling of mustangs, the barking of dogs, the bleating of sheep told of his reception. And presently Shefford was in the midst of an animated scene. Great, woolly, fierce dogs, like wolves, ran out to meet the visitors. Sheep and goats were everywhere, and little lambs scarcely able to walk, with others frisky and frolicsome. There were pure-white lambs, and some that appeared to be painted, and some so beautiful with their fleecy white all except black faces or ears or tails or feet. They ran right under Nack-yal's legs and bumped against Shefford, and kept bleating their thin-piped welcome. Under the cedars surrounding the several hogans were mustangs that took Shefford's eye. He saw an iron-gray with white mane and tail sweeping to the ground; and a fiery black, wilder than any other beast he had ever seen; and a pinto as wonderfully painted as the little lambs; and, most striking of all, a pure, cream-colored mustang with grace and fine lines and beautiful mane and tail, and, strange to see, eyes as blue as azure. This albino mustang came right up to Shefford, an action in singular contrast with that of the others, and showed a tame and friendly spirit toward him and Nack-yal. Indeed, Shefford had reason to feel ashamed of Nack-yal's temper or jealousy.

The first Indians to put in an appearance were a flock of children, half naked, with tangled manes of raven-black hair and skin like gold bronze.

They appeared bold and shy by turns. Then a little, sinewy man, old and beaten and gray, came out of the principal hogan. He wore a blanket round his bent shoulders. His name was Hosteen Doetin, and it meant gentle man. His fine, old, wrinkled face lighted with a smile of kindly interest. His squaw followed him, and she was as venerable as he. Shefford caught a glimpse of the shy, dark Glen Naspa, Nas Ta Bega's sister, but she did not come out. Other Indians appeared, coming from adjacent hogans.

Nas Ta Bega turned the mustangs loose among those Shefford had noticed, and presently there rose a snorting, whistling, kicking, plunging melée. A cloud of dust hid them, and then a thudding of swift hoofs told of a run through the cedars. Joe Lake began picking over stacks of goat-skins and bags of wool that were piled against the hogan.

"Reckon we'll have one grand job packing out this load," he growled. "It's not so heavy, but awkward to pack."

It developed, presently, from talk with the old Navajo, that this pile was only a half of the load to be packed to Kayenta, and the other half was round the corner of the mountain in the camp of Piutes. Hosteen Doetin said he would send to the camp and have the Piutes bring their share over. The suggestion suited Joe, who wanted to save his burros as much as possible. Accordingly, a messenger was despatched to the Piute camp. And Shefford, with time on his hands and poignant memory to combat, decided to recall his keen interest in the Navajo, and learn, if possible, what the Indian's life was like. What would a day of his natural life be?

In the gray of dawn, when the hush of the desert night still lay deep over the land, the Navajo stirred in his blanket and began to chant to the morning light. It began very soft and low, a strange, broken murmur, like the music of a brook, and as it swelled that weird and mournful tone was slowly lost in one of hope and joy. The Indian's soul was coming out of night, blackness, the sleep that resembled death, into the day, the light that was life.

Then he stood in the door of his hogan, his blanket around him, and faced the east.

Night was lifting out of the clefts and ravines; the rolling cedar ridges and the sage flats were softly gray, with thin veils like smoke mysteriously rising and vanishing; the colorless rocks were changing. A long, horizonwide gleam of light, rosiest in the center, lay low down in the east and momentarily brightened. One by one the stars in the deep-blue sky paled and went out and the blue dome changed and lightened. Night had vanished on invisible wings and silence broke to the music of a mocking-bird. The rose in the east deepened; a wisp of cloud turned gold; dim distant mountains showed dark against the red; and low down in a notch a rim of fire appeared. Over the soft ridges and valleys crept a wondrous transfiguration. It was as if every blade of grass, every leaf of sage, every twig of cedar, the flowers, the trees, the rocks came to life at sight of the sun. The red disk rose, and a golden fire burned over the glowing face of that lonely waste.

The Navajo, dark, stately, inscrutable, faced the sun—his god. This was his Great Spirit. The desert was his mother, but the sun was his life. To the keeper of the winds and rains, to the master of light, to the maker of fire, to the giver of life the Navajo sent up his prayer:

> Of all the good things of the Earth let me always have plenty.
> Of all the beautiful things of the Earth let me always have
>   plenty.
> Peacefully let my horses go and peacefully let my sheep go.
> God of the Heavens, give me many sheep and horses.
> God of the Heavens, help me to talk straight.
> Goddess of the Earth, my Mother, let me walk straight.
> Now all is well, now all is well, now all is well, now all is well.

Hope and faith were his.

A chief would be born to save the vanishing tribe of Navajos. A bride would rise from a wind—kiss of the lilies in the moonlight.

He drank from the clear, cold spring bubbling from under mossy rocks. He went into the cedars, and the tracks in the trails told him of the visitors of night. His mustangs whistled to him from the ridge-tops, standing clear with heads up and manes flying, and then trooped down through the sage. The shepherd-dogs, guardians of the flocks, barked him a welcome, and the sheep bleated and the lambs pattered round him.

In the hogan by the warm, red fire his women baked his bread and cooked his meat. And he satisfied his hunger. Then he took choice meat to the hogan of a sick relative, and joined in the song and the dance and the prayer that drove away the evil spirit of illness. Down in the valley, in a sandy, sunny place, was his cornfield, and here he turned in the water from the ditch, and worked awhile, and went his contented way.

He loved his people, his women, and his children. To his son he said: "Be bold and brave. Grow like the pine. Work and ride and play that you may be strong. Talk straight. Love your brother. Give half to your friend. Honor your mother that you may honor your wife. Pray and listen to your gods."

Then with his gun and his mustang he climbed the slope of the mountain. He loved the solitude, but he was never alone. There were voices on the wind and steps on his trail. The lofty pine, the lichened rock, the tiny bluebell, the seared crag—all whispered their secrets. For him their spirits spoke. In the morning light Old Stone Face, the mountain, was a red god calling him to the chase. He was a brother of the eagle, at home on the heights where the winds swept and the earth lay revealed below.

In the golden afternoon, with the warm sun on his back and the blue canyons at his feet, he knew the joy of doing nothing. He did not need rest, for he was never tired. The sage-sweet breath of the open was thick in his nostrils, the silence that had so many whisperings was all about him, the loneliness of the wild was his. His falcon eye saw mustang and sheep, the puff of dust down on the cedar level, the Indian riding on a distant ridge, the gray walls, and the blue clefts. Here was home, still free, still wild, still untainted. He saw with the eyes of his ancestors. He felt them around him. They had gone into the elements from which their voices came on the wind. They were the watchers on his trails.

At sunset he faced the west, and this was his prayer:

> Great Spirit, God of my Fathers,
> Keep my horses in the night.
> Keep my sheep in the night.
> Keep my family in the night.
> Let me wake to the day.
> Let me be worthy of the light.
> Now all is well, now all is well,
> Now all is well, now all is well.

And he watched the sun go down and the gold sink from the peaks and the red die out of the west and the gray shadows creep out of the canyons to meet the twilight and the slow, silent, mysterious approach of night with its gift of stars.

Night fell. The white stars blinked. The wind sighed in the cedars. The sheep bleated. The shepherd-dogs bayed the mourning coyotes. And the Indian lay down in his blankets with his dark face tranquil in the star-light. All was well in his lonely world. Phantoms hovered, illness lingered, injury and pain and death were there, the shadow of a strange white hand flitted across the face of the moon—but now all was well— the Navajo had prayed to the god of his fathers. Now all was well!

And this, thought Shefford in revolt, was what the white man had killed in the Indian tribes, was reaching out now to kill in this wild remnant of the Navajos. The padre, the trapper, the trader, the prospector, and the missionary—so the white man had come, some of him good, no doubt, but more of him evil; and the young brave learned a thirst that could never be quenched at the cold, sweet spring of his forefathers, and the young maiden burned with a fever in her blood, and lost the sweet, strange, wild fancies of her tribe.

Joe Lake came to Shefford and said, "Withers told me you had a mix-up with a missionary at Red Lake."

"Yes, I regret to say," replied Shefford.

"About Glen Naspa?"

"Yes, Nas Ta Bega's sister."

"Withers just mentioned it. Who was the missionary?"

"Willetts, so Presbrey, the trader, said."

"What'd he look like?"

Shefford recalled the smooth, brown face, the dark eyes, the weak chin, the mild expression, and the soft, lax figure of the missionary.

"Can't tell by what you said," went on Joe. "But I'll bet a peso to a horse-hair that's the fellow who's been here. Old Hosteen Doetin just told me. First visits he ever had from the priest with the long gown. That's what he called the missionary. These old fellows will never forget what's come down from father to son about the Spanish padres. Well, anyway, Willetts has been here twice after Glen Naspa. The old chap is impressed, but he doesn't want to let the girl go. I'm inclined to think Glen Naspa would as lief go as stay. She may be a Navajo, but she's a girl. She won't talk much."

"Where's Nas Ta Bega?" asked Shefford.

"He rode off somewhere yesterday. Perhaps to the Piute camp. These Indians are slow. They may take a week to pack that load over here. But if Nas Ta Bega or someone doesn't come with a message today I'll ride over there myself."

"Joe, what do you think about this missionary?" queried Shefford, bluntly.

"Reckon there's not much to think, unless you see him or find out something. I heard of Willetts before Withers spoke of him. He's friendly with Mormons. I understand he's worked for Mormon interests, someway or other. That's on the quiet. Savvy? This matter of him coming after Glen Naspa, reckon that's all right. The missionaries all go after the young people. What'd be the use to try to convert the old Indians? No, the missionary's work is to educate the Indian, and, of course, the younger he is the better."

"You approve of the missionary?"

"Shefford, if you understood a Mormon you wouldn't ask that. Did you ever read or hear of Jacob Hamblin? . . . Well, he was a Mormon missionary among the Navajos. The Navajos were as fierce as Apaches till Hamblin worked among them. He made them friendly to the white man."

"That doesn't prove he made converts of them," replied Shefford, still bluntly.

"No. For the matter of that, Hamblin let religion alone. He made presents, then traded with them, then taught them useful knowledge. Mormon or not, Shefford, I'll admit this: a good man, strong with his body, and learned in ways with his hands, with some knowledge of medicine, can better the condition of these Indians. But just as soon as he begins to preach his religion, then his influence wanes. That's natural. These heathen have their ideals, their gods."

"Which the white man should leave them!" replied Shefford, feelingly.

"That's a matter of opinion. But don't let's argue. . . . Willetts is after Glen Naspa. And if I know Indian girls he'll persuade her to go to his school."

"Persuade her!" Then Shefford broke off and related the incident that had occurred at Red Lake.

"Reckon any means justifies the end," replied Joe, imperturbably. "Let him talk love to her or rope her or beat her, so long as he makes a Christian of her."

Shefford felt a hot flush and had difficulty in controlling himself. From this single point of view the Mormon was impossible to reason with.

"That, too, is a matter of opinion. We won't discuss it," continued Shefford. "But—if old Hosteen Doetin objects to the girl leaving, and if Nas Ta Bega does the same, won't that end the matter?"

"Reckon not. The end of the matter is Glen Naspa. If she wants to go she'll go."

Shefford thought best to drop the discussion. For the first time he had occasion to be repelled by something in this kind and genial Mormon, and he wanted to forget it. Just as he had never talked about men to the sealed wives in the hidden valley, so he could not talk of women to Joe Lake.

Nas Ta Bega did not return that day, but next morning a messenger came calling Lake to the Piute camp. Shefford spent the morning high on the slope, learning more with every hour in the silence and loneliness, that he was stronger of soul than he had dared to hope, and that the added pain which had come to him could be borne.

Upon his return toward camp, in the cedar grove, he caught sight of Glen Naspa with a white man. They did not see him. When Shefford recognized Willetts an embarrassment as well as an instinct made him halt and step into a bushy, low-branched cedar. It was not his intention to spy on them. He merely wanted to avoid a meeting. But the missionary's hand on the girl's arm, and her uplifted head, her pretty face, strange, intent, troubled, struck Shefford with an unusual and irresistible curiosity. Willetts was talking earnestly; Glen Naspa was listening intently. Shefford watched long enough to see that the girl loved the missionary, and that he reciprocated or was pretending. His manner scarcely savored of pretense, Shefford concluded, as he slipped away under the trees.

He did not go at once into camp. He felt troubled, and wished that he had not encountered the two. His duty in the matter, of course, was to tell Nas Ta Bega what he had seen. Upon reflection Shefford decided to give the missionary the benefit of a doubt; and if he really cared for the Indian girl, and admitted or betrayed it, to think all the better of him for the fact. Glen Naspa was certainly pretty enough, and probably lovable enough, to please any lonely man in this desert. The pain and the yearning in Shefford's heart made him lenient. He had to fight himself—not to forget, for that was impossible—but to keep rational and sane when a white flowerlike face haunted him and a voice called.

The cracking of hard hoofs on stones caused him to turn toward camp, and as he emerged from the cedar grove he saw three Indian horsemen ride into the cleared space before the hogans. They were superbly mounted and well armed, and impressed him as being different from Navajos. Perhaps they were Piutes. They dismounted and led the mustangs down to the pool below the spring. Shefford saw another mustang, standing bridle down and carrying a pack behind the saddle. Some squaws with children hanging behind their skirts were standing at the door of Hosteen Doetin's hogan. Shefford glanced in to see Glen Naspa, pale, quiet, almost sullen. Willetts stood with his hands spread. The old Navajo's seamed face worked convulsively as he tried to lift his bent form to some semblance of dignity, and his voice rolled out, sonorously: "Me no savvy Jesus Christ! Me hungry! . . . Me no eat Jesus Christ!"

Shefford drew back as if he had received a blow. That had been Hosteen Doetin's reply to the importunities of the missionary. The old Navajo could work no longer. His sons were gone. His squaw was worn out. He had no one save Glen Naspa to help him. She was young, strong. He was hungry. What was the white man's religion to him?

With long, swift stride Shefford entered the hogan. Willetts, seeing him, did not look so mild as Shefford had him pictured in memory, nor did he appear surprised. Shefford touched Hosteen Doetin's shoulder and said, "Tell me."

The aged Navajo lifted a shaking hand.

"Me no savvy Jesus Christ! Me hungry! . . . Me no eat Jesus Christ!"

Shefford then made signs that indicated the missionary's intention to take the girl away.

"Him come—big talk—Jesus—all Jesus. . . . Me no want Glen Naspa go," replied the Indian.

Shefford turned to the missionary.

"Willetts, is he a relative of the girl?"

"There's some blood tie, I don't know what. But it's not close," replied Willetts.

"Then don't you think you'd better wait till Nas Ta Bega returns? He's her brother."

"What for?" demanded Willetts. "That Indian may be gone a week. She's willing to go."

Shefford looked at the girl.

"Glen Naspa, do you want to go?"

She was shy, ashamed, and silent, but manifestly willing to accompany the missionary. Shefford pondered a moment. How he hoped Nas Ta Bega would come back! It was thought of the Indian that made Shefford stubborn. What his stand ought to be was hard to define, unless he answered to impulse; and here in the wilds he had become imbued with the idea that his impulses and instincts were no longer false.

"Willetts, what do you want with the girl?" queried Shefford, coolly, and at the question he seemed to find himself. He peered deliberately and searchingly into the other's face. The missionary's gaze shifted and a tinge of red crept up from under his collar.

"Absurd thing to ask a missionary!" he burst out, impatiently.

"Do you care for Glen Naspa?"

"I care as God's disciple—who cares to save the soul of heathen," he replied, with the lofty tone of prayer.

"Has Glen Naspa no—no other interest in you—except to be taught religion?"

The missionary's face flamed, and his violent tremor showed that under his exterior there was a different man.

"What right have you to question me?" he demanded. "You're an adventurer—an outcast. I've my duty here. I'm a missionary with church and state and government behind me."

"Yes, I'm an outcast," replied Shefford, bitterly. "And you may be all you say. But we're alone now out here on the desert. And this girl's brother is absent. You haven't answered me yet. . . . Is there anything between you and Glen Naspa except religion?"

"No, you insulting beggar!"

Shefford had forced the reply that he had expected and which damned the missionary beyond any consideration.

"Willetts, you are a liar!" said Shefford, steadily.

"And what are you?" cried Willetts, in shrill fury. "I've heard all about you. Heretic! Atheist! Driven from your church! Hated and scorned for your blasphemy!"

Then he gave way to ungovernable rage, and cursed Shefford as a religious fanatic might have cursed the most debased of sinners. Shefford heard with the blood beating, strangling the pulse in his ears. Somehow this missionary had learned his secret—most likely from the Mormons in Stonebridge. And the terms of disgrace were coals of fire upon Shefford's head. Strangely, however, he did not bow to them, as had been his humble act in the past, when his calumniators had arraigned and flayed him. Passion burned in him now, and hate, for the first time in his life, made a tiger of him. And these raw emotions, new to him, were difficult to control.

"You can't take the girl," he replied, when the other had ceased. "Not without her brother's consent."

"I will take her!"

Shefford threw him out of the hogan and strode after him. Willetts had stumbled. When he straightened up he was white and shaken. He groped for the bridle of his horse while keeping his eyes upon Shefford, and when he found it he whirled quickly, mounted, and rode off. Shefford saw him halt a moment under the cedars to speak with the three strange Indians, and then he galloped away. It came to Shefford then that he had been unconscious of the last strained moment of that encounter. He seemed all cold, tight, locked, and was amazed to find his hand on his gun. Verily the wild environment had liberated strange instincts and impulses, which he had answered. That he had no regrets proved how he had changed.

Shefford heard the old woman scolding. Peering into the hogan, he saw Glen Naspa flounce sullenly down, for all the world like any other thwarted girl. Hosteen Doetin came out and pointed down the slope at the departing missionary.

"Heap talk Jesus—all talk—all Jesus!" he exclaimed, contemptuously. Then he gave Shefford a hard rap on the chest. "Small talk—heap man!"

The matter appeared to be adjusted for the present. But Shefford felt that he had made a bitter enemy, and perhaps a powerful one.

He prepared and ate his supper alone that evening, for Joe Lake and Nas Ta Bega did not put in an appearance. He observed that the three strange Indians, whom he took for Piutes, kept to themselves, and, so far as he knew, had no intercourse with anyone at the camp. This would not have seemed unusual, considering the taciturn habit of Indians, had he not remembered seeing Willetts speak to the trio. What had he to do with them? Shefford was considering the situation with vague doubts when, to his relief, the three strangers rode off into the twilight. Then he went to bed.

He was awakened by violence. It was the gray hour before dawn. Dark forms knelt over him. A cloth pressed down hard over his mouth. Strong hands bound it while other strong hands held him. He could not cry out. He could not struggle. A heavy weight, evidently a man, held down his feet. Then he was rolled over, securely bound, and carried, to be thrown like a sack over the back of a horse.

All this happened so swiftly as to be bewildering. He was too astounded to be frightened. As he hung head downward he saw the legs of a horse and a dim trail. A stirrup swung to and fro, hitting him in the face. He began to feel exceedingly uncomfortable, with a rush of blood to his head, and cramps in his arms and legs. This kept on and grew worse for what seemed a long time. Then the horse was stopped and a rude hand tumbled him to the ground. Again he was rolled over on his face. Strong fingers plucked at his clothes, and he believed he was being searched. His captors were as silent as if they had been dumb. He felt when they took his pocketbook and his knife and all that he had. Then they cut, tore, and stripped off all his clothing. He was lifted, carried a few steps, and dropped upon what seemed a soft, low mound, and left lying there, still tied and naked. Shefford heard the rustle of sage and the dull thud of hoofs as his assailants went away.

His first sensation was one of immeasurable relief. He had not been murdered. Robbery was nothing. And though roughly handled, he had not been hurt. He associated the assault with the three strange visitors of the preceding day. Still, he had no proof of that. Not the slightest clue remained to help him ascertain who had attacked him.

It might have been a short while or a long one, his mind was so filled with growing conjectures, but a time came when he felt cold. As he lay face down, only his back felt cold at first. He was grateful that he had not been thrown upon the rocks. The ground under him appeared soft, spongy, and gave somewhat as he breathed. He had really sunk down a little in this pile of soft earth. The day was not far off, as he could tell by the brightening of the gray. He began to suffer with the cold, and then slowly he seemed to freeze and grow numb. In an effort to roll over upon his back he discovered that his position, or his being bound, or the numbness of his muscles was responsible for the fact that he could not move. Here was a predicament. It began to look serious. What would a few hours of the powerful sun do to his uncovered skin? Somebody would trail and find him: still, he might not be found soon.

He saw the sky lighten, turn rosy and then gold. The sun shone upon him, but some time elapsed before he felt its warmth. All of a sudden a pain, like a sting, shot through his shoulder. He could not see what caused it; probably a bee. Then he felt another upon his leg, and about simultaneously with it a tiny, fiery stab in his side. A sickening sensation pervaded his body, slowly moving, as if poison had entered the blood of his veins. Then a puncture, as from a hot wire, entered the skin of his breast. Unmistakably it was a bite. By dint of great effort he twisted his head to see a big red ant on his breast. Then he heard a faint sound, so exceedingly faint that he could not tell what it was like. But presently his strained ears detected a low, swift, rustling, creeping sound, like the slipping rattle of an infinite number of tiny bits of moving gravel. Then it was a sound like the seeping of wind-blown sand. Several hot bites occurred at once. And then with his head twisted he saw a red stream of ants pour out of the mound and spill over his quivering flesh.

In an instant he realized his position. He had been dropped intentionally upon an ant-heap, which had sunk with his weight, wedging him between the crusts. At the mercy of those terrible desert ants! A frantic effort to roll out proved futile, as did another and another. His violent muscular contractions infuriated the ants, and in an instant he was writhing in pain so horrible and so unendurable that he nearly fainted. But he was too strong to faint suddenly. A bath of vitriol, a stripping of his skin and red embers of fire thrown upon raw flesh, could not have equaled this. There was fury in the bites and poison in the fangs of these ants. Was this an Indian's brutal trick or was it the missionary's revenge? Shefford realized that it would kill him soon. He sweat what seemed blood, although perhaps the blood came from the bites. A strange, hollow, buzzing roar filled his ears, and it must have been the pouring of the angry ants from their mound.

Then followed a time that was hell—worse than fire, for fire would have given merciful death—agony under which his physical being began spasmodically to jerk and retch—and his eyeballs turned and his breast caved in.

A cry rang through the roar in his ears. "Bi Nai! Bi Nai!"

His fading sight seemed to shade round the dark face of Nas Ta Bega.

Then powerful hands dragged him from the mound, through the grass and sage, rolled him over and over, and brushed his burning skin with strong, swift sweep.

❧ 9 ❧

IN THE
DESERT CRUCIBLE

THAT HARD EXPERIENCE was but the beginning of many cruel trials for John Shefford.

He never knew who his assailants were, nor their motive other than robbery; and they had gotten little, for they had not found the large sum of money sewed in the lining of his coat. Joe Lake declared it was Shadd's work, and the Mormon showed the stern nature that lay hidden under his habitual mild manner. Nas Ta Bega shook his head and would not tell what he thought. But a somber fire burned in his eyes.

The three started with a heavily laden pack-train and went down the mountain slope into West Canyon. The second day they were shot at from the rim walls. Lake was wounded, hindering the swift flight necessary to escape deeper into the canyon. Here they hid for days, while the Mormon recovered and the Indian took stealthy trips to try to locate the enemy. Lack of water and grass for the burros drove them on. They climbed out of a side canyon, losing several burros on a rough trail, and had proceeded to within half a day's journey of Red Lake when they were attacked while making camp in a cedar grove. Shefford sustained an exceedingly painful injury to his leg, but, fortunately, the bullet went through without breaking a bone. With that burning pain there came to

Shefford the meaning of fight, and his rifle grew hot in his hands. Night alone saved the trio from certain fatality. Under the cover of darkness the Indian helped Shefford to escape. Joe Lake looked out for himself. The pack-train was lost, and the mustangs, except Nack-yal.

Shefford learned what it meant to lie out at night, listening for pursuit, cold to his marrow, sick with dread, and enduring frightful pain from a ragged bullet-hole. Next day the Indian led him down into the red basin, where the sun shone hot and the sand reflected the heat. They had no water. A wind arose and the valley became a place of flying sand. Through a heavy, stifling pall Nas Ta Bega somehow got Shefford to the trading-post at Red Lake. Presbrey attended to Shefford's injury and made him comfortable. Next day Joe Lake limped in, surly and somber, with the news that Shadd and eight or ten of his outlaw gang had gotten away with the pack-train.

In short time Shefford was able to ride, and with his companions went over the pass to Kayenta. Withers already knew of his loss, and all he said was that he hoped to meet Shadd some day.

Shefford showed a reluctance to go again to the hidden village in the silent canyon with the rounded walls. The trader appeared surprised, but did not press the point. And Shefford meant sooner or later to tell him, yet never quite reached the point. The early summer brought more work for the little post, and Shefford toiled with the others. He liked the outdoor tasks, and at night was grateful that he was too tired to think. Then followed trips to Durango and Bluff and Monticello. He rode fifty miles a day for many days. He knew how a man fares who packs light and rides far and fast. When the Indian was with him he got along well, but Nas Ta Bega would not go near the towns. Thus many mishaps were Shefford's fortune.

Many and many a mile he trailed his mustang, for Nack-yal never forgot the Sagi, and always headed for it when he broke his hobbles. Shefford accompanied an Indian teamster into Durango with a wagon and four wild mustangs. Upon the return, with a heavy load of supplies, accident put Shefford in charge of the outfit. In despair he had to face the hardest task that could have been given him—to take care of a crippled Indian, catch, water, feed, harness, and drive four wild mustangs that did not know him and tried to kill him at every turn, and to get that precious load of supplies home to Kayenta. That he accomplished it proved to him the possibilities of a man, for both endurance and patience. From that time he never gave up in the front of any duty.

In the absence of an available Indian he rode to Durango and back in record time. Upon one occasion he was lost in a canyon for days, with no food and little water. Upon another he went through a sandstorm in the open desert, facing it for forty miles and keeping to the trail. When he rode into Kayenta that night the trader, in grim praise, said there was no worse to endure. At Monticello Shefford stood off a band of desperadoes, and this time Shefford experienced a strange, sickening shock in the wounding of a man. Later he had other fights, but in none of them did he know whether or not he had shed blood.

The heat of midsummer came, when the blistering sun shone, and a hot blast blew across the sand, and the furious storms made floods in the washes. Day and night Shefford was always in the open, and anyone who had ever known him in the past would have failed to recognize him now.

In the early fall, with Nas Ta Bega as companion, he set out to the south of Kayenta upon long-neglected business of the trader. They visited Red Lake, Blue Canyon, Keams Canyon, Oribi, the Moki villages, Tuba, Moencopie, and Moen Ave. This trip took many weeks and gave Shefford all the opportunity he wanted to study the Indians, and the conditions nearer to the border of civilization. He learned the truth about the Indians and the missionaries.

Upon the return trip he rode over the trail he had followed alone to Red Lake and thence on to the Sagi, and it seemed that years had passed since he first entered this wild region which had come to be home, years that had molded him in the stern and fiery crucible of the desert.

❧ 10 ❧

STONEBRIDGE

IN OCTOBER Shefford arranged for a hunt in the Cresaw Mountains with Joe Lake and Nas Ta Bega. The Indian had gone home for a short visit, and upon his return the party expected to start. But Nas Ta Bega did not come back. Then the arrival of a Piute with news that excited Withers and greatly perturbed Lake convinced Shefford that something was wrong.

The little trading-post seldom saw such disorder; certainly Shefford had never known the trader to neglect work. Joe Lake threw a saddle on a mustang he would have scorned to notice in an ordinary moment, and without a word of explanation or farewell rode hard to the north on the Stonebridge trail.

Shefford had long since acquired patience. He was curious, but he did not care particularly what was in the wind. However, when Withers came out and sent an Indian to drive up the horses Shefford could not refrain from a query.

"I hate to tell you," replied the trader.

"Go on," added Shefford, quickly.

"Did I tell you about the government sending a Supreme Court judge out to Utah to prosecute the polygamists?"

"No," replied Shefford.

"I forgot to, I reckon. You've been away a lot. Well, there's been hell up in Utah for six months. Lately this judge and his men have worked down into southern Utah. He visited Bluff and Monticello a few weeks ago. . . . Now what do you think?"

"Withers! Is he coming to Stonebridge?"

"He's there now. Someone betrayed the whereabouts of the hidden village over in the canyon. All the women have been arrested and taken to Stonebridge. The trial begins today."

"Arrested!" echoed Shefford, blankly. "Those poor, lonely, good women? What on earth for?"

"Sealed wives!" exclaimed Withers, tersely. "This judge is after the polygamists. They say he's absolutely relentless."

"But—women can't be polygamists. Their husbands are the ones wanted."

"Sure. But the prosecutors have got to find the sealed wives—the second wives—to find the law-breaking husbands. That'll be a job, or I don't know Mormons. . . . Are you going to ride over to Stonebridge with me?"

Shefford shrank at the idea. Months of toil and pain and travail had not been enough to make him forget the strange girl he had loved. But he had remembered only at poignant intervals, and the lapse of time had made thought of her a dream like that sad dream which had lured him into the desert. With the query of the trader came a bittersweet regret.

"Better come with me," said Withers. "Have you forgotten the Sago Lily? She'll be put on trial. . . . That girl—that child! . . . Shefford, you know she hasn't any friends. And now no Mormon man dare protect her, for fear of prosecution."

"I'll go," replied Shefford, shortly.

The Indian brought up the horses. Nack-yal was thin from his long travel during the hot summer, but he was as hard as iron, and the way he pointed his keen nose toward the Sagi showed how he wanted to make for the upland country, with its clear springs and valleys of grass. Withers mounted his bay and with a hurried farewell to his wife spurred the mustang into the trail. Shefford took time to get his weapons and the light pack he always carried, and then rode out after the trader.

The pace Withers set was the long, steady lope to which these Indian mustangs had been trained all their lives. In an hour they reached the mouth of the Sagi, and at sight of it it seemed to Shefford that the hard half-year of suffering since he had been there had disappeared. Withers, to Shefford's regret, did not enter the Sagi. He turned off to the north and took a wild trail into a split of the red wall, and wound in and out, and climbed a crack so narrow that the light was obscured and the cliffs could be reached from both sides of a horse.

Once up on the wild plateau, Shefford felt again in a different world from the barren desert he had lately known. The desert had crucified him and had left him to die or survive, according to his spirit and his strength. If he had loved the glare, the endless level, the deceiving distance, the shifting sand, it had certainly not been as he loved this softer, wilder, more intimate upland. With the red peaks shining up into the blue, and the fragrance of cedar and pinyon, and the purple sage and flowers and grass and splash of clear water over stones—with these there came back to him something that he had lost and which had haunted him.

It seemed he had returned to this wild upland of color and canyons and lofty crags and green valleys and silent places with a spirit gained from victory over himself in the harsher and sterner desert below. And, strange to him, he found his old self, the dreamer, the artist, the lover of beauty, the searcher for he knew not what, come to meet him on the fragrant wind.

He felt this, saw the old wildness with glad eyes, yet the greater part of his mind was given over to the thought of the unfortunate women he expected to see in Stonebridge.

Withers was harder to follow, to keep up with, than an Indian. For one thing he was a steady and tireless rider, and for another there were times when he had no mercy on a horse. Then an Indian always found easier steps in a trail and shorter cuts. Withers put his mount to some bad slopes, and Shefford had no choice but to follow. But they crossed the great broken bench of upland without mishap, and came out upon a promontory of a plateau from which Shefford saw a wide valley and the dark-green alfalfa fields of Stonebridge.

Stonebridge lay in the center of a fertile valley surrounded by pink cliffs. It must have been a very old town, certainly far older than Bluff or Monticello, though smaller, and evidently it had been built to last. There was one main street, very wide, that divided the town and was crossed at right angles by a stream spanned by a small natural stone bridge. A line of poplar trees shaded each footpath. The little log cabins and stone houses and cottages were half hidden in foliage now tinted with autumn colors. Toward the center of the town the houses and stores and shops fronted upon the street and along one side of a green square, or plaza. Here were situated several edifices, the most prominent of which was a church built of wood, white-washed, and remarkable, according to Withers, for the fact that not a nail had been used in its construction. Beyond the church was a large, low structure of stone, with a split-shingle roof, and evidently this was the town hall.

Shefford saw, before he reached the square, that this day in Stonebridge was one of singular action and excitement for a Mormon village. The town was full of people and, judging from the horses hitched everywhere and the big canvas-covered wagons, many of the people were visitors. A crowd surrounded the hall—a dusty, booted, spurred, shirt-sleeved and sombreroed assemblage that did not wear the hallmark Shefford had come to associate with Mormons. They were riders, cowboys, horse-wranglers, and some of them Shefford had seen in Durango. Navajos and Piutes were present, also, but they loitered in the background.

Withers drew Shefford off to the side where, under a tree, they hitched their horses.

"Never saw Stonebridge full of a riffraff gang like this today," said Withers. "I'll bet the Mormons are wild. There's a tough outfit from Durango. If they can get anything to drink—or if they've got it—Stonebridge will see smoke today! . . . Come on. I'll get in that hall."

But before Withers reached the hall he started violently and pulled up short, then, with apparent unconcern, turned to lay a hand upon Shefford. The trader's face had blanched and his eyes grew hard and shiny, like flint. He gripped Shefford's arm.

"Look! Over to your left!" he whispered. "See that gang of Indians there—by the big wagon. See the short Indian with the chaps. He's got a face big as a ham, dark, fierce. That's Shadd! . . . You ought to know him. Shadd and his outfit here! How's that for nerve? But he pulls a rein with the Mormons."

Shefford's keen eye took in a lounging group of ten or twelve Indians and several white men. They did not present any great contrast to the other groups except that they were isolated, appeared quiet and watchful, and were all armed. A bunch of lean, racy mustangs, restive and spirited, stood nearby in charge of an Indian. Shefford had to take a second and closer glance to distinguish the half-breed. At once he recognized in Shadd the broad-faced squat Indian who had paid him a threatening visit that night long ago in the mouth of the Sagi. A fire ran along Shefford's veins and seemed to concentrate in his breast. Shadd's dark, piercing eyes alighted upon Shefford and rested there. Then the half-breed spoke to one of his white outlaws and pointed at Shefford. His action attracted the attention of others in the gang, and for a moment Shefford and Withers were treated to a keen-eyed stare.

The trader cursed low. "Maybe I wouldn't like to mix it with that damned breed," he said. "But what chance have we with that gang? Besides, we're here on other and more important business. All the same, before I forget, let me remind you that Shadd has had you spotted ever since you came out here. A friendly Piute told me only lately. Shefford, did any Indian between here and Flagstaff ever see that bunch of money you persist in carrying?"

"Why, yes, I suppose so—'way back in Tuba, when I first came out," replied Shefford.

"Huh! Well, Shadd's after that. . . . Come on now, let's get inside the hall."

The crowd opened for the trader, who appeared to be known to every-body. A huge man with a bushy beard blocked the way to a shut door.

"Hello, Meade!" said Withers. "Let us in."

The man opened the door, permitted Withers and Shefford to enter, and then closed it.

Shefford, coming out of the bright glare of sun into the hall, could not see distinctly at first. His eyes blurred. He heard a subdued murmur of many voices. Withers appeared to be affected with the same kind of blindness, for he stood bewildered a moment. But he recovered sooner than Shefford. Gradually the darkness shrouding many obscure forms lifted. Withers drew him through a crowd of men and women to one side of the hall, and squeezed along a wall to a railing where progress was stopped. Then Shefford raised his head to look with bated breath and strange curiosity.

The hall was large and had many windows. Men were in consultation upon a platform. Women to the number of twenty sat close together upon benches. Back of them stood another crowd. But the women on the benches held Shefford's gaze. They were the prisoners. They made a somber group. Some were hooded, some veiled, all clad in dark garments except one on the front bench, and she was dressed in white. She wore a long hood that concealed her face. Shefford recognized the hood and then the slender shape. She was Mary—she whom her jealous neighbors had named the Sago Lily. At sight of her a sharp pain pierced Shefford's breast. His eyes were blurred when he forced them away from her, and it took a moment for him to see clearly.

Withers was whispering to him or to someone near at hand, but Shefford did not catch the meaning of what was said. He paid more attention; however, Withers ceased speaking. Shefford gazed upon the crowd back of him. The women were hooded and it was not possible to see what they looked like. There were many stalwart, clean-cut, young Mormons of Joe Lake's type, and these men appeared troubled, even distressed and at a loss. There was little about them resembling the stern, quiet, somber austerity of the more matured men, and nothing at all of the strange, aloof, serene impassiveness of the gray-bearded old patriarchs. These venerable men were the Mormons of the old school, the sons of the pioneers, the ruthless fanatics. Instinctively Shefford felt that it was in them that polygamy was embodied; they were the husbands of the sealed wives. He conceived an absorbing curiosity to learn if his instinct was correct; and hard upon that followed a hot, hateful eagerness to see which one was the husband of Mary.

"There's Bishop Kane," whispered Withers, nudging Shefford. "And there's Waggoner with him."

Shefford saw the bishop, and then beside him a man of striking presence.

"Who's Waggoner?" asked Shefford, as he looked.

"He owns more than any Mormon in southern Utah," replied the trader. "He's the biggest man in Stonebridge, that's sure. But I don't know his relation to the church. They don't call him elder or bishop. But I'll bet he's some pumpkins. He never had any use for me or any Gentile. A close-fisted, tight-lipped Mormon—a skinflint if I ever saw one! Just look him over."

Shefford had been looking, and considered it unlikely that he would ever forget this individual called Waggoner. He seemed old, sixty at least, yet at that only in the prime of a wonderful physical life. Unlike most of the others, he wore his grizzled beard close-cropped, so close that it showed the lean, wolfish line of his jaw. All his features were of striking sharpness. His eyes, of a singularly brilliant blue, were yet cold and pale. The brow had a serious, thoughtful cast; long furrows sloped down the cheeks. It was a strange, secretive face, full of a power that Shefford had not seen in another man's, full of intelligence and thought that had not been used as Shefford had known them used among men. The face mystified him. It had so much more than the strange aloofness so characteristic of his fellows.

"Waggoner had five wives and fifty-five children before the law went into effect," whispered Withers. "Nobody knows and nobody will ever know how many he's got now. That's my private opinion."

Somehow, after Withers told that, Shefford seemed to understand the strange power in Waggoner's face. Absolutely it was not the force, the strength given to a man from his years of control of men. Shefford, long schooled now in his fair-mindedness, fought down the feelings of other years, and waited with patience. Who was he to judge Waggoner or any other Mormon? But whenever his glance strayed back to the quiet, slender form in white, when he realized again and again the appalling nature of this court, his heart beat heavy and labored within his breast.

Then a bustle among the men upon the platform appeared to indicate that proceedings were about to begin. Some men left the platform; several sat down at a table upon which were books and papers, and others remained standing. These last were all roughly garbed, in riding boots and spurs, and Shefford's keen eye detected the bulge of hidden weapons. They looked like deputy marshals upon duty.

Somebody whispered that the judge's name was Stone. The name fitted him. He was not young, and looked a man suited to the prosecution of these secret Mormons. He had a ponderous brow, a deep, cavernous eye that emitted gleams but betrayed no color or expression. His mouth was the saving human feature of his stony face.

Shefford took the man upon the judge's right hand to be a lawyer, and the one on his left an officer of court, perhaps a prosecuting attorney. Presently this fellow pounded upon the table and stood up as if to address a courtroom. Certainly he silenced that hallful of people. Then he per-functorily and briefly stated that certain women had been arrested upon suspicion of being sealed wives of Mormon polygamists, and were to be herewith tried by a judge of the United States Court. Shefford felt how the impressive words affected that silent hall of listeners, but he gathered from the brief preliminaries that the trial could not be otherwise than a crude, rapid investigation, and perhaps for that the more sinister.

The first woman on the foremost bench was led forward by a deputy to a vacant chair on the platform just in front of the judge's table. She was told to sit down, and showed no sign that she had heard. Then the judge courteously asked her to take the chair. She refused. And Stone nodded his head as if he had experienced that sort of thing before. He stroked his chin wearily, and Shefford conceived an idea that he was a kind man, if he was a relentless judge.

"Please remove your veil," requested the prosecutor.

The woman did so, and proved to be young and handsome. Shefford had a thrill as he recognized her. She was Ruth, who had been one of his best-known acquaintances in the hidden village. She was pale, angry, almost sullen, and her breast heaved. She had no shame, but she seemed to be outraged. Her dark eyes, scornful and blazing, passed over the judge and his assistants, and on to the crowd behind the railing. Shefford, keen as a blade, with all his faculties absorbed, fancied he saw Ruth stiffen and change slightly as her glance encountered someone in that crowd. Then the prosecutor in deliberate and chosen words enjoined her to kiss the Bible handed to her and swear to tell the truth. How strange for Shefford to see her kiss the book which he had studied for so many years! Stranger still to hear the low murmur from the listening audience as she took the oath!

"What is your name?" asked Judge Stone, leaning back and fixing the cavernous eyes upon her.

"Ruth Jones," was the cool reply.

"How old are you?"

"Twenty."

"Where were you born?" went on the judge. He allowed time for the clerk to record her answers.

"Panguitch, Utah."

"Were your parents Mormons?"

"Yes."

"Are you a Mormon?"

"Yes."

"Are you a married woman?"

"No."

The answer was instant, cold, final. It seemed to the truth. Almost Shefford believed she spoke truth. The judge stroked his chin and waited a moment, and then hesitatingly he went on.

"Have you—any children?"

"No." And the blazing eyes met the cavernous ones.

That about the children was true enough, Shefford thought, and he could have testified to it.

"You live in the hidden village near this town?"

"Yes."

"What is the name of this village?"

"It has none."

"Did you ever hear of Fredonia, another village far west of here?"

"Yes."

"It is in Arizona, near the Utah line. There are few men there. Is it the same kind of village as this one in which you live?"

"Yes."

"What does Fredonia mean? The name—has it any meaning?"

"It means free women."

The judge maintained silence for a moment, turned to whisper to his assistants, and presently, without glancing up, said to the woman:

"That will do."

Ruth was led back to the bench, and the woman next to her brought forward. This was a heavier person, with the figure and step of a matured woman. Upon removing her bonnet she showed the plain face of a woman of forty, and it was striking only in that strange, stony aloofness noted in the older men. Here, Shefford thought, was the real Mormon, different in a way he could not define from Ruth. This woman seated herself in the chair and calmly faced her prosecutors. She manifested no emotion whatever. Shefford remembered her and could not see any change in her deportment. This trial appeared to be of little moment to her and she took the oath as if doing so had been a habit all her life.

"What is your name?" asked Judge Stone, glancing up from a paper he held.

"Mary Danton."

"Family or married name?"

"My husband's name was Danton."

"Was. Is he living?"

"No."

"Where did you live when you were married to him?"

"In St. George, and later here in Stonebridge."

"You were both Mormons?"

"Yes."

"Did you have any children by him?"

"Yes."

"How many?"

"Two."

"Are they living?"

"One of them is living."

Judge Stone bent over his paper and then slowly raised his eyes to her face.

"Are you married now?"

"No."

Again the judge consulted his notes, and held a whispered colloquy with the two men at his table.

"Mrs. Danton, when you were arrested there were five children found in your home. To whom do they belong?"

"Me."

"Are you their mother?"

"Yes."

"Your husband Danton is the father of only one, the eldest, according to your former statement. Is that correct?"

"Yes."

"Who, then, is the father—or who are the fathers—of your other children?"

"I do not know."

She said it with the most stony-faced calmness, with utter disregard of what significance her words had. A strong, mystic wall of cold flint insulated her. Strangely it came to Shefford how impossible either to doubt or believe her. Yet he did both! Judge Stone showed a little heat.

"You don't know the father of one or all of these children?" he queried, with sharp rising inflection of voice.

"I do not."

"Madam, I beg to remind you that you are under oath."

The woman did not reply.

"These children are nameless, then—illegitimate?"

"They are."

"You swear you are not the sealed wife of some Mormon?"

"I swear."

"How do you live—maintain yourself?"

"I work."

"What at?"

"I weave, sew, bake, and work in my garden."

"My men made note of your large and comfortable cabin, even luxurious, considering this country. How is that?"

"My husband left me comfortable."

Judge Stone shook a warning finger at the defendant.

"Suppose I were to sentence you to jail for perjury? For a year? Far from your home and children! Would you speak—tell the truth?"

"I am telling the truth. I can't speak what I don't know. . . . Send me to jail."

Baffled, with despairing, angry impatience, Judge Stone waved the woman away.

"That will do for her. Fetch the next one," he said.

One after another he examined three more women, and arrived, by various questions and answers different in tone and temper, at precisely the same point as had been made in the case of Mrs. Danton. Thereupon the proceedings rested a few moments while the judge consulted with his assistants.

Shefford was grateful for this respite. He had been worked up to an unusual degree of interest, and now, as the next Mormon woman to be examined was she whom he had loved and loved still, he felt rise in him emotion that threatened to make him conspicuous unless it could be hidden. The answers of these Mormon women had been not altogether unexpected by him, but once spoken in cold blood under oath, how tragic, how appallingly significant of the shadow, the mystery, the yoke that bound them! He was amazed, saddened. He felt bewildered. He needed to think out the meaning of the falsehoods of women he knew to be good and noble. Surely religion, instead of fear and loyalty, was the foundation and the strength of this disgrace, this sacrifice. Absolutely, shame was not in these women though they swore to shameful facts. They had been coached to give these baffling answers, every one of which seemed to brand them, not the brazen mothers of illegitimate offspring, but faithful, unfortunate sealed wives. To Shefford the truth was not in their words, but it sat upon their somber brows.

Was it only his heightened imagination, or did the silence and the suspense grow more intense when a deputy led that dark-hooded, white-clad, slender woman to the defendant's chair? She did not walk with the poise that had been manifest in the other women, and she sank into the chair as if she could no longer stand.

"Please remove your hood," requested the prosecutor.

How well Shefford remembered the strong, shapely hands! He saw them tremble at the knot of ribbon, and that tremor was communicated to him in a sympathy which made his pulses beat. He held his breath while she removed the hood. And then there was revealed, he thought, the loveliest and the most tragic face that ever was seen in a courtroom.

A low, whispering murmur that swelled like a wave ran through the hall. And by it Shefford divined, as clearly as if the fact had been blazoned on the walls, that Mary's face had been unknown to these

villagers. But the name Sago Lily had not been unknown; Shefford heard
it whispered on all sides.

The murmuring subsided. The judge and his assistants stared at Mary.
As for Shefford, there was no need of his personal feeling to make the
situation dramatic. Not improbably Judge Stone had tried many Mormon
women. But manifestly this one was different. Unhooded, Mary appeared
to be only a young girl, and a court, confronted suddenly with her youth
and the suspicion attached to her, could not but have been shocked.
Then her beauty made her seem, in that somber company, indeed the
white flower for which she had been named. But, more likely, it was her
agony that bound the court into silence which grew painful. Perhaps the
thought that flashed into Shefford's mind was telepathic; it seemed to him
that every watcher there realized that in this defendant the judge had a
girl of softer mold, of different spirit, and from her the bitter truth could
be wrung.

Mary faced the court and the crowd on that side of the platform.
Unlike the other women, she did not look at or seem to see anyone
behind the railing. Shefford was absolutely sure there was not a man or a
woman who caught her glance. She gazed afar, with eyes strained, humid,
fearful.

When the prosecutor swore her to the oath her lips were seen to move,
but no one heard her speak.

"What is your name?" asked the judge.

"Mary." Her voice was low, with a slight tremor.

"What's your other name?"

"I won't tell."

Her singular reply, the tones of her voice, her manner before the judge,
marked her with strange simplicity. It was evident that she was not
accustomed to questions.

"What were your parents' names?"

"I won't tell," she replied, very low.

Judge Stone did not press the point. Perhaps he wanted to make the
examination as easy as possible for her or to wait till she showed more
composure.

"Were your parents Mormons?" he went on.

"No, sir." She added the sir with a quaint respect, contrasting markedly
with the short replies of the women before her.

"Then you were not born a Mormon?"

"No, sir."

"How old are you?"

"Seventeen or eighteen. I'm not sure."

"You don't know your exact age?"

"No."

"Where were you born?"

"I won't tell."

"Was it in Utah?"

"Yes, sir."

"How long have you lived in this state?"

"Always—except last year."

"And that's been over in the hidden village where you were arrested?"

"Yes."

"But you often visited here—this town Stonebridge?"

"I never was here—till yesterday."

Judge Stone regarded her as if his interest as a man was running counter to his duty as an officer. Suddenly he leaned forward.

"Are you a Mormon *now?*" he queried, forcibly.

"No, sir," she replied, and here her voice rose a little clearer.

It was an unexpected reply. Judge Stone stared at her. The low buzz ran through the listening crowd. And as for Shefford, he was astounded. When his wits flashed back and he weighed her words and saw in her face truth as clear as light, he had the strangest sensation of joy. Almost it flooded away the gloom and pain that attended this ordeal.

The judge bent his head to his assistants as if for counsel. All of them were eager where formerly they had been weary. Shefford glanced around at the dark and somber faces, and a slow wrath grew within him. Then he caught a glimpse of Waggoner. The steel-blue, piercing intensity of the Mormon's gaze impressed him at a moment when all that older generation of Mormons looked as hard and immutable as iron. Either Shefford was overexcited and mistaken or the hour had become fraught with greater suspense. The secret, the mystery, the power, the hate, the religion of a strange people were thick and tangible in that hall. For Shefford the feeling of the presence of Withers on his left was entirely different from that of the Mormon on his other side. If there was not a shadow there, then the sun did not shine so brightly as it had shone when he entered. The air seemed clogged with nameless passion.

"I gather that you've lived mostly in the country—away from people?" the judge began.

"Yes, sir," replied the girl.

"Do you know anything about the government of the United States?"

"No, sir."

He pondered again, evidently weighing his queries, leading up to the fatal and inevitable question. Still, his interest in this particular defendant had become visible.

"Have you any idea of the consequences of perjury?"

"No, sir."

"Do you understand what perjury is?"

"It's to lie."

"Do you tell lies?"

"No, sir."

"Have you ever told a single lie?"

"Not—yet," she replied, almost whispering.

It was the answer of a child and affected the judge. He fussed with his papers. Perhaps his task was not easy; certainly it was not pleasant. Then he leaned forward again and fixed those deep, cavernous eyes upon the sad face.

"Do you understand what a sealed wife is?"

"I've never been told."

"But you know there *are* sealed wives in Utah?"

"Yes, sir; I've been told that."

Judge Stone halted there, watching her. The hall was silent except for faint rustlings and here and there deep breaths drawn guardedly. The vital question hung like a sword over the white-faced girl. Perhaps she divined its impending stroke, for she sat like a stone with dilating, appealing eyes upon her executioner.

"Are you a sealed wife?" he flung at her.

She could not answer at once. She made effort, but the words would not come. He flung the question again, sternly.

"No!" she cried.

And then there was silence. That poignant word quivered in Shefford's heart. He believed it was a lie. It seemed he would have known it if this hour was the first in which he had ever seen the girl. He heard, he felt, he sensed the fatal thing. The beautiful voice had lacked some quality before present. And the thing wanting was something subtle, an essence, a beautiful ring—the truth. What a hellish thing to make that pure girl a liar—a perjurer! The heat deep within Shefford kindled to fire.

"You are not married?" went on Judge Stone.

"No, sir," she answered, faintly.

"Have you ever been married?"

"No, sir."

"Do you expect ever to be married?"

"Oh! No, sir."

She was ashen pale now, quivering all over, with her strong hands clasping the black hood, and she could no longer meet the judge's glance.

"Have you—any—any children?" the judge asked, haltingly. It was a hard question to get out.

"No."

Judge Stone leaned far over the table, and that his face was purple showed Shefford he was a man. His big fist clenched.

"Girl, you're not going to swear you, too, were visited—over there by men . . . You're not going to swear that?"

"Oh—no, sir!"

Judge Stone settled back in his chair, and while he wiped his moist face that same foreboding murmur, almost a menace, moaned through the hall.

Shefford was sick in his soul and afraid of himself. He did not know this spirit that flamed up in him. His helplessness was a most hateful fact.

"Come—confess you are a sealed wife," called her interrogator.

She maintained silence, but shook her head.

Suddenly he seemed to leap forward.

"Unfortunate child! Confess."

That forced her to lift her head and face him, yet still she did not speak. It was the strength of despair. She could not endure much more.

"Who is your husband?" he thundered at her.

She rose wildly, terror-stricken. It was terror that dominated her, not of the stern judge, for she took a faltering step toward him, lifting a shaking hand, but of someone or of something far more terrible than any punishment she could have received in the sentence of a court. Still she was not proof against the judge's will. She had weakened, and the terror must have been because of that weakening.

"Who is the Mormon who visits you?" he thundered, relentlessly.

"I—never—knew—his—name."

"But you'd know his face. I'll arrest every Mormon in this country and bring him before you. You'd know his face?"

"Oh, I wouldn't. I *couldn't* tell! . . . I—never—saw his face—in the light!"

The tragic beauty of her, the certainty of some monstrous crime to youth and innocence, the presence of an agony and terror that unfathomably seemed not to be for herself—these transfixed the court and the audience, and held them silenced, till she reached out blindly and then sank in a heap to the floor.

⁂11⁂

AFTER THE TRIAL

SHEFFORD might have leaped over the railing but for Withers's restraining hand, and when there appeared to be some sign of kindness in those other women for the unconscious girl, Shefford squeezed through the crowd and got out of the hall.

The gang outside that had been denied admittance pressed upon Shefford, with jest and curious query, and a good nature that jarred upon him. He was far from gentle as he jostled off the first importuning fellows; the others, gaping at him, opened a lane for him to pass through.

Then there was a hand laid on his shoulder that he did not shake off. Nas Ta Bega loomed dark and tall beside him. Neither the trader nor Joe Lake nor any white man Shefford had met influenced him as this Navajo.

"Nas Ta Bega! You here, too. I guess the whole country is here. We waited at Kayenta. What kept you so long?"

The Indian, always slow to answer, did not open his lips till he drew Shefford apart from the noisy crowd.

"Bi Nai, there is sorrow in the hogan of Hosteen Doetin," he said.

"Glen Naspa!" exclaimed Shefford.

"My sister is gone from the home of her brother. She went away alone in the summer."

"Blue Canyon! She went to the missionary. Nas Ta Bega, I thought I saw her there. But I wasn't sure. I didn't want to make sure. I was afraid it might be true."

"A brave who loved my sister trailed her there."

"Nas Ta Bega, will you—will we go find her, take her home?"

"No. She will come home some day."

What bitter sadness and wisdom in his words!

"But, my friend, that damned missionary—" began Shefford, passionately. The Indian had met him at a bad hour.

"Willetts is here. I saw him go in there," interrupted Nas Ta Bega, and he pointed to the hall.

"Here! He gets around a good deal," declared Shefford. "Nas Ta Bega, what are you going to do to him?"

The Indian held his peace and there was no telling from his inscrutable face what might be in his mind. He was dark, impassive. He seemed a wise and bitter Indian, beyond any savagery of his tribe, and the suffering Shefford divined was deep.

"He'd better keep out of my sight," muttered Shefford, more to himself than to his companion.

"The half-breed is here," said Nas Ta Bega.

"Shadd? Yes, we saw him. There! He's still with his gang. Nas Ta Bega, what are they up to?"

"They will steal what they can."

"Withers says Shadd is friendly with the Mormons."

"Yes, and with the missionary, too."

"With Willetts?"

"I saw them talk together—strong talk."

"Strange. But maybe it's not so strange. Shadd is known well in Monticello and Bluff. He spends money there. They are afraid of him, but he's welcome just the same. Perhaps everybody knows him. It'd be like him to ride into Kayenta. But, Nas Ta Bega, I've got to look out for him, because Withers says he's after me."

"Bi Nai wears a scar that is proof," said the Indian.

"Then it must be he found out long ago I had a little money."

"It might be. But, Bi Nai, the half-breed has a strange step on your trail."

"What do you mean?" demanded Shefford.

"Nas Ta Bega cannot tell what he does not know," replied the Navajo. "Let that be. We shall know some day. Bi Nai, there is sorrow to tell that is not the Indian's. . . . Sorrow for my brother!"

Shefford lifted his eyes to the Indian's, and if he did not see sadness there he was much deceived.

"Bi Nai, long ago you told a story to the trader. Nas Ta Bega sat before the fire that night. You did not know he could understand your language. He listened. And he learned what brought you to the country of the Indian. That night he made you his brother. . . . All his lonely rides into the canyons have been to find the little golden-haired child, the lost girl—Fay Larkin. . . . Bi Nai, I have found the girl you wanted for your sweetheart."

Shefford was bereft of speech. He could not see steadily, and the last solemn words of the Indian seemed far away.

"Bi Nai, I have found Fay Larkin," repeated Nas Ta Bega.

"Fay Larkin!" gasped Shefford, shaking his head. "But—she's dead."

"It would be less sorrow for Bi Nai if she were dead."

Shefford clutched at the Indian. There was something terrible to be revealed. Like an aspen leaf in the wind he shook all over. He divined the revelation—divined the coming blow—but that was as far as his mind got.

"She's in there," said the Indian, pointing toward the hall.

"Fay Larkin?" whispered Shefford.

"Yes, Bi Nai."

"My God! *How* do you know? Oh, I could have seen. I've been blind. . . . Tell me, Indian. Which one?"

"Fay Larkin is the Sago Lily."

Shefford strode away into a secluded corner of the square, where in the shade and quiet of the trees he suffered a storm of heart and mind. During that short or long time—he had no idea how long—the Indian remained with him. He never lost the feeling of Nas Ta Bega close beside him. When the period of acute pain left him and some order began to replace the tumult in his mind he felt in Nas Ta Bega the same quality—silence or strength or help—that he had learned to feel in the deep canyons and the lofty crags. He realized then that the Indian was indeed a brother. And Shefford needed him. What he had to fight was more fatal than suffering and love—it was hate rising out of the unsuspected dark gulf of his heart—the instinct to kill—the murder in his soul. Only now did he come to understand Jane Withersteen's tragic story and the passion of Venters and what had made Lassiter a gunman.

The desert had transformed Shefford. The elements had entered into his muscle and bone, into the very fiber of his heart. Sun, wind, sand, cold, storm, space, stone, the poison cactus, the racking toil, the terrible loneliness—the iron of the desert man, the cruelty of the desert savage, the wildness of the mustang, the ferocity of hawk and wolf, the bitter struggle of every surviving thing—these were as if they had been melted and merged together and now made a dark and passionate stream that was his throbbing blood. He realized what he had become and gloried in it, yet there, looking on with grave and earnest eyes, was his old self, the man of reason, of intellect, of culture, who had been a good man despite the failure and shame of his life. And he gave heed to the voice of warning, of conscience. Not by revengefully seeking the Mormon who had ruined Fay Larkin and blindly dealing a wild justice could he help this unfortunate girl. This fierce, newborn strength and passion must be tempered by reason, lest he become merely elemental, a man answering wholly to primitive impulses. In the darkness of that hour he mined deep into his heart, understood himself, trembled at the thing he faced, and won his victory. He would go forth from that hour a man. He might fight, and perhaps there was death in the balance, but hate would never overthrow him.

Then when he looked at future action he felt a strange, unalterable purpose to save Fay Larkin. She was very young—seventeen or eighteen, she had said—and there could be, there must be some happiness before her. It had been his dream to chase a rainbow—it had been his determination to find her in the lost Surprise Valley. Well, he had found her. It never occurred to him to ask Nas Ta Bega how he had discovered that the Sago Lily was Fay Larkin. The wonder was, Shefford thought, that he had so long been blind himself. How simply everything worked out now! Every thought, every recollection of her was proof. Her strange beauty like that of the sweet and rare lily, her low voice that showed the habit of silence, her shapely hands with the clasp strong as a man's, her lithe form, her swift step, her wonderful agility upon the smooth, steep walls, and the wildness of her upon the heights, and the haunting, brooding shadow of her eyes when she gazed across the canyons—all these fitted so harmoniously the conception of a child lost in a beautiful Surprise Valley and growing up in its wildness and silence, tutored by the sad love of broken Jane and Lassiter. Yes, to save her had been Shefford's dream, and he had loved that dream. He had loved the dream and he had loved the child. The secret of her hiding-place as revealed by the story told him and his slow growth from dream to action—these had strangely given Fay Larkin to him. Then had come the bitter knowledge that she was dead. In the light of this subsequent revelation how easy to account for his loving

Mary, too. Never would she be Mary again to him! Fay Larkin and the Sago Lily were one and the same. She was here, near him, and he was powerless for the present to help her or to reveal himself. She was held back there in that gloomy hall among those somber Mormons, alien to the women, bound in some fatal way to one of the men, and now, by reason of her weakness in the trial, surely to be hated. Thinking of her past and her present, of the future, and that secret Mormon whose face she had never seen, Shefford felt a sinking of his heart, a terrible cold pang in his breast, a fainting of his spirit. She had sworn she was no sealed wife. But had she not lied? So, then, how utterly powerless he was!

But here to save him, to uplift him, came that strange mystic insight which had been the gift of the desert to him. She was not dead. He had found her. What mattered obstacles, even that implacable creed to which she had been sacrificed, in the face of this blessed and overwhelming truth? It was as mighty as the love suddenly dawning upon him. A strong and terrible and deathly sweet wind seemed to fill his soul with the love of her. It was her fate that had drawn him; and now it was her agony, her innocence, her beauty, that bound him for all time. Patience and cunning and toil, passion and blood, the unquenchable spirit of a man to save—these were nothing to give—life itself were little, could he but free her.

Patience and cunning! His sharpening mind cut these out as his greatest assets for the present. And his thoughts flashed like light through his brain. . . . Judge Stone and his court would fail to convict any Mormon in Stonebridge, just the same as they had failed in the northern towns. They would go away, and Stonebridge would fall to the slow, sleepy tenor of its former way. The hidden village must become known to all men, honest and outlawed, in that country, but this fact would hardly make any quick change in the plans of the Mormons. They did not soon change. They would send the sealed wives back to the canyon and, after the excitement had died down, visit them as usual. Nothing, perhaps, would ever change these old Mormons but death.

Shefford resolved to remain in Stonebridge and ingratiate himself deeper into the regard of the Mormons. He would find work there, if the sealed wives were not returned to the hidden village. In case the women went back to the valley Shefford meant to resume his old duty of driving Withers's pack-trains. Wanting that opportunity, he would find some other work, some excuse to take him there.

In due time he would reveal to Fay Larkin that he knew her. How the thought thrilled him! She might deny, might persist in her fear, might fight to keep her secret. But he would learn it—hear her story—hear what had become of Jane Withersteen and Lassiter—and if they were alive, which now he believed, he would find them—and he would take them and Fay out of the country.

The duty, the great task, held a grim fascination for him. He had a foreboding of the cost; he had a dark realization of the force he meant to oppose. There were duty here and pity and unselfish love, but these alone did not actuate Shefford. Mystically fate seemed again to come like a gleam and bid him follow.

When Shefford and Nas Ta Bega returned to the town hall the trial had been ended, the hall was closed, and only a few Indians and cowboys remained in the square, and they were about to depart. On the street, however, and the paths and in the doorways of stores were knots of people, talking earnestly. Shefford walked up and down, hoping to meet Withers or Joe Lake. Nas Ta Bega said he would take the horses to water and feed and then return.

There were indications that Stonebridge might experience some of the excitement and perhaps violence common to towns like Monticello and Durango. There was only one saloon in Stonebridge, and it was full of roystering cowboys and horse-wranglers. Shefford saw the bunch of mustangs, in charge of the same Indian, that belonged to Shadd and his gang. The men were inside, drinking. Next door was a tavern called Hopewell House, a stone structure of some pretensions. There were Indians lounging outside. Shefford entered through a wide door and found himself in a large bare room, boarded like a loft, with no ceiling except the roof. The place was full of men and noise. Here he encountered Joe Lake talking to Bishop Kane and other Mormons. Shefford got a friendly greeting from the bishop, and then was well received by the strangers, to whom Joe introduced him.

"Have you seen Withers?" asked Shefford.

"Reckon he's around somewhere," replied Joe. "Better hang up here, for he'll drop in sooner or later."

"When are you going back to Kayenta?" went on Shefford.

"Hard to say. We'll have to call off our hunt. Nas Ta Bega is here, too."

"Yes, I've been with him."

The older Mormons drew aside, and then Joe mentioned the fact that he was half starved. Shefford went with him into another clapboard room, which was evidently a dining room. There were half a dozen men at the long table. The seat at the end was a box, and scarcely large enough or safe enough for Joe and Shefford, but they risked it.

"Saw you in the hall," said Joe. "Hell—wasn't it?"

"Joe, I never knew how much I dared say to you, so I don't talk much. But, it *was* hell," replied Shefford.

"You needn't be so scared of me," spoke up Joe, testily.

That was the first time Shefford had heard the Mormon speak that way.

"I'm not scared, Joe. But I like you—respect you. I can't say so much of —of your people."

"Did you stick out the whole mix?" asked Joe.

"No. I had enough when—when they got through with Mary." Shefford spoke low and dropped his head. He heard the Mormon grind his teeth. There was silence for a little space while neither man looked at the other.

"Reckon the judge was pretty decent," presently said Joe.

"Yes, I thought so. He might have—" But Shefford did not finish that sentence. "How'd the thing end?"

"It ended all right."

"Was there no conviction—no sentence?" Shefford felt a curious eagerness.

"Naw," he snorted. "That court might have saved its breath."

"I suppose. Well, Joe, between you and me, as old friends now, that trial established one fact, even if it couldn't be proved. . . . Those women *are* sealed wives."

Joe had no reply for that. He looked gloomy, and there was a stern line in his lips. Today he seemed more like a Mormon.

"Judge Stone knew that as well as I knew," went on Shefford. "Any man of penetration could have seen it. What an ordeal that was for good women to go through! I know they're good. And there they were swearing to—"

"Didn't it make me sick?" interrupted Joe in a kind of growl. "Reckon it made Judge Stone sick, too. After Mary went under he conducted that trial like a man cuttin' out steers at a round-up. He wanted to get it over. He never forced any question. . . . Bad job to ride down Stonebridge way! It's out of creation. There's only six men in the party, with a poor lot of horses. Really, government officers or not, they're not safe. And they've taken a hunch."

"Have they left already?" inquired Shefford.

"Were packed an hour ago. I didn't see them go, but somebody said they went. Took the trail for Bluff, which sure is the only trail they could take, unless they wanted to go to Colorado by way of Kayenta. That might have been the safest trail."

"Joe, what might happen to them?" asked Shefford, quietly, with eyes on the Mormon.

"Aw, you know that rough trail. Bad on horses. Weathered slopes— slipping ledges—a rock might fall on you any time. Then Shadd's here with his gang. And bad Piutes."

"What became of the women?" Shefford asked, presently.

"They're around among friends."

"Where are their children?"

"Left over there with the old women. Couldn't be fetched over. But there are some pretty young babies in that bunch—need their mothers."

"I should—think so," replied Shefford, constrainedly. "When will their mothers get back to them?"

"Tonight, maybe, if this mob of cow-punchers and wranglers get out of town. . . . It's a bad mix, Shefford, here's a hunch on that. These fellows will get full of whisky. And trouble might come if they—approach the women."

"You mean they might get drunk enough to take the oaths of those poor women—take the meaning literally—pretend to believe the women are what they swore they were?"

"Reckon you've got the hunch," replied Joe, gloomily.

"My God, man, that would be horrible!" exclaimed Shefford.

"Horrible or not, it's liable to happen. The women can be kept here yet awhile. Reckon there won't be any trouble here. It'll be over there in the valley. Shefford, getting the women over there safe is a job that's been put to me. I've got a bunch of fellows already. Can I count on you? I'm glad to say you're well thought of. Bishop Kane liked you, and what he says goes."

"Yes, Joe, you can count on me," replied Shefford.

They finished their meal then and repaired to the big office-room of the house. Several groups of men were there and loud talk was going on outside. Shefford saw Withers talking to Bishop Kane and two other Mormons, both strangers to Shefford. The trader appeared to be speaking with unwonted force, emphasizing his words with energetic movements of his hands.

"Reckon something's up," whispered Joe, hoarsely. "It's been in the air all day."

Withers must have been watching for Shefford.

"Here's Shefford now," he said to the trio of Mormons, as Joe and Shefford reached the group. "I want you to hear him speak for himself."

"What's the matter?" asked Shefford.

"Give me a hunch and I'll put in my say-so," said Joe Lake.

"Shefford, it's the matter of a good name more than a job," replied the trader. "A little while back I told the bishop I meant to put you on the pack job over to the valley—same as when you first came to me. Well, the bishop was pleased and said he might put something in your way. Just now I ran in here to find you—not wanted. When I kicked I got the straight hunch. Willetts has said things about you. One of them—the one that sticks in my craw—was that you'd do anything, even pretend to be inclined toward Mormonism, just to be among those Mormon women over there. Willetts is your enemy. And he's worse than I thought. Now I want you to tell Bishop Kane *why* this missionary is bitter toward you."

"Gentlemen, I knocked him down," replied Shefford, simply.

"What for?" inquired the bishop, in surprise and curiosity.

Shefford related the incident which had occurred at Red Lake and that now seemed again to come forward fatefully.

"You insinuate he had evil intent toward the Indian girl?" queried Kane.

"I insinuate nothing. I merely state what led to my acting as I did."

"Principles of religion, sir?"

"No. A man's principles."

Withers interposed in his blunt way, "Bishop, did you ever see Glen Naspa?"

"No."

"She's the prettiest Navajo in the country. Willetts was after her, that's all."

"My dear man, I can't believe that of a Christian missionary. We've known Willetts for years. He's a man of influence. He has money back of him. He's doing a good work. You hint of a love relation."

"No, I don't hint," replied Withers, impatiently. "I know. It's not the first time I've known a missionary to do this sort of thing. Nor is it the first time for Willetts. Bishop Kane, I live among the Indians. I see a lot I never speak of. My work is to trade with the Indians, that's all. But I'll not have Willetts or any other damned hypocrite run down my friend here. John Shefford is the finest young man that ever came to me in the desert. And he's got to be put right before you all or I'll not set foot in Stonebridge again. . . . Willetts was after Glen Naspa. Shefford punched him. And later threw him out of the old Indian's hogan up on the mountain. That explains Willetts's enmity. He was after the girl."

"What's more, gentlemen, he *got* her," added Shefford. "Glen Naspa has not been home for six months. I saw her at Blue Canyon. . . . I would like to face this Willetts before you all."

"Easy enough," replied Withers, with a grim chuckle. "He's just outside."

The trader went out; Joe Lake followed at his heels and the three Mormons were next; Shefford brought up the rear and lingered in the door while his eye swept the crowd of men and Indians. His feeling was in direct contrast to his movements. He felt the throbbing of fierce anger. But it seemed a face came between him and his passion—a sweet and tragic face that would have had power to check him in a vastly more critical moment than this. And in an instant he had himself in hand, and, strangely, suddenly felt the strength that had come to him.

Willetts stood in earnest colloquy with a short, squat Indian—the half-breed Shadd. They leaned against a hitching-rail. Other Indians were there, and outlaws. It was a mixed group, rough and hard-looking.

"Hey, Willetts!" called the trader, and his loud, ringing voice, not pleasant, stilled the movement and sound.

When Willetts turned, Shefford was halfway across the wide walk. The missionary not only saw him, but also Nas Ta Bega, who was striding forward. Joe Lake was ahead of the trader, the Mormons followed with decision, and they all confronted Willetts. He turned pale. Shadd had cautiously moved along the rail, nearer to his gang, and then they, with the others of the curious crowd, drew closer.

"Willetts, here's Shefford. Now say it to his face!" declared the trader. He was angry and evidently wanted the fact known, as well as the situation.

Willetts had paled, but he showed boldness. For an instant Shefford studied the smooth face, with its sloping lines, the dark, wine-colored eyes.

"Willetts, I understand you've maligned me to Bishop Kane and others," began Shefford, curtly.

"I called you an atheist," returned the missionary, harshly.

"Yes, and more than that. And I told these men *why* you vented your spite on me."

Willetts uttered a half-laugh, an uneasy, contemptuous expression of scorn and repudiation.

"The charges of such a man as you are can't hurt me," he said.

The man did not show fear so much as disgust at the meeting. He seemed to be absorbed in thought, yet no serious consideration of the situation made itself manifest. Shefford felt puzzled. Perhaps there was no fire to strike from this man. The desert had certainly not made him flint. He had not toiled or suffered or fought.

"But *I* can hurt you," thundered Shefford, with startling suddenness. "Here! Look at this Indian! Do you know him? Glen Naspa's brother. Look at him. Let us see you face him while I accuse you. . . . You made love to Glen Naspa—took her from her home!"

"Harping infidel!" replied Willetts, hoarsely. "So that's your game. Well, Glen Naspa came to my school of her own accord and she will say so."

"Why will she? Because you blinded the simple Indian girl. . . . Willetts, I'll waste little more time on you."

And swift and light as a panther Shefford leaped upon the man and, fastening powerful hands round the thick neck, bore him to his knees and bent back his head over the rail. There was a convulsive struggle, a hard flinging of arms, a straining wrestle, and then Willetts was in a dreadful position. Shefford held him in iron grasp.

"You damned, white-livered hypocrite—I'm liable to kill you!" cried Shefford. "I watched you and Glen Naspa that day up on the mountain. I saw you embrace her. I saw that she loved you. Tell *that*, you liar! That'll be enough."

The face of the missionary turned purple as Shefford forced his head back over the rail.

"I'll *kill* you, man," repeated Shefford, piercingly. "Do you want to go to your God unprepared? Say you made love to Glen Naspa—tell that you persuaded her to leave her home. Quick!"

Willetts raised a shaking hand and then Shefford relaxed the paralyzing grip and let his head come forward. The half-strangled man gasped out a few incoherent words that his livid, guilty face made unnecessary.

Shefford gave him a shove and he fell into the dust at the feet of the Navajo.

"Gentlemen, I leave him to Nas Ta Bega," said Shefford, with a strange change from passion to calmness.

Late that night, when the roystering visitors had gone or were deep in drunken slumber, a melancholy and strange procession filed out of Stonebridge. Joe Lake and his armed comrades were escorting the Mormon women back to the hidden valley. They were mounted on burros and mustangs, and in all that dark and somber line there was only one figure which shone white under the pale moon.

At the starting, until that white-clad figure had appeared, Shefford's heart had seemed to be in his throat; and thereafter its beat was muffled and painful in his breast. Yet there was some sad sweetness in the knowledge that he could see her now, be near her, watch over her.

By and by the overcast clouds drifted and the moon shone bright. The night was still; the great dark mountain loomed to the stars; the numberless waves of rounded rock that must be crossed and circled lay deep in shadow. There was only a steady pattering of light hoofs.

Shefford's place was near the end of the line, and he kept well back, riding close to one woman and then another. No word was spoken. These sealed wives rode where their mounts were led or driven, as blind in their hoods as veiled Arab women in palanquins. And their heads drooped wearily and their shoulders bent, as if under a burden. It took an hour of steady riding to reach the ascent to the plateau, and here, with the beginning of rough and smooth and shadowed trail, the work of the escort began. The line lengthened out and each man kept to the several women assigned to him. Shefford had three, and one of them was the girl he loved. She rode as if the world and time and life were naught to her. As soon as he dared trust his voice and his control he meant to let her know the man whom perhaps she had not forgotten was there with her, a friend. Six months! It had been a lifetime to him. Surely eternity to her! Had she forgotten? He felt like a coward who had basely deserted her. Oh—had he only known!

She rode a burro that was slow, continually blocking the passage for those behind, and eventually it became lame. Thus the other women forged ahead. Shefford dismounted and stopped her burro. It was a moment before she noted the halt, and twice in that time Shefford tried to speak and failed. What poignant pain, regret, love made his utterance fail!

"Ride my horse," he finally said, and his voice was not like his own.

Obediently and wearily she dismounted from the burro and got up on Nack-yal. The stirrups were long for her and he had to change them. His fingers were all thumbs as he fumbled with the buckles.

Suddenly he became aware that there had been a subtle change in her. He knew it without looking up and he seemed to be unable to go on with his task. If his life had depended upon keeping his head lowered he could not have done it. The listlessness of her drooping form was no longer manifest. The peak of the dark hood pointed toward him. He knew then that she was gazing at him.

Never so long as he lived would that moment be forgotten! They were alone. The others had gotten so far ahead that no sound came back. The stillness was so deep it could be felt. The moon shone with white, cold radiance and the shining slopes of smooth stone waved away, crossed by shadows of pinyons.

Then she leaned a little toward him. One swift hand flew up to tear the black hood back so that she could see. In its place flashed her white face. And her eyes were like the night.

"You!" she whispered.

His blood came leaping to sting neck and cheek and temple. What dared he interpret from that single word? Could any other word have meant so much?

"No—one—else," he replied, unsteadily.

Her white hand flashed again to him, and he met it with his own. He felt himself standing cold and motionless in the moonlight. He saw her, wonderful, with the deep, shadowy eyes, and a silver sheen on her hair. And as he looked she released her hand and lifted it, with the other, to her hood. He saw the shiny hair darken and disappear—and then the lovely face with its sad eyes and tragic lips.

He drew Nack-yal's bridle forward, and led him up the moonlit trail.

❧12❧

THE REVELATION

T HE FOLLOWING afternoon cowboys and horse-wranglers, keen-eyed as Indians for tracks and trails, began to arrive in the quiet valley to which the Mormon women had been returned.

Under every cedar clump there were hobbled horses, packs, and rolled bedding in tarpaulins. Shefford and Joe Lake had pitched camp in the old site near the spring. The other men of Joe's escort went to the homes of the women; and that afternoon, as the curious visitors began to arrive, these homes became barred and dark and quiet, as if they had been closed and deserted for the winter. Not a woman showed herself.

Shefford and Joe, by reason of the location of their camp and their alertness, met all the newcomers. The ride from Stonebridge was a long and hard one, calculated to wear off the effects of the whisky imbibed by the adventure-seekers. This fact alone saved the situation. Nevertheless, Joe expected trouble. Most of the visitors were decent, good-natured fellows, merely curious, and simple enough to believe that this really was what the Mormons had claimed—a village of free women. But there were those among them who were coarse, evil-minded, and dangerous.

By suppertime there were two dozen or more of these men in the valley, camped along the west wall. Fires were lighted, smoke curled up over the cedars, gay songs disturbed the usual serenity of the place. Later in the early twilight the curious visitors, by twos and threes, walked about the village, peering at the dark cabins and jesting among themselves. Joe had informed Shefford that all the women had been put in a limited number of cabins, so that they could be protected. So far as Shefford saw or heard there was no unpleasant incident in the village; however, as the sauntering visitors returned toward their camps they loitered at the spring, and here developments threatened.

In spite of the fact that the majority of these cowboys and their comrades were decent-minded and beginning to see the real relation of things, they were not disposed to be civil to Shefford. They were certainly not Mormons. And his position, apparently as a Gentile, among these Mormons was one open to criticism. They might have been jealous, too; at any rate, remarks were passed in his hearing, meant for his ears, that made it exceedingly trying for him not to resent. Moreover, Joe Lake's increasing impatience rendered the situation more difficult. Shefford welcomed the arrival of Nas Ta Bega. The Indian listened to the loud talk of several loungers round the campfire; and thereafter he was like Shefford's shadow, silent, somber, watchful.

Nevertheless, it did not happen to be one of the friendly and sarcastic cowboys that precipitated the crisis. A horse-wrangler named Hurley, a man of bad repute, as much outlaw as anything, took up the bantering.

"Say, Shefford, what in the hell's your job here, anyway?" he queried as he kicked a cedar branch into the campfire. The brightening blaze showed him swarthy, unshaven, a large-featured, ugly man.

"I've been doing odd jobs for Withers," replied Shefford. "Expect to drive pack-trains in here for a while."

"You must stand strong with these Mormons. Must be a Mormon yerself?"

"No," replied Shefford, briefly.

"Wal, I'm stuck on your job. Do you need a packer? I can throw a diamond-hitch better 'n any feller in this country."

"I don't need help."

"Mebbe you'll take me over to see the ladies," he went on, with a coarse laugh.

Shefford did not show that he had heard. Hurley waited, leering as he looked from the keen listeners to Shefford.

"Want to have them all yourself, eh?" he jeered.

Shefford struck him—sent him tumbling heavily, like a log. Hurley, cursing as he half rose, jerked his gun out. Nas Ta Bega, swift as light, kicked the gun out of his hand. And Joe Lake picked it up.

Deliberately the Mormon cocked the weapon and stood over Hurley.

"Get up!" he ordered, and Shefford heard the ruthless Mormon in him then.

Hurley rose slowly. Then Joe prodded him in the middle with the cocked gun. Shefford, startled, expected the gun to go off. So did the others, especially Hurley, who shrank in panic from the dark Mormon.

"Rustle!" said Joe, and gave the man a harder prod. Assuredly the gun did not have a hair-trigger.

"Joe, mebbe it's loaded!" protested one of the cowboys.

Hurley shrank back, and turned to hurry away, with Joe close after him. They disappeared in the darkness. A constrained silence was maintained around the campfire for a while. Presently some of the men walked off and others began to converse. Everybody heard the sound of hoofs passing down the trail. The patter ceased, and in a few moments Lake returned. He still carried Hurley's gun.

The crowd dispersed then. There was no indication of further trouble. However, Shefford and Joe and Nas Ta Bega divided the night in watches, so that someone would be wide awake.

Early next morning there was an exodus from the village of the better element among the visitors. "No fun hangin' round hyar," one of them expressed it, and as good-naturedly as they had come they rode away. Six or seven of the desperado class remained behind, bent on mischief; and they were reinforced by more arrivals from Stonebridge. They avoided the camp by the spring, and when Shefford and Lake attempted to go to them they gave them a wide berth. This caused Joe to assert that they were up to some dirty work. All morning they lounged around under the cedars, keeping out of sight, and evidently the reinforcement from Stonebridge had brought liquor. When they gathered together at their camp, half drunk, all noisy, some wanting to swagger off into the village and others trying to hold them back, Joe Lake said, grimly, that somebody was going to get shot. Indeed, Shefford saw that there was every likelihood of bloodshed.

"Reckon we'd better take to one of the cabins," said Joe.

Thereupon the three repaired to the nearest cabin, and, entering, kept watch from the windows. During a couple of hours, however, they did not see or hear anything of the ruffians. Then came a shot from over in the village, a single yell, and, after that, a scattering volley. The silence and suspense which followed were finally broken by hoofbeats. Nas Ta Bega called Joe and Shefford to the window he had been stationed at. From here they saw the unwelcome visitors ride down the trail, to disappear in the cedars toward the outlet of the valley. Joe, who had numbered them, said that all but one of them had gone.

"Reckon he got it," added Joe.

So indeed it turned out; one of the men, a well-known rustler named Harker, had been killed, by whom no one seemed to know. He had brazenly tried to force his way into one of the houses, and the act had cost him his life. Naturally Shefford, never free from his civilized habit of thought, remarked apprehensively that he hoped this affair would not cause the poor women to be arrested again and haled before some rude court.

"Law!" grunted Joe. "There ain't any. The nearest sheriff is in Durango. That's Colorado. And he'd give us a medal for killing Harker. It was a good job, for it'll teach these rowdies a lesson."

The Mormons, notwithstanding their indifference to the killing of the desperado, gave him decent burial and prayed for his soul.

Next day the old order of life was resumed in the village. And the arrival of a heavily laden pack-train, under the guidance of Withers, attested to the fact that the Mormons meant not only to continue to live in the valley, but also to build and plant and enlarge. This was good news to Shefford. At least the village could be made less lonely. And there was plenty of work to give him excuse for staying there. Furthermore, Withers brought a message from Bishop Kane to the effect that the young man was offered a place as teacher in the school, in cooperation with the Mormon teachers. Shefford experienced no twinge of conscience when he accepted.

It was the fourth evening after the never-to-be-forgotten moonlight ride to the valley that Shefford passed under the dark pinyon trees on his way to Fay Larkin's cottage. He paused in the gloom and memory beset him. The six months were annihilated, and it was the night he had fled. But now all was silent. He seemed to be trying to drag himself back. A beginning must be made. Only how to meet her—what to say—what to conceal!

He tapped on the door and she came out. After all, it was a meeting vastly different from what his feeling made him imagine it might have been. She was nervous, frightened, as were all the other women, for that matter. She was alone in the cottage. He made haste to reassure her about the improbability of any further trouble such as had befallen the last week. As he had always done on those former visits to her, he talked rapidly, using all his wit, and here his emotion made him eloquent; he avoided personalities, except to tell about his prospects of work in the village, and he sought above all to lead her mind from thought of herself and her condition. Before he left her he had the gladness of knowing he had succeeded.

When he said good night he felt the strange falsity of his position. He did not expect to be able to keep up the deception for long. That roused him, and half the night he lay awake, thinking. Next day he was the life of the work and study and play in that village. Kindness and goodwill did not need inspiration, but it was keen, deep passion that made him a plotter for influence and friendship. Was there a woman in the village whom he might trust, in case he needed one? And his instinct guided him to her whom he had liked well—Ruth. Ruth Jones she had called herself at the trial, and when Shefford used the name she laughed mockingly. Ruth was not very religious, and sometimes she was bitter and hard. She wanted life, and here she was a prisoner in a lonely valley. She welcomed Shefford's visits. He imagined that she had slightly changed, and whether it was the added six months with its trouble and pain or a growing revolt he could not tell. After a time he divined that the inevitable retrogression had set in: she had not enough faith to uphold the burden she had accepted, nor the courage to cast it off. She was ready to love him. That did not frighten Shefford, and if she did love him he was not so sure it would not be an anchor for her. He saw her danger, and then he became what he had never really been in all the days of his ministry—the real helper. Unselfishly, for her sake, he found power to influence her; and selfishly, for the sake of Fay Larkin, he began slowly to win her to a possible need.

The days passed swiftly. Mormons came and went, though in the open day, as laborers; new cabins went up, and a store, and other improvements. Some part of every evening Shefford spent with Fay, and these visits were no longer unknown to the village. Women gossiped, in a friendly way about Shefford, but with jealous tongues about the girl. Joe Lake told Shefford the run of the village talk. Anything concerning the Sago Lily the droll Mormon took to heart. He had been hard hit, and admitted it. Sometimes he went with Shefford to call upon her, but he talked little and never remained long. Shefford had anticipated antagonism on the part of Joe; however, he did not find it.

Shefford really lived through the busy day for that hour with Fay in the twilight. And every evening seemed the same. He would find her in the dark, alone, silent, brooding, hopeless. Her mood did not puzzle him, but how to keep from plunging her deeper into despair baffled him. He exhausted all his powers trying to do for her what he had been able to do for Ruth. Yet he failed. Something had blunted her. The shadow of that baneful trial hovered over her, and he came to sense a strange terror in her. It was mostly always present. Was she thinking of Jane Withersteen and Lassiter, left dead or imprisoned in the valley from which she had been brought so mysteriously? Shefford wearied his brain revolving these questions. The fate of her friends, and the cross she bore—of these was tragedy born, but the terror—that Shefford divined came of waiting for the visit of the Mormon whose face she had never seen. Shefford prayed that he might never meet this man. Finally he grew desperate. When he first arrived at the girl's home she would speak, she showed gladness, relief, and then straightway she dropped back into the shadow of her gloom. When he got up to go then there was a wistfulness, an unspoken need, an unconscious reliance, in her reluctant good night.

Then the hour came when he reached his limit. He must begin his revelation.

"You never ask me anything—let alone about myself," he said.

"I'd like to hear," she replied, timidly.

"Do I strike you as an unhappy man?"

"No, indeed."

"Well, how *do* I strike you?"

This was an entirely new tack he had veered to.

"Very good and kind to us women," she said.

"I don't know about that. If I am so, it doesn't bring me happiness. . . . Do you remember what I told you once, about my being a preacher—disgrace, ruin, and all that—and my rainbow-chasing dream out here after a—a lost girl?"

"I—remember all—you said," she replied, very low.

"Listen." His voice was a little husky, but behind it there seemed a tide of resistless utterance. "Loss of faith and name did not send me to this wilderness. But I had love—love for that lost girl, Fay Larkin. I dreamed about her till I loved her. I dreamed that I would find her—my treasure—at the foot of a rainbow. Dreams! . . . When you told me she was dead I accepted that. There was truth in your voice. I respected your reticence. But something died in me then. I lost myself, the best of me, the good that might have uplifted me. I went away, down upon the barren desert, and there I rode and slept and grew into another and a harder man. Yet, strange to say, I never forgot her, though my dreams were done. As I toiled and suffered and changed I loved her—if not her, the thought of her—more and more. Now I have come back to these walled valleys—to the smell of pinyon, to the flowers in the nooks, to the wind on the heights, to the silence and loneliness and beauty. And here the dreams come back and *she* is *with* me always. Her spirit is all that keeps me kind and good, as you say I am. But I suffer, I long for her alive. If I love her dead, how could I love her living! Always I torture myself with the vain dream that—that she *might* not be dead. I have never been anything but a dreamer. And here I go about my work by day and lie awake at night with that lost girl in my mind. . . . I love her. Does that seem strange to you? But it would not if you understood. Think. I had lost faith, hope. I set myself a great work—to find Fay Larkin. And by the fire and the iron and the blood that I felt it would cost to save her some faith must come to me again. . . . My work is undone—I've never saved her. But listen, how strange it is to feel—now—as I let myself go—that just the loving her and the living here in the wildness that holds her somewhere have brought me hope again. Some faith must come, too. It was through her that I met this Indian, Nas Ta Bega. He has saved my life—taught me much. What would I ever have learned of the naked and vast earth, of the sublimity of the wild uplands, of the storm and night and sun, if I had not followed a gleam she inspired? In my hunt for a lost girl perhaps I wandered into a place where I shall find a God and my salvation. Do you marvel that I love Fay Larkin—that she is not dead to me? Do you marvel that I love her, when I *know*, were she alive, chained in a canyon, or bound, or lost in any way, my destiny would lead me to her, and she should be saved?"

Shefford ended, overcome with emotion. In the dusk he could not see the girl's face, but the white form that had drooped so listlessly seemed now charged by some vitalizing current. He knew he had spoken irrationally; still he held it no dishonor to have told her he loved her as one dead. If she took that love to the secret heart of living Fay Larkin, then perhaps a spirit might light in her darkened soul. He had no thought yet that Fay Larkin might ever belong to him. He divined a crime—he had seen her agony. And this avowal of his was only one step toward her deliverance.

Softly she rose, retreating into the shadow.

"Forgive me if I—I disturb you, distress you," he said. "I wanted to tell you. She was—somehow known to you. I am not happy. And are *you* happy? . . . Let her memory be a bond between us. . . . Good night."

"Good night."

Faintly as the faintest whisper breathed her reply, and, though it came from a child forced into womanhood, it whispered of girlhood not dead, of sweet incredulity, of amazed tumult, of a wondering, frantic desire to run and hide, of the bewilderment incident to a first hint of love.

Shefford walked away into the darkness. The whisper filled his soul. Had a word of love ever been spoken to that girl? Never—not the love which had been on his lips. Fay Larkin's lonely life spoke clearly in her whisper.

Next morning as the sun gilded the looming peaks and shafts of gold slanted into the valley she came swiftly down the path to the spring.

Shefford paused in his task of chopping wood. Joe Lake, on his knees, with his big hands in a pan of dough, lifted his head to stare. She had left off the somber black hood, and, although that made a vast difference in her, still it was not enough to account for what struck both men.

"Good morning," she called, brightly.

They both answered, but not spontaneously. She stopped at the spring and with one sweep of her strong arm filled the bucket and lifted it. Then she started back down the path and, pausing opposite the camp, set the bucket down.

"Joe, do you still pride yourself on your sourdough?" she asked.

"Reckon I do," replied Joe, with a grin.

"I've heard your boasts, but never tasted your bread," she went on.

"I'll ask you to eat with us some day."

"Don't forget," she replied.

And then shyly she looked at Shefford. She was like the fresh dawn, and the gold of the sun shone on her head.

"Have you chopped all that wood—so early?" she asked.

"Sure," replied Shefford, laughing. "I have to get up early to keep Joe from doing all the camp chores."

She smiled, and then to Shefford she seemed to gleam, to be radiant.

"It'd be a lovely morning to climb—'way high."

"Why—yes—it would," replied Shefford, awkwardly. "I wish I didn't have my work."

"Joe, will *you* climb with me some day?"

"I should smile I will," declared Joe.

"But I can run right up the walls."

"I reckon. Mary, it wouldn't surprise me to see you fly."

"Do you mean I'm like a canyon swallow or an angel?"

Then, as Joe stared speechlessly, she said goodbye and, taking up the bucket, went on with her swift, graceful step.

"She's perked up," said the Mormon, staring after her. "Never heard her say more'n yes or no till now."

"She did seem—bright," replied Shefford.

He was stunned. What had happened to her? Today this girl had not been Mary, the sealed wife, or the Sago Lily, alien among Mormon women. Then it flashed upon him—she was Fay Larkin. She who had regarded herself as dead had come back to life. In one short night what had transformed her—what had taken place in her heart? Shefford dared not accept, nor allow lodgment in his mind, a thrilling idea that he had made her forget her misery.

"Shefford, did you ever see her like that?" asked Joe.

"Never."

"Haven't you—something to do with it?"

"Maybe I have. I—I hope so."

"Reckon you've seen how she's faded—since the trial?"

"No," replied Shefford, swiftly. "But I've not seen her face in daylight since then."

"Well, take my hunch," said Joe, soberly. "She's begun to fade like the canyon lily when it's broken. And she's going to die unless—"

"Why, man!" ejaculated Shefford. "Didn't you see—"

"Sure I see," interrupted the Mormon. "I see a lot you don't. She's so white you can look through her. She's grown thin, all in a week. She doesn't eat. Oh, I know, because I've made it my business to find out. It's no news to the women. But they'd like to see her die. And she will die unless—"

"My God!" exclaimed Shefford, huskily. "I never noticed—I never thought. . . . Joe, hasn't she any friends?"

"Sure. You and Ruth—and me. Maybe Nas Ta Bega, too. He watches her a good deal."

"We can do so little, when she needs so much."

"Nobody can help her, unless it's you," went on the Mormon. "That's plain talk. She seemed different this morning. Why, she was alive—she talked—she smiled. . . . Shefford, if you cheer her up I'll go to hell for you!"

The big Mormon, on his knees, with his hands in a pan of dough, and his shirt all covered with flour, presented an incongruous figure of a man actuated by pathos and passion. Yet the contrast made his emotion all the simpler and stronger. Shefford grew closer to Joe in that moment.

"Why do you think *I* can cheer her, help her?" queried Shefford.

"I don't know. But she's different with you. It's not that you're a Gentile, though, for all the women are crazy about you. You talk to her. You have power over her, Shefford. I feel that. She's only a kid."

"Who is she, Joe? Where did she come from?" asked Shefford, very low, with his eyes cast down.

"I don't know. I can't find out. Nobody knows. It's a mystery—to all the younger Mormons, anyway."

Shefford burned to ask questions about the Mormon whose sealed wife the girl was, but he respected Joe too much to take advantage of him in a poignant moment like this. Besides, it was only jealousy that made him burn to know the Mormon's identity, and jealousy had become a creeping, insidious, growing fire. He would be wise not to add fuel to it. He rejected many things before he thought of one that he could voice to his friend.

"Joe, it's only her body that belongs to—to . . . Her soul is lost to—"

"John Shefford, let that go. My mind's tired. I've been taught so and so, and I'm not bright. . . . But, after all, men are much alike. The thing with you and me is this—we don't want to see *her* grave!"

Love spoke there. The Mormon had seized upon the single elemental point that concerned him and his friend in their relation to this unfortunate girl. His simple, powerful statement united them; it gave the lie to his hint of denseness; it stripped the truth naked. It was such a wonderful thought-provoking statement that Shefford needed time to ponder how deep the Mormon was. To what limit would he go? Did he mean that here, between two men who loved the same girl, class, duty, honor, creed were nothing if they stood in the way of her deliverance and her life?

"Joe Lake, you Mormons are impossible," said Shefford, deliberately. "You don't want to see her grave. So long as she lives—remains on the earth—white and gold like the flower you call her, that's enough for you. It's her body you think of. And that's the great and horrible error in your religion. . . . But death of the soul is infinitely worse than death of the body. I have been thinking of her soul. . . . So here we stand, you and I. You to save her life—I to save her soul! What will you do?"

"Why, John, I'd turn Gentile," he said, with terrible softness. It was a softness that scorned Shefford for asking, and likewise it flung defiance at his creed and into the face of hell.

Shefford felt the sting and the exaltation.

"And I'd be a Mormon," he said.

"All right. We understand each other. Reckon there won't be any call for such extremes. I haven't an idea what you mean—what can be done. But I say, go slow, so we won't all find graves. First cheer her up somehow. Make her want to live. But go slow, John. *And don't be with her late!"*

That night Shefford found her waiting for him in the moonlight—a girl who was as transparent as crystal-clear water, who had left off the somber gloom with the black hood, who tremulously embraced happiness without knowing it, who was one moment timid and wild like a half-frightened fawn, and the next, exquisitely half-conscious of what it meant to be thought dead, but to be alive, to be awakening, wondering, palpitating, and to be loved.

Shefford lived the hour as a dream and went back to the quiet darkness under the cedars to lie wide-eyed, trying to recall all that she had said. For she had talked as if utterance had long been dammed behind a barrier of silence.

There followed other hours like that one, indescribable hours, so sweet they stung, and in which, keeping pace with his love, was the nobler stride of a spirit that more every day lightened her burden.

The thing he had to do, sooner or later, was to tell her he knew she was Fay Larkin, not dead, but alive, and that, not love nor religion, but sacrifice, nailed her down to her martyrdom. Many and many a time he had tried to force himself to tell her, only to fail. He hated to risk ending this sweet, strange, thoughtless, girlish mood of hers. It might not be soon won back—perhaps never. How could he tell what chains bound her? And so as he vacillated between Joe's cautious advice to go slow and his own pity the days and weeks slipped by.

One haunting fear kept him sleepless half the nights and sick even in his dreams, and it was that the Mormon whose sealed wife she was might come, surely would come, some night. Shefford could bear it. But what would that visit do to Fay Larkin? Shefford instinctively feared the awakening in the girl of womanhood, of deeper insight, of a spiritual realization of what she was, of a physical dawn.

He might have spared himself needless torture. One day Joe Lake eyed him with penetrating glance.

"Reckon you don't have to sleep right on that Stonebridge trail," said the Mormon, significantly.

Shefford felt the blood burn his neck and face. He had pulled his tarpaulin closer to the trail, and his motive was as an open page to the keen Mormon.

"Why?" asked Shefford.

"There won't be any Mormons riding in here soon—by night—to visit the women," replied Joe, bluntly. "Haven't you figured there might be government spies watching the trails?"

"No, I haven't."

"Well, take a hunch, then," added the Mormon, gruffly, and Shefford divined, as well as if he had been told, that warning word had gone to Stonebridge. Gone despite the fact that Nas Ta Bega had reported every trail free of watchers! There was no sign of any spies, cowboys, outlaws, or Indians in the vicinity of the valley. A passionate gratitude to the Mormon overcame Shefford; and the unreasonableness of it, the nature of it, perturbed him greatly. But, something hammered into his brain, if he loved one of these sealed wives, how could he help being jealous?

The result of Joe's hint was that Shefford put off the hour of revelation, lived in his dream, helped the girl grow farther and farther away from her trouble, until that inevitable hour arrived when he was driven by accumulated emotion as much as the exigency of the case.

He had not often walked with her beyond the dark shade of the pinyons round the cottage, but this night, when he knew he must tell her, he led her away down the path, through the cedar grove to the west end of the valley where it was wild and lonely and sad and silent.

The moon was full and the great peaks were crowned as with snow. A coyote uttered his cutting cry. There were a few melancholy notes from a night bird of the stone walls. The air was clear and cold, with a tang of frost in it. Shefford gazed about him at the vast, uplifted, insulating walls, and that feeling of his which was more than a sense told him how walls like these and the silence and shadow and mystery had been nearly all of Fay Larkin's life. He felt them all in her.

He stopped out in the open, near the line where dark shadow of the wall met the silver moonlight on the grass, and here, by a huge flat stone where he had come often alone and sometimes with Ruth, he faced Fay Larkin in the spirit to tell her gently that he knew her, and sternly to force her secret from her.

"Am I your friend?" he began.

"Ah! My only friend," she said.

"Do you trust me, believe I mean well by you, want to help you?"

"Yes, indeed."

"Well, then, let me speak of you. You know one topic we've never touched upon. You!"

She was silent, and looked wonderingly, a little fearfully, at him, as if vague, disturbing thoughts were entering the fringe of her mind.

"Our friendship is a strange one, is it not?" he went on.

"How do I know? I never had any other friendship. What do you mean by strange?"

"Well, I'm a young man. You're a—a married woman. We are together a good deal—and like to be."

"Why is that strange?" she asked.

Suddenly Shefford realized that there was nothing strange in what was natural. A remnant of sophistication clung to him and that had spoken. He needed to speak to her in a way which in her simplicity she would understand.

"Never mind strange. Say that I am interested in you, and, as you're not happy, I want to help you. And say that your neighbors are curious and oppose my idea. Why do they?"

"They're jealous and want you themselves," she replied, with sweet directness. "They've said things I don't understand. But I felt they—they hated in me what would be all right in themselves."

Here to simplicity she added truth and wisdom, as an Indian might have expressed them. But shame was unknown to her, and she had as yet only vague perceptions of love and passion. Shefford began to realize the quickness of her mind, that she was indeed awakening.

"They are jealous—were jealous before I ever came here. That's only human nature. I was trying to get to a point. Your neighbors are curious. They oppose me. They hate you. It's all bound up in the—the fact of your difference from them, your youth, beauty, that you're not a Mormon, that you nearly betrayed their secret at the trial in Stonebridge."

"Please—please don't—speak of that!" she faltered.

"But I must," he replied, swiftly. "That trial was a torture to you. It revealed so much to me. . . . I know you are a sealed wife. I know there has been a crime. I know you've sacrificed yourself. I know that love and religion have nothing to do with—what you are. . . . Now, is not all that true?"

"I must not tell," she whispered.

"But I shall *make* you tell," he replied, and his voice rang.

"Oh no, you cannot," she said.

"I can—with just one word!"

Her eyes were great, starry, shadowy gulfs, dark in the white beauty of her face. She was calm now. She had strength. She invited him to speak the word, and the wistful, tremulous quiver of her lips was for his earnest thought of her.

"Wait—a—little," said Shefford, unsteadily. "I'll come to that presently. Tell me this—have you ever thought of being free?"

"Free!" she echoed, and there was singular depth and richness in her voice. That was the first spark of fire he had struck from her. "Long ago, the minute I was unwatched, I'd have leaped from a wall had I dared. Oh, I wasn't afraid. I'd love to die that way. But I never dared."

"Why?" queried Shefford, piercingly.

She was silent then.

"Suppose I offered to give you freedom that meant life?"

"I—couldn't—take it."

"Why?"

"Oh, my friend, don't ask me any more."

"I know, I can see—you want to tell me—you need to tell."

"But I daren't."

"Won't you trust me?"

"I do—I do."

"Then tell me."

"No—no—oh no!"

The moment had come. How sad, tragic, yet glorious for him! It would be like a magic touch upon this lovely, cold, white ghost of Fay Larkin, transforming her into a living, breathing girl. He held his love as a thing aloof, and, as such, intangible because of the living death she believed she lived, it had no warmth and intimacy for them. What might it not become with a lightning flash of revelation? He dreaded, yet he was driven to speak. He waited, swallowing hard, fighting the tumultuous storm of emotion, and his eyes dimmed.

"What did I come to this country for?" he asked, suddenly, in ringing, powerful voice.

"To find a girl," she whispered.

"I've found her!"

She began to shake. He saw a white hand go to her breast.

"Where is Surprise Valley? . . . How were you taken from Jane Withersteen and Lassiter? . . . I know they're alive. But where?"

She seemed to turn to stone.

"Fay! *Fay Larkin! . . . I know you!*" he cried, brokenly.

She slipped off the stone to her knees, swayed forward blindly with her hands reaching out, her head falling back to let the moon fall full upon the beautiful, snow-white, tragically convulsed face.

·13·

THE STORY
OF SURPRISE VALLEY

O
H, I REMEMBER so well! Even now I dream of it sometimes. I hear the roll and crash of falling rock—like thunder. . . ."

"We rode and rode. Then the horses fell. Uncle Jim took me in his arms and started up the cliff. Mother Jane climbed close after us. They kept looking back. Down there in the gray valley came the Mormons. I see the first one now. He rode a white horse. That was Tull. Oh, I remember so well! And I was five or six years old.

"We climbed up and up and into dark canyons and wound in and out. Then there was the narrow white trail, straight up, with the little cut steps and the great, red, ruined walls. I looked down over Uncle Jim's shoulder. I saw Mother Jane dragging herself up. Uncle Jim's blood spotted the trail. He reached a flat place at the top and fell with me. Mother Jane crawled up to us.

"Then she cried out and pointed. Tull was 'way below, climbing the trail. His men came behind him. Uncle Jim went to a great, tall rock and leaned against it. There was a bloody hole in his hand. He pushed the rock. It rolled down, banging the loose walls. They crashed and crashed—then all was terrible thunder and red smoke. I couldn't hear—I couldn't see.

"Uncle Jim carried me down and down out of the dark and dust into a beautiful valley all red and gold, with a wonderful arch of stone over the entrance.

"I don't remember well what happened then for what seemed a long, long time. I can feel how the place looked, but not so clear as it is now in my dreams. I seem to see myself with the dogs, and with Mother Jane, learning my letters, marking with red stone on the walls.

"But I remember now how I felt when I first understood we were shut in forever. Shut in Surprise Valley where Venters had lived so long. I was glad. The Mormons would never get me. I was seven or eight years old then. From that time all is clear in my mind.

"Venters had left supplies and tools and grain and cattle and burros, so we had a good start to begin life there. He had killed off the wildcats and kept the coyotes out, so the rabbits and quail multiplied till there were

346

thousands of them. We raised corn and fruit, and stored what we didn't use. Mother Jane taught me to read and write with the soft red stone that marked well on the walls.

"The years passed. We kept track of time pretty well. Uncle Jim's hair turned white and Mother Jane grew gray. Every day was like the one before. Mother Jane cried sometimes and Uncle Jim was sad because they could never be able to get me out of the valley. It was long before they stopped looking and listening for someone. Venters would come back, Uncle Jim always said. But Mother Jane did not think so.

"I loved Surprise Valley. I wanted to stay there always. I remembered Cottonwoods, how the children there hated me, and I didn't want to go back. The only unhappy times I ever had in the valley were when Ring and Whitie, my dogs, grew old and died. I roamed the valley. I climbed to every nook upon the mossy ledges. I learned to run up the steep cliffs. I could almost stick on the straight walls. Mother Jane called me a wild girl. We had put away the clothes we wore when we got there, to save them, and we made clothes of skins. I always laughed when I thought of my little dress—how I grew out of it. I think Uncle Jim and Mother Jane talked less as the years went by. And after I'd learned all she could teach me we didn't talk much. I used to scream into the caves just to hear my voice, and the echoes would frighten me.

"The older I grew the more I was alone. I was always running round the valley. I would climb to a high place and sit there for hours, doing nothing. I just watched and listened. I used to stay in the cliff-dwellers' caves and wonder about them. I loved to be out in the wind. And my happiest time was in the summer storms with the thunder echoes under the walls. At evening it was such a quiet place—after the night bird's cry, no sound. The quiet made me sad, but I loved it. I loved to watch the stars as I lay awake.

"So it was beautiful and happy for me there till—till . . .

"Two years or more ago there was a bad storm, and one of the great walls caved. The walls were always weathering, slipping. Many and many a time have I heard the rumble of an avalanche, but most of them were in other canyons. This slide in the valley made it possible, Uncle Jim said, for men to get down into the valley. But we could not climb out unless helped from above. Uncle Jim never rested well after that. But it never worried me.

"One day, over a year ago, while I was across the valley, I heard strange shouts, and then screams. I ran to our camp. I came upon men with ropes and guns. Uncle Jim was tied, and a rope was round his neck. Mother Jane was lying on the ground. I thought she was dead until I heard her moan. I was not afraid. I screamed and flew at Uncle Jim to tear the ropes off him. The men held me back. They called me a pretty cat. Then they talked together, and some were for hanging Lassiter—that was the first time I ever knew any name for him but Uncle Jim—and some were for leaving

him in the valley. Finally they decided to hang him. But Mother Jane
pleaded so and I screamed and fought so that they left off. Then they
went away and we saw them climb out of the valley.

"Uncle Jim said they were Mormons, and some among them had been
born in Cottonwoods. I was not told why they had such a terrible hate for
him. He said they would come back and kill him. Uncle Jim had no guns
to fight with.

"We watched and watched. In five days they did come back, with more
men, and some of them wore black masks. They came to our cave with
ropes and guns. One was tall. He had a cruel voice. The others ran to
obey him. I could see white hair and sharp eyes behind the mask. The
men caught me and brought me before him.

"He said Lassiter had killed many Mormons. He said Lassiter had killed
his father and should be hanged. But Lassiter would be let live and
Mother Jane could stay with him, both prisoners there in the valley, if I
would marry the Mormon. I must marry him, accept the Mormon faith,
and bring up my children as Mormons. If I refused they would hang
Lassiter, leave the heretic Jane Withersteen alone in the valley, and take
me and break me to their rule.

"I agreed. But Mother Jane absolutely forbade me to marry him. Then
the Mormons took me away. It nearly killed me to leave Uncle Jim and
Mother Jane. I was carried and lifted out of the valley, and rode a long
way on a horse. They brought me here, to the cabin where I live, and I
have never been away except that—that time—to—Stonebridge. Only
little by little did I learn my position. Bishop Kane was kind, but stern,
because I could not be quick to learn the faith.

"I am not a sealed wife. But they're trying to make me one. The master
Mormon—he visited me often—at night—till lately. He threatened me.
He never told me a name—except Saint George. I don't—know him—
except his voice. I never—saw his face—in the light!"

Fay Larkin ended her story. Toward its close Shefford had grown involuntarily restless, and when her last tragic whisper ceased all his body seemed
shaken with a terrible violence of his joy. He strode to and fro in the dark
shadow of the stone. The receding blood left him cold, with a pricking,
sickening sensation over his body, but there seemed to be an overwhelming tide accumulating deep in his breast—a tide of passion and pain. He
dominated the passion, but the ache remained. And he returned to the
quiet figure on the stone.

"Fay Larkin!" he exclaimed, with a deep breath of relief that the secret
was disclosed. "So you're not a wife! . . . You're free! Thank heaven!
But I felt it was sacrifice. I knew there had been a crime. For crime it is.
You child! You can't understand what crime. Oh, almost I wish you and
Jane and Lassiter had never been found. But that's wrong of me. One year
of agony—that shall not ruin your life. Fay, I will take you away."

"Where?" she whispered.

"Away from this Mormon country—to the East," he replied, and he spoke of what he had known, of travel, of cities, of people, of happiness possible for a young girl who had spent all her life hidden between the narrow walls of a silent, lonely valley—he spoke swiftly and eloquently till he lost his breath.

There was an instant of flashing wonder and joy on her white face, and then the radiance paled, the glow died. Her soul was the darker for that one strange, leaping glimpse of a glory not for such as she.

"I must stay here," she said, shudderingly.

"Fay!—How strange to *say* Fay aloud to *you!*—Fay, do you know the way to Surprise Valley?"

"I don't know where it is, but I could go straight to it," she replied.

"Take me there. Show me your beautiful valley. Let me see where you ran and climbed and spent so many lonely years."

"Ah, how I'd love to! But I dare not. And why should you want me to take you? We can run and climb here."

"I want to—I mean to save Jane Withersteen and Lassiter," he declared.

She uttered a little cry of pain. "Save them?"

"Yes, save them. Get them out of the valley, take them out of the country, far away where they and *you*—"

"But I can't go," she wailed. "I'm afraid. I'm bound. It *can't* be broken. If I dared—if I tried to go they would catch me. They would hang Uncle Jim and leave Mother Jane alone there to starve."

"Fay, Lassiter and Jane both will starve—at least they will die there if we do not save them. You have been terribly wronged. You're a slave. You're not a wife."

"They—said I'll be burned in hell if I don't marry him. . . . Mother Jane never taught me about God. I don't know. But *he*—he said God was there. I dare not break it."

"Fay, you have been deceived by old men. Let them have their creed. But *you* mustn't accept it."

"John, what is God to you?"

"Dear child, I—I am not sure of that myself," he replied, huskily. "When all this trouble is behind us, surely I can help you to understand and you can help me. The fact that you are alive—that Lassiter and Jane are alive—that I shall save you all—that lifts me up. I tell you—Fay Larkin will be my salvation."

"Your words trouble me. Oh, I shall be torn one way and another. . . . But, John, I daren't run away. I will not tell you where to find Lassiter and Mother Jane."

"I shall find them. I have the Indian. He found you for me. Nas Ta Bega will find Surprise Valley."

"Nas Ta Bega! . . . Oh, I remember. There was an Indian with the Mormons who found us. But he was a Piute."

"Nas Ta Bega never told me how he learned about you. That he learned was enough. And, Fay, he will find Surprise Valley. He will save Uncle Jim and Mother Jane."

Fay's hands clasped Shefford's in strong, trembling pressure; the tears streamed down her white cheeks; a tragic and eloquent joy convulsed her face.

"Oh, my friend, save them! But I can't go. . . . Let them keep me! Let him kill me!"

"Him! Fay—he shall not harm you," replied Shefford in passionate earnestness.

She caught the hand he had struck out with.

"You talk—you look like Uncle Jim when he spoke of the Mormons," she said. "Then I used to be afraid of him. He was so different. John, you must not do anything about me. Let me be. It's too late. He—and his men —they would hang you. And I couldn't bear that. I've enough to bear without losing my friend. Say you won't watch and wait—for—for him."

Shefford had to promise her. Like an Indian she gave expression to primitive feeling, for it certainly never occurred to her that, whatever Shefford might do, he was not the kind of man to wait in hiding for an enemy. Fay had faltered through her last speech and was now weak and nervous and frightened. Shefford took her back to the cabin.

"Fay, don't be distressed," he said. "I won't do anything right away. You can trust me. I won't be rash. I'll consult you before I make a move. I haven't any idea what I could do, anyway. . . . You must bear up. Why, it looks as if you're sorry I found you."

"Oh! I'm glad!" she whispered.

"Then if you're glad you mustn't break down this way again. Suppose some of the women happened to run into us."

"I won't again. It's only you—you surprised me so. I used to think how I'd like you to know—I wasn't really dead. But now—it's different. It hurts me here. Yet I'm glad if my being alive makes you a little happier."

Shefford felt that he had to go then. He could not trust himself any further.

"Good night, Fay," he said.

"Good night, John," she whispered. "I promise—to be good tomorrow."

She was crying softly when he left her. Twice he turned to see the dim, white, slender form against the gloom of the cabin. Then he went on under the pinyons, blindly down the path, with his heart as heavy as lead. That night as he rolled in his blanket and stretched wearily he felt that he would never be able to sleep. The wind in the cedars made him shiver. The great stars seemed relentless, passionless, white eyes, mocking his little destiny and his pain. The huge shadow of the mountain resembled the shadow of the insurmountable barrier between Fay and him.

Her pitiful, childish promise to be good was in his mind when he went to her home on the next night. He wondered how she would be, and he realized a desperate need of self-control.

But that night Fay Larkin was a different girl. In the dark, before she spoke, he felt a difference that afforded him surprise and relief. He greeted her as usual. And then it seemed, though not at all clearly, that he was listening to a girl, strangely and unconsciously glad to see him, who spoke with deeper note in her voice, who talked where always she had listened, whose sadness was there under an eagerness, a subdued gaiety as new to her, as sweet as it was bewildering. And he responded with emotion, so that the hour passed swiftly, and he found himself back in camp, in a kind of dream, unable to remember much of what she had said, sure only of this strange sweetness suddenly come to her.

Upon the following night, however, he discovered what had wrought this singular change in Fay Larkin. She loved him and she did not know it. How passionately sweet and sad and painful was that realization for Shefford! The hour spent with her then was only a moment.

He walked under the stars that night and they shed a glorious light upon him. He tried to think, to plan, but the sweetness of remembered word or look made mental effort almost impossible. He got as far as the thought that he would do well to drift, to wait till she learned she loved him, and then, perhaps, she could be persuaded to let him take her and Lassiter and Jane away together.

And from that night he went at his work and the part he played in the village with a zeal and a cunning that left him free to seek Fay when he chose.

Sometimes in the afternoon, always for a while in the evening, he was with her. They climbed the walls, and sat upon a lonely height to look afar; they walked under the stars, and the cedars, and the shadows of the great cliffs. She had a beautiful mind. Listening to her, he imagined he saw down into beautiful Surprise Valley with all its weird shadows, its colored walls and painted caves, its golden shafts of morning light and the red haze at sunset; and he felt the silence that must have been there, and the singing of the wind in the cliffs, and the sweetness and fragrance of the flowers, and the wildness of it all. Love had worked a marvelous transformation in this girl who had lived her life in a canyon. The burden upon her did not weigh heavily. She could not have an unhappy thought. She spoke of the village, of her Mormon companions, of daily happenings, of Stonebridge, of many things in a matter-of-fact way that showed how little they occupied her mind. She even spoke of sealed wives in a kind of dreamy abstraction. Something had possession of her, something as strong as the nature which had developed her, and in its power she, in her simplicity, was utterly unconscious, a watching and feeling girl. A strange, witching, radiant beauty lurked in her smile. And Shefford heard her laugh in his dreams.

The weeks slipped by. The black mountain took on a white cap of snow; in the early mornings there was ice in the crevices on the heights and frost in the valley. In the sheltered canyons where sunshine seemed to linger it was warm and pleasant, so that winter did not kill the flowers.

Shefford waited so long for Fay's awakening that he believed it would never come, and, believing, had not the heart to force it upon her. Then there was a growing fear with him. What would Fay Larkin do when she awakened to the truth? Fay was indeed like that white and fragile lily which bloomed in the silent, lonely canyons, but the same nature that had created it had created her. Would she droop as the lily would in a furnace blast? More than that, he feared a sudden flashing into life of strength, power, passion, hate. She did not hate yet because she did not yet realize love. She was utterly innocent of any wrong having been done her. More and more he began to fear, and a foreboding grew upon him. He made up his mind to broach the subject of Surprise Valley and of escaping with Lassiter and Jane; still, every time he was with Fay the girl and her beauty and her love were so wonderful that he put off the ordeal till the next night. As time flew by he excused his vacillation on the score that winter was not a good time to try to cross the desert. There was no grass for the mustangs, except in well-known valleys, and these he must shun. Spring would soon come. So the days passed, and he loved Fay more all the time, desperately living out to its limit the sweetness of every moment with her, and paying for his bliss in the increasing trouble that beset him when once away from her charm.

One starry night, about ten o'clock, he went, as was his custom, to drink at the spring. Upon his return to the cedars Nas Ta Bega, who slept under the same tree with him, had arisen, with his blanket hanging half off his shoulder.

"Listen," said the Indian.

Shefford took one glance at the dark, somber face, with its inscrutable eyes, now so strange and piercing, and then, with a kind of cold excitement, he faced the way the Indian looked, and listened. But he heard only the soft moan of the night wind in the cedars.

Nas Ta Bega kept the rigidity of his position for a moment, and then he relaxed, and stood at ease. Shefford knew the Indian had made a certainty of what must have been a doubtful sound. And Shefford leaned his ear to the wind and strained his hearing.

Then the soft night breeze brought a faint patter—the slow trot of horses on a hard trail. Someone was coming into the village at a late hour. Shefford thought of Joe Lake. But Joe lay right behind him, asleep in his blankets. It could not be Withers, for the trader was in Durango at that time. Shefford thought of Willetts and Shadd.

"Who's coming?" he asked low of the Indian.

Nas Ta Bega pointed down the trail without speaking.

Shefford peered through the white dim haze of starlight and presently he made out moving figures. Horses, with riders—a string of them—one—two—three—four—five—and he counted up to eleven. Eleven horsemen riding into the village! He was amazed, and suddenly keenly anxious. This visit might be one of Shadd's raids.

"Shadd's gang!" he whispered.

"No, Bi Nai," replied Nas Ta Bega, and he drew Shefford farther into the shade of the cedars. His voice, his action, the way he kept a hand on Shefford's shoulder, all this told much to the young man.

Mormons come on a night visit! Shefford realized it with a slight shock. Then swift as a lightning flash he was rent by another shock—one that brought cold moisture to his brow and to his heart a flame of hell.

He was shaking when he sank down to find the support of a log. Like a shadow the Indian silently moved away. Shefford watched the eleven horses pass the camp, go down the road, to disappear in the village. They vanished, and the soft clip-clops of hoofs died away. There was nothing left to prove he had not dreamed.

Nothing to prove it except this sudden terrible demoralization of his physical and spiritual being! While he peered out into the valley, toward the black patch of cedars and pinyons that hid the cabins, moments and moments passed, and in them he was gripped with cold and fire.

Was the Mormon who had abducted Fay—the man with the cruel voice—was he among those eleven horsemen? He might not have been. What a torturing hope! But vain—vain, for inevitably he must be among them. He was there in the cabin already. He had dismounted, tied his horse, had knocked on her door. Did he need to knock? No, he would go in, he would call her in that cruel voice, and then . . .

Shefford pulled a blanket from his bed and covered his cold and trembling body. He had sunk down off the log, was leaning back upon it. The stars were pale, far off, and the valley seemed unreal. He found himself listening—listening with sick and terrible earnestness, trying to hear against the thrum and beat of his heart, straining to catch a sound in all that cold, star-blanched, silent valley. But he could hear no sound. It was as if death held the valley in its perfect silence. How he hated that silence! There ought to have been a million horrible, bellowing demons making the night hideous. Did the stars serenely look down upon the lonely cabins of these exiles? Was there no thunderbolt to drop down from that dark and looming mountain upon the silent cabin where tragedy had entered? In all the world, under the sea, in the abysmal caves, in the vast spaces of the air, there was no such terrible silence as this. A scream, a long cry, a moan—these were natural to a woman, and why did

not one of these sealed wives, why did not Fay Larkin, damn this everlasting acquiescent silence? Perhaps she would fly out of her cabin, come
running along the path. Shefford peered into the bright patches of starlight and into the shadows of the cedars. But he saw no moving form in
the open, no dim white shape against the gloom. And he heard no sound
—not even a whisper of wind in the branches overhead.

Nas Ta Bega returned to the shade of the cedars and, lying down on his
blankets, covered himself and went to sleep. The fact seemed to bring
bitter reality to Shefford. Nothing was going to happen. The valley was to
be the same this night as any other night. Shefford accepted the truth. He
experienced a kind of self-pity. The night he had thought so much about,
prepared for, and had forgotten had now arrived. Then he threw another
blanket round him, and, cold, dark, grim, he faced that lonely vigil,
meaning to sit there, wide-eyed, to endure and to wait.

Jealousy and pain, following his frenzy, abided with him long hours,
and when they passed he divined that selfishness passed with them. What
he suffered then was for Fay Larkin and for her sisters in misfortune. He
grew big enough to pity these fanatics. The fiery, racing tide of blood that
had made of him only an animal had cooled with thought of others. Still
he feared that stultifying thing which must have been hate. What a
tempest had raged within him! This blood of his, that had received a
stronger strain from his desert life, might in a single moment flood out
reason and intellect and make him a vengeful man. So in those starlit
hours that dragged interminably he looked deep into his heart and tried
to fortify himself against a dark and evil moment to come.

Midnight—and the valley seemed a tomb! Did he alone keep wakeful?
The sky was a darker blue, the stars burned a whiter fire, the peaks stood
looming and vast, tranquil sentinels of that valley, and the wind rose to
sigh, to breathe, to mourn through the cedars. It was a sad music. The
Indian lay prone, dark face to the stars. Joe Lake lay prone, sleeping as
quietly, with his dark face exposed to the starlight. The gentle movement
of the cedar branches changed the shape of the bright patches on the
grass where shadow and light met. The walls of the valley waved upward,
dark below and growing paler, to shine faintly at the rounded rims. And
there was a tiny, silvery tinkle of running water over stones.

Here was a little nook of the vast world. Here were tranquillity, beauty,
music, loneliness, life. Shefford wondered—did he alone keep watchful?
Did he feel that he could see dark, wide eyes peering into the gloom? And
it came to him after a time that he was not alone in his vigil, nor was Fay
Larkin alone in her agony. There was someone else in the valley, a great
and breathing and watchful spirit. It entered into Shefford's soul and he
trembled. What had come to him? And he answered—only added pain
and new love, and a strange strength from the firmament and the peaks
and the silence and the shadows.

The bright belt with its three radiant stars sank behind the western wall and there was a paler gloom upon the valley.

Then a few lights twinkled in the darkness that enveloped the cabins; a woman's laugh strangely broke the silence, profaning it, giving the lie to that somber yoke which seemed to consist of the very shadows; the voices of men were heard, and then the slow clip-clop of trotting horses on the hard trail.

Shefford saw the Mormons file out into the paling starlight, ride down the valley, and vanish in the gray gloom. He was aware that the Indian sat up to watch the procession ride by, and that Joe turned over, as if disturbed.

One by one the stars went out. The valley became a place of gray shadows. In the east a light glowed. Shefford sat there, haggard and worn, watching the coming of the dawn, the kindling of the light; and had the power been his the dawn would never have broken and the rose and gold never have tipped the lofty peaks.

Shefford attended to his camp chores as usual. Several times he was aware of Joe's close scrutiny, and finally, without looking at him, Shefford told of the visit of the Mormons. A violent expulsion of breath was Joe's answer and it might have been a curse. Straightway Joe ceased his cheery whistling and became as somber as the Indian. The camp was silent; the men did not look at one another. While they sat at breakfast Shefford's back was turned toward the village; he had not looked in that direction since dawn.

"Ugh!" suddenly exclaimed Nas Ta Bega.

Joe Lake muttered low and deep, and this time there was no mistake about the nature of his speech. Shefford did not have the courage to turn to see what had caused these exclamations. He knew since today had dawned that there was calamity in the air.

"Shefford, I reckon if I know women there's a little hell coming to you," said the Mormon, significantly.

Shefford wheeled as if a powerful force had turned him on a pivot. He saw Fay Larkin. She seemed to be almost running. She was unhooded and her bright hair streamed down. Her swift, lithe action was without its usual grace. She looked wild, and she almost fell crossing the stepping-stones of the brook.

Joe hurried to meet her, took hold of her arm and spoke, but she did not seem to hear him. She drew him along with her, up the little bench under the cedars straight toward Shefford. Her face held a white, mute agony, as if in the hour of strife it had hardened into marble. But her eyes were dark-purple fire—windows of an extraordinarily intense and vital life. In one night the girl had become a woman. But the blight Shefford had dreaded to see—the withering of the exquisite soul and spirit and purity he had considered inevitable, just as inevitable as the death of something similar in the flower she resembled, when it was broken and defiled—nothing of this was manifest in her. Straight and swiftly she came to him back in the shade of the cedars and took hold of his hands.

"Last night—*he came!*" she said.

"Yes—Fay—I—I know," replied Shefford, haltingly.

He was tremblingly conscious of amaze at her—of something wonderful in her. She did not heed Joe, who stepped aside a little; she did not see Nas Ta Bega, who sat motionless on a log, apparently oblivious to her presence.

"You knew he came?"

"Yes, Fay. I was awake when—they rode in. I watched them. I sat up all night. I saw them ride away."

"If you knew when he came why didn't you run to me—to get to me before he did?"

Her question was unanswerable. It had the force of a blow. It stunned him. Its sharp, frank directness sprang from a simplicity and a strength that had not been nurtured in the life he had lived. So far men had wandered from truth and nature!

"I came to you as soon as I was able," she went on. "I must have fainted. I just had to drag myself around. . . . And now I can tell you."

He was powerless to reply, as if she had put another unanswerable question. What did she mean to tell him? What might she not tell him? She loosed her hands from his and lifted them to his shoulders, and that was the first conscious action of feeling, of intimacy, which she had ever shown. It quite robbed Shefford of strength, and in spite of his sorrow there was an indefinable thrill in her touch. He looked at her, saw the white-and-gold beauty that was hers yesterday and seemed changed today, and he recognized Fay Larkin in a woman he did not know.

"Listen! He came—"

"Fay, don't—tell me," interrupted Shefford.

"I *will* tell you," she said.

Did the instinct of love teach her how to mitigate his pain? Shefford felt that, as he felt the new-born strength in her.

"Listen," she went on. "He came when I was undressing for bed. I heard the horse. He knocked on the door. Something terrible happened to me then. I felt sick and my head wasn't clear. I remember next—his being in the room—the lamp was out—I couldn't see very well. He thought I was sick and he gave me a drink and let the air blow in on me through the window. I remember I lay back in the chair and I thought. And I listened. When would you come? I didn't feel that you could leave me there alone with him. For his coming was different this time. That pain like a blade in my side! . . . When it came I was not the same. I loved you. I understood then. I belonged to you. I couldn't let him touch me. I had never been his wife. When I realized this—that he was there, that you might suffer for it—I cried right out.

"He thought I was sick. He worked over me. He gave me medicine. And then he prayed. I saw him, in the dark, on his knees, praying for me. That seemed strange. Yet he was kind, so kind that I begged him to let me go. I was not a Mormon. I couldn't marry him. I begged him to let me go.

"Then he thought I had been deceiving him. He fell into a fury. He talked for a long time. He called upon God to visit my sins upon me. He tried to make me pray. But I wouldn't. And then—I fought him. I'd have screamed for you had he not smothered me. I got weak. . . . And you never came. I know I thought you would come. But you didn't. Then I—I gave out. And after—some time—I must have fainted."

"Fay! For Heaven's sake, how could I come to you?" burst out Shefford, hoarse and white with remorse, passion, pain.

"If I'm any man's wife I'm yours. It's a thing you *feel*, isn't it? I know that now. . . . But I want to know what to do!"

"Fay!" he cried, huskily.

"I'm sick of it all. If it weren't for you I'd climb the wall and throw myself off. That would be easy for me. I'd love to die that way. All my life I've been high up on the walls. To fall would be nothing!"

"Oh, you mustn't talk like that!"

"Do you love me?" she asked, with a low and deathless sweetness.

"Love you? With all my heart! Nothing can change that!"

"Do you want me—as you used to want the Fay Larkin lost in Surprise Valley? Do you love me that way? I understand things better than before, but still—not all. I *am* Fay Larkin. I think I must have dreamed of you all my life. I was glad when you came here. I've been happy lately. I forgot— till last night. Maybe it needed that to make me see I've loved you all the time. . . . And I fought him like a wildcat! . . . Tell me the truth. I *feel* I'm yours. Is that true? If I'm not—I'll not live another hour. Something holds me up. I am the same. . . . Do you want me?"

"Yes, Fay Larkin, I want you," replied Shefford, steadily, with his grip on her arms.

"Then take me away. I don't want to live here another hour."

"Fay, I'll take you. But it can't be done at once. We must plan. I need help. There are Lassiter and Jane to get out of Surprise Valley. Give me time, dear—give me time. It'll be a hard job. And we must plan so we can positively get away. Give me time, Fay."

"Suppose *he* comes back?" she queried, with a singular depth of voice.

"We'll have to risk that," replied Shefford, miserably. "But—he won't come soon."

"He said he would," she flashed.

Shefford seemed to freeze inwardly with her words. Love had made her a woman and now the woman in her was speaking. She saw the truth as he could not see it. And the truth was nature. She had been hidden all her life from the world, from knowledge as he had it, yet when love betrayed her womanhood to her she acquired all its subtlety.

"If I wait and he *does* come will you keep me from him?" she asked.

"How can I? I'm staking all on the chance of his not coming soon. . . . But, Fay, if he does come and I don't give up our secret—how on earth can I keep you from him?" demanded Shefford.

"If you love me you will do it," she said, as simply as if she were fate.

"But how?" cried Shefford, almost beside himself.

"You are a man. Any man would save the woman who loves him from —from—Oh, from a beast! . . . How would Lassiter do it?"

"Lassiter!"

"You can kill him!"

It was there, deep and full in her voice, the strength of the elemental forces that had surrounded her, primitive passion and hate and love, as they were in woman in the beginning.

"My God!" Shefford cried aloud with his spirit when all that was red in him sprang again into a flame of hell. That was what had been wrong with him last night. He could kill this stealthy night-rider, and now, face to face with Fay, who had never been so beautiful and wonderful as in this hour when she made love the only and the sacred thing of life, now he had it in him to kill. Yet, murder—even to kill a brute—that was not for John Shefford, not the way for him to save a woman. Reason and wisdom still fought the passion in him. If he could but cling to them—have them with him in the dark and contending hour!

She leaned against him now, exhausted, her soul in her eyes, and they saw only him. Shefford was all but powerless to resist the longing to take her into his arms, to hold her to his heart, to let himself go. Did not her love give her to him? Shefford gazed helplessly at the stricken Joe Lake, at the somber Indian, as if from them he expected help.

"I know him now," said Fay, breaking the silence with startling suddenness.

"What!"

"I've seen him in the light. I flashed a candle in his face. I saw it. I know him now. He was there at Stonebridge with us, and I never knew him. But I know him now. His name is—"

"For God's sake don't tell me who he is!" implored Shefford.

Ignorance was Shefford's safeguard against himself. To make a name of this heretofore intangible man, to give him an identity apart from the crowd, to be able to recognize him—that for Shefford would be fatal.

"Fay—tell me—no more," he said, brokenly. "I love you and I will give you my life. Trust me. I swear I'll save you."

"Will you take me away soon?"

"Yes."

She appeared satisfied with that and dropped her hands and moved back from him. A light flitted over her white face, and her eyes grew dark and humid, losing their fire in changing, shadowing thought of submission, of trust, of hope.

"I can lead you to Surprise Valley," she said. "I feel the way. It's there!" And she pointed to the west.

"Fay, we'll go—soon. I must plan. I'll see you tonight. Then we'll talk. Run home now, before some of the women see you here."

She said goodbye and started away under the cedars, out into the open where her hair shone like gold in the sunlight, and she took the stepping-stones with her old free grace, and strode down the path swift and lithe as an Indian. Once she turned to wave a hand.

Shefford watched her with a torture of pride, love, hope, and fear contending within him.

⅓14⅔

THE NAVAJO

THAT MORNING a Piute rode into the valley. Shefford recognized him as the brave who had been in love with Glen Naspa. The moment Nas Ta Bega saw this visitor he made a singular motion with his hands—a motion that somehow to Shefford suggested despair—and then he waited, somber and statuesque, for the messenger to come to him. It was the Piute who did all the talking, and that was brief. Then the Navajo stood motionless, with his hands crossed over his breast. Shefford drew near and waited.

"Bi Nai," said the Navajo, "Nas Ta Bega said his sister would come home some day. . . . Glen Naspa is in the hogan of her grandfather."

He spoke in his usual slow, guttural voice, and he might have been bronze for all the emotion he expressed; yet Shefford instinctively felt the despair that had been hinted to him, and he put his hand on the Indian's shoulder.

"If I am the Navajo's brother, then I am brother to Glen Naspa," he said. "I will go with you to the hogan of Hosteen Doetin."

Nas Ta Bega went away into the valley for the horses. Shefford hurried to the village, made his excuses at the school, and then called to explain to Fay that trouble of some kind had come to the Indian.

Soon afterward he was riding Nack-yal on the rough and winding trail up through the broken country of cliffs and canyons to the great league-long sage and cedar slope of the mountain. It was weeks since he had ridden the mustang. Nack-yal was fat and lazy. He loved his master, but he did not like the climb, and so fell far behind the lean and wiry pony that carried Nas Ta Bega. The sage levels were as purple as the haze of the distance, and there was a bittersweet tang on the strong, cool wind. The sun was gold behind the dark line of fringe on the mountaintop. A flock of sheep swept down one of the sage levels, looking like a narrow stream of white and black and brown. It was always amazing for Shefford to see how swiftly these Navajo sheep grazed along. Wild mustangs plunged out of the cedar clumps and stood upon the ridges, whistling defiance or curiosity, and their manes and tails waved in the wind.

Shefford mounted slowly to the cedar bench in the midst of which were hidden the few hogans. And he halted at the edge to dismount and take a look at that downward-sweeping world of color, of wide space, at the wild desert upland which from there unrolled its magnificent panorama.

Then he passed on into the cedars. How strange to hear the lambs bleating again! Lambing-time had come early, but still spring was there in the new green of grass, in the bright upland flower. He led his mustang out of the cedars into the cleared circle. It was full of colts and lambs, and there were the shepherd-dogs and a few old rams and ewes. But the circle was a quiet place this day. There were no Indians in sight. Shefford loosened the saddle-girths on Nack-yal and, leaving him to graze, went toward the hogan of Hosteen Doetin. A blanket was hung across the door. Shefford heard a low chanting. He waited beside the door till the covering was pulled in, then he entered.

Hosteen Doetin met him, clasped his hand. The old Navajo could not speak; his fine face was working in grief; tears streamed from his dim old eyes and rolled down his wrinkled cheeks. His sorrow was no different from a white man's sorrow. Beyond him Shefford saw Nas Ta Bega standing with folded arms, somehow terrible in his somber impassiveness. At his feet crouched the old woman, Hosteen Doetin's wife, and beside her, prone and quiet, half covered with a blanket, lay Glen Naspa.

She was dead. To Shefford she seemed older than when he had last seen her. And she was beautiful. Calm, cold, dark, with only bitter lips to give the lie to peace! There was a story in those lips.

At her side, half hidden under the fold of blanket, lay a tiny bundle. Its human shape startled Shefford. Then he did not need to be told the tragedy. When he looked again at Glen Naspa's face he seemed to understand all that had made her older, to feel the pain that had lined and set her lips.

She was dead, and she was the last of Nas Ta Bega's family. In the old grandfather's agony, in the wild chant of the stricken grandmother, in the brother's stern and terrible calmness Shefford felt more than the death of a loved one. The shadow of ruin, of doom, of death hovered over the girl and her family and her tribe and her race. There was no consolation to offer these relatives of Glen Naspa. Shefford took one more fascinated gaze at her dark, eloquent, prophetic face, at the tragic tiny shape by her side, and then with bowed head he left the hogan.

Outside he paced to and fro, with an aching heart for Nas Ta Bega, with something of the white man's burden of crime toward the Indian weighing upon his soul.

Old Hosteen Doetin came to him with shaking hands and words memorable of the time Glen Naspa left his hogan.

"Me no savvy Jesus Christ. Me hungry. Me no eat Jesus Christ!"

That seemed to be all of his trouble that he could express to Shefford. He could not understand the religion of the missionary, this Jesus Christ who had called his granddaughter away. And the great fear of an old Indian was not death, but hunger. Shefford remembered a custom of the Navajos, a thing barbarous looked at with a white man's mind. If an old Indian failed on a long march he was enclosed by a wall of stones, given plenty to eat and drink, and left there to die in the desert. Not death did he fear, but hunger! Old Hosteen Doetin expected to starve, now that the young and strong squaw of his family was gone.

Shefford spoke in his halting Navajo and assured the old Indian that Nas Ta Bega would never let him starve.

At sunset Shefford stood with Nas Ta Bega facing the west. The Indian was magnificent in repose. He watched the sun go down upon the day that had seen the burial of the last of his family. He resembled an impassive destiny, upon which no shocks fell. He had the light of that flaring golden sky in his face, the majesty of the mountain in his mien, the silence of the great gulf below on his lips. This educated Navajo, who had reverted to the life of his ancestors, found in the wildness and loneliness of his environment a strength no white teaching could ever have given him. Shefford sensed in him a measureless grief, an impenetrable gloom, a tragic acceptance of the meaning of Glen Naspa's ruin and death—the vanishing of his race from the earth. Death had written the law of such bitter truth round Glen Naspa's lips, and the same truth was here in the grandeur and gloom of the Navajo.

"Bi Nai," he said, with the beautiful sonorous roll in his voice, "Glen Naspa is in her grave and there are no paths to the place of her sleep. Glen Naspa is gone."

"Gone! Where? Nas Ta Bega, remember I lost my own faith, and I have not yet learned yours."

"The Navajo has one mother—the earth. Her body has gone to the earth and it will become dust. But her spirit is in the air. It shall whisper to me from the wind. I shall hear it on running waters. It will hide in the morning music of a mockingbird and in the lonely night cry of the canyon hawk. Her blood will go to make the red of the Indian flowers and her soul will rest at midnight in the lily that opens only to the moon. She will wait in the shadow for me, and live in the great mountain that is my home, and forever step behind me on the trail."

"You will kill Willetts?" demanded Shefford.

"The Navajo will not seek the missionary."

"But if you meet him you'll kill him?"

"Bi Nai, would Nas Ta Bega kill after it is too late? What good could come? The Navajo is above revenge."

"If he crosses my trail I think I couldn't help but kill him," muttered Shefford in a passion that wrung the threat from him.

The Indian put his arm round the white man's shoulders.

"Bi Nai, long ago I made you my brother. And now you make me your brother. Is it not so? Glen Naspa's spirit calls for wisdom, not revenge. Willetts must be a bad man. But we'll let him live. Life will punish him. Who knows if he was all to blame? Glen Naspa was only one pretty Indian girl. There are many white men in the desert. She loved a white man when she was a baby. The thing was a curse. . . . Listen, Bi Nai, and the Navajo will talk.

"Many years ago the Spanish padres, the first white men, came into the land of the Indian. Their search was for gold. But they were not wicked men. They did not steal and kill. They taught the Indian many useful things. They brought him horses. But when they went away they left him unsatisfied with his life and his god.

"Then came the pioneers. They crossed the great river and took the pasture-lands and the hunting-grounds of the Indian. They drove him backward, and the Indian grew sullen. He began to fight. The white man's government made treaties with the Indian, and these were broken. Then war came—fierce and bloody war. The Indian was driven to the waste places. The stream of pioneers, like a march of ants, spread on into the desert. Every valley where grass grew, every river, became a place for farms and towns. Cattle chocked the waterholes where the buffalo and deer had once gone to drink. The forests in the hills were cut and the springs dried up. And the pioneers followed to the edge of the desert.

"Then came the prospectors, mad, like the padres, for the gleam of gold. The day was not long enough for them to dig in the creeks and the canyons; they worked in the night. And they brought weapons and rum to the Indian, to buy from him the secret of the places where the shining gold lay hidden.

"Then came the traders. And they traded with the Indian. They gave him little for much, and that little changed his life. He learned a taste for the sweet foods of the white man. Because he could trade for a sack of flour he worked less in the field. And the very fiber of his bones softened.

"Then came the missionaries. They were proselytizers for converts to their religion. The missionaries are good men. There may be a bad missionary, like Willetts, the same as there are bad men in other callings, or bad Indians. They say Shadd is a half-breed. But the Piutes can tell you he is a full-blood, and he, like me, was sent to a white man's school. In the beginning the missionaries did well for the Indian. They taught him cleaner ways of living, better farming, useful work with tools—many good things. But the wrong to the Indian was the undermining of his faith. It was not humanity that sent the missionary to the Indian. Humanity would have helped the Indian in his ignorance of sickness and work, and left him his god. For to trouble the Indian about his god worked at the roots of his nature.

"The beauty of the Indian's life is in his love of the open, of all that is nature, of silence, freedom, wildness. It is a beauty of mind and soul. The Indian would have been content to watch and feel. To a white man he might be dirty and lazy—content to dream life away without trouble or what the white man calls evolution. The Indian might seem cruel because he leaves his old father out in the desert to die. But the old man wants to die that way, alone with his spirits and the sunset. And the white man's medicine keeps his old father alive days and days after he ought to be dead. Which is more cruel? The Navajos used to fight with other tribes, and then they were stronger men than they are today.

"But leaving religion, greed, and war out of the question, contact with the white man would alone have ruined the Indian. The Indian and the white man cannot mix. The Indian brave learns the habits of the white man, acquires his diseases, and has not the mind or body to withstand them. The Indian girl learns to love the white man—and that is death of her Indian soul, if not of life.

"So the red man is passing. Tribes once powerful have died in the life of Nas Ta Bega. The curse of the white man is already heavy upon my race in the south. Here in the north, in the wildest corner of the desert, chased here by the great soldier, Carson, the Navajo has made his last stand.

"Bi Nai, you have seen the shadow in the hogan of Hosteen Doetin. Glen Naspa has gone to her grave, and no sisters, no children, will make paths to the place of her sleep. Nas Ta Bega will never have a wife—a child. He sees the end. It is the sunset of the Navajo. . . . Bi Nai, the Navajo is dying—dying—dying!"

⁘15⁘

WILD JUSTICE

A CRESCENT moon hung above the lofty peak over the valley and a train of white stars ran along the bold rim of the western wall. A few young frogs peeped plaintively. The night was cool, yet had a touch of balmy spring, and a sweeter fragrance, as if the cedars and pinyons had freshened in the warm sun of that day.

Shefford and Fay were walking in the aisles of moonlight and the patches of shade, and Nas Ta Bega, more than ever a shadow of his white brother, followed them silently.

"Fay, it's growing late. Feel the dew?" said Shefford. "Come, I must take you back."

"But the time's so short. I have said nothing that I wanted to say," she replied.

"Say it quickly, then, as we go."

"After all, it's only—will you take me away soon?"

"Yes, very soon. The Indian and I have talked. But we've made no plan yet. There are only three ways to get out of this country. By Stonebridge, by Kayenta and Durango, and by Red Lake. We must choose one. All are dangerous. We must lose time finding Surprise Valley. I hoped the Indian could find it. Then we'd bring Lassiter and Jane here and hide them near till dark, then take you and go. That would give us a night's start. But you must help us to Surprise Valley."

"I can go right to it, blindfolded, or in the dark. . . . Oh, John, hurry! I dread the wait. *He* might come again."

"Joe says—they won't come very soon."

"Is it far—where we're going—out of the country?"

"Ten days' hard riding."

"Oh! That night ride to and from Stonebridge nearly killed me. But I could walk very far, and climb forever."

"Fay, we'll get out of the country if I have to carry you."

When they arrived at the cabin Fay turned on the porch step and, with her face nearer a level with his, white and sweet in the moonlight, with her eyes shining and unfathomable, she was more than beautiful.

"You've never been inside my house," she said. "Come in. I've something for you."

"But it's late," he remonstrated. "I suppose you've got me a cake or pie —something to eat. You women all think Joe and I have to be fed."

"No. You'd never guess. Come in," she said, and the rare smile on her face was something Shefford would have gone far to see.

"Well, then, for a minute."

He crossed the porch, the threshold, and entered her home. Her dim, white shape moved in the darkness. And he followed into a room where the moon shone through the open window, giving soft, mellow, shadowy light. He discerned objects, but not clearly, for his senses seemed absorbed in the strange warmth and intimacy of being for the first time with her in her home.

"No, it's not good to eat," she said, and her laugh was happy. "Here—"

Suddenly she abruptly ceased speaking. Shefford saw her plainly, and the slender form had stiffened, alert and strained. She was listening.

"What was that?" she whispered.

"I didn't hear anything," he whispered back.

He stepped softly nearer the open window and listened.

Clip-clop! clip-clop! clip-clop! Hard hoofs on the hard path outside!

A strong and rippling thrill went over Shefford. In the soft light her eyes seemed unnaturally large and black and fearful.

Clip-clop! clip-clop!

The horse stopped outside. Then followed a metallic clink of spur against stirrup—thud of boots on hard ground—heavy footsteps upon the porch.

A swift, cold contraction of throat, of breast, convulsed Shefford. His only thought was that he could not think.

"Ho—Mary!"

A voice liberated both Shefford's muscle and mind—a voice of strange, vibrant power. Authority of religion and cruelty of will—these Mormon attributes constituted that power. And Shefford suffered a transformation which must have been ordered by demons. That sudden flame seemed to curl and twine and shoot along his veins with blasting force. A rancorous and terrible cry leaped to his lips.

"Ho—Mary!" Then came a heavy tread across the threshold of the outer room.

Shefford dared not look at Fay. Yet, dimly, from the corner of his eye, he saw her, a pale shadow, turned to stone, with her arms out. If he looked, if he made sure of that, he was lost. When had he drawn his gun? It was there, a dark and glinting thing in his hand. He must fly—not through cowardice and fear, but because in one more moment he would kill a man. Swift as the thought he dove through the open window. And, leaping up, he ran under the dark pinyons toward camp.

Joe Lake had been out late himself. He sat by the fire, smoking his pipe. He must have seen or heard Shefford coming, for he rose with unwonted alacrity, and he kicked the smoldering logs into a flickering blaze.

Shefford, realizing his deliverance, came panting, staggering into the light. The Mormon uttered an exclamation. Then he spoke, anxiously, but what he said was not clear in Shefford's thick and throbbing ears. He dropped his pipe, a sign of perturbation, and he stared.

But Shefford, without a word, lunged swiftly away into the shadow of the cedars. He found relief in action. He began a steep ascent of the east wall, a dangerous slant he had never dared even in daylight, and he climbed it without a slip. Danger steep walls, perilous heights, night, and black canyon the same—these he never thought of. But something drove him to desperate effort, that the hours might seem short.

The red sun was tipping the eastern wall when he returned to camp, and he was neither calm nor sure of himself nor ready for sleep or food. Only he had put the night behind him.

The Indian showed no surprise. But Joe Lake's jaw dropped and his eyes rolled. Moreover, Joe bore a singular aspect, the exact nature of which did not at once dawn upon Shefford.

"By God! You've got nerve—or you're crazy!" he ejaculated, hoarsely.

Then it was Shefford's turn to stare. The Mormon was haggard, grieved, frightened, and utterly amazed. He appeared to be trying to make certain of Shefford's being there in the flesh and then to find reason for it.

"I've no nerve and I am crazy," replied Shefford. "But, Joe—what do you mean? Why do you look at me like that?"

"I reckon if I get your horse that'll square us. Did you come back for him? You'd better hit the trail quick."

"It's you now who're crazy," burst out Shefford.

"Wish to God I was," replied Joe.

It was then Shefford realized catastrophe, and cold fear gnawed at his vitals, so that he was sick.

"Joe, what has happened?" he asked, with the blood thick in his heart.

"Hadn't you better tell me?" demanded the Mormon, and a red wave blotted out the haggard shade of his face.

"You talk like a fool," said Shefford, sharply, and he strode right up to Joe.

"See here, Shefford, we've been pards. You're making it hard for me. Reckon you ain't square."

Shefford shot out a long arm and his hand clutched the Mormon's burly shoulder.

"Why am I not square? What do you mean?"

Joe swallowed hard and gave himself a shake. Then he eyed his comrade steadily.

"I was afraid you'd kill him. I reckon I can't blame you. I'll help you get away. . . . And I'm a Mormon! Do you take the hunch? . . . But don't deny you killed him!"

"Killed whom?" gasped Shefford.

"Her husband!"

Shefford seemed stricken by a slow, paralyzing horror. The Mormon's changing face grew huge and indistinct and awful in his sight. He was clutched and shaken in Joe's rude hands, yet scarcely felt them. Joe seemed to be bellowing at him, but the voice was far off. Then Shefford began to see, to hear through some cold and terrible deadness that had come between him and everything.

"Say *you* killed him!" hoarsely supplicated the Mormon.

Shefford had not yet control of speech. Something in his gaze appeared to drive Joe frantic.

"Damn you! Tell me quick. Say *you* killed him! . . . If you want to know my stand, why, I'm glad! . . . Shefford, don't look so stony! . . . For *her* sake, say you killed him!"

Shefford stood with a face as gray and still as stone. With a groan the Mormon drew away from him and sank upon a log. He bowed his head; his broad shoulders heaved; husky sounds came from him. Then with a violent wrench he plunged to his feet and shook himself like a huge, savage dog.

"Reckon it's no time to weaken," he said, huskily, and with the words a dark, hard, somber bitterness came to his face.

"Where—is—she?" whispered Shefford.

"Shut up in the schoolhouse," he replied.

"Did she—did she—"

"She neither denied nor confessed."

"Have you—seen her?"

"Yes."

"How did—she look?"

"Cool and quiet as the Indian there. . . . Game as hell! She always had stuff in her."

"Oh, Joe! . . . It's unbelievable!" cried Shefford. "That lovely, innocent girl! She couldn't—she couldn't."

"She's fixed him. Don't think of that. It's too late. We ought to have saved her."

"God! . . . She begged me to hurry—to take her away."

"Think what we can do *now* to save her," cut in the Mormon.

Shefford sustained a vivifying shock. "To save her?" he echoed.

"Think, man!"

"Joe, I can hit the trail and let you tell them I killed him," burst out Shefford in panting excitement.

"Reckon I can."

"So help me God I'll do it!"

The Mormon turned a dark and austere glance upon Shefford.

"You mustn't leave her. She killed him for your sake. . . . You must fight for her now—save her—take her away."

"But the law!"

"Law!" scoffed Joe. "In these wilds men get killed and there's no law. But if she's taken back to Stonebridge those iron-jawed old Mormons will make law enough to—to . . . Shefford, the thing is—get her away. Once out of the country, she's safe. Mormons keep their secrets."

"I'll take her. Joe, will you help me?"

Shefford, even in his agitation, felt the Mormon's silence to be a consent that need not have been asked. And Shefford had a passionate gratefulness toward his comrade. That stultifying and blinding prejudice which had always seemed to remove a Mormon outside the pale of certain virtue suffered final eclipse; and Joe Lake stood out a man, strange and crude, but with a heart and a soul.

"Joe, tell me what to do," said Shefford, with a simplicity that meant he needed only to be directed.

"Pull yourself together. Get your nerve back," replied Joe. "Reckon you'd better show yourself over there. No one saw you come in this morning—your absence from camp isn't known. It's better you seem curious and shocked like the rest of us. Come on. We'll go over. And afterward we'll get the Indian, and plan."

They left camp and, crossing the brook, took the shaded path toward the village. Hope of saving Fay, the need of all his strength and nerve and cunning to effect that end, gave Shefford the supreme courage to overcome his horror and fear. On that short walk under the pinyons to Fay's cabin he had suffered many changes of emotion, but never anything like this change which made him fierce and strong to fight, deep and crafty to plan, hard as iron to endure.

The village appeared very quiet, though groups of women stood at the doors of cabins. If they talked, it was very low. Henninger and Smith, two of the three Mormon men living in the village, were standing before the closed door of the schoolhouse. A tigerish feeling thrilled Shefford when he saw them on guard there. Shefford purposely avoided looking at Fay's cabin as long as he could keep from it. When he had to look he saw several hooded, whispering women in the yard, and Beal, the other Mormon man, standing in the cabin door. Upon the porch lay the long shape of a man, covered with blankets.

Shefford experienced a horrible curiosity.

"Say, Beal, I've fetched Shefford over," said Lake. "He's pretty much cut up."

Beal wagged a solemn head, but said nothing. His mind seemed absent or steeped in gloom, and he looked up as one silently praying.

Joe Lake strode upon the little porch and, reaching down, he stripped the blanket from the shrouded form.

Shefford saw a sharp, cold, ghastly face. "*Waggoner!*" he whispered.

"Yes," replied Lake.

Waggoner! Shefford remembered the strange power in his face, and, now that life had gone, that power was stripped of all disguise. Death, in

Shefford's years of ministry, had lain under his gaze many times and in a multiplicity of aspects, but never before had he seen it stamped so strangely. Shefford did not need to be told that here was a man who believed he had conversed with God on earth, who believed he had a divine right to rule women, who had a will that would not yield itself to death utterly. Waggoner, then, was the devil who had come masked to Surprise Valley, had forced a martyrdom upon Fay Larkin. And this was the Mormon who had made Fay Larkin a murderess. Shefford had hated him living, and now he hated him dead. Death here was robbed of all nobility, of pathos, of majesty. It was only retribution. Wild justice! But alas! That it had to be meted out by a white-souled girl whose innocence was as great as the unconscious savagery which she had assimilated from her lonely and wild environment. Shefford laid a despairing curse upon his own head, and a terrible remorse knocked at his heart. He had left her alone, this girl in whom love had made the great change—like a coward he had left her alone. That curse he visited upon himself because he had been the spirit and the motive of this wild justice, and his should have been the deed.

Joe Lake touched Shefford's arm and pointed at the haft of a knife protruding from Waggoner's breast. It was a wooden haft. Shefford had seen it before somewhere.

Then he was struck with what perhaps Joe meant him to see—the singular impression the haft gave of one sweeping, accurate, powerful stroke. A strong arm had driven that blade home. The haft was sunk deep; there was a little depression in the cloth; no blood showed; and the weapon looked as if it could not be pulled out. Shefford's thought went fatally and irresistibly to Fay Larkin's strong arm. He saw her flash that white arm and lift the heavy bucket from the spring with an ease he wondered at. He felt the strong clasp of her hand as she had given it to him in a flying leap across a crevice upon the walls. Yes, her fine hand and the round, strong arm possessed the strength to have given that blade its singular directness and force. The marvel was not in the physical action. It hid inscrutably in the mystery of deadly passion rising out of a gentle and sad heart.

Joe Lake drew up the blanket and shut from Shefford's fascinated gaze that spare form, that accusing knife, that face of strange, cruel power.

"Anybody been sent for?" asked Lake of Beal.

"Yes. An Indian boy went for the Piute. We'll send him to Stonebridge," replied the Mormon.

"How soon do you expect anyone here from Stonebridge?"

"Tomorrow, mebbe by noon."

"Meantime what's to be done with—this?"

"Elder Smith thinks the body should stay right here where it fell till they come from Stonebridge."

"Waggoner was found here, then?"

"Right here."

"Who found him?"

"Mother Smith. She came over early. An' the sight made her scream. The women all came runnin'. Mother Smith had to be put to bed."

"Who found—Mary?"

"See here, Joe, I told you all I knowed once before," replied the Mormon, testily.

"I've forgotten. Was sort of bewildered. Tell me again. . . . Who found—her?"

"The women folks. She laid right inside the door, in a dead faint. She hadn't undressed. There was blood on her hands an' a cut or scratch. The women fetched her to. But she wouldn't talk. Then Elder Smith come an' took her. They've got her locked up."

Then Joe led Shefford away from the cabin farther on into the village. When they were halted by the somber, grieving women it was Joe who did the talking. They passed the schoolhouse, and here Shefford quickened his step. He could scarcely bear the feeling that rushed over him. And the Mormon gripped his arm as if he understood.

"Shefford, which one of these younger women do you reckon your best friend? Ruth?" asked Lake, earnestly.

"Ruth, by all means. Just lately I haven't seen her often. But we've been close friends. I think she'd do much for me."

"Maybe there'll be a chance to find out. Maybe we'll need Ruth. Let's have a word with her. I haven't seen her out among the women."

They stopped at the door of Ruth's cabin. It was closed. When Joe knocked there came a sound of footsteps inside, a hand drew aside the window-blind, and presently the door opened. Ruth stood there, dressed in somber hue. She was a pretty, slender, blue-eyed, brown-haired young woman. Shefford imagined from her pallor and the set look of shock upon her face, that the tragedy had affected her more powerfully than it had the other women. When he remembered that she had been more friendly with Fay Larkin than any other neighbor, he made sure he was right in his conjecture.

"Come in," was Ruth's greeting.

"No. We just wanted to say a word. I noticed you've not been out. Do you know—all about it?"

She gave them a strange glance.

"Any of the women folks been in?" added Joe.

"Hester ran over. She told me through the window. Then I barred my door to keep the other women out."

"What for?" asked Joe, curiously.

"Please come in," she said, in reply.

They entered, and she closed the door after them. The change that came over her then was the loosing of restraint.

"Joe—what will they do with Mary?" she queried, tensely.

The Mormon studied her with dark, speculative eyes. "Hang her!" he rejoined in brutal harshness.

"O Mother of Saints!" she cried, and her hands went up.

"You're sorry for Mary, then?" asked Joe, bluntly.

"My heart is breaking for her."

"Well, so's Shefford's," said the Mormon, huskily. "And mine's kind of damn shaky."

Ruth glided to Shefford with a woman's swift softness.

"You've been my good—my best friend. You were hers, too. Oh, I know! . . . Can't you do something for her?"

"I hope to God I can," replied Shefford.

Then the three stood looking from one to the other, in a strong and subtly realizing moment, drawn together.

"Ruth," whispered Joe, hoarsely, and then he glanced fearfully around, at the window and door, as if listeners were there. It was certain that his dark face had paled. He tried to whisper more, only to fail. Shefford divined the weight of Mormonism that burdened Joe Lake then. Joe was faithful to a love for Fay Larkin, noble in friendship to Shefford, desperate in a bitter strait with his own manliness, but the power of that creed by which he had been raised struck his lips mute. For to speak on meant to be false to that creed. Already in his heart he had decided, yet he could not voice the thing.

"Ruth"—Shefford took up the Mormon's unfinished whisper—"if we plan to save her—if we need you—will you help?"

Ruth turned white, but an instant and splendid fire shone in her eyes.

"Try me," she whispered back. "I'll change places with her—so you can get her away. They can't do much to me."

Shefford wrung her hands. Joe licked his lips and found his voice: "We'll come back later." Then he led the way out and Shefford followed. They were silent all the way back to camp.

Nas Ta Bega sat in repose where they had left him, a thoughtful, somber figure. Shefford went directly to the Indian, and Joe tarried at the campfire, where he raked out some red embers and put one upon the bowl of his pipe. He puffed clouds of white smoke, then found a seat beside the others.

"Shefford, go ahead. Talk. It'll take a deal of talk. I'll listen. Then I'll talk. It'll be Nas Ta Bega who makes the plan out of it all."

Shefford launched himself so swiftly that he scarcely talked coherently. But he made clear the points that he must save Fay, get her away from the village, let her lead him to Surprise Valley, rescue Lassiter and Jane Withersteen, and take them all out of the country.

Joe Lake dubiously shook his head. Manifestly the Surprise Valley part of the situation presented a new and serious obstacle. It changed the

whole thing. To try to take the three out by way of Kayenta and Durango
was not to be thought of, for reasons he briefly stated. The Red Lake trail
was the only one left, and if that were taken the chances were against
Shefford. It was five days over sand to Red Lake—impossible to hide a
trail—and even with a day's start Shefford could not escape the hard-
riding men who would come from Stonebridge. Besides, after reaching
Red Lake, there were days and days of desert-travel needful to avoid
places like Blue Canyon, Tuba, Moencopie, and the Indian villages.

"We'll have to risk all that," declared Shefford, desperately.

"It's a fool risk," retorted Joe. "Listen. By tomorrow noon all of
Stonebridge, more or less, will be riding in here. You've got to get away
tonight with the girl—or never! And tomorrow you've got to find that
Lassiter and the woman in Surprise Valley. This valley must be back, deep
in the canyon country. Well, you've got to come out this way again.
No trail through here would be safe. Why, you'd put all your heads in a
rope! . . . You mustn't come through this way. It'll have to be tried
across country, off the trails, and that means hell—day-and-night travel,
no camp, no feed for horses—maybe no water. Then you'll have the best
trackers in Utah like hounds on your trail."

When the Mormon ceased his forceful speech there was a silence
fraught with hopeless meaning. He bowed his head in gloom. Shefford,
growing sick again to his marrow, fought a cold, hateful sense of despair.

"Bi Nai!" In his extremity he called to the Indian.

"The Navajo has heard," replied Nas Ta Bega, strangely speaking in his
own language.

With a long, slow heave of breast Shefford felt his despair leave him. In
the Indian lay his salvation. He knew it. Joe Lake caught the subtle spirit
of the moment and looked up eagerly.

Nas Ta Bega stretched an arm toward the east, and spoke in Navajo.
But Shefford, owing to the hurry and excitement of his mind, could not
translate. Joe Lake listened, gave a violent start, leaped up with all his big
frame quivering, and then fired question after question at the Indian.
When the Navajo had replied to all, Joe drew himself up as if facing an
irrevocable decision which would wring his very soul. What did he cast
off in that moment? What did he grapple with? Shefford had no means to
tell, except by the instinct which baffled him. But whether the Mormon's
trial was one of spiritual rending or the natural physical fear of a perilous,
virtually impossible venture, the fact was he was magnificent in his acceptance of it. He turned to Shefford, white, cold, yet glowing.

"Nas Ta Bega believes he can take you down a canyon to the big river
—the Colorado. He knows the head of this canyon. Nonnezoshe Boco it's
called—canyon of the rainbow bridge. He has never been down it. Only
two or three living Indians have ever seen the great stone bridge. But all
have heard of it. They worship it as a god. There's water runs down this

canyon and water runs to the river. Nas Ta Bega thinks he can take you down to the river."

"Go on," cried Shefford, breathlessly, as Joe paused.

"The Indian plans this way. God, it's great! . . . If only I can do my end! . . . He plans to take mustangs today and wait with them for you tonight or tomorrow till you come with the girl. You'll go get Lassiter and the woman out of Surprise Valley. Then you'll strike east for Nonnezoshe Boco. If possible, you must take a pack of grub. You may be days going down—and waiting for me at the mouth of the canyon, at the river."

"Joe! Where will you be?"

"I'll ride like hell for Kayenta, get another horse there, and ride like hell for the San Juan River. There's a big flatboat at the Durango crossing. I'll go down the San Juan in that—into the big river. I'll drift down by day, tie up by night, and watch for you at the mouth of every canyon till I come to Nonnezoshe Boco."

Shefford could not believe the evidence of his ears. He knew the treacherous San Juan River. He had heard of the great, sweeping, terrible red Colorado and its roaring rapids.

"Oh, it seems impossible!" he gasped. "You'll just lose your life for nothing."

"The Indian will turn the trick, I tell you. Take my hunch. It's nothing for me to drift down a swift river. I worked a ferryboat once."

Shefford, to whom flying straws would have seemed stable, caught the inflection of defiance and daring and hope of the Mormon's spirit.

"What then—after you meet us at the mouth of Nonnezoshe Boco?" he queried.

"We'll all drift down to Lee's Ferry. That's at the head of Marble Canyon. We'll get out on the south side of the river, thus avoiding any Mormons at the ferry. Nas Ta Bega knows the country. It's open desert—on the other side of these plateaus. He can get horses from Navajos. Then you'll strike south for Willow Springs."

"Willow Springs? That's Presbrey's trading-post," said Shefford.

"Never met him. But he'll see you safe out of the Painted Desert. . . . The thing that worries me most is how not to miss you all at the mouth of Nonnezoshe. You must have sharp eyes. But I forget the Indian. A bird couldn't pass him. . . . And suppose Nonnezoshe Boco has a steep-walled, narrow mouth opening into a rapids! . . . Whew! Well, the Indian will figure that, too. Now, let's put our heads together and plan how to turn this end of the trick here. Getting the girl!"

After a short colloquy it was arranged that Shefford would go to Ruth and talk to her of the aid she had promised. Joe averred that this aid could be best given by Ruth going in her somber gown and hood to the school-house, and there, while Joe and Shefford engaged the guards outside, she would change apparel and places with Fay and let her come forth.

"What'll they do to Ruth?" demanded Shefford. "We can't accept her sacrifice if she's to suffer—or be punished."

"Reckon Ruth has a strong hunch that she can get away with it. Did you notice how strange she said that? Well, they can't do much to her. The bishop may damn her soul. But—Ruth—"

Here Lake hesitated and broke off. Not improbably he had meant to say that of all the Mormon women in the valley Ruth was the least likely to suffer from punishment inflicted upon her soul.

"Anyway, it's our only chance," went on Joe, "unless we kill a couple of men. Ruth will gladly take what comes to help you."

"All right; I consent," replied Shefford, with emotion. "And now after she comes out—the supposed Ruth—what then?"

"You can be natural-like. Go with her back to Ruth's cabin. Then stroll off into the cedars. Then climb the west wall. Meanwhile Nas Ta Bega will ride off with a pack of grub and Nack-yal and several other mustangs. He'll wait for you or you'll wait for him, as the case may be, at some appointed place. When you're gone I'll jump my horse and hit the trail for Kayenta and the San Juan."

"Very well; that's settled," said Shefford, soberly. "I'll go at once to see Ruth. You and Nas Ta Bega decide on where I'm to meet him."

"Reckon you'd do just as well to walk round and come up to Ruth's from the other side—instead of going through the village," suggested Joe.

Shefford approached Ruth's cabin in a roundabout way; nevertheless, she saw him coming before he got there and, opening the door, stood pale, composed, and quietly bade him enter. Briefly, in low and earnest voice, Shefford acquainted her with the plan.

"You love her so much," she said, wistfully, wonderingly.

"Indeed I do. Is it too much to ask of you to do this thing?" he asked.

"Do it?" she queried, with a flash of spirit. "Of course I'll do it."

"Ruth, I can't thank you. I can't. I've only a faint idea what you're risking. That distresses me. I'm afraid of what may happen to you."

She gave him another of the strange glances. "I don't risk so much as you think," she said, significantly.

"Why?"

She came close to him, and her hands clasped his arms and she looked up at him, her eyes darkening and her face growing paler. "Will you swear to keep my secret?" she asked, very low.

"Yes, I swear."

"I was one of Waggoner's sealed wives!"

"God Almighty!" broke out Shefford, utterly overwhelmed.

"Yes. That's why I say I don't risk so much. I will make up a story to tell the bishop and everybody. I'll tell that Waggoner was jealous, that he was brutal to Mary, that I believed she was goaded to her mad deed, that I thought she ought to be free. They'll be terrible. But what can they do to me? My husband is dead . . . and if I have to go to hell to keep from marrying another married Mormon, I'll go!"

In that low, passionate utterance Shefford read the deathblow to the old Mormon polygamous creed. In the uplift of his spirit, in the joy at this revelation, he almost forgot the stern matter at hand. Ruth and Joe Lake belonged to a younger generation of Mormons. Their nobility in this instance was in part a revolt at the conditions of their lives. Doubt was knocking at Joe Lake's heart, and conviction had come to this young sealed wife, bitter and hopeless while she had been fettered, strong and mounting now that she was free. In a flash of inspiration Shefford saw the old order changing. The Mormon creed might survive, but that part of it which was an affront to nature, a horrible yoke on women's necks, was doomed. It could not live. It could never have survived more than a generation or two of religious fanatics. Shefford had marked a different force and religious fervor in the younger Mormons, and now he understood them.

"Ruth, you talk wildly," he said. "But I understand. I see. You are free and you're going to stay free. . . . It stuns me to think of that man of many wives. What did you feel when you were told he was dead?"

"I dare not think of that. It makes me wicked. And he was good to me. . . . Listen. Last night about midnight he came to my window and woke me. I got up and let him in. He was in a terrible state. I thought he was crazy. He walked the floor and called on his saints and prayed. When I wanted to light a lamp he wouldn't let me. He was afraid I'd see his face. But I saw well enough in the moonlight. And I knew something had happened. So I soothed and coaxed him. He had been a man as close-mouthed as a stone. Yet then I got him to talk. . . . He had gone to Mary's, and upon entering, thought he heard someone with her. She didn't answer him at first. When he found her in her bedroom she was like a ghost. He accused her. Her silence made him furious. Then he berated her, brought down the wrath of God upon her, threatened her with damnation. All of which she never seemed to hear. But when he tried to touch her she flew at him like a she-panther. That's what he called her. She said she'd kill him! And she drove him out of her house. . . . He was all weak and unstrung, and I believe scared, too, when he came to me. She must have been a fury. Those quiet, gentle women are furies when they're once roused. Well, I was hours up with him and finally he got over it. He didn't pray anymore. He paced the room. It was just daybreak when he said the wrath of God had come to him. I tried to keep him from going back to Mary. But he went. . . . An hour later the women ran to tell me he had been found dead at Mary's door."

"Ruth—she was mad—driven—she didn't know what she—was do-ing," said Shefford, brokenly.

"She was always a strange girl, more like an Indian than anyone I ever knew. We called her the Sago Lily. I gave her the name. She was so sweet, lovely, white and gold, like those flowers. . . . And to think! Oh, it's horrible for her! You must save her. If you get her away there never will be anything come of it. The Mormons will hush it up."

"Ruth, time is flying," rejoined Shefford, hurriedly. "I must go back to Joe. You be ready for us when we come. Wear something loose, easily thrown off, and don't forget the long hood."

"I'll be ready and watching," she said. "The sooner the better, I'd say."

He left her and returned toward camp in the same circling route by which he had come. The Indian had disappeared and so had his mustang. This significant fact augmented Shefford's hurried, thrilling excitement. But one glance at Joe's face changed all that to a sudden numbness, a sinking of his heart.

"What is it?" he queried.

"Look there!" exclaimed the Mormon.

Shefford's quick eye caught sight of horses and men down the valley. He saw several Indians and three or four white men. They were making camp.

"Who are they?" demanded Shefford.

"Shadd and some of his gang. Reckon that Piute told the news. By tomorrow the valley will be full as a horse-wrangler's corral. . . . Lucky Nas Ta Bega got away before that gang rode in. Now things won't look as queer as they might have looked. The Indian took a pack of grub, six mustangs, and my guns. Then there was your rifle in your saddle-sheath. So you'll be well heeled in case you come to close quarters. Reckon you can look for a running fight. For now, as soon as your flight is discovered, Shadd will hit your trail. He's in with the Mormons. You know him— what you'll have to deal with. But the advantage will all be yours. You can ambush the trail."

"We're in for it. And the sooner we're off the better," replied Shefford, grimly.

"Reckon that's gospel. Well—come on!"

The Mormon strode off, and Shefford, catching up with him, kept at his side. Shefford's mind was full, but Joe's dark and gloomy face did not invite communication. They entered the pinyon grove and passed the cabin where the tragedy had been enacted. A tarpaulin had been stretched across the front porch. Beal was not in sight, nor were any of the women.

"I forgot," said Shefford, suddenly. "Where am I to meet the Indian?"

"Climb the west wall, back of camp," replied Joe. "Nas Ta Bega took the Stonebridge trail. But he'll leave that, climb the rocks, then hide the outfit and come back to watch for you. Reckon he'll see you when you top the wall."

They passed on into the heart of the village. Joe tarried at the window of a cabin, and passed a few remarks to a woman there, and then he inquired for Mother Smith at her house. When they left here the Mormon gave Shefford a nudge. Then they separated, Joe going toward the schoolhouse, while Shefford bent his steps in the direction of Ruth's home.

Her door opened before he had a chance to knock. He entered. Ruth, white and resolute, greeted him with a wistful smile.

"All ready?" she asked.

"Yes. Are you?" he replied, low-voiced.

"I've only to put on my hood. I think luck favors you. Hester was here and she said Elder Smith told someone that Mary hadn't been offered anything to eat yet. So I'm taking her a little. It'll be a good excuse for me to get in the schoolhouse to see her. I can throw off this dress and she can put it on in a minute. Then the hood. I mustn't forget to hide her golden hair. You know how it flies. But this is a big hood. . . . Well, I'm ready now. And—this's our last time together."

"Ruth, what can I say—how can I thank you?"

"I don't want any thanks. It'll be something to think of always—to make me happy. . . . Only I'd like to feel you—you cared a little."

The wistful smile was there, a tremor on the sad lips, and a shadow of soul-hunger in her eyes. Shefford did not misunderstand her. She did not mean love, although it was a yearning for real love that she mutely expressed.

"Care! I shall care all my life," he said, with strong feeling. "I shall never forget you."

"It's not likely I'll forget you. . . . Goodbye, John!"

Shefford took her in his arms and held her close. "Ruth—goodbye!" he said, huskily.

Then he released her. She adjusted the hood and, taking up a little tray which held food covered with a napkin, she turned to the door. He opened it and they went out.

They did not speak another word.

It was not a long walk from Ruth's home to the schoolhouse, yet if it were to be measured by Shefford's emotion the distance would have been unending. The sacrifice offered by Ruth and Joe would have been noble under any circumstances had they been Gentiles or persons with no particular religion, but, considering that they were Mormons, that Ruth had been a sealed wife, that Joe had been brought up under the strange, secret and binding creed, their action was no less than tremendous in its import. Shefford took it to mean vastly more than loyalty to him and pity for Fay Larkin. As Ruth and Joe had arisen to this height, so perhaps would other young Mormons have arisen. It needed only the situation, the climax, to focus these long-insulated, slow-developing and inquiring minds upon the truth—that one wife, one mother of children, for one man at one time was a law of nature, love and righteousness. Shefford felt as if he were marching with the whole younger generation of Mormons, as if somehow he had been a humble instrument in the working out of their destiny, in the awakening that was to eliminate from their religion the only thing which kept it from being as good for man, and perhaps as true, as any other religion.

And then suddenly he turned the corner of the schoolhouse to encounter Joe talking with the Mormon Henninger. Elder Smith was not present.

"Why, hello, Ruth!" greeted Joe. "You've fetched Mary some dinner. Now that's good of you."

"May I go in?" asked Ruth.

"Reckon so," replied Henninger, scratching his head. He appeared to be tractable, and probably was good-natured under pleasant conditions. "She ought to have somethin' to eat. An' nobody 'pears to have remembered thet—we're so set up."

He unbarred the huge, clumsy door and allowed Ruth to pass in.

"Joe, you can go in if you want," he said. "But hurry out before Elder Smith comes back from his dinner."

Joe mumbled something, gave a husky cough, and then went in.

Shefford experienced great difficulty in presenting to this mild Mormon a natural and unagitated front. When all his internal structure seemed to be in a state of turmoil he did not see how it was possible to keep the fact from showing in his face. So he turned away and took aimless steps here and there.

" 'Pears like we'd hev rain," observed Henninger. "It's right warm an' them clouds are onseasonable."

"Yes," replied Shefford. "Hope so. A little rain would be good for the grass."

"Joe tells me Shadd rode in, an' some of his fellers."

"So I see. About eight in the party."

Shefford was gritting his teeth and preparing to endure the ordeal of controlling his mind and expression when the door opened and Joe stalked out. He had his sombrero pulled down so that it hid the upper half of his face. His lips were a shade off healthy color. He stood there with his back to the door.

"Say, what Mary needs is quiet—to be left alone," he said. "Ruth says if she rests, sleeps a little, she won't get fever. . . . Henninger, don't let anybody disturb her till night."

"All right, Joe," replied the Mormon. "An' I take it good of Ruth an' you to concern yourselves."

A slight tap on the inside of the door sent Shefford's pulses to throbbing. Joe opened it with a strong and vigorous sweep that meant more than the mere action.

"Ruth—reckon you didn't stay long," he said, and his voice rang clear. "Sure you feel sick and weak. Why, seeing her flustered even me!"

A slender, dark-garbed woman wearing a long black hood stepped uncertainly out. She appeared to be Ruth. Shefford's heart stood still because she looked so like Ruth. But she did not step steadily, she seemed dazed, she did not raise the hooded head.

"Go home," said Joe, and his voice rang a little louder. "Take her home, Shefford. Or, better, walk her round some. She's faintish. . . . And see here, Henninger—"

Shefford led the girl away with a hand in apparent carelessness on her arm. After a few rods she walked with a freer step and then a swifter. He found it necessary to make that hold on her arm a real one, so as to keep her from walking too fast. No one, however, appeared to observe them. When they passed Ruth's house then Shefford began to lose his fear that this was not Fay Larkin. He was far from being calm or clear-sighted. He thought he recognized that free step; nevertheless, he could not make sure. When they passed under the trees, crossed the brook, and turned down along the west wall, then doubt ceased in Shefford's mind. He knew this was not Ruth. Still, so strange was his agitation, so keen his suspense, that he needed confirmation of ear, of eye. He wanted to hear her voice, to see her face. Yet just as strangely there was a twist of feeling, a reluctance, a sadness that kept off the moment.

They reached the low, slow-swelling slant of wall and started to ascend. How impossible not to recognize Fay Larkin now in that swift grace and skill on the steep wall! Still, though he knew her, he perversely clung to the unreality of the moment. But when a long braid of dead-gold hair tumbled from under the hood, then his heart leaped. That identified Fay Larkin. He had freed her. He was taking her away. Then a sadness embittered his joy.

As always before, she distanced him in the ascent to the top. She went on without looking back. But Shefford had an irresistible desire to look again and the last time at this valley where he had suffered and loved so much.

⁂16⁂

SURPRISE VALLEY

FROM THE SUMMIT of the wall the plateau waved away in red and yellow ridges, with here and there little valleys green with cedar and pinyon.

Upon one of these ridges, silhouetted against the sky, appeared the stalking figure of the Indian. He had espied the fugitives. He disappeared in a niche, and presently came again into view round a corner of cliff. Here he waited, and soon Shefford and Fay joined him.

"Bi Nai, it is well," he said.

Shefford eagerly asked for the horses, and Nas Ta Bega silently pointed down the niche, which was evidently an opening into one of the shallow canyons. Then he led the way, walking swiftly. It was Shefford, and not Fay, who had difficulty in keeping close to him. This speed caused Shefford to become more alive to the business, instead of the feeling, of the flight. The Indian entered a crack between low cliffs—a very narrow canyon full of rocks and clumps of cedars—and in a half-hour or less he came to where the mustangs were halted among some cedars. Three of the mustangs, including Nack-yal, were saddled; one bore a small pack, and the remaining two had blankets strapped on their backs.

"Fay, can you ride in that long skirt?" asked Shefford. How strange it seemed that his first words to her were practical when all his impassioned thought had been only mute! But the instant he spoke he experienced a relief, a relaxation.

"I'll take it off," replied Fay, just as practically. And in a twinkling she slipped out of both waist and skirt. She had worn them over the short white-flannel dress with which Shefford had grown familiar.

As Nack-yal appeared to be the safest mustang for her to ride, Shefford helped her upon him and then attended to the stirrups. When he had adjusted them to the proper length he drew the bridle over Nack-yal's head and, upon handing it to her, found himself suddenly looking into her face. She had taken off the hood, too. The instant their eyes met he realized that she was strangely afraid to meet his glance, as he was to meet hers. That seemed natural. But her face was flushed and there were unmistakable signs upon it of growing excitement, of mounting happiness. Save for that fugitive glance she would have been the Fay Larkin of yesterday.

How he had expected her to look he did not know, but it was not like this. And never had he felt her strange quality of simplicity so powerfully.

"Have you ever been here—through this little canyon?" he asked.

"Oh yes, lots of times."

"You'll be able to lead us to Surprise Valley, you think?"

"I know it. I shall see Uncle Jim and Mother Jane before sunset!"

"I hope—you do," he replied, a little shakily. "Perhaps we'd better not tell them of the—the—about what happened last night."

Her beautiful, grave, and troubled glance returned to meet his, and he received a shock that he considered was amaze. And after more swift consideration he believed he was amazed because that look, instead of betraying fear or gloom or any haunting shadow of darkness, betrayed apprehension for him—grave, sweet, troubled love for him. She was not thinking of herself at all—of what he might think of her, of a possible gulf between them, of a vast and terrible change in the relation of soul to soul. He experienced a profound gladness. Though he could not understand her, he was happy that the horror of Waggoner's death had escaped her. He loved her, he meant to give his life to her, and right then and there he accepted the burden of her deed and meant to bear it without ever letting her know of the shadow between them.

"Fay, we'll forget—what's behind us," he said. "Now to find Surprise Valley. Lead on. Nack-yal is gentle. Pull him the way you want to go. We'll follow."

Shefford mounted the other saddled mustang, and they set off, Fay in advance. Presently they rode out of this canyon up to level cedar-patched, solid rock, and here Fay turned straight west. Evidently she had been over the ground before. The heights to which he had climbed with her were up to the left, great slopes and looming promontories. And the course she chose was as level and easy as any he could have picked out in that direction.

When a mile or more of this up-and-down travel had been traversed Fay halted and appeared to be at fault. The plateau was losing its rounded, smooth, wavy characteristics, and to the west grew bolder, more rugged, more cut up into low crags and buttes. After a long, sweeping glance Fay headed straight for this rougher country. Thereafter from time to time she repeated this action.

"Fay, how do you know you're going in the right direction?" asked Shefford, anxiously.

"I never forget any ground I've been over. I keep my eyes close ahead. All that seems strange to me is the wrong way. What I've seen before must be the right way, because I saw it when they brought me from Surprise Valley."

Shefford had to acknowledge that she was following an Indian's instinct for ground he had once covered.

Still Shefford began to worry, and finally dropped back to question Nas Ta Bega.

"Bi Nai, she has the eye of a Navajo," replied the Indian. "Look! Iron-shod horses have passed here. See the marks in the stone?"

Shefford indeed made out faint cut tracks that would have escaped his own sight. They had been made long ago, but they were unmistakable.

"She's following the trail by memory—she must remember the stones, trees, sage, cactus," said Shefford in surprise.

"Pictures in her mind," replied the Indian.

Thereafter the farther she progressed the less at fault she appeared and the faster she traveled. She made several miles an hour, and about the middle of the afternoon entered upon the more broken region of the plateau. Views became restricted. Low walls, and ruined cliffs of red rock with cedars at their base, and gullies growing into canyons and canyons opening into larger ones—these were passed and crossed and climbed and rimmed in travel that grew more difficult as the going became wilder. Then there was a steady ascent, up and up all the time, though not steep, until another level, green with cedar and pinyon, was reached.

It reminded Shefford of the forest near the mouth of the Sagi. It was so dense he could not see far ahead of Fay, and often he lost sight of her entirely. Presently he rode out of the forest into a strip of purple sage. It ended abruptly, and above that abrupt line, seemingly far away, rose a long, red wall. Instantly he recognized that to be the opposite wall of a canyon which as yet he could not see.

Fay was acting strangely and he hurried forward. She slipped off Nack-yal and fell, sprang up and ran wildly, to stand upon a promontory, her arms uplifted, her hair a mass of moving gold in the wind, her attitude one of wild and eloquent significance.

Shefford ran, too, and as he ran the red wall in his eager sight seemed to enlarge downward, deeper and deeper, and then it merged into a strip of green.

Suddenly beneath him yawned a red-walled gulf, a deceiving gulf seen through transparent haze, a softly shining green-and-white valley, strange, wild, beautiful, like a picture in his memory.

"Surprise Valley!" he cried, in wondering recognition.

Fay Larkin waved her arms as if they were wings to carry her swiftly downward, and her plaintive cry fitted the wildness of her manner and the lonely height where she leaned.

Shefford drew her back from the rim.

"Fay, we are here," he said. "I recognize the valley. I miss only one thing—the arch of stone."

His words seemed to recall her to reality.

"The arch? That fell when the wall slipped, in the great avalanche. See! There is the place. We can get down there. Oh, let us hurry!"

The Indian reached the rim and his falcon gaze swept the valley.

"Ugh!" he exclaimed. He, too, recognized the valley that he had vainly sought for half a year.

"Bring the lassos," said Shefford.

With Fay leading, they followed the rim toward the head of the valley. Here the wall had caved in, and there was a slope of jumbled rock a thousand feet wide and more than that in depth. It was easy to descend because there were so many rocks waist-high that afforded a handhold. Shefford marked, however, that Fay never took advantage of these. More than once he paused to watch her. Swiftly she went down; she stepped from rock to rock; lightly she crossed cracks and pits; she ran along the sharp and broken edge of a long ledge; she poised on a pointed stone and, sure-footed as a mountain-sheep, she sprang to another that had scarce surface for a foothold; her moccasins flashed, seemed to hold wondrously on any angle; and when a rock tipped or slipped with her she leaped to a surer stand. Shefford watched her performance, so swift, agile, so perfectly balanced, showing such wonderful accord between eye and foot; and then when he swept his gaze down upon that wild valley where she had roamed alone for twelve years he marveled no more.

The farther down he got the greater became the size of rocks, until he found himself amid huge pieces of cliff as large as houses. He lost sight of Fay entirely, and he anxiously threaded a narrow, winding, descending way between the broken masses. Finally he came out upon flat rock again. Fay stood on another rim, looking down. He saw that the slide had moved far out into the valley, and the lower part of it consisted of great sections of wall. In fact, the base of the great wall had just moved out with the avalanche, and this much of it held its vertical position. Looking upward, Shefford was astounded and thrilled to see how far he had descended, how the walls leaned like a great, wide, curving, continuous rim of mountain.

"Here! Here!" called Fay. "Here's where they got down—where they brought me up. Here are the sticks they used. They stuck them in this crack, down to that ledge."

Shefford ran to her side and looked down. There was a narrow split in this section of wall and it was perhaps sixty feet in depth. The floor of rock below led out in a ledge, with a sheer drop to the valley level.

As Shefford gazed, pondering on a way to descend lower, the Indian reached his side. He had no sooner looked than he proceeded to act. Selecting one of the sticks, which were strong pieces of cedar, well hewn and trimmed, he jammed it between the walls of the crack till it stuck fast. Then sitting astride this one he jammed in another some three feet below. When he got down upon that one it was necessary for Shefford to drop him a third stick. In a comparatively short time the Indian reached the ledge below. Then he called for the lassos. Shefford threw them down. His next move was an attempt to assist Fay, but she slipped out of his grasp and descended the ladder with a swiftness that made him hold

his breath. Still, when his turn came, her spirit so governed him that he
went down as swiftly, and even leaped sheer the last ten feet.

Nas Ta Bega and Fay were leaning over the ledge.

"Here's the place," she said, excitedly. "Let me down on the rope."

It took two thirty-foot lassos tied together to reach the floor of the
valley. Shefford folded his vest, put it round Fay, and slipped a loop of the
lasso under her arms. Then he and Nas Ta Bega lowered her to the grass
below. Fay, throwing off the loop, bounded away like a wild creature,
uttering the strangest cries he had ever heard, and she disappeared along
the wall.

"I'll go down," said Shefford to the Indian. "You stay here to help pull
us up."

Hand over hand Shefford descended, and when his feet touched the
grass he experienced a shock of the most singular exultation.

"In Surprise Valley!" he breathed, softly. The dream that had come to
him with his friend's story, the years of waiting, wondering, and then the
long, fruitless, hopeless search in the desert uplands—these were in his
mind as he turned along the wall where Fay had disappeared. He faced a
wide terrace, green with grass and moss and starry with strange white
flowers, and dark-foliaged, spear-pointed spruce trees. Below the terrace
sloped a bench covered with thick copse, and this merged into a forest of
dwarf oaks, and beyond that was a beautiful strip of white aspens, their
leaves quivering in the stillness. The air was close, sweet, warm, fragrant,
and remarkably dry. It reminded him of the air he had smelled in dry
caves under cliffs. He reached a point from where he saw a meadow
dotted with red-and-white-spotted cattle and little black burros. There
were many of them. And he remembered with a start the agony of toil
and peril Venters had endured bringing the progenitors of this stock into
the valley. What a strange, wild, beautiful story it all was! But a story
connected with this valley could not have been otherwise.

Beyond the meadow, on the other side of the valley, extended the
forest, and that ended in the rising bench of thicket, which gave place to
green slope and mossy terrace of sharp-tipped spruces—and all this led
the eye irresistibly up to the red wall where a vast, dark, wonderful cavern
yawned, with its rust-colored streaks of stain on the wall, and the queer
little houses of the cliff-dwellers, with their black, vacant, silent windows
speaking so weirdly of the unknown past.

Shefford passed a place where the ground had been cultivated, but not
as recently as the last six months. There was a scant shock of corn and
many meager standing stalks. He became aware of a low, whining hum
and a fragrance overpowering in its sweetness. And there round another
corner of wall he came upon an orchard all pink and white in blossom and
melodious with the buzz and hum of innumerable bees.

He crossed a little stream that had been dammed, went along a pond,
down beside an irrigation ditch that furnished water to orchard and vine-

yard, and from there he strode into a beautiful cove between two jutting corners of red wall. It was level and green and the spruces stood gracefully everywhere. Beyond their dark trunks he saw caves in the wall.

Suddenly the fragrance of blossom was overwhelmed by the stronger fragrance of smoke from a wood fire. Swiftly he strode under the spruces. Quail fluttered before him as tame as chickens. Big gray rabbits scarcely moved out of his way. The branches above him were full of mockingbirds. And then—there before him stood three figures.

Fay Larkin was held close to the side of a magnificent woman, barbarously clad in garments made of skins and pieces of blanket. Her face worked in noble emotion. Shefford seemed to see the ghost of that fair beauty Venters had said was Jane Withersteen's. Her hair was gray. Near her stood a lean, stoop-shouldered man whose long hair was perfectly white. His gaunt face was bare of beard. It had strange, sloping, sad lines. And he was staring with mild, surprised eyes.

The moment held Shefford mute till sight of Fay Larkin's tear-wet face broke the spell. He leaped forward and his strong hands reached for the woman and the man.

"Jane Withersteen! . . . Lassiter! I have found you!"

"Oh, sir, who are you?" she cried, with rich and deep and quivering voice. "This child came running—screaming. She could not speak. We thought she had gone mad—and escaped to come back to us."

"I am John Shefford," he replied, swiftly. "I am a friend of Bern Venters —of his wife Bess. I learned your story. I came west. I've searched a year. I found Fay. And we've come to take you away."

"You found Fay? But that masked Mormon who forced her to sacrifice herself to save us! . . . What of him? It's not been so many long years—I remember what my father was—and Dyer and Tull—all those cruel churchmen."

"Waggoner is dead," replied Shefford.

"Dead? She is free! Oh, what—how did he die?"

"He was killed."

"Who did it?"

"That's no matter," replied Shefford, stonily, and he met her gaze with steady eyes. "He's out of the way. Fay was never his wife. Fay's free. We've come to take you out of the country. We must hurry. We'll be tracked— pursued. But we've horses and an Indian guide. We'll get away. . . . I think it better to leave here at once. There's no telling how soon we'll be hunted. Get what things you want to take with you."

"Oh—yes—Mother Jane, let us hurry!" cried Fay. "I'm so full—I can't talk—my heart hurts so!"

Jane Withersteen's face shone with an exceedingly radiant light, and a glory blended with a terrible fear in her eyes.

"Fay! My little Fay!"

Lassiter had stood there with his mild, clear blue eyes upon Shefford.

"I shore am glad to see you-all," he drawled, and extended his hand as if the meeting were casual. "What'd you say your name was?"

Shefford repeated it as he met the proffered hand.

"How's Bern an' Bess?" Lassiter inquired.

"They were well, prosperous, happy when last I saw them. . . . They had a baby."

"Now ain't thet fine? . . . Jane, did you hear? Bess has a baby. An', Jane, didn't I always say Bern would come back to get us out? Shore it's just the same."

How cool, easy, slow, and mild this Lassiter seemed! Had the man grown old, Shefford wondered? The past to him manifestly was only yesterday, and the danger of the present was as nothing. Looking in Lassiter's face, Shefford was baffled. If he had not remembered the greatness of this old gunman he might have believed that the lonely years in the valley had unbalanced his mind. In an hour like this coolness seemed inexplicable—assuredly would have been impossible in an ordinary man. Yet what hid behind that drawling coolness? What was the meaning of those long, sloping, shadowy lines of the face? What spirit lay in the deep, mild, clear eyes? Shefford experienced a sudden check to what had been his first growing impression of a drifting, broken old man.

"Lassiter, pack what little you can carry—mustn't be much—and we'll get out of here," said Shefford.

"I shore will. Reckon I ain't a-goin' to need a pack-train. We saved the clothes we wore in here. Jane never thought it no use. But I figgered we might need them some day. They won't be stylish, but I reckon they'll do better 'n these skins. An' there's an old coat thet was Venters's."

The mild, dreamy look became intensified in Lassiter's eyes.

"Did Venters have any hosses when you knowed him?" he asked.

"He had a farm full of horses," replied Shefford, with a smile. "And there were two blacks—the grandest horses I ever saw. Black Star and Night! You remember, Lassiter?"

"Shore. I was wonderin' if he got the blacks out. They must be growin' old by now. . . . Grand hosses, they was. But Jane had another hoss, a big devil of a sorrel. His name was Wrangle. Did Venters ever tell you about him—an' thet race with Jerry Card?"

"A hundred times!" replied Shefford.

"Wrangle run the blacks off their legs. But Jane never would believe thet. An' I couldn't change her all these years. . . . Reckon mebbe we'll get to see them blacks?"

"Indeed, I hope—I believe you will," replied Shefford, feelingly.

"Shore won't thet be fine. Jane, did you hear? Black Star an' Night are livin' an' we'll get to see them."

But Jane Withersteen only clasped Fay in her arms, and looked at Lassiter with wet and glistening eyes.

Shefford told them to hurry and come to the cliff where the ascent from the valley was to be made. He thought best to leave them alone to make their preparations and bid farewell to the cavern home they had known for so long.

Then he strolled back along the wall, loitering here to gaze into a cave, and there to study crude red paintings in the nooks. And sometimes he halted thoughtfully and did not see anything. At length he rounded a corner of cliff to espy Nas Ta Bega sitting upon the ledge, reposeful and watchful as usual. Shefford told the Indian they would be climbing out soon, and then he sat down to wait and let his gaze rove over the valley.

He might have sat there a long while, so sad and reflective and wondering was his thought, but it seemed a very short time till Fay came in sight with her free, swift grace, and Lassiter and Jane some distance behind. Jane carried a small bundle and Lassiter had a sack over his shoulder that appeared no inconsiderable burden.

"Them beans shore is heavy," he drawled, as he deposited the sack upon the ground.

Shefford curiously took hold of the sack and was amazed to find that a second and hard muscular effort was required to lift it.

"Beans?" he queried.

"Shore," replied Lassiter.

"That's the heaviest sack of beans I ever saw. Why—it's not possible it can be. . . . Lassiter, we've a long, rough trail. We've got to pack light."

"Wal, I ain't a-goin' to leave this here sack behind. Reckon I've been all of twelve years in fillin' it," he declared, mildly.

Shefford could only stare at him.

"Fay may need them beans," went on Lassiter.

"Why?"

"Because they're gold."

"Gold!" ejaculated Shefford.

"Shore. An' they represent some work. Twelve years of diggin' an' washin'!"

Shefford laughed constrainedly. "Well, Lassiter, that alters the case considerably. A sack of gold nuggets or grains, or beans, as you call them, certainly must not be left behind. . . . Come, now, we'll tackle this climbing job."

He called up to the Indian and, grasping the rope, began to walk up the first slant, and then by dint of hand-over-hand effort and climbing with knees and feet he succeeded, with Nas Ta Bega's help, in making the ledge. Then he let down the rope to haul up the sack and bundle. That done, he directed Fay to fasten the noose round her as he had fixed it before. When she had complied he called to her to hold herself out from the wall while he and Nas Ta Bega hauled her up.

"Hold the rope tight," replied Fay. "I'll walk up."

And to Shefford's amaze and admiration, she virtually walked up that almost perpendicular wall by slipping her hands along the rope and stepping as she pulled herself up. There, if never before, he saw the fruit of her years of experience on steep slopes. Only such experience could have made the feat possible.

Jane had to be hauled up, and the task was a painful one for her. Lassiter's turn came then, and he showed more strength and agility than Shefford had supposed him capable of. From the ledge they turned their attention to the narrow crack with its ladder of sticks. Fay had already ascended and now hung over the rim, her white face and golden hair framed vividly in the narrow stream of blue sky above.

"Mother Jane! Uncle Jim! You are so slow," she called.

"Wal, Fay, we haven't been second cousins to a canyon squirrel all these years," replied Lassiter.

This upper half of the climb bid fair to be as difficult for Jane, if not so painful, as the lower. It was necessary for the Indian to go up and drop the rope, which was looped around her, and then, with him pulling from above and Shefford assisting Jane as she climbed, she was finally gotten up without mishap. When Lassiter reached the level they rested a little while and then faced the great slide of jumbled rocks. Fay led the way, light, supple, tireless, and Shefford never ceased looking at her. At last they surmounted the long slope and, winding along the rim, reached the point where Fay had led out of the cedars.

Nas Ta Bega, then, was the one to whom Shefford looked for every decision or action of the immediate future. The Indian said he had seen a pool of water in a rocky hole, that the day was spent, that here was a little grass for the mustangs, and it would be well to camp right there. So while Nas Ta Bega attended to the mustangs Shefford set about such preparations for camp and supper as their light pack afforded. The question of beds was easily answered, for the mats of soft needles under pinyon and cedar would be comfortable places to sleep.

When Shefford felt free again the sun was setting. Lassiter and Jane were walking under the trees. The Indian had returned to camp. But Fay was missing. Shefford imagined he knew where to find her, and upon going to the edge of the forest he saw her sitting on the promontory. He approached her, drawn in spite of a feeling that perhaps he ought to stay away.

"Fay, would you rather be alone?" he asked.

His voice startled her.

"I want you," she replied, and held out her hand.

Taking it in his own, he sat beside her.

The red sun was at their backs. Surprise Valley lay hazy, dusky, shadowy beneath them. The opposite wall seemed fired by crimson flame, save far down at its base, which the sun no longer touched. And the dark line of red slowly rose, encroaching upon the bright crimson. Changing, transparent, yet dusky veils seemed to float between the walls; long, red rays, where the sun shone through notch or crack in the rim, split the darker spaces; deep down at the floor the forest darkened, the strip of aspen paled, the meadow turned gray; and all under the shelves and in the great caverns a purple gloom deepened. Then the sun set. And swiftly twilight was there below while day lingered above. On the opposite wall the fire died and the stone grew cold.

A canyon night-hawk voiced his lonely, weird, and melancholy cry, and it seemed to pierce and mark the silence.

A pale star, peering out of a sky that had begun to turn blue, marked the end of twilight. And all the purple shadows moved and hovered and changed till, softly and mysteriously, they embraced black night.

Beautiful, wild, strange, silent Surprise Valley! Shefford saw it before and beneath him, a dark abyss now, the abode of loneliness. He imagined faintly what was in Fay Larkin's heart. For the last time she had seen the sun set there and night come with its dead silence and sweet mystery and phantom shadows, its velvet blue sky and white trains of stars.

He, who had dreamed and longed and searched, found that the hour had been incalculable for him in its import.

❧17❧

THE TRAIL
TO NONNEZOSHE

WHEN SHEFFORD awoke next morning and sat up on his bed of pinyon boughs the dawn had broken cold with a ruddy gold brightness under the trees. Nas Ta Bega and Lassiter were busy around a campfire; the mustangs were haltered nearby; Jane Withersteen combed out her long, tangled tresses with a crude wooden comb; and Fay Larkin was not in sight. As she had been missing from the group at sunset, so she was now at sunrise. Shefford went out to take his last look at Surprise Valley.

On the evening before the valley had been a place of dusky red veils and purple shadows, and now it was pink-walled, clear and rosy and green and white, with wonderful shafts of gold slanting down from the notched eastern rim. Fay stood on the promontory, and Shefford did not break the spell of her silent farewell to her wild home. A strange emotion abided with him and he knew he would always, all his life, regret leaving Surprise Valley.

Then the Indian called.

"Come, Fay," said Shefford, gently.

And she turned away with dark, haunted eyes and a white, still face.

The somber Indian gave a silent gesture for Shefford to make haste. While they had breakfast the mustangs were saddled and packed. And soon all was in readiness for the flight. Fay was given Nack-yal, Jane the saddled horse Shefford had ridden, and Lassiter the Indian's roan. Shefford and Nas Ta Bega were to ride the blanketed mustangs, and the sixth and last one bore the pack. Nas Ta Bega set off, leading this horse; the others of the party lined in behind with Shefford at the rear.

Nas Ta Bega led at a brisk trot, and sometimes, on level stretches of ground, at an easy canter; and Shefford had a grim realization of what this flight was going to be for these three fugitives, now so unaccustomed to riding. Jane and Lassiter, however, needed no watching, and showed they had never forgotten how to manage a horse. The Indian back-trailed yesterday's path for an hour, then headed west to the left, and entered a low pass. All parts of this plateau country looked alike, and Shefford was at some pains to tell the difference of this strange ground from that which he had been over. In another hour they got out of the rugged, broken rock to the wind-worn and smooth, shallow canyon Shefford calculated that they were coming to the end of the plateau. The low walls slanted lower; the canyon made a turn; Nas Ta Bega disappeared; and then the others of the party. When Shefford turned the corner of wall he saw a short strip of bare, rocky ground with only sky beyond. The Indian and his followers had halted in a group. Shefford rode to them, halted himself, and in one sweeping glance realized the meaning of their silent gaze. But immediately Nas Ta Bega started down, and the mustangs, without word or touch, followed him. Shefford, however, lingered on the promontory.

His gaze seemed impelled and held by things afar—the great yellow-and-purple corrugated world of distance, now on a level with his eyes. He was drawn by the beauty and the grandeur of that scene and transfixed by the realization that he had dared to venture to find a way through this vast, wild, and unflung fastness. He kept looking afar, sweeping the three-quartered circle of horizon till his judgment of distance was confounded and his sense of proportion dwarfed one moment and magnified the next. Then he withdrew his fascinated gaze to adopt the Indian's method of studying unlimited spaces in the desert—to look with slow, contracted eyes from near to far.

His companions had begun to zigzag down a long slope, bare of rock, with yellow gravel patches showing between the scant strips of green, and here and there a scrub-cedar. Half a mile down, the slope merged into green level. But close, keen gaze made out this level to be a rolling plain, growing darker green, with blue lines of ravines, and thin, undefined spaces that might be mirage. Miles and miles it swept and rolled and heaved to lose its waves in apparent darker level. A round, red rock stood isolated, marking the end of the barren plain, and farther on were other round rocks, all isolated, all of different shape. They resembled huge grazing cattle. But as Shefford gazed, and his sight gained strength from steadily holding it to separate features, these rocks were strangely magnified. They grew and grew into mounds, castles, domes, crags—great, red, wind-carved buttes. One by one they drew his gaze to the wall of upflung rock. He seemed to see a thousand domes of a thousand shapes and colors, and among them a thousand blue clefts, each one a little mark in his sight, yet which he knew was a canyon.

So far he gained some idea of what he saw. But beyond this wide area of curved lines rose another wall, dwarfing the lower, dark red, horizon-long, magnificent in frowning boldness, and because of its limitless deceiving surfaces, breaks, and lines, incomprehensible to the sight of man. Away to the eastward began a winding, ragged, blue line, looping back upon itself, and then winding away again, growing wider and bluer. This line was the San Juan Canyon. Where was Joe Lake at that moment? Had he embarked yet on the river—did that blue line, so faint, so deceiving, hold him and the boat? Almost it was impossible to believe. Shefford followed the blue line all its length, a hundred miles, he fancied, down toward the west where it joined a dark, purple, shadowy cleft. And this was the Grand Canyon of the Colorado. Shefford's eye swept along with that winding mark, farther and farther to the west, round to the left, until the cleft, growing larger and coming closer, losing its deception, was seen to be a wild and winding canyon. Still farther to the left, as he swung in fascinated gaze, it split the wonderful wall—a vast plateau now with great red peaks and yellow mesas. The canyon was full of purple smoke. It turned, it closed, it gaped, it lost itself and showed again in that chaos of a million cliffs. And then farther on it became again a cleft, a purple line, at last to fail entirely in deceiving distance.

Shefford imagined there was no scene in all the world to equal that. The tranquillity of lesser spaces was not here manifest. Sound, movement, life, seemed to have no fitness here. Ruin was there and desolation and decay. The meaning of the ages was flung at him, and a man became nothing. When he had gazed at the San Juan Canyon he had been appalled at the nature of Joe Lake's Herculean task. He had lost hope, faith. The thing was not possible. But when Shefford gazed at that sublime and majestic wilderness, in which the Grand Canyon was only a dim line, he strangely lost his terror and something else came to him from across the shining spaces. If Nas Ta Bega led them safely down to the river, if Joe Lake met them at the mouth of Nonnezoshe Boco, if they survived the rapids of that terrible gorge, then Shefford would have to face his soul and the meaning of this spirit that breathed on the wind.

He urged his mustang to the descent of the slope, and as he went down, slowly drawing nearer to the other fugitives, his mind alternated between this strange intimation of faith, this subtle uplift of his spirit, and the growing gloom and shadow in his love for Fay Larkin. Not that he loved her less, but more! A possible God hovering near him, like the Indian's spirit-step on the trail, made his soul the darker for Fay's crime, and he saw with clearer sight, with deeper sadness, with sterner truth.

More than once the Indian turned on his mustang to look up the slope and the light flashed from his dark, somber face. Shefford instinctively looked back himself, and then realized the unconscious motive of the action. Deep within him there had been a premonition of certain pursuit, and the Indian's reiterated backward glance had at length brought the feeling upward. Thereafter, as they descended, Shefford gradually added to his already wrought emotions a mounting anxiety.

No sign of a trail showed where the base of the slope rolled out to meet the green plain. The earth was gravelly, with dark patches of heavy silt, almost like cinders; and round, black rocks, flinty and glassy, cracked away from the hoofs of the mustangs. There was a level bench a mile wide, then a ravine, and then an ascent, and after that, rounded ridge and ravine, one after the other, like huge swells of a monstrous sea. Indian paint-brush vied in its scarlet hue with the deep magenta of cactus. There was no sage. Soapweed and meager grass and a bunch of cactus here and there lent the green to that barren; and it was green only at a distance. Nas Ta Bega kept on a steady, even trot. The sun climbed. The wind rose and whipped dust from under the mustangs.

Shefford looked back often, and the farther out in the plain he reached the higher loomed the plateau they had descended; and as he faced ahead again the lower sank the red-domed and castled horizon to the fore. The ravines became deeper, with dry rock bottoms, and the ridge-tops sharper, with outcroppings of yellow, crumbling ledges. Once across the central depression of that wide plain a gradual ascent became evident, and the red, round rocks grew clearer in sight, began to rise and shine and grow. And thereafter every slope brought them nearer.

The sun was straight overhead and hot when Nas Ta Bega halted the party under the first lonely scrub-cedar. They all dismounted to stretch their limbs and rest the horses. It was not a talkative group. Lassiter's comments on the never-ending green plain elicited no response. Jane Withersteen looked afar with the past in her eyes. Shefford felt Fay's wistful glance and could not meet it; indeed, he seemed to want to hide something from her. The Indian bent a falcon gaze on the distant slope, and Shefford did not like that intent, searching, steadfast watchfulness. Suddenly Nas Ta Bega stiffened and whipped the halter he held.

"Ugh!" he exclaimed.

All eyes followed the direction of his dark hand. Puffs of dust rose from the base of the long slope they had descended; tiny dark specks moved with the pace of a snail.

"Shadd!" added the Indian.

"I expected it," said Shefford, darkly, as he rose.

"An' who's Shadd?" drawled Lassiter in his cool, slow speech.

Briefly Shefford explained, and then, looking at Nas Ta Bega, he added:

"The hardest-riding outfit in the country! We can't get away from them."

Jane Withersteen was silent, but Fay uttered a low cry. Shefford did not look at either of them. The Indian began swiftly to tighten the saddle-cinches of his roan, and Shefford did likewise for Nack-yal. Then Shefford drew his rifle out of the saddle-sheath and Joe Lake's big guns from the saddle-bag.

"Here, Lassiter, maybe you haven't forgotten how to use these," he said.

The old gunman started as if he had seen ghosts. His hands grew clawlike as he reached for the guns. He threw open the cylinders, spilled out the shells, snapped back the cylinders. Then he went through motions too swift for Shefford to follow. But Shefford heard the hammers falling so swiftly they blended their clicks almost in one sound. Lassiter reloaded the guns with a speed comparable with the other actions. A remarkable transformation had come over him. He did not seem the same man. The mild eyes had changed; the long, shadowy, sloping lines were tense cords; and there was a cold, ashy shade on his face.

"Twelve years!" he muttered to himself. "I dropped them old guns back there where I rolled the rock. . . . Twelve years!"

Shefford realized the twelve years were as if they had never been. And he would rather have had this old gunman with him than a dozen ordinary men.

The Indian spoke rapidly in Navajo, saying that once in the rocks they were safe. Then, after another look at the distant dust-puffs, he wheeled his mustang.

It was doubtful if the party could have kept near him had they been responsible for the gait of their mounts. The fact was that the way the Indian called to his mustang or some leadership in the one he rode drew the others to a like trot or climb or canter. For a long time Shefford did not turn round; he knew what to expect. And when he did turn he was startled at the gain made by the pursuers. But he was encouraged as well by the looming, red, rounded peaks seemingly now so close. He could see the dark splits between the sloping curved walls, the pinyon patches in the amphitheater under the circled walls. That was a wild place they were approaching, and, once in there, he believed pursuit would be useless. However, there were miles to go still, and those hard-riding devils behind made alarming decrease in the intervening distance. Shefford could see

the horses plainly now. How they made the dust fly! He counted up to six
—and then the dust and moving line caused the others to be indistinguishable.

At last only a long, gently rising slope separated the fugitives from that
labyrinthine network of wildly carved rock. But it was the clear air that
made the distance seem short. Mile after mile the mustangs climbed, and
when they were perhaps halfway across that last slope to the rocks the first
horse of the pursuers mounted to the level behind. In a few moments the
whole band was strung out in sight. Nas Ta Bega kept his mustang at a
steady walk, in spite of the gaining pursuers. There came a point, however, when the Indian, reaching comparatively level ground, put his
mount to a swinging canter. The other mustangs broke into the same gait.

It became a race then, with the couple of miles between fugitives and
pursuers only imperceptibly lessened. Nas Ta Bega had saved his mustangs
and Shadd had ridden his to the limit. Shefford kept looking back, gripping his rifle, hoping it would not come to a fight, yet slowly losing that
reluctance.

Sage began to show on the slope, and other kinds of brush and cedars
straggled everywhere. The great rocks loomed closer, the red color mixed
with yellow, and the slopes lengthening out, not so steep, yet infinitely
longer than they had seemed at a distance.

Shefford ceased to feel the dry wind in his face. They were already in
the lee of the wall. He could see the rock-squirrels scampering to their
holes. The mustangs valiantly held to the gait, and at last the Indian
disappeared between two rounded corners of cliff. The others were close
behind. Shefford wheeled once more. Shadd and his gang were a mile in
the rear, but coming fast, despite winded horses.

Shefford rode around the wall into a widening space thick with cedars.
It ended in a bare slope of smooth rock. Here the Indian dismounted.
When the others came up with him he told them to lead their horses and
follow. Then he began the ascent of the rock.

It was smooth and hard, though not slippery. There was not a crack.
Shefford did not see a broken piece of stone. Nas Ta Bega climbed straight
up for a while, and then wound around a swell, to turn this way and that,
always going up. Shefford began to see similar mounds of rock all around
him, of every shape that could be called a curve. There were yellow domes
far above, and small red domes far below. Ridges ran from one hill of rock
to another. There were no abrupt breaks, but holes and pits and caves
were everywhere, and occasionally, deep down, an amphitheater green
with cedar and pinyon. The Indian appeared to have a clear idea of where
he wanted to go, though there was no vestige of a trail on those bare
slopes. At length Shefford was high enough to see back upon the plain,
but the pursuers were no longer in sight.

Nas Ta Bega led to the top of that wall, only to disclose to his followers another and a higher wall beyond, with a ridged, bare, wild, and scalloped depression between. Here footing began to be precarious for both man and beast. When the ascent of the second wall began it was necessary to zigzag up, slowly and carefully, taking advantage of every level bulge or depression. They must have consumed half an hour mounting this slope to the summit. Once there, Shefford drew a sharp breath with both backward and forward glances. Shadd and his gang, in single file, showed dark upon the bare stone ridge behind. And to the fore there twisted and dropped and curved the most dangerous slopes Shefford had ever seen. The fugitives had reached the height of stone wall, of the divide, and many of the drops upon this side were perpendicular and too steep to see the bottom.

Nas Ta Bega led along the ridge-top and then started down, following the waves in the rock. He came out upon a round promontory from which there could not have been any turning of a horse. The long slant leading down was at an angle Shefford declared impossible for the animals. Yet the Indian started down. His mustang needed urging, but at last edged upon the steep descent. Shefford and the others had to hold back and wait. It was thrilling to see the intelligent mustang. He did not step. He slid his fore hoofs a few inches at a time and kept directly behind the Indian. If he fell he would knock Nas Ta Bega off his feet and they would both roll down together. There was no doubt in Shefford's mind that the mustang knew this as well as the Indian. Foot by foot they worked down to a swelling bulge, and here Nas Ta Bega left his mustang and came back for the pack-horse. It was even more difficult to get this beast down. Then the Indian called for Lassiter and Jane and Fay to come down. Shefford began to keep a sharp lookout behind and above, and did not see how the three fared on the slope, but evidently there was no mishap. Nas Ta Bega mounted the slope again, and at the moment sight of Shadd's dark bays silhouetted against the sky caused Shefford to call out:

"We've got to hurry!"

The Indian led one mustang and called to the others. Shefford stepped close behind. They went down in single file, inch by inch, foot by foot, and safely reached the comparative level below.

"Shadd's gang are riding their horses up and down these walls!" exclaimed Shefford.

"Shore," replied Lassiter.

Both the women were silent.

Nas Ta Bega led the way swiftly to the right. He rounded a huge dome, climbed a low, rolling ridge, descended and ascended, and came out upon the rim of a steep-walled amphitheater. Along the rim was a yard-wide level, with the chasm to the left and steep slope to the right. There was no time to flinch at the danger, when an even greater danger menaced from the rear. Nas Ta Bega led, and his mustang kept at his heels. One misstep would have plunged the animal to his death. But he was sure-footed and his confidence helped the others. At the apex of the curve the only course led away from the rim, and here there was no level. Four of the mustangs slipped and slid down the smooth rock until they stopped in a shallow depression. It cost time to get them out, to straighten pack and saddles. Shefford thought he heard a yell in the rear, but he could not see anything of the gang.

They rounded this precipice only to face a worse one. Shefford's nerve was sorely tried when he saw steep slants everywhere, all apparently leading down into chasms, and no place a man, let alone a horse, could put a foot with safety. Nevertheless the imperturbable Indian never slacked his pace. Always he appeared to find a way, and he never had to turn back. His winding course, however, did not now cover much distance in a straight line, and herein lay the greatest peril. Any moment Shadd and his men might come within range.

Upon a particularly tedious and dangerous side of rocky hill the fugitives lost so much time that Shefford grew exceedingly alarmed. Still, they accomplished it without accident, and their pursuers did not heave in sight. Perhaps they were having trouble in a bad place.

The afternoon was waning. The red sun hung low above the yellow mesa to the left, and there was a perceptible shading of light.

At last Nas Ta Bega came to a place that halted him. It did not look so bad as places they had successfully passed. Yet upon closer study Shefford did not see how they were to get around the neck of the gully at their feet. Presently the Indian put the bridle over the head of his mustang and left him free. He did likewise for two more mustangs, while Lassiter and Shefford rendered a like service to theirs. Then the Indian started down, with his mustang following him. The pack-animal came next, then Fay and Nack-yal, then Lassiter and his mount, with Jane and hers next, and Shefford last. They followed the Indian, picking their steps swiftly, looking nowhere except at the stone under their feet. The right side of the chasm was rimmed, the curve at the head crossed, and then the real peril of this trap had to be faced. It was a narrow slant of ledge, doubling back parallel with the course already traversed.

A sharp warning cry from Nas Ta Bega scarcely prepared Shefford for hoarse yells, and then a rattling rifle-volley from the top of the slope opposite. Bullets thudded on the cliff, whipped up red dust, and spanged and droned away.

Fay Larkin screamed and staggered back against the wall. Nack-yal was hit, and with frightened snort he reared, pawed the air, and came down, pounding the stone. The mustang behind him went to his knees, sank with his head over the rim, and, slipping off, plunged into the depths. In an instant a dull crash came up.

For a moment there was imminent peril for the horses, more in the yawning hole than in the spanging of badly aimed bullets. Lassiter drew Jane up a little slope out of the way of the frightened mustangs, and Shefford, risking his neck, rushed to Fay. She was holding her arm, which was bleeding. Unheeding the rain of bullets, he half carried, half dragged her along the slope of the low bluff, where he hid behind a corner till the Indian drove the mustangs round it. Shefford's swift fingers were wet and red with the blood from Fay's arm when he had bound the wound with his scarf. Lassiter had gotten around with Jane and was calling Shefford to hurry.

It had been Shefford's idea to halt there and fight. But he did not want to send Fay on alone, so he hurried ahead with her. The Indian had the horses going fast on a long level, overhung by bulging wall. Lassiter and Jane were looking back. Shefford, becoming aware of a steep slope to his left, looked down to see a narrow chasm and great crevices in the cliffs, with bunches of cedars here and there.

Presently Nas Ta Bega disappeared with the mustangs. He had evidently turned off to go down behind the split cliffs. Shefford and Fay caught up with Lassiter and Jane, and, panting, hurrying, looking backward and then forward, they kept on, as best they could, in the Indian's course. Shefford made sure they had lost him, when he appeared down to the left. Then they all ran to catch up with him. They went around the chasm, and then through one of the narrow cracks to come out upon the rim, among cedars. Here the Indian waited for them. He pointed down another long swell of naked stone to a narrow green split which was evidently different from all these curved pits and holes and abysses, for this one had straight walls and wound away out of sight. It was the head of a canyon.

"Nonnezoshe Boco!" said the Indian.

"Nas Ta Bega, go on!" replied Shefford. "When Shadd comes out on that slope above he can't see you—where you go down. Hurry on with the horses and women. Lassiter, you go with them. And if Shadd passes me and comes up with you—do your best. . . . I'm going to ambush that Piute and his gang!"

"Shore you've picked out a good place," replied Lassiter.

In another moment Shefford was alone. He heard the light, soft pat and slide of the hoofs of the mustangs as they went down. Presently that sound ceased.

He looked at the red stain on his hands—from the blood of the girl he loved. And he had to stifle a terrible wrath that shook his frame. In regard to Shadd's pursuit, it had not been blood that he had feared, but capture for Fay. He and Nas Ta Bega might have expected a shot if they resisted, but to wound that unfortunate girl—it made a tiger out of him. When he had stilled the emotions that weakened and shook him and reached cold and implacable control of himself, he crawled under the cedars to the rim and, well hidden, he watched and waited.

Shadd appeared to be slow for the first time since he had been sighted. With keen eyes Shefford watched the corner where he and the others had escaped from that murderous volley. But Shadd did not come.

The sun had lost its warmth and was tipping the lofty mesa to his right. Soon twilight would make travel on those walls more perilous and darkness would make it impossible. Shadd must hurry or abandon the pursuit for that day. Shefford found himself grimly hopeful.

Suddenly he heard the click of hoofs. It came, faint yet clear, on the still air. He glued his sight upon that corner where he expected the pursuers to appear. More cracks of hoofs pierced his ear, clearer and sharper this time. Presently he gathered that they could not possibly come from beyond the corner he was watching. So he looked far to the left of that place, seeing no one, then far to the right. Out over a bulge of stone he caught sight of the bobbing head of a horse—then another—and still another.

He was astounded. Shadd had gone below that place where the attack had been made and he had come up this steep slope. More horses appeared—to the number of eight. Shefford easily recognized a low, broad, squat rider to be Shadd. Assuredly the Piute did not know this country. Possibly, however, he had feared an ambush. But Shefford grew convinced that Shadd had not expected an ambush, or at least did not fear it, and had mistaken the Indian's course. Moreover, if he led his gang a few rods farther up that slope he would do worse than make a mistake—he would be facing a double peril.

What fearless horsemen these Indians were! Shadd was mounted, as were three others of his gang. Evidently the white men, the outlaws, were the ones on foot. Shefford thrilled and his veins stung when he saw these pursuers come passing what he considered the danger mark. But manifestly they could not see their danger. Assuredly they were aware of the chasm; however, the level upon which they were advancing narrowed gradually, and they could not tell that very soon they could not go any farther nor could they turn back. The alternative was to climb the slope, and that was a desperate chance.

They came up, now about on a level with Shefford, and perhaps three hundred yards distant. He gripped his rifle with a fatal assurance that he could kill one of them now. Still he waited. Curiosity consumed him because every foot they advanced heightened their peril. Shefford wondered if Shadd would have chosen that course if he had not supposed the Navajo had chosen it first. It was plain that one of the walking Piutes stooped now and then to examine the rock. He was looking for some faint sign of a horse track.

Shadd halted within two hundred yards of where Shefford lay hidden. His keen eye had caught the significance of the narrowing level before he had reached the end. He pointed and spoke. Shefford heard his voice.

The others replied. They all looked up at the steep slope, down into the chasm right below them, and across into the cedars. The Piute in the rear succeeded in turning his horse, went back, and began to circle up the slope. The others entered into an argument and they became more closely grouped upon the narrow bench. Their mustangs were lean, wiry, wild, vicious, and Shefford calculated grimly upon what a stampede might mean in that position.

Then Shadd turned his mustang up the slope. Like a goat he climbed. Another Indian in the rear succeeded in pivoting his steed and started back, apparently to circle round and up. The others of the gang appeared uncertain. They yelled hoarsely at Shadd, who halted on the steep slant some twenty paces above them. He spoke and made motions that evidently meant the climb was easy enough. It looked easy for him. His dark face flashed red in the rays of the sun.

At this critical moment Shefford decided to fire. He meant to kill Shadd, hoping if the leader was gone the others would abandon the pursuit. The rifle wavered a little as he aimed, then grew still. He fired. Shadd never flinched. But the fiery mustang, perhaps wounded, certainly terrified, plunged down with piercing, horrid scream. Shadd fell under him. Shrill yells rent the air. Like a thunderbolt the sliding horse was upon men and animals below.

A heavy shock, wild snorts, upflinging heads and hoofs, a terrible tramping, thudding, shrieking mélée, then a brown, twisting, tangled mass shot down the slant over the rim!

Shefford dazedly thought he saw men running. He did see plunging horses. One slipped, fell, rolled, and went into the chasm.

Then up from the depths came a crash, a long, slipping roar. In another instant there was a lighter crash and a lighter sliding roar.

Two horses, shaking, paralyzed with fear, were left upon the narrow level. Beyond them a couple of men were crawling along the stone. Up on the level stood the two Indians, holding down frightened horses, and staring at the fatal slope.

And Shefford lay there under the cedar, in the ghastly grip of the moment, hardly comprehending that his ill-aimed shot had been a thunderbolt.

He did not think of shooting at the Piutes; they, however, recovering from their shock, evidently feared the ambush, for they swiftly drew up the slope and passed out of sight. The frightened horses below whistled and tramped along the lower level, finally vanishing. There was nothing left on the bare wall to prove to Shefford that it had been the scene of swift and tragic death. He leaned from his covert and peered over the rim. Hundreds of feet below he saw dark growths of pinyons. There was no sign of a pile of horses and men, and then he realized that he could not tell the number that had perished. The swift finale had been as stunning to him as if lightning had struck near him.

Suddenly it flashed over him what state of suspense and torture Fay and Jane must be in at that very moment. And, leaping up, he ran out of the cedars to the slope behind and hurried down at risk of limb. The sun had set by this time. He hoped he could catch up with the party before dark. He went straight down, and the end of the slope was a smooth, low wall. The Indian must have descended with the horses at some other point. The canyon was about fifty yards wide and it headed under the great slope of Navajo Mountain. These smooth, rounded walls appeared to end at its low rim.

Shefford slid down upon a grassy bank, and finding the tracks of the horses, he followed them. They led along the wall. As soon as he had assured himself that Nas Ta Bega had gone down the canyon he abandoned the tracks and pushed ahead swiftly. He heard the soft rush of running water. In the center of the canyon wound heavy lines of bright-green foliage, bordering a rocky brook. The air was close, warm, and sweet with perfume of flowers. The walls were low and shelving, and soon lost that rounded appearance peculiar to the wind-worn slopes above. Shefford came to where the horses had plowed down a gravelly bank into the clear, swift water of the brook. The little pools of water were still muddy. Shefford drank, finding the water cold and sweet, without the bitter bite of alkali. He crossed and pushed on, running on the grassy levels. Flowers were everywhere, but he did not notice them particularly. The canyon made many leisurely turns, and its size, if it enlarged at all, was not perceptible to him yet. The rims above him were perhaps fifty feet high. Cottonwood trees began to appear along the brook, and blossoming buck-brush in the corners of wall.

He had traveled perhaps a mile when Nas Ta Bega, appearing to come out of the thicket, confronted him.

"Hello!" called Shefford. "Where're Fay—and the others?"

The Indian made a gesture that signified the rest of the party were beyond a little way. Shefford took Nas Ta Bega's arm, and as they walked, and he panted for breath, he told what had happened back on the slopes.

The Indian made one of his singular speaking sweeps of hand, and he scrutinized Shefford's face, but he received the news in silence. They turned a corner of wall, crossed a wide, shallow, boulder-strewn place in the brook, and mounted the bank to a thicket. Beyond this, from a clump of cottonwoods, Lassiter strode out with a gun in each hand. He had been hiding.

"Shore I'm glad to see you," he said, and the eyes that piercingly fixed on Shefford were now as keen as formerly they had been mild.

"Gone! Lassiter—they're gone," broke out Shefford. "Where's Fay—and Jane?"

Lassiter called, and presently the women came out of the thick brake, and Fay bounded forward with her swift stride, while Jane followed with eager step and anxious face. Then they all surrounded Shefford.

"It was Shadd—and his gang," panted Shefford. "Eight in all. Three or four Piutes—the others outlaws. They lost track of us. Went below the place—where they shot at us. And they came up—on a bad slope."

Shefford described the slope and the deep chasm and how Shadd led up to the point where he saw his mistake and then how the catastrophe fell.

"I shot—and missed," repeated Shefford, with the sweat in beads on his pale face. "I missed Shadd. Maybe I hit the horse. He plunged—reared—fell back—a terrible fall—right upon that bunch of horses and men be-low. . . . In a horrible, wrestling, screaming tangle they slid over the rim! I don't know how many. I saw some men running along. I saw three other horses plunging. One slipped and went over. . . . I have no idea how many, but Shadd and some of his gang went to destruction."

"Shore that's fine!" said Lassiter. "But mebbe I won't get to use them guns, after all."

"Hardly on that gang," laughed Shefford. "The two Piutes and what others escaped turned back. Maybe they'll meet a posse of Mormons—for of course the Mormons will track us, too—and come back to where Shadd lost his life. That's an awful place. Even the Piute got lost—couldn't follow Nas Ta Bega. It would take any pursuers some time to find how we got in here. I believe we need not fear further pursuit. Certainly not tonight or tomorrow. Then we'll be far down the canyon."

When Shefford concluded his earnest remarks the faces of Fay and Jane had lost the signs of suppressed dread.

"Nas Ta Bega, make camp here," said Shefford. "Water—wood—grass—why, this's something like. . . . Fay, how's your arm?"

"It hurts," she replied, simply.

"Come with me down to the brook and let me wash and bind it properly."

They went, and she sat upon a stone while he knelt beside her and untied his scarf from her arm. As the blood had hardened, it was necessary to slit her sleeve to the shoulder. Using his scarf, he washed the blood from the wound, and found it to be merely a cut, a groove, on the surface.

"That's nothing," Shefford said, lightly. "It'll heal in a day. But there'll always be a scar. And when we—we get back to civilization, and you wear a pretty gown without sleeves, people will wonder what made this mark on your beautiful arm."

Fay looked at him with wonderful eyes. "Do women wear gowns with-out sleeves?" she asked.

"They do."

"Have I a—beautiful arm?"

She stretched it out, white, blue-veined, the skin fine as satin, the lines graceful and flowing, a round, firm, strong arm.

"The most beautiful I ever saw," he replied.

But the pleasure his compliment gave her was not communicated to him. His last impression of that right arm had been of its strength, and his mind flashed with lightning swiftness to a picture that haunted him— Waggoner lying dead on the porch with that powerfully driven knife in his breast. Shefford shuddered through all his being. Would this phantom come often to him like that? Hurriedly he bound up her arm with the scarf and did not look at her, and was conscious that she felt a subtle change in him.

The short twilight ended with the fugitives comfortable in a camp that for natural features could not have been improved upon. Darkness found Fay and Jane asleep on a soft mossy bed, a blanket tucked around them, and their faces still and beautiful in the flickering campfire light. Lassiter did not linger long awake. Nas Ta Bega, seeing Shefford's excessive fatigue, urged him to sleep. Shefford demurred, insisting that he share the night watch. But Nas Ta Bega, by agreeing that Shefford might have the following night's duty, prevailed upon him.

Shefford seemed to shut his eyes upon darkness and to open them immediately to the light. The stream of blue sky above, the gold tints on the western rim, the rosy, brightening colors down in the canyon, were proofs of the sunrise. This morning Nas Ta Bega proceeded leisurely, and his manner was comforting. When all was in readiness for a start he gave the mustang he had ridden to Shefford, and walked, leading the pack-animal.

The mode of travel here was a selection of the best levels, the best places to cross the brook, the best banks to climb, and it was a process of continual repetition. As the Indian picked out the course and the mustangs followed his lead there was nothing for Shefford to do but take his choice between reflection that seemed predisposed toward gloom and an absorption in the beauty, color, wildness, and changing character of Nonnezoshe Boco.

Assuredly his experience in the desert did not count in it a trip down into a strange, beautiful, lost canyon such as this. It did not widen, though the walls grew higher. They began to lean and bulge, and the narrow strip of sky above resembled a flowing blue river. Huge caverns had been hollowed out by some work of nature, what, he could not tell, though he was sure it could not have been wind. And when the brook ran close under one of these overhanging places the running water made a singular, indescribable sound. A crack from a hoof on a stone rang like a hollow bell and echoed from wall to wall. And the croak of a frog—the only living creature he had so far noted in the canyon was a weird and melancholy thing.

Fay rode close to him, and his heart seemed to rejoice when she spoke, when she showed how she wanted to be near him, yet, try as he might, he could not respond. His speech to her—what little there was—did not come spontaneously. And he suffered a remorse that he could not be honestly natural to her. Then he would drive away the encroaching gloom, trusting that a little time would dispel it.

"We are deeper down than Surprise Valley," said Fay.

"How do you know?" he asked.

"Here are the pink and yellow sago-lilies. You remember we went once to find the white ones? I have found white lilies in Surprise Valley, but never any pink or yellow."

Shefford had seen flowers all along the green banks, but he had not marked the lilies. Here he dismounted and gathered several. They were larger than the white ones of higher altitudes, of the same exquisite beauty and fragility, of such rare pink and yellow hues as he had never seen. He gave the flowers to Fay.

"They bloom only where it's always summer," she said.

That expressed their nature. They were the orchids of the summer canyons. They stood up everywhere starlike out of the green. It was impossible to prevent the mustangs treading them under hoof. And as the canyon deepened, and many little springs added their tiny volume to the brook, every grassy bench was dotted with lilies, like a green sky star-spangled. And this increasing luxuriance manifested itself in the banks of purple moss and clumps of lavender daisies and great clusters of yellow violets. The brook was lined by blossoming buck-rush; the rocky corners showed the crimson and magenta of cactus; ledges were green with shining moss that sparkled with little white flowers. The hum of bees filled the air.

But by and by this green and colorful and verdant beauty, the almost level floor of the canyon, the banks of soft earth, the thickets and the clumps of cottonwoods, the shelving caverns and the bulging walls—these features gradually were lost, and Nonnezoshe Boco began to deepen in bare red and white stone steps, the walls sheered away from one another, breaking into sections and ledges, and rising higher and higher, and there began to be manifested a dark and solemn concordance with the nature that had created this rent in the earth.

There was a stretch of miles where steep steps in hard red rock alternated with long levels of round boulders. Here one by one the mustangs went lame. And the fugitives, dismounting to spare the faithful beasts, slipped and stumbled over these loose and treacherous stones. Fay was the only one who did not show distress. She was glad to be on foot again and the rolling boulders were as stable as solid rock for her.

The hours passed; the toil increased; the progress diminished; one of the mustangs failed entirely and was left; and all the while the dimensions of Nonnezoshe Boco magnified and its character changed. It became a thousand-foot walled canyon, leaning, broken, threatening, with great yellow slides blocking passage, with huge sections split off from the main wall, with immense dark and gloomy caverns. Strangely, it had no intersecting canyons. It jealously guarded its secret. Its unusual formations of cavern and pillar and half-arch led the mind to expect any monstrous stone-shape left by an avalanche or cataclysm.

Down and down the fugitives toiled. And now the streambed was bare of boulders, and the banks of earth. The floods that had rolled down that canyon had here borne away every loose thing. All the floor was bare red and white stone, polished, glistening, slippery, affording treacherous foothold. And the time came when Nas Ta Bega abandoned the streambed to take to the rock-strewn and cactus-covered ledges above.

Jane gave out and had to be assisted upon the weary mustang. Fay was persuaded to mount Nack-yal again. Lassiter plodded along. The Indian bent tired steps far in front. And Shefford traveled on after him, footsore and hot.

The canyon widened ahead into a great, ragged, iron-hued amphitheater, and from there apparently turned abruptly at right angles. Sunset rimmed the walls. Shefford wondered dully when the Indian would halt to camp. And he dragged himself onward with eyes down on the rough ground.

When he raised them again the Indian stood on a point of slope with folded arms, gazing down where the canyon veered. Something in Nas Ta Bega's pose quickened Shefford's pulse and then his steps. He reached the Indian and the point where he, too, could see beyond that vast jutting wall that had obstructed his view.

A mile beyond all was bright with the colors of sunset, and spanning the canyon in the graceful shape and beautiful hues of a rainbow was a magnificent stone bridge.

"Nonnezoshe!" exclaimed the Navajo, with a deep and sonorous roll in his voice.

⚜18⚜

AT THE FOOT
OF THE RAINBOW

THE RAINBOW BRIDGE was the one great natural phenomenon, the one grand spectacle, which Shefford had ever seen that did not at first give vague disappointment, a confounding of reality, a disenchantment of contrast with what the mind had conceived.

But this thing was glorious. It silenced him, yet did not awe or stun. His body and brain, weary and dull from the toil of travel, received a singular and revivifying freshness. He had a strange, mystic perception of this rosy-hued stupendous arch of stone, as if in a former life it had been a goal he could not reach. This wonder of nature, though all-satisfying, all-fulfilling to his artist's soul, could not be a resting-place for him, a destination where something awaited him, a height he must scale to find peace, the end of his strife. But it seemed all these. He could not understand his perception or his emotion. Still, here at last, apparently, was the rainbow of his boyish dreams and of his manhood—a rainbow magnified even beyond those dreams, no longer transparent and ethereal, but solidified, a thing of ages, sweeping up majestically from the red walls, its iris-hued arch against the blue sky.

Nas Ta Bega led on down the ledge and Shefford plodded thoughtfully after him. The others followed. A jutting corner of wall again hid the canyon. The Indian was working round to circle the huge amphitheater. It was slow, irritating, strenuous toil, for the way was on a steep slant, rough and loose and dragging. The rocks were as hard and jagged as lava. And the cactus further hindered progress. When at last the long half-circle had been accomplished the golden and rosy lights had faded.

Again the canyon opened to view. All the walls were pale and steely and the stone bridge loomed dark. Nas Ta Bega said camp would be made at the bridge, which was now close. Just before they reached it the Navajo halted with one of his singular actions. Then he stood motionless. Shefford realized that Nas Ta Bega was saying his prayer to this great stone god. Presently the Indian motioned for Shefford to lead the others and the horses on under the bridge. Shefford did so, and, upon turning, was amazed to see the Indian climbing the steep and difficult slope on the other side. All the party watched him until he disappeared behind the

huge base of cliff that supported the arch. Shefford selected a level place
for camp, some few rods away, and here, with Lassiter, unsaddled and
unpacked the lame, drooping mustangs. When this was done twilight had
fallen. Nas Ta Bega appeared, coming down the steep slope on this side of
the bridge. Then Shefford divined why the Navajo had made that arduous
climb. He would not go under the bridge. Nonnezoshe was a Navajo god.
And Nas Ta Bega, though educated as a white man, was true to the
superstition of his ancestors.

Nas Ta Bega turned the mustangs loose to fare for what scant grass grew
on bench and slope. Firewood was even harder to find than grass. When
the camp duties had been performed and the simple meal eaten there was
gloom gathering in the canyon and the stars had begun to blink in the
pale strip of blue above the lofty walls. The place was oppressive and the
fugitives mostly silent. Shefford spread a bed of blankets for the women,
and Jane at once lay wearily down. Fay stood beside the flickering fire, and
Shefford felt her watching him. He was conscious of a desire to get away
from her haunting gaze. To the gentle good night he bade her she made
no response.

Shefford moved away into a strange dark shadow cast by the bridge
against the pale starlight. It was a weird, black belt, where he imagined he
was invisible, but out of which he could see. There was a slab of rock near
the foot of the bridge, and here Shefford composed himself to watch, to
feel, to think the unknown thing that seemed to be inevitably coming to
him.

A slight stiffening of his neck made him aware that he had been
continually looking up at the looming arch. And he found that insensibly
it had changed and grown. It had never seemed the same any two moments, but that was not what he meant. Near at hand it was too vast a
thing for immediate comprehension. He wanted to ponder on what had
formed it—to reflect upon its meaning as to age and force of nature, yet
all he could do at each moment was to see. White stars hung along the
dark curved line. The rim of the arch seemed to shine. The moon must be
up there somewhere. The far side of the canyon was now a blank, black
wall. Over its towering rim showed a pale glow. It brightened. The shades
in the canyon lightened, then a white disk of moon peered over the dark
line. The bridge turned to silver, and the gloomy, shadowy belt it had cast
blanched and vanished.

Shefford became aware of the presence of Nas Ta Bega. Dark, silent,
statuesque, with inscrutable eyes uplifted, with all that was spiritual of the
Indian suggested by a somber and tranquil knowledge of his place there,
he represented the same to Shefford as a solitary figure of human life
brought out the greatness of a great picture. Nonnezoshe Boco needed
life, wild life, life of its millions of years—and here stood the dark and
silent Indian.

There was a surge in Shefford's heart and in his mind a perception of a moment of incalculable change to his soul. And at that moment Fay Larkin stole like a phantom to his side and stood there with her uncovered head shining and her white face lovely in the moonlight.

"May I stay with you—a little?" she asked, wistfully. "I can't sleep."

"Surely you may," he replied. "Does your arm hurt too badly, or are you too tired to sleep?"

"No—it's this place. I—I—can't tell you how I feel."

But the feeling was there in her eyes for Shefford to read. Had he too great an emotion—did he read too much—did he add from his soul? For him the wild, starry, haunted eyes mirrored all that he had seen and felt under Nonnezoshe. And for herself they shone eloquently of courage and love.

"I need to talk—and I don't know how," she said.

He was silent, but he took her hands and drew her closer.

"Why are you so—so different?" she asked, bravely.

"Different?" he echoed.

"Yes. You are kind—you speak the same to me as you used to. But since we started you've been different, somehow."

"Fay, think how hard and dangerous the trip's been! I've been worried —and sick with dread—with— Oh, you can't imagine the strain I'm under! How could I be my old self?"

"It isn't worry I mean."

He was too miserable to try to find out what she did mean; besides, he believed, if he let himself think about it, he would know what troubled her.

"I—I am almost happy," she said, softly.

"Fay! . . . Aren't you at all afraid?"

"No. You'll take care of me. . . . Do—do you love me—like you did before?"

"Why, child! Of course—I love you," he replied, brokenly, and he drew her closer. He had never embraced her, never kissed her. But there was a whiteness about her then—a wraith—a something from her soul, and he could only gaze at her.

"I love you," she whispered. "I thought I knew it that—that night. But I'm only finding it out now. . . . And somehow I had to tell you here."

"Fay, I haven't said much to you," he said, hurriedly, huskily. "I haven't had a chance. I love you. I—I ask you—will you be my wife?"

"Of course," she said, simply, but the white, moon-blanched face colored with a dark and leaping blush.

"We'll be married as soon as we get out of the desert," he went on. "And we'll forget—all—all that's happened. You're so young. You'll forget."

"I'd forgotten already, till this difference came in you. And pretty soon —when I can say something more to you—I'll forget all except Surprise Valley—and my evenings in the starlight with you."

"Say it then—quick!"

She was leaning against him, holding his hands in her strong clasp, soulful, tender, almost passionate.

"You couldn't help it. . . . I'm to blame. . . . I remember what I said."

"What?" he queried in amaze.

" 'You can kill him!' . . . I said that. I made you kill him."

"Kill—whom?" cried Shefford.

"Waggoner. I'm to blame. . . . That must be what's made you different. And, oh, I've wanted you to know it's all my fault. . . . But I wouldn't be sorry if you weren't. . . . I'm glad he's dead."

"You—think—I—" Shefford's gasping whisper failed in the shock of the revelation that Fay believed he had killed Waggoner. Then with the inference came the staggering truth—her guiltlessness; and a paralyzing joy held him stricken.

A powerful hand fell upon Shefford's shoulder, startling him. Nas Ta Bega stood there, looking down upon him and Fay. Never had the Indian seemed so dark, inscrutable of face. But in his magnificent bearing, in the spirit that Shefford sensed in him, there were nobility and power and a strange pride.

The Indian kept one hand on Shefford's shoulder, and with the other he struck himself on the breast. The action was that of an Indian, impressive and stern, significant of an Indian's prowess.

"My God!" breathed Shefford, very low.

"Oh, what does he mean?" cried Fay.

Shefford held her with shaking hands, trying to speak, to fight a way out of these stultifying emotions.

"Nas Ta Bega—you heard. She thinks—I killed Waggoner!"

All about the Navajo then was dark and solemn disproof of her belief. He did not need to speak. His repetition of that savage, almost boastful blow on his breast added only to the dignity, and not to the denial, of a warrior.

"Fay, he means he killed the Mormon," said Shefford. "He must have, for I did not!"

"Ah!" murmured Fay, and she leaned to him with passionate, quivering gladness. It was the woman—the human—the soul born in her that came uppermost then; now, when there was no direct call to the wild and elemental in her nature, she showed a heart above revenge, the instinct of a saving right, of truth as Shefford knew them. He took her into his arms and never had he loved her so well.

"Nas Ta Bega, you killed the Mormon," declared Shefford, with a voice that had gained strength. No silent Indian suggestion of a deed would suffice in that moment. Shefford needed to hear the Navajo speak—to have Fay hear him speak. "Nas Ta Bega, I know—I understand. But tell her. Speak so she will know. Tell it as a white man would!"

"I heard her cry out," replied the Indian, in his slow English. "I waited. When he came I killed him."

A poignant "Why?" was wrenched from Shefford. Nas Ta Bega stood silent.

"Bi Nai!" And when that sonorous Indian name rolled in dignity from his lips he silently stalked away into the gloom. That was his answer to the white man.

Shefford bent over Fay, and as the strain on him broke he held her closer and closer and his tears streamed down and his voice broke in exclamations of tenderness and thanksgiving. It did not matter what she had thought, but she must never know what he had thought. He clasped her as something precious he had lost and regained. He was shaken with a passion of remorse. How could he have believed Fay Larkin guilty of murder? Women less wild and less justified than she had been driven to such a deed, yet how could he have believed it of her, when for two days he had been with her, had seen her face, and deep into her eyes? There was a mystery in his very blindness. He cast the whole thought from him forever. There was no shadow between Fay and him. He had found her. He had saved her. She was free. She was innocent. And suddenly, as he seemed delivered from contending tumults within, he became aware that it was no unresponsive creature he had folded to his breast.

He became suddenly alive to the warm, throbbing contact of her bosom, to her strong arms clinging round his neck, to her closed eyes, to the rapt whiteness of her face. And he bent to cold lips that seemed to receive his first kisses as new and strange; but tremulously changed, at last to meet his own, and then to burn with sweet and thrilling fire.

"My darling, my dream's come true," he said. "You are my treasure. I found you here at the foot of the rainbow! . . . What if it is a stone rainbow—if all is not as I had dreamed? I followed a gleam. And it's led me to love and faith!"

Hours afterward Shefford walked alone to and fro under the bridge. His trouble had given place to serenity. But this night of nights he must live out wide-eyed to its end.

The moon had long since crossed the streak of star-fired blue above and the canyon was black in shadow. At times a current of wind, with all the strangeness of that strange country in its hollow moan, rushed through the great stone arch. At other times there was silence such as Shefford imagined dwelt deep under this rocky world. At still other times an owl hooted, and the sound was nameless. But it had a mocking echo that never ended. An echo of night, silence, gloom, melancholy death, age, eternity!

The Indian lay asleep with his dark face upturned, and the other sleepers lay calm and white in the starlight.

Shefford saw in them the meaning of life and the past—the illimitable train of faces that had shone under the stars. There was a spirit in the canyon, and whether or not it was what the Navajo embodied in the great Nonnezoshe, or the life of the present, or the death of the ages, or the nature so magnificently manifested in those silent, dreaming, waiting walls—the truth for Shefford was that this spirit was God.

Life was eternal. Man's immortality lay in himself. Love of a woman was hope—happiness. Brotherhood—that mystic and grand "Bi Nai!" of the Navajo—that was religion.

❧19❧

THE GRAND CANYON
OF THE COLORADO

THE NIGHT passed, the gloom turned gray, the dawn stole cool and pale into the canyon. When Nas Ta Bega drove the mustangs into camp the lofty ramparts of the walls were rimmed with gold and the dark arch of Nonnezoshe began to lose its steely gray.

The women had rested well and were in better condition to travel. Jane was cheerful and Fay radiant one moment and in a dream the next. She was beginning to live in that wonderful future. They talked more than usual at breakfast, and Lassiter made droll remarks. Shefford, with his great and haunting trouble ended for ever, with now only danger to face ahead, was a different man, but thoughtful and quiet.

This morning the Indian leisurely made preparations for the start. For all the concern he showed he might have known every foot of the canyon below Nonnezoshe. But, for Shefford, with the dawn had returned anxiety, a restless feeling of the need of hurry. What obstacles, what impassable gorges, might lie between this bridge and the river! The Indian's inscrutable serenity and Fay's trust, her radiance, the exquisite glow upon her face, sustained Shefford and gave him patience to endure and conceal his dread.

At length the flight was resumed, with Nas Ta Bega leading on foot, and Shefford walking in the rear. A quarter of a mile below camp the Indian led down a declivity into the bottom of the narrow gorge, where the stream ran. He did not gaze backward for a last glance at Nonnezoshe;

nor did Jane or Lassiter. Fay, however, checked Nack-yal at the rim of the descent and turned to look behind. Shefford contrasted her tremulous smile, her half-happy goodbye to this place, with the white stillness of her face when she had bade farewell to Surprise Valley. Then she rode Nack-yal down into the gorge.

Shefford knew that this would be his last look at the rainbow bridge. As he gazed the tip of the great arch lost its cold, dark stone color and began to shine. The sun had just arisen high enough over some low break in the wall to reach the bridge. Shefford watched. Slowly, in wondrous transformation, the gold and blue and rose and pink and purple blended their hues, softly, mistily, cloudily, until once again the arch was a rainbow.

Ages before life had evolved upon the earth it had spread its grand arch from wall to wall, black and mystic at night, transparent and rosy in the sunrise, at sunset a flaming curve limned against the heavens. When the race of man had passed it would, perhaps, stand there still. It was not for many eyes to see. Only by toil, sweat, endurance, blood could any man ever look at Nonnezoshe. So it would always be alone, grand, silent, beautiful, unintelligible.

Shefford bade Nonnezoshe a mute, reverent farewell. Then plunging down the weathered slope of the gorge to the stream below, he hurried forward to join the others. They had progressed much farther than he imagined they would have, and this was owing to the fact that the floor of the gorge afforded easy travel. It was gravel on rock bottom, tortuous, but open, with infrequent and shallow downward steps. The stream did not now rush and boil along and tumble over rock-encumbered ledges. In corners the water collected in round, green, eddying pools. There were patches of grass and willows and mounds of moss. Shefford's surprise equaled his relief, for he believed that the violent descent of Nonnezoshe Boco had been passed. Any turn now, he imagined, might bring the party out upon the river. When he caught up with them he imparted this conviction, which was received with cheer. The hopes of all, except the Indian, seemed mounting; and if he ever hoped or despaired it was never manifest.

Shefford's anticipation, however, was not soon realized. The fugitives traveled miles farther down Nonnezoshe Boco, and the only changes were that the walls of the lower gorge heightened and merged into those above and that these upper ones towered ever loftier. Shefford had to throw his head straight back to look up at the rims, and the narrow strip of sky was now indeed a flowing stream of blue.

Difficult steps were met, too, yet nothing compared to those of the upper canyon. Shefford calculated that this day's travel had advanced several hours; and more than ever now he was anticipating the mouth of Nonnezoshe Boco. Still another hour went by. And then came striking changes. The canyon narrowed till the walls were scarcely twenty paces apart; the color of stone grew dark red above and black down low; the light of day became shadowed, and the floor was a level, gravelly, winding lane, with the stream meandering slowly and silently.

Suddenly the Indian halted. He turned his ear down the canyon lane. He had heard something. The others grouped round him, but did not hear a sound except the soft flow of water and the heave of the mustangs. Then the Indian went on. Presently he halted again. And again he listened. This time he threw up his head and upon his dark face shone a light which might have been pride.

"Tse ko-n-tsa-igi," he said.

The others could not understand, but they were impressed.

"Shore he means somethin' big," drawled Lassiter.

"Oh, what did he say?" queried Fay in eagerness.

"Nas Ta Bega, tell us," said Shefford. "We are full of hope."

"Grand Canyon," replied the Indian.

"How do you know?" asked Shefford.

"I hear the roar of the river."

But Shefford, listen as he might, could not hear it. They traveled on, winding down the wonderful lane. Every once in a while Shefford lagged behind, let the others pass out of hearing, and then he listened. At last he was rewarded. Low and deep, dull and strange, with some quality to incite dread, came a roar. Thereafter, at intervals, usually at turns in the canyon, and when a faint stir of warm air fanned his cheeks, he heard the sound, growing clearer and louder.

He rounded an abrupt corner to have the roar suddenly fill his ears, to see the lane extend straight to a ragged vent, and beyond that, at some distance, a dark, ragged, bulging wall, like iron. As he hurried forward he was surprised to find that the noise did not increase. Here it kept a strange uniformity of tone and volume. The others of the party passed out of the mouth of Nonnezoshe Boco in advance of Shefford, and when he reached it they were grouped upon a bank of sand. A dark-red canyon yawned before them, and through it slid the strangest river Shefford had ever seen. At first glance he imagined the strangeness consisted of the dark-red color of the water, but at the second he was not so sure. All the others, except Nas Ta Bega, eyed the river blankly, as if they did not know what to think. The roar came from round a huge bulging wall downstream. Up the canyon, half a mile, at another turn, there was a leaping rapid of dirty red-white waves, and the sound of this, probably, was drowned in the unseen but nearer rapid.

"This is the Grand Canyon of the Colorado," said Shefford. "We've come out at the mouth of Nonnezoshe Boco. . . . And now to wait for Joe Lake!"

They made camp on a dry, level sandbar under a shelving wall. Nas Ta Bega collected a pile of driftwood to be used for fire, and then he took the mustangs back up the side canyon to find grass for them. Lassiter appeared unusually quiet, and soon passed from weary rest on the sand to deep slumber. Fay and Jane succumbed to an exhaustion that manifested itself the moment relaxation set in, and they, too, fell asleep. Shefford patrolled the long strip of sand under the wall, and watched up the river for Joe Lake. The Indian returned and went along the river, climbed over the jutting, sharp slopes that reached into the water, and passed out of sight upstream toward the rapid.

Shefford had a sense that the river and the canyon were too magnificent to be compared with others. Still, all his emotions and sensations had been so wrought upon, he seemed not to have any left by which he might judge of what constituted the difference. He would wait. He had a grim conviction that before he was safely out of this earth-riven crack he would know. One thing, however, struck him, and it was that up the canyon, high over the lower walls, hazy and blue, stood other walls, and beyond and above them, dim in purple distance, upreared still other walls. The haze and the blue and the purple meant great distance, and, likewise, the height seemed incomparable.

The red river attracted him most. Since this was the medium by which he must escape with his party, it was natural that it absorbed him, to the neglect of the gigantic cliffs. And the more he watched the river, studied it, listened to it, imagined its nature, its power, its relentlessness, the more he dreaded it. As the hours of the afternoon wore away, and he strolled along and rested on the banks, his first impressions, and what he realized might be his truest ones, were gradually lost. He could not bring them back. The river was changing, deceitful. It worked upon his mind. The low, hollow roar filled his ears and seemed to mock him. Then he endeavored to stop thinking about it, to confine his attention to the gap upstream where sooner or later he prayed that Joe Lake and his boat would appear. But, though he controlled his gaze, he could not his thought, and his strange, impondering dread of the river augmented.

The afternoon waned. Nas Ta Bega came back to camp and said any likelihood of Joe's arrival was past for that day. Shefford could not get over an impression of strangeness—of the impossibility of the reality presented to his naked eyes. These lonely fugitives in the huge-walled canyon waiting for a boatman to come down that river! Strange and wild —those were the words which, inadequately at best, suited this country and the situations it produced.

After supper he and Fay walked along the bars of smooth, red sand. There were a few moments when the distant peaks and domes and turrets were glorified in changing sunset hues. But the beauty was fleeting. Fay still showed lassitude. She was quiet, yet cheerful, and the sweetness of her smile, her absolute trust in him, stirred and strengthened anew his spirit. Yet he suffered torture when he thought of trusting Fay's life, her soul, and her beauty to this strange red river.

Night brought him relief. He could not see the river; only the low roar

made its presence known out there in the shadows. And, there being no
need to stay awake, he dropped at once into heavy slumber. He was
roused by hands dragging at him. Nas Ta Bega bent over him. It was broad
daylight. The yellow wall high above was glistening. A fire was crackling
and pleasant odors were wafted to him. Fay and Jane and Lassiter sat
around the tarpaulin at breakfast. After the meal suspense and strain were
manifested in all the fugitives, even the imperturbable Indian being more
than usually watchful. His eyes scarcely ever left the black gap where the
river slid round the turn above. Soon, as on the preceding day, he disappeared up the ragged, iron-bound shore. There was scarcely an attempt at
conversation. A controlling thought bound that group into silence—if
Joe Lake was ever going to come he would come today.

Shefford asked himself a hundred times if it were possible, and his
answer seemed to be in the low, sullen, muffled roar of the river. And as
the morning wore on toward noon his dread deepened until all chance
appeared hopeless. Already he had begun to have vague and unformed
and disquieting ideas of the only avenue of escape left—to return up
Nonnezoshe Boco—and that would be to enter a trap.

Suddenly a piercing cry pealed down the canyon. It was followed by
echoes, weird and strange, that clapped from wall to wall in mocking
concatenation. Nas Ta Bega appeared high on the ragged slope. The cry
had been the Indian's. He swept an arm out, pointing upstream, and stood
like a statue on the iron rocks.

Shefford's keen gaze sighted a moving something in the bend of the
river. It was long, low, dark, and flat, with a lighter object upright in the
middle. A boat and a man!

"Joe! It's Joe!" yelled Shefford madly. "There! . . . Look!"

Jane and Fay were on their knees in the sand, clasping each other, pale
faces toward that bend in the river.

Shefford ran up the shore toward the Indian. He climbed the jutting
slant of rock. The boat was now full in the turn—it moved faster—it was
nearing the smooth incline above the rapid. There! It glided down—
heaved darkly up—settled back—and disappeared in the frothy, muddy
roughness of water. Shefford held his breath and watched. A dark, bobbing object showed, vanished, showed again to enlarge—to take the
shape of a big flatboat—and then it rode the swift, choppy current out of
the lower end of the rapid.

Nas Ta Bega began to make violent motions, and Shefford, taking his
cue, frantically waved his red scarf. There was a five-mile-an-hour current
right before them, and Joe must needs see them so that he might sheer the
huge and clumsy craft into the shore before it drifted too far down.

Presently Joe did see them. He appeared to be half-naked; he raised
aloft both arms, and bellowed down the canyon. The echoes boomed
from wall to wall, every one stronger with the deep, hoarse triumph in the
Mormon's voice, till they passed on, growing weaker, to die away in the

roar of the river below. Then Joe bent to a long oar that appeared to be fastened to the stern of the boat, and the craft drifted out of the swifter current toward the shore. It reached a point opposite to where Shefford and the Indian waited, and, though Joe made prodigious efforts, it slid on. Still, it also drifted shoreward, and halfway down to the mouth of Non-nezoshe Boco Joe threw the end of a rope to the Indian.

"Ho! Ho!" yelled the Mormon, again setting into motion the fiendish echoes. He was naked to the waist; he had lost flesh; he was haggard, worn, dirty, wet. While he pulled on a shirt Nas Ta Bega made the rope fast to a snag of a log of driftwood embedded in the sand, and the boat swung to shore. It was perhaps thirty feet long by half as many wide, crudely built of rough-hewn boards. The steering-gear was a long pole with a plank nailed to the end. The craft was empty save for another pole and plank, Joe's coat, and a broken-handled shovel. There were water and sand on the flooring.

Joe stepped ashore and he was gripped first by Shefford and then by the Indian. He was an unkempt and gaunt giant, yet how steadfast and reliable, how grimly strong to inspire hope!

"Reckon most of me's here," he said in reply to greetings. "I've had water aplenty. My God! I've had *water!*" He rolled out a grim laugh. "But no grub for three days. . . . Forgot to fetch some!"

How practical he was! He told Fay she looked good for sore eyes, but he needed a biscuit most of all. There was just a second of singular hesitation when he faced Lassiter, and then the big, strong hand of the young Mormon went out to meet the old gunman's. While they fed him and he ate like a starved man Shefford told of the flight from the village, the rescuing of Jane and Lassiter from Surprise Valley, the descent from the plateau, the catastrophe to Shadd's gang—and, concluding, Shefford, without any explanation, told that Nas Ta Bega had killed the Mormon Waggoner.

"Reckon I had that figured," replied Joe. "First off I didn't think so. . . . So Shadd went over the cliff. That's good riddance. It beats me, though. Never knew that Piute's like with a horse. And he had some grand horses in his outfit. Pity about them."

Later when Joe had a moment alone with Shefford he explained that during his ride to Kayenta he had realized Fay's innocence and who had been responsible for the tragedy. He took Withers, the trader, into his confidence, and they planned a story, which Withers was to carry to Stonebridge, that would exculpate Fay and Shefford of anything more serious than flight. If Shefford got Fay safely out of the country at once that would end the matter for all concerned.

"Reckon I'm some ferry-boatman, too—a *fairy* boatman. Haw! Haw!" he added. "And we're going through. . . . Now I want you to help me rig this tarpaulin up over the bow of the boat. If we can fix it up strong it'll keep the waves from curling over. They filled her four times for me."

They folded the tarpaulin three times, and with stout pieces of split plank and horseshoe nails from Shefford's saddle-bags and pieces of rope they rigged up a screen around bow and front corners.

Nas Ta Bega put the saddles in the boat. The mustangs were far up Nonnezoshe Boco and would work their way back to green and luxuriant canyons. The Indian said they would soon become wild and would never be found. Shefford regretted Nack-yal, but was glad the faithful little mustang would be free in one of those beautiful canyons.

"Reckon we'd better be off," called Joe. "All aboard!" He placed Fay and Jane in a corner of the bow, where they would be spared sight of the rapids. Shefford loosed the rope and sprang aboard. "Pard," said Joe, "it's one hell of a river! And now with the snow melting up in the mountains it's twenty feet above normal and rising fast. But that's well for us. It covers the stones in the rapids. If it hadn't been in flood Joe would be an angel now!"

The boat cleared the sand, lazily wheeled in the eddying water, and suddenly seemed caught by some powerful gliding force. When it swept out beyond the jutting wall Shefford saw a quarter of a mile of sliding water that appeared to end abruptly. Beyond lengthened out the gigantic gap between the black and frowning cliffs.

"Wow!" ejaculated Joe. "Drops out of sight there. But that one ain't much. I can tell by the roar. When you see my hair stand up straight— then watch out! . . . Lassiter, you look after the women. Shefford, you stand ready to bail out with the shovel, for we'll sure ship water. Nas Ta Bega, you help here with the oar."

The roar became a heavy, continuous rumble; the current quickened; little streaks and ridges seemed to race along the boat; strange gurglings rose from under the bow. Shefford stood on tiptoe to see the break in the river below. Swiftly it came into sight—a wonderful, long, smooth, red slant of water, a swelling mound, a huge back-curling wave, another and another, a sea of frothy, uplifting crests, leaping and tumbling and diminishing down to the narrowing apex of the rapid. It was a frightful sight, yet it thrilled Shefford. Joe worked the steering-oar back and forth and headed the boat straight for the middle of the incline. The boat reached the round rim, gracefully dipped with a heavy sop, and went shooting down. The wind blew wet in Shefford's face. He stood erect, thrilling, fascinated, frightened. Then he seemed to feel himself lifted; the curling wave leaped at the boat; there was a shock that laid him flat; and when he rose to his knees all about him was roar and spray and leaping, muddy waves. Shock after shock jarred the boat. Splashes of water stung his face. And then the jar and the motion, the confusion and roar, gradually lessened until presently Shefford rose to see smooth water ahead and the long, trembling rapid behind.

"Get busy, bailer," yelled Joe. "Pretty soon you'll be glad you have to bail—so you *can't* see!"

There were several inches of water in the bottom of the boat and Shefford learned for the first time the expediency of a shovel in the art of bailing.

"That tarpaulin worked powerful good," went on Joe. "And it saves the women. Now if it just don't bust on a big wave! That one back there was little."

When Shefford had scooped out all the water he went forward to see how Fay and Jane and Lassiter had fared. The women were pale, but composed. They had covered their heads.

"But the dreadful roar!" exclaimed Fay.

Lassiter looked shaken for once.

"Shore I'd rather taken a chance meetin' them Mormons on the way out," he said.

Shefford spoke with an encouraging assurance which he did not himself feel. Almost at the moment he marked a silence that had fallen into the canyon; then it broke to a low, dull, strange roar.

"Aha! Hear that?" The Mormon shook his shaggy head. "Reckon we're in Cataract Canyon. We'll be standing on end from now on. Hang on to her, boys!"

Danger of this unusual kind had brought out a peculiar levity in the somber Mormon—a kind of wild, gay excitement. His eyes rolled as he watched the river ahead and he puffed out his cheek with his tongue.

The rugged, overhanging walls of the canyon grew sinister in Shefford's sight. They were jaws. And the river—that made him shudder to look down into it. The little whirling pits were eyes peering into his, and they raced on with the boat, disappeared, and came again, always with the little, hollow gurgles.

The craft drifted swiftly and the roar increased. Another rapid seemed to move up into view. It came at a bend in the canyon. When the breeze struck Shefford's cheeks he did not this time experience exhilaration. The current accelerated its sliding motion and bore the flatboat straight for the middle of the curve. Shefford saw the bend, a long, dark, narrow, gloomy canyon, and a stretch of contending waters, then, crouching low, he waited for the dip, the race, the shock. They came—the last stopping the boat—throwing it aloft—letting it drop—and crests of angry waves curled over the side. Shefford, kneeling, felt the water slap around him, and in his ears was a deafening roar. There were endless moments of strife and hell and flying darkness of spray all about him, and under him the rocking boat. When they lessened—ceased in violence—he stood ankle-deep in water, and then madly he began to bail.

Another roar deadened his ears, but he did not look up from his toil. And when he had to get down to avoid the pitch he closed his eyes. That rapid passed and with more water to bail, he resumed his share in the manning of the crude craft. It was more than a share—a tremendous responsibility to which he bent with all his might. He heard Joe yell—and again—and again. He heard the increasing roars one after another till they seemed one continuous bellow. He felt the shock, the pitch, the beating waves, and then the lessening power of sound and current. That set him to his task. Always in these long intervals of toil he seemed to see, without looking up, the growing proportions of the canyon. And the river had become a living, terrible thing. The intervals of his tireless effort when he scooped the water overboard were fleeting, and the rides through rapid after rapid were endless periods of waiting terror. His spirit and his hope were overwhelmed by the rush and roar and fury.

Then, as he worked, there came a change—a rest to deafened ears—a stretch of river that seemed quiet after chaos—and here for the first time he bailed the boat clear of water.

Jane and Fay were huddled in a corner, with the flapping tarpaulin now half fallen over them. They were wet and muddy. Lassiter crouched like a man dazed by a bad dream, and his white hair hung, stained and bedraggled, over his face. The Indian and the Mormon, grim, hard, worn, stood silent at the oar.

The afternoon was far advanced and the sun had already descended below the western ramparts. A cool breeze blew up the canyon, laden with a sound that was the same, yet not the same, as those low, dull roars which Shefford dreaded more and more.

Joe Lake turned his ear to the breeze. A stronger puff brought a heavy, quivering rumble. This time he did not vent his gay and wild defiance to the river. He bent lower—listened. Then as the rumble became a strange, deep, reverberating roll, as if the monstrous river were rolling huge stones down a subterranean canyon, Shefford saw with dilating eyes that the Mormon's hair was rising stiff upon his head.

"Hear that?" said Joe, turning an ashen face to Shefford. "We'll drop off the earth now. Hang on to the girl, so if we go you can go together. . . . And, pard, if you've a God—*pray!*"

Nas Ta Bega faced the bend from whence that rumble came, and he was the same dark, inscrutable, impassive Indian as of old. What was death to him?

Shefford felt the strong, rushing love of life surge in him, and it was not for himself he thought, but for Fay and the happiness she merited. He went to her, patted the covered head, and tried with words choking in his throat to give hope. And he leaned with hands gripping the gunwale, with eyes wide open, ready for the unknown.

The river made a quick turn and from round the bend rumbled a terrible uproar. The current racing that way was divided or uncertain, and it gave strange motion to the boat. Joe and Nas Ta Bega shoved desperately upon the oar, all to no purpose. The currents had their will. The bow of the boat took the place of the stern. Then swift at the head of a curved incline it shot beyond the bulging wall.

And Shefford saw an awful place before them. The canyon had narrowed to half its width, and turned almost at right angles. The huge clamor of appalling sound came from under the cliff where the swollen river had to pass and where there was not space. The rapid rushed in gigantic swells right upon the wall, boomed against it, climbed and spread and fell away, to recede and gather new impetus, to leap madly on down the canyon.

Shefford went to his knees, clasped Fay, and Jane, too. But facing this appalling thing he had to look. Courage and despair came to him at the last. This must be the end. With long, buoyant swing the boat sailed down, shot over the first waves, was caught and lifted upon the great swell and impelled straight toward the cliff. Huge whirlpools raced alongside, and from them came a horrible, engulfing roar. Monstrous bulges rose on the other side. All the stupendous power of that mighty river of down-ward-rushing silt swung the boat aloft, up and up, as the swell climbed the wall. Shefford, with transfixed eyes and harrowed soul, watched the wet black wall. It loomed down upon him. The stern of the boat went high. Then when the crash that meant doom seemed imminent the swell spread and fell back from the wall and the boat never struck at all. By some miraculous chance it had been favored by a strange and momentary receding of the huge spent swell. Then it slid back, was caught and whirled by the current into a red, frothy, up-flung rapids below. Shefford bowed his head over Fay and saw no more, nor felt nor heard. What seemed a long time after that the broken voice of the Mormon recalled him to his labors.

The boat was half full of water. Nas Ta Bega scooped out great sheets of it with his hands. Shefford sprang to aid him, found the shovel, and plunged into the task. Slowly but surely they emptied the boat. And then Shefford saw that twilight had fallen. Joe was working the craft toward a narrow bank of sand, to which, presently, they came, and the Indian sprang out to moor to a rock.

The fugitives went ashore and, weary and silent and drenched, they dropped in the warm sand.

But Shefford could not sleep. The river kept him awake. In the dis-tance it rumbled, low, deep, reverberating, and near at hand it was a thing of mutable mood. It moaned, whined, mocked, and laughed. It had the soul of a devil. It was a river that had cut its way to the bowels of the earth, and its nature was destructive. It harbored no life. Fighting its way through those dead walls, cutting and tearing and wearing, its heavy burden of silt was death, destruction, and decay. A silent river, a murmur-ing, strange, fierce, terrible, thundering river of the desert! Even in the dark it seemed to wear the hue of blood.

All night long Shefford heard it, and toward the dark hours before dawn, when a restless, broken sleep came to him, his dreams were dreams of a river of sounds.

All the beautiful sounds he knew and loved he heard—the sigh of the wind in the pines, the mourn of the wolf, the cry of the laughing-gull, the murmur of running brooks, the song of a child, the whisper of a woman. And there were the boom of the surf, the roar of the north wind in the forest, the roll of thunder. And there were the sounds not of earth—a river of the universe rolling the planets, engulfing the stars, pouring the sea of blue into infinite space.

Night with its fitful dreams passed. Dawn lifted the ebony gloom out of the canyon and sunlight far up on the ramparts renewed Shefford's spirit. He rose and awoke the others. Fay's wistful smile still held its faith. They ate of the gritty, water-soaked food. Then they embarked. The current carried them swiftly down and out of hearing of the last rapid. The character of the river and the canyon changed. The current lessened to a slow, smooth, silent, eddying flow. The walls grew straight, sheer, gloomy, and vast. Shefford noted these features, but he was listening so hard for the roar of the next rapid that he scarcely appreciated them. All the fugitives were listening. Every bend in the canyon—and now the turns were numerous—might hold a rapid. Shefford strained his ears. He imagined the low, dull, strange rumble. He had it in his ears, yet there was the growing sensation of silence.

"Shore this's a dead place," muttered Lassiter.

"She's only slowed up for a bigger plunge," replied Joe. "Listen! Hear that?"

But there was no true sound. Joe only imagined what he expected and hated and dreaded to hear.

Mile after mile they drifted through the silent gloom between those vast and magnificent walls. After the speed, the turmoil, the whirling, shrieking, thundering, the never-ceasing sound and change and motion of the rapids above, this slow, quiet drifting, this utter, absolute silence, these eddying stretches of still water below, worked strangely upon Shefford's mind and he feared he was going mad.

There was no change to the silence, no help for the slow drift, no lessening of the strain. And the hours of the day passed as moments, the sun crossed the blue gap above, the golden lights hung on the upper walls, the gloom returned, and still there was only the dead, vast, insupportable silence.

There came bends where the current quickened, ripples widened, long lanes of little waves roughened the surface, but they made no sound.

And then the fugitives turned through a V-shaped vent in the canyon. The ponderous walls sheered away from the river. There was space and sunshine, and far beyond this league-wide open rose vermilion-colored cliffs. A mile below the river disappeared in a dark, boxlike passage from which came a rumble that made Shefford's flesh creep.

The Mormon flung high his arms and let out the stentorian yell that had rolled down to the fugitives as they waited at the mouth of Nonnezoshe Boco. But now it had a wilder, more exultant note. Strange how he shifted his gaze to Fay Larkin!

"Girl! Get up and look!" he called. "The Ferry! The Ferry!"

Then he bent his brawny back over the steering-oar, and the clumsy craft slowly turned toward the left-hand shore, where a long, low bank of green willows and cottonwoods gave welcome relief to the eyes. Upon the opposite side of the river Shefford saw a boat, similar to the one he was in, moored to the bank.

"Shore, if I ain't losin' my eyes, I seen an Injun with a red blanket," said Lassiter.

"Yes, Lassiter," cried Shefford. "Look, Fay! Look, Jane! See! Indians—hogans—mustangs—there above the green bank!"

The boat glided slowly shoreward. And the deep, hungry, terrible rumble of the remorseless river became something no more to dread.

⁂20⁂

WILLOW SPRINGS

TWO DAYS' travel from the river, along the saw-toothed range of Echo Cliffs, stood Presbrey's trading-post, a little red-stone square house in a green and pretty valley called Willow Springs.

It was nearing the time of sunset—that gorgeous hour of color in the Painted Desert—when Shefford and his party rode down upon the post.

The scene lacked the wildness characteristic of Kayenta or Red Lake. There were wagons and teams, white men and Indians, burros, sheep, lambs, mustangs saddled and unsaddled, dogs and chickens. A young, sweet-faced woman stood in the door of the post and she it was who first sighted the fugitives. Presbrey was weighing bags of wool on a scale, and when she called he lazily turned, as if to wonder at her eagerness.

Then he flung up his head, with its shock of heavy hair, in a start of surprise, and his florid face lost its lazy indolence to become wreathed in a huge smile.

"Haven't seen a white person in six months!" was his extraordinary greeting.

An hour later Shefford, clean-shaven, comfortably clothed once more, found himself a different man; and when he saw Fay in white again, with

a new and indefinable light shining through that old, haunting shadow in
her eyes, then the world changed and he embraced perfect happiness.

There was a dinner such as Shefford had not seen for many a day, and
such as Fay had never seen, and that brought to Jane Withersteen's eyes
the dreamy memory of the bountiful feasts which, long years ago, had
been her pride. And there was a story told to the curious trader and his
kind wife—a story with its beginning back in those past years, of riders of
the purple sage, of Fay Larkin as a child and then as a wild girl in Surprise
Valley, of the flight down Nonnezoshe Boco and the canyon, of a great
Mormon and a noble Indian.

Presbrey stared with his deep-set eyes and wagged his tousled head and
stared again; then with the quick perception of the practical desert man
he said:

"I'm sending teamsters into Flagstaff tomorrow. Wife and I will go
along with you. We've light wagons. Three days, maybe—or four—and
we'll be there. . . . Shefford, I'm going to see you marry Fay Larkin!"

Fay and Jane and Lassiter showed strangely against this background of
approaching civilization. And Shefford realized more than ever the loneliness and isolation and wildness of so many years for them.

When the women had retired Shefford and the men talked awhile.
Then Joe Lake rose to stretch his big frame.

"Friends, reckon I'm all in," he said. "Goodnight." In passing he laid a
heavy hand on Shefford's shoulder. "Well, you got out. I've only a queer
notion how. But *Some One* besides an Indian and a Mormon guided you
out! . . . Be good to the girl. . . . Goodbye, pard!"

Shefford grasped the big hand and in the emotion of the moment did
not catch the significance of Joe's last words.

Later Shefford stepped outside into the starlight for a few moments'
quiet walk and thought before he went to bed. It was a white night. The
coyotes were yelping. The stars shone steadfast, bright, cold. Nas Ta Bega
stalked out of the shadow of the house and joined Shefford. They walked
in silence. Shefford's heart was too full for utterance and the Indian
seldom spoke at any time. When Shefford was ready to go in Nas Ta Bega
extended his hand.

"Goodbye—Bi Nai!" he said, strangely, using English and Navajo in
what Shefford supposed to be merely good night. The starlight shone full
upon the dark, inscrutable face of the Indian. Shefford bade him good
night and then watched him stride away in the silver gloom.

But next morning Shefford understood. Nas Ta Bega and Joe Lake were
gone. It was a shock to Shefford. Yet what could he have said to either?
Joe had shirked saying goodbye to him and Fay. And the Indian had gone
out of Shefford's life as he had come into it.

What these two men represented in Shefford's uplift was too great for
the present to define, but they and the desert that had developed them
had taught him the meaning of life. He might fail often, since failure was

the lot of his kind, but could he ever fail again in faith in man or God while he had mind to remember the Indian and the Mormon?

Still, though he placed them on a noble height and loved them well, there would always abide with him a sorrow for the Mormon and a sleepless and eternal regret for that Indian on his lonely cedar slope with the spirits of his vanishing race calling him.

Willow Springs appeared to be a lively place that morning. Presbrey was happy and his sweet-faced wife was excited. The teamsters were a jolly, whistling lot. And the lean mustangs kicked and bit at one another. The trader had brought out two light wagons for the trip, and, after the manner of desert men, desired to start at sunrise.

Far across the Painted Desert towered the San Francisco peaks, black-timbered, blue-canyoned, purple-hazed, with white snow, like the clouds, around their summits.

Jane Withersteen looked at the radiant Fay and lived again in her happiness. And at last excitement had been communicated to the old gunman.

"Shore we're goin' to live with Fay an' John, an' be near Venters an' Bess, an' see the blacks again, Jane. . . . An' Venters will tell you, as he did me, how Wrangle run Black Star off his legs!"

All connected with that early start was sweet, sad, hopeful.

And so they rode away from Willow Springs, through the green fields of alfalfa and cottonwood, down the valley with its smoking hogans and whistling mustangs and scarlet-blanketed Indians, and out upon the bare, ridgy, colorful desert toward the rosy sunrise.

EPILOGUE

O N THE OUTSKIRTS of a little town in Illinois there was a farm of rolling pasture-land. And here a beautiful meadow, green and red in clover, merged upon an orchard in the midst of which a brown-tiled roof showed above the trees.

One afternoon in May a group of people, strangely agitated, walked down a shady lane toward the meadow.

"Wal, Jane, I always knew we'd get a look at them hosses again—I shore knew," Lassiter was saying in the same old, cool, careless drawl. But his clawlike hands shook a little.

"Oh! Will they know me?" asked Jane Withersteen, turning to a stalwart man—no other than the dark-faced Venters, her rider of other days.

"Know you? I'll bet they will," replied Venters. "What do you say, Bess?"

The shadow brightened in Bess's somber blue eyes, as if his words had recalled her from a sad and memorable past.

"Black Star will know her, surely," replied Bess. "Sometimes he points his nose toward the west and watches as if he saw the purple slopes and smelt the sage of Utah! He has never forgotten. But Night has grown deaf and partly blind of late. I doubt if he'll remember."

Shefford and Fay walked arm in arm in the background.

Out in the meadow two horses were grazing. They were sleek, shiny, long-maned, long-tailed, black as coal, and, though old, still splendid in every line.

"Do you remember them?" whispered Shefford.

"Oh, I only needed to see Black Star," murmured Fay, her voice quivering. "I can remember being lifted on his back. . . . How strange! It seems so long ago. . . . Look! Mother Jane is going out to them."

Jane Withersteen advanced alone through the clover, and it was with unsteady steps. Presently she halted. What glorious and bitter memories were expressed in her strange, poignant call!

Black Star started and swept up his noble head and looked. But Night went on calmly grazing. Then Jane called again—the same strange call, only louder, and this time broken. Black Star raised his head higher and he whistled a piercing blast. He saw Jane; he knew her as he had remembered the call; and he came pounding toward her. She met him, encircled his neck with her arms, and buried her face in his mane.

"Shore I reckon I'd better never say any more about Wrangle runnin' the blacks off their legs thet time," muttered Lassiter, as if to himself.

"Lassiter, you only dreamed that race," replied Venters, with a smile.

"Oh, Bern, isn't it good that Black Star remembered her—that she'll have him—something left of her old home?" asked Bess, wistfully.

"Indeed it is good. But, Bess, Jane Withersteen will find a new spirit and new happiness here."

Jane came toward them, leading both horses. "Dear friends, I am happy. Today I bury all regrets. Of the past I shall remember only—my riders of the purple sage."

Venters smiled his gladness. "And you—Lassiter—what shall you remember?" he queried.

The old gunman looked at Jane and then at his clawlike hands and then at Fay. His eyes lost their shadow and began to twinkle.

"Wal, I rolled a stone once, but I reckon now thet time Wrangle—"

"Lassiter, I said you dreamed that race. Wrangle never beat the blacks," interrupted Venters. . . . "And you, Fay, what shall you remember?"

"Surprise Valley," replied Fay, dreamily.

"And you—Shefford?"

Shefford shook his head. For him there could never be one memory only. In his heart there would never change or die memories of the wild uplands, of the great towers and walls, of the golden sunsets on the canyon ramparts, of the silent, fragrant valleys where the cedars and the sago-lilies grew, of those starlit nights when his love and faith awoke, of grand and lonely Nonnezoshe, of that red, sullen, thundering, mysterious Colorado River, of a wonderful Indian and a noble Mormon—of all that was embodied for him in the meaning of the rainbow trail.

THE
LONE STAR
RANGER

CONTENTS

BOOK ONE
THE OUTLAW

❧1❧

So it was in him, then—an inherited fighting instinct, a driving intensity to kill. He was the last of the Duanes, that old fighting stock of Texas. But not the memory of his dead father, nor the pleading of his soft-voiced mother, nor the warning of this uncle who stood before him now, had brought to Buck Duane so much realization of the dark, passionate strain in his blood. It was the recurrence, a hundredfold increased in power, of a strange emotion that for the last three years had arisen in him.

"Yes, Cal Bain's in town, full of bad whisky an' huntin' for you," repeated the elder man, gravely.

"It's the second time," muttered Duane, as if to himself.

"Son, you can't avoid a meetin'. Leave town till Cal sobers up. He ain't got it in for you when he's not drinkin'."

"But what's he want me for?" demanded Duane. "To insult me again? I won't stand that twice."

"He's got a fever that's rampant in Texas these days, my boy. He wants gunplay. If he meets you he'll try to kill you."

Here it stirred in Duane again, that bursting gush of blood, like a wind of flame shaking all his inner being, and subsiding to leave him strangely chilled.

"Kill me! What for?" he asked.

"Lord knows there ain't any reason. But what's that to do with most of the shootin' these days? Didn't five cowboys over to Everall's kill one another dead all because they got to jerkin' at a quirt among themselves? An' Cal has no reason to love you. His girl was sweet on you."

"I quit when I found out she was his girl."

"I reckon she ain't quit. But never mind her or reasons. Cal's here, just drunk enough to be ugly. He's achin' to kill somebody. He's one of them four-flush gunfighters. He'd like to be thought bad. There's a lot of wild cowboys who're ambitious for a reputation. They talk about how quick they are on the draw. They ape Bland an' King Fisher an' Hardin an' all the big outlaws. They make threats about joinin' the gangs along the Rio Grande. They laugh at the sheriffs an' brag about how they'd fix the rangers. Cal's sure not much for you to bother with, if you only keep out of his way."

"You mean for me to run?" asked Duane, in scorn.

"I reckon I wouldn't put it that way. Just avoid him. Buck, I'm not afraid Cal would get you if you met down there in town. You've your father's eye an' his slick hand with a gun. What I'm most afraid of is that you'll kill Bain."

Duane was silent, letting his uncle's earnest words sink in, trying to realize their significance.

"If Texas ever recovers from that fool war an' kills off these outlaws, why, a young man will have a lookout," went on the uncle. "You're twenty-three now, an' a powerful sight of a fine fellow, barrin' your temper. You've a chance in life. But if you go gunfightin', if you kill a man, you're ruined. Then you'll kill another. It'll be the same old story. An' the rangers would make you an outlaw. The rangers mean law an' order for Texas. This even-break business doesn't work with them. If you resist arrest they'll kill you. If you submit to arrest, then you go to jail, an' mebbe you hang."

"I'd never hang," muttered Duane, darkly.

"I reckon you wouldn't," replied the old man. "You'd be like your father. He was ever ready to draw—too ready. In times like these, with the Texas rangers enforcin' the law, your Dad would have been driven to the river. An', son, I'm afraid you're a chip off the old block. Can't you hold in—keep your temper—run away from trouble? Because it'll only result in you gettin' the worst of it in the end. Your father was killed in a streetfight. An' it was told of him that he shot twice after a bullet had passed through his heart. Think of the terrible nature of a man to be able to do that. If you have any such blood in you, never give it a chance."

"What you say is all very well, Uncle," returned Duane, "but the only way out for me is to run, and I won't do it. Cal Bain and his outfit have already made me look like a coward. He says I'm afraid to come out and face him. A man simply can't stand that in this country. Besides, Cal would shoot me in the back someday if I didn't face him."

"Well, then, what're you goin' to do?" inquired the elder man.

"I haven't decided—yet."

"No, but you're comin' to it mighty fast. That damned spell is workin' in you. You're different today. I remember how you used to be moody an' lose your temper an' talk wild. Never was much afraid of you then. But now you're gettin' cool an' quiet, an' you think deep, an' I don't like the light in your eye. It reminds me of your father."

"I wonder what Dad would say to me today if he were alive and here," said Duane.

"What do you think? What could you expect of a man who never wore a glove on his right hand for twenty years?"

"Well, he'd hardly have said much. Dad never talked. But he would have done a lot. And I guess I'll go downtown and let Cal Bain find me."

Then followed a long silence, during which Duane sat with downcast eyes, and the uncle appeared lost in sad thought of the future. Presently he turned to Duane with an expression that denoted resignation, and yet a spirit which showed wherein they were of the same blood.

"You've got a fast horse—the fastest I know of in this country. After you meet Bain hurry back home. I'll have a saddle-bag packed for you and the horse ready."

With that he turned on his heel and went into the house, leaving Duane to revolve in his mind his singular speech. Buck wondered presently if he shared his uncle's opinion of the result of a meeting between himself and Bain. His thoughts were vague. But on the instant of final decision, when he had settled with himself that he would meet Bain, such a storm of passion assailed him that he felt as if he was being shaken with ague. Yet it was all internal, inside his breast, for his hand was like a rock and, for all he could see, not a muscle about him quivered. He had no fear of Bain or of any other man; but a vague fear of himself, of this strange force in him, made him ponder and shake his head. It was as if he had not all to say in this matter. There appeared to have been in him a reluctance to let himself go, and some voice, some spirit from a distance, something he was not accountable for, had compelled him. That hour of Duane's life was like years of actual living, and in it he became a thoughtful man.

He went into the house and buckled on his belt and gun. The gun was a Colt .45, six-shot, and heavy, with an ivory handle. He had packed it, on and off, for five years. Before that it had been used by his father. There were a number of notches filed in the bulge of the ivory handle. This gun was the one his father had fired twice after being shot through the heart, and his hand had stiffened so tightly upon it in the death-grip that his fingers had to be pried open. It had never been drawn upon any man since it had come into Duane's possession. But the cold, bright polish of the weapon showed how it had been used. Duane could draw it with inconceivable rapidity, and at twenty feet he could split a card pointing edgewise toward him.

Duane wished to avoid meeting his mother. Fortunately, as he thought, she was away from home. He went out and down the path toward the gate. The air was full of the fragrance of blossoms and the melody of birds. Outside in the road a neighbor woman stood talking to a countryman in a

wagon; they spoke to him; and he heard, but did not reply. Then he began
to stride down the road toward the town.

Wellston was a small town, but important in that unsettled part of the
great state because it was the trading center of several hundred miles of
territory. On the main street there were perhaps fifty buildings, some
brick, some frame, mostly adobe, and one-third of the lot, and by far the
most prosperous, were saloons. From the road Duane turned into this
street. It was a wide thoroughfare lined by hitching-rails and saddled
horses and vehicles of various kinds. Duane's eyes ranged down the street,
taking in all at a glance, particularly persons moving leisurely up and
down. Not a cowboy was in sight. Duane slackened his stride, and by the
time he reached Sol White's place, which was the first saloon, he was
walking slowly. Several people spoke to him and turned to look back after
they had passed. He paused at the door of White's saloon, took a sharp
survey of the interior, then stepped inside.

The saloon was large and cool, full of men and noise and smoke. The
noise ceased upon his entrance, and the silence ensuing presently broke
to the clink of Mexican silver dollars at a monte table. Sol White, who
was behind the bar, straightened up when he saw Duane; then, without
speaking, he bent over to rinse a glass. All eyes except those of the
Mexican gamblers were turned upon Duane; and these glances were keen,
speculative, questioning. These men knew Bain was looking for trouble;
they probably had heard his boasts. But what did Duane intend to do?
Several of the cowboys and ranchers present exchanged glances. Duane
had been weighed by unerring Texas instinct, by men who all packed
guns. The boy was the son of his father. Whereupon they greeted him and
returned to their drinks and cards. Sol White stood with his big red hands
out upon the bar; he was a tall, raw-boned Texan with a long mustache
waxed to sharp points.

"Howdy, Buck," was his greeting to Duane. He spoke carelessly and
averted his dark gaze for an instant.

"Howdy, Sol," replied Duane, slowly. "Say, Sol, I hear there's a gent in
town looking for me bad."

"Reckon there is, Buck," replied White. "He came in heah aboot an
hour ago. Shore he was some riled an' a-roarin' for gore. Told me confi-
dential a certain party had given you a white silk scarf, an' he was hell-
bent on wearin' it home spotted red."

"Anybody with him?" queried Duane.

"Burt an' Sam Outcalt an' a little cowpuncher I never seen before.
They-all was coaxin' him to leave town. But he's looked on the flowin'
glass, Buck, an' he's heah for keeps."

"Why doesn't Sheriff Oaks lock him up if he's that bad?"

"Oaks went away with the rangers. There's been another raid at
Flesher's ranch. The King Fisher gang, likely. An' so the town's shore
wide open."

Duane stalked outdoors and faced down the street. He walked the whole length of the long block, meeting many people—farmers, ranchers, clerks, merchants, Mexicans, cowboys, and women. It was a singular fact that when he turned to retrace his steps the street was almost empty. He had not returned a hundred yards on his way when the street was wholly deserted. A few heads protruded from doors and around corners. That main street of Wellston saw some such situation every few days. If it was an instinct for Texans to fight, it was also instinctive for them to sense with remarkable quickness the signs of a coming gunplay. Rumor could not fly so swiftly. In less than ten minutes everybody who had been on the street or in the shops knew that Buck Duane had come forth to meet his enemy.

Duane walked on. When he came to within fifty paces of a saloon he swerved out into the middle of the street, stood there for a moment, then went ahead and back to the sidewalk. He passed on in this way the length of the block. Sol White was standing in the door of his saloon.

"Buck, I'm a-tippin' you off," he said, quick and low-voiced. "Cal Bain's over at Everall's. If he's a-huntin' you bad, as he brags, he'll show there."

Duane crossed the street and started down. Notwithstanding White's statement Duane was wary and slow at every door. Nothing happened, and he traversed almost the whole length of the block without seeing a person. Everall's place was on the corner.

Duane knew himself to be cold, steady. He was conscious of a strange fury that made him want to leap ahead. He seemed to long for this encounter more than anything he had ever wanted. But, vivid as were his sensations, he felt as if in a dream.

Before he reached Everall's he heard loud voices, one of which was raised high. Then the short door swung outward as if impelled by a vigorous hand. A bow-legged cowboy wearing woolly chaps burst out upon the sidewalk. At sight of Duane he seemed to bound into the air, and he uttered a savage roar.

Duane stopped in his tracks at the outer edge of the sidewalk, perhaps a dozen rods from Everall's door.

If Bain was drunk he did not show it in his movement. He swaggered forward, rapidly closing up the gap. Red, sweaty, disheveled, and hatless, his face distorted and expressive of the most malignant intent, he was a wild and sinister figure. He had already killed a man, and this showed in his demeanor. His hands were extended before him, the right hand a little lower than the left. At every step he bellowed his rancor in speech mostly curses. Gradually he slowed his walk, then halted. A good twenty-five paces separated the men.

"Won't nothin' make you draw, you ——!" he shouted, fiercely.

"I'm waitin' on you, Cal," replied Duane.

Bain's right hand stiffened—moved. Duane threw his gun as a boy throws a ball underhand—a draw his father had taught him. He pulled twice, his shots almost as one. Bain's big Colt boomed while it was pointed downward and he was falling. His bullet scattered dust and gravel at Duane's feet. He fell loosely, without contortion.

In a flash all was reality for Duane. He went forward and held his gun ready for the slightest movement on the part of Bain. But Bain lay upon his back, and all that moved were his breast and his eyes. How strangely the red had left his face—and also the distortion! The devil that had showed in Bain was gone. He was sober and conscious. He tried to speak, but failed. His eyes expressed something pitifully human. They changed —rolled—set blankly.

Duane drew a deep breath and sheathed his gun. He felt calm and cool, glad the fray was over. One violent expression burst from him. "The fool!"

When he looked up there were men around him.

"Plumb center," said one.

Another, a cowboy who evidently had just left the gaming table, leaned down and pulled open Bain's shirt. He had the ace of spades in his hand. He laid it on Bain's breast, and the black figure on the card covered the two bullet holes just over Bain's heart.

Duane wheeled and hurried away. He heard another man say:

"Reckon Cal got what he deserved. Buck Duane's first gunplay. Like father like son!"

2

A THOUGHT kept repeating itself to Duane, and it was that he might have spared himself concern through his imagining how awful it would be to kill a man. He had no such feeling now. He had rid the community of a drunken, bragging, quarrelsome cowboy.

When he came to the gate of his home and saw his uncle there with a mettlesome horse, saddled, with canteen, rope, and bags all in place, a subtle shock pervaded his spirit. It had slipped his mind—the consequence of his act. But sight of the horse and the look of his uncle recalled the fact that he must now become a fugitive. An unreasonable anger took hold of him.

"The d——d fool!" he exclaimed, hotly. "Meeting Bain wasn't much,

Uncle Jim. He dusted my boots, that's all. And for that I've got to go on the dodge."

"Son, you killed him—then?" asked the uncle, huskily.

"Yes. I stood over him—watched him die. I did as I would have been done by."

"I knew it. Long ago I saw it comin'. But now we can't stop to cry over spilt blood. You've got to leave town an' this part of the country."

"Mother!" exclaimed Duane.

"She's away from home. You can't wait. I'll break it to her—what she always feared."

Suddenly Duane sat down and covered his face with his hands.

"My God! Uncle, what have I done?" His broad shoulders shook.

"Listen, son, an' remember what I say," replied the elder man, earnestly. "Don't ever forget. You're not to blame. I'm glad to see you take it this way, because maybe you'll never grow hard an' callous. You're not to blame. This is Texas. You're your father's son. These are wild times. The law as the rangers are laying it down now can't change life all in a minute. Even your mother, who's a good, true woman, has had her share in making you what you are this moment. For she was one of the pioneers— the fightin' pioneers of this state. Those years of wild times, before you was born, developed in her instinct to fight, to save her life, her children, an' that instinct has cropped out in you. It will be many years before it dies out of the boys born in Texas."

"I'm a murderer," said Duane, shuddering.

"No, son, you're not. An' you never will be. But you've got to be an outlaw till time makes it safe for you to come home."

"An outlaw?"

"I said it. If we had money an' influence we'd risk a trial. But we've neither. An' I reckon the scaffold or jail is no place for Buckley Duane. Strike for the wild country, an' wherever you go an' whatever you do—be a man. Live honestly, if that's possible. If it isn't, be as honest as you can. If you have to herd with outlaws try not to become bad. There are outlaws who're not all bad—many who have been driven to the river by such a deal as this you had. When you get among these men avoid brawls. Don't drink; don't gamble. I needn't tell you what to do if it comes to gunplay, as likely it will. You can't come home. When this thing is lived down, if that time ever comes, I'll get word into the unsettled country. It'll reach you someday. That's all. Remember, be a man. Goodbye."

Duane, with blurred sight and contracting throat, gripped his uncle's hand and bade him a wordless farewell. Then he leaped astride the black and rode out of town.

As swiftly as was consistent with a care for his steed, Duane put a distance of fifteen or eighteen miles behind him. With that he slowed up, and the matter of riding did not require all his faculties. He passed several ranches and was seen by men. This did not suit him, and he took an old trail across country. It was a flat region with a poor growth of mesquite and prickly-pear cactus. Occasionally he caught a glimpse of low hills in the distance. He had hunted often in that section, and knew where to find grass and water. When he reached this higher ground he did not, however, halt at the first favorable camping spot, but went on and on. Once he came out upon the brow of a hill and saw a considerable stretch of country beneath him. It had the gray sameness characterizing all that he had traversed. He seemed to want to see wide spaces—to get a glimpse of the great wilderness lying somewhere beyond to the southwest. It was sunset when he decided to camp at a likely spot he came across. He led the horse to water, and then began searching through the shallow valley for a suitable place to camp. He passed by old campsites that he well remembered. These, however, did not strike his fancy this time, and the significance of the change in him did not occur at the moment. At last he found a secluded spot, under cover of thick mesquites and oaks, at a goodly distance from the old trail. He took saddle and pack off the horse. He looked among his effects for a hobble, and, finding that his uncle had failed to put one in, he suddenly remembered that he seldom used a hobble, and never on this horse. He cut a few feet off the end of his lasso and used that. The horse, unused to such hampering of his free movements, had to be driven out upon the grass.

Duane made a small fire, prepared and ate his supper. This done, ending the work of that day, he sat down and filled his pipe. Twilight had waned into dusk. A few wan stars had just begun to show and brighten. Above the low continuous hum of insects sounded the evening carol of robins. Presently the birds ceased their singing, and then the quiet was more noticeable. When night set in and the place seemed all the more isolated and lonely for that Duane had a sense of relief.

It dawned upon him all at once that he was nervous, watchful, sleepless. The fact caused him surprise, and he began to think back, to take note of his late actions and their motives. The change one day had wrought amazed him. He who had always been free, easy, happy, especially when out alone in the open, had become in a few short hours bound, serious, preoccupied. The silence that had once been sweet now meant nothing to him except a medium whereby he might the better hear the sounds of pursuit. The loneliness, the night, the wild that had always been beautiful to him, now only conveyed a sense of safety for the present. He watched, he listened, he thought. He felt tired, yet had no inclination to rest. He intended to be off by dawn, heading toward the southwest. Had he a destination? It was vague as his knowledge of that great waste of mesquite and rock bordering the Rio Grande. Somewhere out there was a refuge. For he was a fugitive from justice, an outlaw.

This being an outlaw then meant eternal vigilance. No home, no rest, no sleep, no content, no life worth the living! He must be a lone wolf or he must herd among men obnoxious to him. If he worked for an honest living he still must hide his identity and take risks of detection. If he did not work on some distant outlying ranch, how was he to live? The idea of stealing was repugnant to him. The future seemed gray and somber enough. And he was twenty-three years old.

Why had this hard life been imposed upon him?

The bitter question seemed to start a strange iciness that stole along his veins. What was wrong with him? He stirred the few sticks of mesquite into a last flickering blaze. He was cold, and for some reason he wanted some light. The black circle of darkness weighed down upon him, closed in around him. Suddenly he sat bolt upright and then froze in that position. He had heard a step. It was behind him—no—on the side. Someone was there. He forced his hand down to his gun, and the touch of cold steel was another icy shock. Then he waited. But all was silent— silent as only a wilderness arroyo can be, with its low murmuring of wind in the mesquite. Had he heard a step? He began to breathe again.

But what was the matter with the light of his campfire? It had taken on a strange green luster and seemed to be waving off into the outer shadows. Duane heard no step, saw no movement; nevertheless, there was another present at that campfire vigil. Duane saw him. He lay there in the middle of the green brightness, prostrate, motionless, dying. Cal Bain! His features were wonderfully distinct, clearer than any cameo, more sharply outlined than those of any picture. It was a hard face softening at the threshold of eternity. The red tan of sun, the coarse signs of drunkenness, the ferocity and hate so characteristic of Bain were no longer there. This face represented a different Bain, showed all that was human in him fading, fading as swiftly as it blanched white. The lips wanted to speak, but had not the power. The eyes held an agony of thought. They revealed what might have been possible for this man if he lived—that he saw his mistake too late. Then they rolled, set blankly, and closed in death.

That haunting visitation left Duane sitting there in a cold sweat, a remorse gnawing at his vitals, realizing the curse that was on him. He divined that never would he be able to keep off that phantom. He remembered how his father had been eternally pursued by the furies of accusing guilt, how he had never been able to forget in work or in sleep those men he had killed.

The hour was late when Duane's mind let him sleep, and then dreams troubled him. In the morning he bestirred himself so early that in the gray gloom he had difficulty in finding his horse. Day had just broken when he struck the old trail again.

He rode hard all morning and halted in a shady spot to rest and graze his horse. In the afternoon he took to the trail at an easy trot. The country grew wilder. Bald, rugged mountains broke the level of the monotonous horizon. About three in the afternoon he came to a little river which marked the boundary line of his hunting territory.

The decision he made to travel upstream for a while was owing to two facts: the river was high with quicksand bars on each side, and he felt reluctant to cross into that region where his presence alone meant that he was a marked man. The bottom-lands through which the river wound to the southwest were more inviting than the barrens he had traversed. The rest of that day he rode leisurely upstream. At sunset he penetrated the brakes of willow and cottonwood to spend the night. It seemed to him that in this lonely cover he would feel easy and content. But he did not. Every feeling, every imagining he had experienced the previous night returned somewhat more vividly and accentuated by newer ones of the same intensity and color.

In this kind of travel and camping he spent three more days, during which he crossed a number of trails, and one road where cattle—stolen cattle, probably—had recently passed. This time exhausted his supply of food, except salt, pepper, coffee, and sugar, of which he had a quantity. There were deer in the brakes; but, as he could not get close enough to kill them with a revolver, he had to satisfy himself with a rabbit. He knew he might as well content himself with the hard fare that assuredly would be his lot.

Somewhere up this river there was a village called Huntsville. It was distant about a hundred miles from Wellston, and had a reputation throughout southwestern Texas. He had never been there. The fact was this reputation was such that honest travelers gave the town a wide berth. Duane had considerable money for him in his possession, and he concluded to visit Huntsville, if he could find it, and buy a stock of provisions.

The following day, toward evening, he happened upon a road which he believed might lead to the village. There were a good many fresh horse-tracks in the sand, and these made him thoughtful. Nevertheless, he followed the road, proceeding cautiously. He had not gone very far when the sound of rapid hoofbeats caught his ears. They came from his rear. In the darkening twilight he could not see any great distance back along the road. Voices, however, warned him that these riders, whoever they were, had approached closer than he liked. To go farther down the road was not to be thought of, so he turned a little way in among the mesquites and halted, hoping to escape being seen or heard. As he was now a fugitive, it seemed every man was his enemy and pursuer.

The horsemen were fast approaching. Presently they were abreast of Duane's position, so near that he could hear the creak of saddles, the clink of spurs.

"Shore he crossed the river below," said one man.

"I reckon you're right, Bill. He's slipped us," replied another.

Rangers or a posse of ranchers in pursuit of a fugitive! The knowledge gave Duane a strange thrill. Certainly they could not have been hunting him. But the feeling their proximity gave him was identical to what it would have been had he been this particular hunted man. He held his breath; he clenched his teeth; he pressed a quieting hand upon his horse. Suddenly he became aware that these horsemen had halted. They were whispering. He could just make out a dark group closely massed. What had made them halt so suspiciously?

"You're wrong, Bill," said a man, in a low but distinct voice. "The idee of hearin' a hoss heave! You're wuss'n a ranger. An' you're hell-bent on killin' that rustler. Now I say let's go home an' eat."

"Wal, I'll just take a look at the sand," replied the man called Bill.

Duane heard the clink of spurs on steel stirrup and the thud of boots on the ground. There followed a short silence which was broken by a sharply breathed exclamation.

Duane waited for no more. They had found his trail. He spurred his horse straight into the brush. At the second crashing bound there came yells from the road, and then shots. Duane heard the hiss of a bullet close by his ear, and as it struck a branch it made a peculiar singing sound. These shots and the proximity of that lead missile roused in Duane a quick, hot resentment which mounted into a passion almost ungovernable. He must escape, yet it seemed that he did not care whether he did or not. Something grim kept urging him to halt and return the fire of these men. After running a couple of hundred yards he raised himself from over the pommel, where he had bent to avoid the stinging branches, and tried to guide his horse. In the dark shadows under mesquites and cottonwoods he was hard put to it to find open passage; however, he succeeded so well and made such little noise that gradually he drew away from his pursuers. The sound of their horses crashing through the thickets died away. Duane reined in and listened. He had distanced them. Probably they would go into camp till daylight, then follow his tracks. He started on again, walking his horse, and peered sharply at the ground, so that he might take advantage of the first trail he crossed. It seemed a long while until he came upon one. He followed it until a late hour, when, striking the willow brakes again and hence the neighborhood of the river, he picketed his horse and lay down to rest. But he did not sleep. His mind bitterly revolved the fate that had come upon him. He made efforts to think of other things, but in vain. Every moment he expected the chill, the sense of loneliness that yet was ominous of a strange visitation, the peculiarly imagined lights and shades of the night—these things that presaged the coming of Cal Bain. Doggedly Duane fought against the insidious phantom. He kept telling himself that it was just imagination, that it would wear off in time. Still in his heart he did not believe what he hoped. But he would not give up; he would not accept the ghost of his victim as a reality.

Gray dawn found him in the saddle again headed for the river. Half an hour of riding brought him to the dense chaparral and willow thickets. These he threaded to come at length to the ford. It was a gravel bottom, and therefore an easy crossing. Once upon the opposite shore he reined in his horse and looked darkly back. This action marked his acknowledgment of his situation: he had voluntarily sought the refuge of the outlaws; he was beyond the pale. A bitter and passionate curse passed his lips as he spurred his horse into the brakes on that alien shore.

He rode perhaps twenty miles, not sparing his horse nor caring whether or not he left a plain trail.

"Let them hunt me!" he muttered.

When the heat of the day began to be oppressive, and hunger and thirst made themselves manifest, Duane began to look about him for a place to halt for the noon hours. The trail led into a road which was hard packed and smooth from the tracks of cattle. He doubted not that he had come across one of the roads used by border raiders. He headed into it, and had scarcely traveled a mile when, turning a curve, he came point-blank upon a single horseman riding toward him. Both riders wheeled their mounts sharply and were ready to run and shoot back. Not more than a hundred paces separated them. They stood then for a moment watching each other.

"Mawnin', stranger," called the man, dropping his hand from his hip.

"Howdy," replied Duane, shortly.

They rode toward each other, closing half the gap, then they halted again.

"I seen you ain't no ranger," called the rider, "an' shore I ain't none."

He laughed loudly, as if he had made a joke.

"How'd you know I wasn't a ranger?" asked Duane, curiously. Somehow he had instantly divined that this horseman was no officer, or even a rancher trailing stolen stock.

"Wal," said the fellow, starting his horse forward at a walk, "a ranger'd never git ready to run the other way from one man."

He laughed again. He was small and wiry, slouchy of attire, and armed to the teeth, and he bestrode a fine bay horse. He had quick, dancing brown eyes, at once frank and bold, and a coarse, bronzed face. Evidently he was a good-natured ruffian.

Duane acknowledged the truth of the assertion, and turned over in his mind how shrewdly the fellow had guessed him to be a hunted man.

"My name's Luke Stevens, an' I hail from the river. Who're you?" said this stranger.

Duane was silent.

"I reckon you're Buck Duane," went on Stevens. "I heerd you was a damn bad man with a gun."

This time Duane laughed, not at the doubtful compliment, but at the idea that the first outlaw he met should know him. Here was proof of how swiftly facts about gunplay traveled on the Texas border.

"Wal, Buck," said Stevens, in a friendly manner, "I ain't presumin' on your time or company. I see you're headin' fer the river. But will you stop long enough to stake a feller to a bite of grub?"

"I'm out of grub, and pretty hungry myself," admitted Duane.

"Been pushin' your hoss, I see. Wal, I reckon you'd better stock up before you hit thet stretch of country."

He made a wide sweep of his right arm, indicating the southwest, and there was that in his action which seemed significant of a vast and barren region.

"Stock up?" queried Duane, thoughtfully.

"Shore. A feller has jest got to eat. I can rustle along without whisky, but not without grub. Thet's what makes it so embarrassin' travelin' these parts dodgin' your shadow. Now, I'm on my way to Mercer. It's a little two-bit town up the river a ways. I'm goin' to pack out some grub."

Stevens's tone was inviting. Evidently he would welcome Duane's companionship, but he did not openly say so. Duane kept silence, however, and then Stevens went on.

"Stranger, in this here country two's a crowd. It's safer. I never was much on this lone-wolf dodgin', though I've done it of necessity. It takes a damn good man to travel alone any length of time. Why, I've been thet sick I was jest achin' fer some ranger to come along an' plug me. Give me a pardner any day. Now, mebbe you're not thet kind of a feller, an' I'm shore not presumin' to ask. But I jest declares myself sufficient."

"You mean you'd like me to go with you?" asked Duane.

Stevens grinned. "Wal, I should smile. I'd be particular proud to be braced with a man of your reputation."

"See here, my good fellow, that's all nonsense," declared Duane, in some haste.

"Shore I think modesty becomin' to a youngster," replied Stevens. "I hate a brag. An' I've no use fer these four-flush cowboys thet're always lookin' fer trouble an' talkin' gunplay. Buck, I don't know much about you. But every man who's lived along the Texas border remembers a lot about your Dad. It was expected of you, I reckon, an' much of your rep was established before you throwed your gun. I jest heerd thet you was lightnin' on the draw, an' when you cut loose with a gun, why the figger on the ace of spades would cover your cluster of bullet holes. Thet's the word thet's gone down the border. It's the kind of reputation most sure to fly far an' swift ahead of a man in this country. An' the safest, too; I'll gamble on thet. It's the land of the draw. I see now you're only a boy, though you're shore a strappin' husky one. Now, Buck, I'm not a spring chicken, an' I've been long on the dodge. Mebbe a little of my society won't hurt you none. You'll need to learn the country."

There was something sincere and likable about this outlaw.

"I dare say you're right," replied Duane, quietly. "And I'll go to Mercer with you."

Next moment he was riding down the road with Stevens. Duane had never been much of a talker, and now he found speech difficult. But his companion did not seem to mind that. He was a jocose, voluble fellow, probably glad now to hear the sound of his own voice. Duane listened, and sometimes he thought with a pang of the distinction of name and heritage of blood his father had left to him.

3

L ATE THAT DAY, a couple of hours before sunset, Duane and Stevens, having rested their horses in the shade of some mesquites near the town of Mercer, saddled up and prepared to move.

"Buck, as we're lookin' fer grub, an' not trouble, I reckon you'd better hang up out here," Stevens was saying, as he mounted. "You see, towns an' sheriffs an' rangers are always lookin' fer new fellers gone bad. They sort of forget most of the old boys, except those as are plumb bad. Now, nobody in Mercer will take notice of me. Reckon there's been a thousand men run into the river country to become outlaws since yours truly. You jest wait here an' be ready to ride hard. Mebbe my besettin' sin will go operatin' in spite of my good intentions. In which case there'll be—"

His pause was significant. He grinned, and his brown eyes danced with a kind of wild humor.

"Stevens, have you got any money?" asked Duane.

"Money!" exclaimed Luke, blankly. "Say, I haven't owned a two-bit piece since—wal, fer some time."

"I'll furnish money for grub," returned Duane. "And for whisky, too, providing you hurry back here . . . without making trouble."

"Shore you're a downright good pard," declared Stevens, in admiration, as he took the money. "I give my word, Buck, an' I'm here to say I never broke it yet. Lay low, an' look fer me back quick."

With that he spurred his horse and rode out of the mesquites toward the town. At that distance, about a quarter of a mile, Mercer appeared to be a cluster of low adobe houses set in a grove of cottonwoods. Pastures of alfalfa were dotted by horses and cattle. Duane saw a sheepherder driving in a meager flock.

Presently Stevens rode out of sight into the town. Duane waited, hoping the outlaw would make good his word. Probably not a quarter of an hour had elapsed when Duane heard the clear reports of a Winchester rifle, the clatter of rapid hoofbeats, and yells unmistakably the kind to mean danger for a man like Stevens. Duane mounted and rode to the edge of the mesquites.

He saw a cloud of dust down the road and a bay horse running fast. Stevens apparently had not been wounded by any of the shots, for he had a steady seat in his saddle and his riding, even at that moment, struck Duane as admirable. He carried a large pack over the pommel, and he kept looking back. The shots had ceased, but the yells increased. Duane saw several men running and waving their arms. Then he spurred his horse and got into a swift stride, so Stevens would not pass him. Presently the outlaw caught up with him. Stevens was grinning, but there was now no fun in the dancing eyes. It was a devil that danced in them. His face seemed a shade paler.

"Was jest comin' out of the store," yelled Stevens. "Run plumb into a rancher—who knowed me. He opened up with a rifle. Think they'll chase us."

They covered several miles before there were any signs of pursuit, and when horsemen did move into sight out of the cottonwoods Duane and his companion steadily drew farther away.

"No hosses in thet bunch to worry us," called out Stevens.

Duane had the same conviction, and he did not look back again. He rode somewhat to the fore, and was constantly aware of the rapid thudding of hoofs behind, as Stevens kept close to him. At sunset they reached the willow brakes and the river. Duane's horse was winded and lashed with sweat and lather. It was not until the crossing had been accomplished that Duane halted to rest his animal. Stevens was riding up the low, sandy bank. He reeled in the saddle. With an exclamation of surprise Duane leaped off and ran to the outlaw's side.

Stevens was pale, and his face bore beads of sweat. The whole front of his shirt was soaked with blood.

"You're shot!" cried Duane.

"Wal, who'n hell said I wasn't? Would you mind givin' me a lift—on this here pack?"

Duane lifted the heavy pack down and then helped Stevens to dismount. The outlaw had a bloody foam on his lips, and he was spitting blood.

"Oh, why didn't you *say* so!" cried Duane. "I never thought. You seemed all right."

"Wal, Luke Stevens may be as gabby as an old woman, but sometimes he doesn't say anythin'. It wouldn't have done no good."

Duane bade him sit down, removed his shirt, and washed the blood from his breast and back. Stevens had been shot in the breast, fairly low down, and the bullet had gone clear through him. His ride, holding himself and that heavy pack in the saddle, had been a feat little short of marvelous. Duane did not see how it had been possible, and he felt no hope for the outlaw. But he plugged the wounds and bound them tightly.

"Feller's name was Brown," Stevens said. "Me an' him fell out over a hoss I stole from him over in Huntsville. We had a shootin'-scrape then. Wal, as I was straddlin' my hoss back there in Mercer I seen this Brown, an' seen him before he seen me. Could have killed him, too. But I wasn't breakin' my word to you. I kind of hoped he wouldn't spot me. But he did —an' fust shot he got me here. What do you think of this hole?"

"It's pretty bad," replied Duane; and he could not look the cheerful outlaw in the eyes.

"I reckon it is. Wal, I've had some bad wounds I lived over. Guess mebbe I can stand this one. Now, Buck, get me some place in the brakes, leave me some grub an' water at my hand, an' then you clear out."

"Leave you here alone?" asked Duane, sharply.

"Shore. You see, I can't keep up with you. Brown an' his friends will foller us acrost the river a ways. You've got to think of number one in this game."

"What would you do in my case?" asked Duane, curiously.

"Wal, I reckon I'd clear out an' save my hide," replied Stevens.

Duane felt inclined to doubt the outlaw's assertion. For his own part he decided his conduct without further speech. First he watered the horses, filled canteens and water-bag, and then tied the pack upon his own horse. That done, he lifted Stevens upon his horse, and, holding him in the saddle, turned into the brakes, being careful to pick out hard or grassy ground that left little signs of tracks. Just about dark he ran across a trail that Stevens said was a good one to take into the wild country.

"Reckon we'd better keep right on in the dark—till I drop," concluded Stevens, with a laugh.

All that night Duane, gloomy and thoughtful, attentive to the wounded outlaw, walked the trail and never halted till daybreak. He was tired then and very hungry. Stevens seemed in bad shape, although he was still spirited and cheerful. Duane made camp. The outlaw refused food, but asked for both whisky and water. Then he stretched out.

"Buck, will you take off my boots?" he asked, with a faint smile on his pallid face.

Duane removed them, wondering if the outlaw had the thought that he did not want to die with his boots on. Stevens seemed to read his mind.

"Buck, my old daddy used to say thet I was born to be hanged. But I wasn't . . . an' dyin' with your boots on is the next wust way to croak."

"You've a chance to—to get over this," said Duane.

"Shore. But I want to be correct about the boots—an' say, pard, if I do go over, jest you remember thet I was appreciatin' of your kindness."

Then he closed his eyes and seemed to sleep.

Duane could not find water for the horses, but there was an abundance of dew-wet grass upon which he hobbled them. After that was done he prepared himself a much-needed meal. The sun was getting warm when he lay down to sleep, and when he awoke it was sinking in the west. Stevens was still alive, for he breathed heavily. The horses were in sight. All was quiet except the hum of insects in the brush. Duane listened awhile, then rose and went for the horses.

When he returned with them he found Stevens awake, bright-eyed, cheerful as usual, and apparently stronger.

"Wal, Buck, I'm still with you an' good fer another night's ride," he said. "Guess about all I need now is a big pull on thet bottle. Help me, will you? There! Thet was bully. I ain't swallowin' my blood this evenin'. Mebbe I've bled all there was in me."

While Duane got a hurried meal for himself, packed up the little outfit, and saddled the horses Stevens kept on talking. He seemed to be in a hurry to tell Duane all about the country. Another night ride would put them beyond fear of pursuit, within striking distance of the Rio Grande and the hiding-places of the outlaws.

When it came time for mounting the horses Stevens said, "Reckon you can pull on my boots once more." In spite of the laugh accompanying the words Duane detected a subtle change in the outlaw's spirit.

On this night travel was facilitated by the fact that the trail was broad enough for two horses abreast, enabling Duane to ride while upholding Stevens in the saddle.

The difficulty most persistent was in keeping the horses in a walk. They were used to a trot, and that kind of gait would not do for Stevens. The red died out of the west; a pale afterglow prevailed for a while; darkness set in; then the broad expanse of blue darkened and the stars brightened. After a while Stevens ceased talking and drooped in his saddle. Duane kept the horses going, however, and the slow hours wore away. Duane thought the quiet night would never break to dawn, that there was no end to the melancholy, brooding plain. But at length a grayness blotted out the stars and mantled the level of mesquite and cactus.

Dawn caught the fugitives at a green camping-site on the bank of a rocky little stream. Stevens fell a dead weight into Duane's arms, and one look at the haggard face showed Duane that the outlaw had taken his last ride. He knew it, too. Yet that cheerfulness prevailed.

"Buck, my feet are orful tired packin' them heavy boots," he said, and seemed immensely relieved when Duane had removed them.

This matter of the outlaw's boots was strange, Duane thought. He made Stevens as comfortable as possible, then attended to his own needs. And the outlaw took up the thread of his conversation where he had left off the night before.

"This trail splits up a ways from here, an' every branch of it leads to a hole where you'll find men—a few, mebbe, like yourself—some like me— an' gangs of no-good hoss-thieves, rustlers, an' such. It's easy livin', Buck. I reckon, though, that you'll not find it easy. You'll never mix in. You'll be a lone wolf. I seen that right off. Wal, if a man can stand the loneliness, an' if he's quick on the draw, mebbe lone-wolfin' it is the best. Shore I don't know. But these fellers in here will be suspicious of a man who goes it alone. If they get a chance they'll kill you."

Stevens asked for water several times. He had forgotten or he did not want the whisky. His voice grew perceptibly weaker.

"Be quiet," said Duane. "Talking uses up your strength."

"Aw, I'll talk till—I'm done," he replied, doggedly. "See here, pard, you can gamble on what I'm tellin' you. An' it'll be useful. From this camp we'll—you'll meet men right along. An' none of them will be honest men. All the same, some are better 'n others. I've lived along the river fer twelve years. There's three big gangs of outlaws. King Fisher—you know him, I reckon, fer he's half the time livin' among respectable folks. King is a pretty good feller. It'll do to tie up with him an' his gang. Now, there's Cheseldine, who hangs out in the Rim Rock way up the river. He's an outlaw chief. I never seen him, though I stayed once right in his camp. Late years he's got rich an' keeps back pretty well hid. But Bland—I knowed Bland fer years. An' I haven't any use fer him. Bland has the biggest gang. You ain't likely to miss strikin' his place sometime or other. He's got a regular town, I might say. Shore there's some gamblin' an' gunfightin' goin' on at Bland's camp all the time. Bland has killed some twenty men, an' thet's not countin' Mexicans."

Here Stevens took another drink and then rested for a while.

"You ain't likely to get on with Bland," he resumed, presently. "You're too strappin' big an' good-lookin' to please the chief. Fer he's got women in his camp. Then he'd be jealous of your possibilities with a gun. Shore I reckon he'd be careful, though. Bland's no fool, an' he loves his hide. I reckon any of the other gangs would be better fer you when you ain't goin' it alone."

Apparently that exhausted the fund of information and advice Stevens had been eager to impart. He lapsed into silence and lay with closed eyes. Meanwhile the sun rose warm; the breeze waved the mesquites; the birds came down to splash in the shallow stream; Duane dozed in a comfortable seat. By and by something roused him. Stevens was once more talking, but with a changed tone.

"Feller's name—was Brown," he rambled. "We fell out—over a hoss I stole from him—in Huntsville. He stole it fust. Brown's one of them sneaks—afraid of the open—he steals an' pretends to be honest. Say, Buck, mebbe you'll meet Brown someday . . . you an' me are pards now."

"I'll remember, if I ever meet him," said Duane.

That seemed to satisfy the outlaw. Presently he tried to lift his head, but had not the strength. A strange shade was creeping across the bronzed rough face.

"My feet are pretty heavy. Shore you got my boots off?"

Duane held them up, but was not certain that Stevens could see them.

The outlaw closed his eyes again and muttered incoherently. Then he fell asleep. Duane believed that sleep was final. The day passed, with Duane watching and waiting. Toward sundown Stevens awoke, and his eyes seemed clearer. Duane went to get some fresh water, thinking his comrade would surely want some. When he returned Stevens made no sign that he wanted anything. There was something bright about him, and suddenly Duane realized what it meant.

"Pard, you—stuck—to me!" the outlaw whispered.

Duane caught a hint of gladness in the voice; he traced a faint surprise in the haggard face. Stevens seemed like a little child.

To Duane the moment was sad, elemental, big, with a burden of mystery he could not understand.

Duane buried him in a shallow arroyo and heaped up a pile of stones to mark the grave. That done, he saddled his comrade's horse, hung the weapons over the pommel; and, mounting his own steed, he rode down the trail in the gathering twilight.

4

TWO DAYS later, about the middle of the forenoon, Duane dragged the two horses up the last ascent of an exceedingly rough trail and found himself on top of the Rim Rock, with a beautiful green valley at his feet, the yellow, sluggish Rio Grande shining in the sun, and the great, wild, mountainous barren of Mexico stretching to the south.

Duane had not fallen in with any travelers. He had taken the likeliest-looking trail he had come across. Where it had led him he had not the slightest idea, except that here was the river, and probably the enclosed valley was the retreat of some famous outlaw.

No wonder outlaws were safe in that wild refuge! Duane had spent the last two days climbing the roughest and most difficult trail he had ever seen. From the looks of the descent he imagined the worst part of his travel was yet to come. Not improbably it was two thousand feet down to the river. The wedge-shaped valley, green with alfalfa and cottonwood, and nestling down amid the bare walls of yellow rock, was a delight and a relief to his tired eyes. Eager to get down to a level and to find a place to rest, Duane began the descent.

The trail proved to be the kind that could not be descended slowly. He kept dodging rocks which his horses loosed behind him. And in a short time he reached the valley, entering at the apex of the wedge. A stream of clear water tumbled out of the rocks here, and most of it ran into irrigation ditches. His horses drank thirstily. And he drank with that fullness and gratefulness common to the desert traveler finding sweet water. Then he mounted and rode down the valley wondering what would be his reception.

The valley was much larger than it had appeared from the high elevation. Well watered, green with grass and tree, and farmed evidently by good hands, it gave Duane a considerable surprise. Horses and cattle were everywhere. Every clump of cottonwoods surrounded a small adobe house. Duane saw Mexicans working in the fields and horsemen going to and fro. Presently he passed a house bigger than the others with a porch attached. A woman, young and pretty he thought, watched him from a door. No one else appeared to notice him.

Presently the trail widened into a road, and that into a kind of square lined by a number of adobe and log buildings of rudest structure. Within sight were horses, dogs, a couple of steers, Mexican women with children, and white men, all of whom appeared to be doing nothing. His advent created no interest until he rode up to the white men, who were lolling in the shade of a house. This place evidently was a store and saloon, and from the inside came a lazy hum of voices.

As Duane reined to a halt one of the loungers in the shade rose with a loud exclamation.

"Bust me if thet ain't Luke's hoss!"

The others accorded their interest, if not assent, by rising to advance toward Duane.

"How about it, Euchre? Ain't thet Luke's bay?" queried the first man.

"Plain as your nose," replied the fellow called Euchre.

"There ain't no doubt about thet, then," laughed another, "fer Bosomer's nose is shore plain on the landscape."

These men lined up before Duane, and as he coolly regarded them he thought they could have been recognized anywhere as desperadoes. The man called Bosomer, who had stepped forward, had a forbidding face which showed yellow eyes, an enormous nose, and a skin the color of dust, with a thatch of sandy hair.

"Stranger, who are you an' where in the hell did you git thet bay hoss?" he demanded. His yellow eyes took in Stevens's horse, then the weapons hung on the saddle, and finally turned their glinting, hard light upward to Duane.

Duane did not like the tone in which he had been addressed, and he remained silent. At least half his mind seemed busy with curious interest in regard to something that leaped inside him and made his breast feel tight. He recognized it as that strange emotion which had shot through him often of late, and which had decided him to go out to the meeting with Bain. Only now it was different, more powerful.

"Stranger, who are you?" asked another man, somewhat more civilly.

"My name's Duane," replied Duane, curtly.

"An' how'd you come by the hoss?"

Duane answered briefly, and his words were followed by a short silence, during which the men looked at him. Bosomer began to twist the ends of his beard.

"Reckon he's dead, all right, or nobody'd hev his hoss an' guns," presently said Euchre.

"Mister Duane," began Bosomer, in low, stinging tones, "I happen to be Luke Stevens's side-pardner."

Duane looked him over, from dusty, worn-out boots to his slouchy sombrero. That look seemed to inflame Bosomer.

"An' I want the hoss an' them guns," he shouted.

"You or anybody else can have them, for all I care. I just fetched them in. But the pack is mine," replied Duane. "And say, I befriended your pard. If you can't use a civil tongue you'd better cinch it."

"Civil? Haw, haw!" rejoined the outlaw. "I don't know you. How do we know you didn't plug Stevens, an' stole his hoss, an' jest happened to stumble down here?"

"You'll have to take my word, that's all," replied Duane, sharply.

"—— ——! I ain't takin' your word! Savvy thet? An' I was Luke's pard!"

With that Bosomer wheeled and, pushing his companions aside, he stamped into the saloon, where his voice broke out in a roar.

Duane dismounted and threw his bridle.

"Stranger, Bosomer is shore hot-headed," said the man Euchre. He did not appear unfriendly, nor were the others hostile.

At this juncture several more outlaws crowded out of the door, and the one in the lead was a tall man of stalwart physique. His manner proclaimed him a leader. He had a long face, a flaming red beard, and clear, cold blue eyes that fixed in close scrutiny upon Duane. He was not a Texan; in truth, Duane did not recognize one of these outlaws as native to his state.

"I'm Bland," said the tall man, authoritatively. "Who're you and what're you doing here?"

Duane looked at Bland as he had at the others. This outlaw chief appeared to be reasonable, if he was not courteous. Duane told his story again, this time a little more in detail.

"I believe you," replied Bland, at once. "Think I know when a fellow is lying."

"I reckon you're on the right trail," put in Euchre. "Thet about Luke wantin' his boots took off—thet satisfies me. Luke hed a mortal dread of dyin' with his boots on."

At this sally the chief and his men laughed.

"You said Duane—Buck Duane?" queried Bland. "Are you a son of that Duane who was a gunfighter some years back?"

"Yes," replied Duane.

"Never met him, and glad I didn't," said Bland, with a grim humor. "So you got in trouble and had to go on the dodge? What kind of trouble?"

"Had a fight."

"Fight? Do you mean gunplay?" questioned Bland. He seemed eager, curious, speculative.

"Yes. It ended in gunplay, I'm sorry to say," answered Duane.

"Guess I needn't ask the son of Duane if he killed his man," went on Bland, ironically. "Well, I'm sorry you bucked against trouble in my camp. But as it is, I guess you'd be wise to make yourself scarce."

"Do you mean I'm politely told to move on?" asked Duane, quietly.

"Not exactly that," said Bland, as if irritated. "If this isn't a free place there isn't one on earth. Every man is equal here. Do you want to join my band?"

"No, I don't."

"Well, even if you did I imagine that wouldn't stop Bosomer. He's an ugly fellow. He's one of the few gunmen I've met who wants to kill somebody all the time. Most men like that are four-flushes. But Bosomer is all one color, and that's red. Merely for your own sake I advise you to hit the trail."

"Thanks. But if that's all I'll stay," returned Duane. Even as he spoke he felt that he did not know himself.

Bosomer appeared at the door, pushing men who tried to detain him, and as he jumped clear of a last reaching hand he uttered a snarl like an angry dog. Manifestly the short while he had spent inside the saloon had been devoted to drinking and talking himself into a frenzy. Bland and the other outlaws quickly moved aside, letting Duane stand alone. When Bosomer saw Duane standing motionless and watchful a strange change passed quickly in him. He halted in his tracks, and as he did that the men who had followed him out piled over one another in their hurry to get to one side.

Duane saw all the swift action, felt intuitively the meaning of it, and in Bosomer's sudden change of front. The outlaw was keen, and he had expected a shrinking, or at least a frightened antagonist. Duane knew he was neither. He felt like iron, and yet thrill after thrill ran through him. It was almost as if this situation had been one long familiar to him. Somehow he understood this yellow-eyed Bosomer. The outlaw had come out to kill him. And now, though somewhat checked by the stand of a stranger, he still meant to kill. Like so many desperadoes of his ilk, he was victim of a passion to kill for the sake of killing. Duane divined that no sudden animosity was driving Bosomer. It was just his chance. In that moment murder would have been joy to him. Very likely he had forgotten his pretext for a quarrel. Very probably his faculties were absorbed in conjecture as to Duane's possibilities.

But he did not speak a word. He remained motionless for a long moment, his eyes pale and steady, his right hand like a claw.

That instant gave Duane a power to read in his enemy's eyes the thought that preceded action. But Duane did not want to kill another man. Still he would have to fight, and he decided to cripple Bosomer. When Bosomer's hand moved Duane's gun was spouting fire. Two shots only—both from Duane's gun—and the outlaw fell with his right arm shattered. Bosomer cursed harshly and floundered in the dust, trying to reach the gun with his left hand. His comrades, however, seeing that Duane would not kill unless forced, closed in upon Bosomer and prevented any further madness on his part.

5

OF THE OUTLAWS present Euchre appeared to be the one most inclined to lend friendliness to curiosity; and he led Duane and the horses away to a small adobe shack. He tied the horses in an open shed and removed their saddles. Then, gathering up Stevens's weapons, he invited his visitor to enter the house.

It had two rooms—windows without coverings—bare floors. One room contained blankets, weapons, saddles, and bridles; the other a stone fireplace, rude table and bench, two bunks, a box cupboard, and various blackened utensils.

"Make yourself at home as long as you want to stay," said Euchre. "I ain't rich in this world's goods, but I own what's here, an' you're welcome."

"Thanks. I'll stay awhile and rest. I'm pretty well played out," replied Duane.

Euchre gave him a keen glance.

"Go ahead an' rest. I'll take your horses to grass."

Euchre left Duane alone in the house. Duane relaxed then, and mechanically he wiped the sweat from his face. He was laboring under some kind of a spell or shock which did not pass off quickly. When it had worn away he took off his coat and belt and made himself comfortable on the blankets. And he had a thought that if he rested or slept what difference would it make on the morrow? No rest, no sleep could change the gray outlook of the future. He felt glad when Euchre came bustling in, and for the first time he took notice of the outlaw.

Euchre was old in years. What little hair he had was gray, his face clean-shaven and full of wrinkles; his eyes were half shut from long gazing through the sun and dust. He stooped. But his thin frame denoted strength and endurance still unimpaired.

"Hev a drink or a smoke?" he asked.

Duane shook his head. He had not been unfamiliar with whisky, and he had used tobacco moderately since he was sixteen. But now, strangely, he felt a disgust at the idea of stimulants. He did not understand clearly what he felt. There was that vague idea of something wild in his blood, something that made him fear himself.

Euchre wagged his old head sympathetically. "Reckon you feel a little sick. When it comes to shootin' I run. What's your age?"

"I'm twenty-three," replied Duane.

Euchre showed surprise. "You're only a boy! I thought you thirty anyways. Buck, I heard what you told Bland, an' puttin' thet with my own figgerin', I reckon you're no criminal yet. Throwin' a gun in self-defense— thet ain't no crime!"

Duane, finding relief in talking, told more about himself.

"Huh," replied the old man. "I've been on this river fer years, an' I've seen hundreds of boys come in on the dodge. Most of them, though, was no good. An' thet kind don't last long. This river country has been an' is the refuge fer criminals from all over the states. I've bunked with bank cashiers, forgers, plain thieves, an' out-an'-out murderers, all of which had no bizness on the Texas border. Fellers like Bland are exceptions. He's no Texan—you seen thet. The gang he rules here come from all over, an' they're tough cusses, you can bet on thet. They live fat an' easy. If it wasn't fer the fightin' among themselves they'd shore grow populous. The Rim Rock is no place for a peaceable, decent feller. I heard you tell Bland you wouldn't join his gang. Thet'll not make him take a likin' to you. Have you any money?"

"Not much," replied Duane.

"Could you live by gamblin'? Are you any good at cards?"

"No."

"You wouldn't steal hosses or rustle cattle?"

"No."

"When your money's gone how 'n hell will you live? There ain't any work a decent feller could do. You can't herd with greasers. Why, Bland's men would shoot at you in the fields. What'll you do, son?"

"God knows," replied Duane, hopelessly. "I'll make my money last as long as possible—then starve."

"Wal, I'm pretty pore, but you'll never starve while I got anythin'."

Here it struck Duane again—that something human and kind and eager which he had seen in Stevens. Duane's estimate of outlaws had lacked this quality. He had not accorded them any virtues. To him, as to the outside world, they had been merely vicious men without one redeeming feature.

"I'm much obliged to you, Euchre," replied Duane. "But of course I won't live with anyone unless I can pay my share."

"Have it any way you like, my son," said Euchre, good-humoredly. "You make a fire, an' I'll set about gettin' grub. I'm a sour-dough, Buck. Thet man doesn't live who can beat my bread."

"How do you ever pack supplies in here?" asked Duane, thinking of the almost inaccessible nature of the valley.

"Some comes across from Mexico, an' the rest down the river. Thet river trip is a bird. It's more'n five hundred miles to any supply point. Bland has *mozos*, greaser boatmen. Sometimes, too, he gets supplies in from down-river. You see, Bland sells thousands of cattle in Cuba. An' all this stock has to go down by boat to meet the ships."

"Where on earth are the cattle driven down to the river?" asked Duane.

"Thet's not my secret," replied Euchre, shortly. "Fact is, I don't know. I've rustled cattle for Bland, but he never sent me through the Rim Rock with them."

Duane experienced a sort of pleasure in the realization that interest had been stirred in him. He was curious about Bland and his gang, and glad to have something to think about. For every once in a while he had a sensation that was almost like a pang. He wanted to forget. In the next hour he did forget, and enjoyed helping in the preparation and eating of the meal. Euchre, after washing and hanging up the several utensils, put on his hat and turned to go out.

"Come along or stay here, as you want," he said to Duane.

"I'll stay," rejoined Duane, slowly.

The old outlaw left the room and trudged away, whistling cheerfully.

Duane looked around him for a book or paper, anything to read; but all the printed matter he could find consisted of a few words on cartridge-boxes and an advertisement on the back of a tobacco pouch. There seemed to be nothing for him to do. He had rested; he did not want to lie down any more. He began to walk to and fro, from one end of the room to the other. And as he walked he fell into the lately acquired habit of brooding over his misfortune.

Suddenly he straightened up with a jerk. Unconsciously he had drawn his gun. Standing there with the bright cold weapon in his hand, he looked at it in consternation. How had he come to draw it? With difficulty he traced his thoughts backward, but could not find any that was accountable for his act. He discovered, however, that he had a remarkable tendency to drop his hand to his gun. That might have come from the habit long practice in drawing had given him. Likewise, it might have come from a subtle sense, scarcely thought of at all, of the late, close, and inevitable relation between that weapon and himself. He was amazed to find that, bitter as he had grown at fate, the desire to live burned strong in him. If he had been as unfortunately situated, but with the difference that no man wanted to put him in jail or take his life, he felt that this burning passion to be free, to save himself, might not have been so powerful. Life certainly held no bright prospects for him. Already he had begun to despair of ever getting back to his home. But to give up like a white-hearted coward, to let himself be handcuffed and jailed, to run from a drunken, bragging cowboy, or be shot in cold blood by some border brute who merely wanted to add another notch to his gun—these things were impossible for Duane because there was in him the temper to fight. In that hour he yielded only to fate and the spirit inborn in him. Hereafter this gun must be a living part of him. Right then and there he returned to a practice he had long discontinued—the draw. It was now a stern, bitter, deadly business with him. He did not need to fire the gun, for accuracy was a gift and had become assured. Swiftness on the draw, however, could be improved, and he set himself to acquire the limit of speed possible to any man. He stood still in his tracks; he paced the room; he sat down, lay down, put himself in awkward positions; and from every position he practiced throwing his gun—practiced it till he was hot and tired and his arm ached and his hand burned. That practice he determined to keep up every day. It was one thing, at least, that would help pass the weary hours.

Later he went outdoors to the cooler shade of the cottonwoods. From this point he could see a good deal of the valley. Under different circumstances Duane felt that he would have enjoyed such a beautiful spot. Euchre's shack sat against the first rise of the slope of the wall, and Duane, by climbing a few rods, got a view of the whole valley. Assuredly it was an outlaw settlement. He saw a good many Mexicans, who, of course, were hand and glove with Bland. Also he saw enormous flat-boats, crude of structure, moored along the banks of the river. The Rio Grande rolled away between high bluffs. A cable, sagging deep in the middle, was stretched over the wide yellow stream, and an old scow, evidently used as a ferry, lay anchored on the far shore.

The valley was an ideal retreat for an outlaw band operating on a big scale. Pursuit scarcely need be feared over the broken trails of the Rim Rock. And the open end of the valley could be defended against almost any number of men coming down the river. Access to Mexico was easy and quick. What puzzled Duane was how Bland got cattle down to the river, and he wondered if the rustler really did get rid of his stolen stock by use of boats.

Duane must have idled considerable time up on the hill, for when he returned to the shack Euchre was busily engaged around the campfire.

"Wal, glad to see you ain't so pale about the gills as you was," he said, by way of greeting. "Pitch in an' we'll soon have grub ready. There's shore one consolin' fact round this here camp."

"What's that?" asked Duane.

"Plenty of good juicy beef to eat. An' it doesn't cost a short bit."

"But it costs hard rides and trouble, bad conscience, and life, too, doesn't it?"

"I ain't shore about the bad conscience. Mine never bothered me none. An' as for life, why, thet's cheap in Texas."

"Who is Bland?" asked Duane, quickly changing the subject. "What do you know about him?"

"We don't know who he is or where he hails from," replied Euchre. "Thet's always been somethin' to interest the gang. He must have been a young man when he struck Texas. Now he's middle-aged. I remember how years ago he was soft-spoken an' not rough in talk or act like he is now. Bland ain't likely his right name. He knows a lot. He can doctor you, an' he's shore a knowin' feller with tools. He's the kind thet rules men. Outlaws are always ridin' in here to join his gang, an' if it hadn't been fer the gamblin' an' gunplay he'd have a thousand men around him."

"How many in his gang now?"

"I reckon there's short of a hundred now. The number varies. Then Bland has several small camps up an' down the river. Also he has men back on the cattle-ranges."

"How does he control such a big force?" asked Duane. "Especially when his band's composed of bad men. Luke Stevens said he had no use for Bland. And I heard once somewhere that Bland was a devil."

"Thet's it. He is a devil. He's as hard as flint, violent in temper, never made any friends except his right-hand men, Dave Rugg an' Chess Alloway. Bland 'll shoot at a wink. He's killed a lot of fellers, an' some fer nothin'. The reason thet outlaws gather round him an' stick is because he's a safe refuge, an' then he's well heeled. Bland is rich. They say he has a hundred thousand pesos hid somewhere, an' lots of gold. But he's free with money. He gambles when he's not off with a shipment of cattle. He throws money around. An' the fact is there's always plenty of money where he is. Thet's what holds the gang. Dirty, bloody money!"

"It's a wonder he hasn't been killed. All these years on the border!" exclaimed Duane.

"Wal," replied Euchre, dryly, "he's been quicker on the draw than the other fellers who hankered to kill him, thet's all."

Euchre's reply rather chilled Duane's interest for the moment. Such remarks always made his mind revolve round facts pertaining to himself.

"Speakin' of this here swift wrist game," went on Euchre, "there's been considerable talk in camp about your throwin' of a gun. You know, Buck, thet among us fellers—us hunted men—there ain't anythin' calculated to rouse respect like a slick hand with a gun. I heard Bland say this afternoon

—an' he said it serious-like an' speculative—thet he'd never seen your equal. He was watchin' of you close, he said, an' just couldn't follow your hand when you drawed. All the fellers who seen you meet Bosomer had somethin' to say. Bo was about as handy with a gun as any man in this camp, barrin' Chess Alloway an' mebbe Bland himself. Chess is the captain with a Colt—or he was. An' he shore didn't like the references made about your speed. Bland was honest in acknowledgin' it, but he didn't like it, neither. Some of the fellers allowed your draw might have been just accident. But most of them figgered different. An' they all shut up when Bland told who an' what your Dad was. 'Pears to me I once seen your Dad in a gun-scrape over at Santone, years ago. Wal, I put my oar in today among the fellers, an' I says: 'What ails you locoed gents? Did young Duane budge an inch when Bo came roarin' out, blood in his eye? Wasn't he cool an' quiet, steady of lips, an' weren't his eyes readin' Bo's mind? An' thet lightnin' draw—can't you-all see thet's a family gift?' "

Euchre's narrow eyes twinkled, and he gave the dough he was rolling a slap with his flour-whitened hand. Manifestly he had proclaimed himself a champion and partner of Duane's, with all the pride an old man could feel in a young one whom he admired.

"Wal," he resumed, presently, "thet's your introduction to the border, Buck. An' your card was a high trump. You'll be let severely alone by real gunfighters an' men like Bland, Alloway, Rugg, an' the bosses of the other gangs. After all, these real men *are* men, you know, an' onless you cross them they're no more likely to interfere with you than you are with them. But there's a sight of fellers like Bosomer in the river country. They'll all want your game. An' every town you ride into will scare up some cowpuncher full of booze or a long-haired four-flush gunman or a sheriff—an' these men will be playin' to the crowd an' yellin' for your blood. Thet's the Texas of it. You'll have to hide ferever in the brakes or you'll have to *kill* such men. Buck, I reckon this ain't cheerful news to a decent chap like you. I'm only tellin' you because I've taken a likin' to you, an' I seen right off thet you ain't border-wise. Let's eat now, an' afterward we'll go out so the gang can see you're not hidin'."

When Duane went out with Euchre the sun was setting behind a blue range of mountains across the river in Mexico. The valley appeared to open to the southwest. It was a tranquil, beautiful scene. Somewhere in a house near at hand a woman was singing. And in the road Duane saw a little Mexican boy driving home some cows, one of which wore a bell. The sweet, happy voice of a woman and a whistling barefoot boy—these seemed utterly out of place here.

Euchre presently led to the square and the row of rough houses Duane remembered. He almost stepped on a wide imprint in the dust where Bosomer had confronted him. And a sudden fury beset him that he should be affected strangely by the sight of it.

"Let's have a look in here," said Euchre.

Duane had to bend his head to enter the door. He found himself in a very large room enclosed by adobe walls and roofed with brush. It was full of rude benches, tables, seats. At one corner a number of kegs and barrels lay side by side in a rack. A Mexican boy was lighting lamps hung on posts that sustained the log rafters of the roof.

"The only feller who's goin' to put a close eye on you is Benson," said Euchre. "He runs the place an' sells drinks. The gang calls him Jackrabbit Benson, because he's always got his eye peeled an' his ear cocked. Don't notice him if he looks you over, Buck. Benson is scared to death of every newcomer who rustles into Bland's camp. An' the reason, I take it, is because he's done somebody dirt. He's hidin'. Not from a sheriff or ranger —men who hide from them don't act like Jackrabbit Benson. He's hidin' from some guy who's huntin' him to kill him. Wal, I'm always expectin' to see some feller ride in here an' throw a gun on Benson. Can't say I'd be grieved."

Duane casually glanced in the direction indicated, and he saw a spare, gaunt man with a face strikingly white beside the red and bronze and dark skins of the men around him. It was a cadaverous face. The black mustache hung down; a heavy lock of black hair dropped down over the brow; deep-set, hollow, staring eyes looked out piercingly. The man had a restless, alert, nervous manner. He put his hands on the board that served as a bar and stared at Duane. But when he met Duane's glance he turned hurriedly to go on serving out liquor.

"What have you got against him?" inquired Duane, as he sat down beside Euchre. He asked more for something to say than from real interest. What did he care about a mean, haunted, craven-faced criminal?

"Wal, mebbe I'm crossgrained," replied Euchre, apologetically. "Shore an outlaw an' rustler such as me can't be touchy. But I never stole nothin' but cattle from some rancher who never missed 'em anyway. Thet sneak Benson—he was the means of puttin' a little girl in Bland's way."

"Girl?" queried Duane, now with real attention.

"Shore. Bland's great on women. I'll tell you about this girl when we get out of here. Some of the gang are goin' to be sociable, an' I can't talk about the chief."

During the ensuing half-hour a number of outlaws passed by Duane and Euchre, halted for a greeting or sat down for a moment. They were all gruff, loud-voiced, merry, and good-natured. Duane replied civilly and agreeably when he was personally addressed; but he refused all invitations to drink and gamble. Evidently he had been accepted, in a way, as one of their clan. No one made any hint of an allusion to his affair with Bosomer. Duane saw readily that Euchre was well liked. One outlaw borrowed money from him: another asked for tobacco.

By the time it was dark the big room was full of outlaws and Mexicans, most of whom were engaged at monte. These gamblers, especially the

Mexicans, were intense and quiet. The noise in the place came from the
drinkers, the loungers. Duane had seen gambling-resorts—some of the
famous ones in San Antonio and El Paso, a few in border towns where
license went unchecked. But this place of Jackrabbit Benson's impressed
him as one where guns and knives were accessories to the game. To his
perhaps rather distinguishing eye the most prominent thing about the
gamesters appeared to be their weapons. On several of the tables were
piles of silver—Mexican pesos—as large and high as the crown of his hat.
There were also piles of gold and silver in United States coin. Duane
needed no experienced eyes to see that betting was heavy and that heavy
sums exchanged hands. The Mexicans showed a sterner obsession, an
intenser passion. Some of the Americans staked freely, nonchalantly, as
befitted men to whom money was nothing. These latter were manifestly
winning, for there were brother outlaws there who wagered coin with
grudging, sullen, greedy eyes. Boisterous talk and laughter among the
drinking men drowned, except at intervals, the low, brief talk of the
gamblers. The clink of coin sounded incessantly, sometimes just low,
steady musical rings; and again, when a pile was tumbled quickly, there
was a silvery crash. Here an outlaw pounded on a table with the butt of
his gun; there another noisily palmed a roll of dollars while he studied his
opponent's face. The noises, however, in Benson's den did not contribute
to any extent to the sinister aspect of the place. That seemed to come
from the grim and reckless faces, from the bent, intent heads, from the
dark lights and shades. There were bright lights, but these served only to
make the shadows. And in the shadows lurked unrestrained lust of gain, a
spirit ruthless and reckless, a something at once suggesting lawlessness,
theft, murder, and hell.

"Bland's not here tonight," Euchre was saying. "He left today on one of
his trips, takin' Alloway an' some others. But his other man, Rugg, he's
here. See him standin' with them three fellers, all close to Benson. Rugg's
the little bowlegged man with the half of his face shot off. He's one-eyed.
But he can shore see out of the one he's got. An', darn me! There's
Hardin. You know him? He's got an outlaw gang as big as Bland's. Hardin
is standin' next to Benson. See how quiet an' unassumin' he looks. Yes,
thet's Hardin. He comes here once in a while to see Bland. They're
friends, which's shore strange. Do you see thet greaser there—the one
with gold an' lace on his sombrero? Thet's Manuel, a Mexican bandit.
He's a great gambler. Comes here often to drop his coin. Next to him is
Bill Marr—the feller with the bandana round his head. Bill rode in the
other day with some fresh bullet holes. He's been shot more'n any feller I
ever heard of. He's full of lead. Funny, because Bill's no trouble-hunter,
an', like me, he'd rather run than shoot. But he's the best rustler Bland's
got—a grand rider, an' a wonder with cattle. An' see the tow-headed
youngster. Thet's Kid Fuller, the kid of Bland's gang. Fuller has hit the
pace hard, an' he won't last the year out on the border. He killed his

sweetheart's father, got run out of Staceytown, took to stealin' hosses. An' next he's here with Bland. Another boy gone wrong, an' now shore a hard nut."

Euchre went on calling Duane's attention to other men, just as he happened to glance over them. Any one of them would have been a marked man in a respectable crowd. Here each took his place with more or less distinction, according to the record of his past wild prowess and his present possibilities. Duane, realizing that he was tolerated there, received in careless friendly spirit by this terrible class of outcasts, experienced a feeling of revulsion that amounted almost to horror. Was his being there not an ugly dream? What had he in common with such ruffians? Then in a flash of memory came the painful proof—he was a criminal in sight of Texas law; he, too, was an outcast.

For the moment Duane was wrapped up in painful reflections; but Euchre's heavy hand, clapping with a warning hold on his arm, brought him back to outside things.

The hum of voices, the clink of coin, the loud laughter had ceased. There was a silence that manifestly had followed some unusual word or action sufficient to still the room. It was broken by a harsh curse and the scrape of a bench on the floor. Some man had risen.

"You stacked the cards, you ——!"

"Say that twice," another voice replied, so different in its cool, ominous tone from the other.

"I'll say it twice," returned the first gamester, in hot haste. "I'll say it three times. I'll whistle it. Are you deaf? You light-fingered gent! You stacked the cards!"

Silence ensued, deeper than before, pregnant with meaning. For all that Duane saw, not an outlaw moved for a full moment. Then suddenly the room was full of disorder as men rose and ran and dived everywhere.

"Run or duck!" yelled Euchre, close to Duane's ear. With that he dashed for the door. Duane leaped after him. They ran into a jostling mob. Heavy gun-shots and hoarse yells hurried the crowd Duane was with pell-mell out into the darkness. There they all halted, and several peeped in at the door.

"Who was the Kid callin'?" asked one outlaw.

"Bud Marsh," replied another.

"I reckon them fust shots was Bud's. *Adios*, Kid. It was comin' to him," went on yet another.

"How many shots?"

"Three or four, I counted."

"Three heavy an' one light. Thet light one was the Kid's .38. Listen! There's the Kid hollerin' now. He ain't cashed, anyway."

At this juncture most of the outlaws began to file back into the room. Duane thought he had seen and heard enough in Benson's den for one night and he started slowly down the walk. Presently Euchre caught up with him.

"Nobody hurt much, which's shore some strange," he said. "The Kid— young Fuller thet I was tellin' you about—he was drinkin' an' losin'. Lost his nut, too, callin' Bud Marsh thet way. Bud's as straight at cards as any of 'em. Somebody grabbed Bud, who shot into the roof. An' Fuller's arm was knocked up. He hit a Mexican."

❖ 6 ❖

NEXT morning Duane found that a moody and despondent spell had fastened on him. Wishing to be alone, he went out and walked a trail leading round the river bluff. He thought and thought. After a while he made out that the trouble with him probably was that he could not resign himself to his fate. He abhorred the possibility chance seemed to hold in store for him. He could not believe there was no hope. But what to do appeared beyond his power to tell.

Duane had intelligence and keenness enough to see his peril—the danger threatening his character as a man, just as much as that which threatened his life. He cared vastly more, he discovered, for what he considered honor and integrity than he did for life. He saw that it was bad for him to be alone. But, it appeared, lonely months and perhaps years inevitably must be his. Another thing puzzled him. In the bright light of day he could not recall the state of mind that was his at twilight or dusk or in the dark night. By day these visitations became to him what they really were—phantoms of his conscience. He could dismiss the thought of them then. He could scarcely remember or believe that this strange feat of fancy or imagination had troubled him, pained him, made him sleepless and sick.

That morning Duane spent an unhappy hour wrestling decision out of the unstable condition of his mind. But at length he determined to create interest in all that he came across and so forget himself as much as possible. He had an opportunity now to see just what the outlaw's life really was. He meant to force himself to be curious, sympathetic, clear-sighted. And he would stay there in the valley until its possibilities had been exhausted or until circumstances sent him out upon his uncertain way.

When he returned to the shack Euchre was cooking dinner.

"Say, Buck, I've news for you," he said; and his tone conveyed either pride in his possession of such news or pride in Duane. "Feller named Bradley rode in this mornin'. He's heard some about you. Told about the ace of spades they put over the bullet holes in thet cowpuncher Bain you plugged. Then there was a rancher shot at a water hole twenty miles south of Wellston. Reckon you didn't do it?"

"No, I certainly did not," replied Duane.

"Wal, you get the blame. It ain't nothin' for a feller to be saddled with gunplays he never made. An', Buck, if you ever get famous, as seems likely, you'll be blamed for many a crime. The border 'll make an outlaw an' murderer out of you. Wal, thet's enough of thet. I've more news. You're goin' to be popular."

"Popular? What do you mean?"

"I met Bland's wife this mornin'. She seen you the other day when you rode in. She shore wants to meet you, an' so do some of the other women in camp. They always want to meet the new fellers who've just come in. It's lonesome for women here, an' they like to hear news from the towns."

"Well, Euchre, I don't want to be impolite, but I'd rather not meet any women," rejoined Duane.

"I was afraid you wouldn't. Don't blame you much. Women are hell. I was hopin', though, you might talk a little to thet poor lonesome kid."

"What kid?" inquired Duane, in surprise.

"Didn't I tell you about Jennie—the girl Bland's holdin' here—the one Jackrabbit Benson had a hand in stealin'?"

"You mentioned a girl. That's all. Tell me now," replied Duane, abruptly.

"Wal, I got it this way. Mebbe it's straight, an' mebbe it ain't. Some years ago Benson made a trip over the river to buy mescal an' other drinks. He'll sneak over there once in a while. An' as I get it he run across a gang of greasers with some gringo prisoners. I don't know, but I reckon there was some barterin', perhaps murderin'. Anyway, Benson fetched the girl back. She was more dead than alive. But it turned out she was only starved an' scared half to death. She hadn't been harmed. I reckon she was then about fourteen years old. Benson's idee, he said, was to use her in his den sellin' drinks an' the like. But I never went much on Jackrabbit's word. Bland seen the kid right off and took her—bought her from Benson. You can gamble Bland didn't do thet from notions of chivalry. I ain't gainsayin', however, but thet Jennie was better off with Kate Bland. She's been hard on Jennie, but she's kept Bland an' the other men from treatin' the kid shameful. Late Jennie has growed into an all-fired pretty girl, an' Kate is powerful jealous of her. I can see hell brewin' over there in Bland's cabin. Thet's why I wish you'd come over with me. Bland's hardly ever home. His wife's invited you. Shore, if she gets sweet on you, as she has on— Wal, thet'd complicate matters. But you'd get to see Jennie, an'

mebbe you could help her. Mind, I ain't hintin' nothin'. I'm just wantin'
to put her in your way. You're a man an' can think fer yourself. I had a
baby girl once, an' if she'd lived she be as big as Jennie now, an', by Gawd,
I wouldn't want her here in Bland's camp."

"I'll go, Euchre. Take me over," replied Duane. He felt Euchre's eyes
upon him. The old outlaw, however, had no more to say.

In the afternoon Euchre set off with Duane, and soon they reached
Bland's cabin. Duane remembered it as the one where he had seen the
pretty woman watching him ride by. He could not recall what she looked
like. The cabin was the same as the other adobe structures in the valley,
but it was larger and pleasantly located rather high up in a grove of
cottonwoods. In the windows and upon the porch were evidences of a
woman's hand. Through the open door Duane caught a glimpse of bright
Mexican blankets and rugs.

Euchre knocked upon the side of the door.

"Is that you, Euchre?" asked a girl's voice, low, hesitatingly. The tone
of it, rather deep and with a note of fear, struck Duane. He wondered
what she would be like.

"Yes, it's me, Jennie. Where's Mrs. Bland?" answered Euchre.

"She went over to Deger's. There's somebody sick," replied the girl.

Euchre turned and whispered something about luck. The snap of the
outlaw's eyes was added significance to Duane.

"Jennie, come out or let us come in. Here's the young man I was tellin'
you about," Euchre said.

"Oh, I can't! I look so—so—"

"Never mind how you look," interrupted the outlaw, in a whisper. "It
ain't no time to care fer thet. Here's young Duane. Jennie, he's no rustler,
no thief. He's different. Come out, Jennie, an' mebbe he'll—"

Euchre did not complete his sentence. He had spoken low, with his
glance shifting from side to side.

But what he said was sufficient to bring the girl quickly. She appeared
in the doorway with downcast eyes and a stain of red in her white cheek.
She had a pretty, sad face and bright hair.

"Don't be bashful, Jennie," said Euchre. "You an' Duane have a chance
to talk a little. Now I'll go fetch Mrs. Bland, but I won't be hurryin'."

With that Euchre went away through the cottonwoods.

"I'm glad to meet you, Miss—Miss Jennie," said Duane. "Euchre didn't
mention your last name. He asked me to come over to—"

Duane's attempt at pleasantry halted short when Jennie lifted her
lashes to look at him. Some kind of a shock went through Duane. Her
gray eyes were beautiful, but it had not been beauty that cut short his
speech. He seemed to see a tragic struggle between hope and doubt that
shone in her piercing gaze. She kept looking, and Duane could not break
the silence. It was no ordinary moment.

"What did you come here for?" she asked, at last.

"To see you," replied Duane, glad to speak.

"Why?"

"Well—Euchre thought—he wanted me to talk to you, cheer you up a bit," replied Duane, somewhat lamely. The earnest eyes embarrassed him.

"Euchre's good. He's the only person in this awful place who's been good to me. But he's afraid of Bland. He said you were different. Who are you?"

Duane told her.

"You're not a robber or rustler or murderer or some bad man come here to hide?"

"No, I'm not," replied Duane, trying to smile.

"Then why are you here?"

"I'm on the dodge. You know what that means. I got in a shooting-scrape at home and had to run off. When it blows over I hope to go back."

"But you can't be honest here?"

"Yes, I can."

"Oh, I know what these outlaws are. Yes, you're different." She kept the strained gaze upon him, but hope was kindling, and the hard lines of her youthful face were softening.

Something sweet and warm stirred deep in Duane as he realized the unfortunate girl was experiencing a birth of trust in him.

"O God! Maybe you're the man to save me . . . to take me away before it's too late!"

Duane's spirit leaped.

"Maybe I am," he replied, instantly.

She seemed to check a blind impulse to run into his arms. Her cheek flamed, her lips quivered, her bosom swelled under her ragged dress. Then the glow began to fade; doubt once more assailed her.

"It can't be. You're only—after me, too, like Bland—like all of them."

Duane's long arms went out and his hands clasped her shoulders. He shook her.

"Look at me—straight in the eye. There are decent men. Haven't you a father—a brother?"

"They're dead—killed by raiders. We lived in Dimmit County. I was carried away," Jennie replied, hurriedly. She put up an appealing hand to him. "Forgive me. I believe—I know you're good. It was only—I live so much in fear—I'm half crazy—I've almost forgotten what good men are like. Mr. Duane, you'll help me?"

"Yes, Jennie, I will. Tell me how. What must I do? Have you any plan?"

"Oh no. But take me away."

"I'll try," said Duane, simply. "That won't be easy, though. I must have time to think. You must help me. There are many things to consider. Horses, food, trails, and then the best time to make the attempt. Are you watched—kept prisoner?"

"No. I could have run off lots of times. But I was afraid. I'd only have fallen into worse hands. Euchre has told me that. Mrs. Bland beats me, half starves me, but she has kept me from her husband and these other dogs. She's been as good as that, and I'm grateful. She hasn't done it for love of me, though. She always hated me. And lately she's growing jealous. There was a man came here by the name of Spence—so he called himself. He tried to be kind to me. But she wouldn't let him. She was in love with him. She's a bad woman. Bland finally shot Spence, and that ended that. She's been jealous ever since. I hear her fighting with Bland about me. She swears she'll kill me before he gets me. And Bland laughs in her face. Then I've heard Chess Alloway try to persuade Bland to give me to him. But Bland doesn't laugh then. Just lately before Bland went away things almost came to a head. I couldn't sleep. I wished Mrs. Bland would kill me. I'll certainly kill myself if they ruin me. Duane, you must be quick if you'd save me."

"I realize that," replied he, thoughtfully. "I think my difficulty will be to fool Mrs. Bland. If she suspected me she'd have the whole gang of outlaws on me at once."

"She would that. You've got to be careful . . . and quick."

"What kind of woman is she?" inquired Duane.

"She's—she's brazen. I've heard her with her lovers. They get drunk sometimes when Bland's away. She's got a terrible temper. She's vain. She likes flattery. Oh, you could fool her easy enough if you'd lower yourself to —to—"

"To make love to her?" interrupted Duane.

Jennie bravely turned shamed eyes to meet his.

"My girl, I'd do worse than that to get you away from here," he said, bluntly.

"But—Duane," she faltered, and again she put out the appealing hand. "Bland will kill you."

Duane made no reply to this. He was trying to still a rising strange tumult in his breast. The old emotion—the rush of an instinct to kill! He turned cold all over.

"Chess Alloway will kill you if Bland doesn't," went on Jennie, with her tragic eyes on Duane's.

"Maybe he will," replied Duane. It was difficult for him to force a smile. But he achieved one.

"Oh, better take me off at once," she said. "Save me without risking so much—without making love to Mrs. Bland!"

"Surely, if I can. There! I see Euchre coming with a woman."

"That's her. Oh, she mustn't see me with you."

"Wait—a moment," whispered Duane, as Jennie slipped indoors. "We've settled it. Don't forget. I'll find some way to get word to you, perhaps through Euchre. Meanwhile keep up your courage. Remember I'll save you somehow. We'll try strategy first. Whatever you see or hear me do, don't think less of me . . ."

Jennie checked him with a gesture and a wonderful gray flash of eyes.

"I'll bless you with every drop of blood in my heart," she whispered, passionately.

It was only as she turned away into the room that Duane saw she was lame and that she wore Mexican sandals over bare feet.

He sat down upon a bench on the porch and directed his attention to the approaching couple. The trees of the grove were thick enough for him to make reasonably sure that Mrs. Bland had not seen him talking to Jennie. When the outlaw's wife drew near, Duane saw that she was a tall, strong, full-bodied woman, rather good-looking, with a full-blown, bold attractiveness. Duane was more concerned with her expression than with her good looks; and as she appeared unsuspicious he felt relieved. The situation then took on a singular zest.

Euchre came up on the porch and awkwardly introduced Duane to Mrs. Bland. She was young, probably not over twenty-five, and not quite so prepossessing at close range. Her eyes were large, rather prominent, and brown in color. Her mouth, too, was large, with the lips full, and she had white teeth.

Duane took her proffered hand and remarked frankly that he was glad to meet her.

Mrs. Bland appeared pleased; and her laugh, which followed, was loud and rather musical.

"Mr. Duane—Buck Duane, Euchre said, didn't he?" she asked.

"Buckley," corrected Duane. "The nickname's not of my choosing."

"I'm certainly glad to meet you, Buckley Duane," she said, as she took the seat Duane offered her. "Sorry to have been out. Kid Fuller's lying over at Deger's. You know he was shot last night. He's got fever today. When Bland's away I have to nurse all these shot-up boys, and it sure takes my time. Have you been waiting here alone? Didn't see that slattern girl of mine?"

She gave him a sharp glance. The woman had an extraordinary play of feature, Duane thought, and unless she was smiling was not pretty at all.

"I've been alone," replied Duane. "Haven't seen anybody but a sick-looking girl with a bucket. And she ran when she saw me."

"That was Jen," said Mrs. Bland. "She's the kid we keep here, and she sure hardly pays her keep. Did Euchre tell you about her?"

"Now that I think of it, he did say something or other."

"What did he tell you about me?" bluntly asked Mrs. Bland.

"Wal, Kate," replied Euchre, speaking for himself, "you needn't worry none, for I told Buck nothin' but compliments."

Evidently the outlaw's wife liked Euchre, for her keen glance rested with amusement upon him.

"As for Jen, I'll tell you her story someday," went on the woman. "It's a common enough story along this river. Euchre here is a tender-hearted old fool, and Jen has taken him in."

"Wal, seein' as you've got me figgered correct," replied Euchre, dryly, "I'll go in an' talk to Jennie, if I may."

"Certainly. Go ahead. Jen calls you her best friend," said Mrs. Bland, amiably. "You're always fetching some Mexican stuff, and that's why, I guess."

When Euchre had shuffled into the house Mrs. Bland turned to Duane with curiosity and interest in her gaze.

"Bland told me about you."

"What did he say?" queried Duane, in pretended alarm.

"Oh, you needn't think he's done you dirt. Bland's not that kind of a man. He said: 'Kate, there's a young fellow in camp—rode in here on the dodge. He's no criminal, and he refused to join my band. Wish he would. Slickest hand with a gun I've seen for many a day! I'd like to see him and Chess meet out there in the road.' Then Bland went on to tell how you and Bosomer came together."

"What did you say?" inquired Duane, as she paused.

"Me? Why, I asked him what you looked like," she replied, gaily.

"Well?" went on Duane.

"Magnificent chap, Bland said. Bigger than any man in the valley. Just a great blue-eyed, sunburned boy!"

"Humph!" exclaimed Duane. "I'm sorry he led you to expect somebody worth seeing."

"But I'm not disappointed," she returned, archly. "Duane, are you going to stay long here in camp?"

"Yes, till I run out of money and have to move. Why?"

Mrs. Bland's face underwent one of the singular changes. The smiles and flushes and glances, all that had been coquettish about her, had lent her a certain attractiveness, almost beauty and youth. But with some powerful emotion she changed and instantly became a woman of discontent, Duane imagined, of deep, violent nature.

"I'll tell you, Duane," she said, earnestly, "I'm sure glad if you mean to bide here awhile. I'm a miserable woman, Duane. I'm an outlaw's wife, and I hate him and the life I have to lead. I come of a good family in Brownsville. I never knew Bland was an outlaw till long after he married me. We were separated at times, and I imagined he was away on business. But the truth came out. Bland shot my own cousin, who told me. My family cast me off, and I had to flee with Bland. I was only eighteen then. I've lived here since. I never see a decent woman or man. I never hear anything about my old home or folks or friends. I'm buried here—buried alive with a lot of thieves and murderers. Can you blame me for being glad to see a young fellow—a gentleman—like the boys I used to go with?

I tell you it makes me feel full—I want to cry. I'm sick for somebody to talk to. I have no children, thank God! If I had I'd not stay here. I'm sick of this hole. I'm lonely . . ."

There appeared to be no doubt about the truth of all this. Genuine emotion checked, then halted the hurried speech. She broke down and cried. It seemed strange to Duane that an outlaw's wife—and a woman who fitted her consort and the wild nature of their surroundings—should have weakness enough to weep. Duane believed and pitied her.

"I'm sorry for you," he said.

"Don't be *sorry* for me," she said. "That only makes me see the—the difference between you and me. And don't pay any attention to what these outlaws say about me. They're ignorant. They couldn't understand me. You'll hear that Bland killed men who ran after me. But that's a lie. Bland, like all the other outlaws along this river, is always looking for somebody to kill. He *swears* not, but I don't believe him. He explains that gunplay gravitates to men who are the real thing—that it is provoked by the four-flushes, the bad men. I don't know. All I know is that somebody is being killed every other day. He hated Spence before Spence ever saw me."

"Would Bland object if I called on you occasionally?" inquired Duane.

"No, he wouldn't. He likes me to have friends. Ask him yourself when he comes back. The trouble has been that two or three of his men fell in love with me, and when half drunk got to fighting. You're not going to do that."

"I'm not going to get half drunk, that's certain," replied Duane.

He was surprised to see her eyes dilate, then glow with fire. Before she could reply Euchre returned to the porch, and that put an end to the conversation.

Duane was content to let the matter rest there, and had little more to say. Euchre and Mrs. Bland talked and joked, while Duane listened. He tried to form some estimate of her character. Manifestly she had suffered a wrong, if not worse, at Bland's hands. She was bitter, morbid, overemotional. If she was a liar, which seemed likely enough, she was a frank one, and believed herself. She had no cunning. The thing which struck Duane so forcibly was that she thirsted for respect. In that, better than in her weakness of vanity, he thought he had discovered a trait through which he could manage her.

Once, while he was revolving these thoughts, he happened to glance into the house, and deep in the shadow of a corner he caught a pale gleam of Jennie's face with great, staring eyes on him. She had been watching him, listening to what he said. He saw from her expression that she had realized what had been so hard for her to believe. Watching his chance, he flashed a look at her; and then it seemed to him the change in her face was wonderful.

Later, after he had left Mrs. Bland with a meaning "*Adios—mañana,*" and was walking along beside the old outlaw, he found himself thinking of the girl instead of the woman, and of how he had seen her face blaze with hope and gratitude.

⸭7⸭

THAT NIGHT Duane was not troubled by ghosts haunting his waking and sleeping hours. He awoke feeling bright and eager, and grateful to Euchre for having put something worthwhile into his mind. During breakfast, however, he was unusually thoughtful, working over the idea of how much or how little he would confide in the outlaw. He was aware of Euchre's scrutiny.

"Wal," began the old man, at last, "how'd you make out with the kid?"

"Kid?" inquired Duane, tentatively.

"Jennie, I mean. What'd you an' she talk about?"

"We had a little chat. You know you wanted me to cheer her up."

Euchre sat with coffee cup poised and narrow eyes studying Duane.

"Reckon you cheered her, all right. What I'm afeared of is mebbe you done the job too well."

"How so?"

"Wal, when I went in to Jen last night I thought she was half crazy. She was burstin' with excitement, an' the look in her eyes hurt me. She wouldn't tell me a darn word you said. But she hung onto my hands, an' showed every way without speakin' how she wanted to thank me fer bringin' you over. Buck, it was plain to me thet you'd either gone the limit or else you'd been kinder prodigal of cheer an' hope. I'd hate to think you'd led Jennie to hope more'n ever would come true."

Euchre paused, and, as there seemed no reply forthcoming, he went on:

"Buck, I've seen some outlaws whose word was good. Mine is. You can trust me. I trusted you, didn't I, takin' you over there an' puttin' you wise to my tryin' to help thet poor kid?"

Thus enjoined by Euchre, Duane began to tell the conversations with Jennie and Mrs. Bland word for word. Long before he had reached an end Euchre set down the coffee cup and began to stare, and at the conclusion of the story his face lost some of its red color and beads of sweat stood out thickly on his brow.

"Wal, if thet doesn't floor me!" he ejaculated, blinking at Duane.

"Young man, I figgered you was some swift, an' sure to make your mark on this river; but I reckon I missed your real caliber. So thet's what it means to be a man! I guess I'd forgot. Wal, I'm old, an' even if my heart was in the right place I never was built fer big stunts. Do you know what it'll take to do all you promised Jen?"

"I haven't any idea," replied Duane, gravely.

"You'll have to pull the wool over Kate Bland's eyes, an' even if she falls in love with you, which's shore likely, thet won't be easy. An' she'd kill you in a minnit, Buck, if she ever got wise. You ain't mistaken her none, are you?"

"Not me, Euchre. She's a woman. I'd fear her more than any man."

"Wal, you'll have to kill Bland an' Chess Alloway an' Rugg, an' mebbe some others, before you can ride off into the hills with thet girl."

"Why? Can't we plan to be nice to Mrs. Bland and then at an opportune time sneak off without any gunplay?"

"Don't see how on earth," returned Euchre, earnestly. "When Bland's away he leaves all kinds of spies an' scouts watchin' the valley trails. They've all got rifles. You couldn't git by them. But when the boss is home there's a difference. Only, of course, him an' Chess keep their eyes peeled. They both stay to home pretty much, except when they're playin' monte or poker over at Benson's. So I say the best bet is to pick out a good time in the afternoon, drift over careless-like with a couple of hosses, choke Mrs. Bland or knock her on the head, take Jennie with you, an' make a rush to git out of the valley. If you had luck you might pull thet stunt without throwin' a gun. But I reckon the best figgerin' would include dodgin' some lead an' leavin' at least Bland or Alloway dead behind you. I'm figgerin', of course, thet when they come home an' find out you're visitin' Kate frequent they'll jest naturally look fer results. Chess don't like you, fer no reason except you're swift on the draw . . . mebbe swifter 'n him. Thet's the hell of this gunplay business. No one can ever tell who's the swifter of two gunmen till they meet. Thet fact holds a fascination mebbe you'll learn someday. Bland would treat you civil onless there was reason not to, an' then I don't believe he'd invite himself to a meetin' with you. He'd set Chess or Rugg to put you out of the way. Still Bland's no coward, an' if you came across him at a bad moment you'd have to be quicker 'n you was with Bosomer."

"All right. I'll meet what comes," said Duane, quietly. "The great point is to have horses ready and pick the right moment, then rush the trick through."

"Thet's the *only* chance fer success. An' you can't do it alone."

"I'll have to. I wouldn't ask you to help me. Leave you behind!"

"Wal, I'll take my chances," replied Euchre, gruffly. "I'm goin' to help Jennie, you can gamble your last peso on thet. There's only four men in this camp who would shoot me—Bland, an' his right-hand pards, an' thet rabbit-faced Benson. If you happened to put out Bland and Chess, I'd stand a good show with the other two. Anyway, I'm old an' tired—what's the difference if I do git plugged? I can risk as much as you, Buck, even if I am afraid of gunplay. You said correct, 'Hosses ready, the right minnit, then rush the trick.' Thet much's settled. Now let's figger all the little details."

They talked and planned, though in truth it was Euchre who planned, Duane who listened and agreed. While awaiting the return of Bland and his lieutenants it would be well for Duane to grow friendly with the other outlaws, to sit in a few games of monte, or show a willingness to spend a little money. The two schemers were to call upon Mrs. Bland every day— Euchre to carry messages of cheer and warning to Jennie, Duane to blind the elder woman at any cost. These preliminaries decided upon, they proceeded to put them into action.

No hard task was it to win the friendship of the most of those good-natured outlaws. They were used to men of a better order than theirs coming to the hidden camps and sooner or later sinking to their lower level. Besides, with them everything was easy come, easy go. That was why life itself went on so carelessly and usually ended so cheaply. There were men among them, however, that made Duane feel that terrible inexplicable wrath rise in his breast. He could not bear to be near them. He could not trust himself. He felt that any instant a word, a deed, something might call too deeply to that instinct he could no longer control. Jackrabbit Benson was one of these men. Because of him and other outlaws of his ilk Duane could scarcely ever forget the reality of things. This was a hidden valley, a robbers' den, a rendezvous for murderers, a wild place stained red by deeds of wild men. And because of that there was always a charged atmosphere. The merriest, idlest, most careless moment might in the flash of an eye end in ruthless and tragic action. In an assemblage of desperate characters it could not be otherwise. The terrible thing that Duane sensed was this. The valley was beautiful, sunny, fragrant, a place to dream in; the mountain-tops were always blue or gold rimmed, the yellow river slid slowly and majestically by, the birds sang in the cottonwoods, the horses grazed and pranced, children played and women longed for love, freedom, happiness; the outlaws rode in and out, free with money and speech; they lived comfortably in their adobe homes, smoked, gambled, talked, laughed, whiled away the idle hours—and all the time life there was wrong, and the simplest moment might be precipitated by that evil into the most awful of contrasts. Duane felt rather than saw a dark, brooding shadow over the valley.

Then, without any solicitation or encouragement from Duane, the Bland woman fell passionately in love with him. His conscience was never troubled about the beginning of that affair. She launched herself. It took no great perspicuity on his part to see that. And the thing which evidently held her in check was the newness, the strangeness, and for the moment the all-satisfying fact of his respect for her. Duane exerted himself to please, to amuse, to interest, to fascinate her, and always with deference. That was his strong point, and it had made his part easy so far. He believed he could carry the whole scheme through without involving himself any deeper.

He was playing at a game of love—playing with life and death! Sometimes he trembled, not that he feared Bland or Alloway or any other man, but at the deeps of life he had come to see into. He was carried out of his old mood. Not once since this daring motive had stirred him had he been haunted by the phantom of Bain beside his bed. Rather had he been haunted by Jennie's sad face, her wistful smile, her eyes. He never was able to speak a word to her. What little communication he had with her was through Euchre, who carried short messages. But he caught glimpses of her every time he went to the Bland house. She contrived somehow to pass door or window, to give him a look when chance afforded. And Duane discovered with surprise that these moments were more thrilling to him than any with Mrs. Bland. Often Duane knew Jennie was sitting just inside the window, and then he felt inspired in his talk, and it was all made for her. So at least she came to know him while as yet she was almost a stranger. Jennie had been instructed by Euchre to listen, to understand that this was Duane's only chance to help keep her mind from constant worry, to gather the import of every word which had a double meaning.

Euchre said that the girl had begun to wither under the strain, to burn up with intense hope which had flamed within her. But all the difference Duane could see was a paler face and darker, more wonderful eyes. The eyes seemed to be entreating him to hurry, that time was flying, that soon it might be too late. Then there was another meaning in them, a light, a strange fire wholly inexplicable to Duane. It was only a flash gone in an instant. But he remembered it because he had never seen it in any other woman's eyes. And all through those waiting days he knew that Jennie's face, and especially the warm, fleeting glance she gave him, was responsible for a subtle and gradual change in him. This change, he fancied, was only that through remembrance of her he got rid of his pale, sickening ghosts.

One day a careless Mexican threw a lighted cigarette up into the brush matting that served as a ceiling for Benson's den, and there was a fire which left little more than the adobe walls standing. The result was that while repairs were being made there was no gambling and drinking. Time hung very heavily on the hands of some twoscore outlaws. Days passed by without a brawl, and Bland's valley saw more successive hours of peace than ever before. Duane, however, found the hours anything but empty. He spent more time at Mrs. Bland's; he walked miles on all the trails leading out of the valley; he had a care for the condition of his two horses.

Upon his return from the latest of these tramps Euchre suggested that they go down to the river to the boat landing.

"Ferry couldn't run ashore this mornin'," said Euchre. "River gettin' low an' sandbars makin' it hard fer hosses. There's a greaser freight wagon stuck in the mud. I reckon we might hear news from the freighters. Bland's supposed to be in Mexico."

Nearly all the outlaws in camp were assembled on the river-bank, lolling in the shade of the cottonwoods. The heat was oppressive. Not an outlaw offered to help the freighters, who were trying to dig a heavily freighted wagon out of the quicksand. Few outlaws would work for themselves, let alone for the despised Mexicans.

Duane and Euchre joined the lazy group and sat down with them. Euchre lighted a black pipe, and, drawing his hat over his eyes, lay back in comfort after the manner of the majority of the outlaws. But Duane was alert, observing, thoughtful. He never missed anything. It was his belief that any moment an idle word might be of benefit to him. Moreover, these rough men were always interesting.

"Bland's been chased acrost the river," said one.

"Naw, he's deliverin' cattle to thet Cuban ship," replied another.

"Big deal on, hey?"

"Some big. Rugg says the boss hed an order fer fifteen thousand."

"Say, that order'll take a year to fill."

"Naw. Hardin is in cahoots with Bland. Between 'em they'll fill orders bigger 'n thet."

"Wondered what Hardin was rustlin' in here fer."

Duane could not possibly attend to all the conversation among the outlaws. He endeavored to get the drift of talk nearest to him.

"Kid Fuller's goin' to cash," said a sandy-whiskered little outlaw.

"So Jim was tellin' me. Blood-poison, ain't it? Thet hole wasn't bad. But he took the fever," rejoined a comrade.

"Deger says the Kid might pull through if he hed nursin'."

"Wal, Kate Bland ain't nursin' any shot-up boys these days. She hasn't got time."

A laugh followed this sally; then came a penetrating silence. Some of the outlaws glanced good-naturedly at Duane. They bore him no ill will. Manifestly they were aware of Mrs. Bland's infatuation.

"Pete, 'pears to me you've said thet before."

"Shore. Wal, it's happened before."

This remark drew louder laughter and more significant glances at Duane. He did not choose to ignore them any longer.

"Boys, poke all the fun you like at me, but don't mention any lady's name again. My hand is nervous and itchy these days."

He smiled as he spoke, and his speech was drawled; but the good humor in no wise weakened it. Then his latter remark was significant to a class of men who from inclination and necessity practiced at gun-drawing until they wore callous and sore places on their thumbs and inculcated in the very deeps of their nervous organization a habit that made even the simplest and most innocent motion of the hand end at or near the hip. There was something remarkable about a gunfighter's hand. It never seemed to be gloved, never to be injured, never out of sight or in an awkward position.

There were grizzled outlaws in that group, some of whom had many notches on their gun handles, and they, with their comrades, accorded Duane silence that carried conviction of the regard in which he was held.

Duane could not recall any other instance where he had let fall a familiar speech to these men, and certainly he had never before hinted of his possibilities. He saw instantly that he could not have done better.

"Orful hot, ain't it?" remarked Bill Black, presently. Bill could not keep quiet for long. He was a typical Texas desperado, had never been anything else. He was stoop-shouldered and bow-legged from much riding; a wiry little man, all muscle, with a square head, a hard face partly black from scrubby beard and red from sun, and a bright, roving, cruel eye. His shirt was open at the neck, showing a grizzled breast.

"Is there any guy in this heah outfit sport enough to go swimmin'?" he asked.

"My Gawd, Bill, you ain't agoin' to wash!" exclaimed a comrade.

This raised a laugh in which Black joined. But no one seemed eager to join him in a bath.

"Laziest outfit I ever rustled with," went on Bill, discontentedly. "Nuthin' to do! Say, if nobody wants to swim maybe some of you'll gamble?"

He produced a dirty pack of cards and waved them at the motionless crowd.

"Bill, you're too good at cards," replied a lanky outlaw.

"Now, Jasper, you say thet powerful sweet, an' you look sweet, er I might take it to heart," replied Black, with a sudden change of tone.

Here it was again—that upflashing passion. What Jasper saw fit to reply would mollify the outlaw or it would not. There was an even balance.

"No offense, Bill," said Jasper, placidly, without moving.

Bill grunted and forgot Jasper. But he seemed restless and dissatisfied. Duane knew him to be an inveterate gambler. And as Benson's place was out of running-order, Black was like a fish on dry land.

"Wal, if you-all are afraid of the cairds, what will you bet on?" he asked, in disgust.

"Bill, I'll play you a game of mumbly peg fer two bits," replied one.

Black eagerly accepted. Betting to him was a serious matter. The game obsessed him, not the stakes. He entered into the mumbly-peg contest with a thoughtful mien and a corded brow. He won. Other comrades tried their luck with him and lost. Finally, when Bill had exhausted their supply of two-bit pieces or their desire for that particular game, he offered to bet on anything.

"See thet turtle-dove there?" he said, pointing. "I'll bet he'll scare at one stone or he won't. Five pesos he'll fly or he won't fly when someone chucks a stone. Who'll take me up?"

That appeared to be more than the gambling spirit of several outlaws could withstand.

"Take thet. Easy money," said one.

"Who's goin' to chuck the stone?" asked another.

"Anybody," replied Bill.

"Wal, I'll bet you I can scare him with one stone," said the first outlaw.

"We're in on thet, Jim to fire the darnick," chimed in the others.

The money was put up, the stone thrown. The turtle-dove took flight, to the great joy of all the outlaws except Bill.

"I'll bet you-all he'll come back to thet tree inside of five minnits," he offered, imperturbably.

Hereupon the outlaws did not show any laziness in their alacrity to cover Bill's money as it lay on the grass. Somebody had a watch, and they all sat down, dividing attention between the timepiece and the tree. The minutes dragged by to the accompaniment of various jocular remarks anent a fool and his money. When four and three-quarter minutes had passed a turtle-dove alighted in the cottonwood. Then ensued an impressive silence while Bill calmly pocketed the fifty dollars.

"But it hain't the same dove!" exclaimed one outlaw, excitedly. "This 'n' is smaller, dustier, not so purple."

Bill eyed the speaker loftily.

"Wal, you'll have to ketch the other one to prove thet. Sabe, pard? Now I'll bet any gent heah the fifty I won thet I can scare thet dove with one stone."

No one offered to take his wager.

"Wal, then, I'll bet any of you even money thet you can't scare him with one stone."

Not proof against this chance, the outlaws made up a purse, in no wise disconcerted by Bill's contemptuous allusions to their banding together. The stone was thrown. The dove did not fly. Thereafter, in regard to that bird, Bill was unable to coax or scorn his comrades into any kind of wager.

He tried them with a multiplicity of offers, and in vain. Then he appeared at a loss for some unusual and seductive wager. Presently a little ragged Mexican boy came along the river trail, a particularly starved and poor-looking little fellow. Bill called to him and gave him a handful of silver coins. Speechless, dazed, he went his way hugging the money.

"I'll bet he drops some before he gits to the road," declared Bill. "I'll bet he runs. Hurry, you four-flush gamblers."

Bill failed to interest any of his companions, and forthwith became sullen and silent. Strangely his good humor departed in spite of the fact that he had won considerable.

Duane, watching the disgruntled outlaw, marveled at him and wondered what was in his mind. These men were more variable than children, as unstable as water, as dangerous as dynamite.

"Bill, I'll bet you ten you can't spill whatever's in the bucket thet peon's packin'," said the outlaw called Jim.

Black's head came up with the action of a hawk about to swoop.

Duane glanced from Black to the road, where he saw a crippled peon carrying a tin bucket toward the river. This peon was a half-witted Indian who lived in a shack and did odd jobs for the Mexicans. Duane had met him often.

"Jim, I'll take you up," replied Black.

Something, perhaps a harshness in his voice, caused Duane to whirl. He caught a leaping gleam in the outlaw's eye.

"Aw, Bill, thet's too fur a shot," said Jasper, as Black rested an elbow on his knee and sighted over the long, heavy Colt. The distance to the peon was about fifty paces, too far for even the most expert shot to hit a moving object so small as a bucket.

Duane, marvelously keen in the alignment of sights, was positive that Black held too high. Another look at the hard face, now tense and dark with blood, confirmed Duane's suspicion that the outlaw was not aiming at the bucket at all. Duane leaped and struck the leveled gun out of his hand. Another outlaw picked it up.

Black fell back astounded. Deprived of his weapon, he did not seem the same man, or else he was cowed by Duane's significant and formidable front. Sullenly he turned away without even asking for his gun.

8

WHAT A CONTRAST, Duane thought, the evening of that day presented to the state of his soul. The sunset lingered in golden glory over the distant Mexican mountains; twilight came slowly; a faint breeze blew from the river cool and sweet; the late cooing of a dove and the tinkle of a cowbell were the only sounds; a serene and tranquil peace lay over the valley.

Inside Duane's body there was strife. This third facing of a desperate man had thrown him off his balance. It had not been fatal, but it threatened so much. The better side of his nature seemed to urge him to die rather than to go on fighting or opposing ignorant, unfortunate, savage men. But the perversity of him was so great that it dwarfed reason, conscience. He could not resist it. He felt something dying in him. He suffered. Hope seemed far away. Despair had seized upon him and was driving him into a reckless mood when he thought of Jennie.

He had forgotten her. He had forgotten that he had promised to save her. He had forgotten that he meant to snuff out as many lives as might stand between her and freedom. The very remembrance sheered off his morbid introspection. She made a difference. How strange for him to realize that! He felt grateful to her. He had been forced into outlawry; she had been stolen from her people and carried into captivity. They had met in the river fastness, he to instill hope into her despairing life, she to be the means, perhaps, of keeping him from sinking to the level of her captors. He became conscious of a strong and beating desire to see her, talk with her.

These thoughts had run through his mind while on his way to Mrs. Bland's house. He had let Euchre go on ahead because he wanted more time to compose himself. Darkness had about set in when he reached his destination. There was no light in the house. Mrs. Bland was waiting for him on the porch.

She embraced him, and the sudden, violent, unfamiliar contact sent such a shock through him that he all but forgot the deep game he was playing. She, however, in her agitation did not notice his shrinking. From her embrace and the tender, incoherent words that flowed with it he gathered that Euchre had acquainted her of his action with Black.

"He might have killed you!" she whispered, more clearly; and if Duane had ever heard love in a voice he heard it then. It softened him. After all, she was a woman, weak, fated through her nature, unfortunate in her experience of life, doomed to unhappiness and tragedy. He met her advance so far that he returned the embrace and kissed her. Emotion such as she showed would have made any woman sweet, and she had a certain charm. It was easy, even pleasant, to kiss her; but Duane resolved that, whatever her abandonment might become, he would not go further than the lie she made him act.

"Buck, you love me?" she whispered.

"Yes—yes," he burst out, eager to get it over, and even as he spoke he caught the pale gleam of Jennie's face through the window. He felt a shame he was glad she could not see. Did she remember that she had promised not to misunderstand any action of his? What did she think of him, seeing him out there in the dusk with this bold woman in his arms? Somehow that dim sight of Jennie's pale face, the big dark eyes, thrilled him, inspired him to his hard task of the present.

"Listen, dear," he said to the woman, and he meant his words for the girl. "I'm going to take you away from this outlaw den if I have to kill Bland, Alloway, Rugg—anybody who stands in my path. You were dragged here. You are good—I know it. There's happiness for you some-where—a home among good people who will care for you. Just wait till . . ."

His voice trailed off and failed from excess of emotion. Kate Bland closed her eyes and leaned her head on his breast. Duane felt her heart beat against his, and conscience smote him a keen blow. If she loved him so much! But memory and understanding of her character hardened him again, and he gave her such commiseration as was due her sex, and no more.

"Boy, that's good of you," she whispered, "but it's too late. I'm done for. I can't leave Bland. All I ask is that you love me a little and stop your gun-throwing."

The moon had risen over the eastern bulge of dark mountain, and now the valley was flooded with mellow light, and shadows of cottonwoods wavered against the silver.

Suddenly the clip-clop, clip-clop of hoofs caused Duane to raise his head and listen. Horses were coming down the road from the head of the valley. The hour was unusual for riders to come in. Presently the narrow, moonlit lane was crossed at its far end by black moving objects. Two horses Duane discerned.

"It's Bland!" whispered the woman, grasping Duane with shaking hands. "You must run! No, he'd see you. That'd be worse. It's Bland! I know his horse's trot."

"But you said he wouldn't mind my calling here," protested Duane. "Euchre's with me. It 'll be all right."

"Maybe so," she replied, with visible effort at self-control. Manifestly she had a great fear of Bland. "If I could only think!"

Then she dragged Duane to the door, pushed him in.

"Euchre, come out with me! Duane, you stay with the girl! I'll tell Bland you're in love with her. Jen, if you give us away I'll wring your neck."

The swift action and fierce whisper told Duane that Mrs. Bland was herself again. Duane stepped close to Jennie, who stood near the window. Neither spoke, but her hands were outstretched to meet his own. They were small, trembling hands, cold as ice. He held them close, trying to convey what he felt—that he would protect her. She leaned against him, and they looked out of the window. Duane felt calm and sure of himself. His most pronounced feeling besides that for the frightened girl was a curiosity as to how Mrs. Bland would rise to the occasion. He saw the riders dismount down the lane and wearily come forward. A boy led away the horses. Euchre, the old fox, was talking loud and with remarkable ease, considering what he claimed was his natural cowardice.

". . . that was way back in the sixties, about the time of the war," he was saying. "Rustlin' cattle wasn't nuthin' then to what it is now. An' times is rougher these days. This gun-throwin' has come to be a disease. Men have an itch for the draw same as they used to have fer poker. The only real gambler outside of greasers we ever had here was Bill, an' I presume Bill is burnin' now."

The approaching outlaws, hearing voices, halted a rod or so from the porch. Then Mrs. Bland uttered an exclamation, ostensibly meant to express surprise, and hurried out to meet them. She greeted her husband warmly and gave welcome to the other man. Duane could not see well enough in the shadow to recognize Bland's companion, but he believed it was Alloway.

"Dog-tired we are and starved," said Bland, heavily. "Who's here with you?"

"That's Euchre on the porch. Duane is inside at the window with Jen," replied Mrs. Bland.

"Duane!" he exclaimed. Then he whispered low—something Duane could not catch.

"Why, I asked him to come," said the chief's wife. She spoke easily and naturally and made no change in tone. "Jen has been ailing. She gets thinner and whiter every day. Duane came here one day with Euchre, saw Jen, and went loony over her pretty face, same as all you men. So I let him come."

Bland cursed low and deep under his breath. The other man made a violent action of some kind and apparently was quieted by a restraining hand.

"Kate, you let Duane make love to Jennie?" queried Bland, incredulously.

"Yes, I did," replied the wife, stubbornly. "Why not? Jen's in love with him. If he takes her away and marries her she can be a decent woman."

Bland kept silent a moment, then his laugh pealed out loud and harsh.

"Chess, did you get that? Well, by God! What do you think of my wife?"

"She's lyin' or she's crazy," replied Alloway, and his voice carried an unpleasant ring.

Mrs. Bland promptly and indignantly told her husband's lieutenant to keep his mouth shut.

"Ho, ho, ho!" rolled out Bland's laugh.

Then he led the way to the porch, his spurs clinking, the weapons he was carrying rattling, and he flopped down on a bench.

"How are you, boss?" asked Euchre.

"Hello, old man. I'm well, but all in."

Alloway slowly walked on to the porch and leaned against the rail. He answered Euchre's greeting with a nod. Then he stood there a dark, silent figure.

Mrs. Bland's full voice in eager questioning had a tendency to ease the situation. Bland replied briefly to her, reporting a remarkably successful trip.

Duane thought it time to show himself. He had a feeling that Bland and Alloway would let him go for the moment. They were plainly nonplussed, and Alloway seemed sullen, brooding.

"Jennie," whispered Duane, "that was clever of Mrs. Bland. We'll keep up the deception. Any day now be ready!"

She pressed close to him, and a barely audible "Hurry!" came breathing into his ear.

"Good night, Jennie," he said, aloud. "Hope you feel better tomorrow."

Then he stepped out into the moonlight and spoke. Bland returned the greeting, and, though he was not amiable, he did not show resentment.

"Met Jasper as I rode in," said Bland, presently. "He told me you made Bill Black mad, and there's liable to be a fight. What did you go off the handle about?"

Duane explained the incident. "I'm sorry I happened to be there," he went on. "It wasn't my business."

"Scurvy trick that'd been," muttered Bland. "You did right. All the same, Duane, I want you to stop quarreling with my men. If you were one of us—that 'd be different. I can't keep my men from fighting. But I'm not called on to let an outsider hang around my camp and plug my rustlers."

"I guess I'll have to be hitting the trail for somewhere," said Duane.

"Why not join my band? You've got a bad start already, Duane, and if I know this border you'll never be a respectable citizen again. You're a born killer. I know every bad man on this frontier. More than one of them have told me that something exploded in their brain, and when sense came back there lay another dead man. It's not so with me. I've done a little shooting, too, but I never wanted to kill another man just to rid myself of the last one. My dead men don't sit on my chest at night. That's the gunfighter's trouble. He's crazy. He has to kill a new man—he's driven to it to forget the last one."

"But I'm no gunfighter," protested Duane. "Circumstances made me—"

"No doubt," interrupted Bland, with a laugh. "Circumstances made me a rustler. You don't know yourself. You're young; you've got a temper; your father was one of the most dangerous men Texas ever had. I don't see any other career for you. Instead of going it alone—a lone wolf, as the Texans say—why not make friends with other outlaws? You'll live longer."

Euchre squirmed in his seat.

"Boss, I've been givin' the boy egzactly thet same line of talk. Thet's why I took him in to bunk with me. If he makes pards among us there won't be any more trouble. An' he'd be a grand feller fer the gang. I've seen Wild Bill Hickok throw a gun, an' Billy the Kid, an' Hardin, an'

Chess here—all the fastest men on the border. An' with apologies to
present company, I'm here to say Duane has them all skinned. His draw is
different. You can't see how he does it."

Euchre's admiring praise served to create an effective little silence.
Alloway shifted uneasily on his feet, his spurs jangling faintly, and did not
lift his head. Bland seemed thoughtful.

"That's about the only qualification I have to make me eligible for your
band," said Duane, easily.

"It's good enough," replied Bland, shortly. "Will you consider the
idea?"

"I'll think it over. Good night."

He left the group, followed by Euchre. When they reached the end of
the lane, and before they had exchanged a word, Bland called Euchre
back. Duane proceeded slowly along the moonlit road to the cabin and sat
down under the cottonwoods to wait for Euchre. The night was intense
and quiet, a low hum of insects giving the effect of a congestion of life.
The beauty of the soaring moon, the ebony canyons of shadow under the
mountain, the melancholy serenity of the perfect night, made Duane
shudder in the realization of how far aloof he now was from enjoyment of
these things. Never again so long as he lived could he be natural. His
mind was clouded. His eye and ear henceforth must register impressions of
nature, but the joy of them had fled.

Still, as he sat there with a foreboding of more and darker work ahead
of him there was yet a strange sweetness left to him, and it lay in thought
of Jennie. The pressure of her cold little hands lingered in his. He did not
think of her as a woman, and he did not analyze his feelings. He just had
vague, dreamy thoughts and imaginations that were interspersed in the
constant and stern revolving of plans to save her.

A shuffling step roused him. Euchre's dark figure came crossing the
moonlit grass under the cottonwoods. The moment the outlaw reached
him Duane saw that he was laboring under great excitement. It scarcely
affected Duane. He seemed to be acquiring patience, calmness, strength.

"Bland kept you pretty long," he said.

"Wait till I git my breath," replied Euchre. He sat silent a little while,
fanning himself with a sombrero, though the night was cool, and then he
went into the cabin to return presently with a lighted pipe.

"Fine night," he said; and his tone further acquainted Duane with
Euchre's quaint humor. "Fine night for love affairs, by gum!"

"I'd noticed that," rejoined Duane, dryly.

"Wal, I'm a son of a gun if I didn't stand an' watch Bland choke his
wife till her tongue stuck out an' she got black in the face."

"No!" ejaculated Duane.

"Hope to die if I didn't. Buck, listen to this here yarn. When I got back
to the porch I seen Bland was wakin' up. He'd been too fagged out to

figger much. Alloway an' Kate had gone in the house, where they lit up the lamps. I heard Kate's high voice, but Alloway never chirped. He's not the talkin' kind, an' he's damn dangerous when he's thet way. Bland asked me some questions right from the shoulder. I was ready for them, an' I swore the moon was green cheese. He was satisfied. Bland always trusted me, an' liked me, too, I reckon. I hated to lie black thet way. But he's a hard man with bad intentions toward Jennie, an' I'd doublecross him any day.

"Then we went into the house. Jennie had gone to her little room, an' Bland called her to come out. She said she was undressin'. An' he ordered her to put her clothes back on. Then, Buck, his next move was some surprisin'. He deliberately throwed a gun on Kate. Yes sir, he pointed his big blue Colt right at her, an' he says:

" 'I've a mind to blow out your brains.'

" 'Go ahead,' says Kate, cool as could be.

" 'You lied to me,' he roars.

"Kate laughed in his face. Bland slammed the gun down an' made a grab fer her. She fought him, but wasn't a match fer him, an' he got her by the throat. He choked her till I thought she was strangled. Alloway made him stop. She flopped down on the bed an' gasped fer a while. When she come to them hard-shelled cusses went after her, trying to make her give herself away. I think Bland was jealous. He suspected she'd got thick with you an' was foolin' him. I reckon thet's a sore feelin' fer a man to have— to guess pretty nice, but not to *be* sure. Bland gave it up after a while. An' then he cussed an' raved at her. One sayin' of his is worth pinnin' in your sombrero: 'It ain't nuthin' to kill a man. I don't need much fer thet. But I want to *know*, you hussy!'

"Then he went in an' dragged poor Jen out. She'd had time to dress. He was so mad he hurt her sore leg. You know Jen got thet injury fightin' off one of them devils in the dark. An' when I seen Bland twist her—hurt her—I had a queer hot feelin' deep down in me, an' fer the only time in my life I wished I was a gunfighter.

"Wal, Jen amazed me. She was whiter 'n a sheet, an' her eyes were big and stary, but she had nerve. Fust time I ever seen her show any.

" 'Jennie,' he said, 'my wife said Duane came here to see you. I believe she's lyin'. I think she's been carryin' on with him, an' I want to *know*. If she's been an' you tell me the truth I'll let you go. I'll send you out to Huntsville, where you can communicate with your friends. I'll give you money.'

"Thet must hev been a hell of a minnit fer Kate Bland. If ever I seen death in a man's eye I seen it in Bland's. He loves her. Thet's the strange part of it.

" 'Has Duane been comin' here to see my wife?' Bland asked, fierce-like.

" 'No,' said Jennie.

" 'He's been after you?'

" 'Yes.'

" 'He has fallen in love with you? Kate said thet.'

" 'I—I'm not—I don't know—he hasn't told me.'

" 'But you're in love with him?'

" 'Yes,' she said; an', Buck, if you only could have seen her! She threwed up her head, an' her eyes were full of fire. Bland seemed dazed at sight of her. An' Alloway, why, thet little skunk of an outlaw cried right out. He was hit plumb center. He's in love with Jen. An' the look of her then was enough to make any feller quit. He jest slunk out of the room. I told you, mebbe, thet he'd been tryin' to git Bland to marry Jen to him. So even a tough like Alloway can love a woman!

"Bland stamped up an' down the room. He sure was dyin' hard.

" 'Jennie,' he said, once more turnin' to her. 'You swear in fear of your life thet you're tellin' truth. Kate's not in love with Duane? She's let him come to see *you*? There's been nuthin' between them?'

" 'No. I swear,' answered Jennie; an' Bland sat down like a man licked.

" 'Go to bed, you white-faced—' Bland choked on some word or other —a bad one, I reckon—an' he positively shook in his chair.

"Jennie went then, an' Kate began to have hysterics. An' your Uncle Euchre ducked his nut out of the door an' come home."

Duane did not have a word to say at the end of Euchre's long harangue. He experienced relief. As a matter of fact, he had expected a good deal worse. He thrilled at the thought of Jennie perjuring herself to save that abandoned woman. What mysteries these feminine creatures were!

"Wal, there's where our little deal stands now," resumed Euchre, meditatively. "You know, Buck, as well as me thet if you'd been some feller who hadn't shown he was a wonder with a gun you'd now be full of lead. If you'd happen to kill Bland an' Alloway, I reckon you'd be as safe on this here border as you would in Santone. Such is gun fame in this land of the draw."

❦ 9 ❦

BOTH MEN were awake early, silent with the premonition of trouble ahead, thoughtful of the fact that the time for the long-planned action was at hand. It was remarkable that a man as loquacious as Euchre could hold his tongue so long; and this was significant of the deadly nature of the intended deed. During breakfast he said a few words customary in the service of food. At the conclusion of the meal he seemed to come to an end of deliberation.

"Buck, the sooner the better now," he declared, with a glint in his eye. "The more time we use up now the less surprised Bland'll be."

"I'm ready when you are," replied Duane, quietly, and he rose from the table.

"Wal, saddle up, then," went on Euchre, gruffly. "Tie on them two packs I made, one fer each saddle. You can't tell—mebbe either hoss will be carryin' double. It's good they're both big, strong hosses. Guess thet wasn't a wise move of your Uncle Euchre's—bringin' in your hosses an' havin' them ready?"

"Euchre, I hope you're not going to get in bad here. I'm afraid you are. Let me do the rest now," said Duane.

The old outlaw eyed him sarcastically.

"Thet'd be turrible now, wouldn't it? If you want to know, why, I'm in bad already. I didn't tell you thet Alloway called me last night. He's gettin' wise pretty quick."

"Euchre, you're going with me?" queried Duane, suddenly divining the truth.

"Wal, I reckon. Either to hell or safe over the mountain! I wisht I was a gunfighter. I hate to leave here without takin' a peg at Jackrabbit Benson. Now, Buck, you do some hard figgerin' while I go nosin' round. It's pretty early, which's all the better."

Euchre put on his sombrero, and as he went out Duane saw that he wore a gun-and-cartridge belt. It was the first time Duane had ever seen the outlaw armed.

Duane packed his few belongings into his saddle-bags, and then carried the saddles out to the corral. An abundance of alfalfa in the corral showed that the horses had fared well. They had gotten almost fat during his stay in the valley. He watered them, put on the saddles loosely cinched, and then the bridles. His next move was to fill the two canvas water-bottles. That done, he returned to the cabin to wait.

At the moment he felt no excitement or agitation of any kind. There was no more thinking and planning to do. The hour had arrived, and he was ready. He understood perfectly the desperate chances he must take. His thoughts became confined to Euchre and the surprising loyalty and goodness in the hardened old outlaw. Time passed slowly. Duane kept glancing at his watch. He hoped to start the thing and get away before the outlaws were out of their beds. Finally he heard the shuffle of Euchre's boots on the hard path. The sound was quicker than usual.

When Euchre came around the corner of the cabin Duane was not so astounded as he was concerned to see the outlaw white and shaking. Sweat dripped from him. He had a wild look.

"Luck ours . . . so . . . fur, Buck!" he panted.

"You don't look it," replied Duane.

"I'm turrible sick. Jest killed a man. Fust one I ever killed!"

"Who?" asked Duane, startled.

"Jackrabbit Benson. An' sick as I am, I'm gloryin' in it. I went nosin' round up the road. Saw Alloway goin' into Deger's. He's thick with the Degers. Reckon he's askin' questions. Anyway, I was sure glad to see him away from Bland's. An' he didn't see me. When I dropped into Benson's there wasn't nobody there but Jackrabbit an' some greasers he was startin' to work. Benson never had no use fer me. An' he up an' said he wouldn't give a two-bit piece fer my life. I asked him why.

" 'You're double-crossin' the boss an' Chess,' he said.

" 'Jack, what'd you give fer your own life?' I asked him.

"He straightened up surprised an' mean-lookin'. An' I let him have it, plumb center! He wilted, an' the greasers run. I reckon I'll never sleep again. But I had to do it."

Duane asked if the shot had attracted any attention outside.

"I didn't see anybody but the greasers, an' I sure looked sharp. Comin' back I cut across through the cottonwoods past Bland's cabin. I meant to keep out of sight, but somehow I had an idee I might find out if Bland was awake yet. Sure enough I run plumb into Beppo, the boy who tends Bland's hosses. Beppo likes me. An' when I inquired of his boss he said Bland had been up all night fightin' with the *señora*. An', Buck, here's how I figger. Bland couldn't let up last night. He was sore, an' he went after Kate again, tryin' to wear her down. Jest as likely he might have went after Jennie, with wuss intentions. Anyway, he an' Kate must have had it hot an' heavy. We're pretty lucky."

"It seems so. Well, I'm going," said Duane, tersely.

"Lucky! I should smile! Bland's been up all night after a most draggin' ride home. He'll be fagged out this mornin', sleepy, sore, an' he won't be expectin' hell before breakfast. Now, you walk over to his house. Meet him how you like. Thet's your game. But I'm suggestin', if he comes out an' you want to parley, you can jest say you'd thought over his proposition an' was ready to join his band, or you ain't. You'll have to kill him, an' it'd save time to go fer your gun on sight. Might be wise, too, fer it's likely he'll do thet same."

"How about the horses?"

"I'll fetch them an' come along about two minnits behind you. 'Pears to me you ought to have the job done an' Jennie outside by the time I git there. Once on them hosses, we can ride out of camp before Alloway or anybody else gits into action. Jennie ain't much heavier 'n a rabbit. Thet big black will carry you both."

"All right. But once more let me persuade you to stay—not to mix any more in this," said Duane, earnestly.

"Nope. I'm goin'. You heard what Benson told me. Alloway wouldn't give me the benefit of any doubts. Buck, a last word—look out fer thet Bland woman!"

Duane merely nodded, and then, saying that the horses were ready, he strode away through the grove. Accounting for the short-cut across grove and field, it was about five minutes' walk up to Bland's house. To Duane it seemed long in time and distance, and he had difficulty in restraining his pace. As he walked there came a gradual and subtle change in his feelings. Again he was going out to meet a man in conflict. He could have avoided this meeting. But despite the fact of his courting the encounter he had not as yet felt that hot, inexplicable rush of blood. The motive of this deadly action was not personal, and somehow that made a difference.

No outlaws were in sight. He saw several Mexican herders with cattle. Blue columns of smoke curled up over some of the cabins. The fragrant smell of it reminded Duane of his home and cutting wood for the stove. He noted a cloud of creamy mist rising above the river, dissolving in the sunlight.

Then he entered Bland's lane.

While yet some distance from the cabin he heard loud, angry voices of man and woman. Bland and Kate still quarreling! He took a quick survey of the surroundings. There was now not even a Mexican in sight. Then he hurried a little. Halfway down the lane he turned his head to peer through the cottonwoods. This time he saw Euchre coming with the horses. There was no indication that the old outlaw might lose his nerve at the end. Duane had feared this.

Duane now changed his walk to a leisurely saunter. He reached the porch and then distinguished what was said inside the cabin.

"If you do, Bland, by heaven I'll fix you and her!" That was panted out in Kate Bland's full voice.

"Let me loose! I'm going in there, I tell you!" replied Bland, hoarsely. "What for?"

"I want to make a little love to her. Ha, ha! It 'll be fun to have the laugh on her new lover."

"You lie!" cried Kate Bland.

"I'm not saying what I'll do to her *afterward!*" His voice grew hoarser with passion. "Let me go now!"

"No, no! I won't let you go. You'll choke the—the truth out of her—you'll kill her."

"The *truth!*" hissed Bland.

"Yes. I lied. Jen lied. But she lied to save me. You needn't—murder her —for that."

Bland cursed horribly. Then followed a wrestling sound of bodies in violent straining contact—the scrape of feet—the jangle of spurs—a crash of sliding table or chair, and then the cry of a woman in pain.

Duane stepped into the open door, inside the room. Kate Bland lay half across a table where she had been flung, and she was trying to get to her feet. Bland's back was turned. He had opened the door into Jennie's room and had one foot across the threshold. Duane caught the girl's low, shuddering cry. Then he called out loud and clear.

With catlike swiftness Bland wheeled, then froze on the threshold. His sight, quick as his action, caught Duane's menacing, unmistakable position.

Bland's big frame filled the door. He was in a bad place to reach for his gun. But he would not have time for a step. Duane read in his eyes the desperate calculation of chances. For a fleeting instant Bland shifted his glance to his wife. Then his whole body seemed to vibrate with the swing of his arm.

Duane shot him. He fell forward, his gun exploding as it hit into the floor, and dropped loose from stretching fingers. Duane stood over him, stooped to turn him on his back. Bland looked up with clouded gaze, then gasped his last.

"Duane, you've killed him!" cried Kate Bland, huskily. "I knew you'd have to!"

She staggered against the wall, her eyes dilating, her strong hands clenching, her face slowly whitening. She appeared shocked, half stunned, but showed no grief.

"Jennie!" called Duane, sharply.

"Oh—Duane!" came a halting reply.

"Yes. Come out. Hurry!"

She came out with uneven steps, seeing only him, and she stumbled over Bland's body. Duane caught her arm, swung her behind him. He feared the woman when she realized how she had been duped. His action was protective, and his movement toward the door equally as significant.

"Duane!" cried Mrs. Bland.

It was no time for talk. Duane edged on, keeping Jennie behind him. At that moment there was a pounding of iron-shod hoofs out in the lane. Kate Bland bounded to the door. When she turned back her amazement was changing to realization.

"Where're you taking Jen?" she cried, her voice like a man's.

"Get out of my way," replied Duane. His look perhaps, without speech, was enough for her. In an instant she was transformed into a fury.

"You hound! All the time you were fooling me! You made love to me! You let me believe—you swore you loved me! Now I see what was queer about you. All for that girl! But you can't have her. You'll never leave here alive. Give me that girl! Let me—get at her! She'll never win any more men in this camp."

She was a powerful woman, and it took all Duane's strength to ward off her onslaughts. She clawed at Jennie over his upheld arm. Every second her fury increased.

"*Help! help! help!*" she shrieked, in a voice that must have penetrated to the remotest cabin in the valley.

"Let go! Let go!" cried Duane, low and sharp. He still held his gun in his right hand, and it began to be hard for him to ward the woman off. His coolness had gone with her shriek for help. "Let go!" he repeated, and he shoved her fiercely.

Suddenly she snatched a rifle off the wall and backed away, her strong hands fumbling at the lever. As she jerked it down, throwing a shell into the chamber and cocking the weapon, Duane leaped upon her. He struck up the rifle as it went off, the powder burning his face.

"Jennie, run out! Get on a horse!" he said.

Jennie flashed out of the door.

With an iron grasp Duane held to the rifle barrel. He had grasped it with his left hand, and he gave such a pull that he swung the crazed woman off the floor. But he could not loose her grip. She was as strong as he.

"Kate! Let go!"

He tried to intimidate her. She did not see his gun thrust in her face, or reason had given way to such an extent to passion that she did not care. She cursed. Her husband had used the same curses, and from her lips they seemed strange, unsexed, more deadly. Like a tigress she fought him; her face no longer resembled a woman's. The evil of that outlaw life, the wildness and rage, the meaning to kill, was even in such a moment terribly impressed upon Duane.

He heard a cry from outside—a man's cry, hoarse and alarming.

It made him think of loss of time. This demon of a woman might yet block his plan.

"Let go!" he whispered, and felt his lips stiff. In the grimness of that instant he relaxed his hold on the rifle barrel.

With sudden, redoubled, irresistible strength she wrenched the rifle down and discharged it. Duane felt a blow—a shock—a burning agony tearing through his breast. Then in a frenzy he jerked so powerfully upon the rifle that he threw the woman against the wall. She fell and seemed stunned.

Duane leaped back, whirled, flew out of the door to the porch. The sharp cracking of a gun halted him. He saw Jennie holding to the bridle of his bay horse. Euchre was astride the other, and he had a Colt leveled, and he was firing down the lane. Then came a single shot, heavier, and Euchre's ceased. He fell from the horse.

A swift glance back showed to Duane a man coming down the lane. Chess Alloway! His gun was smoking. He broke into a run. Then in an instant he saw Duane, and tried to check his pace as he swung up his arm. But that slight pause was fatal. Duane shot, and Alloway was falling when his gun went off. His bullet whistled close to Duane and thudded into the cabin.

Duane bounded down to the horses. Jennie was trying to hold the plunging bay. Euchre lay flat on his back, dead, a bullet-hole in his shirt, his face set hard, and his hands twisted round gun and bridle.

"Jennie, you've nerve, all right!" cried Duane, as he dragged down the horse she was holding. "Up with you now! There! Never mind—long stirrups! Hang on somehow!"

He caught his bridle out of Euchre's clutching grip and leaped astride. The frightened horses jumped into a run and thundered down the lane into the road. Duane saw men running from cabins. He heard shouts. But there were no shots fired. Jennie seemed able to stay on her horse, but without stirrups she was thrown about so much that Duane rode closer and reached out to grasp her arm.

Thus they rode through the valley to the trail that led up over the steep and broken Rim Rock. As they began to climb Duane looked back. No pursuers were in sight.

"Jennie, we're going to get away!" he cried, exultation for her in his voice.

She was gazing horror-stricken at his breast, as in turning to look back he faced her.

"Oh, Duane, your shirt's all bloody!" she faltered, pointing with trembling fingers.

With her words Duane became aware of two things—the hand he instinctively placed to his breast still held his gun, and he had sustained a terrible wound.

Duane had been shot through the breast far enough down to give him grave apprehension of his life. The clean-cut hole made by the bullet bled freely both at its entrance and where it had come out, but with no signs of hemorrhage. He did not bleed at the mouth; however, he began to cough up a reddish-tinged foam.

As they rode on Jennie, with pale face and mute lips, looked at him.

"I'm badly hurt, Jennie," he said, "but I guess I'll stick it out."

"The woman—did she shoot you?"

"Yes. She was a devil. Euchre told me to look out for her. I wasn't quick enough."

"You didn't have to—to—" shivered the girl.

"No, no!" he replied.

They did not stop climbing while Duane tore a scarf and made compresses, which he bound tightly over his wounds. The fresh horses made fast time up the rough trail. From open places Duane looked down. When they surmounted the steep ascent and stood on top of the Rim Rock, with no signs of pursuit down in the valley, and with the wild, broken fastnesses before them, Duane turned to the girl and assured her that they now had every chance of escape.

"But—your—wound!" she faltered, with dark, troubled eyes. "I see— the blood—dripping from your back!"

"Jennie, I'll take a lot of killing," he said.

Then he became silent and attended to the uneven trail. He was aware presently that he had not come into Bland's camp by this route. But that did not matter; any trail leading out beyond the Rim Rock was safe enough. What he wanted was to get far away into some wild retreat where he could hide till he recovered from his wound. He seemed to feel a fire inside his breast, and his throat burned so that it was necessary for him to take a swallow of water every little while. He began to suffer considerable pain, which increased as the hours went by and then gave way to a numbness. From that time on he had need of his great strength and endurance. Gradually he lost his steadiness and his keen sight; and he realized that if he were to meet foes, or if pursuing outlaws should come up with him, he could make only a poor stand. So he turned off on a trail that appeared seldom traveled.

Soon after this move he became conscious of a further thickening of his senses. He felt able to hold on to his saddle for a while longer, but he was failing. Then he thought he ought to advise Jennie, so in case she was left alone she would have some idea of what to do.

"Jennie, I'll give out soon," he said. "No—I don't mean—what you think. But I'll drop soon. My strength's going. If I die—you ride back to the main trail. Hide and rest by day. Ride at night. That trail goes to water. I believe you could get across the Nueces, where some rancher will take you in."

Duane could not get the meaning of her incoherent reply. He rode on, and soon he could not see the trail or hear his horse. He did not know whether they traveled a mile or many times that far. But he was conscious when the horse stopped, and had a vague sense of falling and feeling Jennie's arms before all became dark to him.

When consciousness returned he found himself lying in a little hut of mesquite branches. It was well built and evidently some years old. There were two doors or openings, one in front and the other at the back. Duane imagined it had been built by a fugitive—one who meant to keep an eye both ways and not to be surprised. Duane felt weak and had no desire to move. Where was he, anyway? A strange, intangible sense of time, distance, of something far behind weighed upon him. Sight of the two packs

Euchre had made brought his thought to Jennie. What had become of her? There was evidence of her work in a smoldering fire and a little blackened coffeepot. Probably she was outside looking after the horses or getting water. He thought he heard a step and listened, but he felt tired, and presently his eyes closed and he fell into a doze.

Awakening from this, he saw Jennie sitting beside him. In some way she seemed to have changed. When he spoke she gave a start and turned eagerly to him.

"Duane!" she cried.

"Hello. How're you, Jennie, and how am I?" he said, finding it a little difficult to talk.

"Oh, I'm all right," she replied. "And you've come to—your wound's healed; but you've been sick. Fever, I guess. I did all I could."

Duane saw now that the difference in her was a whiteness and tightness of skin, a hollowness of eye, a look of strain.

"Fever? How long have we been here?" he asked.

She took some pebbles from the crown of his sombrero and counted them.

"Nine. Nine days," she answered.

"Nine days!" he exclaimed, incredulously. But another look at her assured him that she meant what she said. "I've been sick all the time? You nursed me?"

"Yes."

"Bland's men didn't come along here?"

"No."

"Where are the horses?"

"I keep them grazing down in a gorge back of here. There's good grass and water."

"Have you slept any?"

"A little. Lately I couldn't keep awake."

"Good Lord! I should think not. You've had a time of it sitting here day and night nursing me, watching for the outlaws. Come, tell me all about it."

"There's nothing much to tell."

"I want to know, anyway, just what you did—how you felt."

"I can't remember very well," she replied, simply. "We must have ridden forty miles that day we got away. You bled all the time. Toward evening you lay on your horse's neck. When we came to this place you fell out of the saddle. I dragged you in here and stopped your bleeding. I thought you'd die that night. But in the morning I had a little hope. I had forgotten the horses. But luckily they didn't stray far. I caught them and kept them down in the gorge. When your wounds closed and you began to breathe stronger I thought you'd get well quick. It was fever that put you back. You raved a lot, and that worried me, because I couldn't stop you. Anybody trailing us could have heard you a good ways. I don't know whether I was scared most then or when you were quiet, and it was so dark and lonely and still all around. Every day I put a stone in your hat."

"Jennie, you saved my life," said Duane.

"I don't know. Maybe. I did all I knew how to do," she replied. "You saved mine—more than my life."

Their eyes met in a long gaze, and then their hands in a close clasp.

"Jennie, we're going to get away," he said, with gladness. "I'll be well in a few days. You don't know how strong I am. We'll hide by day and travel by night. I can get you across the river."

"And then?" she asked.

"We'll find some honest rancher."

"And then?" she persisted.

"Why," he began, slowly, "that's as far as my thoughts ever got. It was pretty hard, I tell you, to assure myself of so much. It means your safety. You'll tell your story. You'll be sent to some village or town and taken care of until a relative or friend is notified."

"And you?" she inquired, in a strange voice.

Duane kept silent.

"What will you do?" she went on.

"Jennie, I'll go back to the brakes. I daren't show my face among respectable people. I'm an outlaw."

"You're no criminal!" she declared, with deep passion.

"Jennie, on this border the little difference between an outlaw and a criminal doesn't count for much."

"You won't go back among those terrible men? You, with your gentleness and sweetness—all that's good about you? Oh, Duane, don't—don't go!"

"I can't go back to the outlaws, at least not Bland's band. No, I'll go alone. I'll lone-wolf it, as they say on the border. What else can I do, Jennie?"

"Oh, I don't know. Couldn't you hide? Couldn't you slip out of Texas —go far away?"

"I could never get out of Texas without being arrested. I could hide, but a man must live. Never mind about me, Jennie."

In three days Duane was able with great difficulty to mount his horse. During daylight, by short relays, he and Jennie rode back to the main trail, where they hid again till he had rested. Then in the dark they rode out of the canyons and gullies of the Rim Rock, and early in the morning halted at the first water to camp.

From that point they traveled after nightfall and went into hiding during the day. Once across the Nueces River, Duane was assured of safety for her and great danger for himself. They had crossed into a country he did not know. Somewhere east of the river there were scattered ranches. But he was as liable to find the rancher in touch with the outlaws as he was likely to find him honest. Duane hoped his good fortune would not desert him in this last service to Jennie. Next to the worry of that was realization of his condition. He had gotten up too soon; he had ridden too far and hard, and now he felt that any moment he might fall from his saddle. At last, far ahead over a barren mesquite-dotted stretch of dusty ground, he espied a patch of green and a little flat, red ranch-house. He headed his horse for it and turned a face he tried to make cheerful for Jennie's sake. She seemed both happy and sorry.

When near at hand he saw that the rancher was a thrifty farmer. And thrift spoke for honesty. There were fields of alfalfa, fruit trees, corrals, windmill pumps, irrigation ditches, all surrounding a neat little adobe house. Some children were playing in the yard. The way they ran at sight of Duane hinted of both the loneliness and the fear of their isolated lives. Duane saw a woman come to the door, then a man. The latter looked keenly, then stepped outside. He was a sandy-haired, freckled Texan.

"Howdy, stranger," he called, as Duane halted. "Get down, you an' your woman. Say, now, air you sick or shot or what? Let me—"

Duane, reeling in his saddle, bent searching eyes upon the rancher. He thought he saw goodwill, kindness, honesty. He risked all on that one sharp glance. Then he almost plunged from the saddle.

The rancher caught him, helped him to a bench.

"Martha, come out here!" he called. "This man's sick. No; he's shot, or I don't know blood stains."

Jennie had slipped off her horse and to Duane's side. Duane appeared about to faint.

"Air you his wife?" asked the rancher.

"No. I'm only a girl he saved from outlaws. Oh, he's so pale! Duane, Duane!"

"Buck Duane!" exclaimed the rancher, excitedly. "The man who killed Bland an' Alloway? Say, I owe him a good turn, an' I'll pay it, young woman."

The rancher's wife came out, and with a manner at once kind and practical essayed to make Duane drink from a flask. He was not so far gone that he could not recognize its contents, which he refused, and weakly asked for water. When that was given him he found his voice.

"Yes, I'm Duane. I've only overdone myself—just all in. The wounds I got at Bland's are healing. Will you take this girl in—hide her awhile till the excitement's over among the outlaws?"

"I shore will," replied the Texan.

"Thanks. I'll remember you—I'll square it."

"What're you goin' to do?"

"I'll rest a bit—then go back to the brakes."

"Young man, you ain't in any shape to travel. See here—any rustlers on your trail?"

"I think we gave Bland's gang the slip."

"Good. I'll tell you what. I'll take you in along with the girl, an' hide both of you till you get well. It'll be safe. My nearest neighbor is five miles off. We don't have much company."

"You risk a great deal. Both outlaws and rangers are hunting me," said Duane.

"Never seen a ranger yet in these parts. An' have always got along with outlaws, mebbe exceptin' Bland. I tell you I owe you a good turn."

"My horses might betray you," added Duane.

"I'll hide them in a place where there's water an' grass. Nobody goes to it. Come now, let me help you indoors."

Duane's last fading sensations of that hard day were the strange feel of a bed, a relief at the removal of his heavy boots, and of Jennie's soft, cool hands on his hot face.

He lay ill for three weeks before he began to mend, and it was another week then before he could walk out a little in the dusk of the evenings. After that his strength returned rapidly. And it was only at the end of this long siege that he recovered his spirits. During most of his illness he had been silent, moody.

"Jennie, I'll be riding off soon," he said, one evening. "I can't impose on this good man Andrews much longer. I'll never forget his kindness. His wife, too—she's been so good to us. Yes, Jennie, you and I will have to say goodbye very soon."

"Don't hurry away," she replied.

Lately Jennie had appeared strange to him. She had changed from the girl he used to see at Mrs. Bland's house. He took her reluctance to say goodbye as another indication of her regret that he must go back to the brakes. Yet somehow it made him observe her more closely. She wore a plain, white dress made from material Mrs. Andrews had given her. Sleep and good food had improved her. If she had been pretty out there in the outlaw den, now she was more than that. But she had the same paleness, the same strained look, the same dark eyes full of haunting shadows. After Duane's realization of the change in her he watched her more, with a growing certainty that he would be sorry not to see her again.

"It's likely we won't ever see each other again," he said. "That's strange to think of. We've been through some hard days, and I seem to have known you a long time."

Jennie appeared shy, almost sad, so Duane changed the subject to something less personal.

Andrews returned one evening from a several days' trip to Huntsville.

"Duane, everybody's talkin' about how you cleaned up the Bland outfit," he said, important and full of news. "It's some exaggerated, accordin' to what you told me; but you've shore made friends on this side of the Nueces. I reckon there ain't a town where you wouldn't find people to welcome you. Huntsville, you know, is some divided in its ideas. Half the people are crooked. Likely enough, all them who was so loud in praise of you are the crookedest. For instance, I met King Fisher, the boss outlaw of these parts. Well, King thinks he's a decent citizen. He was tellin' me what a grand job yours was for the border an' honest cattlemen. Now that Bland and Alloway are done for, King Fisher will find rustlin' easier. There's talk of Hardin movin' his camp over to Bland's. But I don't know how true it is. I reckon there ain't much to it. In the past when a big outlaw chief went under, his band almost always broke up an' scattered. There's no one left who could run thet outfit."

"Did you hear of any outlaws hunting me?" asked Duane.

"Nobody from Bland's outfit is huntin' you, thet's shore," replied Andrews. "Fisher said there never was a hoss straddled to go on your trail. Nobody had any use for Bland. Anyhow, his men would be afraid to trail you. An' you could go right in to Huntsville, where you'd be some popular. Reckon you'd be safe, too, except when some of them fool saloon loafers or bad cowpunchers would try to shoot you for the glory in it. Them kind of men will bob up everywhere you go, Duane."

"I'll be able to ride and take care of myself in a day or two," went on Duane. "Then I'll go. . . . I'd like to talk to you about Jennie."

"She's welcome to a home here with us."

"Thank you, Andrews. You're a kind man. But I want Jennie to get farther away from the Rio Grande. She'd never be safe here. Besides, she may be able to find relatives. She has some, though she doesn't know where they are."

"All right, Duane. Whatever you think best. I reckon now you'd better take her to some town. Go north an' strike for Shelbyville or Crockett. Them's both good towns. I'll tell Jennie the names of men who'll help her. You needn't ride into town at all."

"Which place is nearer, and how far is it?"

"Shelbyville. I reckon about two days' ride. Poor stock country, so you ain't liable to meet rustlers. All the same, better hit the trail at night an' go careful."

At sunset two days later Duane and Jennie mounted their horses and said goodbye to the rancher and his wife. Andrews would not listen to Duane's thanks.

"I tell you I'm beholden to you yet," he declared.

"Well, what can I do for you?" asked Duane. "I may come along here again someday."

"Get down an' come in, then, or you're no friend of mine. I reckon there ain't nothin' I can think of—I just happen to remember—" Here he led Duane out of earshot of the women and went on in a whisper. "Buck, I used to be well-to-do. Got skinned by a man named Brown—Rodney Brown. He lives in Huntsville, an' he's my enemy. I never was much on fightin', or I'd fixed him. Brown ruined me—stole all I had. He's a hoss an' cattle thief an' he has pull enough at home to protect him. I reckon I needn't say any more."

"Is this Brown a man who shot an outlaw named Stevens?" queried Duane, curiously.

"Shore, he's the same. I heard thet story. Brown swears he plugged Stevens through the middle. But the outlaw rode off, an' nobody ever knew for shore."

"Luke Stevens died of that shot. I buried him," said Duane.

Andrews made no further comment, and the two men returned to the women.

"The main road for about three miles, then where it forks take the left-hand road and keep on straight. That what you said, Andrews?"

"Shore. An' good luck to you both!"

Duane and Jennie trotted away into the gathering twilight. At the moment an insistent thought bothered Duane. Both Luke Stevens and the rancher Andrews had hinted to Duane to kill a man named Brown. Duane wished with all his heart that they had not mentioned it, let alone taken for granted the execution of the deed. What a bloody place Texas was! Men who robbed and men who were robbed both wanted murder. It was in the spirit of the country. Duane certainly meant to avoid ever meeting this Rodney Brown. And that very determination showed Duane how dangerous he really was—to men and to himself. Sometimes he had a feeling of how little stood between his sane and better self and a self utterly wild and terrible. He reasoned that only intelligence could save him—only a thoughtful understanding of his danger and a hold upon some ideal.

Then he fell into low conversation with Jennie, holding out hopeful views of her future, and presently darkness set in. The sky was overcast with heavy clouds; there was no air moving; the heat and oppression threatened storm. By and by Duane could not see a rod in front of him, though his horse had no difficulty in keeping to the road. Duane was bothered by the blackness of the night. Traveling fast was impossible, and any moment he might miss the road that led off to the left. So he was compelled to give all his attention to peering into the thick shadows ahead. As good luck would have it, he came to higher ground where there was less mesquite, and therefore not such impenetrable darkness; and at this point he came to where the road split.

Once headed in the right direction, he felt easier in mind. To his annoyance, however, a fine, misty rain set in. Jennie was not well dressed for wet weather; and, for that matter, neither was he. His coat, which in that dry warm climate he seldom needed, was tied behind his saddle, and he put it on Jennie.

They traveled on. The rain fell steadily—if anything, growing thicker. Duane grew uncomfortably wet and chilly. Jennie, however, fared somewhat better by reason of the heavy coat. The night passed quickly despite the discomfort, and soon a gray, dismal, rainy dawn greeted the travelers.

Jennie insisted that he find some shelter where a fire could be built to dry his clothes. He was not in a fit condition to risk catching cold. In fact, Duane's teeth were chattering. To find a shelter in that barren waste seemed a futile task. Quite unexpectedly, however, they happened upon a deserted adobe cabin situated a little off the road. Not only did it prove to have a dry interior, but also there was firewood. Water was available in pools everywhere; however, there was no grass for the horses.

A good fire and hot food and drink changed the aspect of their condition as far as comfort went. And Jennie lay down to sleep. For Duane, however, there must be vigilance. This cabin was no hiding-place. The rain fell harder all the time, and the wind changed to the north. "It's a norther, all right," muttered Duane. "Two or three days." And he felt that his extraordinary luck had not held out. Still one point favored him, and it was that travelers were not likely to come along during the storm.

Jennie slept while Duane watched. The saving of this girl meant more to him than any task he had ever assumed. First it had been partly from a human feeling to succor an unfortunate woman, and partly a motive to establish clearly to himself that he was no outlaw. Lately, however, had come a different sense, a strange one, with something personal and warm and protective in it.

As he looked down upon her, a slight, slender girl with bedraggled dress and disheveled hair, her face, pale and quiet, a little stern in sleep, and her long, dark lashes lying on her cheek, he seemed to see her fragility, her prettiness, her femininity as never before. But for him she might at that very moment have been a broken, ruined girl lying back in that cabin of the Blands'. The fact gave him a feeling of his importance in this shifting of her destiny. She was unharmed, still young; she would forget and be happy; she would live to be a good wife and mother. Somehow the thought swelled his heart. His act, death-dealing as it had been, was a noble one, and helped him to hold on to his drifting hopes. Hardly once since Jennie had entered into his thoughts had those ghosts returned to torment him.

Tomorrow she would be gone among good, kind people with a possibility of finding her relatives. He thanked God for that; nevertheless, he felt a pang.

She slept more than half the day. Duane kept guard, always alert, whether he was sitting, standing, or walking. The rain pattered steadily on the roof and sometimes came in gusty flurries through the door. The horses were outside in a shed that afforded poor shelter, and they stamped restlessly. Duane kept them saddled and bridled.

About the middle of the afternoon Jennie awoke. They cooked a meal and afterward sat beside the little fire. She had never been, in his observation of her, anything but a tragic figure, an unhappy girl, the farthest removed from serenity and poise. That characteristic capacity for agitation struck him as stronger in her this day. He attributed it, however, to the long strain, the suspense nearing an end. Yet sometimes when her eyes were on him she did not seem to be thinking of her freedom, of her future.

"This time tomorrow you'll be in Shelbyville," he said.

"Where will you be?" she asked, quickly.

"Me? Oh, I'll be making tracks for some lonesome place," he replied. The girl shuddered.

"I've been brought up in Texas. I remember what a hard lot the men of my family had. But poor as they were, they had a roof over their heads, a hearth with a fire, a warm bed—somebody to love them. And you, Duane —oh, my God! What must your life be? You must ride and hide and watch eternally. No decent food, no pillow, no friendly word, no clean clothes, no woman's hand! Horses, guns, trails, rocks, holes—these must be the important things in your life. You must go on riding, hiding, killing until you meet—"

She ended with a sob and dropped her head on her knees. Duane was amazed, deeply touched.

"My girl, thank you for that thought of me," he said, with a tremor in his voice. "You don't know how much that means to me."

She raised her face, and it was tear-stained, eloquent, beautiful.

"I've heard tell—the best of men go to the bad out there. You won't. Promise me you won't. I never—knew any man—like you. I—I—we may never see each other again—after today. I'll never forget you. I'll pray for you, and I'll never give up trying to—to do something. Don't despair. It's never too late. It was my hope that kept me alive—out there at Bland's— before you came. I was only a poor weak girl. But if I could hope—so can you. Stay away from men. Be a lone wolf. Fight for your life. Stick out your exile—and maybe—someday—"

Then she lost her voice. Duane clasped her hand and with feeling as deep as hers promised to remember her words. In her despair for him she had spoken wisdom—pointed out the only course.

Duane's vigilance, momentarily broken by emotion, had no sooner reasserted itself than he discovered the bay horse, the one Jennie rode, had broken his halter and gone off. The soft, wet earth had deadened the sound of his hoofs. His tracks were plain in the mud. There were clumps of mesquite in sight, among which the horse might have strayed. It turned out, however, that he had not done so.

Duane did not want to leave Jennie alone in the cabin so near the road. So he put her up on his horse and bade her follow. The rain had ceased for the time being, though evidently the storm was not yet over. The tracks led up a wash to a wide flat where mesquite, prickly pear, and thorn-bush grew so thickly that Jennie could not ride into it. Duane was thoroughly concerned. He must have her horse. Time was flying. It would soon be night. He could not expect her to scramble quickly through that brake on foot. Therefore he decided to risk leaving her at the edge of the thicket and go in alone.

As he went in a sound startled him. Was it the breaking of a branch he had stepped on or thrust aside? He heard the impatient pound of his horse's hoofs. Then all was quiet. Still he listened, not wholly satisfied. He was never satisfied in regard to safety; he knew too well that there never could be safety for him in this country.

The bay horse had threaded the aisles of the thicket. Duane wondered what had drawn him there. Certainly it had not been grass, for there was none. Presently he heard the horse tramping along, and then he ran. The mud was deep, and the sharp thorns made going difficult. He came up with the horse, and at the same moment crossed a multitude of fresh horse-tracks.

He bent lower to examine them, and was alarmed to find that they had been made very recently, even since it had ceased raining. They were tracks of well-shod horses. Duane straightened up with a cautious glance all around. His instant decision was to hurry back to Jennie. But he had come a goodly way through the thicket, and it was impossible to rush back. Once or twice he imagined he heard crashings in the brush, but did not halt to make sure. Certain he was now that some kind of danger threatened.

Suddenly there came an unmistakable thump of horses' hoofs off somewhere to the fore. Then a scream rent the air. It ended abruptly. Duane leaped forward, tore his way through the thorny brake. He heard Jennie cry again—an appealing call quickly hushed. It seemed more to his right, and he plunged that way. He burst into a glade where a smoldering fire and ground covered with footprints and tracks showed that campers had lately been. Rushing across this, he broke his passage out to the open. But he was too late. His horse had disappeared. Jennie was gone. There were no riders in sight. There was no sound. There was a heavy trail of horses going north. Jennie had been carried off—probably by outlaws. Duane realized that pursuit was out of the question—that Jennie was lost.

...mong them occasionally was a man, human in his way,
...ld be, not yet lost to good.

...m were akin in one sense—their outlawry; and that starry
...with their dark faces up, some in packs like wolves, others
...e gray wolf who knew no mate. It did not make much
...Duane's thought of them that the majority were steeped in
...rutality, more often than not stupid from rum, incapable of a
..., just lost wild dogs.

...doubted that there was a man among them who did not realize
...wreck and ruin. He had met poor, half-witted wretches who
...He believed he could enter into their minds and feel the truth of
...lives—the hardened outlaw, coarse, ignorant, bestial, who mur-
...as Bill Black had murdered, who stole for the sake of stealing, who
...d money to gamble and drink, defiantly ready for death, like that
...le outlaw Helm, who cried out on the scaffold, "Let her rip!"

...he wild youngsters seeking notoriety and reckless adventure; the cow-
...ys with a notch on their guns, with boastful pride in the knowledge
...at they were marked by rangers; the crooked men from the North,
...efaulters, forgers, murderers, all pale-faced, flat-chested men not fit for
that wilderness and not surviving; the dishonest cattlemen, hand and
glove with outlaws, driven from their homes; the old grizzled, bow-legged
genuine rustlers—all these Duane had come in contact with, had watched
and known, and as he felt with them he seemed to see that as their lives
were bad, sooner or later to end dismally or tragically, so they must pay
some kind of earthly penalty—if not of conscience, then of fear; if not of
fear, then of that most terrible of all things to restless, active men—pain,
the pang of flesh and bone.

Duane knew, for he had seen them pay. Best of all, moreover, he knew
the internal life of the gunfighter of that select but by no means small
class of which he was representative. The world that judged him and his
kind judged him as a machine, a killing-machine, with only mind enough
to hunt, to meet, to slay another man. It had taken three endless years for
Duane to understand his own father. Duane knew beyond all doubt that
the gunfighters like Bland, like Alloway, like Sellers, men who were evil
and had no remorse, no spiritual accusing Nemesis, had something far
more torturing to mind, more haunting, more murderous of rest and sleep
and peace; and that something was abnormal fear of death. Duane knew
this, for he had shot these men; he had seen the quick, dark shadow in
eyes, the presentiment that the will could not control, and then the
horrible certainty. These men must have been in agony at every meeting
with a possible or certain foe—more agony than the hot rend of a bullet.
They were haunted, too, haunted by this fear, by every victim calling
from the grave that nothing was so inevitable as death, which lurked
behind every corner, hid in every shadow, lay deep in the dark tube of
every gun. These men could not have a friend; they could not love or

❖ 10 ❖

A HUNDRED MILES from the haunts most familiar with Duane's
deeds, far up where the Nueces ran a trickling clear stream between yellow cliffs, stood a small deserted shack of covered mesquite
poles. It had been made long ago, but was well preserved. A door faced
the overgrown trail, and another faced down into a gorge of dense thickets. On the border fugitives from law and men who hid in fear of someone
they had wronged never lived in houses with only one door.

It was a wild spot, lonely, not fit for human habitation except for the
outcast. He, perhaps, might have found it hard to leave for most of the
other wild nooks in that barren country. Down in the gorge there was
never-failing sweet water, grass all the year round, cool, shady retreats,
deer, rabbits, turkeys, fruit, and miles and miles of narrow-twisting, deep
canyon full of broken rocks and impenetrable thickets. The scream of the
panther was heard there, the squall of the wildcat, the cough of the
jaguar. Innumerable bees buzzed in the spring blossoms, and, it seemed,
scattered honey to the winds. All day there was continuous song of birds,
that of the mockingbird loud and sweet and mocking above the rest.

On clear days—and rare indeed were cloudy days—with the subsiding
of the wind at sunset a hush seemed to fall around the little hut. Far-
distant dim-blue mountains stood gold-rimmed, gradually to fade with the
shading of light.

At this quiet hour a man climbed up out of the gorge and sat in the
westward door of the hut. This lonely watcher of the west and listener to
the silence was Duane. And this hut was the one where, three years
before, Jennie had nursed him back to life.

The killing of a man named Sellers, and the combination of circumstances that had made the tragedy a memorable regret, had marked, if not
a change, at least a cessation in Duane's activities. He had trailed Sellers
to kill him for the supposed abducting of Jennie. He had trailed him long
after he had learned Sellers traveled alone. Duane wanted absolute assurance of Jennie's death. Vague rumors, a few words here and there, unauthenticated stories, were all Duane had gathered in years to substantiate
his belief—that Jennie died shortly after the beginning of her second
captivity. But Duane did not know surely. Sellers might have told him.
Duane expected, if not to force it from him at the end, to read it in his
eyes. But the bullet went too unerringly; it locked his lips and fixed
his eyes.

After that meeting Duane lay long at the ranch-house of a friend, and when he recovered from the wound Sellers had given him he started with two horses and a pack for the lonely gorge on the Nueces. There he had been hidden for months, a prey to remorse, a dreamer, a victim of phantoms.

It took work for him to find subsistence in that rocky fastness. And work, action, helped to pass the hours. But he could not work all the time, even if he had found it to do. Then in his idle moments and at night his task was to live with the hell in his mind.

The sunset and the twilight hour made all the rest bearable. The little hut on the rim of the gorge seemed to hold Jennie's presence. It was not as if he felt her spirit. If it had been he would have been sure of her death. He hoped Jennie had not survived her second misfortune; and that intense hope had burned into belief, if not surety. Upon his return to that locality, on the occasion of his first visit to the hut, he had found things just as they had left them, and a poor, faded piece of ribbon Jennie had used to tie around her bright hair. No wandering outlaw or traveler had happened upon the lonely spot, which further endeared it to Duane.

A strange feature of this memory of Jennie was the freshness of it—the failure of years, toil, strife, death-dealing to dim it—to deaden the thought of what might have been. He had a marvelous gift of visualization. He could shut his eyes and see Jennie before him just as clearly as if she had stood there in the flesh. For hours he did that, dreaming, dreaming of life he had never tasted and now never would taste. He saw Jennie's slender, graceful figure, the old brown ragged dress in which he had seen her first at Bland's, her little feet in Mexican sandals, her fine hands coarsened by work, her round arms and swelling throat, and her pale, sad, beautiful face with its staring dark eyes. He remembered every look she had given him, every word she had spoken to him, every time she had touched him. He thought of her beauty and sweetness, of the few things which had come to mean to him that she must have loved him; and he trained himself to think of these in preference to her life at Bland's, the escape with him, and then her recapture, because such memories led to bitter, fruitless pain. He had to fight suffering because it was eating out his heart.

Sitting there, eyes wide open, he dreamed of the old homestead and his white-haired mother. He saw the old home life, sweetened and filled by dear new faces and added joys, go on before his eyes with him a part of it.

Then in the inevitable reaction, in the reflux of bitter reality, he would send out a voiceless cry no less poignant because it was silent: "Poor fool! No, I shall never see Mother again—never go home—never have a home. I am Duane, the Lone Wolf! Oh, God! I wish it were over! These dreams torture me! What have I to do with a mother, a home, a wife? No bright-haired boy, no dark-eyed girl will ever love me. I am an outlaw, an outcast, dead to the good and decent world. I am alone—alone. Better be a callous brute or better dead! I shall go mad thinking! Man, what is left

to you? A hiding-place like a wol____ with phantoms! Or the trail an___ then the hard ride, the sleer____ brakes. What hellish thing____ Only that damned unqu____ on to miserable life—to ha____ to die as gunfighters seldom d____ you're long avenged. I'd change w____ you're avenged. And you others—yo____ and give me peace!"

But they did not lie quiet in their grav____

A group of specters trooped out of the sha____ round him, escorted him to his bed.

When Duane had been riding the trails passion____ ers, or passion-bent in his search, the constant actio____ haustion made him sleep. But when in hiding, as time ____ he required less rest and sleep, and his mind became more a____ little his phantoms gained hold on him, and at length, but fo____ power of his dreams, they would have claimed him utterly.

How many times he had said to himself: "I am an intelligent n____ not crazy. I'm in full possession of my faculties. All this is fancy—____ nation—conscience. I've no work, no duty, no ideal, no hope . . . ____ my mind is obsessed, thronged with images. And these images natura____ are of the men with whom I have dealt. I can't forget them. They come back to me, hour after hour; and when my tortured mind grows weak, then maybe I'm not just right till the mood wears out and lets me sleep."

So he reasoned as he lay down in his comfortable camp. The night was star-bright above the canyon-walls, darkly shadowing down between them. The insects hummed and chirped and thrummed a continuous thick song, low and monotonous. Slow-running water splashed softly over stones in the stream-bed. From far down the canyon came the mournful hoot of an owl. The moment he lay down, thereby giving up action for the day, all these things weighed upon him like a great heavy mantle of loneliness. In truth, they did not constitute loneliness.

And he could no more have dispelled thought than he could have reached out to touch a cold, bright star.

He wondered how many outcasts like him lay under this star-studded, velvety sky across the fifteen hundred miles of wild country between El Paso and the mouth of the river. A vast wild territory—a refuge for outlaws! Somewhere he had heard or read that the Texas Rangers kept a book with names and records of outlaws—three thousand known outlaws! Yet these could scarcely be half of that unfortunate horde which had been recruited from all over the states. Duane had traveled from camp to camp, den to den, hiding-place to hiding-place, and he knew these men. Most of them were hopeless criminals; some were avengers; a few were wronged

☙10❧

A HUNDRED MILES from the haunts most familiar with Duane's deeds, far up where the Nueces ran a trickling clear stream between yellow cliffs, stood a small deserted shack of covered mesquite poles. It had been made long ago, but was well preserved. A door faced the overgrown trail, and another faced down into a gorge of dense thickets. On the border fugitives from law and men who hid in fear of someone they had wronged never lived in houses with only one door.

It was a wild spot, lonely, not fit for human habitation except for the outcast. He, perhaps, might have found it hard to leave for most of the other wild nooks in that barren country. Down in the gorge there was never-failing sweet water, grass all the year round, cool, shady retreats, deer, rabbits, turkeys, fruit, and miles and miles of narrow-twisting, deep canyon full of broken rocks and impenetrable thickets. The scream of the panther was heard there, the squall of the wildcat, the cough of the jaguar. Innumerable bees buzzed in the spring blossoms, and, it seemed, scattered honey to the winds. All day there was continuous song of birds, that of the mockingbird loud and sweet and mocking above the rest.

On clear days—and rare indeed were cloudy days—with the subsiding of the wind at sunset a hush seemed to fall around the little hut. Far-distant dim-blue mountains stood gold-rimmed, gradually to fade with the shading of light.

At this quiet hour a man climbed up out of the gorge and sat in the westward door of the hut. This lonely watcher of the west and listener to the silence was Duane. And this hut was the one where, three years before, Jennie had nursed him back to life.

The killing of a man named Sellers, and the combination of circumstances that had made the tragedy a memorable regret, had marked, if not a change, at least a cessation in Duane's activities. He had trailed Sellers to kill him for the supposed abducting of Jennie. He had trailed him long after he had learned Sellers traveled alone. Duane wanted absolute assurance of Jennie's death. Vague rumors, a few words here and there, unauthenticated stories, were all Duane had gathered in years to substantiate his belief—that Jennie died shortly after the beginning of her second captivity. But Duane did not know surely. Sellers might have told him. Duane expected, if not to force it from him at the end, to read it in his eyes. But the bullet went too unerringly; it locked his lips and fixed his eyes.

After that meeting Duane lay long at the ranch-house of a friend, and when he recovered from the wound Sellers had given him he started with two horses and a pack for the lonely gorge on the Nueces. There he had been hidden for months, a prey to remorse, a dreamer, a victim of phantoms.

It took work for him to find subsistence in that rocky fastness. And work, action, helped to pass the hours. But he could not work all the time, even if he had found it to do. Then in his idle moments and at night his task was to live with the hell in his mind.

The sunset and the twilight hour made all the rest bearable. The little hut on the rim of the gorge seemed to hold Jennie's presence. It was not as if he felt her spirit. If it had been he would have been sure of her death. He hoped Jennie had not survived her second misfortune; and that intense hope had burned into belief, if not surety. Upon his return to that locality, on the occasion of his first visit to the hut, he had found things just as they had left them, and a poor, faded piece of ribbon Jennie had used to tie around her bright hair. No wandering outlaw or traveler had happened upon the lonely spot, which further endeared it to Duane.

A strange feature of this memory of Jennie was the freshness of it—the failure of years, toil, strife, death-dealing to dim it—to deaden the thought of what might have been. He had a marvelous gift of visualization. He could shut his eyes and see Jennie before him just as clearly as if she had stood there in the flesh. For hours he did that, dreaming, dreaming of life he had never tasted and now never would taste. He saw Jennie's slender, graceful figure, the old brown ragged dress in which he had seen her first at Bland's, her little feet in Mexican sandals, her fine hands coarsened by work, her round arms and swelling throat, and her pale, sad, beautiful face with its staring dark eyes. He remembered every look she had given him, every word she had spoken to him, every time she had touched him. He thought of her beauty and sweetness, of the few things which had come to mean to him that she must have loved him; and he trained himself to think of these in preference to her life at Bland's, the escape with him, and then her recapture, because such memories led to bitter, fruitless pain. He had to fight suffering because it was eating out his heart.

Sitting there, eyes wide open, he dreamed of the old homestead and his white-haired mother. He saw the old home life, sweetened and filled by dear new faces and added joys, go on before his eyes with him a part of it.

Then in the inevitable reaction, in the reflux of bitter reality, he would send out a voiceless cry no less poignant because it was silent: "Poor fool! No, I shall never see Mother again—never go home—never have a home. I am Duane, the Lone Wolf! Oh, God! I wish it were over! These dreams torture me! What have I to do with a mother, a home, a wife? No bright-haired boy, no dark-eyed girl will ever love me. I am an outlaw, an outcast, dead to the good and decent world. I am alone—alone. Better be a callous brute or better dead! I shall go mad thinking! Man, what is left to you? A hiding-place like a wolf's—lonely, silent days, lonely nights with phantoms! Or the trail and the road with their bloody tracks, and then the hard ride, the sleepless, hungry ride to some hole in rocks or brakes. What hellish thing drives me? Why can't I end it all? What is left? Only that damned unquenchable spirit of the gunfighter to live—to hang on to miserable life—to have no fear of death, yet to cling like a leach— to die as gunfighters seldom die, with boots off! Bain, you were first, and you're long avenged. I'd change with you. And Sellers, you were last, and you're avenged. And you others—you're avenged. Lie quiet in your graves and give me peace!"

But they did not lie quiet in their graves and give him peace.

A group of specters trooped out of the shadows of dusk and, gathering round him, escorted him to his bed.

When Duane had been riding the trails passion-bent to escape pursuers, or passion-bent in his search, the constant action and toil and exhaustion made him sleep. But when in hiding, as time passed, gradually he required less rest and sleep, and his mind became more active. Little by little his phantoms gained hold on him, and at length, but for the saving power of his dreams, they would have claimed him utterly.

How many times he had said to himself: "I am an intelligent man. I'm not crazy. I'm in full possession of my faculties. All this is fancy—imagination—conscience. I've no work, no duty, no ideal, no hope . . . and my mind is obsessed, thronged with images. And these images naturally are of the men with whom I have dealt. I can't forget them. They come back to me, hour after hour; and when my tortured mind grows weak, then maybe I'm not just right till the mood wears out and lets me sleep."

So he reasoned as he lay down in his comfortable camp. The night was star-bright above the canyon-walls, darkly shadowing down between them. The insects hummed and chirped and thrummed a continuous thick song, low and monotonous. Slow-running water splashed softly over stones in the stream-bed. From far down the canyon came the mournful hoot of an owl. The moment he lay down, thereby giving up action for the day, all these things weighed upon him like a great heavy mantle of loneliness. In truth, they did not constitute loneliness.

And he could no more have dispelled thought than he could have reached out to touch a cold, bright star.

He wondered how many outcasts like him lay under this star-studded, velvety sky across the fifteen hundred miles of wild country between El Paso and the mouth of the river. A vast wild territory—a refuge for outlaws! Somewhere he had heard or read that the Texas Rangers kept a book with names and records of outlaws—three thousand known outlaws! Yet these could scarcely be half of that unfortunate horde which had been recruited from all over the states. Duane had traveled from camp to camp, den to den, hiding-place to hiding-place, and he knew these men. Most of them were hopeless criminals; some were avengers; a few were wronged wanderers; and among them occasionally was a man, human in his way, honest as he could be, not yet lost to good.

But all of them were akin in one sense—their outlawry; and that starry night they lay with their dark faces up, some in packs like wolves, others alone like the gray wolf who knew no mate. It did not make much difference in Duane's thought of them that the majority were steeped in crime and brutality, more often than not stupid from rum, incapable of a fine feeling, just lost wild dogs.

Duane doubted that there was a man among them who did not realize his moral wreck and ruin. He had met poor, half-witted wretches who knew it. He believed he could enter into their minds and feel the truth of all their lives—the hardened outlaw, coarse, ignorant, bestial, who murdered as Bill Black had murdered, who stole for the sake of stealing, who craved money to gamble and drink, defiantly ready for death, like that terrible outlaw Helm, who cried out on the scaffold, "Let her rip!"

The wild youngsters seeking notoriety and reckless adventure; the cowboys with a notch on their guns, with boastful pride in the knowledge that they were marked by rangers; the crooked men from the North, defaulters, forgers, murderers, all pale-faced, flat-chested men not fit for that wilderness and not surviving; the dishonest cattlemen, hand and glove with outlaws, driven from their homes; the old grizzled, bow-legged genuine rustlers—all these Duane had come in contact with, had watched and known, and as he felt with them he seemed to see that as their lives were bad, sooner or later to end dismally or tragically, so they must pay some kind of earthly penalty—if not of conscience, then of fear; if not of fear, then of that most terrible of all things to restless, active men—pain, the pang of flesh and bone.

Duane knew, for he had seen them pay. Best of all, moreover, he knew the internal life of the gunfighter of that select but by no means small class of which he was representative. The world that judged him and his kind judged him as a machine, a killing-machine, with only mind enough to hunt, to meet, to slay another man. It had taken three endless years for Duane to understand his own father. Duane knew beyond all doubt that the gunfighters like Bland, like Alloway, like Sellers, men who were evil and had no remorse, no spiritual accusing Nemesis, had something far more torturing to mind, more haunting, more murderous of rest and sleep and peace; and that something was abnormal fear of death. Duane knew this, for he had shot these men; he had seen the quick, dark shadow in eyes, the presentiment that the will could not control, and then the horrible certainty. These men must have been in agony at every meeting with a possible or certain foe—more agony than the hot rend of a bullet. They were haunted, too, haunted by this fear, by every victim calling from the grave that nothing was so inevitable as death, which lurked behind every corner, hid in every shadow, lay deep in the dark tube of every gun. These men could not have a friend; they could not love or trust a woman. They knew their one chance of holding on to life lay in their own distrust, watchfulness, dexterity, and that hope, by the very nature of their lives, could not be lasting. They had doomed themselves. What, then, could possibly have dwelt in the depths of their minds as they went to their beds on a starry night like this, with mystery in silence and shadow, with time passing surely, and the dark future and its secret approaching every hour—what, then, but hell?

The hell in Duane's mind was not fear of man or fear of death. He would have been glad to lay down the burden of life, providing death came naturally. Many times he had prayed for it. But that over-developed, superhuman spirit of defense in him precluded suicide or the inviting of an enemy's bullet. Sometimes he had a vague, scarcely analyzed idea that this spirit was what had made the Southwest habitable for the white man.

Every one of his victims, singly and collectively, returned to him forever, it seemed, in cold, passionless, accusing domination of these haunted hours. They did not accuse him of dishonor or cowardice or brutality or murder; they only accused him of death. It was as if they knew more than when they were alive, had learned that life was a divine mysterious gift not to be taken. They thronged about him with their voiceless clamoring, drifted around him with their fading eyes.

⊰11⊱

AFTER NEARLY six months in the Nueces gorge the loneliness and inaction of his life drove Duane out upon the trails seeking anything rather than to hide longer alone, a prey to the scourge of his thoughts. The moment he rode into sight of men a remarkable transformation occurred in him. A strange warmth stirred in him—a longing to see the faces of people, to hear their voices—a pleasurable emotion sad and strange. But it was only a precursor of his old bitter, sleepless, and eternal vigilance. When he hid alone in the brakes he was safe from all except his deeper, better self; when he escaped from this into the haunts of men his force and will went to the preservation of his life.

Mercer was the first village he rode into. He had many friends there. Mercer claimed to owe Duane a debt. On the outskirts of the village there was a grave overgrown by brush so that the rude-lettered post which marked it was scarcely visible to Duane as he rode by. He had never read the inscription. But he thought now of Hardin, no other than the erst-while ally of Bland. For many years Hardin had harassed the stockmen and ranchers in and around Mercer. On an evil day for him he or his outlaws had beaten and robbed a man who once succored Duane when sore in need. Duane met Hardin in the little plaza of the village, called him every name known to border men, taunted him to draw, and killed him in the act.

Duane went to the house of one Jones, a Texan who had known his father, and there he was warmly received. The feel of an honest hand, the voice of a friend, the prattle of children who were not afraid of him or his gun, good wholesome food, and change of clothes—these things for the time being made a changed man of Duane. To be sure, he did not often speak. The price of his head and the weight of his burden made him silent. But eagerly he drank in all the news that was told him. In the years of his absence from home he had never heard a word about his mother or uncle. Those who were his real friends on the border would have been the last to make inquiries, to write or receive letters that might give a clue to Duane's whereabouts.

Duane remained all day with this hospitable Jones, and as twilight fell was loath to go and yielded to a pressing invitation to remain overnight. It was seldom indeed that Duane slept under a roof. Early in the evening, while Duane sat on the porch with two awed and hero-worshiping sons of the house, Jones returned from a quick visit down to the post office. Summarily he sent the boys off. He labored under intense excitement.

"Duane, there's rangers in town," he whispered. "It's all over town, too, that you're here. You rode in long after sunup. Lots of people saw you. I don't believe there's a man or boy that'd squeal on you. But the women might. They gossip, and these rangers are handsome fellows—devils with the women."

"What company of rangers?" asked Duane, quietly.

"Company A, under Captain MacNelly, that new ranger. He made a big name in the war. And since he's been in the ranger service he's done wonders. He's cleaned up some bad places south, and he's working north."

"MacNelly. I've heard of him. Describe him to me."

"Slight-built chap, but wiry and tough. Clean face, black mustache and hair. Sharp black eyes. He's got a look of authority. MacNelly's a fine man, Duane. Belongs to a good Southern family. I'd hate to have him look you up."

Duane did not speak.

"MacNelly's got nerve, and his rangers are all experienced men. If they find out you're here they'll come after you. MacNelly's no gunfighter, but he wouldn't hesitate to do his duty, even if he faced sure death. Which he would in this case. Duane, you mustn't meet Captain MacNelly. Your record is clean, if it is terrible. You never met a ranger or any officer except a rotten sheriff now and then, like Rod Brown."

Still Duane kept silence. He was not thinking of danger, but of the fact of how fleeting must be his stay among friends.

"I've already fixed up a pack of grub," went on Jones. "I'll slip out to saddle your horse. You watch here."

He had scarcely uttered the last words when soft, swift footsteps sounded on the hard path. A man turned in at the gate. The light was dim, yet clean enough to disclose an unusually tall figure. When it appeared nearer he was seen to be walking with both arms raised, hands high. He slowed his stride.

"Does Burt Jones live here?" he asked, in a low, hurried voice.

"I reckon. I'm Burt. What can I do for you?" replied Jones.

The stranger peered around, stealthily came closer, still with his hands up.

"It is known that Buck Duane is here. Captain MacNelly's camping on the river just out of town. He sends word to Duane to come out there after dark."

The stranger wheeled and departed as swiftly and strangely as he had come.

"Bust me! Duane, whatever do you make of that?" exclaimed Jones.

"A new one on me," replied Duane, thoughtfully.

"First fool thing I ever heard of MacNelly doing. Can't make head nor tails of it. I'd have said offhand that MacNelly wouldn't double-cross anybody. He struck me as a square man, sand all through. But, hell! he must mean treachery. I can't see anything else in that deal."

"Maybe the captain wants to give me a fair chance to surrender without bloodshed," observed Duane. "Pretty decent of him, if he meant that."

"He *invites* you out to his camp *after dark*. Something strange about this, Duane. But MacNelly's a new man out here. He does some queer things. Perhaps he's getting a swelled head. Well, whatever his intentions, his presence around Mercer is enough for us. Duane, you hit the road and put some miles between you and the amiable captain before daylight. Tomorrow I'll go out there and ask him what in the devil he meant."

"That messenger he sent—he was a ranger," said Duane.

"Sure he was, and a nervy one! It must have taken sand to come bracing you that way. Duane, the fellow didn't pack a gun. I'll swear to that. Pretty odd, this trick. But you can't trust it. Hit the road, Duane."

A little later a black horse with muffled hoofs, bearing a tall, dark rider who peered keenly into every shadow, trotted down a pasture lane back of Jones's house, turned into the road, and then, breaking into swifter gait, rapidly left Mercer behind.

Fifteen or twenty miles out Duane drew rein in a forest of mesquite, dismounted, and searched about for a glade with a little grass. Here he staked his horse on a long lariat; and, using his saddle for a pillow, his saddle-blanket for covering, he went to sleep.

Next morning he was off again, working south. During the next few days he paid brief visits to several villages that lay in his path. And in each some one particular friend had a piece of news to impart that made Duane profoundly thoughtful. A ranger had made a quiet, unobtrusive call upon these friends and left this message, "Tell Buck Duane to ride into Captain MacNelly's camp sometime after night."

Duane concluded, and his friends all agreed with him, that the new ranger's main purpose in the Nueces country was to capture or kill Buck Duane, and that this message was simply an original and striking ruse, the daring of which might appeal to certain outlaws.

But it did not appeal to Duane. His curiosity was aroused; it did not, however, tempt him to any foolhardy act. He turned southwest and rode a hundred miles until he again reached the sparsely settled country. Here he heard no more of rangers. It was a barren region he had never but once ridden through, and that ride had cost him dear. He had been compelled to shoot his way out. Outlaws were not in accord with the few ranchers and their cowboys who ranged there. He learned that both outlaws and Mexican raiders had long been at bitter enmity with these ranchers. Being unfamiliar with roads and trails, Duane had pushed on into the heart of this district, when all the time he really believed he was traveling around it. A rifle shot from a ranch-house, a deliberate attempt to kill him because he was an unknown rider in those parts, discovered to Duane his mistake; and a hard ride to get away persuaded him to return to his old methods of hiding by day and traveling by night.

He got into rough country, rode for three days without covering much ground, but believed that he was getting on safer territory. Twice he came to a wide bottom-land green with willow and cottonwood and thick as chaparral, somewhere through the middle of which ran a river he decided must be the lower Nueces.

One evening, as he stole out from a covert where he had camped, he saw the lights of a village. He tried to pass it on the left, but was unable to because the brakes of this bottom-land extended in almost to the outskirts of the village, and he had to retrace his steps and go round to the right. Wire fences and horses in pasture made this a task, so it was well after midnight before he accomplished it. He made ten miles or more then by daylight, and after that proceeded cautiously along a road which appeared to be well worn from travel. He passed several thickets where he would have halted to hide during the day but for the fact that he had to find water.

He was a long while in coming to it, and then there was no thicket or clump of mesquite near the waterhole that would afford him covert. So he kept on.

The country before him was ridgy and began to show cottonwoods here and there in the hollows and yucca and mesquite on the higher ground. As he mounted a ridge he noted that the road made a sharp turn, and he could not see what was beyond it. He slowed up and was making the turn, which was downhill between high banks of yellow clay, when his mettlesome horse heard something to frighten him or shied at something and bolted.

The few bounds he took before Duane's iron arm checked him were enough to reach the curve. One flashing glance showed Duane the open once more, a little valley below with a wide, shallow, rocky stream, a clump of cottonwoods beyond, a somber group of men facing him, and two dark, limp, strangely grotesque figures hanging from branches.

The sight was common enough in southwest Texas, but Duane had never before found himself so unpleasantly close.

A hoarse voice pealed out: "By hell! There's another one!"

"Stranger, ride down an' account fer yourself!" yelled another.

"Hands up!"

"Thet's right, Jack; don't take no chances. Plug him!"

These remarks were so swiftly uttered as almost to be continuous. Duane was wheeling his horse when a rifle cracked. The bullet struck his left forearm and, he thought, broke it, for he dropped the rein. The frightened horse leaped. Another bullet whistled past Duane. Then the bend in the road saved him probably from certain death. Like the wind his fleet steed went down the long hill.

Duane was in no hurry to look back. He knew what to expect. His chief concern of the moment was for his injured arm. He found that the bones were still intact; but the wound, having been made by a soft bullet, was an exceedingly bad one. Blood poured from it. Giving the horse his head, Duane wound his scarf tightly round the holes, and with teeth and hand tied it tightly. That done, he looked back over his shoulder.

Riders were making the dust fly on the hillside road. There were more coming round the cut where the road curved. The leader was perhaps a quarter of a mile back, and the others strung out behind him. Duane needed only one glance to tell him that they were fast and hard-riding cowboys in a land where all riders were good. They would not have owned any but strong, swift horses. Moreover, it was a district where ranchers had suffered beyond all endurance the greed and brutality of outlaws. Duane had simply been so unfortunate as to run right into a lynching party at a time of all times when any stranger would be in danger and any outlaw put to his limit to escape with his life.

Duane did not look back again till he had crossed the ridgy piece of ground and had gotten to the level road. He had gained upon his pursuers. When he ascertained this he tried to save his horse, to check a little that killing gait. This horse was a magnificent animal, big, strong, fast; but his endurance had never been put to a grueling test. And that worried Duane. His life had made it impossible to keep one horse very long at a time, and this one was an unknown quantity.

Duane had only one plan—the only plan possible in this case—and that was to make the river-bottoms, where he might elude his pursuers in the willow brakes. Fifteen miles or so would bring him to the river, and this was not a hopeless distance for any good horse if not too closely pressed. Duane concluded presently that the cowboys behind were losing a little in the chase because they were not extending their horses. It was decidedly unusual for such riders to save their mounts. Duane pondered over this, looking backward several times to see if their horses were stretched out. They were not, and the fact was disturbing. Only one reason presented itself to Duane's conjecturing, and it was that with him headed straight on that road his pursuers were satisfied not to force the running. He began to hope and look for a trail or a road turning off to right or left. There was none. A rough, mesquite-dotted and yucca-spired country extended away on either side. Duane believed that he would be compelled to take to this hard going. One thing was certain—he had to go round the village. The river, however, was on the outskirts of the village; and once in the willows, he would be safe.

Dust-clouds far ahead caused his alarm to grow. He watched with his eyes strained; he hoped to see a wagon, a few stray cattle. But no, he soon descried several horsemen. Shots and yells behind him attested to the fact that his pursuers likewise had seen these newcomers on the scene. More than a mile separated these two parties, yet that distance did not keep them from soon understanding each other. Duane waited only to see this new factor show signs of sudden quick action, and then, with a muttered curse, he spurred his horse off the road into the brush.

He chose the right side, because the river lay nearer that way. There were patches of open sandy ground between clumps of cactus and mesquite, and he found that despite a zigzag course he made better time. It was impossible for him to locate his pursuers. They would come together, he decided, and take to his tracks.

What, then, was his surprise and dismay to run out of a thicket right into a low ridge of rough, broken rock, impossible to get a horse over. He wheeled to the left along its base. The sandy ground gave place to a harder soil, where his horse did not labor so. Here the growths of mesquite and cactus became scanter, affording better travel but poor cover. He kept sharp eyes ahead, and, as he had expected, soon saw moving dust-clouds and the dark figures of horses. They were half a mile away, and swinging obliquely across the flat, which fact proved that they had entertained a fair idea of the country and the fugitive's difficulty.

Without an instant's hesitation Duane put his horse to his best efforts, straight ahead. He had to pass those men. When this was seemingly made impossible by a deep wash from which he had to turn, Duane began to feel cold and sick. Was this the end? Always there had to be an end to an outlaw's career. He wanted then to ride straight at these pursuers. But reason outweighed instinct. He was fleeing for his life; nevertheless, the strongest instinct at the time was his desire to fight.

He knew when these three horsemen saw him, and a moment afterward he lost sight of them as he got into the mesquite again. He meant now to try to reach the road, and pushed his mount severely, though still saving him for a final burst. Rocks, thickets, bunches of cactus, washes—all operated against his following a straight line. Almost he lost his bearings, and finally would have ridden toward his enemies had not good fortune favored him in the matter of an open burned-over stretch of ground.

Here he saw both groups of pursuers, one on each side and almost within gunshot. Their sharp yells, as much as his cruel spurs, drove his horse into that pace which now meant life or death for him. And never had Duane bestrode a gamer, swifter, stancher beast. He seemed about to accomplish the impossible. In the dragging sand he was far superior to any horse in pursuit, and on this sandy open stretch he gained enough to spare a little in the brush beyond. Heated now and thoroughly terrorized, he kept the pace through thickets that almost tore Duane from his saddle. Something weighty and grim eased off Duane. He was going to get out in front! The horse had speed, fire, stamina.

Duane dashed out into another open place dotted by few trees, and here, right in his path, within pistol-range, stood horsemen waiting. They yelled, they spurred toward him, but did not fire at him. He turned his horse—faced to the right. Only one thing kept him from standing his ground to fight it out. He remembered those dangling limp figures hanging from the cottonwoods. These ranchers would rather hang an outlaw than do anything. They might draw all his fire and then capture him. His horror of hanging was so great as to be all out of proportion compared to his gunfighter's instinct of self-preservation.

A race began then, a dusty, crashing drive through gray mesquite. Duane could scarcely see, he was so blinded by stinging branches across his eyes. The hollow wind roared in his ears. He lost his sense of the nearness of his pursuers. But they must have been close. Did they shoot at him? He imagined he heard shots. But that might have been the cracking of dead snags. His left arm hung limp, almost useless; he handled the rein with his right; and most of the time he hung low over the pommel. The gray walls flashing by him, the whip of twigs, the rush of wind, the heavy, rapid pound of hoofs, the violent motion of his horse—these vied in sensation with the smart of sweat in his eyes, the rack of his wound the cold, sick cramp in his stomach. With these also was dull, raging fury. He had to run when he wanted to fight. It took all his mind to force back that bitter hate of himself, of his pursuers, of this race for his useless life.

Suddenly he burst out of a line of mesquite into the road—a long stretch of lonely road! How fiercely, with hot, strange joy, he wheeled his horse upon it! Then he was sweeping along, sure now that he was out in front. His horse still had strength and speed, but showed signs of breaking. Presently Duane looked back. Pursuers—he could not count how many—

were loping along in his rear. He paid no more attention to them, and with teeth set he faced ahead, grimmer now in his determination to foil them.

He passed a few scattered ranch-houses where horses whistled from corrals, and men curiously watched him fly past. He saw one rancher running, and he felt intuitively that this fellow was going to join in the chase. Duane's steed pounded on, not noticeably slower, but with a lack of former smoothness, with a strained, convulsive, jerking stride which showed he was almost done.

Sight of the village ahead surprised Duane. He had reached it sooner than he expected. Then he made a discovery—he had entered the zone of wire fences. As he dared not turn back now, he kept on, intending to ride through the village. Looking backward, he saw that his pursuers were half a mile distant, too far to alarm any villagers in time to intercept him in his flight. As he rode by the first houses his horse broke and began to labor. Duane did not believe he would last long enough to go through the village.

Saddled horses in front of a store gave Duane an idea, not by any means new, and one he had carried out successfully before. As he pulled in his heaving mount and leaped off, a couple of ranchers came out of the place, and one of them stepped to a clean-limbed, fiery bay. He was about to get into his saddle when he saw Duane, and then he halted, a foot in the stirrup.

Duane strode forward, grasped the bridle of this man's horse.

"Mine's done—but not killed," he panted. "Trade with me."

"Wal, stranger, I'm shore always ready to trade," drawled the man. "But ain't you a little swift?"

Duane glanced back up the road. His pursuers were entering the village.

"I'm Duane—Buck Duane," he cried, menacingly. "Will you trade? Hurry!"

The rancher, turning white, dropped his foot from the stirrup and fell back.

"I reckon I'll trade," he said.

Bounding up, Duane dug spurs into the bay's flanks. The horse snorted in fright, plunged into a run. He was fresh, swift, half wild. Duane flashed by the remaining houses on the street out into the open. But the road ended at that village or else led out from some other quarter, for he had ridden straight into the fields and from them into rough desert. When he reached the cover of mesquite once more he looked back to find six horsemen within rifle-shot of him, and more coming behind them.

His new horse had not had time to get warm before Duane reached a high sandy bluff below which lay the willow brakes. As far as he could see extended an immense flat strip of red-tinged willow. How welcome it was to his eye! He felt like a hunted wolf that, weary and lame, had reached his hole in the rocks. Zigzagging down the soft slope, he put the bay to the dense wall of leaf and branch. But the horse balked.

There was little time to lose. Dismounting, he dragged the stubborn beast into the thicket. This was harder and slower work than Duane cared to risk. If he had not been rushed he might have had better success. So he had to abandon the horse—a circumstance that only such sore straits could have driven him to. Then he went slipping swiftly through the narrow aisles.

He had not gotten under cover any too soon. For he heard his pursuers piling over the bluff, loud-voiced, confident, brutal. They crashed into the willows.

"Hi, Sid! Heah's your hoss!" called one, evidently to the man Duane had forced into a trade.

"Say, if you locoed gents'll hold up a little I'll tell you somethin'," replied a voice from the bluff.

"Come on, Sid! We got him corralled," said the first speaker.

"Wal, mebbe, an' if you hev it's liable to be damn hot. *Thet feller was Buck Duane!*"

Absolute silence followed that statement. Presently it was broken by a rattling of loose gravel and then low voices.

"He can't git acrost the river, I tell you," came to Duane's ears. "He's corralled in the brake. I know thet hole."

Then Duane, gliding silently and swiftly through the willows, heard no more from his pursuers. He headed straight for the river. Threading a passage through a willow brake was an old task for him. Many days and nights had gone to the acquiring of a skill that might have been envied by an Indian.

The Rio Grande and its tributaries for the most of their length in Texas ran between wide, low, flat lands covered by a dense growth of willow. Cottonwood, mesquite, prickly pear, and other growths mingled with the willow, and altogether they made a matted, tangled copse, a thicket that an inexperienced man would have considered impenetrable. From above, these wild brakes looked green and red; from the inside they were gray and yellow—a striped wall. Trails and glades were scarce. There were a few deer-runways and sometimes little paths made by peccaries—the *jabali*, or wild pigs, of Mexico. The ground was clay and unusually dry, sometimes baked so hard that it left no imprint of a track. Where a growth of cottonwood had held back the encroachment of the willows there usually was thick grass and underbrush. The willows were short, slender poles with stems so close together that they almost touched, and with the leafy foliage forming a thick covering.

The depths of this brake Duane had penetrated was a silent, dreamy, strange place. In the middle of the day the light was weird and dim. When a breeze fluttered the foliage, then slender shafts and spears of sunshine pierced the green mantle and danced like gold on the ground.

Duane had always felt the strangeness of this kind of place, and likewise he had felt a protecting, harboring something which always seemed to him to be the sympathy of the brake for a hunted creature. Any unwounded creature, strong and resourceful, was safe when he had glided under the low, rustling green roof of this wild covert. It was not hard to conceal tracks; the springy soil gave forth no sound; and men could hunt each other for weeks, pass within a few yards of each other and never know it. The problem of sustaining life was difficult; but, then, hunted men and animals survived on very little.

Duane wanted to cross the river if that was possible, and, keeping in the brake, work his way upstream till he had reached country more hospitable. Remembering what the man had said in regard to the river, Duane had his doubts about crossing. But he would take any chance to put the river between him and his hunters. He pushed on. His left arm had to be favored, as he could scarcely move it. Using his right to spread the willows, he slipped sideways between them and made fast time. There were narrow aisles and washes and holes low down and paths brushed by animals, all of which he took advantage of, running, walking, crawling, stooping any way to get along. To keep in a straight line was not easy—he did it by marking some bright sunlit stem or tree ahead, and when he reached it looked straight on to mark another. His progress necessarily grew slower, for as he advanced the brake became wilder, denser, darker. Mosquitoes began to whine about his head. He kept on without pause. Deepening shadows under the willows told him that the afternoon was far advanced. He began to fear he had wandered in a wrong direction. Finally a strip of light ahead relieved his anxiety, and after a toilsome penetration of still denser brush he broke through to the bank of the river.

He faced a wide, shallow, muddy stream with brakes on the opposite bank extending like a green and yellow wall. Duane perceived at a glance the futility of his trying to cross at this point. Everywhere the sluggish water laved quicksand bars. In fact, the bed of the river was all quicksand, and very likely there was not a foot of water anywhere. He could not swim; he could not crawl; he could not push a log across. Any solid thing touching that smooth yellow sand would be grasped and sucked down. To prove this he seized a long pole and, reaching down from the high bank, thrust it into the stream. Right there near shore there apparently was no bottom to the treacherous quicksand. He abandoned any hope of crossing the river. Probably for miles up and down it would be just the same as here. Before leaving the bank he tied his hat upon the pole and lifted enough water to quench his thirst. Then he worked his way back to where thinner growth made advancement easier, and kept on upstream till the shadows were so deep he could not see. Feeling around for a place big enough to stretch out on, he lay down. For the time being he was as safe there as he would have been beyond in the Rim Rock. He was tired, though not exhausted, and in spite of the throbbing pain in his arm he dropped at once into sleep.

⚜12⚜

SOMETIME during the night Duane awoke. A stillness seemingly so thick and heavy as to have substance blanketed the black willow brake. He could not see a star or a branch or tree trunk or even his hand before his eyes. He lay there waiting, listening, sure that he had been awakened by an unusual sound. Ordinary noises of the night in the wilderness never disturbed his rest. His faculties, like those of old fugitives and hunted creatures, had become trained to a marvelous keenness. A long low breath of slow wind moaned through the willows, passed away; some stealthy, soft-footed beast trotted by him in the darkness; there was a rustling among dry leaves; a fox barked lonesomely in the distance. But none of these sounds had broken his slumber.

Suddenly, piercing the stillness, came a bay of a bloodhound. Quickly Duane sat up, chilled to his marrow. The action made him aware of his crippled arm. Then came other bays, lower, more distant. Silence enfolded him again, all the more oppressive and menacing in his suspense. Bloodhounds had been put on his trail, and the leader was not far away. All his life Duane had been familiar with bloodhounds; and he knew that if the pack surrounded him in this impenetrable darkness he would be held at bay or dragged down as wolves dragged a stag. Rising to his feet, prepared to flee as best he could, he waited to be sure of the direction he should take.

The leader of the hounds broke into cry again, a deep, full-toned, ringing bay, strange, ominous, terribly significant in its power. It caused a cold sweat to ooze out all over Duane's body. He turned from it, and with his uninjured arm outstretched to feel for the willows he groped his way along. As it was impossible to pick out the narrow passages, he had to slip and squeeze and plunge between the yielding stems. He made such a crashing that he no longer heard the baying of the hounds. He had no hope to elude them. He meant to climb the first cottonwood that he stumbled upon in his blind flight. But it appeared he never was going to be lucky enough to run against one. Often he fell, sometimes flat, at others upheld by the willows. What made the work so hard was the fact that he had only one arm to open a clump of close-growing stems and his feet would catch or tangle in the narrow crotches, holding him fast. He had to struggle desperately. It was as if the willows were clutching hands, his enemies, fiendishly impeding his progress. He tore his clothes on sharp branches and his flesh suffered many a prick. But in a terrible earnestness he kept on until he brought up hard against a cottonwood tree.

There he leaned and rested. He found himself as nearly exhausted as he had ever been, wet with sweat, his hands torn and burning, his breast laboring, his legs stinging from innumerable bruises. While he leaned there to catch his breath he listened for the pursuing hounds. For a long time there was no sound from them. This, however, did not deceive him into any hopefulness. There were bloodhounds that bayed often on a trail, and others that ran mostly silent. The former were more valuable to their owner and the latter more dangerous to the fugitive. Presently Duane's ears were filled by a chorus of short ringing yelps. The pack had found where he had slept, and now the trail was hot. Satisfied that they would soon overtake him, Duane set about climbing the cottonwood, which in his condition was difficult of ascent.

It happened to be a fairly large tree with a fork about fifteen feet up, and branches thereafter in succession. Duane climbed until he got above the enshrouding belt of blackness. A pale gray mist hung above the brake, and through it shone a line of dim lights. Duane decided these were bonfires made along the bluff to render his escape more difficult on that side. Away round in the direction he thought was north he imagined he saw more fires, but, as the mist was thick, he could not be sure. While he sat there pondering the matter, listening for the hounds, the mist and the gloom on one side lightened; and this side he concluded was east and meant that dawn was near. Satisfying himself on this score, he descended to the first branch of the tree.

His situation now, though still critical, did not appear to be so hopeless as it had been. The hounds would soon close in on him, and he would kill them or drive them away. It was beyond the bounds of possibility that any men could have followed running hounds through that brake in the night. The thing that worried Duane was the fact of the bonfires. He had gathered from the words of one of his pursuers that the brake was a kind of trap, and he began to believe there was only one way out of it, and that was along the bank where he had entered, and where obviously all night long his pursuers had kept fires burning. Further conjecture on this point, however, was interrupted by a crashing in the willows and the rapid patter of feet.

Underneath Duane lay a gray, foggy obscurity. He could not see the ground, nor any object but the black trunk of the tree. Sight would not be needed to tell him when the pack arrived. With a pattering rush through the willows the hounds reached the tree; and then high above crash of brush and thud of heavy paws rose a hideous clamor. Duane's pursuers far off to the south would hear that and know what it meant. And at daybreak, perhaps before, they would take a short cut across the brake, guided by the baying of hounds that had treed their quarry.

It wanted only a few moments, however, till Duane could distinguish the vague forms of the hounds in the gray shadow below. Still he waited. He had no shots to spare. And he knew how to treat bloodhounds. Gradually the obscurity lightened, and at length Duane had good enough sight of the hounds for his purpose. His first shot killed the huge brute leader of the pack. Then, with unerring shots, he crippled several others. That stopped the baying. Piercing howls arose. The pack took fright and fled, its course easily marked by the howls of the crippled members. Duane reloaded his gun, and, making certain all the hounds had gone, he descended to the ground and set off at a rapid pace to the northward.

The mist had dissolved under a rising sun when Duane made his first halt some miles north of the scene where he had waited for the hounds. A barrier to further progress, in shape of a precipitous rocky bluff, rose sheer from the willow brake. He skirted the base of the cliff, where walking was comparatively easy, around in the direction of the river. He reached the end finally to see there was absolutely no chance to escape from the brake at that corner. It took extreme labor, attended by some hazard and considerable pain to his arm, to get down where he could fill his sombrero with water. After quenching his thirst he had a look at his wound. It was caked over with blood and dirt. When washed off the arm was seen to be inflamed and swollen around the bullet hole. He bathed it, experiencing a soothing relief in the cool water. Then he bandaged it as best he could and arranged a sling round his neck. This mitigated the pain of the injured member and held it in a quiet and restful position, where it had a chance to begin mending.

As Duane turned away from the river he felt refreshed. His great strength and endurance had always made fatigue something almost unknown to him. However, tramping on foot day and night was as unusual to him as to any other riders of the Southwest, and it had begun to tell on him. Retracing his steps, he reached the point where he had abruptly come upon the bluff, and here he determined to follow along its base in the other direction until he found a way out or discovered the futility of such effort.

Duane covered ground rapidly. From time to time he paused to listen. But he was always listening, and his eyes were ever roving. This alertness had become second nature with him, so that except in extreme cases of caution he performed it while he pondered his gloomy and fateful situation. Such habit of alertness and thought made time fly swiftly.

By noon he had rounded the wide curve of the brake and was facing south. The bluff had petered out from a high, mountainous wall to a low

abutment of rock, but it still held to its steep, rough nature and afforded
no crack or slope where quick ascent could have been possible. He pushed
on, growing warier as he approached the danger zone, finding that as he
neared the river on this side it was imperative to go deeper into the
willows. In the afternoon he reached a point where he could see men
pacing to and fro on the bluff. This assured him that whatever place was
guarded was one by which he might escape. He headed toward these men
and approached to within a hundred paces of the bluff where they were.
There were several men and several boys, all armed and, after the manner
of Texans, taking their task leisurely. Farther down Duane made out black
dots on the horizon of the bluff-line, and these he concluded were more
guards stationed at another outlet. Probably all the available men in the
district were on duty. Texans took a grim pleasure in such work. Duane
remembered that upon several occasions he had served such duty himself.

Duane peered through the branches and studied the lay of the land. For
several hundred yards the bluff could be climbed. He took stock of those
careless guards. They had rifles, and that made vain any attempt to pass
them in daylight. He believed an attempt by night might be successful;
and he was swiftly coming to a determination to hide there till dark and
then try it, when the sudden yelping of a dog betrayed him to the guards
on the bluff.

The dog had likely been placed there to give an alarm, and he was
lustily true to his trust. Duane saw the men run together and begin to talk
excitedly and peer into the brake, which was a signal for him to slip away
under the willows. He made no noise, and he assured himself he must be
invisible. Nevertheless, he heard shouts, then the cracking of rifles, and
bullets began to zip and swish through the leafy covert. The day was hot
and windless, and Duane concluded that whenever he touched a willow
stem, even ever so slightly, it vibrated to the top and sent a quiver among
the leaves. Through this the guards had located his position. Once a
bullet hissed by him; another thudded into the ground before him. This
shooting loosed a rage in Duane. He had to fly from these men, and he
hated them and himself because of it. Always in the fury of such moments
he wanted to give back shot for shot. But he slipped on through the
willows, and at length the rifles ceased to crack.

He sheered to the left again, in line with the rocky barrier, and kept
on, wondering what the next mile would bring.

It brought worse, for he was seen by sharp-eyed scouts, and a hot
fusillade drove him to run for his life, luckily to escape with no more than
a bullet-creased shoulder.

Later that day, still undaunted, he sheered again toward the trap-wall,
and found that the nearer he approached to the place where he had come
down into the brake the greater his danger. To attempt to run the block-
ade of that trail by day would be fatal. He waited for night, and after the
brightness of the fires had somewhat lessened he assayed to creep out of

the brake. He succeeded in reaching the foot of the bluff, here only a bank, and had begun to crawl stealthily up under cover of a shadow when a hound again betrayed his position. Retreating to the willows was as perilous a task as had ever confronted Duane, and when he had accomplished it, right under what seemed a hundred blazing rifles, he felt that he had indeed been favored by Providence. This time men followed him a goodly ways into the brake, and the ripping of lead through the willows sounded on all sides of him.

When the noise of pursuit ceased Duane sat down in the darkness, his mind clamped between two things—whether to try again to escape or wait for possible opportunity. He seemed incapable of decision. His intelligence told him that every hour lessened his chances for escape. He had little enough chance in any case, and that was what made another attempt so desperately hard. Still it was not love of life that bound him. There would come an hour, sooner or later, when he would wrench decision out of this chaos of emotion and thought. But that time was not yet.

When he had remained quiet long enough to cool off and recover from his run he found that he was tired. He stretched out to rest. But the swarms of vicious mosquitoes prevented sleep. This corner of the brake was low and near the river, a breeding-ground for the blood-suckers. They sang and hummed and whined around him in an ever-increasing horde. He covered his head and hands with his coat and lay there patiently. That was a long and wretched night. Morning found him still strong physically, but in a dreadful state of mind.

First he hurried for the river. He could withstand the pangs of hunger, but it was imperative to quench thirst. His wound made him feverish, and therefore more than usually hot and thirsty. Again he was refreshed. That morning he was hard put to it to hold himself back from attempting to cross the river. If he could find a light log it was within the bounds of possibility that he might ford the shallow water and bars of quicksand. But not yet! Wearily, doggedly he faced about toward the bluff.

All that day and all that night, all the next day and all the next night, he stole like a hunted savage from river to bluff; and every hour forced upon him the bitter certainty that he was trapped.

Duane lost track of days, of events. He had come to an evil pass. There arrived an hour when, closely pressed by pursuers at the extreme southern corner of the brake, he took to a dense thicket of willows, driven to what he believed was his last stand.

If only these human bloodhounds would swiftly close in on him! Let him fight to the last bitter gasp and have it over! But these hunters, eager as they were to get him, had care of their own skins. They took few risks. They had him cornered.

It was the middle of the day, hot, dusty, oppressive, threatening storm. Like a snake Duane crawled into a little space in the darkest part of the thicket and lay still. Men had cut him off from the bluff, from the river, seemingly from all sides. But he heard voices only from in front and toward his left. Even if his passage to the river had not been blocked, it might just as well have been.

"Come on fellers—down hyar," called one man from the bluff.

"Got him corralled at last," shouted another.

"Reckon ye needn't be too shore. We thought thet more'n once," taunted another.

"I seen him, I tell you."

"Aw, thet was a deer."

"But Bill found fresh tracks an' blood on the willows."

"If he's winged we needn't hurry."

"Hold on thar, you boys," came a shout in authoritative tones from farther up the bluff. "Go slow. You-all air gittin' foolish at the end of a long chase."

"Thet's right, Colonel. Hold 'em back. There's nothin' shorer than somebody'll be stoppin' lead pretty quick. He'll be huntin' us soon!"

"Let's surround this corner an' starve him out."

"Fire the brake."

How clearly all this talk pierced Duane's ears! In it he seemed to hear his doom. This, then, was the end he had always expected, which had been close to him before, yet never like now.

"By God!" whispered Duane. "The thing for me to do now—is go out —meet them!"

That was prompted by the fighting, the killing instinct in him. In that moment it had almost superhuman power. If he must die, that was the way for him to die. What else could be expected of Buck Duane? He got to his knees and drew his gun. With his swollen and almost useless hand he held what spare ammunition he had left. He ought to creep out noiselessly to the edge of the willows, suddenly face his pursuers, then, while there was a beat left in his heart, kill, kill, kill. These men all had rifles. The fight would be short. But the marksmen did not live on earth who could make such a fight go wholly against him. Confronting them suddenly he could kill a man for every shot in his gun.

Thus Duane reasoned. So he hoped to accept his fate—to meet this end. But when he tried to step forward something checked him. He forced himself; yet he could not go. The obstruction that opposed his will was as insurmountable as it had been physically impossible for him to climb the bluff.

Slowly he fell back, crouched low, and then lay flat. The grim and ghastly dignity that had been his a moment before fell away from him. He lay there stripped of his last shred of self-respect. He wondered was he afraid—had he, the last of the Duanes, had he come to feel fear? No! Never in all his wild life had he so longed to go out and meet men face to face. It was not fear that held him back. He hated this hiding, this eternal vigilance, this hopeless life. The damnable paradox of the situation was that if he went out to meet these men there was absolutely no doubt of his doom. If he clung to his covert there was a chance, a merest chance, for his life. These pursuers, dogged and unflagging as they had been, were mortally afraid of him. It was his fame that made them cowards. Duane's keenness told him that at the very darkest and most perilous moment there was still a chance for him. And the blood in him, the temper of his father, the years of his outlawry, the pride of his unsought and hated career, the nameless, inexplicable something in him made him accept that slim chance.

Waiting then became a physical and mental agony. He lay under the burning sun, parched by thirst, laboring to breathe, sweating and bleeding. His uncared-for wound was like a red-hot prong in his flesh. Blotched and swollen from the never-ending attack of flies and mosquitoes his face seemed twice its natural size, and it ached and stung.

On one side, then, was this physical torture; on the other the old hell, terribly augmented at this crisis, in his mind. It seemed that thought and imagination had never been so swift. If death found him presently, how would it come? Would he get decent burial or be left for the peccaries and the coyotes? Would his people ever know where he had fallen? How wretched, how miserable his state! It was cowardly, it was monstrous for him to cling longer to this doomed life. Then the hate in his heart, the hellish hate of these men on his trail—that was like a scourge. He felt no longer human. He had degenerated into an animal that could think. His heart pounded, his pulse beat, his breast heaved; and this internal strife seemed to thunder into his ears. He was now enacting the tragedy of all crippled, starved, hunted wolves at bay in their dens. Only his tragedy was infinitely more terrible because he had mind enough to see his plight, his resemblance to a lonely wolf, bloody-fanged, dripping, snarling, fire-eyed in a last instinctive defiance.

Mounted upon the horror of Duane's thought was a watching, listening intensity so supreme that it registered impressions which were creations of his imagination. He heard stealthy steps that were not there; he saw shadowy moving figures that were only leaves. A hundred times when he was about to pull trigger he discovered his error. Yet voices came from a distance, and steps and crackings in the willows, and other sounds real enough. But Duane could not distinguish the real from the false. There were times when the wind which had arisen sent a hot, pattering breath down the willow aisles, and Duane heard it as an approaching army.

This straining of Duane's faculties brought on a reaction which in itself was a respite. He saw the sun darkened by thick slow-spreading clouds. A storm appeared to be coming. How slowly it moved! The air was like steam. If there broke one of those dark, violent storms common though rare to the country, Duane believed he might slip away in the fury of wind and rain. Hope, that seemed unquenchable in him, resurged again. He hailed it with a bitterness that was sickening.

Then at a rustling step he froze into the old strained attention. He heard a slow patter of soft feet. A tawny shape crossed a little opening in the thicket. It was that of a dog. The moment while that beast came into full view was an age. The dog was not a bloodhound, and if he had a trail or a scent he seemed to be at fault on it. Duane waited for the inevitable discovery. Any kind of a hunting-dog could have found him in that thicket. Voices from outside could be heard urging on the dog. Rover they called him. Duane sat up at the moment the dog entered the little shaded covert. Duane expected a yelping, a baying, or at least a bark that would tell of his hiding-place. A strange relief swiftly swayed over Duane. The end was near now. He had no further choice. Let them come—a quick fierce exchange of shots—and then this torture past! He waited for the dog to give the alarm.

But the dog looked at him and trotted by into the thicket without a yelp. Duane could not believe the evidence of his senses. He thought he had suddenly gone deaf. He saw the dog disappear, heard him running to and fro among the willows, getting farther and farther away, till all sound from him ceased.

"Thar's Rover," called a voice from the bluff-side. "He's been through thet black patch."

"Nary a rabbit in there," replied another.

"Bah! Thet pup's no good," scornfully growled another man. "Put a hound at thet clump of willows."

"Fire's the game. Burn the brake before the rain comes."

The voices droned off as their owners evidently walked up the ridge.

Then upon Duane fell the crushing burden of the old waiting, watching, listening spell. After all, it was not to end just now. His chance still persisted—looked a little brighter—led him on, perhaps, to forlorn hope.

All at once twilight settled quickly down upon the willow brake, or else Duane noted it suddenly. He imagined it to be caused by the approaching storm. But there was little movement of air or cloud, and thunder still muttered and rumbled at a distance. The fact was the sun had set, and at this time of overcast sky night was at hand.

Duane realized it with the awakening of all his old force. He would yet elude his pursuers. That was the moment when he seized the significance of all these fortunate circumstances which had aided him. Without haste and without sound he began to crawl in the direction of the river. It was not far, and he reached the bank before darkness set in. There were men up on the bluff carrying wood to build a bonfire. For a moment he half yielded to a temptation to try to slip along the river-shore, close in under the willows. But when he raised himself to peer out he saw that an attempt of this kind would be liable to failure. At the same moment he saw a rough-hewn plank lying beneath him, lodged against some willows.

The end of the plank extended in almost to a point beneath him. Quick as a flash he saw where a desperate chance invited him. Then he tied his gun in an oilskin bag and put it in his pocket.

The bank was steep and crumbly. He must not break off any earth to splash into the water. There was a willow growing back some few feet from the edge of the bank. Cautiously he pulled it down, bent it over the water so that when he released it there would be no springing back. Then he trusted his weight to it, with his feet sliding carefully down the bank. He went into the water almost up to his knees, felt the quicksand grip his feet; then, leaning forward till he reached the plank, he pulled it toward him and lay upon it.

Without a sound one end went slowly under water and the farther end appeared lightly braced against the overhanging willows. Very carefully then Duane began to extricate his right foot from the sucking sand. It seemed as if his foot was incased in solid rock. But there was a movement upward, and he pulled with all the power he dared use. It came slowly and at length was free. The left one he released with less difficulty. The next few moments he put all his attention on the plank to ascertain if his weight would sink it into the sand. The far end slipped off the willows with a little splash and gradually settled to rest upon the bottom. But it sank no farther, and Duane's greatest concern was relieved. However, as it was manifestly impossible for him to keep his head up for long he carefully crawled out upon the plank until he could rest an arm and shoulder upon the willows.

When he looked up it was to find the night strangely luminous with fires. There was a bonfire on the extreme end of the bluff, another a hundred paces beyond. A great flare extended over the brake in that direction. Duane heard a roaring on the wind, and he knew his pursuers had fired the willows. He did not believe that would help them much. The brake was dry enough, but too green to burn readily. And as for the bonfires he discovered that the men, probably having run out of wood, were keeping up the light with oil and stuff from the village. A dozen men kept watch on the bluff scarcely fifty paces from where Duane lay concealed by the willows. They talked, cracked jokes, sang songs, and manifestly considered this outlaw-hunting a great lark. As long as the bright light lasted Duane dared not move. He had the patience and the endurance to wait for the breaking of the storm, and if that did not come, then the early hour before dawn when the gray fog and gloom were over the river.

Escape was now in his grasp. He felt it. And with that in his mind he waited, strong as steel in his conviction, capable of withstanding any strain endurable by the human frame.

The wind blew in puffs, grew wilder, and roared through the willows, carrying bright sparks upward. Thunder rolled down over the river, and lightning began to flash. Then the rain fell in heavy sheets, but not steadily. The flashes of lightning and the broad flares played so incessantly that Duane could not trust himself out on the open river. Certainly the storm rather increased the watchfulness of the men on the bluff. He knew how to wait, and he waited, grimly standing pain and cramp and chill. The storm wore away as desultorily as it had come, and the long night set in. There were times when Duane thought he was paralyzed, others when he grew sick, giddy, weak from the strained posture. The first paling of the stars quickened him with a kind of wild joy. He watched them grow paler, dimmer, disappear one by one. A shadow hovered down, rested upon the river, and gradually thickened. The bonfire on the bluff showed as through a foggy veil. The watchers were mere groping dark figures.

Duane, aware of how cramped he had become from long inaction, began to move his legs and uninjured arm and body, and at length overcame a paralyzing stiffness. Then, digging his hand in the sand and holding the plank with his knees, he edged it out into the river. Inch by inch he advanced until clear of the willows. Looking upward, he saw the shadowy figures of the men on the bluff. He realized they ought to see him, feared that they would. But he kept on, cautiously, noiselessly, with a heart-numbing slowness. From time to time his elbow made a little gurgle and splash in the water. Try as he might, he could not prevent this. It got to be like the hollow roar of a rapid filling his ears with mocking sound. There was a perceptible current out in the river, and it hindered straight advancement. Inch by inch he crept on, expecting to hear the bang of rifles, the spattering of bullets. He tried not to look backward, but failed. The fire appeared a little dimmer, the moving shadows a little darker.

Once the plank stuck in the sand and felt as if it were settling. Bringing feet to aid his hand, he shoved it over the treacherous place. This way he made faster progress. The obscurity of the river seemed to be enveloping him. When he looked back again the figures of the men were coalescing with the surrounding gloom, the fires were streaky, blurred patches of light. But the sky above was brighter. Dawn was not far off.

To the west all was dark. With infinite care and implacable spirit and waning strength, Duane shoved the plank along, and when at last he discerned the black border of bank it came in time, he thought, to save him. He crawled out, rested till the gray dawn broke, and then headed north through the willows.

❧13❧

How long Duane was traveling out of that region he never knew. But he reached familiar country and found a rancher who had before befriended him. Here his arm was attended to; he had food and sleep; and in a couple of weeks he was himself again.

When the time came for Duane to ride away on his endless trail his friend reluctantly imparted the information that some thirty miles south, near the village of Shirley, there was posted at a certain crossroad a reward for Buck Duane dead or alive. Duane had heard of such notices, but he had never seen one. His friend's reluctance and refusal to state for what particular deed this reward was offered roused Duane's curiosity. He had never been any closer to Shirley than this rancher's home. Doubtless some post-office burglary, some gun-shooting scrape had been attributed to him. And he had been accused of worse deeds. Abruptly Duane decided to ride over there and find out who wanted him dead or alive, and why.

As he started south on the road he reflected that this was the first time he had ever deliberately hunted trouble. Introspection awarded him this knowledge; during that last terrible flight on the lower Nueces and while he lay abed recuperating he had changed. A fixed, immutable, hopeless bitterness abided with him. He had reached the end of his rope. All the power of his mind and soul were unavailable to turn him back from his fate. That fate was to become an outlaw in every sense of the term, to be what he was credited with being—that is to say, to embrace evil. He had never committed a crime. He wondered now was crime close to him? He reasoned finally that the desperation of crime had been forced upon him, if not its motive; and that if driven, there was no limit to his possibilities. He understood now many of the hitherto inexplicable actions of certain noted outlaws—why they had returned to the scene of the crime that had outlawed them; why they took such strangely fatal chances; why life was no more to them than a breath of wind; why they rode straight into the jaws of death to confront wronged men or hunting rangers, vigilantes, to laugh in their very faces. It was such bitterness as his that drove these men.

Toward afternoon, from the top of a long hill, Duane saw the green fields and trees and shining roofs of a town he considered must be Shirley. And at the bottom of the hill he came upon an intersecting road. There was a placard nailed on the crossroad signpost. Duane drew rein near it and leaned close to read the faded print: $1,000 Reward for Buck Duane

DEAD OR ALIVE. Peering closer to read the finer, more faded print, Duane learned that he was wanted for the murder of Mrs. Jeff Aiken at her ranch near Shirley. The month September was named, but the date was illegible. The reward was offered by the woman's husband, whose name appeared with that of a sheriff's at the bottom of the placard.

Duane read the thing twice. When he straightened he was sick with the horror of his fate, wild with passion at those misguided fools who could believe that he had harmed a woman. Then he remembered Kate Bland, and, as always when she returned to him, he quaked inwardly. Years before word had gone abroad that he had killed her, and so it was easy for men wanting to fix a crime to name him. Perhaps it had been done often. Probably he bore on his shoulders a burden of numberless crimes.

A dark, passionate fury possessed him. It shook him like a storm shakes the oak. When it passed, leaving him cold, with clouded brow and piercing eye, his mind was set. Spurring his horse, he rode straight toward the village.

Shirley appeared to be a large, pretentious country town. A branch of some railroad terminated there. The main street was wide, bordered by trees and commodious houses, and many of the stores were of brick. A large plaza shaded by giant cottonwood trees occupied a central location.

Duane pulled his running horse and halted him, plunging and snorting, before a group of idle men who lounged on benches in the shade of a spreading cottonwood. How many times had Duane seen just that kind of lazy shirt-sleeved Texas group! Not often, however, had he seen such placid, lolling, good-natured men change their expression, their attitude so swiftly. His advent apparently was momentous. They evidently took him for an unusual visitor. So far as Duane could tell, not one of them recognized him, had a hint of his identity.

He slid off his horse and threw the bridle.

"I'm Buck Duane," he said. "I saw that placard—out there on a signpost. It's a damn lie! Somebody find this man Jeff Aiken. I want to see him."

His announcement was taken in absolute silence. That was the only effect he noted, for he avoided looking at these villagers. The reason was simple enough; Duane felt himself overcome with emotion. There were tears in his eyes. He sat down on a bench, put his elbows on his knees and his hands to his face. For once he had absolutely no concern for his fate. This ignominy was the last straw.

Presently, however, he became aware of some kind of commotion among these villagers. He heard whisperings, low, hoarse voices, then the shuffle of rapid feet moving away. All at once a violent hand jerked his gun from its holster. When Duane rose a gaunt man, livid of face, shaking like a leaf, confronted him with his own gun.

"Hands up, thar, you Buck Duane!" he roared, waving the gun.

That appeared to be the cue for pandemonium to break loose. Duane opened his lips to speak, but if he had yelled at the top of his lungs he could not have made himself heard. In weary disgust he looked at the gaunt man, and then at the others, who were working themselves into a frenzy. He made no move, however, to hold up his hands. The villagers surrounded him, emboldened by finding him now unarmed. Then several men lay hold of his arms and pinioned them behind his back. Resistance was useless even if Duane had had the spirit. Some one of them fetched his halter from his saddle, and with this they bound him helpless.

People were running now from the street, the stores, the houses. Old men, cowboys, clerks, boys, ranchers came on the trot. The crowd grew. The increasing clamor began to attract women as well as men. A group of girls ran up, then hung back in fright and pity.

The presence of cowboys made a difference. They split up the crowd, got to Duane, and lay hold of him with rough, business-like hands. One of them lifted his fists and roared at the frenzied mob to fall back, to stop the racket. He beat them back into a circle; but it was some little time before the hubbub quieted down so a voice could be heard.

"Shut up, will you-all?" he was yelling. "Give us a chance to hear somethin'. Easy now—soho. There ain't nobody goin' to be hurt. Thet's right; everybody quiet now. Let's see what's come off."

This cowboy, evidently one of authority, or at least one of strong personality, turned to the gaunt man, who still waved Duane's gun.

"Abe, put the gun down," he said. "It might go off. Here, give it to me. Now, what's wrong? Who's this roped gent, an' what's he done?"

The gaunt fellow, who appeared now about to collapse, lifted a shaking hand and pointed.

"Thet thar feller—he's Buck Duane!" he panted.

An angry murmur ran through the surrounding crowd.

"The rope! The rope! Throw it over a branch! String him up!" cried an excited villager.

"Buck Duane! Buck Duane!"

"Hang him!"

The cowboy silenced these cries.

"Abe, how do you know this fellow is Buck Duane?" he asked, sharply.

"Why—he said so," replied the man called Abe.

"What!" came the exclamation, incredulously.

"It's a tarnal fact," panted Abe, waving his hands importantly. He was an old man and appeared to be carried away with the significance of his deed. "He like to rid' his hoss right over us-all. Then he jumped off, says he was Buck Duane, an' he wanted to see Jeff Aiken bad."

This speech caused a second commotion as noisy though not so enduring as the first. When the cowboy, assisted by a couple of his mates, had restored order again, someone had slipped the noose-end of Duane's rope over his head.

"Up with him!" screeched a wild-eyed youth.

The mob surged closer was shoved back by the cowboys.

"Abe, if you ain't drunk or crazy tell thet over," ordered Abe's interlocutor.

With some show of resentment and more of dignity Abe reiterated his former statement.

"If he's Buck Duane how'n hell did you get hold of his gun?" bluntly queried the cowboy.

"Why—he set down thar—an' he kind of hid his face on his hand. An' I grabbed his gun an' got the drop on him."

What the cowboy thought of this was expressed in a laugh. His mates likewise grinned broadly. Then the leader turned to Duane.

"Stranger, I reckon you'd better speak up for yourself," he said.

That stilled the crowd as no command had done.

"I'm Buck Duane, all right," said Duane, quietly. "It was this way—"

The big cowboy seemed to vibrate with a shock. All the ruddy warmth left his face; his jaw began to bulge; the corded veins in his neck stood out in knots. In an instant he had a hard, stern, strange look. He shot out a powerful hand that fastened in the front of Duane's blouse.

"Somethin' queer here. But if you're Duane you're sure in bad. Any fool ought to know that. You mean it, then?"

"Yes."

"Rode in to shoot up the town, eh? Same old stunt of you gun-fighters? Meant to kill the man who offered a reward? Wanted to see Jeff Aiken bad, huh?"

"No," replied Duane. "Your citizen here misrepresented things. He seems a little off his head."

"Reckon he is. Somebody is, that's sure. You claim Buck Duane, then, an' all his doings?"

"I'm Duane; yes. But I won't stand for the blame of things I never did. That's why I'm here. I saw that placard out there offering the reward. Until now I never was within half a day's ride of this town. I'm blamed for what I never did. I rode in here, told who I was, asked somebody to send for Jeff Aiken."

"An' then you set down an' let this old guy throw your own gun on you?" queried the cowboy in amazement.

"I guess that's it," replied Duane.

"Well, it's powerful strange, if you're really Buck Duane."

A man elbowed his way into the circle.

"It's Duane. I recognize him. I seen him in more'n one place," he said. "Sibert, you can rely on what I tell you. I don't know if he's locoed or what. But I do know he's the genuine Buck Duane. Anyone who'd ever seen him onct would never forget him."

"What do you want to see Aiken for?" asked the cowboy Sibert.

"I want to face him, to tell him I never harmed his wife."

"Why?"

"Because I'm innocent, that's all."

"Suppose we send for Aiken an' he hears you an' doesn't believe you; what then?"

"If he won't believe me—why, then my case's so bad—I'd be better off dead."

A momentary silence was broken by Sibert.

"If this isn't a queer deal! Boys, reckon we'd better send for Jeff."

"Somebody went fer him. He'll be comin' soon," replied a man.

Duane stood a head taller than that circle of curious faces. He gazed out above and beyond them. It was in this way that he chanced to see a number of women on the outskirts of the crowd. Some were old, with hard faces, like the men. Some were young and comely, and most of these seemed agitated by excitement or distress. They cast fearful, pitying glances upon Duane as he stood there with that noose round his neck. Women were more human than men, Duane thought. He met eyes that dilated, seemed fascinated at his gaze, but were not averted. It was the old women who were voluble, loud in expression of their feelings.

Near the trunk of the cottonwood stood a slender woman in white. Duane's wandering glance rested upon her. Her eyes were riveted upon him. A soft-hearted woman, probably, who did not want to see him hanged!

"Thar comes Jeff Aiken now," called a man, loudly.

The crowd shifted and trampled in eagerness.

Duane saw two men coming fast, one of whom, in the lead, was of stalwart build. He had a gun in his hand, and his manner was that of fierce energy.

The cowboy Sibert thrust open the jostling circle of men.

"Hold on, Jeff," he called, and he blocked the man with the gun. He spoke so low Duane could not hear what he said, and his form hid Aiken's face. At that juncture the crowd spread out, closed in, and Aiken and Sibert were caught in the circle. There was a pushing forward, a pressing of many bodies, hoarse cries and flinging hands—again the insane tumult was about to break out—the demand for an outlaw's blood, the call for a wild justice executed a thousand times before on Texas's bloody soil.

Sibert bellowed at the dark encroaching mass. The cowboys with him beat and cuffed in vain.

"Jeff, will you listen?" broke in Sibert, hurriedly, his hand on the other man's arm.

Aiken nodded coolly. Duane, who had seen many men in perfect control of themselves under circumstances like these, recognized the spirit that dominated Aiken. He was white, cold, passionless. There were lines of bitter grief deep round his lips. If Duane ever felt the meaning of death he felt it then.

"Sure this's your game, Aiken," said Sibert. "But hear me a minute.

Reckon there's no doubt about this man bein' Buck Duane. He seen the placard out at the crossroads. He rides in to Shirley. He says he's Buck Duane an' he's lookin' for Jeff Aiken. That's all clear enough. You know how these gunfighters go lookin' for trouble. But here's what stumps me. Duane sits down there on the bench and lets old Abe Strickland grab his gun an' get the drop on him. More'n that, he gives me some strange talk about how, if he couldn't make you believe he's innocent, he'd better be dead. You see for yourself Duane ain't drunk or crazy or locoed. He doesn't strike me as a man who rode in here huntin' blood. So I reckon you'd better hold on till you hear what he has to say."

Then for the first time the drawn-faced, hungry-eyed giant turned his gaze upon Duane. He had intelligence which was not yet subservient to passion. Moreover, he seemed the kind of man Duane would care to have judge him in a critical moment like this.

"Listen," said Duane, gravely, with his eyes steady on Aiken's, "I'm Buck Duane. I never lied to any man in my life. I was forced into out-lawry. I've never had a chance to leave the country. I've killed men to save my own life. I never intentionally harmed any woman. I rode thirty miles today—deliberately to see what this reward was, who made it, what for. When I read the placard I went sick to the bottom of my soul. So I rode in here to find you—to tell you this: I never saw Shirley before today. It was impossible for me to have . . . killed your wife. Last September I was two hundred miles north of here on the upper Nueces. I can prove that. Men who know me will tell you I couldn't murder a woman. I haven't any idea why such a deed should be laid at my hands. It's just that wild border gossip. I have no idea what reasons you have for holding me responsible. I only know . . . you're wrong. You've been deceived. And see here, Aiken. You understand I'm a miserable man. I'm about broken, I guess. I don't care anymore for life, for anything. If you can't look me in the eyes, man to man, and believe what I say—why, by God! You can kill me!"

Aiken heaved a great breath.

"Buck Duane, whether I'm impressed or not by what you say needn't matter. You've had accusers, justly or unjustly, as will soon appear. The thing is we can prove you innocent or guilty. My girl Lucy saw my wife's assailant."

He motioned for the crowd of men to open up.

"Somebody—you, Sibert—go for Lucy. That'll settle this thing."

Duane heard as a man in an ugly dream. The faces around him, the hum of voices, all seemed far off. His life hung by the merest thread. Yet he did not think of that so much as of the brand of a woman-murderer which might be soon sealed upon him by a frightened, imaginative child.

The crowd trooped apart and closed again. Duane caught a blurred image of a slight girl clinging to Sibert's hand. He could not see distinctly.

Aiken lifted the child, whispered soothingly to her not to be afraid. Then he fetched her closer to Duane.

"Lucy, tell me. Did you ever see this man before?" asked Aiken, huskily and low. "Is he the one—who came in the house that day—struck you down—and dragged Mama—?"

Aiken's voice failed.

A lightning flash seemed to clear Duane's blurred sight. He saw a pale, sad face and violet eyes fixed in gloom and horror upon his. No terrible moment in Duane's life ever equaled this one of silence—of suspense.

"It ain't him!" cried the child.

Then Sibert was flinging the noose off Duane's neck and unwinding the bonds round his arms. The spellbound crowd awoke to hoarse exclamations.

"See there, my locoed gents, how easy you'd hang the wrong man," burst out the cowboy, as he made the rope-end hiss. "You-all are a lot of wise rangers. Haw! haw!"

He freed Duane and thrust the bone-handled gun back in Duane's holster.

"You Abe, there. Reckon you pulled a stunt! But don't try the like again. And, men, I'll gamble there's a hell of a lot of bad work Buck Duane's named for—which all he never done. Clear away there. Where's his hoss? Duane, the road's open out of Shirley."

Sibert swept the gaping watchers aside and pressed Duane toward the horse, which another cowboy held. Mechanically Duane mounted, felt a lift as he went up. Then the cowboy's hard face softened in a smile.

"I reckon it ain't uncivil of me to say—hit that road quick!" he said, frankly.

He led the horse out of the crowd. Aiken joined him, and between them they escorted Duane across the plaza. The crowd appeared irresistibly drawn to follow.

Aiken paused with his big hand on Duane's knee. In it, unconsciously probably, he still held the gun.

"Duane, a word with you," he said. "I believe you're not so black as you've been painted. I wish there was time to say more. Tell me this, anyway. Do you know the ranger, Captain MacNelly?"

"I do not," replied Duane, in surprise.

"I met him only a week ago over in Fairfield," went on Aiken, hurriedly. "He declared you never killed my wife. I didn't believe him— argued with him. We almost had hard words over it. Now—I'm sorry. The last thing he said was: 'If you ever see Duane don't kill him. Send him into my camp after dark!' He meant something strange. What—I can't say. But he was right, and I was wrong. If Lucy had batted an eye I'd have killed you. Still, I wouldn't advise you to hunt up MacNelly's camp. He's clever. Maybe he believes there's no treachery in his new ideas of ranger tactics. I tell you for all it's worth. Goodbye. May God help you further as he did this day!"

Duane said goodbye and touched the horse with his spurs.

"So long, Buck!" called Sibert, with that frank smile breaking warm over his brown face; and he held his sombrero high.

⁑14⁑

WHEN DUANE reached the crossing of the roads the name Fairfield on the signpost seemed to be the thing that tipped the oscillating balance of decision in favor of that direction.

He answered here to unfathomable impulse. If he had been driven to hunt up Jeff Aiken, now he was called to find this unknown ranger captain. In Duane's state of mind clear reasoning, common sense or keenness were out of the question. He went because he felt he was compelled.

Dusk had fallen when he rode into a town which inquiry discovered to be Fairfield. Captain MacNelly's camp was stationed just out of the village limits on the other side.

No one except the boy Duane questioned appeared to notice his arrival. Like Shirley, the town of Fairfield was large and prosperous, compared to the innumerable hamlets dotting the vast extent of southwestern Texas. As Duane rode through, being careful to get off the main street, he heard the tolling of a churchbell that was a melancholy reminder of his old home.

There did not appear to be any camp on the outskirts of the town. But as Duane sat his horse, peering around and undecided what further move to make, he caught the glint of flickering lights through the darkness. Heading toward them, he rode perhaps a quarter of a mile to come upon a grove of mesquite. The brightness of several fires made the surrounding darkness all the blacker. Duane saw the moving forms of men and heard horses. He advanced naturally, expecting any moment to be halted.

"Who goes there?" came the sharp call out of the gloom.

Duane pulled his horse. The gloom was impenetrable.

"One man . . . alone," replied Duane.

"A stranger?"

"Yes."

"What do you want?"

"I'm trying to find the ranger camp."

"You've struck it. What's your errand?"

"I want to see Captain MacNelly."

"Get down and advance. Slow. Don't move your hands. It's dark, but I can see."

Duane dismounted, and, leading his horse, slowly advanced a few paces. He saw a dully bright object—a gun—before he discovered the man who held it. A few more steps showed a dark figure blocking the trail. Here Duane halted.

"Come closer, stranger. Let's have a look at you," the guard ordered, curtly.

Duane advanced again until he stood before the man. Here the rays of light from the fires flickered upon Duane's face.

"Reckon you're a stranger, all right. What's your name and your business with the captain?"

Duane hesitated, pondering what best to say.

"Tell Captain MacNelly I'm the man he's been asking to ride into his camp—after dark," finally said Duane.

The ranger bent forward to peer hard at this night visitor. His manner had been alert, and now it became tense.

"Come here, one of you men, quick," he called, without turning in the least toward the campfire.

"Hello! What's up, Pickens?" came the swift reply. It was followed by a rapid thud of boots on soft ground. A dark form crossed the gleams from the firelight. Then a ranger loomed up to reach the side of the guard. Duane heard whispering, the purport of which he could not catch. The second ranger swore under his breath. Then he turned away and started back.

"Here, Ranger, before you go, understand this. My visit is peaceful—friendly, if you'll let it be. Mind, I was asked to come here—after dark."

Duane's clear, penetrating voice carried far. The listening rangers at the campfire heard what he said.

"Ho, Pickens! Tell that fellow to wait," replied an authoritative voice. Then a slim figure detached itself from the dark, moving group at the campfire and hurried out.

"Better be foxy, Cap," shouted a ranger, in warning.

"Shut up—all of you," was the reply.

This officer, obviously Captain MacNelly, soon joined the two rangers who were confronting Duane. He had no fear. He strode straight up to Duane.

"I'm MacNelly," he said. "If you're my man, don't mention your name —yet."

All this seemed so strange to Duane, in keeping with much that had happened lately.

"I met Jeff Aiken today," said Duane. "He sent me—"

"You've met Aiken!" exclaimed MacNelly, sharp, eager, low. "By all that's bully!" Then he appeared to catch himself, to grow restrained.

"Men, fall back, leave us alone a moment."

The rangers slowly withdrew.

"Buck Duane! It's you?" he whispered, eagerly.

"Yes."

"If I give my word you'll not be arrested—you'll be treated fairly—will you come into camp and consult with me?"

"Certainly."

"Duane, I'm sure glad to meet you," went on MacNelly; and he extended his hand.

Amazed and touched, scarcely realizing this actuality, Duane gave his hand and felt no unmistakable grip of warmth.

"It doesn't seem natural, Captain MacNelly, but I believe I'm glad to meet you," said Duane, soberly.

"You will be. Now we'll go back to camp. Keep your identity mum for the present."

He led Duane in the direction of the campfire.

"Pickens, go back on duty," he ordered, "and, Beeson, you look after this horse."

When Duane got beyond the line of mesquite, which had hid a good view of the campsite, he saw a group of perhaps fifteen rangers sitting around the fires, near a long, low shed where horses were feeding, and a small adobe house at one side.

"We've just had grub, but I'll see you get some. Then we'll talk," said MacNelly. "I've taken up temporary quarters here. Have a rustler job on hand. Now, when you've eaten, come right into the house."

Duane was hungry, but he hurried through the ample supper that was set before him, urged on by curiosity and astonishment. The only way he could account for his presence there in a ranger's camp was that MacNelly hoped to get useful information out of him. Still that would hardly have made this captain so eager. There was a mystery here, and Duane could scarcely wait for it to be solved. While eating he had bent keen eyes around him. After a first quiet scrutiny the rangers apparently paid no more attention to him. They were all veterans in service—Duane saw that—and rugged, powerful men of iron constitution. Despite the occasional joke and sally of the more youthful members, and a general conversation of campfire nature, Duane was not deceived about the fact that his advent had been an unusual and striking one, which had caused an undercurrent of conjecture and even consternation among them. These rangers were too well trained to appear openly curious about their captain's guest. If they had not deliberately attempted to be oblivious of his presence Duane would have concluded they thought him an ordinary visitor, somehow of use to MacNelly. As it was, Duane felt a suspense that must have been due to a hint of his identity.

He was not long in presenting himself at the door of the house.

"Come in and have a chair," said MacNelly, motioning for the one other occupant of the room to rise. "Leave us, Russell, and close the door. I'll be through these reports right off."

MacNelly sat at a table upon which was a lamp and various papers. Seen in the light he was a fine-looking, soldierly man of about forty years, dark-haired and dark-eyed, with a bronzed face, shrewd, stern, strong, yet not wanting in kindliness. He scanned hastily over some papers, fussed with them, and finally put them in envelopes. Without looking up he pushed a cigar-case toward Duane, and upon Duane's refusal to smoke he took a cigar, rose to light it at the lamp-chimney, and then, settling back in his chair, he faced Duane, making a vain attempt to hide what must have been the fulfillment of a long-nourished curiosity.

"Duane, I've been hoping for this for two years," he began.

Duane smiled a little—a smile that felt strange on his face. He had never been much of a talker. And speech here seemed more than ordinarily difficult.

MacNelly must have felt that.

He looked long and earnestly at Duane, and his quick, nervous manner changed to grave thoughtfulness.

"I've lots to say, but where to begin," he mused. "Duane, you've had a hard life since you went on the dodge. I never met you before, don't know what you looked like as a boy. But I can see what—well, even ranger life isn't all roses."

He rolled his cigar between his lips and puffed clouds of smoke.

"Ever hear from home since you left Wellston?" he asked, abruptly.

"No."

"Never a word?"

"Not one," replied Duane, sadly.

"That's tough. I'm glad to be able to tell you that up to just lately your mother, sister, uncle—all your folks, I believe—were well. I've kept posted. But haven't heard lately."

Duane averted his face a moment, hesitated till the swelling left his throat, and then said, "It's worth what I went through today to hear that."

"I can imagine how you feel about it. When I was in the war . . . but let's get down to the business of this meeting."

He pulled his chair close to Duane's.

"You've had word more than once in the last two years that I wanted to see you?"

"Three times, I remember," replied Duane.

"Why didn't you hunt me up?"

"I supposed you imagined me one of those gunfighters who couldn't take a dare and expected me to ride up to your camp and be arrested."

"That was natural, I suppose," went on MacNelly. "You didn't know me, otherwise you would have come. I've been a long time getting to you. But the nature of my job, as far as you're concerned, made me cautious. Duane, you're aware of the hard name you bear all over the Southwest?"

"Once in a while I'm jarred into realizing," replied Duane.

"It's the hardest, barring Murrell and Cheseldine, on the Texas border. But there's this difference. Murrell in his day was known to deserve his infamous name. Cheseldine in his day also. But I've found hundreds of men in southwest Texas who're your friends, who swear you never committed a crime. The farther south I get the clearer this becomes. What I want to know is the truth. Have you ever done anything criminal? Tell me the truth, Duane. It won't make any difference in my plan. And when I say crime I mean what *I* would call crime, or any reasonable Texan."

"That way my hands are clean," replied Duane.

"You never held up a man, robbed a store for grub, stole a horse when you needed him bad—never anything like that?"

"Somehow I always kept out of that, just when pressed the hardest."

"Duane, I'm damn glad!" MacNelly exclaimed, gripping Duane's hand. "Glad for your mother's sake! But, all the same, in spite of this, you are a Texas outlaw accountable to the state. You're perfectly aware that under existing circumstances, if you fell into the hands of the law, you'd probably hang, at least go to jail for a long term."

"That's what kept me on the dodge all these years," replied Duane.

"Certainly." MacNelly removed his cigar. His eyes narrowed and glittered. The muscles along his brown cheeks set hard and tense. He leaned closer to Duane, laid sinewy, pressing fingers upon Duane's knee.

"Listen to this," he whispered, hoarsely. "If I place a pardon in your hand—make you a free, honest citizen once more, clear your name of infamy, make your mother, your sister proud of you—will you swear yourself to a service, *any* service I demand of you?"

Duane sat stock still, stunned.

Slowly, more persuasively, with show of earnest agitation, Captain MacNelly reiterated his startling query.

"My God!" burst from Duane. "What's this? MacNelly, you *can't* be in earnest!"

"Never more so in my life. I've a deep game. I'm playing it square. What do you say?"

He rose to his feet. Duane, as if impelled, rose with him. Ranger and outlaw then locked eyes that searched each other's souls. In MacNelly's Duane read truth, strong, fiery purpose, hope, even gladness, and a fugitive mounting assurance of victory.

Twice Duane endeavored to speak, failed of all save a hoarse, incoherent sound, until, forcing back a flood of speech, he found a voice.

"Any service? Every service! MacNelly, I give my word," said Duane.

A light played over MacNelly's face, warming out all the grim darkness. He held out his hand. Duane met it with his in a clasp that men unconsciously give in moments of stress.

When they unclasped and Duane stepped back to drop into a chair MacNelly fumbled for another cigar—he had bitten the other into shreds —and, lighting it as before, he turned to his visitor, now calm and cool. He had the look of a man who had justly won something at considerable cost. His next move was to take a long leather case from his pocket and extract from it several folded papers.

"Here's your pardon from the governor," he said, quietly. "You'll see, when you look it over, that it's conditional. When you sign this paper I have here the condition will be met."

He smoothed out the paper, handed Duane a pen, ran his forefinger along a dotted line.

Duane's hand was shaky. Years had passed since he had held a pen. It was with difficulty that he achieved his signature. Buckley Duane—how strange the name looked!

"Right here ends the career of Buck Duane, outlaw and gunfighter," said MacNelly; and, seating himself, he took the pen from Duane's fingers and wrote several lines in several places upon the paper. Then with a smile he handed it to Duane.

"That makes you a member of Company A, Texas Rangers."

"So that's it!" burst out Duane, a light breaking in upon his bewilderment. "You want me for ranger service?"

"Sure. That's it," replied the Captain, dryly. "Now to hear what that service is to be. I've been a busy man since I took this job, and, as you may have heard, I've done a few things. I don't mind telling you that political influence put me in here and that up Austin way there's a good deal of friction in the Department of State in regard to whether or not the ranger service is any good—whether it should be discontinued or not. I'm on the party side who's defending the ranger service. I contend that it's made Texas habitable. Well, it's been up to me to produce results. So far I have been successful. My great ambition is to break up the outlaw gangs along the river. I have never ventured in there yet because I've been waiting to get the lieutenant I needed. You, of course, are the man I had in mind. It's my idea to start way up the Rio Grande and begin with Cheseldine. He's the strongest, the worst outlaw of the times. He's more than rustler. It's Cheseldine and his gang who are operating on the banks. They're doing bank-robbing. That's my private opinion, but it's not been backed up by any evidence. Cheseldine doesn't leave evidence. He's intelligent, cunning. No one seems to have seen him—to know what he looks like. I assume, of course, that you are a stranger to the country he dominates. It's five hundred miles west of your ground. There's a little town over there called Fairdale. It's the nest of a rustler gang. They rustle and murder at will. Nobody knows who the leader is. I want you to find out. Well, whatever way you decide is best you will proceed to act upon. You are your own boss. You know such men and how they can be approached. You will take all the time needed, if it's months. It will be necessary for you to communicate with me, and that will be a difficult matter. For Cheseldine dominates several whole counties. You must find some way to let me know when I and my rangers are needed. The plan is to break up Cheseldine's gang. It's the toughest job on the border. Arresting him alone isn't to be heard of. He couldn't be brought out. Killing him isn't much better, for his select men, the ones he operates with, are as dangerous to the community as he is. We want to kill or jail this choice selection of robbers and break up the rest of the gang. To find them, to get among them somehow, to learn their movements, to lay your trap for us rangers to spring—that, Duane, is your service to me, and God knows it's a great one!"

"I have accepted it," replied Duane.

"Your work will be secret. You are now a ranger in my service. But no one except the few I choose to tell will know of it until we pull off the job. You will simply be Buck Duane till it suits our purpose to acquaint Texas with the fact that you're a ranger. You'll see there's no date on that paper. No one will ever know just when you entered the service. Perhaps we can make it appear that all or most of your outlawry has really been good service to the state. At that, I'll believe it'll turn out so."

MacNelly paused a moment in his rapid talk, chewed his cigar, drew his brows together in a dark frown, and went on. "No man on the border knows so well as you the deadly nature of this service. It's a thousand to one that you'll be killed. I'd say there was no chance at all for any other man beside you. Your reputation will go far among the outlaws. Maybe that and your nerve and your gunplay will pull you through. I'm hoping so. But it's a long, long chance against your ever coming back."

"That's not the point," said Duane. "But in case I get killed out there —what—"

"Leave that to me," interrupted Captain MacNelly. "Your folks will know at once of your pardon and your ranger duty. If you lose your life out there I'll see your name cleared—the service you render known. You can rest assured of that."

"I am satisfied," replied Duane. "That's so much more than I've dared to hope."

"Well, it's settled, then. I'll give you money for expenses. You'll start as soon as you like—the sooner the better. I hope to think of other suggestions, especially about communicating with me."

Long after the lights were out and the low hum of voices had ceased round the campfire Duane lay wide awake, eyes staring into the blackness, marveling over the strange events of the day. He was humble, grateful to the depths of his soul. A huge and crushing burden had been lifted from his heart. He welcomed this hazardous service to the man who had saved him. Thought of his mother and sister and Uncle Jim, of his home, of old friends came rushing over him the first time in years that he had happiness in the memory. The disgrace he had put upon them would now be removed; and in the light of that, his wasted life of the past, and its probably tragic end in future service as atonement changed their aspects. And as he lay there, with the approach of sleep finally dimming the vividness of his thought, so full of mystery, shadowy faces floated in the blackness around him, haunting him as he had always been haunted.

It was broad daylight when he awakened. MacNelly was calling him to breakfast. Outside sounded voices of men, crackling of fires, snorting and stamping of horses, the barking of dogs. Duane rolled out of his blankets and made good use of the soap and towel and razor and brush nearby on a bench—things of rare luxury to an outlaw on the ride. The face he saw in the mirror was as strange as the past he had tried so hard to recall. Then he stepped to the door and went out.

The rangers were eating in a circle round a tarpaulin spread upon the ground.

"Fellows," said MacNelly, "shake hands with Buck Duane. He's on secret ranger service for me. Service that'll likely make you all hump soon! Mind you, keep mum about it."

The rangers surprised Duane with a roaring greeting, the warmth of which he soon divined was divided between pride of his acquisition to their ranks and eagerness to meet that violent service of which their captain hinted. They were jolly wild fellows, with just enough gravity in their welcome to show Duane their respect and appreciation, while not forgetting his lone-wolf record. When he had seated himself in that circle, now one of them, a feeling subtle and uplifting pervaded him.

After the meal Captain MacNelly drew Duane aside.

"Here's the money. Make it go as far as you can. Better strike straight for El Paso, snook around there and hear things. Then go to Valentine. That's near the river and within fifty miles or so of the edge of the Rim Rock. Somewhere up there Cheseldine holds fort. Somewhere to the north is the town Fairdale. But he doesn't hide all the time in the rocks. Only after some daring raid or hold-up. Cheseldine's got border towns on his staff, or scared of him, and these places we want to know about, especially Fairdale. Write me care of the adjutant at Austin. I don't have to warn you to be careful where you mail letters. Ride a hundred, two hundred miles, if necessary, or go clear to El Paso."

MacNelly stopped with an air of finality, and then Duane slowly rose.

"I'll start at once," he said, extending his hand to the captain. "I wish —I'd like to thank you!"

"Hell, man! Don't thank me!" replied MacNelly, crushing the proffered hand. "I've sent a lot of good men to their deaths, and maybe you're another. But, as I've said, you've one chance in a thousand. And, by heaven! I'd hate to be Cheseldine or any other man you were trailing. No, not goodbye—*Adios*, Duane! May we meet again!"

BOOK TWO

THE RANGER

❖15❖

WEST OF THE PECOS RIVER Texas extended a vast wild region, barren in the north where the Llano Estacado spread its shifting sands, fertile in the south along the Rio Grande. A railroad marked an undeviating course across five hundred miles of this country, and the only villages and towns lay on or near this line of steel. Unsettled as was this western Texas, and despite the acknowledged dominance of the outlaw bands, the pioneers pushed steadily into it. First had come the lone rancher; then his neighbors in near and far valleys; then the hamlets; at last the railroad and the towns. And still the pioneers came, spreading deeper into the valleys, farther and wider over the plains. It was mesquite-dotted, cactus-covered desert, but rich soil upon which water acted like magic. There was little grass to an acre, but there were millions of acres. The climate was wonderful. Cattle flourished and ranchers prospered.

The Rio Grande flowed almost due south along the western boundary for a thousand miles, and then, weary of its course, turned abruptly north, to make what was called the Big Bend. The railroad, running west, cut across this bend, and all that country bounded on the north by the railroad and on the south by the river was as wild as the Staked Plains. It contained not one settlement. Across the face of this Big Bend, as if to isolate it, stretched the Ord mountain range, of which Mount Ord, Cathedral Mount, and Elephant Mount raised bleak peaks above their fellows. In the valleys of the foothills and out across the plains were ranches, and farther north, villages, and the towns of Alpine and Marfa.

Like other parts of the great Lone Star State, this section of Texas was a world in itself—a world where the riches of the rancher were ever enriching the outlaw. The village closest to the gateway of this outlaw-infested region was a little place called Ord, named after the dark peak

541

that loomed some miles to the south. It had been settled originally by Mexicans—there were still the ruins of adobe missions—but with the advent of the rustler and outlaw many inhabitants were shot or driven away, so that at the height of Ord's prosperity and evil sway there were but few Mexicans living there, and these had their choice between holding hand-and-glove with the outlaws or furnishing target practice for that wild element.

Toward the close of a day in September a stranger rode into Ord, and in a community where all men were remarkable for one reason or another he excited interest. His horse, perhaps, received the first and most engaging attention—horses in that region being apparently more important than men. This particular horse did not attract with beauty. At first glance he seemed ugly. But he was a giant, black as coal, rough despite the care manifestly bestowed upon him, long of body, ponderous of limb, huge in every way. A bystander remarked that he had a grand head. True, if only his head had been seen he would have been a beautiful horse. Like men, horses show what they are in the shape, the size, the line, the character of the head. This one denoted fire, speed, blood, loyalty, and his eyes were as soft and dark as a woman's. His face was solid black, except in the middle of his forehead, where there was a round spot of white.

"Say mister, mind tellin' me his name?" asked a ragged urchin, with born love of a horse in his eyes.

"Bullet," replied the rider.

"Thet there's fer the white mark, ain't it?" whispered the youngster to another. "Say, ain't he a whopper? Biggest hoss I ever seen."

Bullet carried a huge black silver-ornamented saddle of Mexican make, a lariat and canteen, and a small pack rolled into a tarpaulin.

This rider apparently put all care of appearances upon his horse. His apparel was the ordinary jeans of the cowboy without vanity, and it was torn and travel-stained. His boots showed evidence of an intimate acquaintance with cactus. Like his horse, this man was a giant in stature, but rangier, not so heavily built. Otherwise the only striking thing about him was his somber face with its piercing eyes, and hair white over the temples. He packed two guns, both low down—but that was too common a thing to attract notice in the Big Bend. A close observer, however, would have noted a singular fact—this rider's right hand was more bronzed, more weather-beaten than his left. He never wore a glove on that right hand!

He had dismounted before a ramshackle structure that bore upon its wide, high-boarded front the sign, "Hotel." There were horsemen coming and going down the wide street between its rows of old stores, saloons, and houses. Ord certainly did not look enterprising. Americans had manifestly assimilated much of the leisure of the Mexicans. The hotel had a wide platform in front, and this did duty as porch and sidewalk. Upon it, and leaning against a hitching-rail, were men of varying ages, most of them slovenly in old jeans and slouched sombreros. Some were booted, belted, and spurred. No man there wore a coat, but all wore vests. The guns in that group would have outnumbered the men.

It was a crowd seemingly too lazy to be curious. Good nature did not appear to be wanting, but it was not the frank and boisterous kind natural to the cowboy or rancher in town for a day. These men were idlers; what else, perhaps, was easy to conjecture. Certainly to this arriving stranger, who flashed a keen eye over them, they wore an atmosphere never associated with work.

Presently a tall man, with a drooping, sandy mustache, leisurely detached himself from the crowd.

"Howdy, stranger," he said.

The stranger had bent over to loosen the cinches; he straightened up and nodded. Then: "I'm thirsty!"

That brought a broad smile to faces. It was characteristic greeting. One and all trooped after the stranger into the hotel. It was a dark, ill-smelling barn of a place, with a bar as high as a short man's head. A bartender with a scarred face was serving drinks.

"Line up, gents," said the stranger.

They piled over one another to get to the bar, with coarse jests and oaths and laughter. None of them noted that the stranger did not appear so thirsty as he had claimed to be. In fact, though he went through the motions, he did not drink at all.

"My name's Jim Fletcher," said the tall man with the drooping, sandy mustache. He spoke laconically, nevertheless there was a tone that showed he expected to be known. Something went with that name. The stranger did not appear to be impressed.

"My name might be Blazes, but it ain't," he replied. "What do you call this burg?"

"Stranger, this heah me-tropoles bears the handle Ord. Is thet new to you?"

He leaned back against the bar, and now his little yellow eyes, clear as crystal, flawless as a hawk's, fixed on the stranger. Other men crowded close, forming a circle, curious, ready to be friendly or otherwise, according to how the tall interrogator marked the newcomer.

"Sure, Ord's a little strange to me. Off the railroad some, ain't it? Funny trails hereabouts."

"How fur was you goin'?"

"I reckon I was goin' as far as I could," replied the stranger, with a hard laugh.

His reply had subtle reaction on that listening circle. Some of the men exchanged glances. Fletcher stroked his drooping mustache, seemed thoughtful, but lost something of that piercing scrutiny.

"Wal, Ord's the jumpin'-off place," he said, presently. "Sure you've heerd of the Big Bend country?"

"I sure have, an' was makin' tracks fer it," replied the stranger.

Fletcher turned toward a man in the outer edge of the group. "Knell, come in heah."

This individual elbowed his way in and was seen to be scarcely more than a boy, almost pale beside those bronzed men, with a long, expressionless face, thin and sharp.

"Knell, this heah's—" Fletcher wheeled to the stranger. "What 'd you call yourself?"

"I'd hate to mention what I've been callin' myself lately."

This sally fetched another laugh. The stranger appeared cool, careless, indifferent. Perhaps he knew, as the others present knew, that this show of Fletcher's, this pretense of introduction, was merely talk while he was looked over.

Knell stepped up, and it was easy to see, from the way Fletcher relinquished his part in the situation, that a man greater than he had appeared upon the scene.

"Any business here?" he queried, curtly. When he spoke his expressionless face was in strange contrast with the ring, the quality, the cruelty of his voice. This voice betrayed an absence of humor, of friendliness, of heart.

"Nope," replied the stranger.

"Know anybody hereabouts?"

"Nary one."

"Jest ridin' through?"

"Yep."

"Slopin' fer back country, eh?"

There came a pause. The stranger appeared to grow a little resentful and drew himself up disdainfully.

"Wal, considerin' you-all seem so damn friendly an' oncurious down here in this Big Bend country, I don't mind sayin' yes—I am in on the dodge," he replied, with deliberate sarcasm.

"From west of Ord—out El Paso way, mebbe?"

"Sure."

"A-huh! Thet so?" Knell's words cut the air, stilled the room. "You're from way down the river. Thet's what they say down there—'on the dodge.' . . . Stranger, you're a liar!"

With swift clink of spur and thump of boot the crowd split, leaving Knell and the stranger in the center.

Wild breed of that ilk never made a mistake in judging a man's nerve. Knell had cut out with the trenchant call, and stood ready. The stranger suddenly lost his every semblance to the rough and easy character before manifest in him. He became bronze. That situation seemed familiar to him. His eyes held a singular piercing light that danced like a compass-needle.

"Sure I lied," he said, "so I ain't takin' offense at the way you called me. I'm lookin' to make friends, not enemies. You don't strike me as one of them four-flushes, achin' to kill somebody. But if you are—go ahead an' open the ball. . . . You see, I never throw a gun on them fellers till they go fer theirs."

Knell coolly eyed his antagonist, his strange face not changing in the least. Yet somehow it was evident in his look that here was metal which rang differently from what he had expected. Invited to start a fight or withdraw, as he chose, Knell proved himself big in the manner character-istic of only the genuine gunman.

"Stranger, I pass," he said, and, turning to the bar, he ordered liquor.

The tension relaxed, the silence broke, the men filled up the gap; the incident seemed closed. Jim Fletcher attached himself to the stranger, and now both respect and friendliness tempered his asperity.

"Wal, fer want of a better handle I'll call you Dodge," he said.

"Dodge's as good as any. . . . Gents, line up again—an' if you can't be friendly, be careful!"

Such was Buck Duane's debut in the little outlaw hamlet of Ord.

Duane had been three months out of the Nueces country. At El Paso he bought the finest horse he could find, and, armed and otherwise outfit-ted to suit him, he had taken to unknown trails. Leisurely he rode from town to town, village to village, ranch to ranch, fitting his talk and his occupation to the impression he wanted to make upon different people whom he met. He was in turn a cowboy, a rancher, a cattleman, a stock-buyer, a boomer, a land-hunter; and long before he reached the wild and inhospitable Ord he had acted the part of an outlaw, drifting into new territory. He passed on leisurely because he wanted to learn the lay of the country, the location of villages and ranches, the work, habit, gossip, pleasures, and fears of the people with whom he came in contact. The one subject most impelling to him—outlaws—he never mentioned; but by talking all around it, sifting the old ranch and cattle story, he acquired a knowledge calculated to aid his plot. In this game time was of no mo-ment; if necessary he would take years to accomplish his task. The stupen-dous and perilous nature of it showed in the slow, wary preparation. When he heard Fletcher's name and faced Knell he knew he had reached the place he sought. Ord was a hamlet on the fringe of the grazing country, of doubtful honesty, from which, surely, winding trails led down into that free and never-disturbed paradise of outlaws—the Big Bend.

Duane made himself agreeable, yet not too much so, to Fletcher and several other men disposed to talk and drink and eat; and then, after having a care for his horse, he rode out of town a couple of miles to a grove he had marked, and there, well hidden, he prepared to spend the night. This proceeding served a double purpose—he was safer, and the habit would look well in the eyes of outlaws, who would be more inclined to see in him the lone-wolf fugitive.

Long since Duane had fought out a battle with himself, won a hard-earned victory. His outer life, the action, was much the same as it had been; but the inner life had tremendously changed. He could never become a happy man, he could never shake utterly those haunting phantoms that had once been his despair and madness; but he had assumed a task impossible for any man save one like him, he had felt the meaning of it grow strangely and wonderfully, and through that flourished up consciousness of how passionately he now clung to this thing which would blot out his former infamy. The iron fetters no more threatened his hands; the iron door no more haunted his dreams. He never forgot that he was free. Strangely, too, along with this feeling of new manhood there gathered the force of imperious desire to run these chief outlaws to their dooms. He never called them outlaws—but rustlers, thieves, robbers, murderers, criminals. He sensed the growth of a relentless driving passion, and sometimes he feared that, more than the newly acquired zeal and pride in this ranger service, it was the old, terrible inherited killing instinct lifting its hydra-head in new guise. But of that he could not be sure. He dreaded the thought. He could only wait.

Another aspect of the change in Duane, neither passionate nor driving, yet not improbably even more potent of new significance to life, was the imperceptible return of an old love of nature dead during his outlaw days.

For years a horse had been only a machine of locomotion, to carry him from place to place, to beat and spur and goad mercilessly in flight; now this giant black, with his splendid head, was a companion, a friend, a brother, a loved thing, guarded jealously, fed and trained and ridden with an intense appreciation of his great speed and endurance. For years the daytime, with its birth of sunrise on through long hours to the ruddy close, had been used for sleep or rest in some rocky hole or willow brake or deserted hut, had been hated because it augmented danger of pursuit, because it drove the fugitive to lonely, wretched hiding; now the dawn was a greeting, a promise of another day to ride, to plan, to remember, and sun, wind, cloud, rain, sky—all were joys to him, somehow speaking his freedom. For years the night had been a black space, during which he had to ride unseen along the endless trails, to peer with cat-eyes through gloom for the moving shape that ever pursued him; now the twilight and the dusk and the shadows of grove and canyon darkened into night with its train of stars, and brought him calm reflection of the day's happenings, of the morrow's possibilities, perhaps a sad, brief procession of the old phantoms, then sleep. For years canyons and valleys and mountains had been looked at as retreats that might be dark and wild enough to hide even an outlaw; now he saw these features of the great desert with something of the eyes of the boy who had once burned for adventure and life among them.

This night a wonderful afterglow lingered long in the west, and against the golden-red of clear sky the bold, black head of Mount Ord reared itself aloft, beautiful but aloof, sinister yet calling. Small wonder that Duane gazed in fascination upon the peak! Somewhere deep in its corrugated sides or lost in a rugged canyon was hidden the secret stronghold of the master outlaw Cheseldine. All down along the ride from El Paso Duane had heard of Cheseldine, of his band, his fearful deeds, his cunning, his widely separated raids, of his flitting here and there like a jack-o'-lantern; but never a word of his den, never a word of his appearance.

Next morning Duane did not return to Ord. He struck off to the north, riding down a rough, slow-descending road that appeared to have been used occasionally for cattle-driving. As he had ridden in from the west, this northern direction led him into totally unfamiliar country. While he passed on, however, he exercised such keen observation that in the future he would know whatever might be of service to him if he chanced that way again.

The rough, wild, brush-covered slope down from the foothills gradually leveled out into plain, a magnificent grazing country, upon which till noon of that day Duane did not see a herd of cattle or a ranch. About that time he made out smoke from the railroad, and after a couple of hours' riding he entered a town which inquiry discovered to be Bradford. It was the largest town he had visited since Marfa, and he calculated must have a thousand or fifteen hundred inhabitants, not including Mexicans. He decided this would be a good place for him to hold up for a while, being the nearest town to Ord, only forty miles away. So he hitched his horse in front of a store and leisurely set about studying Bradford.

It was after dark, however, that Duane verified his suspicions concerning Bradford. The town was awake after dark, and there was one long row of saloons, dance halls, gambling resorts in full blast. Duane visited them all, and was surprised to see wildness and license equal to that of the old river camp of Bland's in its palmiest days. Here it was forced upon him that the farther west one traveled along the river the sparser the respectable settlements, the more numerous the hard characters, and in consequence the greater the element of lawlessness. Duane returned to his lodging-house with the conviction that MacNelly's task of cleaning up the Big Bend country was a stupendous one. Yet, he reflected, a company of intrepid and quick-shooting rangers could have soon cleaned up this Bradford.

The innkeeper had one other guest that night, a long black-coated and wide-sombreroed Texan who reminded Duane of his grandfather. This man had penetrating eyes, a courtly manner, and an unmistakable leaning toward companionship and mint juleps. The gentleman introduced himself as Colonel Webb, of Marfa, and took it as a matter of course that Duane made no comment about himself.

"Sir, it's all one to me," he said, blandly, waving his hand. "I have traveled. Texas is free, and this frontier is one where it's healthier and just as friendly for a man to have no curiosity about his companion. You might be Cheseldine, of the Big Bend, or you might be Judge Little, of El Paso—it's all one to me. I enjoy drinking with you anyway."

Duane thanked him, conscious of a reserve and dignity that he could not have felt or pretended three months before. And then, as always, he was a good listener. Colonel Webb told, among other things, that he had come out to the Big Bend to look over the affairs of a deceased brother who had been a rancher and a sheriff of one of the towns, Fairdale by name.

"Found no affairs, no ranch, not even his grave," said Colonel Webb. "And I tell you, sir, if hell's any tougher than this Fairdale I don't want to expiate my sins there."

"Fairdale. . . . I imagine sheriffs have a hard row to hoe out here," replied Duane, trying not to appear curious.

The colonel swore lustily.

"My brother was the only honest sheriff Fairdale ever had. It was wonderful how long he lasted. But he had nerve, he could throw a gun, and he was on the square. Then he was wise enough to confine his work to offenders of his own town and neighborhood. He let the riding outlaws alone, else he wouldn't have lasted at all. . . . What this frontier needs, sir, is about six companies of Texas Rangers."

Duane was aware of the colonel's close scrutiny.

"Do you know anything about the service?" he asked.

"I used to. Ten years ago when I lived in San Antonio. A fine body of men, sir, and the salvation of Texas."

"Governor Stone doesn't entertain that opinion," said Duane.

Here Colonel Webb exploded. Manifestly the governor was not his choice for a chief executive of the great state. He talked politics for a while, and of the vast territory west of the Pecos that seemed never to get a benefit from Austin. He talked enough for Duane to realize that here was just the kind of intelligent, well-informed, honest citizen that he had been trying to meet. He exerted himself thereafter to be agreeable and interesting; and he saw presently that here was an opportunity to make a valuable acquaintance, if not a friend.

"I'm a stranger in these parts," said Duane, finally. "What is this outlaw situation you speak of?"

"It's damnable, sir, and unbelievable. Not rustling anymore, but just wholesale herd-stealing, in which some big cattlemen, supposed to be honest, are equally guilty with the outlaws. On this border, you know, the rustler has always been able to steal cattle in any numbers. But to get rid of big bunches—that's the hard job. The gang operating between here and Valentine evidently have not this trouble. Nobody knows where the stolen stock goes. But I'm not alone in my opinion that most of it goes to several big stockmen. They ship to San Antonio, Austin, New Orleans, also to El Paso. If you travel the stock-road between here and Marfa and

Valentine you'll see dead cattle all along the line and stray cattle out in the scrub. The herds have been driven fast and far, and stragglers are not rounded up."

"Wholesale business, eh?" remarked Duane. "Who are these—er—big stock-buyers?"

Colonel Webb seemed a little startled at the abrupt query. He bent his penetrating gaze upon Duane and thoughtfully stroked his pointed beard.

"Names, of course, I'll not mention. Opinions are one thing, direct accusation another. This is not a healthy country for the informer."

When it came to the outlaws themselves Colonel Webb was disposed to talk freely. Duane could not judge whether the colonel had a hobby of that subject or the outlaws were so striking in personality and deed that any man would know all about them. The great name along the river was Cheseldine, but it seemed to be a name detached from an individual. No person of veracity known to Colonel Webb had ever seen Cheseldine, and those who claimed that doubtful honor varied so diversely in descriptions of the chief that they confused the reality and lent to the outlaw only further mystery. Strange to say of an outlaw leader, as there was no one who could identify him, so there was no one who could prove he had actually killed a man. Blood flowed like water over the Big Bend country, and it was Cheseldine who spilled it. Yet the fact remained there were no eyewitnesses to connect any individual called Cheseldine with these deeds of violence. But in striking contrast to this mystery was the person, character, and cold-blooded action of Poggin and Knell, the chief's lieutenants. They were familiar figures in all the towns within two hundred miles of Bradford. Knell had a record, but as gunman with an incredible list of victims Poggin was supreme. If Poggin had a friend no one ever heard of him. There were a hundred stories of his nerve, his wonderful speed with a gun, his passion for gambling, his love of a horse—his cold, implacable, inhuman wiping out of his path any man that crossed it.

"Cheseldine is a name, a terrible name," said Colonel Webb. "Sometimes I wonder if he's not only a name. In that case where does the brains of this gang come from? No; there must be a master craftsman behind this border pillage; a master capable of handling those terrors Poggin and Knell. Of all the thousands of outlaws developed by western Texas in the last twenty years these three are the greatest. In southern Texas, down between the Pecos and the Nueces, there have been and are still many bad men. But I doubt if any outlaw there, possibly excepting Buck Duane, ever equaled Poggin. You've heard of this Duane?"

"Yes, a little," replied Duane, quietly. "I'm from southern Texas. Buck Duane, then, is known out here?"

"Why, man, where isn't his name known?" returned Colonel Webb. "I've kept track of his record as I have all the others. Of course, Duane, being a lone outlaw, is somewhat of a mystery also, but not like Cheseldine. Out here there have drifted many stories of Duane, horrible some of them. But despite them a sort of romance clings to that Nueces outlaw. He's killed three great outlaw leaders, I believe—Bland, Hardin, and the other I forgot. Hardin was known in the Big Bend, had friends there. Bland had a hard name at Del Rio."

"Then this man Duane enjoys rather an unusual repute west of the Pecos?" inquired Duane.

"He's considered more of an enemy to his kind than to honest men. I understand Duane had many friends, that whole counties swear by him . . . secretly, of course, for he's a hunted outlaw with rewards on his head. His fame in this country appears to hang on his matchless gunplay and his enmity toward outlaw chiefs. I've heard many a rancher say: 'I wish to God that Buck Duane would drift out here! I'd give a hundred pesos to see him and Poggin meet.' It's a singular thing, stranger, how jealous these great outlaws are of each other."

"Yes, indeed, all about them is singular," replied Duane. "Has Cheseldine's gang been busy lately?"

"No. This section has been free of rustling for months, though there's unexplained movements of stock. Probably all the stock that's being shipped now was rustled long ago. Cheseldine works over a wide section, too wide for news to travel inside of weeks. Then sometimes he's not heard of at all for a spell. These lulls are pretty surely indicative of a big storm sooner or later. And Cheseldine's deals, as they grow fewer and farther between, certainly get bigger, more daring. There are some people who think Cheseldine had nothing to do with the bank robberies and train holdups during the last few years in this country. But that's poor reasoning. The jobs have been too well done, too surely covered, to be the work of greasers or ordinary outlaws."

"What's your view of the outlook? How's all this going to wind up? Will the outlaw ever be driven out?" asked Duane.

"Never. There will always be outlaws along the Rio Grande. All the armies in the world couldn't comb the wild brakes of that fifteen hundred miles of river. But the sway of the outlaw, such as is enjoyed by these great leaders, will sooner or later be past. The criminal element flock to the Southwest. But not so thick and fast as the pioneers. Besides, the outlaws kill themselves, and the ranchers are slowly rising in wrath, if not in action. That will come soon. If they only had a leader to start the fight! But that will come. There's talk of vigilantes, the same that were organized in California and are now in force in Idaho. So far it's only talk. But the time will come. And the days of Cheseldine and Poggin are numbered."

Duane went to bed that night exceedingly thoughtful. The long trail was growing hot. This voluble colonel had given him new ideas. It came to Duane in surprise that he was famous along the upper Rio Grande. Assuredly he would not long be able to conceal his identity. He had no doubt that he would soon meet the chiefs of this clever and bold rustling gang. He could not decide whether he would be safer unknown or known. In the latter case his one chance lay in the fatality connected with his name, in his power to look it and act it. Duane had never dreamed of any sleuth-hound tendency in his nature, but now he felt something like one. Above all others his mind fixed on Poggin—Poggin the brute, the executor of Cheseldine's will, but mostly upon Poggin the gunman. This in itself was a warning to Duane. He felt terrible forces at work within him. There was the stern and indomitable resolve to make MacNelly's boast good to the governor of the state—to break up Cheseldine's gang. Yet this was not in Duane's mind before a strange grim and deadly instinct— which he had to drive away for fear he would find in it a passion to kill Poggin, not for the state, nor for his word to MacNelly, but for himself. Had his father's blood and the hard years made Duane the kind of man who instinctively wanted to meet Poggin? He was sworn to MacNelly's service, and he fought himself to keep that, and that only, in his mind.

Duane ascertained that Fairdale was situated two days' ride from Bradford toward the north. There was a stage which made the journey twice a week.

Next morning Duane mounted his horse and headed for Fairdale. He rode leisurely, as he wanted to learn all he could about the country. There were few ranches. The farther he traveled the better grazing he encountered, and, strange to note, the fewer herds of cattle.

It was just sunset when he made out a cluster of adobe houses that marked the halfway point between Bradford and Fairdale. Here, Duane had learned, was stationed a comfortable inn for wayfarers.

When he drew up before the inn the landlord and his family and a number of loungers greeted him laconically.

"Beat the stage in, hey?" remarked one.

"There she comes now," said another. "Joel shore is drivin' tonight."

Far down the road Duane saw a cloud of dust and horses and a lumbering coach. When he had looked after the needs of his horse he returned to the group before the inn. They awaited the stage with that interest common to isolated people. Presently it rolled up, a large mud-bespattered and dusty vehicle, littered with baggage on top and tied on behind. A number of passengers alighted, three of whom excited Duane's interest. One was a tall, dark, striking-looking man, and the other two were ladies, wearing long gray ulsters and veils. Duane heard the proprietor of the inn address the man as Colonel Longstreth, and as the party entered the inn Duane's quick ears caught a few words which acquainted him with the fact that Longstreth was the mayor of Fairdale.

Duane passed inside himself to learn that supper would soon be ready. At table he found himself opposite the three who had attracted his attention.

"Ruth, I envy the lucky cowboys," Longstreth was saying.

Ruth was a curly-headed girl with gray or hazel eyes.

"I'm crazy to ride bronchos," she said.

Duane gathered she was on a visit to western Texas. The other girl's deep voice, sweet like a bell, made Duane regard her closer. She had beauty as he had never seen it in another woman. She was slender, but the development of her figure gave Duane the impression she was twenty years old or more. She had the most exquisite hands Duane had ever seen. She did not resemble the colonel, who was evidently her father. She looked tired, quiet, even melancholy. A finely chiseled oval face; clear, olive-tinted skin, long eyes set wide apart and black as coal, beautiful to look into; a slender, straight nose that had something nervous and delicate about it which made Duane think of a thoroughbred; and a mouth by no means small, but perfectly curved; and hair like jet—all these features proclaimed her beauty to Duane. Duane believed her a descendant of one of the old French families of eastern Texas. He was sure of it when she looked at him, drawn by his rather persistent gaze. There were pride, fire, and passion in her eyes. Duane felt himself blushing in confusion. His stare at her had been rude, perhaps, but unconscious. How many years had passed since he had seen a girl like her! Thereafter he kept his eyes upon his plate, yet he seemed to be aware that he had aroused the interest of both girls.

After supper the guests assembled in a big sitting-room where an open fireplace with blazing mesquite sticks gave out warmth and a cheery glow. Duane took a seat by a table in the corner, and, finding a paper, began to read. Presently when he glanced up he saw two dark-faced men, strangers who had not appeared before, and were peering in from a doorway. When they saw Duane had observed them they stepped back out of sight.

It flashed over Duane that the strangers acted suspiciously. In Texas in the seventies it was always bad policy to let strangers go unheeded. Duane pondered a moment. Then he went out to look over these two men. The doorway opened into a patio, and across that was a little dingy, dim-lighted barroom. Here Duane found the innkeeper dispensing drinks to the two strangers. They glanced up when he entered, and one of them whispered. He imagined he had seen one of them before. In Texas, where outdoor men were so rough, bronzed, bold, and sometimes grim of aspect, it was no easy task to pick out the crooked ones. But Duane's years on the border had augmented a natural instinct or gift to read character, or at least to sense the evil in men; and he knew at once that these strangers were dishonest.

"Hev somethin'?" one of them asked, leering. Both looked Duane up and down.

"No thanks, I don't drink," Duane replied, and returned their scrutiny with interest. "How's tricks in the Big Bend?"

Both men stared. It had taken only a close glance for Duane to recognize a type of ruffian most frequently met along the river. These strangers had that stamp, and their surprise proved he was right. Here the innkeeper showed signs of uneasiness, and seconded the surprise of his customers. No more was said at the instant, and the two rather hurriedly went out.

"Say, boss, do you know those fellows?" Duane asked the innkeeper.

"Nope."

"Which way did they come?"

"Now I think of it, them fellers rid in from both corners today," he replied, and he put both hands on the bar and looked at Duane. "They nooned heah, comin' from Bradford, they said, an' trailed in after the stage."

When Duane returned to the sitting-room Colonel Longstreth was absent, also several of the other passengers. Miss Ruth sat in the chair he had vacated, and across the table from her sat Miss Longstreth. Duane went directly to them.

"Excuse me," said Duane, addressing them. "I want to tell you there are a couple of rough-looking men here. I've just seen them. They mean evil. Tell your father to be careful. Lock your doors—bar your windows tonight."

"Oh!" cried Ruth, very low. "Ray, do you hear?"

"Thank you; we'll be careful," said Miss Longstreth, gracefully. The rich color had faded in her cheek. "I saw those men watching you from that door. They had such bright black eyes. Is there really danger—here?"

"I think so," was Duane's reply.

Soft swift steps behind him preceded a harsh voice: "Hands up!"

No man quicker than Duane to recognize the intent in those words! His hands shot up. Miss Ruth uttered a little frightened cry and sank into her chair. Miss Longstreth turned white, her eyes dilated. Both girls were staring at someone behind Duane.

"Turn around!" ordered the harsh voice.

The big, dark stranger, the bearded one who had whispered to his comrade in the barroom and asked Duane to drink, had him covered with a cocked gun. He strode forward, his eyes gleaming, pressed the gun against him, and with his other hand dove into his inside coat pocket and tore out his roll of bills. Then he reached low at Duane's hip, felt his gun, and took it. Then he slapped the other hip, evidently in search of another weapon. That done, he backed away, wearing an expression of fiendish satisfaction that made Duane think he was only a common thief, a novice at this kind of game.

His comrade stood in the door with a gun leveled at two other men, who stood there frightened, speechless.

"Git a move on, Bill," called this fellow; and he took a hasty glance backward. A stamp of hoofs came from outside. Of course the robbers had horses waiting. The one called Bill strode across the room, and with brutal, careless haste began to prod the two men with his weapon and to search them. The robber in the doorway called "Rustle!" and disappeared.

Duane wondered where the innkeeper was, and Colonel Longstreth and the other two passengers. The bearded robber quickly got through with his searching, and from his growls Duane gathered he had not been well remunerated. Then he wheeled once more. Duane had not moved a muscle, stood perfectly calm with his arms high. The robber strode back with his bloodshot eyes fastened upon the girls. Miss Longstreth never flinched, but the little girl appeared about to faint.

"Don't yap, there!" he said, low and hard. He thrust the gun close to Ruth. Then Duane knew for sure that he was no knight of the road, but a plain cutthroat robber. Danger always made Duane exult in a kind of cold glow. But now something hot worked within him. He had a little gun in his pocket. The robber had missed it. And he began to calculate chances.

"Any money, jewelry, diamonds!" ordered the ruffian, fiercely.

Miss Ruth collapsed. Then he made at Miss Longstreth. She stood with her hands at her breast. Evidently the robber took this position to mean that she had valuables concealed there. But Duane fancied she had instinctively pressed her hands against a throbbing heart.

"Come out with it!" he said, harshly, reaching for her.

"Don't dare touch me!" she cried, her eyes ablaze. She did not move. She had nerve.

It made Duane thrill. He saw he was going to get a chance. Waiting had been a science with him. But here it was hard. Miss Ruth had fainted, and that was well. Miss Longstreth had fight in her, which fact helped Duane, yet made injury possible to her. She eluded two lunges the man made at her. Then his rough hand caught her waist, and with one pull ripped it asunder, exposing her beautiful shoulder, white as snow.

She cried out. The prospect of being robbed or even killed had not shaken Miss Longstreth's nerve as had this brutal tearing off of half her waist.

The ruffian was only turned partially away from Duane. For himself he could have waited no longer. But for her! That gun was still held dangerously upward close to her. Duane watched only that. Then a bellow made him jerk his head. Colonel Longstreth stood in the doorway in a magnificent rage. He had no weapon. Strange how he showed no fear! He bellowed something again.

Duane's shifting glance caught the robber's sudden movement. It was a kind of start. He seemed stricken. Duane expected him to shoot Longstreth. Instead the hand that clutched Miss Longstreth's torn waist loosened its hold. The other hand with its cocked weapon slowly dropped till it pointed to the floor. That was Duane's chance.

Swift as a flash he drew his gun and fired. Thud! went his bullet, and he could not tell on the instant whether it hit the robber or went into the ceiling. Then the robber's gun boomed harmlessly. He fell with blood spurting over his face. Duane realized he had hit him, but the small bullet had glanced.

Miss Longstreth reeled and might have fallen had Duane not supported her. It was only a few steps to a couch, to which he half led, half carried her. Then he rushed out of the room, across the patio, through the bar to the yard. Nevertheless, he was cautious. In the gloom stood a saddled horse, probably the one belonging to the fellow he had shot. His comrade had escaped. Returning to the sitting-room, Duane found a condition approaching pandemonium.

The innkeeper rushed in, pitchfork in hands. Evidently he had been out at the barn. He was now shouting to find out what had happened. Joel, the stage-driver, was trying to quiet the men who had been robbed. The woman, wife of one of the men, had come in, and she had hysterics. The girls were still and white. The robber Bill lay where he had fallen, and Duane guessed he had made a fair shot, after all. And, lastly, the thing that struck Duane most of all was Longstreth's rage. He never saw such passion. Like a caged lion Longstreth stalked and roared. There came a quieter moment in which the innkeeper shrilly protested:

"Man, what're you ravin' aboot? Nobody's hurt, an' thet's lucky. I swear to God I hadn't nothin' to do with them fellers!"

"I ought to kill you anyhow!" replied Longstreth. And his voice now astounded Duane, it was so full of power.

Upon examination Duane found that his bullet had furrowed the robber's temple, torn a great piece out of his scalp, and, as Duane had guessed, had glanced. He was not seriously injured, and already showed signs of returning consciousness.

"Drag him out of here!" ordered Longstreth; and he turned to his daughter.

Before the innkeeper reached the robber Duane had secured the money and gun taken from him, and presently recovered the property of the other men. Joel helped the innkeeper carry the injured man somewhere outside.

Miss Longstreth was sitting white but composed upon the couch, where lay Miss Ruth, who evidently had been carried there by the colonel. Duane did not think she had wholly lost consciousness, and now she lay very still, with eyes dark and shadowy, her face pallid and wet. The colonel, now that he finally remembered his women-folk, seemed to be gentle and kind. He talked soothingly to Miss Ruth, made light of the adventure, said she must learn to have nerve out here where things happened.

"Can I be of any service?" asked Duane, solicitously.

"Thanks; I guess there's nothing you can do. Talk to these frightened girls while I go see what's to be done with that thick-skulled robber," he replied, and, telling the girls that there was no more danger, he went out.

Miss Longstreth sat with one hand holding her torn waist in place; the other she extended to Duane. He took it awkwardly, and he felt a strange thrill.

"You saved my life," she said, in grave, sweet seriousness.

"No, no!" Duane exclaimed. "He might have struck you, hurt you, but no more."

"I saw murder in his eyes. He thought I had jewels under my dress. I couldn't bear his touch. The beast! I'd have fought. Surely my life was in peril."

"Did you kill him?" asked Miss Ruth, who lay listening.

"Oh no. He's not badly hurt."

"I'm very glad he's alive," said Miss Longstreth, shuddering.

"My intention was bad enough," Duane went on. "It was a ticklish place for me. You see, he was half drunk, and I was afraid his gun might go off. Fool careless he was!"

"Yet you say you didn't save me," Miss Longstreth returned, quickly.

"Well, let it go at that," Duane responded. "I saved you something."

"Tell me all about it?" asked Miss Ruth, who was fast recovering.

Rather embarrassed, Duane briefly told the incident from his point of view.

"Then you stood there all the time with your hands up thinking of nothing—watching for nothing except a little moment when you might draw your gun?" asked Miss Ruth.

"I guess that's about it," he replied.

"Cousin," said Miss Longstreth, thoughtfully, "it was fortunate for us that this gentleman happened to be here. Papa scouts—laughs at danger. He seemed to think there was no danger. Yet he raved after it came."

"Go with us all the way to Fairdale—please?" asked Miss Ruth, sweetly offering her hand. "I am Ruth Herbert. And this is my cousin, Ray Longstreth."

"I'm traveling that way," replied Duane, in great confusion. He did not know how to meet the situation.

Colonel Longstreth returned then, and after bidding Duane a good night, which seemed rather curt by contrast to the graciousness of the girls, he led them away.

Before going to bed Duane went outside to take a look at the injured robber and perhaps to ask him a few questions. To Duane's surprise, he was gone, and so was his horse. The innkeeper was dumbfounded. He said that he left the fellow on the floor in the barroom.

"Had he come to?" inquired Duane.

"Sure. He asked for whisky."

"Did he say anything else?"

"Not to me. I heard him talkin' to the father of them girls."

"You mean Colonel Longstreth?"

"I reckon. He sure was some riled, wasn't he? Jest as if I was to blame fer that two-bit of a hold-up!"

"What did you make of the old gent's rage?" asked Duane, watching the innkeeper. He scratched his head dubiously. He was sincere, and Duane believed in his honesty.

"Wal, I'm doggoned if I know what to make of it. But I reckon he's either crazy or got more nerve than most Texans."

"More nerve, maybe," Duane replied. "Show me a bed now, innkeeper."

Once in bed in the dark, Duane composed himself to think over the several events of the evening. He called up the details of the holdup and carefully revolved them in mind. The colonel's wrath, under circumstances where almost any Texan would have been cool, nonplussed Duane, and he put it down to a choleric temperament. He pondered long on the action of the robber when Longstreth's bellow of rage burst in upon him. This ruffian, as bold and mean a type as Duane had ever encountered, had, from some cause or other, been startled. From whatever point Duane viewed the man's strange indecision he could come to only one conclusion—his start, his check, his fear had been that of recognition. Duane compared this effect with the suddenly acquired sense he had gotten of Colonel Longstreth's powerful personality. Why had that desperate robber lowered his gun and stood paralyzed at sight and sound of the mayor of Fairdale? This was not answerable. There might have been a number of reasons, all to Colonel Longstreth's credit, but Duane could not understand. Longstreth had not appeared to see danger for his daughter, even though she had been roughly handled, and had advanced in front of a cocked gun. Duane probed deep into this singular fact, and he brought to bear on the thing all his knowledge and experience of violent Texas life. And he found that the instant Colonel Longstreth had appeared on the scene there *was* no further danger threatening his daughter. Why? That likewise Duane could not answer. Then his rage, Duane concluded, had been solely at the idea of *his* daughter being assaulted by a robber. This deduction was indeed a thought-disturber, but Duane put it aside to crystallize and for more careful consideration.

Next morning Duane found that the little town was called Sanderson. It was larger than he had at first supposed. He walked up the main street and back again. Just as he arrived some horsemen rode up to the inn and dismounted. And at this juncture the Longstreth party came out. Duane heard Colonel Longstreth utter an exclamation. Then he saw him shake hands with a tall man. Longstreth looked surprised and angry, and he spoke with force; but Duane could not hear what it was he said. The fellow laughed, yet somehow he struck Duane as sullen, until suddenly he espied Miss Longstreth. Then his face changed, and he removed his sombrero. Duane went closer.

"Floyd, did you come with the teams?" asked Longstreth, sharply.

"Not me. I rode a horse, good and hard," was the reply.

"Humph! I'll have a word to say to you later." Then Longstreth turned to his daughter. "Ray, here's the cousin I've told you about. You used to play with him ten years ago—Floyd Lawson. Floyd, my daughter—and my niece, Ruth Herbert."

Duane always scrutinized everyone he met, and now with a dangerous game to play, with a consciousness of Longstreth's unusual and significant personality, he bent a keen and searching glance upon this Floyd Lawson.

He was under thirty, yet gray at his temples—dark, smooth-shaven, with lines left by wildness, dissipation, shadows under dark eyes, a mouth strong and bitter, and a square chin—a reckless, careless, handsome, sinister face strangely losing the hardness when he smiled. The grace of a gentleman clung round him, seemed like an echo in his mellow voice. Duane doubted not that he, like many a young man, had drifted out to the frontier, where rough and wild life had wrought sternly but had not quite effaced the mark of good family.

Colonel Longstreth apparently did not share the pleasure of his daughter and his niece in the advent of this cousin. Something hinged on this meeting. Duane grew intensely curious, but, as the stage appeared ready for the journey, he had no further opportunity to gratify it.

⸙16⸙

DUANE followed the stage through the town, out into the open, onto a wide, hard-packed road showing years of travel. It headed northwest. To the left rose a range of low, bleak mountains he had noted yesterday, and to the right sloped the mesquite-patched sweep of ridge and flat. The driver pushed his team to a fast trot, which gait surely covered ground rapidly.

The stage made three stops in the forenoon, one at a place where the horses could be watered, the second at a chuck-wagon belonging to cowboys who were riding after stock, and the third at a small cluster of adobe and stone houses constituting a hamlet the driver called Longstreth, named after the colonel. From that point on to Fairdale there were only a few ranches, each one controlling great acreage.

Early in the afternoon from a ridge-top Duane sighted Fairdale, a green patch in the mass of gray. For the barrens of Texas it was indeed a fair sight. But he was more concerned with its remoteness from civilization than its beauty. At that time, in the early seventies, when the vast western third of Texas was a wilderness, the pioneer had done wonders to settle there and establish places like Fairdale.

It needed only a glance for Duane to pick out Colonel Longstreth's ranch. The house was situated on the only elevation around Fairdale, and it was not high, nor more than a few minutes' walk from the edge of the town. It was a low, flat-roofed structure made of red adobe bricks, and covered what appeared to be fully an acre of ground. All was green about it, except where the fenced corrals and numerous barns or sheds showed gray and red.

Duane soon reached the shady outskirts of Fairdale, and entered the town with mingled feelings of curiosity, eagerness, and expectation. The street he rode down was a main one, and on both sides of the street was a solid row of saloons, resorts, hotels. Saddled horses stood hitched all along the sidewalk in two long lines, with a buckboard and team here and there breaking the continuity. This block was busy and noisy.

From all outside appearances Fairdale was no different from other frontier towns, and Duane's expectations were scarcely realized. As the afternoon was waning he halted at a little inn. A boy took charge of his horse. Duane questioned the lad about Fairdale and gradually drew to the subject most in mind.

"Colonel Longstreth has a big outfit, eh?"

"Reckon he has," replied the lad. "Doan know how many cowboys. They're always comin' and goin'. I ain't acquainted with half of them."

"Much movement of stock these days?"

"Stock's always movin'," he replied, with a queer look.

"Rustlers?"

But he did not follow up that look with the affirmative Duane expected.

"Lively place, I hear—Fairdale is?"

"Ain't so lively as Sanderson, but it's bigger."

"Yes, I heard it was. Fellow down there was talking about two cowboys who were arrested."

"Sure. I heered all about that. Joe Bean an' Brick Higgins—they belong heah, but they ain't heah much. Longstreth's boys."

Duane did not want to appear overinquisitive, so he turned the talk into other channels.

After getting supper Duane strolled up and down the main street. When darkness set in he went into a hotel, bought cigars, sat around, and

watched. Then he passed out and went into the next place. This was of
rough crude exterior, but the inside was comparatively pretentious and
ablaze with lights. It was full of men coming and going—a dusty-booted
crowd that smelled of horses and smoke. Duane sat down for a while, with
wide eyes and open ears. Then he hunted up the bar, where most of the
guests had been or were going. He found a great square room lighted by
six huge lamps, a bar at one side, and all the floor-space taken up by tables
and chairs. This was the only gambling-place of any size in southern
Texas in which he had noted the absence of Mexicans. There was some
card-playing going on at this moment. Duane stayed in there for a while,
and knew that strangers were too common in Fairdale to be conspicuous.
Then he returned to the inn where he had engaged a room.

Duane sat down on the steps of the dingy little restaurant. Two men
were conversing inside, and they had not noticed Duane.

"Laramie, what's the stranger's name?" asked one.

"He didn't say," replied the other.

"Sure was a strappin' big man. Struck me a little odd, he did. No
cattleman, him. How'd you size him?"

"Well, like one of them cool, easy, quiet Texans who's been lookin' for
a man for years—to kill him when he found him."

"Right you are, Laramie; and, between you an' me, I hope he's lookin'
for Long—"

"S-sh!" interrupted Laramie. "You must be half drunk, to go talkin'
that way."

Thereafter they conversed in too low a tone for Duane to hear, and
presently Laramie's visitor left. Duane went inside, and, making himself
agreeable, began to ask casual questions about Fairdale. Laramie was not
communicative.

Duane went to his room in a thoughtful frame of mind. Had Laramie's
visitor meant he hoped someone had come to kill Longstreth? Duane
inferred just that from the interrupted remark. There was something
wrong about the mayor of Fairdale. Duane felt it. And he felt also, if there
was a crooked and dangerous man, it was this Floyd Lawson. The innkeeper Laramie would be worth cultivating. And last in Duane's thoughts
that night was Miss Longstreth. He could not help thinking of her—how
strangely the meeting with her had affected him. It made him remember
that long-past time when girls had been a part of his life. What a sad and
dark and endless void lay between that past and the present! He had no
right even to dream of a beautiful woman like Ray Longstreth. That
conviction, however, did not dispel her; indeed, it seemed perversely to
make her grow more fascinating. Duane grew conscious of a strange,
unaccountable hunger, a something that was like a pang in his breast.

Next day he lounged about the inn. He did not make any overtures to
the taciturn proprietor. Duane had no need of hurry now. He contented

himself with watching and listening. And at the close of that day he decided Fairdale was what MacNelly had claimed it to be, and that he was on the track of an unusual adventure. The following day he spent in much the same way, though on one occasion he told Laramie he was looking for a man. The innkeeper grew a little less furtive and reticent after that. He would answer casual queries, and it did not take Duane long to learn that Laramie had seen better days—that he was now broken, bitter and hard. Someone had wronged him.

Several days passed. Duane did not succeed in getting any closer to Laramie, but he found the idlers on the corners and in front of the stores unsuspicious and willing to talk. It did not take him long to find out that Fairdale stood parallel with Huntsville for gambling, drinking, and fighting. The street was always lined with dusty, saddled horses, the town full of strangers. Money appeared more abundant than in any place Duane had ever visited; and it was spent with the abandon that spoke forcibly of easy and crooked acquirement. Duane decided that Sanderson, Bradford, and Ord were but notorious outposts to this Fairdale, which was a secret center of rustlers and outlaws. And what struck Duane strangest of all was the fact that Longstreth was mayor here and held court daily. Duane knew intuitively, before a chance remark gave him proof, that this court was a sham, a farce. And he wondered if it were not a blind. This wonder of his was equivalent to suspicion of Colonel Longstreth, and Duane reproached himself. Then he realized that the reproach was because of the daughter. Inquiry had brought him the fact that Ray Longstreth had just come to live with her father. Longstreth had originally been a planter in Louisiana, where his family had remained after his advent in the West. He was a rich rancher; he owned half of Fairdale; he was a cattle-buyer on a large scale. Floyd Lawson was his lieutenant and associate in deals.

On the afternoon of the fifth day of Duane's stay in Fairdale he returned to the inn from his usual stroll, and upon entering was amazed to have a rough-looking young fellow rush by him out of the door. Inside Laramie was lying on the floor, with a bloody bruise on his face. He did not appear to be dangerously hurt.

"Bo Snecker! He hit me and went after the cash-drawer," said Laramie, laboring to his feet.

"Are you hurt much?" queried Duane.

"I guess not. But Bo needn't to have socked me. I've been robbed before without that."

"Well, I'll take a look after Bo," replied Duane.

He went out and glanced down the street toward the center of the town. He did not see anyone he could take for the innkeeper's assailant. Then he looked up the street, and he saw the young fellow about a block away, hurrying along and gazing back.

Duane yelled for him to stop and started to go after him. Snecker broke into a run. Then Duane set out to overhaul him. There were two motives in Duane's action—one of anger, and the other a desire to make a friend of this man Laramie, whom Duane believed could tell him much.

Duane was light on his feet, and he had a giant stride. He gained rapidly upon Snecker, who, turning this way and that, could not get out of sight. Then he took to the open country and ran straight for the green hill where Longstreth's house stood. Duane had almost caught Snecker when he reached the shrubbery and trees and there eluded him. But Duane kept him in sight, in the shade, on the paths, and up the road into the courtyard, and he saw Snecker go straight for Longstreth's house.

Duane was not to be turned back by that, singular as it was. He did not stop to consider. It seemed enough to know that fate had directed him to the path of this rancher Longstreth. Duane entered the first open door on that side of the court. It opened into a corridor which led into a plaza. It had wide, smooth stone porches, and flowers and shrubbery in the center. Duane hurried through to burst into the presence of Miss Longstreth and a number of young people. Evidently she was giving a little party.

Lawson stood leaning against one of the pillars that supported the porch roof; at sight of Duane his face changed remarkably, expressing amazement, consternation, then fear.

In the quick ensuing silence Miss Longstreth rose white as her dress. The young women present stared in astonishment, if they were not equally perturbed. There were cowboys present who suddenly grew intent and still. By these things Duane gathered that his appearance must be disconcerting. He was panting. He wore no hat or coat. His big gun-sheath showed plainly at his hip.

Sight of Miss Longstreth had an unaccountable effect upon Duane. He was plunged into confusion. For the moment he saw no one but her.

"Miss Longstreth—I came—to search—your house," panted Duane.

He hardly knew what he was saying, yet the instant he spoke he realized that that should have been the last thing for him to say. He had blundered. But he was not used to women, and this dark-eyed girl made him thrill and his heart beat thickly and his wits go scattering.

"Search my house!" exclaimed Miss Longstreth; and red succeeded the white in her cheeks. She appeared astonished and angry. "What for? Why, how dare you! This is unwarrantable!"

"A man—Bo Snecker—assaulted and robbed Jim Laramie," replied Duane, hurriedly. "I chased Snecker here—saw him run into the house."

"Here? Oh, sir, you must be mistaken. We have seen no one. In the absence of my father I'm mistress here. I'll not permit you to search."

Lawson appeared to come out of his astonishment. He stepped forward.

"Ray, don't be bothered now," he said, to his cousin. "This fellow's making a bluff. I'll settle him. See here, mister, you clear out!"

"I want Snecker. He's here, and I'm going to get him," replied Duane, quietly.

"Bah! That's all a bluff," sneered Lawson. "I'm onto your game. You just wanted an excuse to break in here—to see my cousin again. When you saw the company you invented that excuse. Now, be off, or it'll be the worse for you."

Duane felt his face burn with a tide of hot blood. Almost he felt that he was guilty of such motive. Had he not been unable to put this Ray Longstreth out of his mind? There seemed to be scorn in her eyes now. And somehow that checked his embarrassment.

"Miss Longstreth, will you let me search the house?" he asked.

"No."

"Then—I regret to say—I'll do so without your permission."

"You'll not dare!" she flashed. She stood erect, her bosom swelling.

"Pardon me—yes, I will."

"Who are you?" she demanded, suddenly.

"I'm a Texas Ranger," replied Duane.

"*A Texas Ranger!*" she echoed.

Floyd Lawson's dark face turned pale.

"Miss Longstreth, I don't need warrants to search houses," said Duane. "I'm sorry to annoy you. I'd prefer to have your permission. A ruffian has taken refuge here—in your father's house. He's hidden somewhere. May I look for him?"

"If you are indeed a ranger."

Duane produced his papers. Miss Longstreth haughtily refused to look at them.

"Miss Longstreth, I've come to make Fairdale a safer, cleaner, better place for women and children. I don't wonder at your resentment. But to doubt me—insult me. Someday you may be sorry."

Floyd Lawson made a violent motion with his hands.

"All stuff! Cousin, go on with your party. I'll take a couple of cowboys and go with this—this Texas Ranger."

"Thanks," said Duane, coolly, as he eyed Lawson. "Perhaps you'll be able to find Snecker quicker than I could."

"What do you mean?" demanded Lawson, and now he grew livid. Evidently he was a man of fierce, quick passions.

"Don't quarrel," said Miss Longstreth. "Floyd, you go with him. Please hurry. I'll be nervous till . . . the man's found or you're sure there's not one."

They started with several cowboys to search the house. They went through the rooms searching, calling out, peering into dark places. It struck Duane more than forcibly that Lawson did all the calling. He was hurried, too, tried to keep in the lead. Duane wondered if he knew his voice would be recognized by the hiding man. Be that as it might, it was Duane who peered into a dark corner and then, with a gun leveled, said, "Come out!"

He came forth into the flare—a tall, slim, dark-faced youth, wearing sombrero, blouse and trousers. Duane collared him before any of the others could move and held the gun close enough to make him shrink. But he did not impress Duane as being frightened just then; nevertheless, he had a clammy face, the pallid look of a man who had just gotten over a shock. He peered into Duane's face, then into that of the cowboy next to him, then into Lawson's, and if ever in Duane's life he beheld relief it was then. That was all Duane needed to know, but he meant to find out more if he could.

"Who're you?" asked Duane, quietly.

"Bo Snecker," he said.

"What 'd you hide here for?"

He appeared to grow sullen.

"Reckoned I'd be as safe in Longstreth's as anywheres."

"Ranger, what'll you do with him?" Lawson queried, as if uncertain, now the capture was made.

"I'll see to that," replied Duane, and he pushed Snecker in front of him out into the court.

Duane had suddenly conceived the idea of taking Snecker before Mayor Longstreth in the court.

When Duane arrived at the hall where court was held there were other men there, a dozen or more, and all seemed excited; evidently, news of Duane had preceded him. Longstreth sat at a table up on a platform. Near him sat a thick-set grizzled man, with deep eyes, and this was Hanford Owens, county judge. To the right stood a tall, angular, yellow-faced fellow with a drooping sandy mustache. Conspicuous on his vest was a huge silver shield. This was Gorsech, one of Longstreth's sheriffs. There were four other men whom Duane knew by sight, several whose faces were familiar, and half a dozen strangers, all dusty horsemen.

Longstreth pounded hard on the table to be heard. Mayor or not, he was unable at once to quell the excitement. Gradually, however, it subsided, and from the last few utterances before quiet was restored Duane gathered that he had intruded upon some kind of a meeting in the hall.

"What 'd you break in here for," demanded Longstreth.

"Isn't this the court? Aren't you the mayor of Fairdale?" interrogated Duane. His voice was clear and loud, almost piercing.

"Yes," replied Longstreth. Like flint he seemed, yet Duane felt his intense interest.

"I've arrested a criminal," said Duane.

"Arrested a criminal!" ejaculated Longstreth. *"You?* Who're you?"

"I'm a ranger," replied Duane.

A significant silence ensued.

"I charge Snecker with assault on Laramie and attempted robbery—if not murder. He's had a shady past here, as this court will know if it keeps a record."

"What's this I hear about you, Bo? Get up and speak for yourself," said Longstreth, gruffly.

Snecker got up, not without a furtive glance at Duane, and he had shuffled forward a few steps toward the mayor. He had an evil front, but not the boldness even of a rustler.

"It ain't so, Longstreth," he began, loudly. "I went in Laramie's place fer grub. Some feller I never seen before come in from the hall an' hit Laramie an' wrastled him on the floor. I went out. Then this big ranger chased me an' fetched me here. I didn't do nothin'. This ranger's hankerin' to arrest somebody. Thet's my hunch, Longstreth."

Longstreth said something in an undertone to Judge Owens, and that worthy nodded his great bushy head.

"Bo, you're discharged," said Longstreth, bluntly. "Now the rest of you clear out of here."

He absolutely ignored the ranger. That was his rebuff to Duane—his slap in the face to an interfering ranger service. If Longstreth was crooked he certainly had magnificent nerve. Duane almost decided he was above suspicion. But his nonchalance, his air of finality, his authoritative assurance—these to Duane's keen and practiced eyes were in significant contrast to a certain tenseness of line about his mouth and a slow paling of his olive skin. In that momentary lull Duane's scrutiny of Longstreth gathered an impression of the man's intense curiosity.

Then the prisoner, Snecker, with a cough that broke the spell of silence, shuffled a couple of steps toward the door.

"Hold on!" called Duane. The call halted Snecker, as if it had been a bullet.

"Longstreth, I saw Snecker attack Laramie," said Duane, his voice still ringing. "What has the court to say to that?"

"The court has this to say. West of the Pecos we'll not aid any ranger service. We don't want you out here. Fairdale doesn't need you."

"That's a lie, Longstreth," retorted Duane. "I've letters from Fairdale citizens all begging for ranger service."

Longstreth turned white. The veins corded at his temples. He appeared about to burst into rage. He was at a loss for quick reply.

Floyd Lawson rushed in and up to the table. The blood showed black and thick in his face; his utterance was incoherent, his uncontrollable outbreak of temper seemed out of all proportion to any cause he should reasonably have had for anger. Longstreth shoved him back with a curse and a warning glare.

"Where's your warrant to arrest Snecker?" shouted Longstreth.

"I don't need warrants to make arrests. Longstreth, you're ignorant of the power of Texas Rangers."

"You'll come none of your damned ranger stunts out here. I'll block you."

That passionate reply of Longstreth's was the signal Duane had been waiting for. He had helped on the crisis. He wanted to force Longstreth's hand and show the town his stand.

Duane backed clear of everybody.

"Men! I call on you all!" cried Duane, piercingly. "I call on you to witness the arrest of a criminal prevented by Longstreth, mayor of Fairdale. It will be recorded in the report to the Adjutant-General at Austin. Longstreth, you'll never prevent another arrest."

Longstreth sat white with working jaw.

"Longstreth, you've shown your hand," said Duane, in a voice that carried far and held those who heard. "Any honest citizen of Fairdale can now see what's plain—yours is a damn poor hand! You're going to hear me call a spade a spade. In the two years you've been mayor you've never arrested one rustler. Strange, when Fairdale's a nest for rustlers! You've never sent a prisoner to Del Rio, let alone to Austin. You have no jail. There have been nine murders during your office—innumerable streetfights and holdups. Not one arrest! But you have ordered arrests for trivial offenses, and have punished these out of all proportion. There have been lawsuits in your court—suits over water rights, cattle deals, property lines. Strange how in these lawsuits you or Lawson or other men close to you were always involved! Strange how it seems the law was stretched to favor your interest!"

Duane paused in his cold, ringing speech. In the silence, both outside and inside the hall, could be heard the deep breathing of agitated men. Longstreth was indeed a study. Yet did he betray anything but rage at this interloper?

"Longstreth, here's plain talk for you and Fairdale," went on Duane. "I don't accuse you and your court of dishonesty. I say *strange!* Law here has been a farce. The motive behind all this laxity isn't plain to me—yet. But I call your hand!"

17

DUANE left the hall, elbowed his way through the crowd, and went down the street. He was certain that on the faces of some men he had seen ill-concealed wonder and satisfaction. He had struck some kind of a hot trail, and he meant to see where it led. It was by no means unlikely that Cheseldine might be at the other end. Duane controlled a mounting eagerness. But ever and anon it was shot through with a remembrance of Ray Longstreth. He suspected her father of being not what he pretended. He might, very probably would, bring sorrow and shame to this young woman. The thought made him smart with pain. She began to haunt him, and then he was thinking more of her beauty and sweetness than of the disgrace he might bring upon her. Some strange emotion, long locked inside Duane's heart, knocked to be heard, to be let out. He was troubled.

Upon returning to the inn he found Laramie there, apparently none the worse for his injury.

"How are you, Laramie?" he asked.

"Reckon I'm feelin' as well as could be expected," replied Laramie. His head was circled by a bandage that did not conceal the lump where he had been struck. He looked pale, but was bright enough.

"That was a good crack Snecker gave you," remarked Duane.

"I ain't accusin' Bo," remonstrated Laramie with eyes that made Duane thoughtful.

"Well, I accuse him. I caught him—took him to Longstreth's court. But they let him go."

Laramie appeared to be agitated by this intimation of friendship.

"See here, Laramie," went on Duane, "in some parts of Texas it's policy to be close-mouthed. Policy and health-preserving! Between ourselves, I want you to know I lean on your side of the fence."

Laramie gave a quick start. Presently Duane turned and frankly met his gaze. He had startled Laramie out of his habitual set taciturnity; but even as he looked the light that might have been amaze and joy faded out of his face, leaving it the same old mask. Still Duane had seen enough. Like a bloodhound he had a scent.

"Talking about work, Laramie, who'd you say Snecker worked for?"

"I didn't say."

"Well, say so now, can't you? Laramie, you're powerful peevish today. It's that bump on your head. Who does Snecker work for?"

"When he works at all, which sure ain't often, he rides for Longstreth."

"Humph! Seems to me that Longstreth's the whole circus round Fairdale. I was some sore the other day to find I was losing good money at Longstreth's faro game. Sure if I'd won I wouldn't have been sore—ha, ha! But I was surprised to hear someone say Longstreth owned the Hope So joint."

"He owns considerable property hereabouts," replied Laramie, constrainedly.

"Humph again! Laramie, like every other fellow I meet in this town, you're afraid to open your trap about Longstreth. Get me straight, Laramie. I don't care a damn for Colonel Mayor Longstreth. And for cause I'd throw a gun on him just as quick as on any rustler in Pecos."

"Talk's cheap," replied Laramie, making light of his bluster, but the red was deeper in his face.

"Sure. I know that," Duane said. "And usually I don't talk. Then it's not well known that Longstreth owns the Hope So?"

"Reckon it's known in Pecos, all right. But Longstreth's name isn't connected with the Hope So. Blandy runs the place."

"That Blandy. His faro game's crooked, or I'm a locoed bronch. Not that we don't have lots of crooked faro-dealers. A fellow can stand for them. But Blandy's mean, back-handed, never looks you in the eyes. That Hope So place ought to be run by a good fellow like you, Laramie."

"Thanks," replied he; and Duane imagined his voice a little husky. "Didn't you hear I used to—run it?"

"No. Did you?" Duane said, quickly.

"I reckon. I built the place, made additions twice, owned it for eleven years."

"Well, I'll be doggoned." It was indeed Duane's turn to be surprised, and with the surprise came a glimmering. "I'm sorry you're not there now. Did you sell out?"

"No. Just lost the place."

Laramie was bursting for relief now—to talk, to tell. Sympathy had made him soft.

"It was two years ago—two years last March," he went on. "I was in a big cattle deal with Longstreth. We got the stock—an' my share, eighteen hundred head, was rustled off. I owed Longstreth. He pressed me. It come to a lawsuit—an' I—was ruined."

It hurt Duane to look at Laramie. He was white, and tears rolled down his cheeks. Duane saw the bitterness, the defeat, the agony of the man. He had failed to meet his obligations; nevertheless, he had been swindled. All that he suppressed, all that would have been passion had the man's spirit not been broken, lay bare for Duane to see. He had now the secret of his bitterness. But the reason he did not openly accuse Longstreth, the secret of his reticence and fear—these Duane thought best to try to learn at some later time.

"Hard luck! It certainly was tough," Duane said. "But you're a good loser. And the wheel turns! Now, Laramie, here's what. I need your advice. I've got a little money. But before I lose it I want to invest some. Buy some stock, or buy an interest in some rancher's herd. What I want you to steer me on is a good square rancher. Or maybe a couple of ranchers, if there happen to be two honest ones. Ha, ha! No deals with ranchers who ride in the dark with rustlers! I've a hunch Fairdale is full of them. Now, Laramie, you've been here for years. Sure you must know a couple of men above suspicion."

"Thank God I do," he replied, feelingly. "Frank Morton an' Si Zimmer, my friends an' neighbors all my prosperous days, an' friends still. You can gamble on Frank an' Si. But if you want advice from me—don't invest money in stock now."

"Why?"

"Because any new feller buyin' stock these days will be rustled quicker 'n he can say Jack Robinson. The pioneers, the new cattlemen—these are easy pickin' for the rustlers. Lord knows all the ranchers are easy enough pickin'. But the new fellers have to learn the ropes. They don't know anythin' or anybody. An' the old ranchers are wise an' sore. They'd fight if they—"

"What?" Duane put in, as he paused. "If they knew who was rustling the stock?"

"Nope."

"If they had the nerve?"

"Not thet so much."

"What then? What'd make them fight?"

"A leader!"

"Howdy thar, Jim," boomed a big voice.

A man of great bulk, with a ruddy, merry face, entered the room.

"Hello, Morton," replied Laramie. "I'd introduce you to my guest here, but I don't know his name."

"Haw! Haw! Thet's all right. Few men out hyar go by their right names."

"Say, Morton," put in Duane, "Laramie gave me a hunch you'd be a good man to tie to. Now, I've a little money and before I lose it I'd like to invest it in stock."

Morton smiled broadly.

"I'm on the square," Duane said, bluntly. "If you fellows never size up your neighbors any better than you have sized me—well, you won't get any richer."

It was enjoyment for Duane to make his remarks to these men pregnant with meaning. Morton showed his pleasure, his interest, but his faith held aloof.

"I've got some money. Will you let me in on some kind of deal? Will you start me up as a stockman with a little herd all my own?"

"Wal, stranger, to come out flat-footed, you'd be foolish to buy cattle now. I don't want to take your money an' see you lose out. Better go back across the Pecos where the rustlers ain't so strong. I haven't had more'n twenty-five hundred herd of stock for ten years. The rustlers let me hang on to a breedin' herd. Kind of them, ain't it?"

"Sort of kind. All I hear is rustlers, Morton," replied Duane, with impatience. "You see, I haven't ever lived long in a rustler-run county. Who heads the gang, anyway?"

Morton looked at Duane with a curiously amused smile, then snapped his big jaw as if to shut in impulsive words.

"Look here, Morton. It stands to reason, no matter how strong these rustlers are, how hidden their work, however involved with supposedly honest men—they *can't* last."

"They come with the pioneers, an' they'll last till thar's a single steer left," he declared.

"Well, if you take that view of circumstances I just figure you as one of the rustlers!"

Morton looked as if he were about to brain Duane with the butt of his whip. His anger flashed by then, evidently as unworthy of him; and, something striking him as funny, he boomed out a laugh.

"It's not so funny," Duane went on. "If you're going to pretend a yellow streak, what else will I think?"

"Pretend?" he repeated.

"Sure. I know men of nerve. And here they're not any different from those in other places. I say if you show anything like a lack of sand it's all bluff. By nature you've got nerve. There are a lot of men around Fairdale who're afraid of their shadows—afraid to be out after dark—afraid to open their mouths. But you're not one. So I say if you claim these rustlers will last you're pretending lack of nerve just to help the popular idea along. For they *can't* last. What you need out here is some new blood. Savvy what I mean?"

"Wal, I reckon I do," he replied, looking as if a storm had blown over him. "Stranger, I'll look you up the next time I come to town."

Then he went out.

Laramie had eyes like flint striking fire.

He breathed a deep breath and looked around the room before his gaze fixed again on Duane.

"Wal," he replied, speaking low. "You've picked the right men. Now, who in the hell are you?"

Reaching into the inside pocket of his buckskin vest, Duane turned the lining out. A star-shaped bright silver object flashed as he shoved it, pocket and all, under Jim's hard eyes.

"*Ranger!*" he whispered, cracking the table with his fist. "You sure rung true to me."

"Laramie, do you know who's boss of this secret gang of rustlers hereabouts?" asked Duane, bluntly. It was characteristic of him to come sharp to the point. His voice—something deep, easy, cool about him—seemed to steady Laramie.

"No," replied Laramie.

"Does anybody know?" went on Duane.

"Wal, I reckon there's not one honest native who *knows.*"

"But you have your suspicions?"

"We have."

"Give me your idea about this crowd that hangs round the saloons—the regulars."

"Jest a bad lot," replied Laramie, with the quick assurance of knowledge. "Most of them have been here years. Others have drifted in. Some of them work, odd times. They rustle a few steers, steal, rob, anythin' for a little money to drink an' gamble. Jest a bad lot!"

"Have you any idea whether Cheseldine and his gang are associated with this gang here?"

"Lord knows. I've always suspected them the same gang. None of us ever seen Cheseldine—an' thet's strange, when Knell, Poggin, Panhandle Smith, Blossom Kane, and Fletcher, they all ride here often. No, Poggin doesn't come often. But the others do. For thet matter, they're around all over west of the Pecos."

"Now I'm puzzled over this," said Duane. "Why do men—apparently honest men—seem to be so close-mouthed here? Is that a fact, or only my impression?"

"It's a sure fact," replied Laramie, darkly. "Men have lost cattle an' property in Fairdale—lost them honestly or otherwise, as hasn't been proved. An' in some cases when they talked—hinted a little—they was found dead. Apparently held up an' robbed. But dead. Dead men don't talk! Thet's why we're close-mouthed."

Duane felt a dark, somber sternness. Rustling cattle was not intolerable. Western Texas had gone on prospering, growing in spite of the hordes of rustlers ranging its vast stretches; but a cold, secret, murderous hold on a little struggling community was something too strange, too terrible for men to stand long.

The ranger was about to speak again when the clatter of hoofs interrupted him. Horses halted out in front, and one rider got down. Floyd Lawson entered. He called for tobacco.

If his visit surprised Laramie he did not show any evidence. But Lawson showed rage as he saw the ranger, and then a dark glint flitted from the eyes that shifted from Duane to Laramie and back again. Duane leaned easily against the counter.

"Say, that was a bad break of yours," Lawson said. "If you come fooling round the ranch again there'll be hell."

It seemed strange that a man who had lived west of the Pecos for ten years could not see in Duane something which forbade that kind of talk. It certainly was not nerve Lawson showed; men of courage were seldom intolerant. With the matchless nerve that characterized the great gunmen of the day there was a cool, unobtrusive manner, a speech brief, almost gentle, certainly courteous. Lawson was a hot-headed Louisianian of French extraction; a man, evidently, who had never been crossed in anything, and who was strong, brutal, passionate, which qualities in the face of a situation like this made him simply a fool.

"I'm saying again, you used your ranger bluff just to get near Ray Longstreth," Lawson sneered. "Mind you, if you come up there again there'll be hell."

"You're right. But not the kind you think," Duane retorted, his voice sharp and cold.

"Ray Longstreth wouldn't stoop to know a dirty blood-tracker like you," said Lawson, hotly. He did not seem to have a deliberate intention to rouse Duane; the man was simply rancorous, jealous. "I'll call you right, you cheap bluffer! You four-flush! You damned interfering, conceited ranger!"

"Lawson, I'll not take offense, because you seem to be championing your beautiful cousin," replied Duane, in slow speech. "But let me return your compliment. You're a fine Southerner! Why, you're only a cheap four-flush—damned, bullheaded *rustler!*"

Duane hissed the last word. Then for him there was the truth in Lawson's working passion-blackened face.

Lawson jerked, moved, meant to draw. But how slow! Duane lunged forward. His long arm swept up. And Lawson staggered backward, knocking table and chairs, to fall hard, in a half-sitting posture against the wall.

"Don't draw!" warned Duane.

"Lawson, git away from your gun!" yelled Laramie.

But Lawson was crazed with fury. He tugged at his hip, his face corded with purple welts, malignant, murderous. Duane kicked the gun out of his hand. Lawson got up, raging, and rushed out.

Laramie lifted his shaking hands.

"What'd you wing him for?" he wailed. "He was drawin' on you. Kickin' men like him won't do out here."

"That bull-headed fool will roar and butt himself with all his gang right into our hands. He's just the man I've needed to meet. Besides, shooting him would have been murder."

"Murder!" exclaimed Laramie.

"Yes, for me," replied Duane.

"That may be true—whoever you are—but if Lawson's the man you think he is he'll begin thet secret underground bizness. Why, Lawson won't sleep of nights now. He an' Longstreth have always been after me."

"Laramie, what are your eyes for?" demanded Duane. "Watch out. And now here. See your friend Morton. Tell him this game grows hot. Together you approach four or five men you know well and can absolutely trust. I may need your help."

Then Duane went from place to place, corner to corner, bar to bar, watching, listening, recording. The excitement had preceded him, and speculation was rife. He thought best to keep out of it. After dark he stole up to Longstreth's ranch. The evening was warm; the doors were open; and in the twilight the only lamps that had been lit were in Longstreth's big sitting-room, at the far end of the house. When a buckboard drove up and Longstreth and Lawson alighted, Duane was well hidden in the bushes, so well screened that he could get but a fleeting glimpse of Longstreth as he went in. For all Duane could see, he appeared to be a calm and quiet man, intense beneath the surface, with an air of dignity under insult. Duane's chance to observe Lawson was lost. They went into the house without speaking and closed the door.

At the other end of the porch, close under a window, was an offset between step and wall, and there in the shadow Duane hid. So Duane waited there in the darkness with patience born of many hours of hiding.

Presently a lamp was lit; and Duane heard the swish of skirts.

"Something's happened surely, Ruth," he heard Miss Longstreth say, anxiously. "Papa just met me in the hall and didn't speak. He seemed pale, worried."

"Cousin Floyd looked like a thundercloud," said Ruth. "For once he didn't try to kiss me. Something's happened. Well, Ray, this has been a bad day."

"Oh, dear! Ruth, what can we do? These are wild men. Floyd makes life miserable for me. And he teases you unmer—"

"I don't call it teasing. Floyd wants to spoon," declared Ruth, emphatically. "He'd run after any woman."

"A fine compliment to me, Cousin Ruth," laughed Ray.

"I don't care," replied Ruth, stubbornly. "It's so. He's mushy. And when he's been drinking and tries to kiss me—I hate him!"

There were steps on the hall floor.

"Hello, girls!" sounded out Lawson's voice, minus its usual gaiety.

"Floyd, what's the matter?" asked Ray, presently. "I never saw Papa as he is tonight, nor you so—so worried. Tell me, what has happened?"

"Well, Ray, we had a jar today," replied Lawson, with a blunt, expressive laugh.

"Jar?" echoed both the girls, curiously.

"We had to submit to a damnable outrage," added Lawson, passionately, as if the sound of his voice augmented his feeling. "Listen, girls; I'll tell you all about it." He coughed, cleared his throat in a way that betrayed he had been drinking.

Duane sunk deeper into the shadow of his covert, and, stiffening his muscles for a protracted spell of rigidity, prepared to listen with all acuteness and intensity. Just one word from this Lawson, inadvertently uttered in a moment of passion, might be the word Duane needed for his clue.

"It happened at the town hall," began Lawson, rapidly. "Your father and Judge Owens and I were there in consultation with three ranchers from out of town. Then that damned ranger stalked in dragging Snecker, the fellow who hid here in the house. He had arrested Snecker for alleged assault on a restaurant-keeper named Laramie. Snecker being obviously innocent, he was discharged. Then this ranger began shouting his insults. Law was a farce in Fairdale. The court was a farce. There was no law. Your father's office as mayor should be impeached. He made arrests only for petty offenses. He was afraid of the rustlers, highwaymen, murderers. He was afraid or—he just let them alone. He used his office to cheat ranchers and cattlemen in lawsuits. All this the ranger yelled for everyone to hear. A damnable outrage. Your father, Ray, insulted in his own court by a rowdy ranger!"

"Oh!" cried Ray Longstreth, in mingled distress and anger.

"The ranger service wants to rule western Texas," went on Lawson. "These rangers are all a low set, many of them worse than the outlaws they hunt. Some of them were outlaws and gunfighters before they became rangers. This is one of the worst of the lot. He's keen, intelligent, smooth, and that makes him more to be feared. For he is to be feared. He wanted to kill. He would kill. If your father had made the least move he would have shot him. He's a cold-nerved devil—the born gunman. My God, any instant I expected to see your father fall dead at my feet!"

"Oh, Floyd! The unspeakable ruffian!" cried Ray Longstreth, passionately.

"You see, Ray, this fellow, like all rangers, seeks notoriety. He made that play with Snecker just for a chance to rant against your father. He tried to inflame all Fairdale against him. That about the lawsuits was the worst! Damn him! He'll make us enemies."

"What do you care for the insinuations of such a man?" said Ray Longstreth, her voice now deep and rich with feeling. "After a moment's thought no one will be influenced by them. Do not worry, Floyd. Tell Papa not to worry. Surely after all these years he can't be injured in reputation by—by an adventurer."

"Yes, he can be injured," replied Floyd, quickly. "The frontier is a queer place. There are many bitter men here—men who have failed at ranching. And your father has been wonderfully successful. The ranger has dropped poison, and it'll spread."

⁘18⁘

STRANGERS rode into Fairdale; and other hard-looking customers, new to Duane if not to Fairdale, helped to create a charged and waiting atmosphere. The saloons did unusual business and were never closed. Respectable citizens of the town were awakened in the early dawn by rowdies carousing in the streets.

Duane kept pretty close under cover during the day. He did not entertain the opinion that the first time he walked down-street he would be a
target for guns. Things seldom happened that way; and when they did
happen so, it was more accident than design. But at night he was not idle.
He met Laramie, Morton, Zimmer, and others of like character; a secret
club had been formed; and all the members were ready for action. Duane
spent hours at night watching the house where Floyd Lawson stayed when
he was not up at Longstreth's. At night he was visited, or at least the
house was, by strange men who were swift, stealthy, mysterious—all that
kindly disposed friends or neighbors would not have been. Duane had not
been able to recognize any of these night visitors; and he did not think
the time was ripe for a bold holding-up of one of them. Nevertheless, he
was sure such an event would discover Lawson, or someone in that house,
to be in touch with crooked men.

Laramie was right. Not twenty-fours hours after his last talk with
Duane, in which he advised quick action, he was found behind the little
bar of his restaurant with a bullet-hole in his breast, dead. No one could
be found who had heard a shot. It had been deliberate murder, for upon
the bar had been left a piece of paper rudely scrawled with a pencil: "All
friends of rangers look for the same."

This roused Duane. His first move, however, was to bury Laramie.
None of Laramie's neighbors evinced any interest in the dead man or the
unfortunate family he had left. Duane saw that these neighbors were held
in check by fear. Mrs. Laramie was ill; the shock of her husband's death
was hard on her; and she had been left almost destitute with five children.
Duane rented a small adobe house on the outskirts of town and moved
the family into it. Then he played the part of provider and nurse and
friend.

After several days Duane went boldly into town and showed that he
meant business. It was his opinion that there were men in Fairdale secretly glad of a ranger's presence. What he intended to do was food for
great speculation. A company of militia could not have had the effect
upon the wild element of Fairdale that Duane's presence had. It got out
that he was a gunman lightning swift on the draw. It was death to face
him. He had killed thirty men—wildest rumor of all. It was actually said
of him he had the gun-skill of Buck Duane or of Poggin.

At first there had not only been great conjecture among the vicious
element, but also a very decided checking of all kinds of action calculated
to be conspicuous to a keen-eyed ranger. At the tables, at the bars and
lounging-places Duane heard the remarks: "Who's thet ranger after?
What'll he do fust off? Is he waitin' fer somebody? Who's goin' to draw on
him fust—an' go to hell? Jest about how soon will he be found somewheres full of lead?"

When it came out somewhere that Duane was openly cultivating the honest stay-at-home citizens to array them in time against the other element, then Fairdale showed its wolf teeth. Several times Duane was shot at in the dark and once slightly injured. Rumor had it that Poggin, the gunman, was coming to meet him. But the lawless element did not rise up in a mass to slay Duane on sight. It was not so much that the enemies of the law awaited his next move, but just a slowness peculiar to the frontier. The ranger was in their midst. He was interesting, if formidable. He would have been welcomed at card-tables, at the bars, to play and drink with the men who knew they were under suspicion. There was a rude kind of good humor even in their open hostility.

Besides, one ranger or a company of rangers could not have held the undivided attention of these men from their games and drinks and quarrels except by some decided move. Excitement, greed, appetite were rife in them. Duane marked, however, a striking exception to the usual run of strangers he had been in the habit of seeing. Snecker had gone or was under cover. Again Duane caught a vague rumor of the coming of Poggin, yet he never seemed to arrive. Moreover, the goings-on among the habitués of the resorts and the cowboys who came in to drink and gamble were unusually mild in comparison with former conduct. This lull, however, did not deceive Duane. It could not last. The wonder was that it had lasted so long.

Duane went often to see Mrs. Laramie and her children. One afternoon while he was there he saw Miss Longstreth and Ruth ride up to the door. They carried a basket. Evidently they had heard of Mrs. Laramie's trouble. Duane felt strangely glad, but he went into an adjoining room rather than meet them.

"Mrs. Laramie, I've come to see you," said Miss Longstreth, cheerfully.

The little room was not very light, there being only one window and the doors, but Duane could see plainly enough. Mrs. Laramie lay, hollow-cheeked and haggard, on a bed. Once she had evidently been a woman of some comeliness. The ravages of trouble and grief were there to read in her worn face; it had not, however, any of the hard and bitter lines that had characterized her husband's.

Duane wondered, considering that Longstreth had ruined Laramie, how Mrs. Laramie was going to regard the daughter of an enemy.

"So you're Granger Longstreth's girl?" queried the woman, with her bright, black eyes fixed on her visitor.

"Yes," replied Miss Longstreth, simply. "This is my cousin, Ruth Herbert. We've come to nurse you, take care of the children, help you in any way you'll let us."

There was a long silence.

"Well, you look a little like Longstreth," finally said Mrs. Laramie, "but you're not *at all* like him. You must take after your mother. Miss Longstreth, I don't know if I can—if I ought accept anything from you. Your father ruined my husband."

"Yes, I know," replied the girl, sadly. "That's all the more reason you should let me help you. Pray don't refuse. It will . . . mean so much to me."

If this poor, stricken woman had any resentment it speedily melted in the warmth and sweetness of Miss Longstreth's manner. Duane's idea was that the impression of Ray Longstreth's beauty was always swiftly succeeded by that of her generosity and nobility. At any rate, she had started well with Mrs. Laramie, and no sooner had she begun to talk to the children than both they and the mother were won. The opening of that big basket was an event. Poor, starved little beggars! Duane's feelings seemed too easily roused. Hard indeed would it have gone with Jim Laramie's slayer if he could have laid eyes on him then. However, Miss Longstreth and Ruth, after the nature of tender and practical girls, did not appear to take the sad situation to heart. The havoc was wrought in that household. The needs now were cheerfulness, kindness, help, action—and these the girls furnished with a spirit that did Duane good.

"Mrs. Laramie, who dressed this baby?" presently asked Miss Longstreth. Duane peeped in to see a dilapidated youngster on her knee. That sight, if any other was needed, completed his full and splendid estimate of Ray Longstreth and wrought strangely upon his heart.

"The ranger," replied Mrs. Laramie.

"The ranger!" exclaimed Miss Longstreth.

"Yes, he's taken care of us all since—since—" Mrs. Laramie choked.

"Oh! So you've had no help but his," replied Miss Longstreth, hastily. "No women. Too bad! I'll send someone, Mrs. Laramie, and I'll come myself."

"It'll be good of you," went on the older woman. "You see, Jim had few friends—that is, right in town. And they've been afraid to help us—afraid they'd get what poor Jim—"

"That's awful!" burst out Miss Longstreth, passionately. "A brave lot of friends! Mrs. Laramie, don't you worry anymore. We'll take care of you. Here, Ruth, help me. Whatever is the matter with baby's dress?"

Manifestly Miss Longstreth had some difficulty in subduing her emotion.

"Why, it's on hind side before," declared Ruth. "I guess Mr. Ranger hasn't dressed many babies."

"He did the best he could," said Mrs. Laramie. "Lord only knows what would have become of us!"

"Then he is—is something more than a ranger?" queried Miss Longstreth, with a little break in her voice.

"He's more than I can tell," replied Mrs. Laramie. "He buried Jim. He paid our debts. He fetched us here. He bought food for us. He cooked for us and fed us. He washed and dressed the baby. He sat with me the first two nights after Jim's death, when I thought I'd die myself. He's so kind, so gentle, so patient. He has kept me up just by being near. Sometimes I'd wake from a doze, an', seeing him there, I'd know how false were all these tales Jim heard about him and believed at first. Why, he plays with the children just—just like any good man might. When he has the baby up I just can't believe he's a bloody gunman, as they say. He's good, but he isn't happy. He has such sad eyes. He looks far off sometimes when the children climb round him. They love him. His life is sad. Nobody need tell me—he sees the good in things. Once he said somebody had to be a ranger. Well, I say, 'Thank God for a ranger like him!' "

Duane did not want to hear more, so he walked into the room.

"It was thoughtful of you," Duane said. "Womankind are needed here. I could do so little. Mrs. Laramie, you look better already. I'm glad. And here's baby, all clean and white. Baby, what a time I had trying to puzzle out the way your clothes went on! Well, Mrs. Laramie, didn't I tell you— friends would come? So will the brighter side."

"Yes, I've more faith than I had," replied Mrs. Laramie. "Granger Longstreth's daughter has come to me. There for a while after Jim's death I thought I'd sink. We have nothing. How could I ever take care of my little ones? But I'm gaining courage to—"

"Mrs. Laramie, do not distress yourself anymore," said Miss Longstreth. "I shall see you are well cared for. I promise you."

"Miss Longstreth, that's fine!" exclaimed Duane. "It's what I'd have— expected of you."

It must have been sweet praise to her, for the whiteness of her face burned out in a beautiful blush.

"And it's good of you, too, Miss Herbert, to come," added Duane. "Let me thank you both. I'm glad I have you girls as allies in part of my lonely task here. More than glad for the sake of this good woman and the little ones. But both of you be careful about coming here alone. There's risk. And now I'll be going. Goodbye, Mrs. Laramie. I'll drop in again tonight. Goodbye."

"Mr. Ranger, wait!" called Miss Longstreth, as he went out. She was white and wonderful. She stepped out of the door close to him.

"I have wronged you!" she said, impulsively.

"Miss Longstreth! How can you say that?" he returned.

"I believed what my father and Floyd Lawson said about you. Now I see . . . I wronged you."

"You make me very glad. But, Miss Longstreth, please don't speak of wronging me. I have been a—a gunman, I am a ranger—and much said of me is true. My duty is hard on others—sometimes on those who are innocent, alas! But God knows that duty is hard, too, on me."

"I did wrong you. If you entered my home again I would think it an honor. I—"

"Please—please don't, Miss Longstreth," interrupted Duane.

"But, sir, my conscience flays me," she went on. There was no other sound like her voice. "Will you take my hand? Will you forgive me?"

She gave it royally, while the other was there pressing at her breast. Duane took the proffered hand. He did not know what else to do.

Then it seemed to dawn upon him that there was more behind this white, sweet, noble intensity of her than just the making amends for a fancied or real wrong. Duane thought the man did not live on earth who could have resisted her then.

"I honor you for your goodness to this unfortunate woman," she said, and now her speech came swiftly. "When she was all alone and helpless you were her friend. It was the deed of a man. But Mrs. Laramie isn't the only unfortunate woman in the world. I, too, am unfortunate. Ah, how *I* may soon need a friend! Will *you* be my friend? I'm so alone. I'm terribly worried. I fear—I fear— Oh, surely I'll need a friend soon—soon. Oh, I'm afraid of what you'll find out sooner or later. I want to help you. Let us save life if not honor. Must I stand alone—all alone? Will you—will you be—" Her voice failed.

It seemed to Duane that she must have discovered what he had begun to suspect—that her father and Lawson were not the honest ranchers they pretended to be. Perhaps she knew more! Her appeal to Duane shook him deeply. He wanted to help her more than he had ever wanted anything. And with the meaning of the tumultuous sweetness she stirred in him there came realization of a dangerous situation.

"I must be true to my duty," he said, hoarsely.

"If you knew me you'd know I could never ask you to be false to it."

"Well, then—I'll do anything for you."

"Oh, thank you! I'm ashamed that I believed my cousin Floyd! He lied —he lied. I'm all in the dark, strangely distressed. My father wants me to go back home. Floyd is trying to keep me here. They've quarreled. Oh, I know something dreadful will happen. I know I'll need you if—if— Will you help me?"

"Yes," replied Duane, and his look brought the blood to her face.

❖19❖

AFTER SUPPER Duane stole out for his usual evening's spying. The night was dark, without starlight, and a stiff wind rustled the leaves. Duane bent his steps toward Longstreth's ranch-house. He had so much to think about that he never knew where the time went. This night when he reached the edge of the shrubbery he heard Lawson's well-known footsteps and saw Longstreth's door open, flashing a broad bar of light in the darkness. Lawson crossed the threshold, the door closed, and all was dark again outside. Not a ray of light escaped from the window.

Little doubt there was that his talk with Longstreth would be interesting to Duane. He tiptoed to the door and listened, but could hear only a murmur of voices. Besides, that position was too risky. He went round the corner of the house.

This side of the big adobe house was of much older construction than the back and larger part. There was a narrow passage between the houses, leading from the outside through to the patio.

This passage now afforded Duane an opportunity, and he decided to avail himself of it in spite of the very great danger. Crawling on very stealthily, he got under the shrubbery to the entrance of the passage. In the blackness a faint streak of light showed the location of a crack in the wall. He had to slip in sidewise. It was a tight squeeze, but he entered without the slightest noise. As he progressed the passage grew a very little wider in that direction, and that fact gave rise to the thought that in case of a necessary and hurried exit he would do best by working toward the patio. It seemed a good deal of time was consumed in reaching a vantage-point. When he did get there the crack he had marked was a foot over his head. There was nothing to do but find toe-holes in the crumbling walls, and by bracing knees on one side, back against the other, hold himself up. Once with his eye there he did not care what risk he ran. Longstreth appeared disturbed; he sat stroking his mustache; his brow was clouded. Lawson's face seemed darker, more sullen, yet lighted by some indomitable resolve.

"We'll settle both deals tonight," Lawson was saying. "That's what I came for."

"But suppose I don't choose to talk here?" protested Longstreth, impatiently. "I never before made my house a place to—"

"We've waited long enough. This place's as good as any. You've lost your nerve since that ranger hit the town. First now, will you give Ray to me?"

580

"Floyd, you talk like a spoiled boy. Give Ray to you! Why, she's a woman, and I'm finding out that she's got a mind of her own. I told you I was willing for her to marry you. I tried to persuade her. But Ray hasn't any use for you now. She liked you at first. But now she doesn't. So what can I do?"

"You can make her marry me," replied Lawson.

"Make that girl do what she doesn't want to? It couldn't be done even if I tried. And I don't believe I'll try. I haven't the highest opinion of you as a prospective son-in-law, Floyd. But if Ray loved you I would consent. We'd all go away together before this damned miserable business is out. Then she'd never know. And maybe you might be more like you used to be before the West ruined you. But as matters stand, you fight your own game with her. And I'll tell you now you'll lose."

"What'd you want to let her come out here for?" demanded Lawson, hotly. "It was a dead mistake. I've lost my head over her. I'll have her or die. Don't you think if she was my wife I'd soon pull myself together? Since she came we've none of us been right. And the gang has put up a holler. No, Longstreth, we've got to settle things tonight."

"Well, we can settle what Ray's concerned in, right now," replied Longstreth, rising. "Come on; we'll ask her. See where you stand."

They went out, leaving the door open. Duane dropped down to rest himself and to wait. He would have liked to hear Miss Longstreth's answer. But he could guess what it would be. Lawson appeared to be all Duane had thought him, and he believed he was going to find out presently that he was worse.

The men seemed to be absent a good while, though that feeling might have been occasioned by Duane's thrilling interest and anxiety. Finally he heard heavy steps. Lawson came in alone. He was leaden-faced, humiliated. Then something abject in him gave place to rage. He strode the room; he cursed. Then Longstreth returned, now appreciably calmer. Duane could not but decide that he felt relief at the evident rejection of Lawson's proposal.

"Don't fuss about it, Floyd," he said. "You see I can't help it. We're pretty wild out here, but I can't rope my daughter and give her to you as I would an unruly steer."

"Longstreth, I can *make* her marry me," declared Lawson, thickly.

"How?"

"You know the hold I got on you—the deal that made you boss of this rustler gang?"

"It isn't likely I'd forget," replied Longstreth, grimly.

"I can go to Ray, tell her that, make her believe I'd tell it broadcast—tell this ranger—unless she'd marry me."

Lawson spoke breathlessly, with haggard face and shadowed eyes. He had no shame. He was simply in the grip of passion.

Longstreth gazed with dark, controlled fury at this relative. In that look Duane saw a strong, unscrupulous man fallen into evil ways, but still a man. It betrayed Lawson to be the wild and passionate weakling. Duane seemed to see also how during all the years of association this strong man had upheld the weak one. But that time had gone forever, both in intent on Longstreth's part and in possibility. Lawson, like the great majority of evil and unrestrained men on the border, had reached a point where influence was futile. Reason had degenerated. He saw only himself.

"But, Floyd, Ray's the one person on earth who must never know I'm a rustler, a thief, a red-handed ruler of the worst gang on the border," replied Longstreth, impressively.

Floyd bowed his head at that, as if the significance had just occurred to him. But he was not long at a loss.

"She's going to find it out sooner or later. I tell you she knows now there's something wrong out here. She's got eyes. Mark what I say."

"Ray has changed, I know. But she hasn't any idea yet that her daddy's a boss rustler. Ray's concerned about what she calls my duty as mayor. Also I think she's not satisfied with my explanations in regard to certain property."

Lawson halted in his restless walk and leaned against the stone mantelpiece. He had his hands in his pockets. He squared himself as if this was his last stand. He looked desperate, but on the moment showed an absence of his usual nervous excitement.

"Longstreth, that may well be true," he said. "No doubt all you say is true. But it doesn't help me. I want the girl. If I don't get her—I reckon we'll all go to hell!"

He might have meant anything, probably meant the worst. He certainly had something more in mind. Longstreth gave a slight start, barely perceptible, like the switch of an awakening tiger. He sat there, head down, stroking his mustache. Almost Duane saw his thought. He had long experience in reading men under stress of such emotion. He had no means to vindicate his judgment, but his conviction was that Longstreth right then and there decided that the thing to do was to kill Lawson. For Duane's part he wondered that Longstreth had not come to such a conclusion before. Not improbably the advent of his daughter had put Longstreth in conflict with himself.

Suddenly he threw off a somber cast of countenance, and he began to talk. He talked swiftly, persuasively, yet Duane imagined he was talking to smooth Lawson's passion for the moment. Lawson no more caught the fateful significance of a line crossed, a limit reached, a decree decided than if he had not been present. He was obsessed with himself. How, Duane wondered, had a man of his mind ever lived so long and gone so far among the exacting conditions of the Southwest? The answer was, perhaps, that Longstreth had guided him, upheld him, protected him.

The coming of Ray Longstreth had been the entering-wedge of dissension.

"You're too impatient," concluded Longstreth. "You'll ruin any chance of happiness if you rush Ray. She might be won. If you told her who I am she'd hate you forever. She might marry you to save me, but she'd hate you. That isn't the way. Wait. Play for time. Be different with her. Cut out your drinking. She despises that. Let's plan to sell out here—stock, ranch, property—and leave the country. Then you'd have a show with her."

"I told you we've got to stick," growled Lawson. "The gang won't stand for our going. It can't be done unless you want to sacrifice everything."

"You mean double-cross the men? Go without their knowing? Leave them here to face whatever comes?"

"I mean just that."

"I'm bad enough, but not that bad," returned Longstreth. "If I can't get the gang to let me off, I'll stay and face the music. All the same, Lawson, did it ever strike you that most of the deals the last few years have been *yours?*"

"Yes. If I hadn't rung them in there wouldn't have been any. You've had cold feet, and especially since this ranger has been here."

"Well, call it cold feet if you like. But I call it sense. We reached our limit long ago. We began by rustling a few cattle—at a time when rustling was laughed at. But as our greed grew so did our boldness. Then came the gang, the regular trips, the one thing and another till, before we knew it —before *I* knew it—we had shady deals, holdups, and *murders* on our record. Then we *had* to go on. Too late to turn back!"

"I reckon we've all said that. None of the gang wants to quit. They all think, and I think, we can't be touched. We may be blamed, but nothing can be proved. We're too strong."

"There's where you're dead wrong," rejoined Longstreth, emphatically. "I imagined that once, not long ago. I was bull-headed. Who would ever connect Granger Longstreth with a rustler gang? I've changed my mind. I've begun to think. I've reasoned out things. We're crooked, and we can't last. It's the nature of life, even here, for conditions to grow better. The wise deal for us would be to divide equally and leave the country, all of us."

"But you and I have all the stock—all the gain," protested Lawson.

"I'll split mine."

"I won't—that settles that," added Lawson, instantly.

Longstreth spread wide his hands as if it was useless to try to convince this man. Talking had not increased his calmness, and he now showed more than impatience. A dull glint gleamed deep in his eyes.

"Your stock and property will last a long time—do you lots of good when this ranger—"

"Bah!" hoarsely croaked Lawson. The ranger's name was a match applied to powder. "Haven't I told you he'd be dead soon—anytime—same as Laramie is?"

"Yes, you mentioned the—the supposition," replied Longstreth, sarcastically. "I inquired, too, just how that very desired event was to be brought about."

"The gang will lay him out."

"Bah!" retorted Longstreth, in turn. He laughed contemptuously.

"Floyd, don't be a fool. You've been on the border for ten years. You've packed a gun and you've used it. You've been with rustlers when they killed their men. You've been present at many fights. But you never in all that time saw a man like this ranger. You haven't got sense enough to see him right if you had a chance. Neither have any of you. The only way to get rid of him is for the gang to draw on him, all at once. Then he's going to drop some of them."

"Longstreth, you say that like a man who wouldn't care much if he did drop some of them," declared Lawson; and now he was sarcastic.

"To tell you the truth, I wouldn't," returned the other, bluntly. "I'm pretty sick of this mess."

Lawson cursed in amazement. His emotions were all out of proportion to his intelligence. He was not at all quick-witted. Duane had never seen a vainer or more arrogant man.

"Longstreth, I don't like your talk," he said.

"If you don't like the way I talk you know what you can do," replied Longstreth, quickly. He stood up then, cool and quiet, with flash of eyes and set of lips that told Duane he was dangerous.

"Well, after all, that's neither here nor there," went on Lawson, unconsciously cowed by the other. "The thing is, do I get the girl?"

"Not by any means except her consent."

"You'll not make her marry me?"

"No. No," replied Longstreth, his voice still cold, low-pitched.

"All right. Then I'll make her."

Evidently Longstreth understood the man before him so well that he wasted no more words. Duane knew what Lawson never dreamed of, and that was that Longstreth had a gun somewhere within reach and meant to use it. Then heavy footsteps sounded outside tramping upon the porch. Duane might have been mistaken, but he believed those footsteps saved Lawson's life.

"There they are," said Lawson, and he opened the door.

Five masked men entered. They all wore coats hiding any weapons. A big man with burly shoulders shook hands with Longstreth, and the others stood back.

The atmosphere of that room had changed. Lawson might have been a nonentity for all he counted. Longstreth was another man—a stranger to

Duane. If he had entertained a hope of freeing himself from this band, of getting away to a safer country, he abandoned it at the very sight of these men. There was power here, and he was bound.

The big man spoke in low, hoarse whispers, and at this all the others gathered around him close to the table. There were evidently some signs of membership not plain to Duane. Then all the heads were bent over the table. Low voices spoke, queried, answered, argued. By straining his ears Duane caught a word here and there. They were planning, and they were brief. Duane gathered they were to have a rendezvous at or near Ord.

Then the big man, who evidently was the leader of the present convention, got up to depart. He went as swiftly as he had come, and was followed by his comrades. Longstreth prepared for a quiet smoke. Lawson seemed uncommunicative and unsociable. He smoked fiercely and drank continually. All at once he straightened up as if listening.

"What's that?" he called, suddenly.

Duane's strained ears were pervaded by a slight rustling sound.

"Must be a rat," replied Longstreth.

The rustle became a rattle.

"Sounds like a rattlesnake to me," said Lawson.

Longstreth got up from the table and peered round the room.

Just at that instant Duane felt an almost inappreciable movement of the adobe wall which supported him. He could scarcely credit his senses. But the rattle inside Longstreth's room was mingling with little dull thuds of falling dirt. The adobe wall, merely dried mud, was crumbling. Duane distinctly felt a tremor pass through it. Then the blood gushed back to his heart.

"What in the hell!" exclaimed Longstreth.

"I smell dust," said Lawson, sharply.

That was the signal for Duane to drop down from his perch, yet despite his care he made a noise.

"Did you hear a step?" queried Longstreth.

No one answered. But a heavy piece of the adobe wall fell with a thud. Duane heard it crack, felt it shake.

"There's somebody between the walls!" thundered Longstreth.

Then a section of the wall fell inward with a crash. Duane began to squeeze his body through the narrow passage toward the patio.

"Hear him!" yelled Lawson. "This side!"

"No, he's going that way," yelled Longstreth.

The tramp of heavy boots lent Duane the strength of desperation. He was not shirking a fight, but to be cornered like a trapped coyote was another matter. He almost tore his clothes off in that passage. The dust nearly stifled him. When he burst into the patio it was not a single instant too soon. But one deep gasp of breath revived him and he was up, gun in hand, running for the outlet into the court. Thumping footsteps turned him back. While there was a chance to get away he did not want to fight. He thought he heard someone running into the patio from the other end. He stole along, and coming to a door, without any idea of where it might lead, he softly pushed it open a little way and slipped in.

⁂20⁂

A LOW CRY greeted Duane. The room was light. He saw Ray Long-streth sitting on her bed in her dressing-gown. With a warning gesture to her to be silent he turned to close the door. It was a heavy door without bolt or bar, and when Duane had shut it he felt safe only for the moment. Then he gazed around the room. There was one window with blind closely drawn. He listened and seemed to hear footsteps retreating, dying away.

Then Duane turned to Miss Longstreth. She had slipped off the bed, half to her knees, and was holding out trembling hands. She was as white as the pillow on her bed. She was terribly frightened. Again with warning hand commanding silence, Duane stepped softly forward, meaning to reassure her.

"Oh!" she whispered, wildly; and Duane thought she was going to faint. When he got close and looked into her eyes he understood the strange, dark expression in them. She was terrified because she believed he meant to kill her, or do worse, probably worse. Duane realized he must have looked pretty hard and fierce bursting into her room with that big gun in hand.

The way she searched Duane's face with doubtful, fearful eyes hurt him.

"Listen. I didn't know this was your room. I came here to get away—to save my life. I was pursued. I was spying on—on your father and his men. They heard me, but did not see me. They don't know who was listening. They're after me now."

Her eyes changed from blank gulfs to dilating, shadowing, quickening windows of thought.

Then she stood up and faced Duane with the fire and intelligence of a woman in her eyes.

"Tell me now. You were spying on my father?"

Briefly Duane told her what had happened before he entered her room, not omitting a terse word as to the character of the men he had watched.

"My God! So it's that? I knew something was terribly wrong here—with him—with the place—the people. And right off I hated Floyd Lawson. Oh, it'll kill me if—if— It's so much worse than I dreamed. What shall I do?"

The sound of soft steps somewhere near distracted Duane's attention, reminded him of her peril, and now, what counted more with him, made clear the probability of being discovered in her room.

"I'll have to get out of here," whispered Duane.

"Wait," she replied. "Didn't you say they were hunting for you?"

"They sure are," he returned, grimly.

"Oh, then you mustn't go. They might shoot you before you got away. Stay. If we hear them you can hide. I'll turn out the light. I'll meet them at the door. You can trust me. Wait till all quiets down, if we have to wait till morning. Then you can slip out."

"I oughtn't to stay. I don't want to—I won't," Duane replied, perplexed and stubborn.

"But you must. It's the only safe way. They won't come here."

"Suppose they should? It's an even chance Longstreth'll search every room and corner in this old house. If they found me here I couldn't start a fight. You might be hurt. Then the fact of my being here . . ."

Duane did not finish what he meant, but instead made a step toward the door. White of face and dark of eye, she took hold of him to detain him. She was as strong and supple as a panther. But she need not have been either resolute or strong, for the clasp of her hand was enough to make Duane weak.

"Up yet, Ray?" came Longstreth's clear voice, too strained, too eager to be natural.

"No. I'm in bed reading. Good night," instantly replied Miss Longstreth, so calmly and naturally that Duane marveled at the difference between man and woman. Then she motioned for Duane to hide in the closet. He slipped in, but the door would not close altogether.

"Are you alone?" went on Longstreth's penetrating voice.

"Yes," she replied. "Ruth went to bed."

The door swung inward with a swift scrape and jar. Longstreth half entered, haggard, flaming-eyed. Behind him Duane saw Lawson, and indistinctly another man.

Longstreth barred Lawson from entering, which action showed control as well as distrust. He wanted to see into the room. When he had glanced around he went out and closed the door.

Then what seemed a long interval ensued. The house grew silent once more. Duane could not see Miss Longstreth, but he heard her quick breathing. How long did she mean to let him stay hidden there? Hard and perilous as his life had been, this was a new kind of adventure. He had divined the strange softness of his feeling as something due to the magnetism of this beautiful woman. It hardly seemed possible that he, who had been outside the pale for so many years, could have fallen in love. Yet that must be the secret of his agitation.

Presently he pushed open the closet door and stepped forth. Miss Longstreth had her head lowered upon her arms and appeared to be in distress. At his touch she raised a quivering face.

"I think I can go now—safely," he whispered.

"Go then, if you must, but you may stay till you're safe," she replied.

"I—I couldn't thank you enough. It's been hard on me—this finding out—and you his daughter. I feel strange. I don't understand myself well. But I want you to know—if I were not an outlaw—a ranger—I'd lay my life at your feet."

"Oh! You have seen so—so little of me," she faltered.

"All the same it's true. And that makes me feel more the trouble my coming caused you."

"You will not fight my father?"

"Not if I can help it. I'm trying to get out of his way."

"But you spied upon him."

"I am a ranger, Miss Longstreth."

"And oh! I am a rustler's daughter," she cried. "That's so much more terrible than I'd suspected. It was tricky cattle deals I imagined he was engaged in. But only tonight I had strong suspicions aroused."

"How? Tell me."

"I overheard Floyd say that men were coming tonight to arrange a meeting for my father at a rendezvous near Ord. Father did not want to go. Floyd taunted him with a name."

"What name?" queried Duane.

"It was Cheseldine."

"*Cheseldine!* My God! Miss Longstreth, why did *you* tell me that?"

"What difference does that make?"

"Your father and Cheseldine are one and the same," whispered Duane, hoarsely.

"I gathered so much myself," she replied, miserably. "But Longstreth is father's real name."

Duane felt so stunned he could not speak at once. It was the girl's part in this tragedy that weakened him. The instant she betrayed the secret Duane realized perfectly that he did love her. The emotion was like a great flood.

"Miss Longstreth, all this seems so unbelievable," he whispered. "Cheseldine is the rustler chief I've come out here to get. He's only a name. Your father is the real man. I've sworn to get him. I'm bound by more than law or oaths. I can't break what binds me. And I must disgrace you—wreck your life! Why, Miss Longstreth, I believe I—I love you. It's all come in a rush. I'd die for you if I could. How fatal—terrible—this is! How things work out!"

She slipped to her knees, with her hands on his.

"You won't kill him?" she implored. "If you care for me—you won't kill him?"

"No. That I promise you."

With a low moan she dropped her head upon the bed.

Duane opened the door and stealthily stole out through the corridor to the court.

When Duane got out into the dark, where his hot face cooled in the wind, his relief equaled his other feelings.

The night was dark, windy, stormy, yet there was no rain. Duane hoped as soon as he got clear of the ranch to lose something of the pain he felt. But long after he had tramped out into the open there was a lump in his throat and an ache in his breast. All his thought centered around Ray Longstreth. What a woman she had turned out to be! He seemed to have a vague, hopeless hope that there might be, there must be, some way he could save her.

⸙21⸙

BEFORE going to sleep that night Duane had decided to go to Ord and try to find the rendezvous where Longstreth was to meet his men. These men Duane wanted even more than their leader. If Longstreth, or Cheseldine, was the brains of that gang, Poggin was the executor. It was Poggin who needed to be found and stopped. Poggin and his right-hand men! Duane experienced a strange, tigerish thrill. It was thought of Poggin more than thought of success for MacNelly's plan. Duane felt dubious over this emotion.

Next day he set out for Bradford. He was glad to get away from Fairdale for a while. But the hours and the miles in no way changed the new pain in his heart. The only way he could forget Miss Longstreth was to let his mind dwell upon Poggin, and even this was not always effective.

He avoided Sanderson, and at the end of a day and a half he arrived at Bradford.

The night of the day before he reached Bradford, No. 6, the mail and express train going east, was held up by train robbers, the Wells Fargo messenger killed over his safe, the mail clerk wounded, the bags carried away. The engine of No. 6 came into town minus even a tender, and engineer and fireman told conflicting stories. A posse of railroad men and citizens, led by a sheriff Duane suspected was crooked, was made up before the engine steamed back to pick up the rest of the train. Duane had the sudden inspiration that he had been cudgeling his mind to find; and, acting upon it, he mounted his horse again and left Bradford unobserved. As he rode out into the night, over a dark trail in the direction of Ord, he uttered a short, grim, sardonic laugh at the hope that he might be taken for a train robber.

He rode at an easy trot most of the night, and when the black peak of Ord Mountain loomed up against the stars he halted, tied his horse, and slept until dawn. He had brought a small pack, and now he took his time cooking breakfast. When the sun was well up he saddled Bullet, and, leaving the trail where his tracks showed plain in the ground, he put his horse to the rocks and brush. He selected an exceedingly rough, round-about, and difficult course to Ord, hid his tracks with the skill of a long-hunted fugitive, and arrived there with his horse winded and covered with lather. It added considerable to his arrival that the man Duane remembered as Fletcher and several others saw him come in the back way through the lots and jump a fence into the road.

Duane led Bullet up to the porch where Fletcher stood wiping his beard. He was hatless, vestless, and evidently had just enjoyed a morning drink.

"Howdy, Dodge," said Fletcher, laconically.

Duane replied, and the other man returned the greeting with interest.

"Jim, my hoss 's done up. I want to hide him from any chance tourists as might happen to ride up curious-like."

"Haw! Haw! Haw!"

Duane gathered encouragement from that chorus of coarse laughter.

"Wal, if them tourists ain't too durned snooky the hoss'll be safe in the 'dobe shack back of Bill's here. Feed thar, too, but you'll hev to rustle water."

Duane led Bullet to the place indicated, had care of his welfare, and left him there. Upon returning to the tavern porch Duane saw the group of men had been added to by others, some of whom he had seen before. Without comment Duane walked along the edge of the road, and wherever one of the tracks of his horse showed he carefully obliterated it. This procedure was attentively watched by Fletcher and his companions.

"Wal, Dodge," remarked Fletcher, as Duane returned, "thet's safer 'n prayin' fer rain."

Duane's reply was a remark as loquacious as Fletcher's, to the effect that a long, slow, monotonous ride was conducive to thirst. They all joined him, unmistakably friendly. But Knell was not there, and most assuredly not Poggin. Fletcher was no common outlaw, but, whatever his ability, it probably lay in execution of orders. Apparently at that time these men had nothing to do but drink and lounge around the tavern. Evidently they were poorly supplied with money, though Duane observed they could borrow a peso occasionally from the bartender. Duane set out to make himself agreeable and succeeded. There was card-playing for small stakes, idle jests of coarse nature, much bantering among the younger fellows, and occasionally a mild quarrel. All morning men came and went, until, all told, Duane calculated he had seen at least fifty. Toward the middle of the afternoon a young fellow burst into the saloon and yelled one word:

"Posse!"

From the scramble to get outdoors Duane judged that word and the ensuing action was rare in Ord.

"What the hell!" muttered Fletcher, as he gazed down the road at a dark, compact bunch of horses and riders. "Fust time I ever seen thet in Ord! We're gettin' popular like them camps out of Valentine. Wish Phil was here or Poggy. Now all you gents keep quiet. I'll do the talkin'."

The posse entered the town, trotted up on dusty horses, and halted in a bunch before the tavern. The party consisted of about twenty men, all heavily armed, and evidently in charge of a clean-cut, lean-limbed cowboy. Duane experienced considerable satisfaction at the absence of the sheriff who he had understood was to lead the posse. Perhaps he was out in another direction with a different force.

"Hello, Jim Fletcher," called the cowboy.

"Howdy," replied Fletcher.

At his short, dry response and the way he strode leisurely out before the posse, Duane found himself modifying his contempt for Fletcher. The outlaw was different now.

"Fletcher, we've tracked a man to all but three miles of this place. Tracks as plain as the nose on your face. Found his camp. Then he hit into the brush, an' we lost the trail. Didn't have no tracker with us. Think he went into the mountains. But we took a chance an' rid over the rest of the way, seein' Ord was so close. Anybody come in here late last night or early this mornin'?"

"Nope," replied Fletcher.

His response was what Duane had expected from his manner, and evidently the cowboy took it as a matter of course. He turned to the others of the posse, entering into a low consultation. Evidently there was difference of opinion, if not real dissension, in that posse.

"Didn't I tell ye this was a wild-goose chase, comin' way out here?" protested an old hawk-faced rancher. "Them hoss tracks we follored ain't like any of them we seen at the water-tank where the train was held up."

"I'm not so sure of that," replied the leader.

"Wal, Guthrie, I've follored tracks all my life . . ."

"But you couldn't keep to the trail this feller made in the brush."

"Gimme time, an' I could. Thet takes time. An' heah you go hell-bent fer election! But it's a wrong lead out this way. If you're right this road-agent, after he killed his pals, would hev rid back right through town. An' with them mail-bags! Supposin' they was greasers? Some greasers has sense, an' when it comes to thievin' they're shore cute."

"But we ain't got any reason to believe this robber who murdered the greasers is a greaser himself. I tell you it was a slick job done by no ordinary sneak. Didn't you hear the facts? One greaser hopped the engine an' covered the engineer an' fireman. Another greaser kept flashin' his gun outside the train. The big man who shoved back the car door an' did the killin'—he was the real gent, an' don't you forget it."

Some of the posse sided with the cowboy leader and some with the old cattleman. Finally the young leader disgustedly gathered up his bridle.

"Aw, hell! Thet sheriff shoved you off this trail. Mebbe he hed reason! Savvy thet? If I hed a bunch of cowboys with me—I tell you what—I'd take a chance an' clean up this hole!"

All the while Jim Fletcher stood quietly with his hands in his pockets.

"Guthrie, I'm shore treasurin' up your friendly talk," he said. The menace was in the tone, not the content of his speech.

"You can—an' be damned to you, Fletcher!" called Guthrie, as the horses started.

Fletcher, standing out alone before the others of his clan, watched the posse out of sight.

"Luck fer you-all thet Poggy wasn't here," he said, as they disappeared. Then with a thoughtful mien he strode up on the porch and led Duane away from the others into the barroom. When he looked into Duane's face it was somehow an entirely changed scrutiny.

"Dodge, where'd you hide the stuff? I reckon I git in on this deal, seein' I staved off Guthrie."

Duane played his part. Here was his opportunity, and like a tiger after prey he seized it. First he coolly eyed the outlaw and then disclaimed any knowledge whatever of the train robbery other than Fletcher had heard himself. Then at Fletcher's persistence and admiration and increasing show of friendliness he laughed occasionally and allowed himself to swell with pride, though still denying. Next he feigned a lack of consistent will-power and seemed to be wavering under Fletcher's persuasion and grew silent, then surly. Fletcher, evidently sure of ultimate victory, desisted for the time being; however, in his solicitous regard and close companionship for the rest of that day he betrayed the bent of his mind.

Later, when Duane started up announcing his intention to get his horse and make for camp out in the brush, Fletcher seemed grievously offended.

"Why don't you stay with me? I've got a comfortable 'dobe over here. Didn't I stick by you when Guthrie an' his bunch come up? Supposin' I hedn't showed down a cold hand to him? You'd be swingin' somewheres now. I tell you, Dodge, it ain't square."

"I'll square it. I pay my debts," replied Duane. "But I can't put up here all night. If I belonged to the gang it'd be different."

"What gang?" asked Fletcher, bluntly.

"Why, Cheseldine's."

Fletcher's beard nodded as his jaw dropped.

Duane laughed. "I run into him the other day. Knowed him on sight. Sure, he's the kingpin rustler. When he seen me an' asked me what reason I had for bein' on earth or some such like—why, I up an' told him."

Fletcher appeared staggered.

"Who in all-fired hell air you talkin' about?"

"Didn't I tell you once? Cheseldine. He calls himself Longstreth over there."

All of Fletcher's face not covered by hair turned a dirty white.

"Cheseldine—Longstreth!" he whispered, hoarsely. "Gord Almighty! You braced the—" Then a remarkable transformation came over the outlaw. He gulped; he straightened his face; he controlled his agitation. But he could not send the healthy brown back to his face. Duane, watching this rude man, marveled at the change in him, the sudden checking movement, the proof of a wonderful fear and loyalty. It all meant Cheseldine, a master of men!

"Who air you?" queried Fletcher, in a queer, strained voice.

"You gave me a handle, didn't you? Dodge. Thet's as good as any. Shore it hits me hard. Jim, I've been pretty lonely for years, an' I'm gettin' in need of pals. Think it over, will you? See you mañana."

The outlaw watched Duane go off after his horse, watched him as he returned to the tavern, watched him ride out into the darkness—all without a word.

Duane left the town, threaded a quiet passage through cactus and mesquite to a spot he had marked before, and made ready for the night. His mind was so full that he found sleep aloof. Luck at last was playing his game. He sensed the first slow heave of a mighty crisis. The end, always haunting, had to be sternly blotted from thought. It was the approach that needed all his mind.

He passed the night there, and late in the morning, after watching trail and road from a ridge, he returned to Ord. If Jim Fletcher tried to disguise his surprise the effort was a failure. Certainly he had not expected to see Duane again. Duane allowed himself a little freedom with Fletcher, an attitude hitherto lacking.

That afternoon a horseman rode in from Bradford, an outlaw evidently well known and liked by his fellows, and Duane heard him say, before he could possibly have been told, the train robber was in Ord, that the loss of money in the holdup was slight. Like a flash Duane saw the luck of this report. He pretended not to have heard.

In the early twilight at an opportune moment he called Fletcher to him, and, linking his arm within the outlaw's, he drew him off in a stroll to a log bridge spanning a little gully. Here after gazing around, he took out a roll of bills, spread it out, split it equally, and without a word handed one half to Fletcher. With clumsy fingers Fletcher ran through the roll.

"Five hundred!" he exclaimed. "Dodge, thet's damn handsome of you, considerin' the job wasn't—

"Considerin' nothin'," interrupted Duane. "I'm makin' no reference to a job here or there. You did me a good turn. I split my pile. If thet doesn't make us pards, good turns an' money ain't no use in this country."

Fletcher was won.

The two men spent much time together. Duane made up a short fictitious history about himself that satisfied the outlaw, only it drew forth a laughing jest upon Duane's modesty. For Fletcher did not hide his belief that this new partner was a man of achievements. Knell and Poggin, and then Cheseldine himself, would be persuaded of this fact, so Fletcher boasted. He had influence. He would use it. He thought he pulled a stroke with Knell. But nobody on earth, not even the boss, had any influence on Poggin. Poggin was concentrated ice part of the time; all the rest he was bursting hell. But Poggin loved a horse. He never loved anything else. He could be won with that black horse Bullet. Cheseldine was already won by Duane's monumental nerve; otherwise he would have killed Duane.

Little by little the next few days Duane learned the points he longed to know—and how indelibly they etched themselves in his memory! Cheseldine's hiding-place was on the far slope of Mount Ord, in a deep, high-walled valley. He always went there just before a contemplated job, where he met and planned with his lieutenants. Then while they executed he basked in the sunshine before one or another of the public places he owned. He was there in the Ord den now, getting ready to plan the biggest job yet. It was a bank robbery; but where, Fletcher had not as yet been advised.

Then when Duane had pumped the now amenable outlaw of all details pertaining to the present he gathered data and facts and places covering a period of ten years Fletcher had been with Cheseldine. And herewith was unfolded a history so dark in its bloody régime, so incredible in its brazen daring, so appalling in its proof of the outlaw's sweep and grasp of the country from Pecos to Rio Grande, that Duane was stunned. Compared to this Cheseldine of the Big Bend, to this rancher, stock buyer, cattle speculator, property holder, all the outlaws Duane had ever known sank into insignificance. The power of the man stunned Duane; the strange fidelity given him stunned Duane; the intricate inside working of his great system was equally stunning. But when Duane recovered from that the old terrible passion to kill consumed him, and it raged fiercely and it could not be checked. If that red-handed Poggin, if that cold-eyed, dead-faced Knell had only been at Ord! But they were not, and Duane with help of time got what he hoped was the upper hand of himself.

✦22✦

AGAIN inaction and suspense dragged at Duane's spirit. Like a leashed hound with a keen scent in his face Duane wanted to leap forth when he was bound. He almost fretted. Something called to him over the bold, wild brow of Mount Ord. But while Fletcher stayed in Ord waiting for Knell and Poggin, or for orders, Duane knew his game was again a waiting one.

But one day there were signs of the long quiet of Ord being broken. A messenger strange to Duane rode in on a secret mission that had to do with Fletcher. When he went away Fletcher became addicted to thoughtful moods and lonely walks. He seldom drank, and this in itself was a striking contrast to former behavior. The messenger came again. Whatever communication he brought, it had a remarkable effect upon the outlaw. Duane was present in the tavern when the fellow arrived, saw the few words whispered, but did not hear them. Fletcher turned white with anger or fear, perhaps both, and he cursed like a madman. The messenger, a lean, dark-faced, hard-riding fellow reminding Duane of the cowboy Guthrie, left the tavern without even a drink and rode away off to the west. This west mystified and fascinated Duane as much as the south beyond Mount Ord. Where were Knell and Poggin? Apparently they were not at present with the leader on the mountain. After the messenger left Fletcher grew silent and surly. He had presented a variety of moods to Duane's observation, and this latest one was provocative of thought. Fletcher was dangerous. It became clear now that the other outlaws of the camp feared him, kept out of his way. Duane let him alone, yet closely watched him.

Perhaps an hour after the messenger had left, not longer, Fletcher manifestly arrived at some decision, and he called for his horse. Then he went to his shack and returned. To Duane the outlaw looked in shape both to ride and to fight. He gave orders for the men in camp to keep close until he returned. Then he mounted.

"Come here, Dodge," he called.

Duane went up and laid a hand on the pommel of the saddle. Fletcher walked his horse, with Duane beside him, till they reached the log bridge, when he halted.

"Dodge, I'm in bad with Knell," he said. "An' it 'pears I'm the cause of friction between Knell an' Poggy. Knell never had any use fer me, but Poggy's been square, if not friendly. The boss has a big deal on, an' here it's been held up because of this scrap. He's waitin' over there on the mountain to give orders to Knell or Poggy, an' neither one's showin' up. I've got to stand in the breach, an' I ain't enjoyin' the prospects."

"What's the trouble about, Jim?" asked Duane.

"Reckon it's a little about you, Dodge," said Fletcher, dryly. "Knell hadn't any use fer you thet day. He ain't got no use fer a man onless he can rule him. Some of the boys here hev blabbed before I edged in with my say, an' there's hell to pay. Knell claims to know somethin' about you that'll make both the boss an' Poggy sick when he springs it. But he's keepin' quiet. Hard man to figger, thet Knell. Reckon you'd better go back to Bradford fer a day or so, then camp out near here till I come back."

"Why?"

"Wal, because there ain't any use fer you to git in bad, too. The gang will ride over here any day. If they're friendly I'll light a fire on the hill there, say three nights from tonight. If you don't see it thet night you hit the trail. I'll do what I can. Jim Fletcher sticks to his pals. So long, Dodge."

Then he rode away.

He left Duane in a quandary. This news was black. Things had been working out so well. Here was a setback. At the moment Duane did not know which way to turn, but certainly he had no idea of going back to Bradford. Friction between the two great lieutenants of Cheseldine! Open hostility between one of them and another of the chief's right-hand men! Among outlaws that sort of thing was deadly serious. Generally such matters were settled with guns. Duane gathered encouragement even from disaster. Perhaps the disintegration of Cheseldine's great band had already begun. But what did Knell know? Duane did not circle around the idea with doubts and hopes; if Knell knew anything it was that this stranger in Ord, this new partner of Fletcher's, was no less than Buck Duane. Well, it was about time, thought Duane, that he made use of his name if it were to help him at all. That name had been MacNelly's hope. He had anchored all his scheme to Duane's fame. Duane was tempted to ride off after Fletcher and stay with him. This, however, would hardly be fair to an outlaw who had been fair to him. Duane concluded to await developments and when the gang rode in to Ord, probably from their various hiding-places, he would be there ready to be denounced by Knell. Duane could not see any other culmination of this series of events than a meeting between Knell and himself. If that terminated fatally for Knell there was all probability of Duane's being in no worse situation than he was now. If Poggin took up the quarrel! Here Duane accused himself again—tried in vain to revolt from a judgment that he was only reasoning out excuses to meet these outlaws.

Meanwhile, instead of waiting, why not hunt up Cheseldine in his mountain retreat? The thought no sooner struck Duane than he was hurrying for his horse.

He left Ord, ostensibly toward Bradford, but, once out of sight, he turned off the road, circled through the brush, and several miles south of town he struck a narrow grass-grown trail that Fletcher had told him led to Cheseldine's camp. The horse tracks along this trail were not less than a week old, and very likely much more. It wound between low, brush-covered foothills, through arroyos and gullies lined with mesquite, cottonwood, and scrub-oak.

In an hour Duane struck the slope of Mount Ord, and as he climbed he got a view of the rolling, black-spotted country, partly desert, partly fertile, with long, bright lines of dry stream-beds winding away to grow dim in the distance. He got among broken rocks and cliffs, and here the open, downward-rolling land disappeared, and he was hard put to it to find the trail. He lost it repeatedly and made slow progress. Finally he climbed into a region of all rock benches, rough here, smooth there, with only an occasional scratch of iron horseshoe to guide him. Many times he had to go ahead and then work to right or left till he found his way again. It was slow work; it took all day; and night found him halfway up the mountain. He halted at a little side-canyon with grass and water, and here he made camp. The night was clear and cool at that height, with a dark-blue sky and a streak of stars blinking across. With this day of action behind him he felt better satisfied than he had been for some time. Here, on this venture, he was answering to a call that had so often directed his movements, perhaps his life, and it was one that logic or intelligence could take little stock of. And on this night, lonely like the ones he used to spend in the Nueces gorge, and memorable of them because of a likeness to that old hiding-place, he felt the pressing return of old haunting things—the past so long ago, wild flights, dead faces—and the places of these were taken by one quiveringly alive, white, tragic, with its dark, intent, speaking eyes—Ray Longstreth's.

That last memory he yielded to until he slept.

In the morning, satisfied that he had left still fewer tracks than he had followed up this trail, he led his horse up to the head of the canyon, there a narrow crack in low cliffs, and with branches of cedar fenced him in. Then he went back and took up the trail on foot.

Without the horse he made better time and climbed through deep clefts, wide canyons, over ridges, up shelving slopes, along precipices—a long, hard climb—till he reached what he concluded was a divide. Going down was easier, though the farther he followed this dim and winding trail the wider the broken battlements of rock. Above him he saw the black fringe of pinyon and pine, and above that the bold peak, bare, yellow, like a desert butte. Once, through a wide gateway between great escarpments, he saw the lower country beyond the range, and beyond this, vast and clear as it lay in his sight, was the great river that made the Big Bend. He went down and down, wondering how a horse could follow that broken trail, believing there must be another better one somewhere into Cheseldine's hiding-place.

He rounded a jutting corner, where view had been shut off, and presently came out upon the rim of a high wall. Beneath, like a green gulf seen through blue haze, lay an amphitheater walled in on the two sides he could see. It lay perhaps a thousand feet below him; and, plain as all the other features of that wild environment, there shone out a big red stone or adobe cabin, white water shining away between great borders, and horses and cattle dotting the levels. It was a peaceful, beautiful scene. Duane could not help grinding his teeth at the thought of rustlers living there in quiet and ease.

Duane worked halfway down to the level, and, well hidden in a niche, he settled himself to watch both trail and valley. He made note of the position of the sun and saw that if anything developed or if he decided to descend any farther there was small likelihood of his getting back to his camp before dark. To try that after nightfall he imagined would be vain effort.

Then he bent his keen eyes downward. The cabin appeared to be a crude structure. Though large in size, it had, of course, been built by outlaws.

There was no garden, no cultivated field, no corral. Excepting for the rude pile of stones and logs plastered together with mud, the valley was as wild, probably, as on the day of discovery. Duane seemed to have been watching for a long time before he saw any sign of man, and this one apparently went to the stream for water and returned to the cabin.

The sun went down behind the wall, and shadows were born in the darker places of the valley. Duane began to want to get closer to that cabin. What had he taken this arduous climb for? He held back, however, trying to evolve further plans.

While he was pondering the shadows quickly gathered and darkened. If he was to go back to camp he must set out at once. Still he lingered. And suddenly his wide-roving eye caught sight of two horsemen riding up the valley. They must have entered at a point below, round the huge abutment of rock, beyond Duane's range of sight. Their horses were tired and stopped at the stream for a long drink.

Duane left his perch, took to the steep trail, and descended as fast as he could without making noise. It did not take him long to reach the valley floor. It was almost level, with deep grass, and here and there clumps of bushes. Twilight was already thick down there. Duane marked the location of the trail, and then began to slip like a shadow through the grass and from bush to bush. He saw a bright light before he made out the dark outline of the cabin. Then he heard voices, a merry whistle, a coarse song, and the clink of iron cooking utensils. He smelled fragrant wood-smoke. He saw moving dark figures cross the light. Evidently there was a wide door, or else the fire was out in the open.

Duane swerved to the left, out of direct line with the light, and thus was able to see better. Then he advanced noiselessly but swiftly toward the back of the house. There were trees close to the wall. He would make no noise, and he could scarcely be seen—if only there was no watchdog! But all his outlaw days he had taken risks with only his useless life at stake; now, with that changed, he advanced stealthy and bold as an Indian. He reached the cover of the trees, knew he was hidden in their shadows, for at few paces' distance he had been able to see only their tops. From there he slipped up to the house and felt along the wall with his hands.

He came to a little window where light shone through. He peeped in. He saw a room shrouded in shadows, a lamp turned low, a table, chairs. He saw an open door, with bright flare beyond, but could not see the fire. Voices came indistinctly. Without hesitation Duane stole farther along— all the way to the end of the cabin. Peeping round, he saw only the flare of light on bare ground. Retracing his cautious steps, he paused at the crack again, saw that no man was in the room, and then he went on round that end of the cabin. Fortune favored him. There were bushes, an old shed, a woodpile, all the cover he needed at that corner. He did not even need to crawl.

Before he peered between the rough corner of wall and the bush growing close to it Duane paused a moment. This excitement was different from that he had always felt when pursued. It had no bitterness, no pain, no dread. There was as much danger here, perhaps more, yet it was not the same. Then he looked.

He saw a bright fire, a red-faced man bending over it, whistling, while he handled a steaming pot. Over him was a roofed shed built against the wall, with two open sides and two supporting posts. Duane's second glance, not so blinded by the sudden bright light, made out other men, three in the shadow, two in the flare, but with backs to him.

"It's a smoother trail by long odds, but ain't so short as this one right over the mountain," one outlaw was saying.

"What's eatin' you, Panhandle?" ejaculated another. "Blossom an' me rode from Faraway Springs, where Poggin is with some of the gang."

"Excuse me, Phil. Shore I didn't see you come in, an' Boldt never said nothin'."

"It took you a long time to get here, but I guess that's just as well," spoke up a smooth, suave voice with a ring in it.

Longstreth's voice—Cheseldine's voice!

Here they were—Cheseldine, Phil Knell, Blossom Kane, Panhandle Smith, Boldt—how well Duane remembered the names!—all here, the big men of Cheseldine's gang, except the biggest—Poggin. Duane had holed them, and his sensations of the moment deadened sight and sound of what was before him. He sank down, controlled himself, silenced a mounting exultation; then from a less-strained position he peered forth again.

The outlaws were waiting for supper. Their conversation might have been that of cowboys in camp, ranchers at a round-up. Duane listened with eager ears, waiting for the business talk that he felt would come. All the time he watched with the eyes of a wolf upon its quarry. Blossom Kane was the lean-limbed messenger who had so angered Fletcher. Boldt was a giant in stature, dark, bearded, silent. Panhandle Smith was the red-faced cook, merry, profane, a short, bow-legged man resembling many rustlers Duane had known, particularly Luke Stevens. And Knell, who sat there, tall, slim, like a boy in build, like a boy in years, with his pale, smooth, expressionless face and his cold, gray eyes. And Longstreth, who leaned against the wall, handsome, with his dark face and beard like an aristocrat, resembled many a rich Louisiana planter Duane had met. The sixth man sat so much in the shadow that he could not be plainly discerned, and, though addressed, his name was not mentioned.

Panhandle Smith carried pots and pans into the cabin, and cheerfully called out: "If you gents air hungry fer grub, don't look fer me to feed you with a spoon."

The outlaws piled inside, made a great bustle and clatter as they sat to their meal. Like hungry men, they talked little.

Duane waited there awhile, then guardedly got up and crept round to the other side of the cabin. After he became used to the dark again he ventured to steal along the wall to the window and peeped in. The outlaws were in the first room and could not be seen.

Duane waited. The moments dragged endlessly. His heart pounded. Longstreth entered, turned up the light, and, taking a box of cigars from the table, he carried it out.

"Here, you fellows, go outside and smoke," he said. "Knell, come on in now. Let's get it over."

He returned, sat down, and lighted a cigar for himself. He put his booted feet on the table.

Duane saw that the room was comfortably, even luxuriously furnished. There must have been a good trail, he thought—else how could all that stuff have been packed in there? Most assuredly it could not have come over the trail he had traveled. Presently he heard the men go outside, and their voices became indistinct. Then Knell came in and seated himself without any of his chief's ease. He seemed preoccupied and, as always, cold.

"What's wrong, Knell? Why didn't you get here sooner?" queried Long-streth.

"Poggin, damn him! We're on the outs again."

"What for?"

"Aw, he needn't have got sore. He's breakin' a new hoss over there at Faraway, an' you know him where a hoss 's concerned. That kept him, I reckon, more than anythin'."

"What else? Get it out of your system so we can go on to the new job."

"Well, it begins back a ways. I don't know how long ago—weeks—a stranger rode into Ord an' got down easy-like as if he owned the place. He seemed familiar to me. But I wasn't sure. We looked him over, an' I left, tryin' to place him in my mind."

"What 'd he look like?"

"Rangy, powerful man, white hair over his temples, still, hard face, eyes like knives. The way he packed his guns, the way he walked an' stood an' swung his right hand showed me what he was. You can't fool me on the gun-sharp. An' he had a grand horse, a big black."

"I've met your man," said Longstreth.

"No!" exclaimed Knell. It was wonderful to hear surprise expressed by this man that did not in the least show it in his strange physiognomy. Knell laughed a short, grim, hollow laugh. "Boss, this here big gent drifts into Ord again an' makes up to Jim Fletcher. Jim, you know, is easy led. He likes men. An' when a posse come along trailin' a blind lead, huntin' the wrong way for the man who held up No. 6, why, Jim—he up an' takes this stranger to be the fly road-agent an' cottons to him. Got money out of him sure. An' that's what stumps me more. What's this man's game? I happen to know, boss, that he couldn't have held up No. 6."

"How do you know?" demanded Longstreth.

"Because I did the job myself."

A dark and stormy passion clouded the chief's face.

"Damn you, Knell! You're incorrigible. You're unreliable. Another break like that queers you with me. Did you tell Poggin?"

"Yes. That's one reason we fell out. He raved. I thought he was goin' to kill me."

"Why did you tackle such a risky job without help or plan?"

"It offered, that's all. An' it was easy. But it was a mistake. I got the country an' the railroad hollerin' for nothin'. I just couldn't help it. You know what idleness means to one of us. You know also that this very life breeds fatality. It's wrong—that's why. I was born of good parents, an' I know what's right. We're wrong, an' we can't beat the end, that's all. An' for my part I don't care a damn when that comes."

"Fine wise talk from you, Knell," said Longstreth, scornfully. "Go on with your story."

"As I said, Jim cottons to the pretender, an' they get chummy. They're together all the time. You can gamble Jim told all he knew an' then some.

A little liquor loosens his tongue. Several of the boys rode over from Ord, an' one of them went to Poggin an' says Jim Fletcher has a new man for the gang. Poggin, you know, is always ready for any new man. He says if one doesn't turn out good he can be shut off easy. He rather liked the way this new pard of Jim's was boosted. Jim an' Poggin always hit it up together. So until I got on the deal Jim's pard was already in the gang, without Poggin or you ever seein' him. Then I got to figurin' hard. Just where had I ever seen that chap? As it turned out, I never had seen him, which accounts for my bein' doubtful. I'd never forget any man I'd seen. I dug up a lot of old papers from my kit an' went over them. Letters, pictures, clippin's, an' all that. I guess I had a pretty good notion what I was lookin' for an' who I wanted to make sure of. At last I found it. An' I knew my man. But I didn't spring it on Poggin. Oh no! I want to have some fun with him when the time comes. He'll be wilder than a trapped wolf. I sent Blossom over to Ord to get word from Jim, an' when he verified all this talk I sent Blossom again with a message calculated to make Jim hump. Poggin got sore, said he'd wait for Jim, an' I could come over here to see you about the new job. He'd meet me in Ord."

Knell had spoken hurriedly and low, now and then with passion. His pale eyes glinted like fire in ice, and now his voice fell to a whisper.

"Who do you think Fletcher's new man is?"

"Who?" demanded Longstreth.

"Buck Duane!"

Down came Longstreth's boots with a crash, then his body grew rigid.

"That Nueces outlaw? That two-shot ace-of-spades gun-thrower who killed Bland, Alloway—?"

"An' Hardin." Knell whispered this last name with more feeling than the apparent circumstance demanded.

"Yes; and Hardin, the best one of the Rim Rock fellows—Buck Duane!"

Longstreth was so ghastly white now that his black mustache seemed outlined against chalk. He eyed his grim lieutenant. They understood each other without more words. It was enough that Buck Duane was there in the Big Bend. Longstreth rose presently and reached for a flask, from which he drank, then offered it to Knell. He waved it aside.

"Knell," began the chief, slowly, as he wiped his lips, "I gathered you have some grudge against this Buck Duane."

"Yes."

"Well, don't be a —— fool now and do what Poggin or almost any of you men would—don't meet this Buck Duane. I've reason to believe he's a Texas Ranger now."

"The hell you say!" exclaimed Knell.

"Yes. Go to Ord and give Jim Fletcher a hunch. He'll get Poggin, and they'll fix even Buck Duane."

"All right. I'll do my best. But if I run into Duane—"

"Don't run into him!" Longstreth's voice fairly rang with the force of its passion and command. He wiped his face, drank again from the flask, sat down, resumed his smoking, and, drawing a paper from his vest pocket, he began to study it.

"Well, I'm glad that's settled," he said, evidently referring to the Duane matter. "Now for the new job. This is October the eighteenth. On or before the twenty-fifth there will be a shipment of gold reaching the Rancher's Bank of Val Verde. After you return to Ord give Poggin these orders. Keep the gang quiet. You, Poggin, Kane, Fletcher, Panhandle Smith, and Boldt to be in on the secret and the job. Nobody else. You'll leave Ord on the twenty-third, ride across country by the trail till you get within sight of Mercer. It's a hundred miles from Bradford to Val Verde—about the same from Ord. Time your travel to get you near Val Verde on the morning of the twenty-sixth. You won't have to more than trot your horses. At two o'clock in the afternoon, sharp, ride into town and up to the Rancher's Bank. Val Verde's a pretty big town. Never been any holdups there. Town feels safe. Make it a clean, fast, daylight job. That's all. Have you got the details?"

Knell did not even ask for the dates again.

"Suppose Poggin or me might be detained?" he asked.

Longstreth bent a dark glance upon his lieutenant.

"You never can tell what'll come off," continued Knell. "I'll do my best."

"The minute you see Poggin, tell him. A job on hand steadies him. And I say again—look to it that nothing happens. Either you or Poggin carry the job through. But I want both of you in it. Break for the hills, and when you get up in the rocks where you can hide your tracks head for Mount Ord. When all's quiet again I'll join you here. That's all. Call in the boys."

Like a swift shadow and as noiseless, Duane stole across the level toward the dark wall of rock. Every nerve was a strung wire. For a little while his mind was cluttered and clogged with whirling thoughts, from which, like a flashing scroll, unrolled the long, baffling order of action. The game was now in his hands. He must cross Mount Ord at night. The feat was improbable, but it might be done. He must ride into Bradford, forty miles from the foothills, before eight o'clock next morning. He must telegraph MacNelly to be in Val Verde on the twenty-fifth. He must ride back to Ord, to intercept Knell, face him, be denounced, kill him, and while the iron was hot strike hard to win Poggin's half-won interest as he had wholly won Fletcher's. Failing that last, he must let the outlaws alone to bide their time in Ord, to be free to ride on to their new job in Val Verde. In the meantime he must plan to arrest Longstreth. It was a magnificent outline, incredible, alluring, unfathomable in its nameless certainty. He felt like fate. He seemed to be the iron consequences falling upon these doomed outlaws.

Under the wall the shadows were black, only the tips of trees and crags showing, yet he went straight to the trail. It was merely a grayness between borders of black. He climbed and never stopped. It did not seem steep. His feet might have had eyes. He surmounted the wall, and, looking down into the ebony gulf pierced by one point of light, he lifted a menacing arm and shook it. Then he strode on and did not falter till he reached the huge shelving cliffs. Here he lost the trail; there was none; but he remembered the shapes, the points, the notches of rock above. Before he reached the ruins of splintered ramparts and jumbles of broken walls the moon topped the eastern slope of the mountain, and the mystifying blackness he had dreaded changed to magic silver light. It seemed as light as day, only soft, mellow, and the air held a transparent sheen. He ran up the bare ridges and down the smooth slopes, and, like a goat, jumped from rock to rock. In this light he knew his way and lost no time looking for a trail. He crossed the divide and then had all downhill before him. Swiftly he descended, almost always sure of his memory of the landmarks. He did not remember having studied them in the ascent, yet here they were, even in changed light, familiar to his sight. What he had once seen was pictured on his mind. And, true as a deer striking for home, he reached the canyon where he had left his horse.

Bullet was quickly and easily found. Duane threw on the saddle and pack, cinched them tight, and resumed his descent. The worst was now to come. Bare downward steps in rock, sliding, weathered slopes, narrow black gullies, a thousand openings in a maze of broken stone—these Duane had to descend in fast time, leading a giant of a horse. Bullet cracked the loose fragments, sent them rolling, slid on the scaly slopes, plunged down the steps, followed like a faithful dog at Duane's heels.

Hours passed as moments. Duane was equal to his great opportunity. But he could not quell that self in him which reached back over the lapse of lonely, searing years and found the boy in him. He who had been worse than dead was now grasping at the skirts of life—which meant victory, honor, happiness. Duane knew he was not just right in part of his mind. Small wonder that he was not insane, he thought! He tramped on downward, his marvelous faculty for covering rough ground and holding to the true course never before even in flight so keen and acute. Yet all the time a spirit was keeping step with him. Thought of Ray Longstreth as he had left her made him weak. But now, with the game clear to its end, with the trap to spring, with success strangely haunting him, Duane could not dispel memory of her. He saw her white face, with its sweet sad lips and the dark eyes so tender and tragic. And time and distance and risk and toil were nothing.

The moon sloped to the west. Shadows of trees and crags now crossed to the other side of him. The stars dimmed. Then he was out of the rocks, with the dim trail pale at his feet. Mounting Bullet, he made short work of the long slope and the foothills and the rolling land leading down to Ord. The little outlaw camp, with its shacks and cabins and row of houses, lay silent and dark under the paling moon. Duane passed by on the lower trail, headed into the road, and put Bullet to a gallop. He watched the dying moon, the waning stars, and the east. He had time to spare, so he saved the horse. Knell would be leaving the rendezvous about the time Duane turned back toward Ord. Between noon and sunset they would meet.

The night wore on. The moon sank behind low mountains in the west. The stars brightened for a while, then faded. Gray gloom enveloped the world, thickened, lay like smoke over the road. Then shade by shade it lightened, until through the transparent obscurity shone a dim light.

Duane reached Bradford before dawn. He dismounted some distance from the tracks, tied his horse, and then crossed over to the station. He heard the clicking of the telegraph instrument, and it thrilled him. An operator sat inside reading. When Duane tapped on the window he looked up with startled glance, then went swiftly to unlock the door.

"Hello. Give me paper and pencil. Quick," whispered Duane.

With trembling hands the operator complied. Duane wrote out the message he had carefully composed.

"Send this—repeat it to make sure—then keep mum. I'll see you again. Goodbye."

The operator stared, but did not speak a word.

Duane left as stealthily and swiftly as he had come. He walked his horse a couple of miles back on the road and then rested him till break of day. The east began to redden, Duane turned grimly in the direction of Ord.

When Duane swung into the wide, grassy square on the outskirts of Ord he saw a bunch of saddled horses hitched in front of the tavern. He knew what that meant. Luck still favored him. If it would only hold! But he could ask no more. The rest was a matter of how greatly he could make his power felt. An open conflict against odds lay in the balance. That would be fatal to him, and to avoid it he had to trust to his name and a presence he must make terrible. He knew outlaws. He knew what qualities held them. He knew what to exaggerate.

There was not an outlaw in sight. The dusty horses had covered distance that morning. As Duane dismounted he heard loud, angry voices inside the tavern. He removed coat and vest, hung them over the pommel. He packed two guns, one belted high on the left hip, the other swinging low on the right side. He neither looked nor listened, but boldly pushed the door and stepped inside.

The big room was full of men, and every face pivoted toward him. Knell's pale face flashed into Duane's swift sight; then Boldt's, then Blossom Kane's, then Panhandle Smith's, then Fletcher's, then others that were familiar, and last that of Poggin. Though Duane had never seen Poggin or heard him described, he knew him. For he saw a face that was a record of great and evil deeds.

There was absolute silence. The outlaws were lined back of a long table upon which were papers, stacks of silver coin, a bundle of bills, and a huge gold-mounted gun.

"Are you gents lookin' for me?" asked Duane. He gave his voice all the ringing force and power of which he was capable. And he stepped back, free of anything, with the outlaws all before him.

Knell stood quivering, but his face might have been a mask. The other outlaws looked from him to Duane. Jim Fletcher flung up his hands.

"My Gawd, Dodge, what'd you bust in here fer?" he said, plaintively, and slowly stepped forward. His action was that of a man true to himself. He meant he had been sponsor for Duane and now he would stand by him.

"Back, Fletcher!" called Duane, and his voice made the outlaw jump.

"Hold on, Dodge, an' you-all, everybody," said Fletcher. "Let me talk, seein' I'm in wrong here."

His persuasions did not ease the strain.

"Go ahead. Talk," said Poggin.

Fletcher turned to Duane. "Pard, I'm takin' it on myself thet you meet enemies here when I swore you'd meet friends. It's my fault. I'll stand by you if you let me."

"No, Jim," replied Duane.

"But what'd you come fer without the signal?" burst out Fletcher, in distress. He saw nothing but catastrophe in this meeting.

"Jim, I ain't pressin' my company none. But when I'm wanted bad—"

Fletcher stopped him with a raised hand. Then he turned to Poggin with a rude dignity.

"Poggy, he's my pard, an' he's riled. I never told him a word thet'd make him sore. I only said Knell hadn't no more use fer him than fer me. Now, what you say goes in this gang. I never failed you in my life. Here's my pard. I vouch fer him. Will you stand fer me? There's goin' to be hell if you don't. An' us with a big job on hand!"

While Fletcher toiled over his slow, earnest persuasion, Duane had his gaze riveted upon Poggin. There was something leonine about Poggin. He was tawny. He blazed. He seemed beautiful as fire was beautiful. But looked at closer, with glance seeing the physical man, instead of that thing which shone from him, he was of perfect build, with muscles that swelled and rippled, bulging his clothes, with the magnificent head and face of the cruel, fierce, tawny-eyed jaguar.

Looking at this strange Poggin, instinctively divining his abnormal and hideous power, Duane had for the first time in his life the inward quaking fear of a man. It was like a cold-tongued bell ringing within him and numbing his heart. The old instinctive firing of blood followed, but did not drive away that fear. He knew. He felt something here deeper than thought could go. And he hated Poggin.

That individual had been considering Fletcher's appeal.

"Jim, I ante up," he said, "an' if Phil doesn't raise us out with a big hand—why, he'll get called, an' your pard can set in the game."

Every eye shifted to Knell. He was dead white. He laughed, and anyone hearing that laugh would have realized his intense anger equally with an assurance which made him master of the situation.

"Poggin, you're a gambler, you are—the ace-high, straight-flush hand of the Big Bend," he said, with stinging scorn. "I'll bet you my roll to a greaser peso that I can deal you a hand you'll be afraid to play."

"Phil, you're talkin' wild," growled Poggin, with both advice and menace in his tone.

"If there's anythin' you hate it's a man who pretends to be somebody else when he's not. Thet so?"

Poggin nodded in slow-gathering wrath.

"Well, Jim's new pard—this man Dodge—he's not who he seems. Oh-ho! He's a hell of a lot different. But I know him. An' when I spring his name on you, Poggin, you'll freeze to your gizzard. Do you get me? You'll freeze, an' your hand'll be stiff when it ought to be lightnin'—all because you'll realize you've been standin' there five minutes—five minutes *alive* before him!"

If not hate, then assuredly great passion toward Poggin manifested itself in Knell's scornful, fiery address, in the shaking hand he thrust before Poggin's face. In the ensuing silent pause Knell's panting could be plainly heard. The other men were pale, watchful, cautiously edging either way to the wall, leaving the principals and Duane in the center of the room.

"Spring his name, then, you—" said Poggin, violently, with a curse.

Strangely Knell did not even look at the man he was about to denounce. He leaned toward Poggin, his hands, his body, his long head all somewhat expressive of what his face disguised.

"*Buck Duane!*" he yelled, suddenly.

The name did not make any great difference in Poggin. But Knell's passionate, swift utterance carried the suggestion that the name ought to bring Poggin to quick action. It was possible, too, that Knell's manner, the import of his denunciation, the meaning back of all his passion held Poggin bound more than the surprise. For the outlaw certainly was surprised, perhaps staggered at the idea that he, Poggin, had been about to stand sponsor with Fletcher for a famous outlaw hated and feared by all outlaws.

Knell waited a long moment, and then his face broke its cold immobility in an extraordinary expression of devilish glee. He had hounded the great Poggin into something that gave him vicious, monstrous joy.

"*Buck Duane!* Yes," he broke out, hotly. "The Nueces gunman! That two-shot, ace-of-spades lone wolf! You an' I—we've heard a thousand times of him—talked about him often. An' here he is *in front* of you! Poggin, you were backin' Fletcher's new pard, Buck Duane. An' he'd fooled you both but for me. But *I* know him. An' I know why he drifted in here. To flash a gun on Cheseldine—on you—on me! Bah! Don't tell me he wanted to join the gang. You know a gunman, for you're one yourself. Don't you always want to kill another man? An' don't you always want to meet a real man, not a four-flush? It's the madness of the gunman, an' I know it. Well, Duane faced you—called you! An' when I sprung his name, what ought you have done? What would the boss—anybody—have expected of Poggin? Did you throw your gun, swift, like you have so often? Naw; you froze. An' why? Because here's a man with the kind of nerve you'd love to have. Because he's great—meetin' us here alone. Because you know he's a wonder with a gun an' you love life. Because you an' I an' every damned man here had to take his front, each to himself. If we all drew we'd kill him. Sure! But who's goin' to lead? Who was goin' to be first? Who was goin' to make him draw? Not you, Poggin! You leave that for a lesser man—me—who've lived to see you a coward. It comes once to every gunman. You've met your match in Buck Duane. An', by God, I'm glad! Here's once I show you up!"

The hoarse, taunting voice failed. Knell stepped back from the comrade he hated. He was wet, shaking, haggard, but magnificent.

"Buck Duane, do you remember Hardin?" he asked, in scarcely audible voice.

"Yes," replied Duane, and a flash of insight made clear Knell's attitude.

"You met him—forced him to draw—killed him?"

"Yes."

"Hardin was the best pard I ever had."

His teeth clicked together tight, and his lips set in a thin line.

The room grew still. Even breathing ceased. The time for words had passed. In that long moment of suspense Knell's body gradually stiffened, and at last the quivering ceased. He crouched. His eyes had a soul-piercing fire.

Duane watched them. He waited. He caught the thought—the breaking of Knell's muscle-bound rigidity. Then he drew.

Through the smoke of his gun he saw two red spurts of flame. Knell's bullets thudded into the ceiling. He fell with a scream like a wild thing in agony.

Duane did not see Knell die. He watched Poggin. And Poggin, like a stricken and astounded man, looked down upon his prostrate comrade.

Fletcher ran at Duane with hands aloft.

"Hit the trail, you liar, or you'll hev to kill me!" he yelled.

With hands still up, he shouldered and bodied Duane out of the room. Duane leaped on his horse, spurred, and plunged away.

⁃23⁃

DUANE returned to Fairdale and camped in the mesquite till the twenty-third of the month. The few days seemed endless. All he could think of was that the hour in which he must disgrace Ray Longstreth was slowly but inexorably coming. In that waiting time he learned what love was and also duty. When the day at last dawned he rode like one possessed down the rough slope, hurdling the stones and crashing through the brush, with a sound in his ears that was not all the rush of the wind. Something dragged at him.

Apparently one side of his mind was unalterably fixed, while the other was a hurrying conglomeration of flashes of thought, reception of sensations. He could not get calmness. By and by, almost involuntarily, he hurried faster on. Action seemed to make his state less oppressive; it eased the weight. But the farther he went on the harder it was to continue. Had he turned his back upon love, happiness, perhaps on life itself?

There seemed no use to go on farther until he was absolutely sure of himself. Duane received a clear warning thought that such work as seemed haunting and driving him could never be carried out in the mood under which he labored. He hung onto that thought. Several times he slowed up, then stopped, only to go on again. At length, as he mounted a low ridge, Fairdale lay bright and green before him not far away, and the sight was a conclusive check. There were mesquites on the ridge, and Duane sought the shade beneath them. It was the noon hour, with hot, glary sun and no wind. Here Duane had to have out his fight. Duane was utterly unlike himself; he could not bring the old self back; he was not the same man he once had been. But he could understand why. It was because of Ray Longstreth. Temptation assailed him. To have her his wife! It was impossible. The thought was insidiously alluring. Duane pictured a home. He saw himself riding through the cotton and rice and cane, home to a stately old mansion, where long-eared hounds bayed him welcome, and a woman looked for him and met him with happy and beautiful smile.

There might—there would be children. And something new, strange, confounding with its emotion, came to life deep in Duane's heart. There would be children! Ray their mother! The kind of life a lonely outcast always yearned for and never had! He saw it all, felt it all.

But beyond and above all other claims came Captain MacNelly's. It was then there was something cold and deathlike in Duane's soul. For he knew, whatever happened, of one thing he was sure—he would have to kill either Longstreth or Lawson. Longstreth might be trapped into arrest; but Lawson had no sense, no control, no fear. He would snarl like a panther and go for his gun, and he would have to be killed. This, of all consummations, was the one to be calculated upon.

Duane came out of it all bitter and callous and sore—in the most fitting of moods to undertake a difficult and deadly enterprise. He had fallen upon his old strange, futile dreams, now rendered poignant by reason of love. He drove away those dreams. In their places came the images of the olive-skinned Longstreth with his sharp eyes, and the dark, evil-faced Lawson, and then returned tenfold more thrilling and sinister the old strange passion to meet Poggin.

It was about one o'clock when Duane rode into Fairdale. The streets for the most part were deserted. He went directly to find Morton and Zimmer. He found them at length, restless, somber, anxious, but unaware of the part he had played at Ord. They said Longstreth was home, too. It was possible that Longstreth had arrived home in ignorance.

Duane told them to be on hand in town with their men in case he might need them, and then with teeth locked he set off for Longstreth's ranch.

Duane stole through the bushes and trees, and when nearing the porch he heard loud, angry, familiar voices. Longstreth and Lawson were quarreling again. How Duane's lucky star guided him! He had no plan of action, but his brain was equal to a hundred lightning-swift evolutions. He meant to take any risk rather than kill Longstreth. Both of the men were out on the porch. Duane wormed his way to the edge of the shrubbery and crouched low to watch for his opportunity.

Longstreth looked haggard and thin. He was in his shirt-sleeves, and he had come out with a gun in his hand. This he laid on a table near the wall. He wore no belt.

Lawson was red, bloated, thick-lipped, all fiery and sweaty from drink, though sober on the moment, and he had the expression of a desperate man in his last stand. It was his last stand, though he was ignorant of that.

"What's your news? You needn't be afraid of my feelings," said Lawson.

"Ray confessed to an interest in this ranger," replied Longstreth.

Duane thought Lawson would choke. He was thick-necked anyway, and the rush of blood made him tear at the soft collar of his shirt. Duane awaited his chance, patient, cold, all his feelings shut in a vise.

"But *why* should your daughter meet this ranger?" demanded Lawson, harshly.

"She's in love with him, and he's in love with her."

Duane reveled in Lawson's condition. The statement might have had the force of a juggernaut. Was Longstreth sincere? What was his game?

Lawson, finding his voice, cursed Ray, cursed the ranger, then Longstreth.

"You damned selfish fool!" cried Longstreth, in deep bitter scorn. "All you think of is yourself—your loss of the girl. Think once of *me*—my home—my life!"

Then the connection subtly put out by Longstreth apparently dawned upon the other. Somehow through this girl her father and cousin were to be betrayed. Duane got that impression, though he could not tell how true it was. Certainly Lawson's jealousy was his paramount emotion.

"To hell with you!" burst out Lawson, incoherently. He was frenzied. "I'll have her, or nobody else will!"

"You never will," returned Longstreth, stridently. "So help me God I'd rather see her the ranger's wife than yours!"

While Lawson absorbed that shock Longstreth leaned toward him, all of hate and menace in his mien.

"Lawson, you made me what I am," continued Longstreth. "I backed you—shielded you. *You're* Cheseldine—if the truth is told! Now it's ended. I quit you. I'm done!"

Their gray passion-corded faces were still as stones.

"Gentlemen!" Duane called in far-reaching voice as he stepped out. *"You're both done!"*

They wheeled to confront Duane.

"Don't move! Not a muscle! Not a finger!" he warned.

Longstreth read what Lawson had not the mind to read. His face turned from gray to ashen.

"What d'ye mean?" yelled Lawson, fiercely, shrilly. It was not in him to obey a command, to see impending death.

All quivering and strung, yet with perfect control, Duane raised his left hand to turn back a lapel of his open vest. The silver star flashed brightly.

Lawson howled like a dog. With barbarous and insane fury, with sheer impotent folly, he swept a clawing hand for his gun. Duane's shot broke his action.

Before Lawson even tottered, before he loosed the gun, Longstreth leaped behind him, clasped him with left arm, quick as lightning jerked the gun from both clutching fingers and sheath. Longstreth protected himself with the body of the dead man. Duane saw red flashes, puffs of smoke; he heard quick reports. Something stung his left arm. Then a blow like wind, light of sound yet shocking in impact, struck him, staggered him. The hot rend of lead followed the blow. Duane's heart seemed to explode, yet his mind kept extraordinarily clear and rapid.

Duane heard Longstreth work the action of Lawson's gun. He heard the hammer click, fall upon empty shells. Longstreth had used up all the loads in Lawson's gun. He cursed as a man cursed at defeat. Duane waited, cool and sure now. Longstreth tried to lift the dead man, to edge him closer toward the table where his own gun lay. But, considering the peril of exposing himself, he found the task beyond him. He bent peering at Duane under Lawson's arm, which flopped out from his side. Longstreth's eyes were the eyes of a man who meant to kill. There was never any mistaking the strange and terrible light of eyes like those. More than once Duane had a chance to aim at them, at the top of Longstreth's head, at a strip of his side.

Longstreth flung Lawson's body off. But even as it dropped, before Longstreth could leap, as he surely intended, for the gun, Duane covered him, called piercingly to him:

"Don't jump for the gun! Don't! I'll kill you! Sure as God I'll kill you!"

Longstreth stood perhaps ten feet from the table where his gun lay. Duane saw him calculating chances. He was game. He had the courage that forced Duane to respect him. Duane just saw him measure the distance to that gun. He was magnificent. He meant to do it. Duane would have to kill him.

"Longstreth, listen," cried Duane, swiftly. "The game's up. You're done. But think of your daughter! I'll spare your life—I'll try to get you freedom on one condition. For her sake! I've got you nailed—all the proofs. There lies Lawson. You're alone. I've Morton and men to my aid. Give up. Surrender. Consent to demands, and I'll spare you. Maybe I can persuade MacNelly to let you go free back to your old country. It's for Ray's sake! Her life, perhaps her happiness, can be saved! Hurry, man! Your answer!"

"Suppose I refuse?" he queried, with a dark and terrible earnestness.

"Then I'll kill you in your tracks! You can't move a hand! Your word or death! Hurry, Longstreth! Be a man! For her sake! Quick! Another second now—I'll kill you!"

"All right, Buck Duane, I give my word," he said, and deliberately walked to the chair and fell into it.

Longstreth looked strangely at the bloody blot on Duane's shoulder.

"There come the girls!" he suddenly exclaimed. "Can you help me drag Lawson inside? They mustn't see him."

Duane was facing down the porch toward the court and corrals. Miss Longstreth and Ruth had come in sight, were swiftly approaching, evidently alarmed. The two men succeeded in drawing Lawson into the house before the girls saw him.

"Duane, you're not hard hit?" said Longstreth.

"Reckon not," replied Duane.

"I'm sorry. If only you could have told me sooner! Lawson, damn him! Always I've split over him!"

"But the last time, Longstreth."

"Yes, and I came near driving you to kill me, too. Duane, you talked me out of it. For Ray's sake! She'll be in here in a minute. This'll be harder than facing a gun."

"Hard now. But I hope it'll turn out all right."

"Duane, will you do me a favor?" he asked, and he seemed shamefaced.

"Sure."

"Let Ray and Ruth think Lawson shot you. He's dead. It can't matter. Duane, the old side of my life is coming back. It's been coming. It'll be here just about when she enters this room. And, by God, I'd change places with Lawson if I could!"

"Glad you—said that, Longstreth," replied Duane. "And sure—Lawson plugged me. It's our secret."

Just then Ray and Ruth entered the room. Duane heard two low cries, so different in tone, and he saw two white faces. Ray came to his side. She lifted a shaking hand to point at the blood upon his breast. White and mute, she gazed from that to her father.

"Papa!" cried Ray, wringing her hands.

"Don't give way," he replied, huskily. "Both you girls will need your nerve. Duane isn't badly hurt. But Floyd is—is dead. Listen. Let me tell it quick. There's been a fight. It—it was Lawson—it was Lawson's gun that shot Duane. Duane let me off. In fact, Ray, he saved me. I'm to divide my property—return so far as possible what I've stolen—leave Texas at once with Duane, under arrest. He says maybe he can get MacNelly, the ranger captain, to let me go. For your sake!"

She stood there, realizing her deliverance, with the dark and tragic glory of her eyes passing from her father to Duane.

"You must rise above this," said Duane to her. "I expected this to ruin you. But your father is alive. He will live it down. I'm sure I can promise you he'll be free. Perhaps back there in Louisiana the dishonor will never be known. This country is far from your old home. And even in San Antonio and Austin a man's evil repute means little. Then the line between a rustler and a rancher is hard to draw in these wild border days. Rustling is stealing cattle, and I once heard a well-known rancher say that all rich cattlemen had done a little stealing. Your father drifted out here, and, like a good many others, he succeeded. It's perhaps just as well not to split hairs, to judge him by the law and morality of a civilized country. Some way or other he drifted in with bad men. Maybe a deal that was honest somehow tied his hands. This matter of land, water, a few stray head of stock had to be decided out of court. I'm sure in his case he never realized where he was drifting. Then one thing led to another, until he was face to face with dealing that took on crooked form. To protect himself he bound men to him. And so the gang developed. Many powerful gangs have developed that way out here. He could not control them.

He became involved with them. And eventually their dealings became deliberately and boldly dishonest. That meant the inevitable spilling of blood sooner or later, and so he grew into the leader because he was the strongest. Whatever he is to be judged for, I think he could have been infinitely worse."

❖24❖

O N   T H E   M O R N I N G   of the twenty-sixth Duane rode into Bradford in time to catch the early train. His wounds did not seriously incapacitate him. Longstreth was with him. And Miss Longstreth and Ruth Herbert would not be left behind. They were all leaving Fairdale forever. Longstreth had turned over the whole of his property to Morton, who was to divide it as he and his comrades believed just. Duane had left Fairdale with his party by night, passed through Sanderson in the early hours of dawn, and reached Bradford as he had planned.

That fateful morning found Duane outwardly calm, but inwardly he was in a tumult. He wanted to rush to Val Verde. Would Captain MacNelly be there with his rangers, as Duane had planned for them to be? Memory of that tawny Poggin returned with strange passion. Duane had borne hours and weeks and months of waiting, had endured the long hours of the outlaw, but now he had no patience. The whistle of the train made him leap.

It was a fast train, yet the ride seemed slow.

Duane, disliking to face Longstreth and the passengers in the car, changed his seat to one behind his prisoner. They had seldom spoken. Longstreth sat with bowed head, deep in thought. The girls sat in a seat nearby and were pale but composed. Occasionally the train halted briefly at a station. The latter half of that ride Duane had observed a wagon-road running parallel with the railroad, sometimes right alongside, at others near or far away. When the train was about twenty miles from Val Verde Duane espied a dark group of horsemen trotting eastward. His blood beat like a hammer at his temples. The gang! He thought he recognized the tawny Poggin and felt a strange inward contraction. He thought he recognized the clean-cut Blossom Kane, the black-bearded giant Boldt, the red-faced Panhandle Smith, and Fletcher. There was another man strange to him. Was that Knell? No! It could not have been Knell.

Duane leaned over the seat and touched Longstreth on the shoulder. "Look!" he whispered. Cheseldine was stiff. He had already seen.

The train flashed by; the outlaw gang receded out of range of sight.

"Did you notice Knell wasn't with them?" whispered Duane.

Duane did not speak to Longstreth again till the train stopped at Val Verde.

They got off the car, and the girls followed as naturally as ordinary travelers. The station was a good deal larger than that at Bradford, and there was considerable action and bustle incident to the arrival of the train.

Duane's sweeping gaze searched faces, rested upon a man who seemed familiar. This fellow's look, too, was that of one who knew Duane, but was waiting for a sign, a cue. Then Duane recognized him—MacNelly, clean-shaven. Without mustache he appeared different, younger.

When MacNelly saw that Duane intended to greet him, to meet him, he hurried forward. A keen light flashed from his eyes. He was glad, eager, yet suppressing himself, and the glances he sent back and forth from Duane to Longstreth were questioning, doubtful. Certainly Longstreth did not look the part of an outlaw.

"Duane! Lord, I'm glad to see you," was the captain's greeting. Then at closer look into Duane's face his warmth fled—something he saw there checked his enthusiasm, or at least its utterance.

"MacNelly, shake hands with Cheseldine," said Duane, low-voiced.

The ranger captain stood dumb, motionless. But he saw Longstreth's instant action, and awkwardly he reached for the outstretched hand.

"Any of your men down here?" queried Duane, sharply.

"No. They're uptown."

"Come. MacNelly, you walk with him. We've ladies in the party. I'll come behind with them."

They set off uptown. Longstreth walked as if he were with friends on the way to dinner. The girls were mute. MacNelly walked like a man in a trance. There was not a word spoken in four blocks.

Presently Duane espied a stone building on a corner of the broad street. There was a big sign, "Rancher's Bank."

"There's the hotel," said MacNelly. "Some of my men are there. We've scattered around."

They crossed the street, went through office and lobby, and then Duane asked MacNelly to take them to a private room. Without a word the captain complied. When they were all inside Duane closed the door, and, drawing a deep breath as if of relief, he faced them calmly.

"Miss Longstreth, you and Miss Ruth try to make yourselves comfortable now," he said. "And don't be distressed." Then he turned to his captain. "MacNelly, this girl is the daughter of the man I've brought to you, and this one is his niece."

Then Duane briefly related Longstreth's story, and, though he did not spare the rustler chief, he was generous.

"When I went after Longstreth," concluded Duane, "it was either to kill him or offer him freedom on conditions. So I chose the latter for his daughter's sake. He has already disposed of all his property. I believe he'll live up to the conditions. He's to leave Texas, never to return. The name Cheseldine has been a mystery, and now it'll fade."

A few moments later Duane followed MacNelly to a large room, like a hall, and here were men reading and smoking. Duane knew them— rangers!

MacNelly beckoned to his men.

"Boys, here he is."

"How many men have you?" asked Duane.

"Fifteen."

MacNelly almost embraced Duane, would probably have done so but for the dark grimness that seemed to be coming over the man. Instead he glowed, he sputtered, he tried to talk, to wave his hands. He was beside himself. And his rangers crowded closer, eager, like hounds ready to run. They all talked at once, and the word most significant and frequent in their speech was "outlaws."

MacNelly clapped his fist in his hand.

"This'll make the adjutant sick with joy. Maybe we won't have it on the governor! We'll show them about the ranger service. Duane! How'd you ever do it?"

"Now, Captain, not the half nor the quarter of this job's done. The gang's coming down the road. I saw them from the train. They'll ride into town on the dot—two-thirty."

"How many?" asked MacNelly.

"Poggin, Blossom Kane, Panhandle Smith, Boldt, Jim Fletcher, and another man I don't know. These are the picked men of Cheseldine's gang. I'll bet they'll be the fastest, hardest bunch you rangers ever faced."

"Poggin—that's the hard nut to crack! I've heard their records since I've been in Val Verde. Where's Knell? They say he's a boy, but hell and blazes!"

"Knell's dead."

"Ah!" exclaimed MacNelly, softly. Then he grew business-like, cool, and of harder aspect. "Duane, it's your game today. I'm only a ranger under orders. We're all under your orders. We've absolute faith in you. Make your plan quick, so I can go around and post the boys who're not here."

"You understand there's no sense in trying to arrest Poggin, Kane, and that lot?" queried Duane.

"No, I don't understand that," replied MacNelly, bluntly.

"It can't be done. The drop can't be got on such men. If you meet them they shoot, and mighty quick and straight. Poggin! That outlaw has no equal with a gun—unless— He's got to be killed quick. They'll all have to be killed. They're all bad, desperate, know no fear, are lightning in action."

"Very well, Duane; then it's a fight. That'll be easier, perhaps. The boys are spoiling for a fight. Out with your plan, now."

"Put one man at each end of this street, just at the edge of town. Let him hide there with a rifle to block the escape of any outlaw that we might fail to get. I had a good look at the bank building. It's well situated for our purpose. Put four men up in that room over the bank—four men, two at each open window. Let them hide till the game begins. They want to be there so in case these foxy outlaws get wise before they're down on the ground or inside the bank. The rest of your men put inside behind the counters, where they'll hide. Now go over to the bank, spring the thing on the bank officials, and don't let them shut up the bank. You want their aid. Let them make sure of their gold. But the clerks and cashier ought to be at their desks or window when Poggin rides up. He'll glance in before he gets down. They make no mistakes, these fellows. We must be slicker than they are, or lose. When you get the bank people wise, send your men over one by one. No hurry, no excitement, no unusual thing to attract notice in the bank."

"All right. That's great. Tell me, where do you intend to wait?"

Duane heard MacNelly's question, and it struck him peculiarly. He had seemed to be planning and speaking mechanically. As he was confronted by the fact it nonplussed him somewhat, and he became thoughtful, with lowered head.

"Where'll you wait, Duane?" insisted MacNelly, with keen eyes speculating.

"I'll wait in front—just inside the door," replied Duane, with an effort.

"Why?" demanded the captain.

"Well," began Duane, slowly, "Poggin will get down first and start in. But the others won't be far behind. They'll not get swift till inside. The thing is—they *mustn't* get clear inside, because the instant they do they'll pull guns. That means death to somebody. If we can we want to stop them just at the door."

"But will you hide?" asked MacNelly.

"Hide!" The idea had not occurred to Duane.

"There's a wide-open doorway, a sort of round hall, a vestibule, with steps leading up to the bank. There's a door in the vestibule, too. It leads somewhere. We can put men in there. You can be there."

Duane was silent.

"See here, Duane," began MacNelly, nervously. "You sha'n't take any undue risk here. You'll hide with the rest of us?"

"No!" The word was wrenched from Duane.

MacNelly stared, and then a strange, comprehending light seemed to flit over his face.

"Duane, I can give you no orders today," he said, distinctly. "I'm only offering advice. Need you take any more risks? You've done a grand job for the service—already. You've paid me a thousand times for that pardon. You've redeemed yourself. The governor, the adjutant-general—the whole state will rise up and honor you. The game's almost up. We'll kill these outlaws, or enough of them to break forever their power. I say, as a ranger, need you take more risk than your captain?"

Still Duane remained silent. He was locked between two forces. And one, a tide that was bursting at its bounds, seemed about to overwhelm him. Finally that side of him, the retreating self, the weaker, found a voice.

"Captain, you want this job to be sure?" he asked.

"Certainly."

"I've told you the way. I alone know the kind of men to be met. Just *what* I'll do or *where* I'll be I can't say yet. In meetings like this the moment decides. But I'll be there!"

MacNelly spread wide his hands, looked helplessly at his curious and sympathetic rangers, and shook his head.

"Now you've done your work—laid the trap—is this strange move of yours going to be fair to Miss Longstreth?" asked MacNelly, in significant low voice.

Like a great tree chopped at the roots Duane vibrated to that. He looked up as if he had seen a ghost.

Mercilessly the ranger captain went on: "You can win her, Duane! Oh, you can't fool me. I was wise in a minute. Fight with us from cover—then go back to her. You will have served the Texas Rangers as no other man has. I'll accept your resignation. You'll be free, honored, happy. That girl loves you! I saw it in her eyes. She's—"

But Duane cut him short with a fierce gesture. He lunged up to his feet, and the rangers fell back. Dark, silent, grim as he had been, still there was a transformation singularly more sinister, stranger.

"Enough. I'm done," he said, somberly. "I've planned. Do we agree—or shall I meet Poggin and his gang alone?"

MacNelly cursed and again threw up his hands, this time in baffled chagrin. There was deep regret in his dark eyes as they rested upon Duane.

Duane was left alone.

Never had his mind been so quick, so clear, so wonderful in its understanding of what had heretofore been intricate and elusive impulses of his strange nature. His determination was to meet Poggin, meet him before anyone else had a chance—Poggin first—and then the others! He was as unalterable in that decision as if on the instant of its acceptance he had become stone.

Why? Then came realization. He was not a ranger now. He cared nothing for the state. He had no thought of freeing the community of a dangerous outlaw, of ridding the country of an obstacle to its progress and prosperity. He wanted to kill Poggin. It was significant now that he forgot the other outlaws. He was the gunman, the gun-thrower, the gunfighter, passionate and terrible. His father's blood, that dark and fierce strain, his mother's spirit, that strong and unquenchable spirit of the surviving pioneer—these had been in him; and the killings, one after another, the wild and haunted years, had made him, absolutely in spite of his will, the gunman. He realized it now, bitterly, hopelessly. The thing he had intelligence enough to hate he had become. At last he shuddered under the driving, ruthless, inhuman blood-lust of the gunman. Long ago he had seemed to seal in a tomb that horror of his kind—the need, in order to forget the haunting, sleepless presence of his last victim, to go out and kill another. But it was still there in his mind, and now it stalked out, worse, more powerful, magnified by its rest, augmented by the violent passions peculiar and inevitable to that strange, wild product of the Texas frontier —the gunfighter. And those passions were so violent, so raw, so base, so much lower than what ought to have existed in a thinking man. Actual pride of his record! Actual vanity in his speed with a gun! Actual jealousy of any rival!

Duane could not believe it. But there he was, without a choice. What he had feared for years had become a monstrous reality. Respect for himself, blindness, a certain honor that he had clung to while in outlawry —all, like scales, seemed to fall away from him. He stood stripped bare, his soul naked—the soul of Cain. Always since the first brand had been forced and burned upon him he had been ruined. But now with conscience flayed to the quick, yet utterly powerless over this tiger instinct, he was lost. He said it. He admitted it. And at the utter abasement the soul he despised suddenly leaped and quivered with the thought of Ray Longstreth.

Then came agony. As he could not govern all the chances of this fatal meeting—as all his swift and deadly genius must be occupied with Poggin, perhaps in vain—as hard-shooting men whom he could not watch would be close behind, this almost certainly must be the end of Buck Duane. That did not matter. But he loved the girl. He wanted her. All her sweetness, her fire, and pleading returned to torture him.

At that moment the door opened, and Ray Longstreth entered.

"Duane," she said, softly. "Captain MacNelly sent me to you."

"But you shouldn't have come," replied Duane.

"As soon as he told me I would have come whether he wished it or not. You left me—all of us—stunned. I had no time to thank you. Oh, I do—

with all my soul. It was noble of you. Father is overcome. He didn't expect so much. And he'll be true. But, Duane, I was told to hurry, and here I'm selfishly using time."

"Go, then—and leave me. You mustn't unnerve me now, when there's a desperate game to finish."

"Need it be desperate?" she whispered, coming close to him.

"Yes; it can't be else."

MacNelly had sent her to weaken him; of that Duane was sure. And he felt that she had wanted to come. Her eyes were dark, strained, beautiful, and they shed a light upon Duane he had never seen before.

"You're going to take some mad risk," she said. "Let me persuade you not to. You said—you cared for me—and I—oh, Duane—don't you—know—?"

The low voice, deep, sweet as an old chord, faltered and broke and failed.

Duane sustained a sudden shock and an instant of paralyzed confusion of thought.

She moved, she swept out her hands, and the wonder of her eyes dimmed in a flood of tears.

"My God! You can't care for me?" he cried, hoarsely.

Then she met him, hands outstretched.

"But I do—I do!"

Swift as light Duane caught her and held her to his breast. He stood holding her tight, with the feel of her warm, throbbing breast and the clasp of her arms as flesh and blood realities to fight a terrible fear. He felt her, and for the moment the might of it was stronger than all the demons that possessed him. And he held her as if she had been his soul, his strength on earth, his hope of heaven, against his lips.

The strife of doubt all passed. He found his sight again. And there rushed over him a tide of emotion unutterably sweet and full, strong like an intoxicating wine, deep as his nature, something glorious and terrible as the blaze of the sun to one long in darkness. He had become an outcast, a wanderer, a gunman, a victim of circumstances; he had lost and suffered worse than death in that loss; he had gone down the endless bloody trail, a killer of men, a fugitive whose mind slowly and inevitably closed to all except the instinct to survive and a black despair; and now, with this woman in his arms, her swelling breast against his, in this moment almost of resurrection, he bent under the storm of passion and joy possible only to him who had endured so much.

"Do you care . . . a little?" he whispered, unsteadily.

He bent over her, looking deep into the dark wet eyes.

She uttered a low laugh that was half sob, and her arms slipped up to his neck.

"A little! Oh, Duane—Duane—a great deal!"

Their lips met in their first kiss. The sweetness, the fire of her mouth seemed so new, so strange, so irresistible to Duane. His sore and hungry heart throbbed with thick and heavy beats. He felt the outcast's need of love. And he gave up to the enthralling moment. She met him halfway, returned kiss for kiss, clasp for clasp, her face scarlet, her eyes closed, till, her passion and strength spent, she fell back upon his shoulder.

Duane suddenly thought she was going to faint. He divined then that she had understood him, would have denied him nothing, not even her life, in that moment. But she was overcome, and he suffered a pang of regret at his unrestraint.

Presently she recovered, and she drew only the closer, and leaned upon him with her face upturned. He felt her hands on his, and they were soft, clinging, strong, like steel under velvet. He felt the rise and fall, the warmth of her breast. A tremor ran over him. He tried to draw back, and if he succeeded a little her form swayed with him, pressing closer. She held her face up, and he was compelled to look. It was wonderful now: white, yet glowing, with the red lips parted, and dark eyes alluring. But that was not all. There was passion, unquenchable spirit, woman's resolve deep and mighty.

"I love you, Duane!" she said. "For my sake don't go out to meet this outlaw face to face. It's something wild in you. Conquer it if you love me."

Duane became suddenly weak, and when he did take her into his arms again he scarcely had strength to lift her to a seat beside him. She seemed more than a dead weight. Her calmness had fled. She was throbbing, palpitating, quivering, with hot wet cheeks and arms that clung to him like vines. She lifted her mouth to him, whispering, "Kiss me!" She meant to change him, hold him.

Duane bent down, and her arms went round his neck and drew him close. With his lips on hers he seemed to float away. That kiss closed his eyes, and he could not lift his head. He sat motionless, holding her, blind and helpless, wrapped in a sweet, dark glory. She kissed him—one long, endless kiss—or else a thousand times. Her lips, her wet cheeks, her hair, the softness, the fragrance of her, the tender clasp of her arms, the swell of her breast—all these seemed to inclose him.

Duane could not put her from him. He yielded to her lips and arms, watching her, involuntarily returning her caresses, sure now of her intent, fascinated by the sweetness of her, bewildered, almost lost. This was what it was to be loved by a woman. His years of outlawry had blotted out any boyish love he might have known. This was what he had to give up—all this wonder of her sweet person, this strange fire he feared yet loved, this mate his deep and tortured soul recognized. Never until that moment had he divined the meaning of a woman to a man. That meaning was physical inasmuch that he learned what beauty was, what marvel in the touch of quickening flesh; and it was spiritual in that he saw there might have been for him, under happier circumstances, a life of noble deeds lived for such a woman.

"Don't go! Don't go!" she cried, as he started violently.

"I must. Dear, goodbye. Remember I loved you!"

He pulled her hands loose from his, stepped back.

"Ray, dearest—I believe—I'll come back!" he whispered.

These last words were falsehood.

He reached the door, gave her one last piercing glance, to fix forever in memory that white face with its dark, staring, tragic eyes.

"*Duane!*"

He fled with that moan like thunder, death, hell in his ears.

To forget her, to get back his nerve, he forced into mind the image of Poggin—Poggin, the tawny-haired, the yellow-eyed, like a jaguar, with his rippling muscles. He brought back his sense of the outlaw's wonderful presence, his own unaccountable fear and hate. Yes, Poggin had sent the cold sickness of fear to his marrow. Why, since he hated life so? Poggin was his supreme test. And this abnormal and stupendous instinct, now deep as the very foundation of his life, demanded its wild and fatal issue. There was a horrible thrill in his sudden remembrance that Poggin likewise had been taunted in fear of him.

So the dark tide overwhelmed Duane, and when he left the room he was fierce, implacable, steeled to any outcome, quick like a panther, somber as death, in the thrall of his strange passion.

There was no excitement in the street. He crossed to the bank corner. A clock inside pointed the hour of two. He went through the door into the vestibule, looked around, passed up the steps into the bank. The clerks were at their desks, apparently busy. But they showed nervousness. The cashier paled at sight of Duane. There were men—the rangers—crouching down behind the low partition. All the windows had been removed from the iron grating before the desks. The safe was closed. There was no money in sight. A customer came in, spoke to the cashier, and was told to come tomorrow.

Duane returned to the door. He could see far down the street, out into the country. There he waited, and minutes were eternities. He saw no person near him; he heard no sound. He was insulated in his unnatural strain.

At a few minutes before half past two a dark, compact body of horsemen appeared far down, turning into the road. They came at a sharp trot —a group that would have attracted attention anywhere at any time. They came a little faster as they entered town; then faster still; now they were four blocks away, now three, now two. Duane backed down the middle of the vestibule, up the steps, and halted in the center of the wide doorway.

There seemed to be a rushing in his ears through which pierced sharp, ringing clip-clop of iron hoofs. He could see only the corner of the street. But suddenly into that shot lean-limbed dusty bay horses. There was a clattering of nervous hoofs pulled to a halt.

Duane saw the tawny Poggin speak to his companions. He dismounted quickly. They followed suit. They had the manner of ranchers about to conduct some business. No guns showed. Poggin started leisurely for the bank door, quickening step a little. The others, close together, came behind him. Blossom Kane had a bag in his left hand. Jim Fletcher was left at the curb, and he had already gathered up the bridles.

Poggin entered the vestibule first, with Kane on one side, Boldt on the other, a little in his rear.

As he strode in he saw Duane.

"Hell's Fire!" he cried.

Something inside Duane burst, piercing all of him with cold. Was it that fear?

"Buck Duane!" echoed Kane.

One instant Poggin looked up and Duane looked down.

Like a striking jaguar Poggin moved. Almost as quickly Duane threw his arm.

The guns boomed almost together.

Duane felt a blow just before he pulled trigger. His thoughts came fast, like the strange dots before his eyes. His rising gun had loosened in his hand. Poggin had drawn quicker! A tearing agony encompassed his breast. He pulled—pulled—at random. Thunder of booming shots all about him! Red flashes, jets of smoke, shrill yells! He was sinking. The end; yes, the end! With fading sight he saw Kane go down, then Boldt. But supreme torture, bitterer than death, Poggin stood, mane like a lion's, back to the wall, bloody-faced, grand, with his guns spouting red!

All faded, darkened. The thunder deadened. Duane fell, seemed floating. There it drifted—Ray Longstreth's sweet face, white, with dark, tragic eyes, fading from his sight . . . fading . . . fading . . .

⁙25⁙

LIGHT shone before Duane's eyes—thick, strange light that came and went. For a long time dull and booming sounds rushed by, filling all. It was a dream in which there was nothing; a drifting under a burden; darkness, light, sound, movement; and vague, obscure sense of time—time that was very long. There was fire—creeping, consuming fire. A dark cloud of flame enveloped him, rolled him away.

He saw then, dimly, a room that was strange, strange people moving about over him, with faint voices, far away, things in a dream. He saw again, clearly, and consciousness returned, still unreal, still strange, full of those vague and faraway things. Then he was not dead. He lay stiff, like a stone, with a weight ponderous as a mountain upon him and all his bound body racked in slow, dull-beating agony.

A woman's face hovered over him, white and tragic-eyed, like one of his old haunting phantoms, yet sweet and eloquent. Then a man's face bent over him, looked deep into his eyes, and seemed to whisper from a distance: "Duane—Duane! Ah, he knew me!"

After that there was another long interval of darkness. When the light came again, clearer this time, the same earnest-faced man bent over him. It was MacNelly. And with recognition the past flooded back.

Duane tried to speak. His lips were weak, and he could scarcely move them.

"Poggin!" he whispered. His first real conscious thought was for Poggin —ruling passion—eternal instinct!

"Poggin is dead, Duane; shot to pieces," replied MacNelly, solemnly. "What a fight he made! He killed two of my men, wounded others. God! he was a tiger. He used up three guns before we downed him."

"Who—got—away?"

"Fletcher, the man with the horses. We downed all the others. Duane, the job's done—it's done! Why, man, you're—"

"What of—of—*her?*"

"Miss Longstreth has been almost constantly at your bedside. She helped the doctor. She watched your wounds. And, Duane, the other night, when you sank low—so low—I think it was her spirit that held yours back. Oh, she's a wonderful girl. Duane, she never gave up, never lost her nerve for a moment. Well, we're going to take you home, and she'll go with us. Colonel Longstreth left for Louisiana right after the fight. I advised it. There was great excitement. It was best for him to leave."

"Have I—a—chance—to recover?"

"Chance? Why, man," exclaimed the Captain, "you'll get well! You'll pack a sight of lead all your life. But you can stand that. Duane, the whole Southwest knows your story. You need never again be ashamed of the name Buck Duane. The brand outlaw is washed out. Texas believes you've been a secret ranger all the time. You're a hero. And now think of home, your mother, of this noble girl—of your future."

The rangers took Duane home to Wellston.

A railroad had been built since Duane had gone into exile. Wellston had grown. A noisy crowd surrounded the station, but it stilled as Duane was carried from the train.

A sea of faces pressed close. Some were faces he remembered—schoolmates, friends, old neighbors. There was an upflinging of many hands. Duane was being welcomed home to the town from which he had fled. A deadness within him broke. This welcome hurt him somehow, quickened him; and through his cold being, his weary mind, passed a change. His sight dimmed.

Then there was a white house, his old home. How strange, yet how real! His heart beat fast. Had so many, many years passed? Familiar yet strange it was, and all seemed magnified.

They carried him in, these ranger comrades, and laid him down, and lifted his head upon pillows. The house was still, though full of people. Duane's gaze sought the open door.

Someone entered—a tall girl in white, with dark, wet eyes and a light upon her face. She was leading an old lady, gray-haired, austere-faced, somber and sad. His mother! She was feeble, but she walked erect. She was pale, shaking, yet maintained her dignity.

The someone in white uttered a low cry and knelt by Duane's bed. His mother flung wide her arms with a strange gesture.

"This man! They've not brought back my boy. This man's his father! Where is my son? My son—oh, my son!"

When Duane grew stronger it was a pleasure to lie by the west window and watch Uncle Jim whittle his stick and listen to his talk. The old man was broken now. He told many interesting things about people Duane had known—people who had grown up and married, failed, succeeded, gone away, and died. But it was hard to keep Uncle Jim off the subject of guns, outlaws, fights. He could not seem to divine how mention of these things hurt Duane. Uncle Jim was childish now, and he had a great pride in his nephew. He wanted to hear of all of Duane's exile. And if there was one thing more than another that pleased him it was to talk about the bullets which Duane carried in his body.

"Five bullets, ain't it?" he asked, for the hundredth time. "Five in that last scrap! By gum! And you had six before?"

"Yes, Uncle," replied Duane.

"Five and six. That makes eleven. By gum! A man's a man, to carry all that lead. But, Buck, you could carry more. There's that fellow Edwards, right here in Wellston. He's got a ton of bullets in him. Doesn't seem to mind them none. And there's Cole Miller. I've seen him. Been a bad man in his day. They say he packs twenty-three bullets. But he's bigger than you—got more flesh. . . . Funny, wasn't it, Buck, about the doctor only bein' able to cut one bullet out of you—that one in your breast-bone? It was a forty-one caliber, an unusual cartridge. I saw it, and I wanted it, but Miss Longstreth wouldn't part with it. Buck, there was a bullet left in one of Poggin's guns, and that bullet was the same kind as the one cut out of you. By gum! Boy, it'd have killed you if it'd stayed there."

"It would indeed, Uncle," replied Duane, and the old, haunting, somber mood returned.

But Duane was not often at the mercy of childish old hero-worshiping Uncle Jim. Miss Longstreth was the only person who seemed to divine Duane's gloomy mood, and when she was with him she warded off all suggestion.

One afternoon, while she was there at the west window, a message came for him. They read it together.

You have saved the ranger service to the Lone Star State.
                                                    MacNelly

Ray knelt beside him at the window, and he believed she meant to speak then of the thing they had shunned. Her face was still white, but sweeter now, warm with rich life beneath the marble; and her dark eyes were still intent, still haunted by shadows, but no longer tragic.

"I'm glad for MacNelly's sake as well as the state's," said Duane.

She made no reply to that and seemed to be thinking deeply. Duane shrank a little.

"The pain—is it any worse today?" she asked, instantly.

"No; it's the same. It will always be the same. I'm full of lead, you know. But I don't mind a little pain."

"Then—it's the old mood—the fear?" she whispered. "Tell me."

"Yes. It haunts me. I'll be well soon—able to go out. Then that—that hell will come back!"

"No, no!" she said, with emotion.

"Some drunken cowboy, some fool with a gun, will hunt me out in every town, wherever I go," he went on, miserably. "Buck Duane! To kill Buck Duane!"

"Hush! Don't speak so. Listen. You remember that day in Val Verde, when I came to you—pleaded with you not to meet Poggin? Oh, that was a terrible hour for me. But it showed me the truth. I saw the struggle between your passion to kill and your love for me. I could have saved you then had I known what I know now. Now I understand that—that thing which haunts you. But you'll never have to draw again. You'll never have to kill another man, thank God!"

Like a drowning man he would have grasped at straws, but he could not voice his passionate query.

She put tender arms round his neck. "Because you'll have me with you always," she replied. "Because always I shall be between you and that—that terrible thing."

It seemed with the spoken thought absolute assurance of her power came to her. Duane realized instantly that he was in the arms of a stronger woman than she who had plead with him that fatal day.

"We'll—we'll be married and leave Texas," she said, softly, with the red blood rising rich and dark in her cheeks.

"Ray!"

"Yes we will, though you're laggard in asking me, sir."

"But, dear—suppose," he replied, huskily, "suppose there might be—be children—a boy. A boy with his father's blood!"

"I pray God there will be. I do not fear what you fear. But even so—he'll be half my blood."

Duane felt the storm rise and break in him. And his terror was that of joy quelling fear. The shining glory of love in this woman's eyes made him weak as a child. How could she love him—how could she so bravely face a future with him? Yet she held him in her arms, twining her hands round his neck, and pressing close to him. Her faith and love and beauty—these she meant to throw between him and all that terrible past. They were her power, and she meant to use them all. He dared not think of accepting her sacrifice.

"But Ray—you dear, noble girl—I'm poor. I have nothing. And I'm a cripple."

"Oh, you'll be well some day," she replied. "And listen. I have money. My mother left me well off. All she had was her father's— Do you understand? We'll take Uncle Jim and your mother. We'll go to Louisiana —to my old home. It's far from here. There's a plantation to work. There are horses and cattle—a great cypress forest to cut. Oh, you'll have much to do. You'll forget there. You'll learn to love my home. It's a beautiful old place. There are groves where the gray moss blows all day and the nightingales sing all night.

"My darling!" cried Duane, brokenly. "No, no, no!"

Yet he knew in his heart that he was yielding to her, that he could not resist her a moment longer. What was this madness of love?

"We'll be happy," she whispered. "Oh, I know. Come!—come!—come!"

Her eyes were closing, heavy-lidded, and she lifted sweet, tremulous, waiting lips.

With bursting heart Duane bent to them. Then he held her, close pressed to him, while with dim eyes he looked out over the line of low hills in the west, down where the sun was setting gold and red, down over the Nueces and the wild brakes of the Rio Grande which he was never to see again.

It was in this solemn and exalted moment that Duane accepted happiness and faced new life, trusting this brave and tender woman to be stronger than the dark and fateful passion that had shadowed his past.

It would come back—that wind of flame, that madness to forget, that driving, relentless instinct for blood. It would come back with those pale, drifting, haunting faces and the accusing fading eyes, but all his life, always between them and him, rendering them powerless, would be the faith and love and beauty of this noble woman.